BY RICHARD S. WHEELER
FROM TOM DOHERTY ASSOCIATES

Going Home

· AND ·

Downriver

RICHARD S.
WHEELER

A TOM DOHERTY ASSOCIATES BOOK · NEW YORK

This is a work of fiction. All of the characters, organizations, and events portrayed in these novels are either products of the author's imagination or are used fictitiously.

GOING HOME AND DOWNRIVER

Going Home copyright © 2000 by Richard S. Wheeler

Downriver copyright © 2001 by Richard S. Wheeler

All rights reserved.

A Forge Book
Published by Tom Doherty Associates
175 Fifth Avenue
New York, NY 10010

www.tor-forge.com

Forge® is a registered trademark of Macmillan Publishing Group, LLC.

ISBN 978-0-7653-9165-0

Our books may be purchased in bulk for promotional, educational, or business use. Please contact your local bookseller or the Macmillan Corporate and Premium Sales Department at 1-800-221-7945, extension 5442, or by e-mail at MacmillanSpecialMarkets@macmillan.com.

First Edition: July 2017

Printed in the United States of America

0 9 8 7 6 5 4 3 2 1

CONTENTS

Going Home

A BARNABY SKYE NOVEL

1

Barnaby Skye did not have a care in the world, except perhaps for those big doings yonder in the shade of a brush arbor. He took his ease on a buffalo robe before his small lodge, watching puffball clouds spin out of the mountains and the gents in the brush arbor divide up the world. The wild times, when every trapper in the beaver country quenched a mighty, yearlong drought, had died, and now in the somnolent mid-July heat, rough trappers played cutthroat games, spun yarns, snored, or flirted with enterprising red hoydens.

His Crow wife, Victoria, had abandoned him to his trapping cronies and gone to drink spirits and tell bawdy jokes with the Flatheads, allies of her people, who were present in force to trade at the Rocky Mountain Fur Company store and sponge up the bacchanal. She had female friends and even distant relatives among the Salish.

The Flatheads and other tribes had swarmed to the great 1832 summer fair, this time in Pierre's Hole, the navel in Mother Earth just west of the Great Breasts, or Grand Tetons, which Barnaby Skye thought was plumb center, the best of all places for the great annual gathering of trappers.

Pierre's Hole offered a mild climate, vast stretches of

lush grazing ground for all the ponies, icy creeks tumbling from the mountains, abundant firewood, plentiful game—though not any buffalo—and saucy breezes eddying out of the Tetons to freshen the spirit as well as body. What better place to bake the year's aches out of the body, swill the Sublettes' firewater with new and old rivals, and engage in nefarious sins that ruined body and soul?

This year, the frosty waters of the Tetons had been mixed with pure grain spirits carried in great casks from St. Louis, and seasoned with some ancient plugs of tobacco and cayenne pepper to produce trade whiskey, the alchemist's potion that set trappers and redskins to baying at the moon and marking trees. Skye had finally had his fill of that, and of the nausea that dogged each binge, and had sunk into a summer of indolence, his mind meandering and untethered and his keen eye observing the daily passage of dusky and predatory females.

These were some doings, all right. For the first time, the American Fur Company had shown up, a big brigade of trappers led by William H. Vanderburgh and Andrew Drips, and they planned to set up a store of their own just as soon as Lucien Fontenelle arrived with that company's trade goods, which were being shipped up the Missouri and then carried by packhorse to the rendezvous. That was the big doings. They were late, which gave the Rocky Mountain Fur Company an edge for the moment. But from a longer perspective, the well-funded opposition probably signaled the end of the outfit.

Nor was that all of it. This year an American army officer named Bonneville, fat with East Coast capital, had ventured west with his own expedition. And an odd Bostonian ice merchant named Nathaniel Wyeth had marched out with a whole troop of idiot *mangeurs du lard* in uniforms. And in addition to that, there was a big party of free trappers in camp, all of them ruthless rivals of the men Skye had allied with for years: Bridger, Fraeb, Gervais, Fitzpatrick, and Sublette.

The new competition troubled Skye. The mountains were his mother and father. He wasn't a Yank, but a pressed seaman who had jumped his Royal Navy frigate at Fort Vancouver in 1826 and ended up in the Rocky Mountains, a man without a country. He had never eyed the settled United States, and had no great wish to.

England was a closed chapter in his young life. He had Victoria, and if he belonged to anything other than the Trappers Nation now, it was the Crow Nation, into which he had married. He could scarcely imagine his slim Crow consort padding the lanes of London in her moccasins. But sometimes, in the still of the night, he wondered how his family fared, and how the streets of his own city would appeal to him now. And he missed those things.

Of his family he knew little. He had been a merchant's son, destined to take over the family export business, when a press gang snatched him from the cobbled streets hard by the London Dock at East End. He never saw his family again. They surely did not know his whereabouts or even whether he was alive. And would never know.

Black Harris folded his lengthy frame beside Skye.

"What's the word?" he asked, nodding in the general direction of that willow-covered brush arbor where the brigade leaders from several outfits dickered with each other.

Skye squinted through the heat, and shrugged. "They'll make my fate, or I'll make my fate," he said.

"Nothing'll change. American Fur will gouge us just as mighty as our outfit for possibles. We'll still fork out mountain prices for every blanket and trap and jug of lightning, and they'll still offer mountain prices for every plew, take it or leave it," Harris said. "Everything changes except prices."

"It reminds me of my first rendezvous, when I walked in

from the sea. That's when Ashley sold out to Smith, Jackson, and Sublette. Now we're seeing big doings again."

Rendezvous was the time to reoutfit, buy some white men's marvels such as calico, knives, ribbons, copper kettles, and thick blankets for his Crow woman. And of course, take the edge off his thirst. Each spring his thirst built up in his parched body like a plugged volcano. And the day the supply caravan rolled in, Barnaby Skye could be found near the head of the line leading toward the kettles of mountain whiskey, ready to pickle his brains for a week.

The Skyes had done well with the old firm.

But Barnaby Skye wasn't sure about the future. Which of these outfits, wrestling with each other under that brush arbor, would survive and which would go under? How would things line up? Suddenly life in the mountains wasn't a sure bet. Maybe he'd be out of salaried work as a camp tender or brigade leader or hunter, his occupations these several years. It nagged him. He didn't like trapping. Trappers lived hard and dangerous lives, wading in icy streams, always in danger of freezing, drowning, starving, and from arrows and scalp knives.

He was the stray dog without a country. A man ought to have a home, a nation, a people, but all his allegiances were nothing more than transitory alliances formed at summer rendezvous like this one. He knew he was set apart in their minds. He spoke the polite English he was born with, and not the bizarre vernacular of the Yanks.

"I think I'm about to become a free trapper again, Black."

"No man'd do better at it. You know which way the stick floats."

"I never much cared for it. But I could make a warm camp and keep men healthy. I can hunt, make meat."

"That's plumb center, Skye."

"*Mister* Skye, mate."

Harris was grinning.

For six years, they had called him Skye and for six years he had told them to preface it with a *mister*. That's what the Royal Navy did to him, all those gentlemen officers calling each other mister, but addressing enlisted men by their last names.

It was the joke of the camps. Call Barnaby Skye anything but mister and watch the response. Trappers would send greenhorns, *mangeurs du lard*, or "pork-eaters," as they were called, over to Skye just to watch him fume at the way they addressed him. That was all right with Skye.

Barnaby Skye had filled out in the mountains until he became a barrel of a man. He still walked with a rolling sailor's gait, as if the mountains were the pitching decks of men-o'-war. He squinted out at the wilderness from deep-set blue eyes, set apart by a formidable ridge his friends swore was the king of all noses, long, thick, mountainous, dominant, and overmastering the rest of his jowly red face.

They made sport of his nose, betting that no one at any rendezvous would ever match it, and he let them. His nose was the fleshly evidence of a thousand sailor brawls, a nose that had been erected by fistic abuse into the lord and viceroy of all mortal noses. The mountaineers treasured his nose even more than they treasured Skye.

His other hallmark was his splendid beaver top hat, black and silky, climbing up from his skull like a cannon's barrel. It was the hat gentlemen habitually wore, and that is why he wore it. In England, and in the Royal Navy, he could not be a true gentleman. In this, the New World, he could be what he chose. And so they called him Mister Skye, and he wore his top hat, much battered now and bearing evidence of the uninvited passage of two arrows, and the whole of this, the royal nose, the top hat, and the way he required others to address him, they saw as crown and scepter and purple and ermine.

"Skye, I'd pass the jug with you tonight, but your nose would get in the way," Harris said. "It wouldn't be fair to the rest. You can snort a whole snifter of firewater and hold it in your nostrils."

"It is a rare English talent, Black," said Skye. "I accept. I will drink your party dry."

Black Harris yawned and headed to his robes for a nap.

Skye thought he'd sleep to dusk, carve some meat off the hanging elk haunch, and then buy another jug of mountain whiskey. The supply had declined alarmingly, and Skye wanted one last celebration before the casks went dry, or the firm began watering the last of its stock, reducing woeful trappers to sniffing a cork and sighing.

Thus passed a July afternoon, while the adventurers who ran the business, took the risks, carted supplies a thousand miles from St. Louis and a fortune in furs back to that gateway of the West, haggled through the day.

Skye snored, until late in the day when a shadow darkened his leisure. In any place other than rendezvous, that shadow would have evoked a lifesaving bolt upward and twist to one side. But here, the one place in the wilderness where it was safe, he contented himself merely to open his eyes and squint upward, past the ridgeback of his nose, to the young man above.

Ogden.

Skye blinked.

"Mister Skye," said Ogden.

"You're the only gent in six years who's addressed me as I wish. For that I am tentatively in your debt."

Skye sat up. Ogden was grinning. They had not seen each other for six years. When Skye was fleeing pell-mell from the Royal Navy, he ran smack into Peter Skene Ogden and his brigade of Hudson's Bay trappers in the Oregon country. He expected to be captured and hauled back to Fort Vancouver and sent in chains to London and a life in durance vile. But this Canadian was no ordinary man, and actually listened to Skye's story rather than scoffing and threatening. In the end, he helped a desperate and hungry seaman escape into the wilderness of North America.

And here was his benefactor, wanting to talk. Ogden was seven hundred miles away from Vancouver. Barnaby Skye sensed that there was portent in all this.

2

Ogden. Barnaby Skye knew he was in the presence of one of the most impressive men in the mountains. He was flattered that this brilliant brigade leader of the Hudson's Bay Company was pausing to say hello. Peter Skene Ogden was a match, maybe more than a match, for any Yank in the wilderness.

Ogden settled himself on the buffalo robe. "Have you a moment, Mister Skye? I should like to talk privately. Your choice. Here or somewhere up the river."

That was no choice. "Here, Mr. Ogden. I don't go sneaking about, and if there's business to be done, let it take place before my mates in the Yank company."

"Here, then." Ogden grinned, obviously liking the decision. Skye saw a man as powerful as himself, stocky and clean-limbed, as lithe as a mountain cat, and as skillful as any in dealing with men, women, animals, weapons, and war. But Ogden had more: he was a thoroughly educated man who kept a journal, knew his way through English literature, and was, above all, a Loyalist. His family had been obdurate Loyalists during the American revolution, and had moved to Canada to remain within the circle of British power. Ogden was bred to those beliefs,

and worked through Hudson's Bay to extend British do-
minion over the North American continent.

"You've come a long way," Skye ventured.

"I came all the way to see you and only you. We always observe these Yank festivals, of course, and the
scoundrels make us welcome even if we're rivals, but
that's not what brought me here. You did."

"I can't go home and I can't work for Hudson's Bay,"
Skye said bluntly.

"I know all about that, Mister Skye. You told me your
story on the banks of the Columbia long ago, and I found
myself believing it entirely." He smiled. "Some others,
you may recall, didn't credit you with an ounce of truth."

How well Skye remembered. He had barely escaped
with his life from one HBC post, Fort Nez Perce, more
commonly called Fort Walla Walla.

"You've risen from a greenhorn to a brigade leader, and
one of the top men in the mountains. Smith, Jackson, and
Sublette put great store in you. So have their successors."

Skye grunted, his gaze resting a moment on that brush
arbor where the fate of his company and his employment
rested.

"Watching me, mate? To snatch me back to England
and a dungeon?"

Ogden shook his head. "John McLoughlin took an interest in you once he heard my report about you. Cursed
the Royal Navy for misleading him."

"An interest, yes. His men chased me five hundred
miles and almost killed me."

"He no longer thinks that way. He sees a gifted Englishman who can't go home, a man who'd be a great asset to HBC, an experienced mountaineer with a proven
ability to lead, stay out of trouble, deal with fractious men,
and bring back the pelts at a profit."

"This is an employment offer? Sorry, mate. I'm beholden

here, and these Yanks have treated me honestly and generously."

"Hear me out, Mister Skye. Let's talk as one Englishman to another."

"I'm a man without a country."

"Because the Royal Navy wants you? That has been looked after."

Now, finally, Skye paused. "Looked after?"

"Yes. Let me tell you the rest. John McLoughlin, a most formidable man known through the West as the White Eagle, a Canadian doctor and indomitable force in the Northwest, took it upon himself to make certain inquiries about you in London. It took some while to get responses. His letters found their way to York Factory, carried by our voyageurs, and were carried in our barks to England, and in London they were slowly acted upon because of the disinterest of the lord directors. But at last Dr. McLoughlin, these three years later, has his reply. Would you like to know what this was about?"

"If it's about working for HBC, or returning to the Crown, no, I don't."

Ogden continued, undaunted. "Well, it's about exactly that. One of his letters asked the directors to make inquiry about your family."

Skye's body stiffened. He wasn't sure he wanted to hear this.

"Everything was as you told me and the others. Your father's in the import and export business, and you vanished from their bosom suddenly and mysteriously. They haven't heard a word about you since."

Skye choked, his throat clamped upon the feelings he had swallowed back all the brutal years in the Royal Navy and all the years of his exile in the American wilderness.

"My father lives?" he said, hoarsely.

"He does, but he's ill and not long for this world, so we hear. Your mother . . . is gone. She went to her grave not knowing whatever became of her son. Your older sister lives and is happily married. Your younger one, a maiden, is with your father."

"And do they, did you . . . ?"

"Yes, the lord directors delegated the Reverend Father Hargreaves, our company chaplain, to visit your father. He told Edward Barnaby Skye you were alive, and what had happened, and gave him to understand where you are."

Skye stood and turned his back, not wanting Ogden to see what was written on his face or the tears welling in his eyes.

"Your father rejoiced at the news, Mister Skye, but was saddened as well. A deserter from the Royal Navy, a blot upon his honorable name. He does not wholly grasp your circumstances."

Skye turned again to Ogden. "What took my mother?"

"Bilious fever. If she had lived six more weeks, Mister Skye, she would have known that her son lives."

Beatrice Marlowe Skye, from whose womb he was torn, gone. "Is there any more bad news?"

"I should think it would be good news, a father restored."

"I am a shame to him."

"No, the company doesn't see it that way. Our Honorable Mr. Leeds took it upon himself to visit the king's privy chancellor about the matter, describing the way a merchant's son was rudely abducted and ill treated, denied the rights of Englishmen or any recourse in the navy, reduced to abject servitude for seven years, which is two years longer than the usual enlistment. It was the failure of the Royal Navy, sir. Desperate men in unjust circumstances shall do what they will, and without blame."

"And what did your company man find out?"

"The pardon is assured, but the navy is objecting and refuses to believe a word of the story. Frankly, it's covering its abuses, hiding them from the Crown."

"So no pardon is assured."

"Not assured, no. But should you present yourself to the king's court of equity, matters will go in your favor. The HBC has been assured of that. You can go home. You can see your father before he passes. You can see your sisters. You can go to London, get redress, and walk away from London entirely a free subject of the Crown. And you will not have to wait, either. HBC has that assurance."

Skye felt torn to pieces. "Mr. Ogden, I'm not a subject. I'm not a piece of baggage to be shuttled about by merchants and bureaucrats. This is the New World, and I am a sovereign man."

Peter Ogden measured his words. "You have the rights of all Englishmen, Mister Skye. Those Magna Carta and common law rights may have been abused, but they exist and your case is now well known and the Crown will make amends. We want you to go to London and then return to the Northwest. HBC wishes to make you a senior man with responsibilities equal to my own. You are a born and bred Englishman, sir. And unless I misunderstand you, a man whose allegiance is unshaken, even by the brutal treatment afforded you by officers who should have known better."

"You know me all too well, sir."

"Dr. McLoughlin sent me on this long passage to lay these matters before you, Mister Skye. We consider it a matter of utmost gravity. You may trust the honor of Hudson's Bay, and we are sworn to do you no wrong. There is no trickery in this. There is not the slightest thought of capturing you and shipping you in chains to England and your fate. Dr. McLoughlin sees only a wronged man and a great talent he wishes to employ.

"You, more than any other Englishman, know the Yanks, their ways, their attitudes, their genius, their failings. Your knowledge would be invaluable to HBC. Your knowledge could help England control the whole of Oregon, now jointly claimed. Your expert knowledge would help England possess the Pacific coast of North America, from the arctic down to Mexican California, from the continental divide here in the Rockies down to the northern most boundaries of Mexico. Your employment by HBC would keep the United States from ever becoming a transcontinental power."

"You have not spoken of my wife, Mr. Ogden."

"We have thought of her. Dr. McLoughlin has a half-Cree wife, understands your sensitivities, and is adamant about protecting your union. If you wish to take her to London, HBC would undertake her passage. When you return, wherever we post you, she would be your helpmeet and be free to visit her people."

"She doesn't think much of HBC, mate. Your company arms the Blackfeet, her people's enemies."

Ogden shrugged. "We cannot deal with all the facets of this. We can only propose. Now, Mister Skye, think on it, but think quickly. It's already too late to go with our voyageurs to York Factory and embark there for England. Nor would we want you to. Our governor, Mr. George Simpson, who resides there, is not persuaded of the soundness of any of this, and might cause trouble."

"So there's trouble, after all."

"Dr. McLoughlin and I prefer another option. Fort Vancouver, you know, is resupplied by sea. Each year a schooner, usually the *Cadboro*, leaves Portsmouth, sails clear around Cape Horn, and works its way up the Pacific Coast to the mouth of the Columbia, there to disgorge the year's supply of trade goods and necessaries, and take on the peltries our voyageurs are unable to canoe and portage and haul across the Canadian wilds. We want you to be on that vessel when it leaves about the middle of September.

"Come at least to interview the man who has done so much on your behalf, and caused you to receive news of your family."

"I will think on it," said Skye.

3

Victoria Skye, named among her Absaroka people as Many Quill Woman, loved the high sweet days of summer most of all. And especially the trappers' rendezvous, when everything new and exciting in the world gathered together to insult the past.

This year she would not see her Kicked-in-the-Belly band, or her chief, Rotten Belly, or her father, Walks Alone, or her second mother, Digs the Roots, or her Otter Clan brother and sisters. They lived far away in the land of the Yellowstone, not here where the Salish and Shoshones hunted and fished. Here the waters drained into the Snake River, and emptied in the western sea somewhere beyond imagining. There, in the land of her people, the waters ran east into the great seas beyond the sunrise.

No woman worked much at the trappers' fairs, so women could be as evil as they chose. She loved being evil. Somehow there was always food aplenty, elk and deer hanging from limbs high above the yapping dogs, and stew boiling in every kettle.

So it was a time for scandalous gossip, jokes, laziness, and sipping firewater while visiting the lodges of the tribes that had come to trade with the white-eyes. The finger-talk sufficed. She did not need to know the Snake people's words to have a merry afternoon with them. She spent one whole day learning new white men's oaths from cheerful trappers who delighted to demonstrate them to her. She marveled that they had so many curses, and wanted to perfect her use of them, so she had them repeat their mighty oaths over and over.

Already, though the rendezvous was young, she had bought yellow ribbons, jingle bells, Venetian glass beads, thread, a new awl and knife, a copper kettle, and a real pair of five-point, thick, warm, Hudson's Bay blankets, gray with red bands at either end. Before she left she would add flannel to her purchases. That is, if Skye didn't squander everything on his whiskey.

She corrected herself. Their whiskey. She enjoyed a good jug just as much as he did, but she didn't indulge herself the way he did. Someone had to look out for him when he visited the other world, so she did. The elders did not approve, but she was young and reckless and willing to try anything. There on the great grassy flats, mountain men and tribesmen alike flouted the wisdom of their fathers, and relished doing it. Later, she would pray to the Above Ones and ask them to come back to her.

She had borne no children, and neither she nor Skye could understand it. But that was what the First Maker had decreed, and she bore this with patience and resignation. It had freed her to help her man during the hard trapping seasons when they sometimes ventured into the lands patrolled by the Siksika, the dangerous Blackfeet. If she could not be a mother of Skye's children, she could be one more warrior and the medicine woman who could divine the future and nurse the ill and steer the grimy, awkward, and buffalo-witted pale men out of trouble.

She had often pondered the greatest of all mysteries: where were the white women? This alone consumed most of the gossip of the Shoshone and Salish women. Where did they hide? Why did white men not bring their women out to this beautiful land? No one could answer it. No one had ever seen a white woman.

Perhaps such women were frail and disease-ridden, or so ugly the men hid them in lodges beyond the sunrise and enjoyed lusty moments with the more beautiful and healthy brown-skinned women of the tribes. She smiled. Skye had enough lust for ten women. She wished he would get another two or three wives so they could all share his manhood.

Once she asked Skye about white women, and he said they were kept away in towns with big houses in them, and they did not like to come to savage places.

That puzzled her. Was this sweet plain beneath the great breasts the trappers called the Tetons a savage place? No woman of the tribes had ever received an answer. But it was rumored that some Lakota, or Sioux, had once traveled far, far east and had seen the cities of the white men, and their women, all pale and so dressed in clothing that only their faces and hands were exposed to view. Something clearly was wrong with white women.

This white men's year of 1832 was different, and she sensed that it boded ill for her man. For all the years they had been together, there had been only one band of mountain men, but now there were several bands, fiercely opposed to one another, and each determined to wreck the prospects of the other. Yet they were all present at this rendezvous, drinking, sporting, bragging, lying, and getting girls pregnant.

This soft evening she padded across the flats, past knots of horses, some of them guarded by Shoshone boys. The new jingle bells on her moccasins delighted her. The yellow ribbons bobbing on her black braids pleased her. She was pretty, though too thin. She wished she could put on some good weight, and be full and round like her mother and sister. She found Skye alone, silent, and lifting a jug, all of which were bad signs. She knew trouble when she saw it, and now Skye exuded trouble.

"You hungry?" she asked.

He stared at the blue band in the west, and nodded.

"I'll make some goddam stew. You gonna get drunk alone?"

He nodded.

"What's wrong?"

"Nothing, Victoria. Got me a job offer from Hudson's Bay."

"An offer? We should not go to them. They put many guns in the hands of the Siksika."

Any friend of the Blackfeet was an enemy of the Absarokas.

"I will tell him no."

"Who?"

"Peter Ogden."

"Him? He is a great chief."

"The best they've got. And he came seven hundred miles to say they want me."

"It is a bad thing. They will catch you and turn you over to the water men looking for you."

"He says it's not so."

A chill ran through her. There was more to this.

"Give me that jug, dammit. I will drink with you."

She sat beside him, took the jug, and poured the fire-water into her throat. It burned like a river of lava as it went down.

"Aaaie!" she cried.

"I got news today. Ogden told me about my family."

This was big doings. Skye had word from this place called London, the many-houses place near the great sea, this place she could not even imagine. This news had traveled far, for many moons, maybe many winters, and found its way to this summer festival.

Slowly, measuring his words, he described Ogden's visit. His mother was dead. His father still lived but was frail. His older sister was fine, married, and had a family. His younger one remained at home. The Hudson's Bay Company had verified everything that Skye had told Ogden long ago, during his flight from the Royal Navy. They had approached the elders, the ones who advised the great chief, the one called king, to see if Skye could be welcomed back to England. They were proposing that Skye return to London, receive his pardon and visit his family, and then work for HBC . . .

With sudden insight, Victoria saw her life with the trapper coming to its end. He would return to his own people. He would resume a life she had heard of but could not imagine, working in big houses, working where there were thousands of people, more people in one big village than in her entire tribe, at home again, happy to be with his own.

"You're going away."

"I haven't decided yet."

"I'll go back to Absaroka. It is a good land. I will find someone. You go back."

"Victoria!"

Some animal feeling seemed to erupt from him, rumbling up his windpipe into a great roar. He had bear medicine, and now the grizzly in him roared. He stood, wobbled, roared at the quiet camp, and roared at the sunset, and roared at the Great Breasts.

"Give me the jug," she said. She took it from him and downed another fierce swallow of firewater. It was eating her belly and stealing through her limbs.

"Go to your people," she said, her soul leaden.

He stared at her, hurt in his eyes. "Is that what you want?"

"No, dammit. But you must do this now."

He settled heavily onto the robe.

"Maybe I have to," he said. "Maybe there's things a man has to do whether he wants to or not."

"I will go to my people."

"I don't want you to go home. You are my wife."

"That was the past. Now your people call you."

"I'm a free man here. I bloody well make my own choices."

"Skye," she said and clasped his hand. "No one is always free."

He nodded. "If I go, it's because of duty. My father's old. He got word of me. He's expecting me. Home, that's what it is. I don't even know what home means any more."

"Home is where your people are."

"This tears me up."

"Wait, then. There is no need to hurry."

"Yes, there is. They want me to meet the factor at Fort Vancouver—that's not far from the western sea—soon. Before their supply ship leaves for England in two moons. They want me on it."

She knew what was tearing at him, and she knew darkly that his decision was beyond her. She could only stand apart and watch and wait, not knowing her own fate. After six winters, was this how her life with the white man would end?

"Skye, we must talk to this Chief Ogden some more. It is dangerous. We must find out everything."

He nodded. "If this goes awry, they'll just pitch me into the gaol," he said. "Hard labor, maybe send me to Australia."

"What is Australia?"

"Another land across the western sea, where England sends it criminals."

"We send bad men to other bands. Your people do this, too."

"I have to go," he said. "And I don't want to. I can't afford to take you. Maybe I'll be back. Maybe not. Maybe I'll never see you again. Maybe you'll be standing on the hillside, waiting for me to ride in some dusk, waiting with the lodgefire lit, waiting for a man who has vanished across the seas. Waiting for your husband who had to do what duty required of him."

She didn't grasp all of that, but she understood all too much.

4

Skye detected a heaviness in the spirit of his Victoria that night. Sometimes she stared solemnly at him. Sometimes she plunged into a leaden silence. He well understood her feelings. She was uncertain of her fate, and likely to see their union come to a painful end.

The fate of "mountain wives," as the Indian spouses of the trappers and traders were called, was well known. Whenever a mountain man wished to return to the States, he abandoned his dusky lady and all his children with untroubled conscience, and they never saw him again. This was not a scandal among the tribes. These things were understood and dealt with. But often a woman who had enjoyed years of happy companionship with a white man suddenly found herself alone, with children and no support.

So Victoria imprisoned within her whatever she was feeling, and only the dour turn of her mouth suggested that this was a painful moment in her life. She had loved, and maybe now would lose.

Skye felt himself being torn to bits, tugged this way and that, unable to reach any shore. He knew that this opportunity cut to his very heart. Through the good offices of the Hudson's Bay Company, he could become an Englishman again, restored to his birthright, his family, his people, his home, his traditions. He could abandon this rough life if he chose. He could keep or abandon Victoria if he chose.

But there was a dark prospect. He knew that she would find only torment in London, the object of vicious curiosity, made fun of behind her back, and regarded as a savage, far below the most brutish of the English. He doubted it would ever change—that the European assumptions about other peoples would ever evolve into anything kinder. It could be a terrible thing to take her with him if he should choose to return to England.

But did he really want to go?

He spent a troubled night, she beside him as always, but somehow separated by an invisible wall. He fathomed only that these things were momentous and could radically change both of their lives. He crawled out of his lodge in the depths of a moonless night, and found solace in the stars, which were always there like faithful friends. The North Star gave direction unless the world was clouded. The fragrance of woodsmoke drifted by. The great encampment slept. Not even the diehard gamblers and drinkers remained awake. Herders guarded the horses against theft, but he did not hear them or the horses. The air stood still, and the breezes told him nothing at all. He wanted decision to come on a breeze, but the air brought nothing upon it. He felt stupid and bewildered.

This encampment lay in a sunny plain in the warmest season of the year, but the mountains were mostly cold and cruel and tortured his flesh. Soon cold would numb his fingers and toes again, and a small buffaloskin lodge would be his sole protection against vicious storm and arctic cold. There would be no refuge from all of nature's onslaught, or the onslaught of hostile tribesmen, or even the wiles of malicious Fate.

In London there would be.

But of course, if he accepted HBC's offer, he would be bound to serve the English company for a time. He would become a top man in the fur trade, but a man with a country, a people, a tradition, a common language.

He didn't have to decide for a day or two. He would see how Victoria felt at dawn, when vision and sun came together, pale and then bright. And he would again talk to Ogden.

He crawled back into his tent, and settled on his robe, upon the hard ground he had never quite gotten used to. Her small brown hand found his and pressed it.

That was all. She always seemed to know where he was, what he was thinking, and what he needed. The still night air, the stars, had schooled him in nothing, and he would await the day.

The next morning he found Ogden touring the great encampment. HBC men usually showed up at the Yank rendezvous and were welcomed heartily, with much joking and raffish humor, for they were all white men in wilderness, even if they all competed ruthlessly. That Ogden was collecting information, counting trappers, counting bales of plews, examining prices in the canvas-sheltered RMFC store, and perhaps trying to entice a few free trappers to take their trade elsewhere, didn't really matter. Bourgeois and trapper alike gabbed with the Englishmen or their Creole employees, and made friends. In the wilds, a friend could be the most precious of all assets.

Ogden, it turned out, had made his own camp with two French Canadians, settling rather closer to the American Fur Company outfit than to the Rocky Mountain partners and their brigades. Now, with the sun lapping up the slopes, breezes danced the breakfast smoke up and away, and filled the camp with that heady scent of pine forest, wilderness, meat, and coffee. It was a fine, hearty smell that stirred something in Barnaby Skye.

Ogden turned to him. "How are you faring this fine morning, Mister Skye?"

Skye grunted a noncommital response.

"Is there anything you wish to know, or which I can do?"

Ogden lifted a blue-enameled pot and poured tea into a tin cup and handed it to Skye, who sipped it gingerly. Skye had rarely had tea since his abduction from England. He wasn't sure he liked it after years of coffee.

"Mr. Ogden, there's a heap of things to think about."

Ogden nodded, but remained silent. Ogden was a realist who knew how easily he could drive Skye away.

"Suppose I go to London, get my name cleared, see my family, and ship back to York Factory, and out here. How long would HBC require me to stay in its employ?"

"Some considerable while, Mister Skye. The company would go to great expense to clear you, and would expect a quid pro quo."

"Suppose I don't go to England."

"We would be pleased to employ you in any case, but as a trapper at one of our outposts."

"Is there danger in that?"

"Considerable. Governor George Simpson, for one, sits on his throne, wondering how to clap you in irons and turn you over to the next royal frigate that makes port. And we are visited frequently, both in Hudson's Bay and at Vancouver, by the Royal Navy. And there probably would be those in the company eager to betray you. The navy's ten-pound reward for your capture still stands."

That was forthright. Peter Skene Ogden didn't waffle or conceal.

"I am a married man, Mr. Ogden. Victoria isn't merely a mountain wife, but my chosen mate."

"John McLoughlin feels exactly as you do, Mister Skye. Marguerite, his part-Indian wife, is his mate and helpmeet, and she's devoted herself to his comforts. She's not particularly distinguishable from white women after many years as the mistress of his hearth."

"Victoria does not wish to be a white woman. She thinks white women are hopeless. Far from trying to become a white woman, she teaches me Absaroka ways and expects me to become her own white Crow."

Ogden smiled. "The company respects such arrangements. Or, again, McLoughlin does. I can't say the same for George Simpson, or for the Anglican clerics they ship out here to enlighten us. That is something you'd have to deal with."

"Would the company finance Victoria's passage to and from England?"

Ogden paused. "Yes, I imagine, if there is genuine commitment on your part. Hudson's Bay is not a charitable society, and wishes to make a profit from its arrangements."

"Five years?"

"Seven. Five is not enough for the investment in you."

"And if matters don't work out, then what?"

"You would be bound for your indentured term."

"With no possibility of buying myself out?"

"I won't ask where you'd find the means."

"Victoria, mate. She works furiously and produces the finest tanned skins and trapper clothes anyone could ask for."

Ogden studied Skye's rabbit-trimmed shirt, leggings, and moccasins. "It's often said that Skye is the best-turned-out man in the mountains. Well, talk to McLoughlin. I imagine he would permit a buyout provision in your contract."

"I don't know, I don't know," Skye muttered.

"Talk with John McLoughlin. It's a long trip, but well worth it. You don't need to commit. From the looks of things here, everything is unstable. More Yank outfits, free trappers, Bonneville, Wyeth, American Fur Company.

This might be your moment to go for the highest bidder. HBC's going to bid high, Mister Skye, not only with a good salary but with your freedom, your honor, your good name, and a future in England. You're an Englishman. You're an Anglican."

"I'm a drunk."

Ogden laughed. "So are we all, at rendezvous, until the jugs run dry."

"I'll think on it, mate," said Skye.

Skye left the brigade leader and wandered through the vast encampment, feeling at home on these grassy flats beneath the Tetons. This was his ground, his people, his weather. This was near the land of his wife.

He discovered that the American Fur packtrain had arrived from the Missouri River, and that AFC men were swiftly setting up shop. He wandered through Nat Wyeth's camp, set up on a military model, everything as rectangular and right-angled as the orderly New England mind could make it. Its contrast to the anarchy of the rest of the camp amused him. Wyeth's bivouac had been the talk of the tribes.

He headed back to his lodge, where Victoria was patiently mending Gabe Bridger's moccasins while he squatted beside her and told crazy stories.

It was morning, but Skye was wandering through the dark.

5

Skye had never felt so torn. Through the mists he saw his father beckoning him urgently, and his sister reaching out. Not since he had been a pressed seaman had the urge to go home risen so strong in him. Something stirred within: he was an Englishman, born to the Island Kingdom, his soul a part of the bone and sinew and soul of his people. He could clear his name, reunite with his family, rejoice to be among his proud people.

But his friends were here, and this land beneath his boots was his, and his woman belonged on this soil, not across the salt sea. He could take her there, but her tears would flood their union.

He knew himself to be one of the most daring breed of men ever born. These mountaineers about him were masters of the wilds, and he admired each of them. They included him among them but he felt like a poor imitation of the likes of Bridger and Meek and Fitzpatrick and the Sublettes. There was, in these awesome fastnesses, a brotherhood forged from danger and joy.

These men were so isolated that most of the world's news never reached their ears. They could survive, even if the fragile supply lines back to civilization were snapped in two. They could endure, even when all the furies of nature were unloosed on them. And they had made him one of them, given him his diploma, magna cum laude. He lived in a small male society where greenhorns approached him with respect and begged advice from him, where veterans slapped him on the back and welcomed him to their campfires. They had saved his life more times than he could remember, and he had rescued so many of them that the bonds they had forged would last as long as they lived.

It hadn't all been pleasant. This extreme life had drawn the misfits and scoundrels, the ones who could not endure ordinary society, the mad, and angry, the desolate, the wounded.

He'd had his fill of trappers who ragged him about the condition of the camps, challenged him to absurd contests, mocked his Englishness, hated him just because he existed, or because he didn't cuss, or because he spoke the true tongue of the English. The mountain men were a vicious breed, and he hoped no one back in the States would ever romanticize them or their squalid, desperate lives.

But on a summer's eve, when the woodsmoke tinted the air with joy, and the tall tales began, and a generous jug found its way around the circle, he knew these men were his brothers, and he was their brother, and this hardy band was his one and only nation.

Thus did he pass a morning in anguish, his glance occasionally falling upon the great men gathered under that brush arbor beneath the wilting cottonwood leaves that shadowed them. This rendezvous was different. Three companies in the field, plus a large and organized band of independent trappers. And they were talking to one another. Who would Wyeth ally himself with? How would they carve up the mountains? What would Hudson's Bay do? What would happen with the muscular American Fur Company in the field, competing for every beaver pelt?

It had been hard enough for one Yank company and one British company to survive; how would things go now?

The answer came that very afternoon, when the pow-wows in the arbor broke up. Skye watched Tom Fitzpatrick, still frail after a harrowing ordeal just before the rendezvous, hobble toward him, leaning heavily on his staff.

"Afternoon, Mister Skye," he said. "Mind if I light a moment?"

Skye waved him to the robe.

Fitzpatrick eased himself slowly to the ground, still sick and weak, pain around his eyes. Just before the rendezvous, the partners sent him out to look for Sublette's packtrain with the resupply, to tell him to hurry up because of the competition from American Fur. Tom Fitzpatrick delivered the message and was hurrying back to Pierre's Hole when he ran into Blackfeet, not once but twice, narrowly escaping both times. He lost everything, including his rifle, and survived only because of his magnificent skills as a mountaineer. By the time he was discovered by two friendly Iroquois hunters he was in rags, his moccasins were used up, and he was starved down to nothing.

But here he was, and a hundred hardy men like him.

"Mister Skye," he said without preamble, "the long and short of it is, we're facing stiff competition and we're cutting back. The only salaries we'll be paying is to the partners and a few top men. We'll not be able to afford camp tenders. The trappers will do that themselves. We're counting on you to stay on as a free trapper. You join one of our brigades, but it'll be mostly the same."

The news stung Skye.

"A trapper's plews, even in a good campaign, won't come close to what I made as a camp tender, will they, Tom?"

"No, I reckon they won't. But we've no choice. We're not alone any more."

"What's Wyeth going to do?"

"He's going west. Wants to talk to HBC, start a fishery on the Columbia, ship preserved salmon east, and trade for a few furs as a sideline. He's going to trade directly with the tribes if he can. His New Englanders don't know the nose of a beaver from the tail, but they can run a store." Fitzpatrick paused. "And he might succeed, and if he does, that's all the more plews we'll never see."

"And Vanderburgh and Drips?"

"Eyeball to eyeball with us at every beaver ground in the Rockies, Mister Skye. And they've got support. The Chouteaus of St. Louis and all their Frenchy cousins are in. And experience. Those people were in the fur business before we were tadpoles."

"It's bad, then."

"We'll give 'em a run for it. It's not the end, but we're going to stay lean. We're going deep in hock just to pay for next year's outfit."

"Who are you keeping on salary?"

"Black Harris, two or three others."

"All Yanks."

"That wasn't considered. You're as good a man as any in the mountains."

"And not a Yank. You're sticking with your own. I'm as good as any, but not one of your countrymen."

"You'll be a free trapper."

"Maybe I won't." Skye's temper boiled upward. "Maybe I'll start my own opposition. I could take ten men with me."

Fitzpatrick stared. "Don't do anything foolish."

"I don't like being cashiered. I was a loyal man."

The RMC man's affability vanished. "Cool down, Mister Skye. We'll talk some more about this. Forget going into opposition. We'll crush all opposition. We have the means and the skills. Don't be dumb."

Tom Fitzpatrick stood slowly, recovered his staff, and hobbled into the sun. Skye watched him go, his mind roiling with bitterness.

Skye felt something hard and cold and ruthless down in his gut. Suddenly he knew he had no flag to follow, and no allegiance to offer. Just when life seemed good, Fate knocked him two rungs down the ladder.

Well, change was in the wind.

He stood and stretched, feeling the power in his limbs, feeling their constancy and obedience to his will. The somnolent camp seemed changed. He could not fathom it. He wandered willy-nilly, going nowhere. He visited with Wyeth's men, clearly more educated and cultivated than the rest of those in the mountains, and yet not one he wanted to befriend. He meandered through the AFC digs, good men, many of them Creoles from St. Louis, brilliant in the mountains, wild in drink, crazy among women, and the best travelers on earth.

He hunted for Peter Skene Ogden and finally found him in earnest conversation with the Sublettes. They waved him off. Company business.

The earth under his feet was no longer his. He no longer owned the sun, or possessed this warm flat nested in the mountain shadows. He could not put a name to this change that had slid quietly into the place. He thought it was something like leaving an inn, where he had visited with friends and had a grand time, and enjoyed fine feasts, and then stepping into a world that no one owned.

The only things that hadn't changed were the buffalo-hide lodges of the Shoshones and Flatheads. But even those portable lodges would be dismantled in a few days and carried away on travois. The various tribes were always at home and had no perception of wilderness.

He thought about going into opposition with a dozen

free trappers, cleaning out beaver before the Yank company even got to the trapping grounds. But he didn't want to devote his life to a small, mean ambition like that. No man worthy of respect could devote himself to revenge.

Skye let his anger drain away. There was no point in nursing it along.

Then at last a decision did gel in him: he would go to Fort Vancouver, discover what the White Eagle really thought and wanted, and make his decision about Hudson's Bay, a trip over the seas to England, and a new life as an HBC brigade leader.

He would read the correspondence about his family, understand what was wanted, assess the man who had set HBC's blood-hounds after him six years before, decide if this legendary prince of the company would be a good man to work for, a man he could trust. He had come to trust and admire his Yank friends—Bridger, Fitzpatrick, Jackson, Smith, the Sublettes—men who now were rejecting him. He would need to be more careful in the future, and take a hard, cold look at the chief factor.

Thus was his decision made, but he was uneasy with it. What would it mean to Victoria, and indeed, to his marriage? She was off among the Shoshones again, so he wandered in that direction until he came upon the gaudily dyed buffalohide lodges of that tribe, and paced among them, enjoying the smiles of the old men and women, the parade of pretty girls flaunting their newly won jingle bells, ribbons, combs, beads, and calico, and their bold flirtations.

It was not hard to find Victoria: she lounged under a majestic cottonwood tree, along with three other matrons, each doing beadwork as they gossiped.

She rose at once upon seeing him. He never came here or interrupted her day, and he beheld worry in her thin, sharp face.

"Yes, what?" she asked.

He touched her arm. "I'm wanting to go to Fort Vancouver and talk with the White Eagle, and I'm wanting you to come with me. If not, I'm wanting you to wait for me because I'll be back, sometime, some way, even if a winter or two winters pass."

"From this place across the sea?"

"Maybe."

"Would you like me to come to this place of your birth?"

"I'm thinking it, if it doesn't scare you. Maybe there's a way."

She laughed. "I'll go. I will see with my own eyes what place this is and what strange people live there, and then we will be closer, eh? Goddam, Skye, do you think an Absaroka woman is afraid? What a big place the world is!"

He squeezed her and rejoiced.

6

Skye found Peter Skene Ogden at dusk enjoying something he poured from a silver flask, along with half a dozen HBC men, all French Canadians.

"Ah, Mister Skye, have a drink. What I have here is single-malt scotch, the likes of which you'll never see again at a Yank rendezvous."

"Can't say as I've ever sampled it."

"Let me pour you one. It's all the smoke and heather of the Highlands in one distilled essence. Have you come to a decision?"

Skye settled himself on the ground and took the proffered tin cup. "A sort of one, Mr. Ogden, a sort of one. We'll go to Vancouver and talk with Dr. McLoughlin, and see."

"Good! See how he stands."

"I'm not entirely persuaded, Mr. Ogden. If I come over to HBC, you'll get a gifted woman, too. She's my mate, and she'll go wherever I go. Will you pay her?"

"Ah, Skye, when I heard you'd named her Victoria, after the royal princess, I knew you belonged with us and I urged it upon McLoughlin. I think, within reason, you can propose terms of employment we'd accept, eh?"

"I have little love of the royal family, mate. Her family's among the finest of the Crows. She's a Crow princess."

Skye sipped the Scottish whiskey, intrigued by its smoky flavor and silkiness. But what did he know? The only whiskey he'd ever sampled in his constricted life had been the outlaw variety manufactured for wild Indians and wilder trappers.

"If you're choosing this course, then it's necessary for you to be off at once, at dawn, so you can sail on the *Cadboro*. You'll be going alone. I can't go with you."

Skye sipped. The scotch was seducing him.

"Why aren't you coming with me?" he asked.

"Because I'm still negotiating some territorial agreements with the Yanks. So far, it's gone badly. We offered to stay out of the country east of the divide if they'd stay out of the west slope. But they have us there. Oregon country's contested, and we can't keep the Yanks out. We're at a disadvantage. HBC won't spill a drop of spirits to acquire a pelt from a savage. There are now two or three Yank companies competing with us, and some freelancers, too. What are we to do? Make alliances. I'm going to talk with Wyeth. He's newest and easiest to deal with."

"Nothing'll come of it, mate. The Yanks go where they please and do what they please, and they don't take kindly to HBC. They know you've been stirring up the Blackfeet against them, and arming them, too."

"Well, that's our trump. We could cut off the Blackfeet—if we get something in return."

"Mr. Ogden, I wonder if you know the Yanks at all. They're spoiling for fights, half of them."

"So it seems," Ogden said.

Doubts and details nagged at Skye. He needed an outfit. He was in debt to the Yank company. Who would supply him and Victoria with suitable attire for London?

He and Ogden dealt with these and other details, and within the space of an hour they had hammered things out. Skye would proceed down the Snake and Columbia rivers with saddle- and packhorses. HBC, in exchange for a term of service, would outfit the Skyes.

Then it was done. He rose stiffly, discovering that night had embraced them. A mountain breeze eddied cold air through the camp, bringing woodsmoke on its wings. Men were crawling into their robes. This rendezvous was growing long of tooth and most of the trappers had squandered a year's income on wild times, whooping it up, outfitting themselves, and now they had little to do at night except play euchre or monte or spin tales.

In a week or so it would all be over, and then the lonelies would crawl into the belly of each man, and the mountaineers would silently pack up and leave. Now the lonelies struck Skye hard. He would be ditching all this, maybe forever.

He made his way past campfires, most of them little more than glowing coals, looking for a certain one. He found the fire he wanted, and spotted Tom Fitzpatrick, Bill Sublette, Davy Jackson, Jed Smith, Gabe Bridger, and others, talking quietly among themselves, no doubt planning the year's campaign. He approached cautiously, top hat in hand, but old Broken Hand Fitzpatrick waved him in.

This was going to be hard.

"I guess I've come to say goodbye, gents," he said.

"You goin' somewheres?" Bridger asked.

"Probably home to England for a spell," he said. "I've a chance to clear my name. I never figured jumping ship was wrong, not when I was pressed in and kept a slave, but the lords in the admiralty feel otherwise."

Briefly, he described the news he had received from Ogden, and finally said that he might be working for HBC. They sat silently. HBC was the enemy, the supplier of the Blackfeet.

"Guess you want to see your family, Mister Skye," said

Jackson. "Now, out here, most of us coons, we don't ever want to see our famblies."

The laughter went thin. He could have announced his move to American Fur and they would have cheered him. But not HBC.

"I owe the store one hundred fifty-four dollars and some cents," he said. "I've come to offer you a good packhorse, worth over a hundred, and my nine-pole lodge. Not many a man gets to stay in a tent with a fire inside it on a January night. It's worth a piece. I figure the package, a good Crow-trained travois and packhorse, and the lodge, well, it comes to my debt."

"Don't know what the company'd do with a lodge," Sublette said.

"Sell it," Fitzpatrick said. "All right, Skye, I'll go for it if the rest will."

Skye saw the nods, lit by flickering flame.

"Done, then." He saw the Yanks distancing themselves from him. "You're good men. Took in a starving limey and let me make my way. Maybe, when I come back, I'll see you. Maybe not. But as long as I live, I'll remember you."

These were great-hearted men and they put aside their differences, just as Skye had set aside his anger.

"You go tell that pa of yourn, and them proper sisters of yourn, how it be in the mountains, and fill 'em full of tall tales," Bridger said.

"Don't need to, mate. The real tales are more than anyone in London'll believe."

"You taking Victoria?"

"Yes."

"Well, that's some. But not the first time. I heard tell, long time gone, some Iroquois shipped over there to France and half them Frenchies went mad just to get a look at 'em. You go run old Victoria down that Piccadilly Circus, and watch the dogs come sniffing!"

Skye didn't like the vector of this. "She's got courage.

Imagine her pulling up from her village and coming with me. She's never even seen a Yank village, much less a city. And the biggest boat she's seen is a canoe. How do you think it'll be to see a three-master?"

"She's some, she is," said Milt Sublette.

Fitzpatrick spoke for them all. "Sorry we couldn't keep you on salary, Mister Skye. Thought you'd be happy enough as a free trapper, you and the missus. But you go on across the sea now, and get your name cleared. And watch out. There's those in HBC that'd sooner skin you alive than call you an Englishman. Stuffy outfit. They won't be calling you mister, like we do." He laughed. "At least like we try to do.

"There'll be those as have long knives out, those naval officers you told us about. And there'll be those who'll think you're a rough man unfit for London. The mountains turn us all rough, and it won't get you into tea parties. But seeing your father who thought ye dead and gone. Ah, there'll be tears aplenty. And seeing the sisters, there'll be tears of joy. You've got your chance, and you're taking it, and there's been no finer man in the mountains."

One by one they stood to pump his hand, give him a bear hug, thump him on the back, and then the shyness came over them, and he wound his way back to his small lodge where Victoria lay in the robes awaiting his news.

"It's all set," he said. "We'll be riding at dawn with just a packhorse. They'll take the other nag and the lodge to clear my debts."

"It's a good lodge," she said. "It has kept us warm and safe. It was given to us by the People."

"They made us a fine lodge, but we made it a safe home," he said. "Now we'll walk into danger. You're a brave woman, Victoria."

"I am not afraid, dammit. I'm Skye's woman, and you honor me by taking me to your people."

Skye stared out the smoke hole at the bright stars, one of which was lying beside him.

7

Skye and Victoria left the rendezvous at first light, following the Teton River northwest. At the edge of the great, somnolent encampment, Skye reined up, lifted his top hat, and settled it over his long hair. That was his farewell to the men of the mountains who had taken him in and made him part of their wild nation. His life with the Yanks was over. Their images came to him: Fitzpatrick, Bridger, Sublette, Smith, Jackson . . . Goodbye, goodbye, to them all.

"We're hell and damn right all alone," Victoria said. Skye nodded and touched heels to his thin, tough mustang, gotten from Victoria's people. They were alone, and shifting from the protection of the rendezvous to danger. From now on they were prey.

It was his fate to be alone, without allegiances. But he was *going home* and that thought reached so deep into his heart that it lifted his sagging spirits. He was going home, but Victoria was traveling farther then ever from her home family. That's how their marriage was, one outbound, one inbound, she never quite happy in the white men's company, he never quite at home among her Crow people. He saw no help for it. And yet they had grown close to each other, a tiny nation of two, separate from the whole world.

She rode beside him along the icy river that deposited the snows of the Tetons into Henry's Fork of the Snake, and ultimately into the Pacific Ocean some short distance beyond Fort Vancouver. It would be a long ride, but not so desperate as his odyssey six years earlier, as a seaman escaping the long arm of the navy.

Home to see his father, home to see his sisters and children he had never met. And his cousins, too. Home to the small vistas and towering majesty of the Island Kingdom. Home to the friends who would have been his classmates at Cambridge, men who would be shocked by him now. No doubt he would repel them, just as he most likely would repel his father and sister and all of his relatives. And if his roughness offended them, Victoria's ways would appall them. But it had to be done.

A good name counted for much, and he wanted his good name and his citizenship back. Then he would be what he had been set upon the earth to be, a free and honorable Englishman.

As the sky lightened behind the eastern mountains, he and Victoria wound their way along grassy parks dotted with mottes of aspen or cottonwood, past long slopes of lodgepole pine, the grades gentle and easy on their horses and the surly packhorse behind them. That beast was not heavily laden. The Skyes could travel light, and on this trip they chose to: at Fort Vancouver, they would shed everything they owned for a very different sort of attire.

Skye paused repeatedly to examine the world behind him.

That was an ironclad rule in the mountains: know what lay before, and what lay behind. He squinted sharply into the dull light, the sun still canceled by the blue mountains, and discovered motion, something yellow and low, probably a coyote.

He nodded to Victoria and pointed. But the movement had ceased, and whatever creature lay a hundred yards back would not reveal itself. He reined the mustang around and headed downstream again, leading the packhorse while Victoria kept to the rear.

Over the next miles they spotted the animal trailing behind, and knew it was either a stalking coyote or a dog. Then, midmorning, when they paused at streambank to water the horses and rest, they beheld a yellow dog on its haunches watching them; some mutt from one of the tribal encampments.

"I hope he goes back," Skye said. "I don't want a dog."

"The sonofabitch isn't gonna get close, anyway," she said.

When Skye concluded, from a ridge, that the land was open and level enough, he cut west, straight for Henry's Fork, abandoning the north-trending Teton River. They rode through lodgepole forests and open grassy parks, across a vast country in which a man couldn't see far because of the trees. But they were far off any trails and didn't expect to run into any trouble except perhaps for a bear.

The yellow dog followed, now approaching to within fifty yards.

"I'll shoot it," Skye growled.

"Dammit, Skye, just leave it."

A few mountaineers put much store in dogs, arguing that they warned their masters of approaching enemies. But most of them found, to their sorrow, that it was the other way around. A barking mutt led stalkers straight into camp, and the dog-lovers lost their scalps and their lives and their mutts.

All that quiet day the cur crawled along behind them, sitting, watching, squirming, hiding in grasses, running through concealing shadows. Skye watched warily, looking for a clear shot.

Victoria disapproved. There were usually dogs in Indian camps, and they were useful, cleaning up offal and guard-

ing against horse raids. For some of the peoples, they
were also a handy source of food.

"Maybe he is a goddam spirit-dog," she said. "Medicine dog, come to help us."

"He's just looking for some vittles," Skye replied. He
would not let his woman soften his decision. Dogs were
dangerous and a burden to feed. A he-dog got into scraps
and had to be doctored.

A she-dog caused more trouble, stirring up all sorts of
headaches, whelping and confronting its owner with pups.

"Horseapples," she said.

Victoria had picked up the trappers' rough lingo in the
brigades, year after year, and had no idea that there was
such a thing as polite society and that such words were
simply unacceptable to them. Skye wondered how he could
prepare her for London, for European ways, and knew he
couldn't. This was her version of English, and that was
how it would be, whether in a Mayfair drawing room or
in the camps of the mountain men. But at least he would
tell her what words to avoid.

They reached Henry's Fork late in the day and camped
in a leafy bower well back from the trails tracing its
banks. This was a sweet land, with stretching vistas and
snowcapped mountains poking through the distant haze.
The yellow dog made itself at home just one rifleshot
away. Skye didn't much care. The mutt wasn't slinking in,
and disappeared for long periods, no doubt hunting.

He was more concerned about Indians. This was sa-
vannah country, with plenty of cover for stalking war
parties. It was best to dodge them all, even the friendly
ones. The loss of one horse would plunge them into trouble. He had ridden over rock and hard ground, walked
down rivulets and creeks, hidden their passage to all but
the most observant eye. But it was never enough, and luck
usually decided who went under and who lived. This was

Bannock country, or so he had heard, traversed by Flatheads and Shoshones and Nez Perce. But it was not unknown to the adventuresome Blackfeet, either, and it wouldn't help him an iota to be in the company of a Crow woman.

Henry's Fork teemed with trout, but Victoria wouldn't touch them. Demons from under the waters she called them and always watched dourly when white men caught and cooked them. It surprised her that they didn't die on the spot. But she always said that they sickened after eating underwater things; she could see it.

They hadn't hunted this day and now Victoria pulled parched corn from the packstores, built a tiny fire against a low bank, and boiled the corn into mush in her kettle. They would eat simply.

"It is lonely, Skye," she said, after scouring the pot and dousing the tiny fire. "One day we are with friends. The next day we are two and a dog."

"Just two. I'm thinking to run that dog off."

"Let us see. It is a spirit-dog."

"It's a mutt."

Skye rose, restlessly, and looked to the horses. He had picketed them close to camp on good grass. Later, when he was ready for the robes, he would bring them in and tie them to the aspen a few feet from his bed.

Some coyotes gossiped somewhere over the horizon and Skye waited for the damned mutt to howl, but it didn't. It lay there, out in the darkness, silent and full of its own purposes.

He had never owned a dog, didn't know whether he wanted one.

The mountaineers argued dogs in camp, often with such heat that men got into brawls. Some claimed that a man and dog made a family, if not an entire nation. Others cursed dogs and said the redskins should eat the whole dog nation for the sake of the world. Skye didn't much care.

After he'd had his pipe of the precious leaf, he knocked out the dottle, tied the horses close, and drew his robes around him against the high country chill. The ground was always hard and his head never enjoyed a pillow and he had never gotten used to the privation.

She joined him. She had always come to him in the night, if only to be held or to hold her man. She held him now, and no word passed between them. He felt the wash of tenderness again, knowing that this union was more important than going home to England. Much would depend on what McLoughlin had to say. But whatever his fate, it would be Victoria's fate as well. He didn't know why that was so. They hadn't spoken of it or pledged it to each other. Perhaps she was his only nation, his only people, and the two of them, molded by danger and hardship into one heart.

He awakened at first light and everything was all right. He could always tell. Some intuitive understanding, honed from years of danger in strange places, told him when things were amiss at the first gray coloration of the eastern sky. His hip was bruised where he had slept on a rock, but that was all.

She slept. He wondered why they had bred no children, but neither of them knew. Something in her slender form, or maybe within him, made her barren. He didn't know whether to regret it. The wilderness was not a place to rear a family. She would disagree with him. She never understood the white men's idea of wilderness, a place apart from civilization. The whole land was her home and the home of her people, so why not an infant in a cradleboard?

The horses stood stock-still, dozing. All was well.

The outfit snugged beside him, untouched. His Hawken lay in its quilled and fringed sheath within reach, covered with dew. His flint and striker lay beside him, his powder horn next to the rest. Moisture lay thick over everything, including his blankets.

The dog lay ten yards distant, staring directly at him. Ugly yellow thing, big scar over one eye, half an ear off, distrustful and ready to bolt. Skye hunted for a rock to pitch, but the dog crawled back and waited.

"Skye, dammit, let it be," she said. "I got feelings about that dog. It's a he-dog, and he's watching us."

"Put an arrow through him," Skye said.

She stared, stonily. He knew she would not reach for her bow and quiver.

The dog stood, stretched, front legs first, and then rear, and waited.

"Well, don't feed him," he said, not yet surrendering.

"He'll quit us if we don't."

But his instincts told him that wasn't true.

8

They spotted game all the next day: an antelope, mallards bobbing on an estuary, a mule deer, beaver, but Skye would not make meat, and he stayed Victoria every time she strung her bow. She complied, but sullenly.

He was not going to surrender to that yellow dog. There would be no offal, no bones, no scraps, no hide for that hideous creature to gnaw on and thus lay claim upon the House of Skye.

No! But the starved and ribby beast never quit, sulking along behind, and then to one flank or the other, sometimes disappearing. They passed an ancient deer carcass, nothing but bone and hide, and the mutt lingered. Skye hoped that foul pile would poison the beast and they would never see him again.

But an hour later, as they rode along Henry's Fork of the Snake, the hellish creature trotted along, just beyond rifle shot. The dog knew full well how Skye felt: time after time, Skye dismounted, gathered a handful of pebbles, and threw them. The dog gauged Skye's accuracy and ignored the missiles. Skye was feeling defeat and climbed into himself.

Victoria turned stony. "It is spirit-dog. You make trouble for us," she said. "He has come to protect us."

He ignored her. He was not going to endanger her, himself, or his property by accepting the company of some disease-shot yellow parasite that would howl at the first sign of trouble. If there was one lesson he had squeezed out of his six years in the wilds, it was to hide from danger. Hide from passing villages, hide from angry bears, hide from unknown bands of horsemen, hide from solitary warriors, hide from storms and wind and cold. If he welcomed that miserable excuse for a dog, he could hide no more.

The bright day invited a sunny heart, but his spirits darkened. Victoria refused to speak to him, her frown beclouding an otherwise perfect summer day spent upon a sweeping grassland surrounded by hazy mountains.

That dawn, when he had discovered the dog lying on the very edge of his camp, he threw off his robes with a roar and plunged barefoot after the cur, his bear-rumblings driving the animal far afield. Two minutes later the dog sat on its haunches laughing at Skye.

Then, midday, the mutt circled around the right side of Skye's small caravan, trotted out ahead, paused occasionally, sniffed, and trotted even farther forward. Skye, always the wary man, unsheathed his Hawken and checked the load. A fresh cap covered the nipple. He preferred the percussion lock version of the Hawken brothers' mountain rifle to the flintlock, even though there was always the danger of running out of caps in a place so far from a resupply. But the caplock Hawkens fired when you wanted them to, and rarely failed in damp weather.

The man meandering through a sunlit meadow ahead clearly was no Indian. He wore a high-collared white muslin shirt, a proper tweed jacket with elbow patches, and laced hightop boots. He carried a rucksack. A panama, tilted at a jaunty angle, covered his head. Skye tugged his reins, the sight of the lone traveler straining credulity.

"Goddam!" muttered Victoria, pulling up beside him.

The yellow cur had frozen ahead, nose and tail pointing, as the man studied the earth and occasionally plucked something from it as if he were hunting for lost gold. Close to him walked a nondescript gray dog carrying a small pack of some sort. It turned toward the yellow dog but did not attack.

"Hello," yelled Skye.

The gentleman straightened up.

"Ah! Company! Come see this. It's a sport variety of the death camas. Look at this. The raceme is really a panicle."

He waved a limp stem at them. The man behind that weed seemed to consider Skye and Victoria old friends.

"Where's your party, sir?" Skye asked.

"Party? Why, I don't believe I know. Back at the camp, I suppose. Wyeth, of course. He'll be along sometime."

"I'm Mister Skye, and this is my wife Victoria."

"Oh, forgive me. When I'm out in the field I forget my manners. Nutmeg here, Alistair Nutmeg, on a small sabbatical."

"You are an herbalist? A doctor?"

"Ah, no, sir, a naturalist. Here we have a whole virgin continent filled with species never collected or recorded, and that's what I'm doing . . . now hold on, Dolly dear, don't growl at our visitors."

He caught the collar of his gray dog and smiled. "Do come down off those steeds and we shall have some Darjeeling, eh? What a jolly coincidence!"

Skye scarcely knew what to make of it. "You came with Wyeth?"

"Yes, a fine little jaunt. He's got twenty of his New Englanders with him, pleasant chaps but timid sorts, and half of them are out of temper and going home. The rest'll come along to the coast. He's got a trading ship going there, you know, the brig, *Sultana,* and I'll return to Boston on it. Visionary fellow. I'm a lecturer at Harvard but actually an Englishman. I didn't get this far last time; that was with the trapper Manuel Lisa in 'aught-ten. But I got a fine bag from it. Hundreds of new species. Wrote it all up. And it's only the beginning."

An Englishman.

"Well, sir, so am I an Englishman. London born. And you?"

"Leicester, sir. I came over here in 'aught-eight, apprenticed as a printer in Philadelphia, but that was a mistake, eh? This is what I was born to do, born, born, born. This pup here, Dolly, carries some good, watertight panniers where I keep my notes and sketches and dried samples."

"You aren't armed?"

"Why should I be, Skye?"

"It's Mister Skye, sir."

"Yes, of course. Professor, here. Professor Nutmeg." He discovered a moth floating by. "Now look at that white beauty. I wish I had my net. But I can only do one thing at a time. We'll leave the bugs and get the herbs. Of course, when a species lands in my lap, I record it. Do you know how many cottonwoods I've found? Three. All unknown to the world. I propose to name one *Populus nutmega*. Vanity, you know."

The professor lifted his panama, and Skye discovered that it had shaded a high-domed pink forehead and receding hairline. The man peered up at Skye with boyish blue eyes, innocence in his countenance. His was the face of a man who'd never heard of evil, a man born before Adam.

The man was a fool.

"When's Wyeth coming?"

"Oh, whenever the rendezvous breaks up, I suppose. He'll find me."

"He knows you're here?"

"He'll catch up with me."

"You're saying you got ahead of him? And he doesn't know it?"

Furrows plowed across Nutmeg's brow. "I suppose I should have notified him."

Skye was aghast. "Don't you suppose he's looking for you? Sending out searchers? Combing the country for a body? Expecting to find a corpse with a scalped head, maybe?"

Nutmeg reddened but held his peace.

"What was the arrangement? Did you tell him you'd be wandering wherever your fancy took you?"

"Why, sir, I scarcely thought of it."

"Did he ask you to stay close?"

The professor nodded.

"There's a rule in this wilderness, Professor. Men stick together always. Lives depend on it. If a man's missing, the whole outfit stops and searches and camps at that place until the missing man is found. Are you aware of that?"

"Oh, yes, they were always talking about it coming out from St. Louis."

"Have you seen any Indians?"

"Well, I believe one sits astride her steed beside you, Mister Skye. Nice specimen, properly dried and pressed she'd last forever. Get into the British Museum. What species?"

"Goddam Absaroka."

"Ah," he said, amusement crinkling the corners of those innocent eyes as he gazed upon her. "She speaks the king's tongue with great vigor."

Skye liked him and laughed in spite of his indignation. "Where do you sleep? What do you eat?"

"Why, this is July, Mister Skye, and this whole continent bursts with wild strawberries, grapes, cherries, huckleberries, blueberries, wild onions, nuts, chokecherries, various tubers that resemble carrots . . ."

"And how do you feed your dog?"

"I don't. She's on her own. She has to use her little dog brain. Sometimes the Indians give me meat. Very pleasant people, these North American Indians. Some fine chaps in black-dyed moccasins dropped by just yesterday and left me some venison for the pooch. But Dolly is quite adept at hunting. Is that your fine canine there, the yellow one?"

"Professor, he's yours. He's loyal to a fault, totally disobedient, and without honor."

Nutmeg sighed. "If I had a pack rig for him, I would, but you see—"

"I'll rig something. He's all yours."

"Why, how extraordinarily kind."

The Skyes and Nutmeg repaired to a grove of noble cottonwoods sheltering the bank of Henry's Fork. There the professor and Victoria ignited a small fire, boiled water, and produced tea, while Skye restlessly watched horizons. He didn't like the news of Blackfeet in the area.

"Professor, how many Blackfeet in that party?"

"Blackfeet were they? Oh, perhaps twenty. Young men, all painted up like a bunch of Zulus."

"On horse?"

"Yes, everyone, and most had a spare."

"What did they do?"

"Jolly fellows. I invited them to step down and see my collection. I pulled out my sketches and pressed flowers and notes, and they had a fine time. I made a sketch of one fellow, and he laughed."

"You damn lucky to have your hair," Victoria grumbled.

"Oh, they were perfectly cordial." He touched his breast. "They have good hearts."

"Painted up means they were going to war, Professor," Skye said. "You should learn that."

"We shouldn't be fussbudgets, Mister Skye. Worry, worry, worry, and all that."

Skye listened dourly. He didn't tell Nutmeg that most Indians leave crazy people alone and some even honor them. He and Victoria exchanged glances.

"Here, try this Darjeeling. I've nursed my little canister of it. A fine brew, I'd say."

It did taste good to Skye, even in a tin cup. "Professor, which direction did they go?"

Nutmeg pointed downstream. The Blackfeet were ahead, then, and that was the answer Skye least wanted to hear.

The professor's gray dog settled in the shade, panting slowly. The damned yellow cur sulked just beyond a stone's throw. Skye didn't know how he would catch the thing and fit a harness to it.

"Professor, your dog's starved, and you're surviving on a few berries that won't be here long. Then what?"

"Yes, poor Dolly's having a time of it. Old carcasses, that sort of thing."

"Where are you heading?"

"Vancouver, of course, and on to the coast. Atlantic to Pacific, gathering botanical specimens. I'll sail home. There's Wyeth's brig to go back on, with Captain Lambert, but also Hudson's Bay runs a supply ship out there each year and back to Liverpool."

Skye pondered that. The man would never make it alive to Vancouver unless Wyeth caught up with him.

"I think, mate, that we'd better have a talk," Skye said. It would be irresponsible to leave this man-child here. He would start Nutmeg toward the rendezvous and hope the man survived.

9

The strange Englishman's dog was starving. Victoria wondered whether the man was even aware of it. It lay miserably at the man's feet, its ribs poking out, its flanks caved in and skeletal. It was in worse shape than the yellow dog, which had some ability to fend for itself.

Victoria itched to put an arrow through the mallards or the Canada geese she saw everywhere and feed the meat to the hungry dogs. But she held her peace. She was Skye's woman and Skye did not want her to feed the dogs.

He obviously didn't want to feed the Englishman, either.

"Professor," said Skye, "I think you'd better bloody well turn around. Go back to the rendezvous and find Wyeth. You owe that to him. He's no doubt worried aplenty about you, and it's your responsibility to inform him of your whereabouts just as fast as you can. You've probably delayed him for several days. You just can't do this to a captain of a brigade."

"Well, I'm sorry, but my work engrosses me. I'll just wander along, then. Don't you worry about old Nutmeg."

Skye visibly pushed back the anger percolating through him. "This isn't safe country. You're unarmed and unable to defend yourself even against an animal. I'll give you some parched corn, and any other necessaries you might need, and I insist you turn back and relieve Nat Wyeth of his worries."

"But Mister Skye. That's the wrong direction. I'm heading for the Pacific coast. Wyeth will catch up."

Skye lifted his black top hat and resettled it. "Professor, you have no idea what lies ahead. I do. Here you're in an Eden. But when you reach the Snake, the country'll turn harsh, dry, volcanic, and there won't be fruits and berries hanging from every tree. Then you'll need to cross the Blue Mountains, and there's nothing much in them but pines and dry meadows. Then it gets worse. You'll pass through desert . . ."

"Your dog, it ain't gonna last two days," Victoria added.

Nutmeg gazed mildly at her through his oval gold-rimmed spectacles. "She does all right, don't you think?"

"Look at her," Victoria snapped.

"Yes, yes, but that yellow dog of yours looks just the same."

"It's not ours, mate. It's a stray."

"Well, I see. But I'm traveling west. Suppose I go with you?" He smiled. "Consider me a stray. The world's full of stray dogs."

Skye shook his head. "We're mounted and we're in a hurry. We've business at Fort Vancouver. Sorry, mate."

"But I can keep up."

"Show me your boots."

The Englishman reluctantly pushed his feet forward. Both soles were worn and the uppers were separating from the soles. This man would be barefoot in a little while. Skye shook his head.

"That's one more reason we can't take you. Sorry."

Victoria didn't like this. Why was Skye treating a man from his own nation this way? She arose, angrily. There were moments when Skye angered her, and this was one.

The yellow mutt watched her.

Nutmeg bowed slightly. "Well, I'll just putter along, then. Much to do. This day I've found two subspecies of grass unknown to botany. I plan to publish, you know. Complete notes, dried specimens to take East, sketches . . ."

"Goddam," she snapped, and hiked away from the men. She could not understand white men, and especially Englishmen. She poked along the banks of the placid river until she reached a widening where cattails thickened and the waters scarcely eddied. There she strung her bow, plucked an arrow, and drove it through a Canada goose, which flapped once and lay still in the water. She waded out, retrieved it, freed her arrow with her skinning knife, and shot another goose just as it lifted into flight. This day the starving dogs would get some meat and she would make sure the two Englishmen didn't get a morsel.

Happy at last, she gathered the geese by their necks and trudged back. Skye would glare at her like a thundercloud, but she didn't care. The two men were fussing with their kits. The professor was settling his little canister of tea in his ruck-sack, while Skye was adjusting the pack on the horse.

They paused, watching her enter the shady bower bearing her big geese. Both dogs stood, alert, aquiver.

"Dammit, this is for the dogs. They deserve meat more than you do," she snapped.

"Why, you have given Dolly a little treat," said Nutmeg. "How pleasant. Thank you."

Skye said nothing, his face a mask.

"The Englishman has thanked me," she said to Skye.

The dogs quivered and crawled, but neither pounced. Angrily she plucked feathers by the fistful and singed away the residue in the dying fire, choking on the foul smoke, turning the birds until the coals had reduced them to naked flesh, while the dogs whined. Then she gave one big bird to each mutt. They each nipped at it, tore gently, whined, and finally clamped their paws over the booty and worked flesh loose with their teeth.

Skye's gaze radiated his anger, but she didn't care.

"You have done Dolly a great service, madam. I am in your debt. I shall name a new species after you."

"Sonofabitch."

"I don't know of any such species, but I'll manage the Latin version."

Skye laughed. Something suddenly eased in her big man, and she saw the merriment in his face.

"Professor, if you're going to tag along I can't stop you. But you'll walk along right smartly and not go chasing daisies. Maybe Victoria and I can see you out to Fort Vancouver and maybe we can put some meat in Dolly's paws now and then. But we're going to leave messages for Wyeth. Lots of them. Starting right here."

That was one of those many moments when Victoria loved her man more than she had words to describe. Something passed between them and she knew that everything had been made true and good again.

"Now, there'll be some rules to follow," Skye said. "We've a Blackfoot war party ahead of us and we'll be traveling as silently as we can. I think Victoria can make meat with her arrows. She's a good and quiet hunter. But we're no match for a dozen Blackfeet and our only refuge is to flee, to hide, to make ourselves invisible."

"Oh, Mister Skye, they're fine fellows. You oughtn't worry a bit."

Skye didn't respond. She could see him swallowing back everything that he wanted to say to Nutmeg. Indeed, she would have pitched in with a few words of warning about the Siksika, ancient enemies of her people, but she didn't. There was something in Nutmeg's innocent eyes that showed them how it went with him.

"Before your boots fall off your feet, you let us know. We can patch. Victoria has an awl and plenty of thong and thread. But above all, we can't delay. That's the one thing I must impress upon you." The storms in his eyes passed. "Here we are, a pair of limeys in paradise."

"I say, you have a humor of your own," Nutmeg said.

"You lead the packhorse, Professor, and I'll have Victoria work ahead of us. She'll be our advance scout."

Skye asked the professor for some paper, wrote a note, wrapped it in a patch of greased buckskin, built a low rock cairn smack in the trail, and placed the note under the top rocks.

"We're going to leave more notes for Wyeth," he said. "I still prefer that you go back, but you won't, and I don't have time to argue. Now let's go."

And so they started. The dogs were still gnawing at their feasts, but would catch up soon enough. Victoria urged her pony forward, solemn and alert, watching the way birds flew, listening for unusual silences, studying the air ahead for dust. She saw and heard nothing unusual, but that didn't mean much. A number of unshod ponies had gone by, leaving faint prints in dusty ground, and these she studied as she rode.

From time to time she paused on a slight rise, examining the great basin they were piercing. She knew Skye was suffering. Nutmeg was zigzagging along, veering from tree to plant to brush, pausing to snatch a leaf or a root or a bloom. Whenever Nutmeg fell too far behind, Skye stopped and waited, his body rigid. She could see him admonishing the professor all that afternoon, but little good it did. The naturalist meandered wherever the breezes took him and the wandering was costing time. She knew they would make barely half of their usual distance on this day.

By late afternoon Skye slouched grimly in his saddle, ignoring the professor, his glare restless. She knew he was worried. Nutmeg would slow them so much that they would never reach Vancouver in time. He rode angrily behind her, glaring at the dogs, at the professor, and trying to stay alert to that war party. If they ran into the Siksika they would be in trouble and it would come so swiftly that there would be little they could do. It was not a land where one could hole up and hide.

They were traveling directly over the tracks of the war party, which worried her more and more as the sunny afternoon dragged by. Evening found them at the confluence of Henry's Fork and the Snake, in a broad basin surrounded by distant benches and bluffs. The tracks of the Blackfoot party headed relentlessly down the Snake.

She paused there, waiting for Skye.

He studied the place and nodded. She and Skye and Nutmeg would camp in this area. A cutbank near the river would permit them to build an unseen fire and cook something.

Nutmeg trudged in, his countenance radiating good cheer.

"We're going to stay here tonight," Skye said.

"Capital. I could use a bit of a break and some tea," the professor said. "Are those rascals still ahead of us?"

"Yes," Victoria said. "We're going to scout after sundown and look for a fire. Then we know."

"We could invite the chaps over," the professor said.

Skye looked as if he was about to lecture the man but held his peace. Swiftly he unloaded the panniers and packframe from the packhorse and put the animals on picket lines. The dogs showed up, looking ready for another feast, but Victoria had nothing to offer them.

She built a small cookfire well concealed from view under arching brush that would dissipate the smoke, and boiled more parched corn. They would not risk a shot on meat, so close to a war party that would love nothing more than to torture them all before killing and scalping them.

Skye urged the professor not to talk. There would be time ahead when they could get acquainted.

Nutmeg nodded. He was accepting Skye's direction, which Victoria thought was a good sign.

She had never seen Skye so miserable and she knew every way in which he was suffering.

And then Nutmeg's dog, Dolly, barked.

10

Skye dipped into deep shadow, cursing the dog. Artfully, Victoria doused the small fire, which hissed and spat its defiance and then faded in a cloud of acrid steam.

"Professor, lie quiet and don't talk," Skye whispered in a voice so low it scarcely traveled ten feet. "Hold that dog. Try to keep her from barking."

"The mosquitos are a bit thick," he said.

He was right. A maddening swarm of them whined around them, poking and probing, lancing Skye's neck. It had been a terrible choice for a campsite.

When his eyes had adjusted to the starlight, he studied the surrounding country but spotted nothing. He knew that Victoria, who had better night vision than he, was padding through the area in search of trouble. She was good at this; something in her Absaroka blood had given her the gift.

She slid down beside him a few minutes later.

"Nothing, Skye. The horses aren't interested, either. They ain't making noises. They aren't even staring the same direction."

"His dog's going to get us into grief," he whispered. "Where's the yellow mutt?"

"Keeping silent, Skye. He's a smart one."

"I should shoot the pair of them."

They hugged the ground for another ten minutes, and then Skye rose quietly.

"These mosquitos. We're moving."

"I'm covered with bites, the bloody devils," Nutmeg said.

Mosquitos had been the ruin of many a man trying to hide. He slapped gently at the whining devils that hovered about his ears. The horses were restless, and when Skye ran a hand over them he knew why. He brushed scores of blood-filled mosquitos off their backs. He had chosen the worst possible place to camp and now they were all paying the price.

He was in a black mood he couldn't shake.

He headed for the open and arid benches, hoping to escape the maddening mosquitos. Twenty minutes later, and several hundred feet higher, they were high above the valley.

On the distant western horizon, at a distance hard to calculate, a campfire flickered.

"There," Skye said.

"Sonofabitch Siksika," Victoria growled.

"I hope those chaps don't suffer the way we did," Nutmeg said.

Victoria grunted.

They walked the bench country through thin grasses, lit only by a new moon and starlight, until they found a sheltered bank, a cleft in rock, actually, and paused there. No mosquitos troubled them. Skye picketed the horses on thin grass, hoping they would crop enough of it to fill their bellies, and they unrolled their robes on stony ground.

Dolly panted beside her master. The yellow mutt was nowhere in sight and Skye devoutly hoped that mosquitos had carried him off to dog Valhalla.

This wasn't so bad. No mosquitos. Absolutely barren approaches in every direction. He knew where the war party had settled for the night. He was hungry, and so were the rest, but they wouldn't cook this night. A night without food would darken his mood even more.

Angrily, he dug out some jerky, one of few pieces he had collected at rendezvous. Jerky never satisfied hunger and usually made it worse.

"Professor," Skye said, "I'm going to give you a piece of jerky. Keep it in your pocket. When Dolly looks ready to bark, stuff jerky in her face. We'd be in trouble now if those Blackfeet were crowding us."

"Why, certainly, but she gave us a warning, didn't she?"

"A false one, and she gave us away."

Slowly, he relaxed. They were safe enough here. The animals were watered. A clean breeze filtered through his buckskins and cooled his bitten flesh. His mood lifted a bit; it always did sooner or later.

Victoria quietly scraped out the cookpot, whose contents had doused the fire, while the professor settled himself against the rock. He dug for his briar pipe, but Skye stayed him. "No, not a match, not a flame," he said.

"It is my one small pleasure," Nutmeg said, desolately.

"Friends of mine have gotten themselves killed for less."

"I should like to be a noncombatant in these wars," the professor said. "Is there no signal I can give them, or sign or banner, that will tell these people I mean them not the slightest harm?"

"No. The best bet is a gift of tobacco. We always carry a few plugs. It's a peace offering."

"I wish to enlist them in a great enterprise," the professor said. "They could all be valuable to me. Would you help?"

Skye peered into the night, listening intently to soft sounds on the wind. "Maybe I can, Professor."

"Well, you see, sir, here's an entire continent whose

flora and fauna are almost unknown. Imagine it: a land larger than western Europe, and science knows very little. Back in Philadelphia, my former colleague, Professor Barton, showed me an armadillo. What an amazing creature. I'd never seen or heard of such a thing. I knew instantly what my life work would be.

"Now, imagine it. I couldn't cover this continent in ten lifetimes, and yet I'm committed to a project so grand that I must find the means. I'm not alone, of course. Our fellow Englishman John Bradbury has taken up the work, too, a most admirable and intrepid soul, who lets nothing, neither disease nor storm nor hostile natives nor disaster stay him. He's sent hundreds of species to the Liverpool Botanical Gardens, you know. I only hope, sir, that I may in some pale way emulate so great a soul."

Skye marveled that a man's passion could lead him into such dangerous corners of the world and render him almost oblivious to that danger.

"Some tribes might help, Professor. Not all."

"Well, sir, the Indians could be my salvation. Tell them that I want at least one of everything that grows, small enough for me to sketch, and to dry between papers. Tell them that I need to know the exact habitat, high or low, moist or dry . . ."

Skye was skeptical. "Unless you know their tongue, you won't get what you want."

"But surely there are translators?"

"Very few. Some French Canadians know Indian tongues, and have intermarried with them."

"Then I must find some!"

"And would you employ them?"

"Oh, I haven't a pence with me. But once they see the importance of this work, the majesty of it, surely they'll bend the oar . . ."

Skye was reluctant to say what he thought. He was still bleak of mind, worried about the delays this man would cause him, worried about shepherding a fool another five hundred miles. This man's passion and dreams towered higher than those of ordinary mortals, and no practical matters would curb his mania. He didn't want to help this impossible man, but he had to.

Things puzzled Skye. "Professor, where's the rest of your collection?"

"Why, sir, back with Wyeth. He'll bring it along. I've a packmule with him, and I'm already running out of room. We'll find another mule, eh? Maybe I could buy yours. I'd like to stay right here. Hardly scratched the surface. We'll meet in Fort Vancouver or some place. Wyeth's going to ship everything."

Skye wondered if the professor had absorbed anything Skye tried to teach him.

"Have you a family, Professor? A wife? Children?"

Nutmeg sighed, happily. "Yes, the old dear. But this is my whole life, Mister Skye, my contribution to human knowledge. I hope to organize and publish in between expeditions. And you, sir. Have you an enterprise?"

"No, nothing except surviving."

"A pity. A good man like you could serve king and country most admirably."

"My dreams are small, Professor. Once they were large, before the Royal Navy robbed me of a life. But yes, I do have a passion. A chance to go home. We're going to see about it. Hudson's Bay is clearing the way for me. My father lives. I yearn to see him while I can; see the old man who remembers only the boy, the pale student. He won't recognize me, sir. Not at all.

"I'll walk into his parlor and he'll think me a tradesman or some such, and I'll tell him who I am, and we'll not say much, not at first, but I know just how it'll be. He'll stare. And I'll be ill-at-ease there, with my wife beside me, and it'll be like a glacier thawing, but then the water's going to flow, Professor."

"That's your goal, then?"

"I didn't know how much England meant to me until I was offered it once again."

"But that's not a goal. You must join me. You and your savage, you come help me. I'll arrange a few dollars if I can from the American Philosophical Society, and then we three'll go on a little field trip across the continent. I want to do a southern trip next, and especially a trip to those deserts of Mexico. Frightful succulents there, you know. Simply frightful. I must dig them up and send them East. I need a strong man built like an ox. This is a work of such importance, such magnitude, such seriousness, that I must have all the help I can manage."

Skye shook his head. "My goals are smaller, Professor. I would give all I possess just to see my family, even for one hour."

Mister Skye turned away from the conversation, his mood so low he couldn't stand another word.

11

The Skyes visibly relaxed when the hoofprints of the Blackfoot war party veered into a ford of the Snake River and death went with it. Just to make sure, Skye forded the river himself, swimming his saddlehorse a few yards to cross a channel, but otherwise walking through shallows. The party, he reported, had headed south toward the Bear River.

"That's how it goes, Professor," he explained. "Most of the time you never see them but you know they're nearby."

"Well, those chaps didn't harm me," Nutmeg said. He privately believed the Skyes' caution was exaggerated and he was growing impatient with them.

They hiked along the Snake, entering a volcanic and arid land. Nutmeg devoted himself to new species he was finding everywhere: a new prickly pear, a new shortgrass, two new sagebrush variations. One of these, which he named *Artemisia tridentata*, he found on the river benches. The new prickly pear he called *Opuntia fragilis* because its lobes fell off so easily. All these he sketched, regretting that he lacked the space to send whole samples back to the American Philosophical Society in Philadelphia.

The Skyes kept pressing him to hurry, but they simply

didn't understand. What he was doing was timeless. Why couldn't they accommodate him?

He felt he was scarcely touching the surface: he ought to be capturing every bug and snake and bird, too, but the Skyes were always pressuring him to hasten. He always agreed to, but then he would discover new things and lose track of time. He roved far from the riverbank trail and his collection bag swelled with divers species, and he sketched furiously, ignoring the dark looks emanating from his trail companions.

This was a harsh land, but it lured him into its wastes with the promise of discovery. Finding something new! He was treading where no naturalist had gone! Was ever there a more joyous occupation? How could he resist when every leaf was a bonanza? Every creek and trail leading out of it seemed to head for cool mountains, forested slopes, and lush meadows, and a dozen new species.

Twice he had strayed far away from the riverbank trail, and Skye had come after him, finding him miles from the river. His guide rebuked him gently, stressing the importance of staying together and never losing sight of one another. And each time, Nutmeg earnestly agreed to be more considerate of his companions. But the whole business, which kept repeating itself, was demeaning. Must he always apologize?

Skye was having trouble subsisting his entourage, and things worsened when game vanished. Nutmeg saw not an antelope, deer, bear, or any other creature larger than a marmot. His dog starved again even though the Skyes did their best, occasionally downing a mud hen or killing a snake. The yellow mutt trailed behind distrustfully, in perpetual sorrow for intruding where he wasn't wanted, and Nutmeg wondered why it was still following the Skyes.

Nutmeg was not a young man, but he brimmed with vigor and the joy of his quest. Behind him, in Boston, his American wife Hattie lived quite alone, though she didn't lack the companionship of faculty wives at Harvard College. She had gotten used to his wanderings, good old sport was she, and resigned herself to a life less domestic than she had hoped for. He occasionally felt a bit guilty about that, but not very. His great North American botanical catalog was the important thing. She understood perfectly, but so far he had not been able to bring the Skyes to the same frame of mind.

The evenings were better. He had come to cherish those campfire times when Skye and Victoria relaxed a bit and even allowed themselves a conversation. Victoria fascinated him: he had never met a woman of such contrasts: fierce, warm, suspicious, generous, loving, savage in her feelings toward other tribes. He learned swiftly to avoid the slightest condescension toward her or Skye, because she responded explosively.

Skye proved to be reticent at first, but Nutmeg drew the man's story out of him. The wretch had been caught by a press gang on the East End, near the London Dock at Wapping, within hailing distance of his father's brick warehouse. His father, it seemed, was an importer of tea, coffee, and spices and an exporter of finished cottons, linen, and Wedgwood. The East End whelped hooligans, and press gangs commonly roved the crowded, crabbed alleys snatching up young billies for service in the Royal Navy. But when they caught Skye, they nabbed a youth who was destined for Cambridge and eventually a vocation in a large merchant firm.

"After that, Professor, it was war. I tried to get word out to my family, fought everyone and everything, got a reputation so bad they wouldn't let me on deck in port because they knew they'd never see me again. I stopped just short of mutiny. That would have been the end of me. They had a way of dealing with a rebel, you know. Tie him in the rigging under the bowsprit and give him a knife to cut himself loose when he can't stand it any more."

Skye told him about his escape after seven years of perdition, and his desperate flight up the Columbia, hounded by the Royal Navy and Hudson's Bay.

"And now you're going straight back? To Fort Vancouver?"

"That's right. It's a risk, but a chance to clear my name and see my family and rejoin the country of my birth. To England I was born, and to England I must return."

Thus did Nutmeg acquire a good grasp of the young man's life, and the more he heard, the more he marveled at Skye.

"I'm going home, sir, but not for long. I'll soon enough have my fill of Fishmonger's Hall and Westminster, and the swans on the Thames, and then I'll sail back and work for the company I once hated so much I spent my hours plotting its ruin in North America. This is all the doing of John McLoughlin, sir. He's a mountain of a man, both physically and mentally, and he took an interest in me."

"So I've heard. But why do you trust him?"

"By his reputation, sir. He is known in the mountains, and there's not a Yank at the rendezvous who doesn't admire him."

"Then you've put your trust in a good man. We must trust; not to trust, not to have faith, is the doom of many a good soul."

Some evenings Nutmeg deliberately focused on Victoria, but she was shy as a field mouse around him and regarded him as some sort of rival, taking Skye into realms of science and white men's learning of which she hadn't the faintest comprehension. But his patience eventually prevailed, and she warmed to him.

She had taken over the task of feeding Dolly and that strange yellow mutt, and that was no easy burden in a land increasingly harsh and volcanic. Yet, by day's end, she usually had speared or shot some sort of vile meat: snakes, fowl, lizards, hares, chucks, once a kit fox, once a wounded coyote, and these morsels she divided between the dogs.

Skye had stopped trying to chase off the yellow dog even though he ritually warned Victoria that the miserable beast would get them into trouble.

"He's a spirit-dog," was all she ever said, and that shut him up properly.

"When we get to Fort Vancouver, that's the end of him," he grumbled. "He does nothing but exploit you. At least Dolly, there, carries a pack for the professor. But that ribby devil's nothing more than a parasite, taking what it can and giving nothing. I've met a few men in the mountains like that and usually they don't last long or win any friends. I've seen trapping brigades drive such men out."

"He's looking out for us," she insisted.

"He'll betray us," he retorted.

Then one day the yellow dog went hunting and returned dragging a three-month-old antelope it had killed up on a bench somewhere above the Snake. This he laid at Victoria's feet, circling wide around Skye, who watched hard-eyed and cold.

The ugly, battle-scarred mutt had not ripped one bite out of the antelope but presented it whole to the Crow woman.

She lifted her arms skyward and sang a warbling song of thanksgiving and praise, her back arched, her fingertips touching the sky, and Nutmeg knew she was blessing the yellow cur and thanking her gods.

Then she reached out to touch the mutt, but it crabbed back violently and watched her with unblinking brown eyes.

They were camping in a wash draining out of the north, with a few scrub cottonwoods in it and she hung the baby antelope from a limb and butchered it. Nutmeg doubted that there was more than ten pounds of usable meat in it. Victoria first fed the yellow dog, cutting prime flank meat for him, and then gave Dolly a good feed, and finally cooked the last of it for the three mortals present at that campfire.

That night the mutt wiggled closer to the camp than it had ever done before. Dolly drifted over for a sniff and the two didn't fight, so Nutmeg let them make their rapprochement. The Skyes had, willy-nilly, acquired a dog. That amused the professor. Skye was a force of nature, but he proved to be the loser of this contest.

As the August days and weeks rolled by uneventfully except for an odd storm that boiled out of the north, an idea began to take form in Professor Nutmeg's mind. The more he shaped it and tested it and argued it, the better he liked it.

"Mister Skye," he said. "I've been observing you almost as closely as I've been observing the flora and fauna here. I hope you don't mind. What I see is just the sort of man and woman I need as assistants. You are naturalists without even knowing it. I have a great enterprise before me, and need help. I think I can arrange some funds from the estate of my friend Smithson. What I propose, sir, is that you become my guides and assistants. Together, sir, we shall advance science."

Skye stared at him, and then at unseen shores.

12

Skye did not say no, although that was what he was thinking.

All that remained of the fire was a circle of embers and an occasional sniff of acrid cottonwood smoke. Below, trapped in a dark deep canyon, the Snake was sawing through volcanic rock. It was like the river of his own life, trapped between walls of black rock. He did not like this country. He didn't much care for the west slope of the Rockies, or the arid lands stretching to the coastal ranges.

The yellow mutt was out patrolling, sniffing the night winds, and Skye grudgingly admitted to himself that maybe the thing was performing a service after all.

"You're a man of exceptional ability," Nutmeg said. "I saw that at once. Your American friends saw it, too, and promoted you. Hudson's Bay Company sees it, and wants you. It's gone to great lengths to get you.

"You have intelligence and will and courage. There's nothing to stop you if you wish to make something of your life. The Royal Navy only delayed the bloom. I suppose what I'm doing here is lifting your sights a bit. Showing you what lies beyond your horizons.

"I have a grand passion, the botanical cataloging of this continent. I lecture at Harvard as a means to stay here, take time off now and then to plunge in again. But as hard as I might struggle, I'll achieve in my lifetime only a fraction of what needs doing. I've been looking for a man to follow me; a man I can train in the field, an intelligent man, able and strong. A man to continue when I no longer can. I've been watching you, Mister Skye, and I think you're the chap."

"I'm not educated."

"Oh, yes you are. You're a man acquainted with books, comfortable with ideas, but practical. You'll take over from me some day, sir, and there'll be some royal recognition: Order of the Garter, maybe knighthood. You have all that in you, and all it takes is a nudge from someone to awaken you to it."

Skye eyed Victoria, her face lit by the last orange glow of the coals, caught in a darkness of knowledge. She sat cross-legged beside him, listening to things of which she had no grasp. There were chasms between her world and the world Nutmeg was opening to them around a faltering fire this nippy August night. He wondered whether she could bridge that chasm. Whether she would be miserable in England and pine away until she died. For now, she was keeping silent. Sometime soon she would pepper questions at him, but he knew he couldn't really explain much to a woman who had never seen a white man's city and could not grasp what lay within a library.

"All that's fine, Professor," he said. "But not bloody likely."

He deliberately used the vulgarity to emphasize the gulf that lay between them. Professor Nutmeg seemed to ignore it, but Skye knew he had drawn the linguistic line between the professor's gentility and whatever it was that Skye had become.

Nutmeg shifted to another tack. "You know, my friend, I need someone to keep me out of trouble. Botany is my passion, and I sometimes forget all else and ignore the dangers of the wilds, and the tribesmen, and the weather. That's why I need you. It's a blindness in me. You're an experienced man in this unsettled land, but at the same time you've a keen intelligence and a grasp of what I'm about.

"I think I can get some funds. My old friend James Smithson died a few years ago, and gave his considerable fortune to his nephew. But he also gave me a letter urging the nephew, Henry Hungerford, to fund any worthwhile project. Quite a man, Smithson. Oxford, best chemist and mineralogist in Europe. A passion for science."

Skye did not share that passion, nor did he intend to work for any man without wilderness sense. He would make a poor botanist, anyway. He was not a sorter by nature, nor a collector, nor organizer. The things that awakened his interests were more spiritual and even aesthetic. There had been sunrises, quiet and still and sublime, that he would never forget, craggy mountain prospects that were etched in his soul, moments when he sensed he was not alone and not abandoned, and seemed to hike effortlessly a foot above the earth. He hadn't a single file drawer in his mind, but sometimes he had a yen to paint. Could he ever capture the ephemera of the wilds on canvas?

"I appreciate your interest, mate," he rumbled. "I've other plans. Visit my family, then come back here and work for a fur company. That's what I want to do."

Nutmeg absorbed that for a moment. "If you should change your mind . . ."

"Time to crawl between my robes," Skye said.

They began their evening ritual. Nutmeg always unrolled blankets at some distance from the Skyes—too far, Skye thought, but it was a sensitive gesture. This man was not so naive after all. Skye and Victoria were given the privacy they sometimes needed. Dolly had taken to shuttling from one bed to the other, and sometimes Skye found himself pinned in, or the dog lying on his ever-ready Hawken beside him. The yellow cur never came close.

There was no such thing as safety in the wilds, and Skye slept lightly, a part of his mind sorting out the faint night-whispers.

Victoria said nothing. Tomorrow, when Nutmeg drifted out of earshot in hot pursuit of a burning bush or the Ten Commandments graven on a petal, she would approach Skye crossly, wrestling with the pain of her ignorance and afraid of losing him if he drifted back to his own world. And then he would reassure her that he had no plan to do that.

Nutmeg's proposition intrigued him. There was an income in it; a sense of building something enduring. But he would probably commit to Hudson's Bay Company. He tossed in his blankets, knowing that the matter would not be settled until he had a long talk with the most formidable man in the Northwest, Dr. McLoughlin.

"You gonna do this?" Victoria whispered.

"I'm thinking on it."

"I don't know what the hell he's talking about."

"You'd pick it up fast in London."

"You do what you want. White man things. Maybe I'll go visit my family."

Maybe she should. Maybe this would tear them apart. Their union might work in the wilderness, but would it survive in London? She would be treated as a great curiosity. She might have trouble finding friends there. On the other hand, maybe she would take London by storm. The trappers loved her; why not Englishmen? After he had completed his service to Hudson's Bay, would she enjoy life in London, his home but not hers?

The more he wrestled with it all, the more perplexed he became. Go back to the world he knew, and work as a trapper? Victoria would be happiest if he did that. Work for Hudson's Bay? He could do that. She wouldn't like it much. Work for Nutmeg? She would soon find herself excluded no matter how hard Skye tried to draw her into the botany.

He had no answers and no wisdom to help him along. He'd never had an employment opportunity before; years of slavery aboard ships of war, then working in a trapping brigade, glad to find some way to feed and shelter himself. Now he felt bewildered.

"You gonna flop around like a fish on the grass or let me sleep?"

"Stuff on my mind."

"You want what I think?"

"Yes."

She didn't answer, but instead pulled herself close to him, and he felt her arms draw him tight, and then he felt her cheek and it was wet.

"You go home," she said. "You're a man with no people. I got people, everyone else got people. You got to go back to the people who make you."

She was offering herself, and their love, as a sacrifice to him. He had no response except to hug her back. What she said was true. He needed his people. He desperately wanted to see his father. He was curious about that. What was his father like now? He remembered a demanding man who didn't have enough time for a boy; a man sometimes testy and usually kinder to his sisters than to him. He remembered being anxious to please his father, and a little afraid, and often feeling he never could win the man's esteem.

But he also remembered his father's confidence in him, and the paternal gaze that rested upon him with pride. His father had not been a harsh man, but not given to much affection, either. Now Skye was a man, inured to hardship, independent, bruised by a painful life. He would be a man visiting a man, not a dutiful son visiting a father . . .

"You're right," he said. "A man needs a country."

He felt the hotness of her tears on his stubbled cheek and knew her anguish. She felt out of place in his world, the world of the English, the people across the Great Waters to the east. She understood the gulf and was immolating herself and her love so that he might return to his home.

"Come with me and see my country," he said. "They'll not be friendly, but your people weren't very friendly to me. That's how the world works. Remember how it was for me in Rotten Belly's village?"

"Yes," she said. Skye had been scorned by most, and derided by the young warriors. Only an old shaman granted him any honor.

"It'll be like that for you."

"I'll go to this England if you want me to," she whispered.

The mutt had crept close, watching in the murky darkness, irritating Skye. Then it growled, so low that Skye could barely hear its throaty menace.

"Sonofabitch," Victoria said, throwing off the four-point blanket.

"What?" said Skye, irked at the dog for wrecking this moment.

Victoria grabbed her bow and strung it with one swift flex. Then she snatched an arrow from her quiver.

The mutt growled again.

"Goddammit, get up, Skye!"

He wallowed around, finding his sheathed Hawken, and extracted it. Damned yellow dog, starting a ruckus.

He heard a swift confusion of sound, a low voice, the snort of nervous horses, and then the sharp clatter of hooves. Skye sprang up, checked the load on his Hawken, peered into a thick gloom looking for a target.

The rattle of hooves diminished. The horses were running straight back from the river and into the arid benches to the north.

He ran after them, seeing nothing but smelling the dust driven into the air by the hooves.

Some damned Indians had stolen the horses. He had watered them and then picketed them on some good bunch grass not ten yards from their camp. He found the place and found the butts of the picket ropes, which had been cut.

"What was all that, eh?" asked Nutmeg.

"Horses gone," Skye said.

"Stolen?"

"They didn't walk off by themselves."

"Long walk to Fort Vancouver," Nutmeg said.

"I'll get our horses back," Skye said. He had done it before and he would do it again. And maybe in ways that would shock the genteel professor.

13

Skye plucked up the Hawken. The sooner he started after the thieves, the better.

"Who were they?" Nutmeg asked.

"Any damned one," Skye replied. "This is Shoshone country. But this river, it could be anyone. Who knows?"

Angrily he scanned the skies, seeing a quarter moon dodging silver-edged clouds. It wasn't the blackest of nights, but there wasn't enough moonlight to help him. It would be too gloomy to see hoofprints, moccasin prints, or much of anything else. He would have to track the thieves mostly by intuition and smell. Horses left an acrid odor and manure behind them.

He reckoned it was still three hours to dawn.

"I'll go with you," Nutmeg volunteered.

"Professor, this is war. Stealing horses is a way of fighting enemies. You'd better let me handle it."

"How can one man deal with a war party?"

"I'll never know until I see what I'm up against."

"If you can't recover the nags, you'll not get to Fort Vancouver in time."

"Not before that ship sails," Skye said.

He watched Victoria tug the pack and gear under the lip of the ledge behind their camp. She would stay and take care of Nutmeg and guard their gear. She would know how to hide herself and Nutmeg if she had to.

She turned to Skye, saying nothing, and touched his hand. That was her goodbye and blessing. They had long since come to the point where they didn't need to say much to each other. He couldn't tell her when he would be back. The thieves were only a few minutes ahead, but on horse, and minutes could be an eternity.

"Professor, if Victoria asks you to do something, you do it. She'll try to keep you safe."

"Oh, I'll just be collecting samples."

Skye's response was sharp. "If she says you can, mate."

There was no answer. He hiked into the gloom, across arid benchland on the right bank of the Snake, directed more by intuition than sign. He would heed the old tracker's wisdom: if there was no sign to guide you, think about where your quarry is going and head that way. Distant in the moonlight was a vague notch. He would go there.

A mile out, he discovered the yellow mutt dragging along behind. A rage built in him and he hunted for rocks to throw, but he knew there was nothing he could do. The hound would simply follow just out of range of his arm. He knew he ought to be grateful: the damned dog had furtively awakened him, growling in his ear instead of barking, and that had given Skye the warning he should have heeded. But he couldn't bring himself to thank the miserable cur.

It would be tough without horses. He'd walked before and would walk again. But being put afoot by some damned savages in some damned wilderness, and being forced to abandon the gear needed to survive—that was hell.

He trudged quietly through the pillowed darkness while the pale moon swung lower in the sky, and vanished behind the drifting night-clouds now and then, plunging him into utter gloom. Still he persevered, fueled by his own fury.

After an hour he struck lava country and knew that unless he was careful, the knife-edged stone would slice his moccasins to bits. But he was hiking along a dry watercourse that had butchered its way through the black rock that tumbled upward on both sides of him, the jumbled volcanic debris spearing the black sky.

This was ambush country, and Skye began to sweat. One warrior with a bow and arrow could wipe out pursuit. He wondered whether he would die suddenly in this remote place, his body never to be found by his wife or anyone else.

But he abolished the thought from mind. He was frightened, yes, but he harnessed his fear to good purpose, studying the jumble of rock, his senses so whetted that he could almost peer around the next bend. He would not be a coward, dying a thousand times before his death.

The cur stayed ten yards ahead. Skye raged at the mutt. The yellow dog would find something, bark, and give Skye away. Once in a while the dog paused, sniffed, and slowly slinked forward. He wasn't a proper dog, slinking like some back-alley thug. He was a sneaking, rotten dog, ugly and scarred, with no manners. Skye knew he could probably kill the stalking animal with one good toss of his Bowie knife, but he didn't do that, either.

He was on the right trail; that's all he knew. The acrid smell that hung in that watercourse, and the occasional manure, told him that.

The eastern skies began to stitch threads of light, and Skye reckoned he had walked five miles. It would be a long hike home if he didn't recover his nags. He was sorry to see daylight, which dashed his hope of sneaking into the Indian camp, finding his ponies and sneaking out with them under the cover of darkness. He persevered, wanting a drink and a rest, but knowing that his quarry might be fleeing even faster than he was chasing.

The yellow mutt paused, sniffed, sprinted ahead, turned

to watch Skye, and vanished from sight. Skye found him ahead, low on the ground, his tail slathering across clay, his nose pointed. This time the mutt didn't bound forward. Skye took that for a caution, and peered around a black rock, discovering a sort of grassy park of several acres where the lava flows had parted. He spotted the dull forms of perhaps twenty horses. His would be among them.

Smart dog.

At first he saw no one, but then, on closer study as the light quickened, he saw several bedrolls and two men sitting up, staring at nothing. Cautiously Skye examined the scene. The men were gathered around a vegetated hollow, probably with a spring supplying water. The dim bulks of the horses ghosted over the grass. He could not tell his from the others.

The mutt whined, but so quietly Skye knew the sound did not carry. Maybe that verminous creature had some sense after all. Skye hunted for an upstream exit. If this was a widening in a watercourse, there would be a gulch stretching toward the distant mountains. He did not see it at first, which worried him. Under siege, these warriors would flee upslope, pushing their ponies before them.

Then things were taken out of his hands. The mutt slithered into the park, heading toward the ponies. Skye wished he could shoot the damned thing. The critter was going to stir up the horses, which Skye didn't want at all. Yet he was powerless to stop what a small canine brain had set in motion. Skye did slip into the park, and drifted to one side of the gulch leading back to the Snake. If the mutt was going to stir trouble, maybe the milling horses would head for the river if he didn't block the way.

It occurred to him that maybe he could turn all this to his advantage, but he hated like the devil to admit it. The slithering dog caught the eye of a horse, which stared at it. The dog bounded a few paces and halted. The mutt was not headed into the horses, but past them, to the upper end of the park. Could it be that this dog was a natural herder, getting around behind the animals?

Skye marveled.

Then one of the savages shouted.

"El coyote! Cuidado!"

Men bounded up, grabbing their rifles. The horses stirred.

These were not savages, but Mexicans, and they were about to shoot the yellow mutt.

"Alto ahi!" Skye bellowed. They turned and stared. Some swung their rifles toward him.

The trouble was, he didn't know more than a dozen Spanish words, and now he was in a jackpot. He ran straight toward them, his big Hawken leveled, and began yelling.

"I'm getting my horses back, and I'll kill the first man that moves," he roared, not knowing or caring whether they understood him. One lifted his rifle but found himself facing the huge bore of the Hawken, and lowered it.

"You stole my nags. Go ahead and try to kill me; one of you'll die and maybe more before you get me," he rumbled.

They spread, making themselves less a target. The yellow dog was cutting through the dancing horses now, nipping at the flanks of one of them, dodging the kicks.

"Drop your rifles and raise your hands," he roared, swinging toward one Mexican whose hands were busy.

They didn't.

Skye didn't stop moving, but circled closer to them, proddy and dangerous. He had caught them in a sleepy moment, but they were gathering their wits.

"I'm getting my horses, and whoever stops me is a goner," he roared.

Keep talking, keep them from doing anything.

One older man raised an arm. "Senor, I talk."

"Tell them I'm taking my ponies. If they try to stop me, they're dead."

He had, for the moment, the upper hand. He faced four Mexicans.

He risked a glance at the yellow mutt, which had cut out two of Skye's horses and started them south. But the rest milled. He marveled at the dog.

There was no need to shout any more and addressed the one who knew a little English. "Go get my other one. If you do, no one gets hurt."

"That is a dog of many wonders, Mister Skye."

Skye turned sharply. "How do you know my name?"

The man shrugged. "Everyone knows the man in the black hat. Mister Skye is the greatest of names." He turned to the others. "Senor Skye," he said. "Senor Skye." Then back to Skye. "We did not know it was you, friend. Come sit with us and we will talk, eh? We are *hermanos*, brothers, from Taos, Nuevo Méjico, and we have come to make our fortune, eh? Gold, silver, beaver, horses, who knows? You do us honor with a visit."

"How do you know me?"

"In the winters, the Yankee trappers stay with us in Taos and you are spoken of."

Skye watched the yellow mutt cut the last of Skye's horses and start it south.

He lowered the Hawken.

14

So they knew him. Skye glowed. His fame as a mountaineer had traveled even to Mexico. He had worked
long and hard for the fur company, done well, and now
he was known as a good man.

But then his glow vanished.

They were laughing, the bores of their big dragoon re-
volvers pointing at him, their eyes lit with glee.

"Ah, Senor Skye, it is so, you are a great hombre. And
now we will honor you. Ah, it is pleasure to honor so great
an hombre. In all the world, under heaven above, there is
not so great a man as *Meester* Skye. This we hear from
Christopher Carson and other Yanqui *hombres grandes*
who live among us."

Skye debated swinging his Hawken upward and shooting the man. But not for long. Three big pistols and a venerable fowling piece would make a swift end of him. His
skin crawled. Rarely had he looked into the black muzzle of a loaded firearm, and the sight of four such bores
pointing at his chest catapulted his pulse and squeezed
his throat.

"You will do us the honor of dropping your Hawken,
very very carefully, to the groun', si?"

Skye did as he was told. At least they weren't shooting

at him. He trembled so much he could not control the spasms in his hands.

"Now, the powder horn, si?"

Skye lifted the horn and deposited it on the grass. It was a beauty, with an ornate box that held his caps.

"Ah, muchas gracias, Senor Skye. This is to pay for your horses. You have bought them back from us, did you know that? A fair trade. One fine rifle for tres caballos. Our papa, he says, there is wealth everywhere. Go get the riches and bring them to me. Make us *ricos grandes*. So, my brothers, we go get the riches. He is right. They are everywhere. Now we will be the envy of Taos, si?"

"You letting me go?"

"It is an honor to meet the mountaineer. Shall we kill you? Only if you are foolish, amigo. Go. You have your horses, we have a fine Hawken, made in St. Louis, the rifle that puts a ball right in the center. Ah, half of Nuevo Méjico would sell their souls to el Diablo for that rifle."

Skye scarcely dared to turn his back, knowing these brigands might have one final surprise for him. But it mattered little whether they shot him from front or rear, so he retreated.

They were silent.

He rounded the bend and smelled the dust raised by his horses.

Shame swept over him. He had succumbed to his own vanity. All they had to do was flatter him, crudely and grossly, and he had lowered his guard. Sugared words. He had heard few of those in his life; not once in the navy had anyone praised him. And his father had not been one to commend him. Only among the Yank trappers had he heard a word about his worth.

He vowed that, if he lived, he would never be tricked again, and the flattery of others would never be of consequence to him for as long as he survived. Rarely did anyone have a second chance in the famous college of the

Rocky Mountains, as his trapper friends called it. He counted this as a lesson learned, and a lesson he would never forget.

He rounded a bend in the black rock and breathed easier. They had had their fun, humiliated a gringo, and let him go. But he was unarmed and facing hundreds of miles of travel.

He walked quietly, knowing the horses were ahead, herded by the yellow cur. He owed that mutt his loyalty. The mutt was more dog than he had supposed.

He focused on the good things. He had the horses. They could ride and pack. Victoria was a gifted hunter, and she had a dozen deadly arrows in her quiver. They would be traveling among friendly tribes and could barter for food.

The August heat rose, and he was parched, but there would be no water anywhere on that long dry gulch. But by the time the sun reached its zenith he would be back in camp, explaining to Victoria his humiliation. He resolved not to hide it. There had never been anything hidden between them, including his defeats.

He walked another mile, abraded by the reproach of his soul, and then came upon the horses, which stood somnolently while the panting dog lay in the dry gulch. The mutt did not rise at his approach. He wondered if he could catch a horse and ride it barebacked. The horses were haltered, but he had nothing with which to make some reins. He could not control his saddler, but it had no place to go but forward, hemmed on both sides by jagged volcanic rock.

He owed the dog something.

"You're better than I allowed," he said. "Like Victoria says, you're looking after me."

The dog stared but made no move toward him. And he feared he'd be bitten hard if he tried to pet the dog. It lay there, sinister, yellow, scarred, vicious, slackjawed, and stupid, except that it wasn't stupid. It had its own approach to life, its ways, and they had kept it alive.

He wondered if his big spotted horse would let him get on, and eased slowly toward it, watching the beasts sidle away from him. But he talked quietly, finally grabbed the halter and tugged the horse toward some rock that would help him mount. The horse obliged him.

It stood quietly while he clambered up the jagged rock and then slid a leg over its hot back. Moments later he was seated, nervous because he had little control. But the yellow dog was on his feet again.

Skye tapped his moccasin heels into the side of the horse, and it walked forward. The dog didn't need to herd the others; they followed naturally.

And so he rode back to camp, relieved not to walk, feeling better because he had gotten his horses.

As he approached the sunken river, which slashed this land into north and south, he found Victoria and Professor Nutmeg nestled under an overhanging slab of rock back from the well-used trail along the north bank. She watched him come in, her gaze surveying the horses and then watching the yellow hound.

Skye slid off, landing awkwardly, while Victoria bridled the horses.

Nutmeg handed him a water flask, and Skye drank greedily.

"They took my rifle," he said.

"Who?" Victoria asked.

"Mexicans from Taos."

"But you got the horses."

"The dog did."

Her eyes lit. "It is as I said."

"You'll have to make meat."

"The dog will feed us."

"I've got to tell you something. I let the Mexicans trick me, Victoria. They told me I was a great man and invited me to sit and visit."

She eyed him solemnly. "I will not condemn you. You are a great one among the trappers. You have not heard this with your own ears. But it is said of you everywhere. The Absaroka know it. My people respect you. The white men I talk to, they know it. So now the stories about you have flown to Taos, in Mexico. That is not bad. It is good. I am proud to be your woman."

He peered at her, amazed.

She busied herself with the horses again. "We are three now. You, me, and the dog."

He peered at the beast, which lay panting again.

"Let's go down to the river, fella," he said.

This time the dog followed him as he descended a steep and treacherous path that took him to the swift-flowing Snake. The mutt lapped the water and then waded into the current. Skye knelt, drank again, sloshed water over his stubbled face, and drank once more.

The dog swam to the bank, clambered up the muck slope, and shook himself.

A bond had been forged. Skye settled himself quietly beside the river and the dog wiggled toward him in short bursts, ever ready to bolt. Skye dared not reach out and kept his big, blunt-fingered hands to himself.

"I owe you," Skye said.

This earned him the first, tentative switch of the dog's scruffy tail.

The dog wiggled closer and Skye knew that this was a long delayed but important moment in the lives of each of them. He eased his hand outward, palm up. The dog squirmed closer and sniffed it. Then, tentatively, the dog licked Skye's hand. The tongue rasped over his flesh and Skye made himself hold still.

"I guess I have a dog in my family," he said.

The dog edged closer and sniffed Skye's moccasins, buckskins, back, and shirt. Skye glanced behind him and discovered Victoria watching from the bank high above.

Then her face vanished. She was leaving this rapprochement to Skye and the dog.

Skye studied the mutt. Its ears had been chewed on. Its face bore scars, so many they formed almost a hatchwork of ridged flesh. One eyelid drooped. There were patches of hair missing, bare gray hide poking through its abused torso.

He scarcely dared move his hand for fear the ugly thing would bite it off. But tentatively he did, slowly, letting the dog see every move in advance. Once the dog went rigid and Skye retreated, but after a moment Skye's hand was running down the dog's neck and over his back.

The cur growled and Skye retreated. That was enough for one day. His hand was still intact.

They clambered up the steep slope together.

"What you gonna name the damned dog?" Victoria asked.

"What do you think?"

"I don't know. He's your dog. You name him." She sounded testy.

"You've domesticated the dog?" Nutmeg asked. "Ah, he and Dolly are a match. You need a name for him."

"I don't have a name," Skye said, irked. "He's just a bloody ugly dog."

"He will tell you his name," Victoria said. "He is a spirit-dog, and his name is secret. But you will get it in a dream. Or maybe a vision quest."

Skye grunted. He didn't put much stock in all that.

"Let's move. We've an appointment at Vancouver," he said.

15

They toiled through blistering August heat, sometimes making little visible progress. The Snake River sulked in a black canyon on their left day after day; the hazy benches and mountains brooding on their right never changed. It seemed to Professor Nutmeg that they were on a treadmill, doing each day's progress over again.

He would have been more assiduous in his botanical collecting, but sheer hunger had enervated him, and so he roamed less far from the trail, conserving his energy. Finding places where they could descend to the river and water their horses became a problem. Few streams entered from the north.

But the overarching worry was hunger. They had only Victoria's bow and arrows, but not even Skye's rifle would have helped much in this arid land. They saw no large animals; only an occasional hare. The dogs stalked gophers and various other small beasts, hunting at night. But they starved, too.

Skye had fallen into silence, his eyes peering from slits in his swollen face, his gaze ceaselessly raking the world for something to eat: antelope, deer, sheep, even a stray horse. But neither he nor Victoria, who rode off now and then to try her luck away from the trail, succeeded. Even the fowl had deserted this stretch of the gloomy river.

The parched corn vanished and then the pemmican and the jerky. They devoured the small hoard of sugar and molasses the Skyes had kept in their gear. They boiled the last of the tea. Victoria showed Nutmeg which berries were edible and after that the professor haunted the river bottoms, hunting for the occasional bitter choke-cherry or wild grape. He found little in that arid land, and the hole in his belly was not filled.

Only the horses flourished. Bunchgrass, unending, fed them, along with lush green shoots in the river bottom. Nutmeg, who was forced to walk for the want of another horse, trudged wearily onward, thinning down each day and aching for any sort of food. He fantasized food, dreamed of sausage and milk and cheese and butter and fresh bread.

Then the river seemed to rise in the canyon, or rather the land and the river reached much the same elevation once again, and the malevolent Snake rolled by, offering them nothing but wetness for their parched bodies and grass for their beasts. Somehow the dogs did better than the humans, but Nutmeg didn't know how they survived. Once he found them carrying chunks of an ancient carcass, which they chewed upon whenever the party rested.

Dolly roved so much he feared he would lose his precious samples and drawings that she bore in a waterproof harness on her skinny back. He didn't have much to add to his collection these days, and regretted that he lacked the strength to roam.

He began to wonder whether he would survive. Then one day Skye stepped down from his mount.

"You're done in, mate. You and I'll share. Victoria needs a fast horse to chase game, but we'll make do. You ever ridden before?"

"Very little."

Gratefully, Nutmeg clambered into the saddle.

"I'll take the reins and lead for a while. You just relax and if you see a specimen, we'll stop and get it. Who knows, maybe it'll be something to eat."

Those were gentle words and arrived unaccustomed.

And so the professor found himself periodically sitting on Skye's horse, conserving his energy. From that high vantage point he saw occasional flora he would have missed, and Skye always obliged him while he plucked up something or other and made some notes and a swift sketch.

Nutmeg had come to admire Skye. The man never complained, never relaxed his vigilance, looked constantly for hiding places now that they were virtually defenseless, and most importantly, tried to accommodate the professor's every botanical need. The more Nutmeg talked to Skye, the more he discovered an emerald waiting for a good cutting and polishing. This was no ordinary wilderness ruffian but a man who might yet serve the Crown and bring glory to himself and to his native England.

Nothing more had been said about Nutmeg's proposal, but Nutmeg knew that Skye was weighing it as an option if the Hudson's Bay arrangement fell through. Nutmeg began to see his guide as a junior partner, a man who, with a few books and some field observation, might make a first-rate naturalist.

Whenever the well-worn trail departed from the river, Victoria patrolled close to the water where game might be. But she found nothing. She tried her luck on a hare, but it fled too fast for her arrows, and she made no meat that day. That bad day she lost two arrows.

They were in serious trouble and weakening daily. Were it not for the strong horses they might have no hope at all.

Then one morning they discovered Victoria sitting her horse dead ahead, waiting for them. When they reached her she pointed.

A mile or so ahead they saw the faintest plume of smoke. It apparently rose from the south bank but they could not say for sure. Maybe succor, maybe trouble.

"I will go look," she said. "You come a little way and wait."

She rode ahead, gaining ground on them while they walked slowly behind. Nutmeg was on foot, although he no longer had the strength to walk much at all. Skye had let him put his backpack on the packhorse, perched on a mound of equipment, but he preferred that the professor hike if at all possible.

Skye settled them in thick reeds close to the river and waited.

"Sorry, mate. I'm unarmed and all we can do is hide," he said. "That's the first rule anyway. Never confront if you can hide."

Dolly sat down beside him, panting and gaunt. Skye's yellow cur settled a yard from Skye and stared. The cur had an odd quality about him: he rarely took his gaze away from Skye, but seemed to focus on the man constantly. So far, no one had named him, and Skye simply called him the mutt.

Victoria materialized from the riverbank.

"It is a fishing village," she said. "Across the river. A stream comes in there from the south. They saw me and some are coming now. We go meet them, yes?"

There would be food if all went well.

Skye brightened visibly. He mounted slowly, while the professor collected his walking stick. They started down the trail once again. Before them, half a mile off, a party of the Shoshones awaited them. Water dripped from their ponies, and that suggested a ford, probably just upstream from the village and the confluence.

A dozen honey-fleshed men on horseback watched them. They were nearly naked, wearing only breechclouts. But they bristled with bows and arrows, lances, war clubs, hatchets, and one of them had a musket and powder horn.

Skye lifted his hand and they lifted theirs. He rode right up to them, and then his fingers began to work. Nutmeg wondered how a few signs could convey much, but apparently they did. One of the Shoshones addressed Victoria, and she responded in her own tongue. Skye dismounted, went back to his packhorse, dug out a twist of tobacco and some jingle bells, and handed the twist to the headman and a jingle bell to each of the others. They smiled and escorted the Skyes and Nutmeg to the village. They crossed a shallow ford at a wide point, and then splashed across the small tributary, and walked in. One of the Indians gave Nutmeg a lift over both fords and deposited him on the far banks where a great crowd of silent Shoshones had congregated. The camp was located in a ravine where a river debouched into the Snake.

"I told 'em we're hungry and would trade some good things. They have plenty of salmon. Told 'em we're all going to Fort Vancouver. Told 'em you're a great wise man among the whites and a healer with herbs. They'll want to see your samples. Probably bring you some."

"But Mister Skye, I'm not a healer."

"It's the closest thing I could think of to say about you, mate."

"They'll want me to heal them!"

"No, you tell 'em you want to learn their secrets."

Nutmeg thought Skye had pushed truth beyond its limits but remained silent about that. What would these people know of academics and naturalists and science?

Their escorts led them through a large village, mostly consisting of buffalohide lodges, but there were other lodges of thatched reeds as well. These were people of medium build and height, many of the women dressed in traders' cloth.

"I'd guess these are the Malad River Snakes—one of

two bands south of the Snake River," Skye said. "And I'd guess this is the Bruneau, up from the south. It cuts through some canyons to get here."

For once Nutmeg didn't much care.

"I need food," he muttered.

"We'll get it. Some ceremony first. They'll welcome us and after that I'll dicker."

The Snakes weren't strong on ceremony. A headman spoke to the assembled villagers. At one point their gazes all rested on Nutmeg, and he wondered what was being said about them.

Victoria responded in her Absaroka tongue, which was translated to the Snake tongue.

"Crows and Snakes are mostly old friends," Skye explained. "Some Crow women live here. It's hard to describe Snakes. They're always shifting around, switching bands. Some are like Plains Indians, living on buffalo, some not. These are mostly fishing people."

The sight of thousands of salmon drying on makeshift racks, and the smell of salmon stew in dozens of kettles dizzied the professor.

"Food, Mister Skye, before I faint."

"They'll feed us in their own good time, mate. I told 'em you're looking for herbs that heal, and I imagine you'll be hearing from plenty of 'em."

"Food, Mister Skye."

Dolly and the yellow cur stole fish from the racks, but the Snakes just laughed.

"You tell them what a fine people they are and how you want to learn from them," Skye said.

Nutmeg did, while Victoria and others transformed his thoughts into things the Snakes would understand.

Then the guests were led to a salmon feast and Nutmeg abandoned spiritual pleasures for the sensual.

16

Skye, Victoria, and Professor Nutmeg tarried for two days in the Snake village. The Skyes had endured starving times in the mountains during the terrible winters, but Nutmeg hadn't, and now he could scarcely stop wolfing any food at hand.

Their hosts fed them bountifully, and with each meal Skye reciprocated with gifts from his trading supplies, mercifully plentiful in the wake of the rendezvous. He had knives, awls, fire steels and flints, vermilion and foofaraw for the women. With each exchange, the potlatch grew more lavish: Skye's larder swelled to include pine nuts traded from the Paiutes to the south, a fish-type pemmican, mounds of sun-dried salmon shredded and sealed in gut; yucca fruit, wild onions, jerky from the meat of mountain sheep, antelope fat rendered and packed in gut, and all sorts of desiccated roots and berries, the half of which he didn't know, all of which lifted Victoria's spirits.

Skye loaded these gustatory treasures into his panniers knowing how fast they would vanish. His burdens had expanded to include two mutts and a pilgrim, five mouths in all. He ached for a beaver trap, just one, knowing that it could be used to catch all sorts of cur cuisine and stewpot

meat while he slept, but he could not talk any of the Snake
men out of theirs. So he faced six hundred miles of travel
with mouths to feed and no way, save for Victoria's arrows,
to make meat.

But Skye was not the cynosure of the village. From the
time Professor Nutmeg greeted the day by scraping away
his blond beard to the time he rolled into his stained blankets, the Snakes crowded about him as if he had descended
from Valhalla. They came to behold his leaf collection and
his sketches, and he patiently turned one page after another,
showing them well-wrought drawings of plants they instantly recognized. He showed them his samples, carefully
pressed between absorbent pages, and they marveled at
this amazing and novel sight.

Then undreamed-of fortune fell to him. Shyly at first,
the Snake women and children presented various species to him. Many were items he could but little use, having been torn from the earth in pieces and without any
caring about their location or the neighboring species. But
then a matron presented him with a whole yucca that
was new to him, and showed him how they made soap
from its roots. With Victoria's help he managed to learn
where it grew. He sketched it while the Snakes watched
diligently, seeing the graphite pencil miraculously repro-
duce the yucca on paper. Then he measured the plant, took
notes, and pressed one of its spiky leaves between his papers to preserve it, but with little success.

Whatever he lacked by way of knowledge of the Snakes,
he made up for with innate courtesy and good cheer, so
that much of the daily life of the village slowed and people
gathered about him.

That suited Skye fine. It was time for a rest. The horses
cropped good grass with the Snake herd. The dogs gorged
themselves and snoozed. The yellow cur stole fish, ate until
bloat set in, and then rolled onto his back, four paws aimed

toward the four winds of heaven. But whenever the cur awakened, it followed Skye as if it were heaven-sent to guard him, his new benefactor.

Skye scarcely knew what to make of that. Dogs were new to him. His London family had none. The Royal Navy had none that he knew of, though an occasional admiral might own one. And his entire experience with dogs was confined to those wretches that lived off the bands of Plains tribes, gorging offal during hunting times and starving the rest.

There were fat dogs running with the Snakes and maybe some of them ended up in the cooking kettles, though he wasn't sure of it. Some tribes were dog-eaters; many weren't, and these despised the ones that did break the neck of a puppy now and then and drop it into the stew.

But Skye knew time was flying and he had to hurry west for his appointment with destiny.

"Professor," he said after a day of feasting and trading and gift-giving, "you know, this is paradise for you and Dolly. Wyeth should be along in a week or two, and you could rest here, fatten up, collect new species, entertain these people, and then rejoin Wyeth's party."

"But, Skye, don't you want me to accompany you?" Nutmeg looked dismayed.

"Of course I do. But I'm always thinking ahead. We have food for a couple of weeks, but we're still six weeks from Fort Vancouver and bloody likely to starve again. With Wyeth you wouldn't have to worry about your meals or Dolly's. And I would have fewer mouths to feed. This has nothing to do with you personally. It's simply a matter of survival. If you choose to stay, I'll give you a few trading items to bargain for food."

"I see," he said. He looked crestfallen and Skye felt as if he were the spoiler of good times. "But what if Wyeth doesn't make it?"

"These are friendly people. You could make a temporary home with them."

Nutmeg sighed. "This is the end, eh? You're rejecting me?"

"Mate, I've got business to attend."

"Very well, then."

Nutmeg turned desolately to his papers, and Skye felt bad. But the wilderness was a hard master and it wasn't as if Skye were abandoning the man to his fate. The village was fat. And Wyeth would be along in a week or two.

That soft August evening, a delegation of the Snakes came to Skye, along with Victoria.

"They gonna talk," she said. "This is Pokotel, Yan Maow . . . that's Big Nose, Tisidimit, and Taihi. These are all headmen, but there ain't no big chiefs among these people. They say they gonna go to Fort Walla Walla, that's some Hudson's Bay fort long way away, over the mountains even, and trade. We go with them."

Skye was surprised. "Escort us?"

"Yeah, go on big trip, see the world, go visit friends, all that."

Skye couldn't quite imagine why, but Victoria clarified that at once. "Professor Nutmeg. They think him big medicine. They gonna go with him, show him new plants he never seen. They gonna teach him Snake mysteries, tell him Snake stories, and maybe he make pictures for them."

A trip to Fort Walla Walla, at the confluence of the Walla Walla River and the Columbia. Skye remembered the place bitterly. He had barely escaped with his life from there, long ago, when he had struggled into the interior after escaping the Royal Navy.

He had learned, since, that he had gone out of his way that first trip. The Umatilla River would have taken him eastward faster. But what was a witless limey to know?

The Snake leaders were waiting for a reply, gathered

about him. They were a formidable bunch, stocky, raw-boned, long-haired, and well-armed.

"What do you think, Victoria?" he asked.

"Dammit, Skye, you are slower than a turtle."

"I just told Nutmeg I'd rather he wait here for Wyeth."

She squinted at him, reading his face. They were all reading his face. Even the yellow mutt was staring up at him. He lifted his top hat and ran weathered fingers through his matted hair.

"I guess I can back up. I know when I'm whipped. But they got to do something for me."

Victoria turned solemn. "Skye, dammit."

"They got to name this yellow mutt."

Victoria cackled and began a monologue at once in her Absaroka tongue, which Pokotel slowly translated. Then they were all grinning.

"Tisidimit says, tonight they name the spirit-dog. Big meeting, big medicine."

They left it to Skye to find the professor. The man was, as usual, surrounded by Snakes, this time mostly shy children who peered at his drawings and squealed happily. They all had wilted leaves and stems to offer this strange white man, and he took each one, examined it, and usually flipped to a sketch of the plant.

"Professor, you can come with us if you want."

"No, Mister Skye, I've learned to take life as it comes and I'll be quite content among these delightful people."

Skye grinned. "A big party's going to escort us to the Columbia just for a lark. It's in your honor, you see. They think you're some."

"Some? Some what?"

"Something special. That's Yank trapper talk. You're some, all right, mate."

"They barbarize the mother tongue, eh?"

"Well, so do the tars in the Royal Navy."

Nutmeg relaxed. "I'll be ready, Mister Skye. I take it that this changes your plans with respect to me?"

"Most likely. That's a mighty bunch of warriors and hunters, and they'll keep us from starving. We're having a little ceremony tonight at dusk. Whole band's saying goodbye and doing a little favor for me."

"A favor?"

"I told them they could escort us if they bestow a name on this yellow mutt of mine. I've been half crazy trying to think of a name. Nothing works. He's a sneaky, snaky dog creeping around, so I won't call him King or Duke or Prince. He's ugly as the devil, so I can't call him Marmaduke. I was thinking of calling him Nutmeg, but you'd be insulted."

"I'd be honored, Mister Skye."

"I suppose it beats naming half a dozen reeds and grasses after yourself in Latin. No, Professor, I won't name this beast. Tonight the Snakes'll do it."

17

The Snakes escorted Skye to an elder, one Tixitl. Skye beheld an ancient man with a piercing stare and seamed countenance. He seemed fragile and half out of his body and into some other world.

He handed the old man a plug of tobacco.

"Grandfather, I have come to ask you to name my dog."

They translated this for the old shaman, who nodded. He spoke briefly to one of the Snake headmen.

"Tixitl wants to see the dog, Mister Skye."

"I don't know where he is."

The old man seemed to understand even without the translating. Then he spoke again.

Victoria translated. "He says you have a dog that knows no laws. He will ask the winds for a name and tonight at dusk he will speak."

"Thank the grandfather for me." Skye said.

That evening they feasted again on a stew made of the flesh of the salmon, with many roots and nuts and stalks in it. He and Victoria packed their kit and prepared for an early departure at dawn. Nutmeg strapped his little leather harness over Dolly, and slid his notes and samples into a waterproof oilcloth satchel.

At the appointed time, Skye ventured to the reed hut of the shaman and discovered most of the Snake village waiting raptly for him to appear. Even fragile grandmothers and newborns had been carried to the place, and laid gently down upon soft robes. The yellow cur had vanished, which annoyed Skye. The miserable mutt refused to show up for his own christening.

The Snakes waited eagerly. Skye realized a naming was an important event for them. A name established many things: kinship, natures, expectations, failings, dangers, virtues. So it was with all the tribes Skye knew of. It had overtones of religion, though the Shoshones cared less about such things than most tribes.

The shaman took his time inside that dark hut, and the crowd waited patiently, knowing that the Mysteries could not be hurried, and that revealed knowledge would come in its own time and season. Maybe he was waiting for portents: comets, falling stars, a thunderclap in a cloudless heaven, the howl of a dragon.

Skye settled on the clay before the silent hovel, and then moved a few feet when he found his legs teeming with black ants. The first stars poked through as the light narrowed to a band of blue in the northwest. And still Tixitl tarried. Skye grew restless. He had the white man's itch for swift decisions in him, but Victoria had sunk into age-old watchfulness.

The crowd had fallen into a holy vigil.

Maybe they were waiting for the yellow cur to walk on stage, but it lingered beyond the camp, making its own way, perhaps an ally in life's adventures but no friend of any living thing.

At last the old man emerged from his hut, stood, stretched, and surveyed the great assemblage. Skye thought that the entire village had come for this event and now the Snakes stood in a great arc, the men in the first ranks, the women and children behind them.

A signal from Tixitl drew the translators and Skye to him.

"I have asked the winds for the name. I have asked the heavens, and the creatures under the earth. I have asked the creatures in the water, and the four-foots that walk. I have asked the before-people, and my own spirit-counselor, whose name is a mystery."

Skye waited patiently, wishing his yellow dog would show up. But the dog stayed well hidden.

"They have given me no name for this dog," Tixitl said. "The heavens give no name. And the winds give no name. And all the spirits give me no name. This dog must not be named. Hairy man, do not give this dog a name. As long as he has no name, his power will watch over you. If you name this dog, you will break him in two, like a twig snapping. Therefore he is No Name. The spirits have spoken to me, and I have spoken to you."

With that, the old man stood silent, letting these words sink into the assemblage, while the translators droned.

"Thank you, grandfather," said Skye, brushing off ants.

He had a nameless dog who would not answer to his call, and yet watched over Skye.

If the Snakes were disappointed they did not show it. Indeed, he walked through faces wreathed in smiles. Forbidding a name was as good as a naming, and maybe all the more medicine because it was so mysterious.

Skye did not see the yellow dog that night and supposed that the cur had found a home among the village mutts and would stay on. At dawn Skye studied the quiet village, still searching for the dog, and missing it badly. His feeling surprised him. But he would be better off without the dog. He would probably have to leave it at Fort Vancouver anyway if he shipped to England. He had no idea whether a wild dog would be welcome on a merchant ship, but he doubted it. So it all was a blessing. He had surrendered a dog and gained a thousand ants in his britches.

Nutmeg was dressed and ready, with his knapsack over his back and fat Dolly beside him, carrying her small pack. Skye yawned, pulled on his thick-soled moccasins, and hiked out to the horse herd under the watchful eyes of the boys who guarded it. His horses were skittish, liking the easy living and the gossipy society of the Snake brethren. He tried to catch the packhorse, but it sidled away from him. He did better with Victoria's little spotted horse, sliding a hackamore over its nose and leading it back to camp.

It took him until sunrise to catch his own wily horse, which dodged through the herd, stirring trouble. It angered him. He vowed he would spend more time with his willful horses and work with them until they were absolutely reliable. When he finally returned with his nags, the travelers were all awaiting him. The escort party of eleven warriors all had their mounts in hand, ready to go. Victoria was ready; the packhorse stood ready.

Skye had had no breakfast but decided to forgo it. He had delayed his own departure.

"All right," he said.

Most of the village was up, and people silently watched the party leave camp, riding beside the broad, purling Snake, carrying its burden of mountain snows to the far Pacific. It was a silent departure. Skye hunted for the no-name yellow cur and saw no canine other than Dolly, and was relieved that the mutt had made his home with this band where it could live to fat old age gorging on salmon and buffalo and the offal of a dozen other animals.

This had been a good stop. In all of his years as a mountaineer, he had found hospitality and succor among friendly tribes.

He turned to the professor, waiting beside Skye's pony. "You rested, Mr. Nutmeg?"

"Entirely, and ready for the next lap. And chock-full of ideas. I can put the Indians to work, Mister Skye! Those people brought me half a dozen items that were new to me; some simple variations, but two were wax-leaf desert shrubs I'd never seen. I hadn't realized I can trade manufactured goods for these things. My work would go twice as fast. I wish I'd thought to stock up at the rendezvous."

Skye nodded. Professor Nutmeg's mind ran one direction.

Their Snake escort set a slow pace, pausing frequently to observe the wonders of their world: the diving eagle, the geese bobbing in estuaries, the track of a mountain lion, the flight of crows, and the ripples in the river that spoke to them of things Skye would never fathom.

The pace at least was more comfortable for Nutmeg, who had time to meander, forgetful of safety and direction as his quest for knowledge took him from plant to plant. But Pokotel and Tisidimit kept an eye on him, sometimes walking their spotted mounts, the famous dappled palouses of the Nez Perce, as outriders well back from the river.

Victoria had slipped into rare melancholia, her dark visions plain upon her sharp face.

"You're gonna find some Englishwoman when we get there, and then I'm no good for you anymore," she said, after reining her pony beside his. "She gonna be like you, big and white, and blue-eyes, and she gonna talk your tongue, not like old Victoria. I don't say things good. I listen to Nutmeg, him big wise man among you, and I know I talk no good, and he thinks you could be big wise man of the English, and then you send me back to the Kicked-in-the-Bellies and you take a young, pretty white woman for wife and make many children. I no damn good at making a baby, so you get none from me. You say so and I will turn around and go back to my people."

He had never heard her talk like that. Always, she had been adventuresome, ready for whatever life brought, fierce and determined. But now he heard despair in her voice.

Skye protested but could not stop this outpouring of

worry. There were a few grains of truth in it. He could not himself say how he would feel about her in England. Maybe the woman he loved so much in this great North American wilderness would strike him as alien in crowded London, and maybe he would regret trying to prolong the union.

Skye had the sense that no matter how much he might vow to stick with her, giant forces, such as his cultural memories, probable condescension in London, future trouble within Hudson's Bay Company, might conspire to tear his sweet, fragile mountain marriage to bits.

He was a strong man, and yet he felt helpless.

He reached over to touch her arm. She saw his big blunt fingers on the sleeve of her tradecloth blouse, and he saw a wetness in her brown eyes.

18

The quickening light stirred Skye out of a dream-tormented sleep. He had won no rest that night. He pulled aside his robes and beheld the no-name dog, lying three feet away, gazing intently at him.

He did not welcome the dog. He marveled that the dog would leave the paradise of the Snake village and follow him to this place, two days distant. He would have to betray the dog at Fort Vancouver, have McLoughlin lock up the mutt when Skye boarded that ship . . . if indeed that was to be his fate.

He didn't want any kin just then. Not Victoria, who would suffer in England, not the dog. Not his friends in the mountains. If he stepped aboard that bark, he would betray them all, exchange his mountain family for his English one.

Last night he had decided, while tossing in his blankets, that Victoria was right: he had to choose. He could have England and his family . . . or her. But not both. There lay an ocean and a continent between them, and not just sea and land, but an ocean that divided white people, English people, from these tribes. As usual, she saw the things he didn't see, the things he wallpapered over and tried not to see. She hadn't seen England, but she knew she would wither there and pine for her free, sunlit prairies, shining mountains, and her people, who lived without fences and hedgerows, who went where they pleased and did whatever came to them.

For her, even a one-year visit would be an eternity that would end in a grave in some dank English burial field outside the yard of any church, for they would not bury her in sacred ground. She had vision; he didn't. And he could see no way out. He could abandon England and citizenship and his father and sisters, and keep her. And the no-name dog.

With daylight he banished the dreads that had bored through his soul all night, and now, in dawn's light, things weren't so bad. She could wait for him. He'd be gone perhaps a year and a half—if all went well. If the bark he sailed on didn't founder at sea, if he didn't sicken and die in London, if the Crown truly restored his name, if Hudson's Bay kept its word, if the returning bark to York Factory in Canada didn't founder, if he didn't sicken and die canoeing and portaging from Hudson's Bay over half a continent to Fort Vancouver.

Would Victoria and the no-name dog wait?

He and the dog were the only ones in camp who were awake.

He arose, stretched, and found the mutt pressing its muzzle against his leg, an act of proprietary interest if not ownership. Gingerly he lowered his big hand and stroked the dog's head. The dog let him.

He didn't know what in bloody hell he would do with the dog, and that made him irritable.

They progressed along the Snake River, and he marveled at the fishing skills of his comrades. They could spear a salmon even though the water tricked the eye into thinking the fish was not where it really was. They had small throw-nets that settled over the fat fish.

He also wondered about their utter lack of caution. They traveled without vedettes, scarcely paying attention to danger. If they had done this on the plains, they would be in mortal danger. But it was as if they had no enemies, and perhaps they didn't, at least when they were getting along with the Nez Perce, which they usually did.

They sang and sometimes danced to the thump of a small drum in the evenings, simply as a way to make the evenings pass. He gradually acquired some grasp of their ways. They had little public religion, other than a belief in a spirit-guardian from the animal world. That was a private matter: some of the Snakes had medicine, others never even sought spirit helpers and counselors. Skye thought they were not as handsome as some tribes, such as the Lakota, but he admired their honeyed flesh and cleanness of limb.

When he sought to find out why they had come along on this journey, Victoria's response was simply that they wanted to; it was adventure, and they loved adventure. They loved to honor the great white wise man who was making pictures of all plants on earth. They were celebrating such a wonder, and also honoring Skye, the greatest of the white fur men, and his fine Absaroka woman.

And that was all the reason they needed.

They came one evening to a point near a great bend of the Snake, and there the headman, Tisidimit, conveyed to Skye, by sign, that here they would leave the river and head westward along various valleys, and finally over the Blue Mountains beyond the horizon.

Now they would hunt rather than fish. This was a land of fine hares, and the Snake people treasured the pelts of rabbits almost as much as the hides of buffalo.

So they turned away from the Snake River and started overland through an arid land that gradually greened as it rose. Skye saw at once that this land would yield its wild grapes and berries, its small game, rich and verdant grasses for the horses, springs and creeks, firewood aplenty, yews and willows and cottonwoods for shade. But now, as they pierced into a wetter country, the mosquitos tormented them all, and Skye began dreading the nights when no robe or smudge fire would protect his vulnerable flesh from a thousand bloodsucking insects.

The yellow dog didn't mind. The horses did, and their tails lashed at the vicious clouds of insects. Victoria's face puffed up with the bites she bore stoically, but they all endured, uncomplaining. For some reason the mosquitos barely bothered the Snakes, and Skye wondered what mysterious potions they used upon themselves.

They made good progress. The Snakes did all the hunting and rarely did they make camp without fresh meat. The yellow dog ate and fattened and studied Skye with opaque eyes that hid the mystery of its origins. When was this ugly thing born, and what had it suffered to be so scarred, and how did it learn to hunt and fight and survive? And always, Skye came back to the great question: why had this miserable beast attached itself to him?

Victoria knew the answer, and Skye stopped laughing at her notions.

He did not know where the Snakes were taking him: only that they would go as far as they wanted, and then turn back, having made a lark of a summer's moon. Maybe they would take the dog with them. The test would soon come at Fort Vancouver, and then Victoria would see whether the no-name mutt was Skye's spirit-dog, or just a beast looking for a handout.

They ascended the Blue mountains, traveling through open pine forest dotted with parks, rather more arid above than in the foothill country. Nutmeg found little to interest him; the vegetation was uniform, limited, and dull. He and Dolly roved wide from the plain and well-worn trail, and had nothing to report except an encounter with a black bear that was berrying under a bluff.

"What are your plans now, Professor?" Skye asked one evening.

"Why, wait for Nat Wyeth, I suppose. When his party arrives at Vancouver, I'll go to the coast with them and board their bark, the *Sultana*, at the mouth of the Columbia, and head back to Boston via Cape Horn. If all goes well, I'll land only a few miles from Harvard Yard. I'm sure there'd be passage for you, Mister Skye, if you wish it."

"I'll see what Dr. McLoughlin has in mind, mate. This whole business is bloody mysterious."

"Why doesn't HBC just make you an offer straight out?"

"Because they know I'd never accept. They're tied to the Crown, administer Crown lands, operate the criminal justice system in their territory, and unless I'm cleared and restored to my rights as an Englishman, they'll never put me officially on their rolls."

They descended into a rich foothill country, and then a grassy plain. This was the Columbia basin, and Skye felt a change. The last of the Rockies were behind him, and this land looked westward to the coastal ranges and the great Pacific. Suddenly he felt wary. The Rockies had been his home for six years. The Yanks had been his friends and offered him the means to survive. Now, suddenly, this country, brooding in the sun, seemed alien, and his future loomed as a large question mark. The West was always the future; the East the past.

They reached a large tributary of the Columbia, whose name Skye did not know, and there the Snakes went their own way. They wished to go up to Fort Walla Walla, the Hudson's Bay post built to trade with the Nez Perce.

Pokotel and Tisidimit clasped their white friends, sang songs, laughed, and started north across a great flat that showed signs of the presence of wild horses. The possibility of capturing some of the cayuses excited them.

Just follow the river, they explained to Victoria, who translated.

And then the Snakes departed in a long line, winding

their way over the undulating grasses, leaving Skye, Victoria, Nutmeg, and their critters suddenly alone.

Skye felt naked. He had no weapon. Only Victoria's bow and quiver protected them. They had, at least, the food they had traded for weeks earlier, but it would not last them to Fort Vancouver, which lay a great distance to the west. Skye was struck, once again, by the vastness of this North America, its size unfathomable.

"We're almost unarmed, and we'll be careful, mate," he said to Nutmeg.

They started down a pleasant stream, abounding with game along its banks.

Now, suddenly, the professor found himself in a new botanical zone, and he worked furiously to harvest the treasures of this intermountain land.

Skye rode ahead, scouting a safe passage, and soon spotted a fishing village. He could only hope its people were friendly. It would probably be Umatilla, Wallawalla, or Cayuse, but without a guide he doubted he could tell which.

He rode straight for the village, hoping for the best.

19

A sea of heavy-boned friendly faces greeted them as they entered the camp. Skye spotted some small, wiry horses picketed close, and thought these were Cayuse Indians, who caught just such ponies on the vast arid plains of the area. He also guessed that they were fishing the Umatilla River. He wished he had a guide to help him put names to places and people.

They wore little clothing this summery day. They were a people of golden flesh, notably bad teeth, but silky straight hair which the women let hang loose over their breasts. Although a great fishery had been erected of poles out of the nearby mountains, including a framework above the river where spearmen could harvest salmon, no one seemed to be working much. Perhaps they didn't need to.

The place stank of fish offal, dung, and kitchen trash. Whirling clouds of green-bellied flies swarmed over everything and everyone, along with bigger and blacker horseflies. Sulky curs circled as Skye and his party rode in, and sniffed Dolly, who stayed beside the professor. Skye saw no lodges, but only a jumble of shacks and arbors thrown together from river brush and a few poles, not enough to slow the wind but enough to provide a little shade. These people might be fine fishermen, but they did

not impress Skye, who preferred the rich culture and hau-
teur of the Plains Indians.

Skye wondered what the ritual might be: did these far-
west people follow the protocols of the Plains tribes? He
dismounted, extracted a plug of tobacco from his pack
and waited for a headman or chief. But none came and
there was no official welcoming. Several old men held out
their hands, plainly wanting the tobacco, but Skye tarried.

Victoria took matters into her own hands: her fingers
danced. But again, these people stared. It was dawning on
Skye that even the universal sign language, which he had
thought was known to tribes everywhere, wasn't much
used here. One young man stood aside, and from his bearing and an elaborate conch-shell necklace dangling from
his neck, Skye thought him to be a leader of some sort, so
he doffed his top hat, approached, and attempted by sign
language to seek the welcome of the village.

The young man nodded but did not otherwise reply.

Skye remembered the jingle bells. He dug out several
and handed them about, first to the young man, and then
to the nearest of these people.

Dogs sniffed, growled at Dolly, and Skye wondered
where his dog had gone. Maybe the beast was so cowardly
that he would not enter a village and was lurking around
at the periphery, waiting for his friend—Skye knew better
than to suppose he was the mutt's master—to escape this
foul place.

But Victoria was busily finding someone she could
talk to, and eventually found a Nez Perce woman, a wife
of one of the young fishers, who was acquainted with the
sign language.

Skye held Victoria's pony while the women sign-talked.
Yes, these were Cayuse people. Fishing now, then catching horses in the fall and training them through the winter.

But it was Nutmeg who found a welcome. Children
flocked to him, fascinated by the canvas packs carried on

Dolly's back. The naturalist sat down, pulled out one of his thick folders filled with pressed leaves and stems and flowers, each between a sheet of soft paper, and his penciled drawings of various species. Sitting crosslegged, he showed these to the children, and then the women who came to see what strange thing the white man possessed, and finally to a throng of Cayuse people, who marveled at each rendering of each plant.

"There, you see?" Nutmeg said. "I collect one of each species and write them up, eh?" He showed them his bulky notes, which they could not in the slightest comprehend. It was the sketches that fascinated the Cayuse people. With each likeness they exclaimed and talked among themselves.

"I have more in my knapsack," he said. He pulled the straps off his shoulders and pulled off the heavy bag. He rummaged in it and pulled out two more folders of pressed plants and sketches.

"See here," he said. "I collect these. I've six notebooks filled with all this."

The village women crowded close so they too could see these amazing drawings.

"No, it's not magic, and I'm a poor hand at drawing, but I have to get things right. Everything perfect and exact, and showing the species to best advantage, eh?"

They listened solemnly, saying nothing. It dawned on Skye that maybe they knew some English but weren't admitting it. They traded, after all, at Fort Walla Walla, and had no doubt spent plenty of time among Englishmen.

"Does anyone speak English?" Skye asked.

A powerful warrior, middle-aged, graying at the temples, his eyes as opaque as basalt, nodded.

"I make trade," he said.

That was good. Skye and Victoria had been trying every way but the obvious to talk to these people.

"I am Skye. We are going to Fort Vancouver," he said.

The man nodded. Then pointed at himself. "Waapita," he said.

"We come in peace."

"You trade?"

"No."

"What people is the woman?"

"Absaroka. Far east, over the mountains. She is my woman."

"You Yank?"

"No, English." He pointed at Professor Nutmeg. "He's English."

"You Hudson Bayee?"

Skye pondered that a moment. "No."

The big man didn't reply and Skye felt him withdrawing. These people were bonded to the great trading company.

"I am going to talk to the White Eagle. Then maybe I am Hudson's Bay."

"White Eagle. Ahhh. You want to trade horse?"

Skye did not like the look of the Cayuse ponies, which were ugly, small, ribby, and deformed. His Plains horses were better stock.

"No," he said. "But maybe buy one?"

He was thinking of a pony for Nutmeg, whose slow passage on foot, in bad boots and on sore feet, was slowing them down to a crawl.

"Trade," said Waapita. "I like you horse."

"No, no trade. But I will give two knives and one awl for a gentle horse with good feet and legs."

"No," said his host, whose gaze flicked to Skye's equipment, and then to the knife at Skye's waist.

Skye suddenly sensed that this was not good. He turned to Victoria. "Get out," he said.

She glanced swiftly at him, and instantly clambered onto her pony.

He walked to the crowd being entertained by Nutmeg.

"We're leaving, Professor."

"But Mister Skye, these people are enjoying my little picture show—"

"Now."

"Oh, pshaw, Skye, don't be in such a dither."

"Gather your things."

Then it happened.

Skye watched some playful urchins unbuckle Dolly's harness and furtively slide Nutmeg's two packs chock-full of his collections and notes into the dense crowd.

"Professor!" he barked. "Your notes!"

"I say, Mister Skye!"

Then Nutmeg's knapsack vanished, and two of the three notebooks vanished, while Skye watched, horrified.

He plunged into the crowd, pushing carefully, fighting his way toward the fleeing children, who dodged, rounded corners, reappeared, and ran free, into the maze of shacks and fish-drying racks and middens of refuse. Astonishingly, the yellow cur followed the boys, a yellow flag for Skye to follow.

Skye sprang after them, a lithe force, and yet he made no headway. The boys separated, one carrying the knapsack going one way, another vanishing into a longhouse, and another bearing Dolly's packs and harness starting for the river. Another boy joyously carried one of the notebooks Nutmeg had exhibited, his laughter a cataract of childish delight. Skye chased that one until suddenly a dark wall of men with leveled fishing spears loomed before him. Skye stood, paralyzed, knowing he was one breath away from death from a dozen iron-pointed lances.

He sat swiftly, knowing that a sitting unarmed man facing warriors is safer than a standing one.

The boys had disappeared.

Skye heard Nutmeg's strangulated bellowing. He sat panting, sensing that he and Nutmeg and Victoria might not leave this village alive.

He gauged the temper of these young fisher-hunter-warriors, and stood slowly, gathering his courage. He elaborately ignored them, turned his back to them, feeling his flesh prickle, and walked wearily across the entire village, in what seemed an eternity, to the silent crowd surrounding the naturalist.

He found the professor slumping at the same place, Dolly at his feet, clutching one remaining folio of species, notes, and sketches. He looked a lot calmer than Skye felt, but Skye knew it wasn't calm. The professor stared, vacant-eyed, into space. Victoria had climbed to her saddle and had grabbed the halter rope of the packhorse.

"You'll get them back, of course, Skye," Nutmeg said in a dreamy whisper. "Five are gone."

"I'll try, Professor."

The crowd had quieted. Skye walked slowly to the one who knew a little English, who stood apart. The man shifted slightly as Skye stopped before him.

Skye lifted his hat and settled it. "Him wise man. Spent many months collecting all plants, for the wisdom of the world. Now you must bring everything back to him, every thing the boys took, or Hudson's Bay very angry."

The big man shrugged.

"I will give you gifts. Everything on my packhorse. You give us everything the boys took."

"They my boys," the man said. "Go away now."

Skye studied the man and knew he meant it. He wondered what he would tell Professor Nutmeg and what faith the naturalist would profess after that.

20

The sun scorched the whole world white, and for a moment Alistair Nutmeg was blinded. He closed his eyes against the pain of the sun, but the whiteness persisted. He heard the yelping dogs, listened to the excited Cayuse people, heard running and shouts. When he opened his eyes again, the crowd had pulled back from him. He clutched one folio. Dolly rubbed his leg, the hair of her neck bristling.

He sensed that he would never see the five stolen folios again, but waited tautly until Skye would return with news. He was a born and bred Englishman, and punctilious about displaying emotion. To all the world he seemed collected and in control of his fate. But in fact, his mind tumbled through loss: months of collecting gone unless Skye worked a miracle. He wished he might sit down on the grass and weep, but that would be unthinkable and a ghastly sign of weakness. An Englishman was he, an Englishman, an Englishman . . .

So he stared numbly, his thoughts frozen by grief. It was all he could do to pay attention, and not drift off somewhere in the clouds, to a meeting of the Royal Academy of Science to honor his great achievements in North America, or his lectern at Harvard, educating eager acned boys about hitherto unknown flora of this vast continent.

He smiled at the savages, holding everything in like a draught of air in his lungs, and pausing only to exhale and inhale again, smiling at these brutes who had observed nature closely but had made no systematic note of what they knew. No one would ever accuse Alistair Nutmeg, lecturer at Harvard, adventuresome naturalist, of losing his composure in a bitter moment.

These were friendly people; the urchins were only doing what daring boys do. But as he stood there, awaiting direction from Skye, he grasped how foolish he had been and how valid were the cautions of his wilderness guides. Nat Wyeth and his men had constantly admonished him to be careful. Skye had warned him so often that Nutmeg had privately raged at the man.

But it wasn't war or death or murderous intent that had caused this loss: it was the gulf that lay between him and these people. They did not know the value of his collection or its purpose. They had yet to encounter science or the arts. They had yet to invent the wheel or an alphabet or mine and refine metal or put their own language on paper. They were Stone Age men.

They could not know what this fateful moment meant to a naturalist who had devoted months simply to planning and financing this expedition, and then months in the actual and difficult work of examining flora, categorizing them, checking them against known botanical specimens, drawing them accurately, describing their habitat in detail, and noting any practical purpose for the plant, whether as medicine or dye or food or fiber.

He stood stoically, with a stiff upper lip, an Englishman to the core, weeping at his fate within, a mask to this raw world.

Skye approached. "We've got to leave at once, mate. No telling what'll happen if we stay."

"The folios?"

"Scattered in the camps, hidden by boys, prizes of war . . . I am sorry."

"Is there the slightest chance?"

"Always a chance, mate. Hudson's Bay is a powerful force. All they have to do is threaten to close the trading window."

"But this won't happen soon. And the specimens may not survive . . ."

Skye led the professor away from the silent Cayuse people, and Dolly followed. Nutmeg, his movements jerky and stiff, like a windup tin soldier, walked away from the rank-smelling camp, walking alongside Skye, feeling as bereft as if he had lost his entire family, his good name, his reputation, and all that he had ever written into the Book of Life.

Skye leaned over the mane of his horse.

"You all right, mate?"

"Never better," Nutmeg replied.

"How much did you lose?"

"Five of six folios. All my notes and sketches. Almost everything. There are a couple folios with Wyeth, but I will have to start over."

"A year lost?"

"Two, actually."

"That is a great loss," Skye said. "You could change your plans, Professor. Head east overland, next spring, after wintering at Fort Vancouver, collecting all the way. Undo the loss, from west to east."

Nutmeg sighed. "I'm afraid it won't succeed, sir. Collecting requires large amounts of soft absorbent paper. I dry my leaves and stems and flowers between the sheets. I should need reams of that, and reams of writing paper for notes, and reams of paper for sketches, you see. And some waterproof folders to store them. I don't suppose I'd find such a trove of paper at Fort Vancouver."

"Likely not," Skye said. "But if you sailed down the coast to Monterey, capital of Mexican California, you might acquire these things, and a guide to take you east."

"With what, sir?"

Something in Nutmeg's voice gave him away, and Skye turned silent. Nutmeg knew he was barely controlling the festering anger within him. He was doubly angry: at himself for ignoring the warnings of experienced wilderness men, and at Skye, whose very concern now rankled him. One more kind inquiry from Skye and Nutmeg would decant a magnum of bitterness.

But Skye had sensed his rage, and pulled ahead of him.

Victoria rode silently beside them, sharing all this without comment. Then, ahead, they beheld the yellow dog lying in the worn riverside path.

Dolly bounded ahead to sniff No Name. She looked happy without the pack she had carted for so many hundreds of miles. The Cayuse boys had liberated her, and she had instantly become less dutiful. And that festered in Nutmeg, too. Everything in his existence was needling and jabbing him, and most of all Skye and his squaw.

He composed himself once again. It would not do to let himself be discovered in a tantrum like some schoolboy, and be laughed at or condescended to by the likes of that ruffian Skye, who may have started as a cultivated London youth, but now was coarse and brutal . . .

Petulantly he forced his mind from that sort of disdain.

Mostly, he felt despair. He had lost scores of genus and subgenus possibilities, several new species. He had lost numerous new pteropsida: ferns, conifers, firs. He had lost several new dicots: elms, peaches, blackberries, mustards, nightshades, and ragweeds. He had lost a rich assortment of new monocots, including endless varieties of grasses, sedges, lilies, and yuccas. He had lost several new mosses, or bryophyta, several mycophyta, or fungi, mushrooms, and toadstools. He knew he could never recover samples of the rare ones. He would always be in the wrong place, or in the wrong season. Some appeared to be so local that he doubted he would ever find them again.

Worse, he had lost a dozen or so specimens of plant life he could not classify: he was not sure of the order or genus or subgenus of any of them. He lacked the taxonomic skills to place them in the botanic universe. Some were tiny. Some were water-borne. One flourished deep in a limestone cave he had explored. And these were the most exciting of all. They might lead anywhere: even to a new order. Losing those was comparable to losing his health, or the crown jewels, or his mind. All gone, gone, gone.

His surviving portfolio contained some fine new peas and sages, as well as a fine collection of lichen. But he no longer cared. He wished the Cayuse boys had taken it, too.

He stumbled forward amid a quietness that radiated more from the Skyes than from nature. They were leaving him alone to come to grips with his loss.

Then he discovered Skye standing just ahead.

"Would you like to ride, Professor? I need to walk."

Nutmeg felt weary but shook his head. "I am not in need of charity," he said.

Skye turned aside, addressing the empty world. "When I was at sea, and the rails of the ship were the bars of my prison, I didn't know why I was set upon this earth," he said quietly. "I lived a futile life, without purpose, serving masters who wanted only the use of my muscle, men who saw me as no more than a problem in the ship's company."

"What are you getting at?" Nutmeg asked, too sharply, and then regretted the tone that erupted from him.

"We are here on earth for some reason," Skye said, "even though we may not understand it at the time."

"I suppose I was put here so that I might lose my life's work? And therefore learn a bit of humility?"

Skye laughed. The rumble began within him, like the

prelude to an earthquake, and then erupted like a volcano, cascading joy and humor over his world.

Nutmeg didn't want to laugh, and loathed himself for starting to laugh, but then he laughed, too, disliking the eruption.

No Name peered at them, sunk its tail between its legs, turned soulfully, and bayed.

"Now you have something to tell your colleagues at Harvard," Skye said, at last.

Victoria was puzzled. She obviously understood very little of this. Whenever the white men's way proved too much for her, she seemed to pull into herself, which was what she was doing now. Nutmeg approached her pony and peered up at her from those wise and guileless eyes.

"What I have lost is very large, and cannot be replaced entirely. But on this trip I have found good things. From you I have learned about the Absaroka, and listened to your wisdom and admired your skills, your beauty, your kindness, and all your fine qualities. These are things that any people, anywhere, from any nation, would admire.

"So all is not lost. You and Mister Skye have been my traveling companions for several weeks, and you have taught me many things I did not know. I was an innocent, wandering a dangerous world without knowing it. Now I have some of your wisdom, and look forward to learning more if you wish to teach me. Maybe, some day, when I am wise in your ways, Victoria of the Crow people, I might successfully prosecute my own work."

She stared down at him softly, smiled, and touched his lips with her slim fingers.

21

Skye found himself admiring Professor Nutmeg, who soldiered on without further complaint. But never more so than one evening at dusk, when he confessed remorse.

"I imagine Wyeth thinks I'm dead," he said. "I shouldn't have done that to him. He must have spent days searching for me, sending men out and about, tracking me. Worse, you tried to get me to wait but I didn't. I insisted on tagging along. No, Mister Skye, I would now have everything safe and secure if I had abided by your counsel."

Skye found himself liking that. The professor was a decent sort, with all the noble qualities of the English. And maybe some of the eccentricities and weaknesses, too.

"That's the past, Professor. We'll look to the future now. Count it a lesson."

"It's that all right," Nutmeg said. "When I see Wyeth at Vancouver, I'll try to make amends."

They had made good time down the Umatilla River, reached its confluence with the mighty Columbia, and headed along the left bank through an arid and depressing land. Skye and Nutmeg traded seats on the horse, while Victoria ranged ahead hunting and scouting. No Name had taken to scouting with her and had proven to be a valuable bird dog, retrieving an occasional goose or duck she pierced with her dwindling supply of arrows. The meat helped extend the shrinking supply of dried salmon.

There was not enough to feed them to the Hudson's Bay post, but there would be fishing villages en route, and Skye still had a handful of trade goods from the cache he had acquired at rendezvous. Somehow they would make it.

They discovered a fishing camp of a people they could not identify, snugged into a wooded ravine that debouched on the river. As was the custom of the northwest tribes, this people welcomed the visitors and fed them. Skye noticed the large river canoes beached along the bank, and for a while played with the idea of trading his three horses for a ride to Fort Vancouver. It was certainly a temptation, letting the current of the great river, and the strength of the oarsmen, take them swiftly to their destination.

And yet he hesitated, and as he thought about it, he realized why he would not do that: nothing was certain. He might not like McLoughlin's proposal. And if he rejected it, he and Victoria would need those horses to return to the interior. Without those horses he would have nothing. He could even trade the packhorse for a rifle and supplies and still have a pair of them to ride. No, as seductive as the idea was of floating to the post, he would resist.

This time, No Name didn't vanish as he had during other visits. He stuck close to Skye, as if finally attaching himself to his new comrade. Skye knew the dog would never accept a master, but welcomed a friend. The thought of abandoning the mutt at Vancouver disturbed him, but there would be no help for it if they wouldn't let him ship the dog to England.

He remembered that fateful moment when the Cayuse boys had merrily divested Nutmeg of his botanical materials and scattered through the complex village. The dog had appeared out of nowhere and traced the passage of the boys through longhouses and huts and drying racks, his yellow coat a flag enabling Skye to keep track of the scampering boys—until he faced a wall of spears. How had the dog known to do that? What intuition did it possess? It was an intelligent creature that had survived on its own for some indeterminate time, avoiding fights, disappearing, and yet willing to war if war was thrust upon it, and eager to serve Skye for reasons that no mortal could ever know.

Now, in the failing light, he surveyed the dog. He could not even guess its age. Its ears had been cut and shredded by a hard life. One bent forward unnaturally. Its face was seamed with scars. But those brown eyes, which seemed to anticipate Skye's every thought, were what touched Skye. He swore the dog seemed to be following his very train of thought. Somehow No Name knew that this evening, more than any that had passed before, Barnaby Skye had accepted the friendship, nay, love, of the hound and had marveled at the dog's uncanny wisdom.

The dog squirmed closer until it could press its muzzle into Skye's lap as he sat cross-legged before the coals. Skye gingerly stroked its head, still fearful of a sudden, snarling explosion of snapping teeth. But that did not happen.

Victoria watched closely, her face a mask. She had long since made her peace with the dog and formed a hunting alliance with him.

They reached the Dalles of the Columbia a few days later, and headed around the rapids and looming cliffs. Tribesmen fished and loitered through the whole area, ready to portage canoes and boats, or demand tribute for passage past the great obstacle in the river. Skye, unarmed, knew he was at great disadvantage and tried to bluff his way past the alert and treacherous Indians. The bandits wanted a horse and everything in the pack for safe passage. Skye countered with a handful of awls and knives. He would not surrender the packhorse. The impasse lasted until a headman found himself staring at Victoria's drawn bow and realized that this small party was not without weapons after all. That gave Skye the moment he needed to draw his Arkansas toothpick. They ended up traversing the well-worn paths around the narrows without harassment. But it had been a close thing.

Victoria finally returned her arrow to its quiver and unstrung her beautifully crafted double-reflex bow, which compounded the force of her arrows. She rode ahead again, through an arid grassland, scouting and hunting, often with No Name rooting out small game for her.

On the western horizon, like a black wall barring them from a future, lay the Cascades, gloomy and forested. And rising into the misty heavens was the forbidding cone of Mount Hood, aloof, frosty, and arrogant. It did not comfort Skye that the volcano had been named for a British admiral, Lord Hood, some four decades earlier. He knew of Lord Hood, and knowing of him was enough to darken his day. The imperious and frigid mountain reminded him of all he wished to forget about England, and every time his gaze was drawn to it, he felt a renewed dread. Was he doing the sensible thing or merely throwing his life away?

They progressed gradually into the Cascade foothills, and now the mighty river ran between gloomy slopes heavily forested and forlorn. They came to the Hood River and found no way across except to swim the horses in the icy water. Skye hewed a small raft for the pack goods, and put Professor Nutmeg on the pack-horse, and hoped for the best. They made the west bank, but only after being chilled to the bone. Increasingly, Skye wondered how he would cross the vast Columbia, running a quarter-mile wide and cruelly cold. He wished he had tackled the river far upstream, where its breadth wasn't so formidable and it seemed friendlier. He had little choice now but to ride opposite Fort Vancouver and try to summon help.

The September nights turned starkly cold in the dripping Cascade Mountains, and suddenly the trip was no longer a summer's lark. Often the trail catapulted upward, negotiated cliffs and promontories, ran hard against the riverbank, and was hemmed by dense, dark forest. In the rare clearings, the travelers often found fishing sites where one or another of the river tribes harvested the salmon that was their food and wealth.

When they reached the west slope it rained continuously, making fires impossible and drenching them to the skin until they were so chilled that Skye feared they would sicken. They holed up under a rock ledge for an entire day trying to avoid the pelting rain, which still found its way to them whenever a breeze whipped the droplets under the ledge. The shelter had been much-used, and not a stick of firewood lay anywhere nearby. But at least they could huddle up. He was increasingly worried about Nutmeg, who shivered unceasingly and looked ashen. The man's few duds had vanished along with his knapsack in the Cayuse camp and not even his stiff English resolve could conceal the blueness of his face, or his suffering. Victoria, unused to such deluges on the plains, was suffering almost as much.

Skye realized that his stores of goods had dwindled almost to nothing and that he could turn a canvas pack-cloth into ponchos for Nutmeg and Victoria, so he set to work with his knife, sawing the canvas into two rectangles and cutting head holes in it. Both of them donned their ponchos, and both soon stopped their shaking. Once Nutmeg had warmed he was able to repair his sodden boots, which were falling apart again.

They were out of most staples and hadn't come to a village in many leagues, and Skye worried about how to feed three mortals and two dogs the remaining distance. Vancouver was not far, but if the bad weather persisted, it could as well be five hundred miles as one hundred.

Brutally, he pushed westward even though the drizzle had not yet halted, and they splashed along the dreary bankside trail, sometimes making only a few miles a day. Shelter was hard to find, and the mist or rain rarely let up. Skye could not remember any time he was so cold, not even on the North Sea, up in the rigging of a warship during a blow.

Sometimes Victoria magically found dry wood and they could make a fire; more often, there was nothing dry enough to burn. Skye cut them back to half-rations and they all fought the gnawing emptiness of their bellies.

Then one day the clouds lifted and they discovered themselves emerging from the vast dark canyon of the Cascades and into a sunlit plain densely foliaged with brush and leafy trees. They paused on a rocky flat to dry out and let the late September sun bake the winter out of their bones. The dogs, hunting together, scared up some geese, which gave Victoria an opportunity she took good advantage of, with her next-to-last arrow. There was just enough meat to feed the mortals sparingly, and the dogs a little better.

Skye had weathered worse, and should have been happy. Instead, he felt taut and irritable, snapping at Nutmeg, glaring at Victoria, and mad at himself. He admitted he was afraid, and that he might be making the most terrible mistake of his life. But there was nothing he could do but go on, his fate not really in his hands.

22

Skye found himself in an Eden, but it didn't feel at all like paradise. He and Victoria and the redoubtable professor toiled westward through a bountiful land, brimming with wild fruits and nuts, with abundant vegetation and the mildest of climates.

Nutmeg was enthralled and busied himself studying the flora, even though he had no means to preserve or describe or sketch any of it. He was like a bright butterfly, alighting on one bloom after another, drinking of its pollen before rushing off to the next delight.

He got lost one day, wandering afield in his old manner, oblivious of his traveling companions, intent on finding more of a berry bush he had never seen before, and for which he had no name. By dusk he was out of sight of the river and his friends, and hungry. He was also guilty, knowing he had betrayed the trust that the Skyes had placed in him. And yet he could not help it: something as new and exciting as an unknown fruit had raptured his mind until nothing else mattered. This greenish berry was sweet, had lobes, and didn't disturb his digestion, and he wanted various samples, taken from various sites, for closer examination in camp.

He was wandering through some grassed and rocky

hills when night fell and he scarcely knew which way to turn. He couldn't help it. He didn't mean to lose track of the Skyes, but his obsessions got the best of him.

That's when the no-name dog found him and Dolly, and moments later Skye loomed out of the dark, the clop of his horse's hooves announcing his approach.

Nutmeg expected rebuke but Skye's voice was gentle. "I'll take you back, Professor," was all he said, but there was a certain tautness in his words.

"Mister Skye, I've strayed and I proffer my sincere apologies," he said.

Skye nodded but said nothing. It took them half the night to reach the camp Victoria had made beside the mighty river. Neither Skye nor Victoria uttered a rebuke, but he knew that the silence itself was reproaching him.

The next morning the sun shone sweetly and all was well.

Even Victoria, who had been melancholic this long journey, had been lifted into smiles and joy as she steered her pony through belly-high grasses and exclaimed at the shimmering blue river rolling gently to the sea.

But Skye felt anxious. His muscles were taut. His temper irritable. His humor liverish. He knew himself not to be an anxious person. In the wilds of the Rockies, he had never let dire circumstance worry and abrade him. That had been one of his strengths. For Skye, there was always a way. So the emotion that inhabited his soul surprised him.

He was not comfortable with the constant worry that exhausted him even as the threesome and the two dogs rambled across the benign plains that formed the heart of the empire of Hudson's Bay. Sometimes he turned around and beheld the strange cone of Mount Hood and thought that the very eye of the Royal Navy was upon him, even in this remote corner of the New World. Admiral Hood stood over him, and had him in his clutches.

They were hand-to-mouth now and yet remained fed, for every bush bore fruit: huckleberries, plums, wild grapes, and a dozen more delights Skye couldn't identify. They had passed several fisheries but all on the north side of the mighty river. And he remembered how he had fled along that bank, six years earlier, fled for his life, fled for his liberty, determined to escape or die. By the grace of God he had lived.

They came at last to a broad valley, which shouldered a great pewter river from the south that he could see from the hill where he stood. That, he concluded, was the Willamette, and this was the place. He gazed across the waters, seeing nothing at first, and then just maybe, the hand of man, on the north bank of the Columbia. Was it a stockade? At such a great distance he could not be sure. It sat well back from the Columbia, and well east of the Willamette.

The place wrought powerful feelings in him. On a cold night in 1826 he had slid overboard, leaving a Royal Navy frigate behind him, and worked swiftly inland, never pausing, knowing he would not be safe for a hundred miles. That proved to be a serious underestimate. He had starved his way east for five hundred before he began to breathe easily.

"Here," he said gently, pointing across the enormous river. "That's Fort Vancouver."

"I don't see a thing," Nutmeg said.

Victoria said nothing. She was as taut as he, and he could well imagine what thoughts flooded her mind just then.

Here indeed was an odd thing: he had no means to get across the river. He did not even have a rifle with which to signal the post. The horses and dogs probably could not swim such a vast flood and would drown. Neither he nor Victoria could swim it, nor could Professor Nutmeg.

He studied the hazy fort closely, and discovered another thing: a vessel lay anchored beside it, its masts barely visible and its sails furled. That would be the ship that Peter Skene Ogden had urged him to catch, the ship of passage to England—if he chose to go to England, which he was not sure he would do even if it meant visiting his family, seeing his father, and clearing his name.

He could make out that it was a schooner, a two-master with fore-and-aft sails rather than square rigging. Had so small a bark traversed the Atlantic, rounded Cape Horn, and then made its way to the Sandwich Islands and across to this misty place? Could that fragile vessel carry the treasure of Hudson's Bay Company, in the form of furs, clear to England?

He didn't know how to cross to the north bank of the Columbia. He hoped to run into a fishing village where he could find a ferry. After that the HBC could come and get the rest, and the horses. But they had passed none as they traversed the last few miles to a point opposite the post. And then it came to him to wait until night and build a signal fire, and that surely would bring a canoe or barge across the waters to investigate.

"All right, mate, we'll camp here," he said to Nutmeg. "Tonight we'll signal. They probably won't start across before dawn."

"Couldn't we try some smoke right now?" Nutmeg asked.

"We could see. But there's a fresh breeze and I think it'll just dissipate."

Even as they talked, Victoria was looking for dry wood, which was scarce in this rain-soaked land. But soon she was pulling driftwood from the shores, and breaking dead branches from trees, and shaving the slimmest imaginable kindling that would form a tiny nest for the embers that would catch under her flint and steel.

Skye helped her. They would need plenty of wood, for only a giant fire would attract attention at such a distance.

Then, when all was ready, she crouched over the tiny nest, sheltering it from the breeze, and deftly struck her steel across the flint, raining sparks down on her flammable thimbleful of fuzz. The first strikes seemed futile, but then a tiny ember burned in one spot. She struck more sparks until several burned, and then crouched over the kindling and blew gently.

That always seemed the agonizing moment to Skye, the moment that would spell life or death in the dead of winter, the moment that would tell whether they would eat raw and vile food, or cook a meal and warm their flesh and feel the life of the fire secure their own perilous lives.

The flame flickered, smouldered, and caught, tiny, fragile, but real. She fed hairlike bits of tinder into it until it bloomed into a three-inch-high blaze. He sighed. They were still a half hour from a fire that would boil smoke, generated by moist grasses, into the air high enough to be spotted from that hazy shore so far distant.

The professor perched himself on a boulder and stared across the empty river. It was the end of a failed journey for him, and yet he had somehow risen above the disaster. Here he would await the arrival of Wyeth in a few days or weeks, and then ride home in Wyeth's ship.

Nutmeg was at ease, but Skye wasn't. He could not sit at all, but paced restlessly, waiting for the fire to build. He headed down to the river bank and watched the innocent waters purl by. He felt a terrible temptation to turn the horses east and flee once again. He was still wanted by the Crown, and the Hudson's Bay Company was the long arm of the Crown. And yet he stayed. He was not a man of little faith, but one of hope and courage. He would see what the White Eagle, McLoughlin, was made of, and what would be laid upon the table.

If he fled now they would be helpless. Victoria had but one arrow, and that was the extent of their weaponry. And yet Skye had endured worse times, over and over, drawing from some singular courage and determination to weather the worst that the wilds could throw at him. He would endure now. As he stood gazing across those shimmering waters, his courage stole back into him, and the anxiety faded. He had left the Royal Navy still a boy; now he was a man, and a man among men.

He turned to observe the flame on the slope behind him, and discovered a fine gray plume, wrought by moist grasses. Surely the men at Fort Vancouver would see it. And yet for the better part of an hour, nothing happened. He watched the far shore alertly, watched the distant ship, watched the hazy stockade, and yet saw nothing.

But at last, late in the day when the westering sun was lighting one side of Victoria's plume of smoke, he saw some movement. It took ten minutes before he knew that a canoe was heading across the waters. They had been discovered at last.

He watched its slow progress, knowing that it held his fate on board. When it was still a hundred yards distant and fighting the current, he made out five men in it, two rowing on each side, while one steered. The big canoe, longer and wider than any he had seen, drove straight at him, and finally beached on a strand just below his perch.

A young man peered upward. Four French-Canadian voyageurs rested on their oars.

"Be ye, by any chance, Barnaby Skye?" he asked.

"I am."

"And this is your party. Who have ye with you?"

"My wife Victoria, and Alistair Nutmeg, a naturalist from Leicester. He lectures at Harvard, in Boston, but he's an Englishman and a gentleman, sir. And who are you?"

"Douglas, sir. Hudson's Bay, at your service."

"Well, Mr. Douglas, we need to carry three horses, two dogs, and three mortals, across those waters."

"We'll manage it. Dr. McLoughlin has been hoping

you'd arrive in time. She's sailing in two days. Hop in, sir, and we'll carry you over."

Skye paused. "I'd prefer to cross with my wife and colleague, Mr. Douglas. We've come a long way together and we'll finish this trip together."

"The factor will be disappointed."

"Only for an hour or two."

"Very well, sir. We'll likely bring the flatboat over. She's slow, but there's a small sail."

"It can board the horses?"

"From that bench there, sir. The channel runs deep there, and they've a long gangway."

"We'll be ready, then."

A voyageur clambered out, grappled the prow of the canoe, and then hopped aboard as the crew rowed into the blue. Skye reckoned that before dark he would know whether he and Victoria would be going to England.

He stared guiltily at No Name, who sulked beside him, accusation in his eyes.

23

As the flatboat closed, Skye beheld McLoughlin standing at the bank. It could be no other. This man towered a foot above everyone else, was built on the model of a keg, and his head was crowned with a burst of white hair, which gave him his name: the White Eagle.

Behind him, well back from the Columbia, stood the imperial Fort Vancouver, a large stockaded fortress Skye had seen once before. Everything about it weighed heavy, from its towering stockades to its huge waterfront gate. This western capital of a pounds-and-pence empire struck awe in him. But it was larger now, double what it had been, and a village surrounded it. In every direction he could see agricultural pursuits: orchards, vineyards, hay- and grainfields, a grist mill.

Scores lined the riverbank, but it was McLoughlin who commanded his gaze. The man radiated something regal, as if he were the true royalty here. At his side stood a dark and stocky woman wearing a dress that no doubt would be fashionable in London. That, no doubt, would be the notorious Marguerite, his consort of many years, the widow of the explorer Alexander McKay, but not before she had taken up with McLoughlin.

This was no outpost but a city. The closer the leaky

flatboat drew, the higher ran Skye's estimates. Several hundred lived in this self-supporting capital. He eyed, as well, the schooner, a trim white ship better suited to coastal trade than navigating oceans. Did the entire resupply of HBC arrive in that small vessel, and did it take a whole year's gathering of pelts and furs to England in that tiny hold?

But it was McLoughlin who riveted him. The man was lord and emperor here, responsible only to Governor George Simpson half across a continent at York Factory, and thus largely sovereign in his lordship over this northwest quarter. As the flatboat slowed and the voyageurs tossed hempen ropes to shore, a swift fear built in Skye; he knew at once he could not brook the awesome will of that sovereign lord of the wilds.

Then the flatboat bumped land, and voyageurs leapt to drag it up a gravelly beach. Amid a great hue and cry, Victoria slipped close to Skye, unnerved by this white men's world she was seeing for the first time. He plucked her hand and held it tight within his rough one, saying things with his fingers that she would understand.

They were helped over the prow and set foot on the shoreline, and people whirled tight like a sliding noose. Professor Nutmeg stepped out, and the two dogs bounded onto land.

Skye found himself staring upward into a probing gaze.

"McLoughlin here. Welcome to our post, Mister Skye!"

Skye found himself shaking hands with the giant.

"There, you see? I know a bit about you. Have I addressed you as you wish?"

"You have, sir. This is my wife Victoria, of the Crow people, and Professor Nutmeg, a naturalist who started with the Wyeth party but joined us."

McLoughlin's gaze bored into Victoria. "Ah, a most lovely consort, Mister Skye. And may I introduce my Marguerite? You women will have much in common."

Marguerite smiled and clasped Victoria's hand.

Victoria found her voice. "Goddam," she muttered.

"Well said, madam. A woman after my own heart. And Nutmeg? I didn't know about you, sir. Welcome."

"A most amazing post, Doctor."

"Do I detect England in your voice, Professor?"

"Leicester, sir, but now a lecturer at Harvard. A naturalist, a botanist."

"And what are your plans, eh?"

"I'll be returning on Wyeth's ship, the *Sultana*."

"I've not heard of it or Wyeth."

"It's a brig sent round the horn, Doctor. Wyeth plans to set up a salmon fishery on the Columbia and send the proceeds back. It's carrying machinery for making casks and processing fish, and also some trade goods to sell to American trappers."

All that was news to Skye. It had never occurred to him to ask Nutmeg what Wyeth was up to. So Wyeth wasn't going to buck the already fierce competition in the fur and peltry business except as a sideline.

McLoughlin paused suddenly, taking stock of the obvious threat to HBC, and then smiled.

"Come in." He turned to some subordinates. "Put these horses up, and bring in our guests' truck."

Skye led the silent Victoria into the jaws of the post, and found himself cloistered by walls he guessed were twenty feet high. Within, he discovered, to his astonishment, a complete settlement, a gracious headquarters and home for the factor, barracks for the single men, great kitchens, and warehouses for the peltries.

And women, even one or two white women. He had not seen a white woman in more years than he could remember. Marguerite was a half-breed, as were most of the well-dressed ladies present there, but there, indeed, across the yard, stood a fair-fleshed woman.

Victoria sucked breath. She had never seen a white woman.

McLoughlin was looking him over, but making no overt move, and Skye realized that not until the amenities of the evening were behind them would he and the factor have a talk, probably closeted somewhere.

Assorted lackeys settled the guests in two rooms, and Victoria gasped at the interior of the one she shared with Skye. She walked over to the bed and pressed it, marveling. She peered through the glass panes, touched the glass, astonished. She studied the washstand and bowl and pitcher, scarcely believing what lay before her eyes. She studied the smooth, polished plank floor. She sat in a chair, surprised that she didn't need to squat on her heels as she usually did. She explored under the bed and discovered a porcelain thundermug, and understood its purpose at once. She pulled back the coverlet and beheld crisp sheets of good English cotton, covered with thick, four-point Hudson's Bay blankets. She poked a pillow and then examined it closely, discovering that it was filled with down, and scowled. Skye wondered whether she would object to sleeping on feathers.

Skye showed her how to pull the shutters tight for privacy, and how to open and close a door by turning the iron knob. He showed her the candles in their holders, and how to light one with a taper sitting near a small iron stove.

He thought she would enjoy these things, but he discovered a fear in her, and understood. All the marvels she had seen in the rendezvous, in the traders' kits, were nothing compared to what she was seeing now.

"Victoria," he said, "don't be afraid of this world. These are all useful things but they are nothing. Dr. McLoughlin's wife is half Cree, and she'll help you with anything you need or wish to learn. I think you'll enjoy these things, but if you don't, say so, and we'll head back to the mountains. If you're unhappy . . ."

"Oh, Skye," she said, pushing tears away with her small brown fists.

He hadn't given much thought to what all this would look like to a Crow Indian woman who had never seen a white man's city. He hadn't expected anything like this; just another roughhewn fort, which it obviously still was, except for this one corner of it, the factor's own home and guest quarters.

But she was showing a brave face, and next he knew she was pouring water from the white porcelain pitcher into the basin, sampling the ball of scented English soap, whose use she understood intuitively, and was washing away her tears and her fear. She found a towel, marveled, wiped her face and hands, and grinned cockily at him.

He cleaned up and waited, not knowing what to expect.

Victoria spent a while prettying herself. From her small kit she withdrew her prized vermilion and ran a streak down her forehead. She smoothed her soft doeskin dress and cleaned her quilled moccasins. She enjoyed the looking glass.

Skye watched gently, loving her, knowing that his Crow wife would be struggling and perhaps distraught when she faced the dinner table.

"Victoria, just enjoy yourself. You'll see how life is lived in the white men's cities and maybe even how it will be in London."

"Well, dammit, Skye, I don't know nothing."

"Be yourself, and if you have doubts, watch."

They found their way to a dining hall where the factor and his wife and their guests had gathered, a place separate from the great mess hall that fed many of their employees.

This was indeed civilization, though only the veneer of it. The long table and chairs had been crafted locally, but good English china and wine goblets rested on it, and candles in pewter holders lit it, and linen serviettes rested beside silver at each place setting. If the walls were hand-sawn plank, the mirrors and art on them were encased in gilt frames.

The women wore brown, or scarlet, or cream, or muted green cotton dresses, some trimmed in white, elaborately sewn and decorated with myriad buttons. No matter whether they were full-bloods, half-bloods, or white, they were all dressed fashionably in the European manner. The gentlemen were, likewise, dressed in frock coats, shirts, and cravats. John McLoughlin cared less about his dress than the underlings, and wore no cravat.

Skye felt out of place in his calico shirt, buckskin britches, and high moccasins, and he supposed that his bear claw necklace didn't help him any. Victoria clung close to him, not frightened but intensely observant, choosing deep silence as her refuge.

Professor Nutmeg remained casually dressed as well, having lost all his clothing in the Cayuse village. His ancient jacket had been patched repeatedly with leather at the elbows. It was not clean, any more than Skye's hard-used buckskins or shirt were clean.

Still, no one seemed to notice. McLoughlin could scarcely expect company dressed to the nines at such a place.

McLoughlin proved a gracious host. He introduced James Douglas, second in command; then the various women, wives or consorts of the post's administrators. He introduced a white-bearded gentleman in a plain but natty blue uniform as Emilius Simpson, master of the HBC schooner, *Cadboro*, which bobbed on the river a hundred yards distant. Several of his merchant vessel officers were in attendance, also.

Skye, in turn, introduced Victoria, and shook hands with the whole lot of these gentlemen and ladies.

Skye could barely remember such a scene, and dredged his memories for youthful recollections of such things in his family's home. His father and mother had occasionally welcomed guests, but Skye could remember nothing like this glittering banquet, with candles in dizzy numbers illumining the great room, and fashionable guests at every hand.

Such dinners as he remembered had been served by his mother and younger sisters, who were barely visible at table, and Skye wondered if these women would do the same. But when McLoughlin invited the company to be seated, the women sat beside their men, with Marguerite McLoughlin at the opposite end of the great table.

Then Indian women poured in from the kitchen, bearing platters burdened with savory meats and vegetables and fresh bread. Skye marveled. He had not had a slice of fresh bread in a decade. Swiftly the women deposited these massive heaps of food on the table.

McLoughlin rose. His wine goblet was filled only with water, and Skye suspected he didn't touch spirits. But the other glasses on the table glowed with ruby wine.

"Ladies and gentlemen, let us welcome our distinguished guests. Mister Barnaby Skye, his wife Victoria, and Professor Alistair Nutmeg, in case any of you have not met them, Englishmen and friends of the HBC."

They toasted the guests, and Skye arose to toast his hosts and their company. Victoria sat quietly, transfixed by all this.

Skye soon found himself wolfing down food that had only been a memory for many years: beefsteak, potatoes and maize swimming in butter, apples and plums and pears, and breads galore.

Then he noticed Victoria sitting primly, her plate of foods untouched, her hands folded in her lap. She was staring at the rest, and he understood. She had never seen Europeans eat at table, had never seen the uses of silverware, had never seen serviettes across laps, or food enter mouths without the aid of fingers. She had never seen people dab their lips with those cloths, nor had she seen people sip daintily from glass goblets. She had never seen serving women hurry empty platters away and bring fresh ones. She had never listened to polite conversation at table.

He didn't know whether she was afraid or simply observing with those sharp eyes of hers. But he paused, slipped a hand over hers, and squeezed.

"Sonofabitch," she said, and began to eat, flawlessly mimicking her hosts and hostesses.

24

Skye found himself closeted with the formidable McLoughlin after the dinner. An oil lamp provided the sole illumination, adding a furtive and sinister quality to the interview. They sat in the factor's study, surrounded by ledgers but barren of books. McLoughlin's mind turned more to curios of the wilderness that had been presented him over the years.

McLoughlin motioned Skye to the cut-glass decanter of spirits—brandy, Skye supposed—but Skye declined. This was the interview that would shape his life. He would walk through the fateful portal as a man pursuing something radically new, or he would gather Victoria and ride back to the mountains.

"Well, Mister Skye, I've been following your case for years. I first thought of you as a criminal and lowlife. That's what the blasted navy had to say of you. But then reports filtered in from my men in our trading houses. They have a keen eye and a good ear, you know. And the two Skyes didn't match up. So, you see, I conducted a small inquiry of my own. I gather Ogden told you the rest."

"Yes, some of it."

"Enough to bring you here. That suggests to me that we may have something to offer. Eh?"

"What do you know of me, Doctor?"

"It's John, if you please. I never was much for ceremony. Especially here." A massive hand swept the air, and the gesture evoked a primal lordship.

But it was too much for Skye to call this man John. McLoughlin was the image of Empire, the king's magistrate, the representative of a vast, royally chartered company, and a man of massive size and ability.

The factor continued. "You are a good man. We want you. You can have a distinguished career with us. That sums it up."

"Why do you think I'm a good man?"

"I don't think it, I know it."

"I would like to hear your proposal in your own words, even though Peter Ogden gave it to me, sir."

"We've kept track. You're a resourceful brigade leader. You inspire your men. You don't stoop to the usual Yank trickery or ruthlessness and yet you do the job better. You have dignity and courage. You've pulled out of scrapes that would sink any man I know of in the mountains except Ogden and maybe Bridger and Fitzpatrick. You've revealed an ethical nature, paying off debts that might easily be forgotten. Your word is your bond.

"Ogden may be leaving us in two or three years. I wish to have you replace him. You're an Englishman. We're an English firm. You don't belong with the Yanks. Of course you had to stick with 'em, but I've been busy about that. You can come back to the Union Jack. I have good men here at the post, but none have the field experience you have. I'd put you out there, knowing you'd keep the Yanks from stealing our trappers, and send back peltries and make us a tidy sum."

"You mustn't listen to trappers' tales, sir."

"Would you deny any of it?"

Skye entertained mixed feelings about that. He knew he and Victoria, together, had survived where most men would go under. But she made the other half of it.

"Yes, sir. My consort Victoria . . ."

"Yes, yes, of course. That's understood. I'll confide in you." He glared at Skye, as if daring him to whisper a word of it elsewhere. "I've been looking for a successor. Someone to fill my position in a half dozen years. HBC has damned good men. But the ones in the field would be poor at governing this unruly empire, and the ones around me have no field experience. Then I was thinking about you . . ."

That stunned Skye.

"Show me that you can do it, Mister Skye."

Swiftly, this lord of the wilds answered Skye's questions even before they were asked. Years earlier, when McLoughlin realized that Skye wasn't cut to the Royal Navy's cloth, he became curious. He dispatched letters to London asking for information, and got it. Yes, Skye was a merchant's son who had vanished, deeply grieving the family. They thought him dead. Yes, the family had destined him for a business life. Yes, the press gang had snatched him near the London Dock. Yes, he had been a rebellious and sullen seaman, always on the brink of getting himself tossed into the sea to feed the sharks. Yes, he had become the joke, the byword, of the admiralty; the ultimate bad actor.

And yes, his father lived, but was failing.

Skye choked.

"Why should I go back there, risk my liberty, sir?"

"Because you must. We've friends in the right places. I had an HBC man approach the king's chancellor, Lord Pims, directly about it. We told his lordship that you'd prospered with the Yanks, that you've a stout heart and the destiny of Empire may hinge on fetching you back and jacking you to command. The Oregon country's up for grabs and jointly claimed by the Yanks and ourselves. We made the case, and Lord Pims will see to the royal pardon. Mere form, actually."

Skye listened, amazed that so much whirled around his person. "Who are my adversaries and what might go wrong?"

"Simpson, George Simpson, up in York Factory. He sees no good in you and he'd clap you in irons the moment he lays eyes on you. He's not only the governor of HBC in America, but he's also the king's man. He rules the territory by leave of King George. If he catches you and sends you off to England, there's not a thing I could do. He's the law. We must obey it. That's why I'm not sending you back via York Factory or Hudson's Bay, but around the Horn."

"Who else?"

"Count on envy to make enemies, Mister Skye. I'm passing over a dozen men."

"Why do you trust me?"

"I don't, entirely. If you go to London, get your pardon, see your family, and fail to return to us, then I'll know the measure of you."

"My circumstance also requires trust. Will I arrive in England and be clapped in irons?"

"The admiralty would like it—if they knew of it. They don't. So far, this is between you, me, my contact on the board of governors of HBC, and Lord Pims. No one else knows."

Skye sighed. This forceful man seemed the soul of honesty, yet a man of cunning and a thousand schemes.

"How will all this happen?" he asked curtly.

"In two days our schooner, under Emilius Simpson, sets sail. You'll be on it. He won't have any idea you're a seaman and you obviously won't reveal it. Your past must remain obscure."

"I have a family here."

"A family, a family?"

"Victoria and our dog."

"Victoria should go with you if you feel she can master it. My women have, easily. Marguerite is, for all intents, a white woman. But the dog, that's up to the master of the *Cadboro*."

"I'll ask him, then."

"By all means. And if he says no, we could subsist the dog here and you'd be reunited in less than two years," the factor added.

Skye didn't like that. Something bad was crawling through his mind.

"We're penniless. I don't even have my rifle. We have nothing for passage."

"Three fine horses, Mister Skye."

Skye nodded.

"Here's what they'll fetch you. A fine suit of clothes and a spare frock coat and boots; two dresses, slippers, shoes, nightgown, and everything else required to outfit a lady for London, including a shawl. A good beaver hat, to replace the, ah, unsuitable one. A few pounds of traveling cash. A mug of soap, brush and razor, and any other toiletries you and Mrs. Skye might require. Good Scottish wool capes to keep you warm around the Horn and in England.

"We'll keep your dog, if need be, and outfit you for work when you return. I'll do an accounting: the value of the saddle horses is considerable here, and we are short and willing to pay a hundred Yank dollars, or twenty pounds, apiece. Sixty pounds will buy you the finest wardrobes this post can supply—and we can do you up, believe me. You'll sail to London and return, debt-free, but with an obligation."

Skye pondered that, half liking it, half itchy and unhappy.

McLoughlin pressed further. "Time's flying, sir. It'll

take every hour of tomorrow to fit you out. The women are fine seamstresses, but not even they could outfit Mrs. Skye in less than a day."

Skye hesitated.

McLoughlin pulled a folder close and extracted a letter. "Here, sir."

Skye held it to the lamp so he could read. He needed spectacles but no such thing could be found in the mountains.

It was dated October, the year previous.

"To my son, Barnaby, wherever you might be . . ."

Barnaby Skye's hand trembled. At the base of the brief letter he discerned his father's own signature, crabbed and thick.

A kind gentleman from Hudson's Bay Company has sought me out to tell me that you live somewhere in North America, and all the rest. We thought you were dead, the victim of some foul waterfront deed. Your mother and I grieved.

But that is the past. She is gone now, having left us in eighteen and twenty-nine, never knowing that you lived. May she rest with the angels. The rest of us live, though my health is precarious, dropsy and gout afflicting me.

I rejoice in this news, and urge you to come home swiftly, while time remains for me to behold you with my own eyes. The gentlemen have apprised me of your difficulties and assure me that the matter can be remedied in the king's chancery. We yearn to see you, and wish you Godspeed in your long journey. With this news, God has granted me my fondest wish.

With most loving affection,
Your father,
Edward Barnaby Skye.

Skye read it, and again, and let the memories of the man who had sired him flood through him. His sire would be old now, and his slim sisters would be fleshy. Something deep and primal stirred in him. He would go. And he would accept the costs and consequences and risks.

25

Victoria marveled at the skill of the several women who swiftly sewed her new clothing. That day they hurried her into a room where seven of them had gathered, measured her and set to work.

"These are the latest fashions from London," explained Marguerite McLoughlin.

"What is latest? This I do not understand."

"White women are forever changing their way of dressing. What is good one year is bad the next."

"That is very strange," Victoria said. "They are all mad."

That evoked some smiles and a giggle or two.

They fitted her first for a woolen winter dress of stiff gray fabric, and then for two dresses of cotton. And several of them had dug into their own chests and given her assorted accessories and underthings. One supplied a broad-brimmed straw hat sporting an extravagant feather much larger than any Victoria had ever seen.

"The feather is from Africa," someone told her.

"What is Africa?"

"I don't know."

Victoria discovered that these women sewed clothing in much the way as her Absaroka sisters made it. Two of these women were white, the rest were women of the Peoples, or breeds, such as Marguerite.

"What is England like?" she asked, but they did not know.

The two white women were Canadians and had never seen England.

"I would not want to go there," said one Cree woman. "They would look down on me."

Victoria supposed that might be true. Skye had desperately tried to tell her everything he could about London, but she only grew confused. She finally realized she didn't know what he was talking about. He could not explain things she could not imagine. She could not even think about their King George, and what he did, and the people surrounding him. And when he described Parliament, she thought of a council of elders passing the pipe and speaking in turn, and that proved to be mostly wrong.

So she would have to see. And learn. But, she reminded herself, he had to learn the ways of her Kicked-in-the-Belly band of Absarokas, and he had been strange and shocking to her people for many months until he learned the ways, the rituals, and especially what was sacred and deserved uttermost respect.

She knew what she would do: be silent. She would not get into much trouble in this London if she said nothing and was careful to imitate the conduct she saw around her.

But the seamstresses at Fort Vancouver tried anyway to explain matters.

"When you enter a church, you should wear a hat or a veil," one said.

"What's this church?"

"A building where they worship God."

"What is worship?"

This went on through the morning, and by noontime she knew less about Skye's people than before, because everything she thought she knew proved untrue. One thing she knew: everything white people did was vastly more complicated than her own ways, especially making medicine and talking to the spirits and the winds. When the women finally dressed her in all the proper underthings and the gray woolen dress, she felt constricted and anchored down. Her own durable, supple fringed doeskin dress with its quillwork was stronger, more comfortable, and more beautiful to the eye, and she didn't have to wear layers of little skirts under it.

But the women swarmed over her, fitting the clothing, adding a hat and gloves, and then led her to a looking glass.

Victoria shrank back from the image. She knew this was not herself.

"What the hell do I do when I must go to the bushes?" she asked. "Three of these little skirts and these pants?" She laughed maliciously.

None of them had been to England, so no one knew. They knew of chamber pots and privies, but little else.

Skye would know and she would ask him.

Later that afternoon she found him but barely recognized him. He wore a dove-gray cutaway coat with a double row of black buttons, black vest, a white shirt, blue britches, black leather shoes, and his battered beaver top hat had been exchanged for a glossy new one. He had lost his beard, too, and gazed at her from a smooth and ruddy face.

"Sonofabitch!" she yelled. "You some big medicine man!"

He grinned.

They laughed. She had never seen Skye looking like this. He had never seen her looking like a white woman. Suddenly Skye was a British gentleman; suddenly she was a dusky British lady. She took his arm and they promenaded round about the confines of the fort, following the footsteps of the bagpiper the night before.

That had been a terror. At sundown that first night she had heard the strangest howl, a noise that sent a chill through the marrow of her bones. Skye was closeted with McLoughlin and she didn't know what to do, so she slammed the door of their small apartment and waited. But the howl droned on, never stopping, like the groan of a dying dog, but there was more to it. She heard a whining melody, soft and cruel, like the wailing of mourners when her people lifted a dead person into its scaffold, and this wail sent chills through her. The yellow cur lifted its nose to the sky and howled.

Still, no one seemed alarmed. She heard no shouts, no running, no clamors, no war-cries. She softly opened the door a crack and peered out upon the dusky yard of the post, and there she beheld a man in a skirt, holding some fiendish device, walking in measured paces about the perimeter of the post. Then she had understood: he was a medicine man, chasing away the devils of the night, scaring the wandering spirits away from the post so the people could sleep in peace. Ah! A holy man!

She had watched this strange man, with the strange skirt and strange cap on his head, and this fiendish machine piping away the evils of the underworld, and she knew it was well. Skye had never mentioned this custom to her and she had planned to ask him about it. But she forgot, because when he returned to their apartment, he was filled with his meeting with McLoughlin, and that is what they babbled about.

But now Skye was strolling with her on the very path the medicine man with the fiendish device had paced so slowly that she had wondered if he were ill.

"What was that noise I heard last night?" she asked.

"What noise?"

"Like a hundred dying wolves."

He brightened. "Bagpiper. An old Scots custom."

"A medicine man?"

"You could say that," he said. "I haven't heard one since I was a lad. Call it a warrior's pipe. It's a big flute."

"Ah! It terrifies the enemy."

He explained what he knew of the piper, but she understood little. Maybe she would learn more in this London.

"You look very beautiful," he said, with some strange feeling in his voice.

"I do?"

"You . . . remind me of my sisters."

That disappointed her. She wanted him to like her as an Absaroka woman, not someone wrapped in these strange clothes that scratched and tortured her.

"I don't like your stuff," she said.

She saw some sadness in his face. He lifted his top hat and settled it. "We'll be coming back soon. Soon you'll be wearing your beautiful doeskin dresses and I'll be very happy."

"And you?"

"I confess I enjoy these clothes. I am, for the moment, a man of parts."

"Well, goddamit, let's go."

No Name found them and growled his disapproval.

Skye turned silent.

The dog chose a path between them, his pace matching theirs as they hiked around the vast yard.

She knew that silence. Whenever Skye was torn, he turned silent, and now he was terribly torn.

"They will feed him," she said.

But she didn't believe it. This yellow dog was a spirit-animal and such a creature had to go wherever its brothers went. But tomorrow they were going somewhere no dog could go.

They pierced the great gate, strolled down the gentle slope to the riverbank, and stared at the schooner bobbing there at anchor. The dog followed, whining once and then trembling.

The ocean canoe looked mighty to her, another wonder of the white men, but Skye was not impressed.

"This isn't much of a ship," he said. "Big merchant ship would be thirty or forty feet longer and ten or fifteen wider at the beam. This is a little thing for a big ocean. I wonder how the company can store a year's worth of furs in that hold."

She couldn't imagine a larger vessel.

"But she's seaworthy," he continued, talking to himself. "And she'll run. She's rigged to run, fore and aft sails . . ."

The dog was trembling.

She reached to touch its head, and the moment her hand touched the dog, it quieted.

"You must find a way to take him, Skye," she said.

"It will be up to the master."

"If he says no, we shouldn't go."

They stopped their stroll.

"Sometimes a man has to do hard things, Victoria. Give up something to receive something larger. I'm prepared to leave the dog behind if I must."

She didn't reply at first. Then she said, "He will not give you up. If he would give you his name, then he would be an ordinary dog you could give up. Any ordinary dog has a name. That is what names are for. If this dog had a name, you could leave him with McLoughlin. But he has withheld his name and that means he is bound to you for all of his life. He is not just a dog. He is a dog appointed to watch over you. He is more important to you than I am."

"That cannot be, Victoria."

"But it is so," she said, her tone adamant.

The dog was trembling again, and her heart was heavy.

26

Skye stood on the teak deck of a fine schooner, feeling joy. He was on his way to London to recover his good name. He was an Englishman returning home. He had a future assured in North America, working for a mighty English company. He could return to his homeland in the future. He would see his father and sisters and cousins and return to the bosom of his family. He would see nephews and nieces he had never seen.

He would not lose Victoria or his new life, either. She would go with him and return to her native land with him, and see her own family and tribe a year or so hence. No Name would remain. Skye had tried to win passage for the dog, but the master, Simpson, had flatly refused.

"I've never shipped a dirty dog, suh, and never will," the master had said.

McLoughlin had agreed to keep the animal. No Name would be waiting for Skye here in this massive post.

As he stood at the rail watching the crew smartly prepare to sail, he beheld almost the whole population of this amazing outpost. Several hundred men and women, not least of them the White Eagle, were watching the departure of the ship that linked them to the Mother Country so far distant; the ship that came but once a year and a half, bearing amenities and news of loved ones, as well as the staples of life. Skye waved one last farewell to Nutmeg, who waved back, full of good cheer.

No Name had tried to follow Skye out the short wharf and up the gangway, but two bosuns turned him back and then the dog slinked back to the riverbank and watched quietly. Skye was relieved: this would be all right. The good doctor would look after the strange creature.

Victoria held his hand, resolute in the midst of her fears.

"You have courage," he whispered to her. "We'll be back."

She didn't smile. This trip was for her like sailing over the lip of the world. But it wasn't the trip that held her; it was the dog, watching them mournfully from the shore, its head tucked between its front paws, forgotten by all the excited crowd of Indians, voyageurs, farmhands, clerks, and laborers collected in knots before the fort.

He knew he would not forget this spectacle, this bright October day, this vast panorama.

A breeze freshened even as Emilius Simpson's topmen raised the canvas. The master wore white kid gloves and stood quietly on the quarterdeck watching his hands twist the capstan that raised the anchor, while others looked to the sails.

Skye watched them carefully, knowing his life would be in the hands of this crew, and was satisfied. Simpson's quiet demeanor said much. The man radiated iron command in a curious way, as if some great reserve of force lay behind his gentle direction. He addressed his chief mate and bosuns, or deck officers, softly, but there would be no questioning this master's order. The kid-gloved hands occasionally squeezed shut, only to open again. It was as if Simpson needed the layer of soft leather to separate the duties of his hands from the rest of himself. Such as holding a whip.

But Simpson's was not the face of a martinet, and Skye knew that Hudson's Bay had chosen well, selecting a top man among a seafaring people.

Then, slowly, the schooner slid free of its anchorage and hove into the wind as the shuddering sails caught the breeze. This trip downriver would rely heavily on the current of the Columbia to take it to sea, but there was nothing like a good two-masted schooner with fore-and-aft sails to employ an adverse wind.

Skye's home would be a cramped cabin on the quarterdeck, behind the master's own. He and Victoria would share a tiny galley with the entire crew, including the master and two mates. There were few amenities. The *Cadboro* was but fifty-six feet from bow to stern, and but seventeen at the beam, and carried a crew of thirty: chief and petty officers, seamen, cooks, navigators and helmsmen, carpenters and sailmakers. It was armed with six brass cannon, good for little other than scaring Indians and saluting passing vessels. But it was a clean ship, well caulked and scraped and enameled, gleaming the pride of its master.

In its eight-foot-high hold rested the entire year's fur catch, the wealth of the HBC borne in a single fragile bark that would sail clear down the Pacific coast of North and South America, round the fearsome Horn, head across the South Atlantic, and then north to England, a journey that would take six or seven months with good winds, longer if beset with troubles. The return, to York Factory on Hudson's Bay and then overland, would fly faster.

Skye felt the ship stir under his feet and heel subtly in the wind as the sails filled and the chattering stopped. The helmsman had measured the wind, checking its direction with a glance at the wooly wind gauge, and quartered north. The river there ran more northerly than west, but eventually would swing west to the sea. That vector made for fast sailing.

Skye said nothing and revealed nothing. His past was a secret known only to Victoria and himself. For the rest of those on board, he was a British gentleman, smartly turned out in serviceable fashion, escorted by a comely Indian maiden he had taken to wife in the fur trade. That suited Skye fine. The less they knew of him, the better.

The shoreline receded and the fort diminished to the rear, and then there was only the glittering river, shooting sparks off its surface, purling toward the sea, cold and hazy on a bright day. The wooded shores seemed small and distant even as the helmsman caught the swiftest current to carry it along.

They strolled the small deck, where temporary disorder reigned. But Skye knew that no master would allow such disarray upon reaching the sea, where great waves would wash anything not tied down or anchored into the rails.

Then Victoria pointed. There on a promontory, small but unmistakable, was the yellow dog, its head high, staring squarely at Skye and Victoria. The dog rested there, its sides heaving, and then started west again, tracing the shore, never stopping because the ship never stopped.

Skye felt a bitter weight. "It'll turn around and go back," he said, not really believing it.

"It will find a way," Victoria replied. She was sincere; he hadn't been.

"It'll wear out. A ship never stops unless fog or haze forces it to. If the moon's full it can run at night. The pup'll come to a river and quit, and find its way back to wait for us."

"No," she said, and he stared at her.

Most of the next hour they didn't see the dog, but every time Skye thought the dog had quit, it reappeared, ghostly and yellow and staring at the distant ship, sometimes half a mile distant when the helmsman skirted the south bank.

Mr. Simpson appeared at their side. "Here's my glass," he said. "He's a fine loyal dog. The watch up there is talking about nothing else."

Skye lifted the telescoping brass spy glass to his eye and failed to see the dog.

"You're behind it, I think," Simpson said.

Skye swung the lens forward and caught a flash of yellow, and then finally focused on No Name, who was running easily, a few hundred yards at a time before sitting on his haunches to rest a moment.

He gave the glass to Victoria, who found the dog and muttered bitterly, keeping her thoughts in Absaroka rather than sharing them with the white men. Then she handed the glass back.

"We'll reach the Pacific about nine this evening. Rough water there, some dangerous bars, and often some fog. With a favorable wind, we should be at sea just before full dark. It's the most dangerous point in the entire journey, more so even than Cape Horn. But once we reach the Pacific, we'll head down the coast, riding the Japan current, doing some trading in Mexican California before we abandon the continent."

Skye nodded. His thoughts were on the dog. Even without the glass, he could occasionally see the movement of a bit of yellow.

"Crew's betting when the dog'll quit," Simpson said. "They're taking odds that the pup will quit at the Lewis River."

"No," said Victoria.

"No dog can keep up for long," Simpson said, gently disagreeing. "We are moving at nine or ten knots."

The master returned to his watch, and Skye and Victoria watched the silent world slide by. A chill rose from the river, but neither of them would leave the rail even to fetch a shawl or a cape from the wardrobes hastily assembled for them.

Skye watched the dog struggle along the shore. It was obviously weary now, pausing to rest frequently. Skye could not see his sides heaving, but he knew exactly how that dog would look close at hand, and he sorrowed. He felt helpless and saddened and finally despairing, feeling that the dog would run itself to death rather than do the sensible thing and turn back.

What had Skye done to deserve such loyalty?

They passed the confluence of the Lewis, a large stream out of the St. Helen's wilderness and the crew lined the rail until a sharp word from the mates sent them to their posts again.

Skye did not see the dog. They sailed past the river. The forest thickened and the shore vaulted upward again. And then, at a rocky point, they saw the yellow dog. The sun caught it until it glowed like gold. It stood proudly in the sun until the *Cadboro* passed, and then ran downstream again.

No one cheered.

27

They saw no more of the yellow dog. By the time they passed the Kalama River, Skye knew the dog had given up. He grieved. No creature had ever loved him so much. He was ashamed at how reluctantly he had come to love the dog, how stupid he had been.

He brooded a while, studying the shore, hoping yet not hoping, wanting the dog to turn back to Fort Vancouver but wanting to see it again, a golden streak pacing the schooner as it cut the tide. The confusion of his mind wearied him.

Still, the future beckoned. He turned at last to his cabin, settling himself for a half-year journey home while Victoria still patrolled the deck of the small ship as if to measure her new world. The thought of England stirred feelings so deep he couldn't even name them. Not all of them were pleasant. His father's warehouse stood deep in East End, surrounded by misery and ignorance and depravity. The cruelties he had seen, even as a boy, had made it easier for him to adapt to the New World, where most people had a chance to fashion a life in a fresh, sweet land.

Maybe he would swiftly weary of London. After making his peace with the Crown and embracing his family, he would itch to escape to this vibrant continent where people were carving out a new life for themselves and severing the chains of Europe. He decided not to worry about all that: he was going home for a while, and what else mattered?

He felt increasingly confident about the weathered master, Simpson, who was sailing swiftly but not recklessly down the river, going faster than a square-rigged ship could but never so fast as to endanger his vessel. The *Cadboro* swung easily from one channel to another, responding instantly to the helmsman. Skye studied the men and the ship, seeing in their conduct more than the master suspected.

Victoria had slid into silence, mourning the dog, but later in the day she recovered her spirits.

She questioned him about everything:

"Why does that tree stick out in front?" she asked.

"That's the bowsprit, and it increases the amount of sail for the wind to catch."

"Why do the master and bosun's mates wear blue clothing?"

"Those are merchant marine uniforms, and they express the master's authority over the men."

"Why do the men obey?"

"Many reasons. They are paid to obey. Their life depends on obeying, working in unison. They could be punished if they don't."

"How?"

"Lashes across the back. That's a common punishment. Starvation and thirst. Execution."

"Death?"

"In the worst cases, yes. The sea kills swiftly."

"No war chief would kill one of his people."

"Unless the warrior tried to kill him. On a long voyage, seamen sometimes mutiny."

She wanted to know the names of things and he supplied them: the foremast, mainmast, taffrail, capstan, hold, and crow's nest.

They struck fog suddenly, late in the afternoon, a white blanket that had boiled inland from the Pacific, swallowing the wide river until they could not see twenty yards ahead. Simpson lowered sail, but the current still drew the ship along too swiftly and he finally ordered the anchors dropped, narrowly avoiding a large island dividing the wide river.

The dank mist penetrated Skye's clothing and chilled his face. They were approaching the sea now, and the mood of the weather changed. He smelled the salt sea in the breeze and sensed that they had reached tidal waters.

"I do not like this," Victoria said, and retreated to the cabin. He knew she would not find warmth or solace there. It was sunlight and fresh air that made the cabin comfortable.

Simpson patrolled the deck, making sure the schooner was well secured.

"Well, Mister Skye, what do you make of the *Cadboro* so far?"

"A tight ship, sir."

"You've been at sea. I imagine it holds no terrors for you."

"The sea always holds terrors for me, sir."

"Then you'd make a good seaman. I imagine you arrived at York Factory, Hudson's Bay, eh?"

"No, sir, I set foot on North America at Fort Vancouver."

"Ah! Then this is all familiar. What bark brought you here?"

"It's a long story, sir, for some other time."

"Well, I'd say you know more of sailing than you let on. You are quite at home aboard."

"As you say, sir."

Skye wished to change the subject. He did not wish to lie.

A mate summoned Simpson to deal with a rent in a sail,

and Skye stared moodily into the whiteness, the whole world cloaked from his eyes by the soft fog.

It would be a miserable night, with cold sweat gathering on the polished interior wood of the cabin. Only the galley and mess, where a cookfire supplied heat, would offer comfort to those aboard.

The monotonous gray faded into blackness and the ship bobbed softly in the dark, hour after hour, nothing visible, not shore or stars or even the tops of the masts. Skye felt isolated, caught in a constricting world and aching for the freedom of the open sea.

A bell summoned them to the mess, but Victoria chose not to eat. He realized then how profoundly this was afflicting her, in spite of her fierce loyalty and bravado.

He thought he would at least salvage a few biscuits for her if she hungered in the night. The cabin contained two narrow bunks and was barely six feet wide. A porthole let in dim light. The climate within was so damp that he suddenly feared for her health. How would a woman of the dry interior, the high plains and arid mountains, endure this cloaked and choking sea mist day after day?

But she said nothing, lying in her lower bunk, her gaze watchful of everything he did.

It was two hours after their simple mess, plum duff and raisin pudding, that he heard the shouting from the deck, and left the cabin to see.

The crew hastened up the hatchways and poured out on the slippery deck. The fog had lifted to some extent, forming a low ceiling. They could peer under it to a dark shore a hundred yards distant. But approaching across those inky waters was a big canoe of some sort, bigger than any Skye had ever seen, with some sort of lantern in its prow. It was propelled not by two paddlers, but a dozen.

"Bring the cannon around," Mr. Simpson said. "Load with grape and be quick. Mr. Burgess, prepare to repel boarders."

Several seamen began charging the brass six-pounders while others grabbed belaying pins, pikes, and axes. The mate and his men assembled at the rail, ready for war.

The canoe glided across the glistening water, those aboard making a considerable commotion. They were certainly not sneaking toward the *Cadboro*.

They were Indians of some sort, maybe Clatsop, but Skye didn't know these people. They were nothing more than names he had heard at Fort Vancouver. He found Victoria beside him, wreathed in smiles, and he wondered why.

"Goddam," she said, grinning.

"Who are they?"

"People who listen to the spirits."

That was no help at all. Skye watched the dimly visible canoe heave to, and swing parallel. One old man stood, speaking in a tongue Skye could not fathom.

"Mister Skye, perhaps you or Mrs. Skye could tell us what he wants," said Simpson. "If it's trade, say no."

But Victoria was nudging Skye, pointing at something gold in the darkness of the canoe.

Skye exhaled slowly, refusing to believe.

"Mr. Simpson, they have brought my dog to me."

"Well, send them off. I will not ship a dog all the way to England."

Even as Skye stared, his heart thudding, the dog uncurled, paced forward, and stood high on the very prow of the canoe, arching as if he would jump.

The seamen exclaimed.

"Can you carry him until we reach Monterey?"

The crew waited in utter silence.

"Oh, I suppose. But you'll have to leave him there."

"Then I will pay for his passage."

Simpson paused, weighing matters. "Your passage is paid for by HBC," he said. "Very well. But you'll be responsible for him. I run a tight ship, and if it's fouled, that dog will be donated to the sharks."

An odd throaty cheer arose. Skye sensed that every seaman aboard would see to the cleaning.

"Dog comes," said the old man. "Dog looking for you. Watches water. We see."

"I will take him," said Skye.

The crew lowered a gangway until it hovered just over the canoe. Several strong bronze men lifted the dog to it. The exhausted dog crawled up the cleats and tumbled onto the deck, too tired to move, except for its tail, which wagged once.

Victoria crouched over the half-dead No Name. The crew's silence amazed Skye.

He worked his way down the pitching gangway that rested on the bobbing canoe and clasped the old man's hand.

"You have made me whole again," he said. Maybe he would not be understood, but maybe this Clatsop, or whoever he was, would grasp something of it.

He could think of no way to say thanks except to dig into his money pouch and pull out one of the shillings that McLoughlin had given him, and hand it to the man.

The Indian fingered the coin, smiled, and nodded. Then, with a quiet command, he set his canoe in motion, as oarsmen backed it away from the schooner. Skye found himself scurrying up the gangway and on board just in time.

Victoria was stroking the inert, shivering, half-dead dog, crooning a lullaby in her Absaroka tongue.

He stared at No Name, knowing he would never learn how the dog made it some eighty miles from Fort Vancouver, swimming two large rivers, and then inspired a Clatsop village or hunting party to take it to the schooner.

Victoria was right. It was no ordinary dog.

28

Skye scarcely dared talk to the bosuns and able seamen manning the *Cadboro*, knowing that he would swiftly give himself away. Their tongue was his. But little by little he did get to know some of them, including the carpenter's mate and the sailmakers and cooks. They told him of their passages around the Horn, of porpoises and sharks and drifting treasures; of scurvy and thirst and starvation and new sails that fell to pieces.

But always, their queries turned to the dog.

"What's his name?" one bosun asked.

"He has none, sir."

"Then the bloody dog's no pet, eh?"

"No, he's no pet. And I'm not his master. He is here because he wishes to take care of me."

"Now that's a bloody strange mutt. Do ye pet him or train him?"

"No, I barely touch him, sir."

"Then what's the use, eh?"

Skye had no answer to that.

Victoria nursed the dog back to health. For a day it lay motionless in the tiny cabin, more dead than alive, acknowledging their presence with a bare flap of the tail, but always watching. Victoria lifted it to her bunk and crooned softly, ancient Absaroka incantations, but the dog paid no heed.

Then, upon the second evening, it ate and drank heartily, and paraded around the small deck with Victoria, sniffing the endless green sea and measuring the constricted world to which it was now committed.

For Skye, the dog remained an unfinished story. He had resolutely abandoned the dog at Fort Vancouver, torn as he was between the dog and the great promise of England. And now he would have to do it all over again when the *Cadboro* dropped anchor at Monterey Harbor and Mr. Simpson did a trade in sea otter skins and other HBC business.

He wondered if he had cash enough to purchase casks of salt pork or beef to feed the dog clear to London, and knew he didn't. He had five pounds, the residue of his horse sale, supplied by McLoughlin's second in command, James Douglas, in a variety of coin, including pieces of eight, Mexican reales, Yank dollars, and English shillings and pence. That would have to sustain Victoria and him in London.

In any case, he knew Simpson would flatly refuse.

So the dog would find itself among the Mexicans, and for that reason Skye stayed aloof, not welcoming the dog, not wanting his heart to be torn to bits once again in a few days.

They had reached the treacherous tidal waters of the Columbia the morning after they received the yellow dog. The river had broadened to three or four miles there, and seemed wrapped in permanent cold haze. Simpson slowed the schooner, raised the keel, and drifted over the ever-changing sand bars where the river dropped its burden into the sea. Then the master wheeled the schooner south, turned the ship over to the master's mate, and ran the Pacific coast, rarely out of sight of land, whipped along by the Japan current and the westerlies.

Skye found himself loving the sea. He had thought he would hate it after his years of captivity. But here the benign sea sparkled and the salt air refreshed him. Gulls alighted in the booms and watched the world travel by. The cutwater prow sliced cleanly, parting the ocean around the smooth hull, leaving an arrow-straight wake behind them. Clean air swelled the headsail anchored to the bowsprit, and whipped into the two mighty gaff sails hung from the masts until every cord and rope grew taut and the ship hummed.

His own bright spirits affected Victoria's and helped her past her nausea and the strange circumstance of being upon a white man's ship, living according to white men's schedules, eating upon the sound of a bell, sleeping by shift, never pausing night and day so long as the horizons and stars and waters were visible to the men stationed high above. The air was never warm but never cold, and Skye found his frock coat suitable while Victoria usually wrapped a shawl over her shoulders during her endless circumnavigation of the short, slim deck, the ribby No Name at her heels. The dog was devouring every scrap the seamen gave it.

Sometimes when land was in sight he thought about the New World, of which this was the westernmost shore. Across a void lay ancient Asia, and ancient Europe beyond that. Here, in the unknown continent, he had grown into a man. The New World had rescued him from a short brutal life of slavery and had filled him with hope. But he did not reject the civilization from whence he sprang, for in its measured law and charity and protections, most people flowered, and in its sacred beliefs most people found courage and a means to transcend their worst instincts. Maybe some day the old and new would be fashioned into a great nation that protected the peoples it harbored even while granting them the chance to make anything they chose of their lives.

Simpson joined him at the rail.

"That's Mexican California, Mister Skye. A vast land, barely settled. One of the most isolated places on earth. Tomorrow I'll be stopping at Yerba Buena briefly; fresh water and whatever sealskins we can buy. An hour or two, if possible. There's an amazing inland sea there, where several rivers converge. Some day it may be among the world's greatest ports." He paused. "You might see about some salt beef for your dog."

"I'll do that, Mr. Simpson."

"You're partial to that dog; is he a good hunter or bird dog?"

"Truth to tell, sir, he's nothing. Just a tagalong."

"Well, tomorrow's your chance to get rid of him."

Skye stared moodily at the foam-girt swells. "I guess I'll wait until Monterey, sir."

"I've the feeling you're an old salt."

"Why would you think that?"

"Oh, I'd say the practiced eye. The way you examine a sail. Only an old salt looks at sails as you do."

"What do I see, sir?"

"Where the sail is weak; where they've been patched. How they hang wrong, sagging and bulgy, defying the wind. How the ship cuts the water. What sort of wake it leaves. What's in the bilge. How the seamen behave. Whether they respect their master. Whether the deck's holystoned. Whether there's rot in the timbers. Whether the cannon are loose. Whether the crew eats gruel or gets a tasty morsel now and then . . ."

Simpson waited, an eyebrow cocked, but Skye did not oblige him with the opening of his past. Skye liked him. He did not rule the way a naval captain ruled, though Skye didn't doubt that Simpson and his chief mate and bosuns could be just as tough as circumstances required.

The next morning they sailed through an amazing fog-shrouded passage into an inland sea, and hove to at Yerba

Buena, a scattered collection of adobes huddled on a chill inland shore. Skye dismissed it at once. Such a mud village had no future.

Simpson launched a jollyboat and was rowed to shore, the Skyes and No Name with him. Skye and Victoria set foot in Mexico for the first time. Yerba Buena was not an impressive village, at least to Skye, but Victoria saw it through other eyes, and exclaimed at the assortment of whitewashed buildings and the brightly clad Mexicans who crowded around the crew and master.

Skye hunted for a butcher, looking for salt beef, and found none. No Name scarcely budged from Skye's shadow.

The negotiations didn't last long. The alcalde, who greeted them on the muddy tidal flat of a small cove, announced that a Yank trader had cleaned out every pelt in town only the day before and had sold numerous trade items, including bolts of calico, at better prices than those of HBC.

Simpson didn't tarry. Within the hour the *Cadboro* set sail, fighting a furious tide as it pushed through the shrouded gate and into the cold Pacific once again.

"I hope things aren't as discouraging in Monterey," he said to Skye once the schooner reached open water. "It's a much larger place and we have consignors and agents there, and those gentlemen have a warehouse and do a regular trade. Did you inquire about salt meat for the dog?"

"I made an effort but without success, sir."

"Well, we can subsist the mutt to Monterey. It's not far down the shore. We'll spend a day there."

The coastal mountains of California erupted high above the Pacific for most of the journey south. Simpson steered far out to sea to avoid hazards, but the coast was usually visible that afternoon. Skye sensed that the weather was moderating a bit; the air seemed more inviting than it had been during the north California passage, where the timbered coast was forbidding and dark.

The second morning found them closing on Monterey Bay.

"What about the dog?" Victoria asked.

"We find a family that'll take him. We've a day to do it."

"He will only die."

Skye sighed. "We will find him a master."

"This dog knows no master. He will run until he dies if we leave without him."

Skye felt bad. "What would you do?" he asked.

She shook her head, not knowing, and he saw the pain in her eyes. He held her, and then supplied the only assurance he could: "I'll see about some preserved meat for a sea voyage. Maybe he'll take the dog if I buy the chow. If Simpson agrees . . ."

She buried her face in his shoulder.

The yellow dog stared, and Skye swore the beast knew every thought crawling through Skye's brain.

They swept into a hook-shaped bay, not a true harbor but enough of a shelter to provide quiet water. Monterey, the rustic capital of the rural province, was indeed a larger place, with whitewashed buildings crawling up steep green slopes, the buildings topped with red-tile roofs.

But that wasn't what caught Skye's eye.

The Royal Navy's Pacific squadron was anchored there.

29

Suddenly Skye's world darkened. He spotted a man-o'-war and two frigates. The Union Jacks fluttered lazily from the mainmasts. He could not tell whether one of the frigates was the *H.M.S. Jaguar*, from which he freed himself years earlier by slipping at night into the icy waters of the Columbia.

The Royal Navy had a long memory.

He watched helplessly as the HBC schooner saluted the king's navy and slid toward an anchorage well off shore. The Mexicans had never built a proper wharf. Simpson anchored the *Cadboro* about a hundred yards from the nearest frigate; too far for Skye to make out its name.

But there would be officers on these ships who would know him, or know of him, and delight in throwing him into irons and dragging him to England, or more likely, arranging for Skye's demise at sea.

The chances of his survival were slim if the navy caught him here. And the likelihood was overwhelming that the navy would. There would be courtesy visits. Simpson and any civilians on board would be piped onto the flagship to meet the commodore and his officers and share some rum. In turn, the officers of all three royal warships would be invited for grog by the master of the merchant ship.

Around him, the crew was anchoring the *Cadboro* fore and aft to avoid collision with the fleet. Others were lowering a jollyboat to take Simpson ashore, even as several Mexican craft were launching themselves toward the merchant vessel.

Skye felt that choking feeling that comes of foreknowledge of ruin, but swallowed it back.

Victoria and the dog stood beside him.

"That's the Royal Navy and I'm in trouble," he said. "We've got to get off this ship, leave everything behind, and make for shore and hide."

Fear lit Victoria's eyes. "So big," she breathed. "I thought this boat big, but now . . ."

"That man-o'-war's four times the length of this, and two or three times wider, and it carries forty-eight cannon."

"Skye—"

"We'll try to get off. Before the visits start. We'll be on foreign soil but not safe even there. If one of those frigates is the *Jaguar*, my shipmates are going to be in every grogshop in the city. And some'll be pleased to turn me in."

Simpson materialized beside them.

"We'll, Mister Skye, it's a sight, eh? The royal presence. It always fills me with a certain awe, seeing the fleet. They're flying the welcome ensigns and we'll run up our own, eh?"

Skye smiled crookedly.

"But those pleasures will come in a bit, eh? I'm heading ashore to do business."

"We'd like to join you, sir. Stretch our legs. I need to do some business."

"I have a boatful this time. I've promised some shore

leave to the men, and of course I'll need to take my bo-suns and master's mate to negotiate."

Skye swallowed back his fear and nodded. "You might employ the other jollyboat, sir," he said softly.

"No, not just now. Later, of course. I'm having my crew clean it out and ready it. We'll take it over to visit the commodore when we're invited. We'll do this by turns."

"Yes, sir," Skye said.

Deckmen lowered the jollyboat from its stanchions and a Jacob's ladder as well, and soon it was bobbing on the azure waters of Monterey Bay. The oarsmen descended, followed by the master and his officers, and the little ves-sel whirled toward the golden shore, the beach divided by outcrops of dark rock. Skye watched it bitterly, as if watch-ing his sole hope for staying alive grow small. On that very beach, seamen wearing whatever they chose, and of-ficers in blue, watched the progress of the little boat. Most of the seamen were loading water casks into longboats, or storing crates of fruit and vegetables and firewood into other longboats. A lighter carried six bawling Mexican cattle to the man-o'-war. Monterey was alive with the navy, and not just those on the waterfront. Every grogshop in town would be pouring rum into the gullets of the limeys.

He watched Simpson's jollyboat tie up at a crowded jetty on the rocky strand, and watched Simpson shake hands with the Royal Navy. He watched the officers con-verse, and remembered that he had never disguised his name. He was Barnaby Skye to the master of the *Cadboro*; the navy's most notorious deserter was Barnaby Skye. Sooner or later, when Simpson described his shipboard complement, he would name Barnaby Skye. It was only a matter of time.

It was but early afternoon. Skye thought the mutual visits wouldn't begin until the dinner hour and would stretch through the evening. Darkness was always a friend of fugitives and maybe darkness would preserve him in its gentle hand. Maybe it was pure luck that Simpson declined to take him and Victoria and the dog on the first shore visit.

"Victoria," he said low and soft and out of earshot, "we have to think this through. We're a hundred fifty yards from shore."

"I can swim that."

"Not in that heavy clothing, dress and petticoats and all. And I can't swim in this getup for long."

"The dog can."

She was smiling tautly.

He felt helpless but determined. He lacked a weapon and carried nothing more than an old Green River knife that he had acquired at his first rendezvous. He and his family had to get off this ship, and do it at night, and escape Monterey. If that meant leaving their entire wardrobe behind, he would do it. If it meant abandoning his vision of England, he would do it. The thought wrought pain in him, but the prospect of capture and probable death at the hands of his former officers, feasting on their triumph, was the vision that controlled his every act.

"Victoria, make a small bundle, nothing obvious, of all the clothing you can carry, whatever we'll need. And one for me as well. We'll be going ashore here. We will never reach England."

She glanced sharply at him and wordlessly headed for the cabin.

His mind whirled with ideas but none of them seemed very good. He watched the navy's seamen load cask after cask of water and row out to the warships; he watched Simpson and the *Cadboro* officers dicker with the Mexicans crowding about on the shore. He watched Simpson signal for the second jollyboat, and watched seamen lower and row it to shore, filled with empty casks. He itched to board that boat with Victoria and the yellow dog, but they would step ashore in the midst of ten or twelve midshipmen and petty officers of the navy, very likely some under whom he had suffered. He told himself to be patient; darkness would tenderly cloak them.

An hour ticked by and then one of the bosuns, Abner Gilbert, approached Skye at the rail.

"Mr. Simpson says to catch the next jollyboat in," Gilbert said. "He's mindful you have business ashore. About the dog, you know. He's met a Mexican who'd take it and he'll introduce you. We'll be loading sealskins and water and vegetables until well after dark. Lift anchor at first light."

There it was. Fate hung. Skye could scarcely refuse. But there was advantage. On shore, on foreign soil, he had a chance. On board, he didn't.

"All right, sir," Skye said.

He found Victoria bundling clothes.

"We're going in. Simpson's invited us. Forget this," he said, waving at the wardrobe in their trunks.

Victoria grinned. That grin, famous and huge in his mind, had lifted him past the worst moments of his life. They would leave everything behind if that's what it took. Who needed clothing like that in the mountains?

Victoria did stuff her doeskin dress, and his buckskins, and the two capes into a carpetbag, and they headed for the rail. The jollyboat bobbed on the water below as they descended the jacob's ladder and set foot in the careening little vessel. Minutes later the oarsmen beached the boat on the sand—the Royal Navy had commandeered the little jetty—and Skye helped Victoria jump the last foot from the prow to the sand.

Land! All about them the Royal Navy was at work. The seamen paid no attention to a burly man in a frock coat and top hat, or his dusky wife and ribby mutt. Skye proffered an arm to Victoria, and they paraded amiably past sailors too busy wrestling kegs to study them. Skye pushed the top hat lower on his face to deepen the shadow. His long dark and graying hair, gathered with a string at the nape of his neck, further altered his face.

They ascended a rocky incline that took them above the tidal shore and walked slowly toward the line of small adobe merchant buildings that disgorged or swallowed the burdens of visiting ships.

He began to relax a little: they had passed, in the bright afternoon sunlight, the thickest concentration of tars and officers unscathed.

He spotted Simpson talking earnestly to a Mexican before the yawning doors of a warehouse, and headed that way, as casually as he could manage.

The Mexican delighted the eye: he wore a short black coat, tight britches of fawn-colored cloth, a bright red sash, and a great sombrero. He was much better dressed than the rest of his people, who toiled barefoot in soiled white cottons, loading long, velvety, tan sealskins upon mule-drawn carts.

"Ah! Mister Skye! And Mrs. Skye! May I introduce Don Emilio Baromillo, a fur merchant here, and also Senor Esteban Larocha, Mexican customs, who's making sure we pay our tuppence for every pelt."

They shook hands. "Mr. Baromillo says he might consider the dog—"

But Skye was watching the swift approach of an ensign posted at the next warehouse, a man he suddenly realized he knew.

"Skye!" bellowed the officer, drawing his bright sword. "I'd know that ugly nose anywhere!"

30

Skye resisted two impulses. One was to run; the other was to bull straight into the skinny ensign—his name was Plover—and wrest the sword from him.

It was too late, anyway. Plover thundered down on Skye as he stood next to Simpson and the two Mexicans, waving his glittering blade and summoning his work detail to join him with his shrill boatswain's pipe.

A half-dozen tars swarmed out of the next building and swiftly surrounded him.

Victoria was aghast and backed away. She had a way of becoming invisible. The world somehow never paid her much attention, which had saved their lives more than once. No Name joined her.

"Got you, Skye, and don't tell me you're someone else. Oh, what a day this'll be for the Pacific squadron!" He bawled at his seamen, "Hold this bloody devil. Don't let him get away. We've been after him for years, and now he's walked into our parlor."

Skye stood as quietly as he could manage, knowing his chances were slim and growing slimmer by the second as the burly seamen circled him, ready to pounce.

"A damned deserter!" Plover cried to those who were watching.

Don Emilio Baromillo observed all this with a frown. The customs man, Esteban Larocha, grew excited.

"Come along, Skye!"

"I think not," said Skye.

"What? What? Grab him, men."

The seamen, none of whom Skye had seen before, swarmed him and tossed him to the rocky ground. Skye fell hard, hurting himself in the shoulder. Victoria was circling around behind the ensign, though Skye could not fathom why unless to grab his sword.

"Alto!" said Baromillo, in a voice that brooked no resistance. "This is Méjico!"

"I don't care where it is, we're taking this man with us," Plover bellowed.

"Alto," the don snapped. "Do you want to taste my sword, ensign?"

"It's none of your bloody business," Plover retorted.

"It is Méjico's business. When a man is forcibly taken from our country, it is our business. Let him go. I will tell you now, release him."

Larocha sprang into the action. "I will get el gobernador. This makes the war! Madre Dios, what insolence!"

That sobered Plover a moment, but his defiance bloomed again. "Go ahead, get your army for all I care. This man's wanted by the Royal Navy and we'll take him."

Baromillo pressed forward and spoke in that low deadly tone that commands instant attention. "This hombre you want to kidnap is a Hudson's Bay man brought here by Capitan Simpson. I will not allow this to happen, not on our soil. England will not be welcome here if you take him without our consent. Go resupply elsewhere. This is not your country. It is the Republica de Méjico. Tell that to your capitan." He turned to Larocha. "Fetch the guardia, and el gobernador, pronto, pronto."

Skye rubbed his aching shoulder and clambered slowly to his feet, well aware of the sharp blade switching back and forth like a cat's tail and hovering inches from his body. He brushed sand off his frock coat, retrieved his top hat, and stood quietly, his mind awhirl with calculation.

"Thank you, Don Emilio," he said quietly. "I would like to have your governor settle this matter. I am indeed Barnaby Skye, and I am in the fur business and associated with the Hudson's Bay Company. I have been in the fur business six years."

"They call you a criminal, Senor Skye."

"I know of no crime that I've committed."

"Desertion!" Plover yelled.

Skye did not deny it. He ignored Plover and addressed the powerful Mexican directly and quietly. "A man pressed into service against his will does what he must. An unbound English freeman who is made a slave at the age of thirteen, snatched off the streets of London, has every right to free himself. I served seven years, and now am a free man on Mexican soil, engaging in an honorable trade, welcomed here by your officials."

"The Crown wants him," Plover blustered. "If you won't let us have him, the Crown will be displeased, and you'll hear from our envoys."

Plover was not going to surrender his prize lightly.

Baromillo waved a hand impatiently, as if to discourage a pesky fly. "That will be up to the authorities. Perhaps they will release him to you. But you will not drag him away, not on Méjican soil. If you do, you will face my own good Toledo sword, and you will regret your conduct the second your beating heart feels my steel. Do you wish to test me?"

That quieted Ensign Plover and his men.

They waited in the bright Monterey sun. Skye calculated his chances of escape and found them nonexistent. Even if he should escape the navy, Mexican soldiers would track him down fast. He had never seen this country and wouldn't know where to go; it was their home and they would catch him. He stared bleakly at Victoria and the dog, and had no answer for them as they watched him.

Some eternity later a squad of uniformed soldiers from the presidio appeared, the tramp of their boots thudding a cadence through the narrow streets of the province's capital. Along with them came a corpulent, dark, warm-eyed man with a cheerful and imperial air. The soldiers were armed with pikes and muskets. Don Baromillo translated.

"El gobernador is not present, but I am Amarilla, his devoted and loyal lieutenant. What is this I hear? Does the British navy snatch a man off the streets of Monterey, the capital of Alta California?"

Plover made his case in vehement terms, talking furiously while the don translated calmly.

Amarilla considered the case only briefly. "We will hold this man for the gobernador. He is due here within a fortnight, having matters to deal with at his estancia, including the birth of a seventh child, the theft of angora goats, the training of a dozen horses, and a daughter who wishes to marry an unworthy lout from the City of the Angels."

"But we're sailing this evening!"

Amarilla shrugged. "El gobernador will be pleased to entertain your petition, and listen as well to this hombre and his petition, si? There is a small fee involved. Perhaps he will turn this man over to you. He wishes for relations between the English and the province of Alta California, en Méjico, to be warm and fruitful, eh?"

"A reward! I'll return to my ship and we'll supply a bounty for this man. Give me two hours and the bounty will be yours. We want him. Ten pounds for this man! I will get it from the strongbox. The commodore will be pleased."

Amarilla shrugged. "Show us the papers against him,

and the amount of the bounty, and perhaps justice will be accomplished in time for your sailing. How could this man be worth so much, eh? He does not look like a criminal, except for that vast and noble nose. Perhaps it is true that evil men are revealed by the size of their noses. That is a theory to look into."

Skye watched his chances diminish to nothing. All this was hard for Victoria to follow, but she signaled to him that she understood. Whatever his chances, everything would be up to her. But to think it was to know that she could do nothing. She was a Crow Indian from the mountains. She had scarcely set foot in such a world as this.

At least he had a better chance among the Mexicans than he did with the navy. The Mexicans might detain him but would not kill him. He was sure of it now: the longstanding resentment at Skye's escape long ago had not diminished, but had become a legend in the admiralty. There would be many a cheerful ensign and lieutenant and captain and commodore toasting Plover this evening. And tomorrow, at sea, they would tie Skye to the webbing under the bowsprit of one of those vessels of war, give him a knife but no water, and let him settle his own fate.

So it had come down to cash. Amarilla was not above a little financial improvement, so long as it could be clothed in bounty and warrants and all the rest of the trappings of international law. Skye knew his life wasn't worth a shilling just then.

They marched him up hill through the dirt streets of Monterey, past lovely whitewashed houses with shuttered windows and red-tile roofs, past staring women and children and old men, all of them dressed in a bright and showy manner, velvet coats and pantaloons, soft slippers, gaudy sashes, thick tortoiseshell combs, and delicate mantillas over jet hair. They were beautiful people, warm-fleshed and handsome, but they eyed him soberly as he

passed, surrounded by the stern blue-and-white uniformed soldiers with the pike poles and muskets.

Skye watched Victoria and No Name follow, unnoticed, for they posed no threat nor did reward hang over
her head. She wore European clothing and her dusky features could not even be distinguished from those of the
Californios. They paid her no heed, and that was good.
She would help if she could, but neither he nor she had
the slightest plan or any place to escape to. He could not
go back to Simpson. The master would probably turn him
over to the navy without a second thought.

They arrived at the presidio, a small whitewashed post
with commanding views of the blue bay. Skye passed
through thick adobe walls into an inner yard, and was
led to a small room guarded by a massive wooden door.
Victoria paused, and then entered the yard, the dog wandering casually at her side. At least she would know
where he was taken, where to find him if she could free
him. The soldiers paid her no heed. The last he saw of her,
she was hovering just a dozen yards away, her eyes drinking him in.

Amarilla ushered him into a small bare room, lit only by
a high barred window, and without any furniture of any
sort. "Senor Skye, welcome to Méjico," he said, smiling
not at all kindly. "A thousand pardons for this indignity.
Perhaps your visit will be brief, or so we both may hope, si?"

31

The old helplessness visited him once again. He had spent more time than he cared to think about confined in one cage or another. The navy was very good at shackling or confining a man. Now he was snared once again, this time in a mean dirt-floored trap with stained and pocked walls and a tiny grilled window, too small to crawl through, high above.

The place stank. A filthy corner served as the latrine. He paced a circle restlessly, knowing it would do no good, but then willed himself to quiet his spirits. His liberty had vanished and there was little he could do but wait. He slumped against the gummy wall as far from the stink-hole as he could. He could see a few inches of blue sky through that window. For six sweet years he had seen all of the heavens each day.

He remembered his ancient vow: he would die rather than live where he could not see the sky without bars between it and his eyes. He had wrestled his way free by placing his liberty ahead of his life. More than once he had told others that he would die before he would be taken. He had meant it. But now, in a lax moment he had let himself be captured.

But this was only the beginning of the story. He did not

know how this would end, but he knew, once again, that he would not board a naval warship alive. If they took him, he would fight them to death. The thought hardened his resolve but didn't console him. His life as a free man had been indescribably sweet, and he had won the respect of the mountaineers, rising to brigade leader. He had come into himself at last.

Time stalled. It always did in confinement. A few minutes seemed like an hour. A day seemed like a month. He had learned that lesson long ago. So he found patience, knowing that all this would come to a head swiftly if what the ensign said was true.

Ten pounds bounty. That puzzled him. He couldn't imagine the pinch-pursed Royal Navy squandering ten pounds to snare a deserter. Ten pounds for a bloody tar who'd slipped overboard six years earlier? For what? To prosecute him as an example to other seamen? Or just because Skye had become a dark legend in the admiralty? He didn't know. He didn't even know why the admiralty had taken such an interest in him. No other seaman in the admiralty's memory had tried longer or harder to escape, and no other sailor had been subjected to such harsh measures to prevent it, and yet Skye had found a way, defeating his lord jailors at last.

Daylight slipped by and no one came. The presidio stayed chill, swept by sea breezes that trumped the mercies of the sun. The coldness and darkness drifted through Skye's body and mind, reducing him to melancholia. He felt raw fear, and hated it.

He wondered where Victoria was. She lacked so much as a shilling to purchase tripe for herself and the dog. She had never bought anything at a market before, never pushed a coin across a counter, but she had seen how white men did things at rendezvous, and again at Fort Vancouver. The warren in which he was confined did not face any street, but stood near the rear of the presidio. He had no way of tossing a coin or two to her. He wondered what she was doing, his lady of miracles. She knew nothing of forts or presidios. They were all fearsome mysteries to her. She had scarcely even seen a permanent building before. But now she knew their uses, including the use put to this bleak closet.

More time drained by, and the light shifted as the sun progressed across the tiny window. He was practiced enough at confinement to know that two, three, maybe four hours had gone by without the arrival of the Royal Navy and its Judas coin.

No one came. No one cracked the door to look in on him. No one delivered water or food. He thirsted, after the morning spent in bright sun. Soon he would hunger, too. He heard nothing without; no soldiers tramping, no shouts, no conversation, no bustle of daily toil, no bugles. Only a mortuary silence, as if the world had forgotten this place or the raging man caged within it.

He began to suffer. His tongue rasped sand. His throat swelled. The light shifted again, darkening to azure by several shades, and he knew the night was stealthily approaching. And still no one came. He rose, paced restlessly to relieve his cramped muscles, round and round his globe, moving nowhere at all, wearing a groove in the earth; a groove already begun by those who had been thrown in here before him. But walking kept him sane.

Darkness fell, and he knew that ten or eleven hours had elapsed since he had been tossed in here and held for ransom, politely described as bounty offered by the king's men for a man who had escaped their control. By dusk, when the light faded and the room plunged into a gloom just shy of blackness, he knew that no bounty was offered for the likes of Skye, and that the commodore of this squadron, whoever that might be, had probably laughed the ensign out of his presence.

Skye hammered on the massive door, thinking perhaps

he had been forgotten. But no one responded. By full dark he was desperate for water, his mouth dusty and his throat seared by every breath.

Maybe they would kill him. Maybe this was some sort of local hospitality. Maybe he would die a slow, anguished death from dehydration. He hammered wildly on the door, thumping it with his boots and fists, and heard only the echoing silence.

The cold filtered in and chilled him. He pressed into a corner to conserve what heat he could, and finally slumped into a long bleak quietness as the minutes and hours ticked by.

Dark thoughts visited him. What would poor Victoria do after they let him die? She knew nothing of these people or their tongue. He thought of his father, the man he would not see. The family he would not see. The lanes of London he would not see. The royal pardon, making him a free subject of the Crown, he would never hold in hand.

The HBC ship must have sailed. Simpson planned to pull out while there was yet daylight and make for Cape Horn, with only provisioning stops en route.

He lost track of time. Thirst tortured him and that was all he thought of.

And then, strangely, he fathomed the clack of bars and bolts, and the door opened. A man holding a small candle-lamp appeared. He carried an earthen jug and handed it to Skye, who drank, and again, and again, and then again as fast as his body could accept the sweet water. Skye drank until he had drained the entire earthen jug.

What a miracle was water. Food a man could do without for some while, but not water. Swiftly Skye's body stopped protesting, and he stood.

That was when Amarilla appeared, sidling through the door like some ghost.

"Senor, may your time in Méjico be blessed and prosperous, and may you enjoy Alta California, which is next to God's own paradise in comforts and consolations. May you be a friend to all Californios, and may we welcome you to our province with honors and true and holy affection, as prescribed by the holy fathers."

"It's about time you came."

"Ah, Senor Skye. The English do not waste uno centavo on you. No bounty. It's a pity. The ensign, he said your price was ten pounds. Ah! That is a fortune, senor. That would make a poor official comfortable. The gobernador pays so little, you know. A few pesos a month, and your servant has a large family to support because my esposa is a lusty woman. It is too bad he is not here to take care of this matter."

"Am I free?"

The governor's lieutenant sighed. "How I wish for your sake that it could be, senor."

"What's holding me here? I'm a visitor."

"Ah, amigo, you are here for the crime of being here too long without permission. Have you papers? Did el gobernador approve that you should be here?"

"I was forcibly brought to this prison."

"Ah, amigo Skye, it is a crime nonetheless. The fine is ten English pounds."

"I don't have that."

"It is a pity, si?"

Skye pulled his small leather purse from his frock coat. "This is what I have. It is something less than five pounds. A lot of money."

Amarilla hoisted the purse and poured out the glinting coins in his hands. "Where is the rest? No gentleman travels without much more. I have seen the English and the Yankees."

"Search," said Skye. He handed his frock coat to the bureaucrat, who made diligent search.

"Is that enough?" Skye demanded sharply.

"Ah, senor, it is enough to satisfy one of the charges, but not the other."

"What other charge?"

"Vagrancy. You are now a man without a centavo, without a home, without means of support, a wanderer among us. Therefore a vagrant. We have laws against it. A pity, senor. Such a fine foreign gentleman. So we must detain you here until you acquire means—"

That was too damned much for Skye. He leapt at Amarillo, grabbed him by the throat, and rattled him.

"Aargh!" the man cried.

The old soldier, who had supplied the water, sprang at Skye, who decked him with one massive blow. The man tumbled to the ground, senseless. His lantern smashed and the candle died. Skye peered swiftly about. He had no idea what time it was, but his best guess was somewhere midway between midnight and dawn. The presidio slept. Everything was so black and unfamiliar that he scarcely knew how to let himself out of the presidio.

He lifted the bureaucrat to his feet and grabbed a handful of shirt.

"Take me to the gate," he said. "And if you make a sound, you'll feel my boot."

This wee-hours visit was odd, and Skye sensed that the man did not want to be seen there, cleaning Skye out of every shilling he possessed. Some things were so shameful that only darkness could cloak them.

The man led him past looming buildings to the gate, which was wide open and unguarded. Now at last Skye could see the whole peninsula and the bay far below in the soft moonglow.

"Give me my purse, you pirate," Skye whispered.

Amarilla resisted, whining like a pig that sees the knife approach its throat, so Skye dug around until he found it.

"Go ahead of me. Down to the waterfront."

"Senor, por favor, I wish to depart your pleasant and treasured company. Consider yourself an honored guest of Méjico."

Skye laughed softly. "Go wake up the soldiers and let them chase me if you dare," he said, releasing the official.

He watched the man hasten away, downhill. Then he peered at the moon-glittered bay. It was empty.

32

Skye watched Amarilla hasten through the night toward a warm bed, no doubt grateful that the distinguished English visitor to Méjico hadn't kicked his ribs in.

The bay caught the moonlight and glittered it back at him, and he studied it. No black hulks bobbed on the waters. No black masts poked the sky. The Royal Navy squadron had sailed. The commodore had better ways to spend the king's purse than purchasing a notorious deserter.

But it was not the sea that caught him, but the dark sky with its pinpricks of light coming from some unimaginably distant place. He could see the whole bowl of heaven; he was free. He possessed himself and his future.

No Name rubbed at his legs. Startled, he beheld the gaunt cur standing guard over him. He knew, intuitively, that if he turned his head just a fraction, he would behold the woman he loved, and suddenly he choked.

"Thank you for waiting for me," he said.

"Goddam, Skye, I thought they take you away. I see these big houses and I think, this is a place of safety. People live behind thick walls and keep the rain and cold away.

But now I see that big houses take away a man's freedom, too. Absaroka don't have big houses."

Skye had never thought of that: that white men's structures were both refuges and prisons.

He slipped an arm about her shoulder and drew her to him and then he kissed her, and she kissed back.

"We should leave here," she whispered. "This bad place."

"We will," he said. "I got my money back from that pirate. Maybe we could buy horses. Maybe outfit ourselves. Five pounds isn't much, though. Twenty-five yank dollars."

"How much is a rifle and bullets, Skye?"

He sighed. "I don't know. I can't even speak their tongue."

"They know finger talk?"

"No."

"What you gonna do, Skye? Go to England?"

Skye studied the dark expanse of heaven and knew that something had changed forever: he would never see England. Nothing was the same.

"No, Victoria, we'll go to the mountains. We'll go home."

"You gonna work for Hudson Bay?"

"They can't employ me as a brigade leader unless I have a pardon. I could probably work for them as a trapper in some obscure post, more or less out of sight."

"How we gonna go from here, eh?"

"I don't know. I know there's mighty mountains all around this place, and winter's coming."

He felt dizzy from lack of food, and walked slowly toward the bay. That seemed the safest place until morning, when the markets opened. Victoria followed him down the slope until they stood at the edge of the sea, watching the ebb tide drain across dark sands. England seemed some impossible distance away; a world and lifetime away now. His fate lay here, in this untouched and merciful continent where hope lived. He sorrowed. He had wanted so much to see his father one last time; to be restored to the freedoms of an Englishman. He saw, in his mind's eye, the image of his father soften and fade and then vanish.

"You not feeling good, Skye."

"I was saying goodbye to my father. I'll be all right in the morning."

He settled against a rocky outcrop and listened to the sea as it flooded hope in and out of the lengthy shoreline. Someplace far away lay China.

The dog had vanished again. Who could say what the yellow cur was doing? And then, after a while, it appeared, carrying something large in its jaw. This burden it brought to Skye, who sat slumped into the hard rock, and laid it upon the sand.

One slow slash of the cur's tail informed Skye that this was a gift.

"Sonofabitch," said Victoria.

Skye lifted up a haunch of meat, discovered that it had been well cooked and was fresh. He did not know what sort of meat, but thought it was lamb. The cur eyed him dolefully.

"Where did you steal this, you rascal?" Skye asked.

The dog waited.

Skye dug into his frock coat and found the small skinning knife sheathed at his waist, his sole memento of the mountains.

Tenderly, he sliced a piece of the cold and tender flesh and handed that first piece to the dog. It accepted gently, settled on a grassy spot, and began gnawing at the food.

"Thank you. No Name," Skye said, sudden feeling blooming in him. This dog was not a pet nor a son nor a child; this dog was his New World father, looking after his son and daughter. The dog looked very old and wise, and much smarter than any mere mortal.

Then Skye cut thin slices for Victoria, who ate each one with relish, licking her fingers and clucking with sheer joy. When it came to good meat, no one was more appreciative than an Absaroka Indian.

Finally he himself ate one piece and then another, and then he fed the dog again and Victoria, and they ate thin, sweet slices of lamb until the moon slid down the bowl of the sky and the eastern sky began to lighten. It was very cold, and they had only the clothing they wore. They huddled together, and then the dog crawled across their laps, warming them a little with his body.

They watched the dark bay of Monterey begin to blue as the sun crept over the distant mountains south and east. The bay looked so empty. Had great events occurred on these serene waters just one day before? Had armed might, a hundred and fifty cannon, anchored there? Had the Union Jack flown there, along with the Hudson's Bay standard?

The sun climbed and no one stirred, and Skye suspected that the Californios lived on a leisurely plan and did not rise early if they could help it. Skye ached, and he knew Victoria did, too. They had suffered much in the past hours.

He hadn't the faintest idea what to do. His few pounds might buy an ancient flintlock, but maybe not. The cash would not equip him and his loved ones for a long hard journey to the Stony Mountains, in the middle of winter.

He knew of two men here who spoke English well enough. One was the fur trader, Don Emilio Baromillo, and the other was the customs man, Esteban Larocha. Of these, Skye preferred to deal with Baromillo. He was not keen on seeing an official, with an official's attitude toward foreigners in California without the permission of the governor.

He would try to find Baromillo, if only to obtain some

advice. How did one leave California for the interior? And what equipment would the don recommend?

No Name slept the sleep of the innocent. Skye felt less innocent and buried the remains of the haunch deep in sand. Around them now, people stirred. An ancient woman in black combed the shore, eyeing the visitors sharply. A group of fishermen gathered about a beached boat and dragged it into the bay. Then they boarded, loaded some supplies, pushed free of land, and raised a venerable sail.

Children flocked by, and the Skyes found themselves objects of curiosity, but when Skye tried to speak to them, they stared solemnly or giggled, and vanished along the strand. Skye was weary: he hadn't slept and he had endured one of the most harrowing nights in years. But he didn't want to move, or wander the town, risking attention. So they watched the turquoise bay, watched puffball clouds float over, watched gulls wheel, and watched Monterey brighten into a bold city with red-tiled roofs, rioting flowers, and whitewashed adobe buildings.

Then Skye saw someone stirring at Baromillo's warehouse, the very place where he had been discovered while conversing with Simpson and the Mexicans. He rose stiffly, and Victoria rose as well. But No Name raised one eyebrow, closed it, and dozed on. Skye brushed sand off his begrimed frock coat and britches, repaired to the warehouse, and found a slender young man there.

"Do you speak English?"

The man shook his head.

"Could you direct me to Don Emilio?"

"Don Emilio? Ah . . ." the man fought for words. "Una hora?"

"One hour." Skye pointed at himself. "Senor Barnaby Skye. Senora Victoria Skye."

"Skye?" Some knowingness lit the man's face. "Ah, si."

"Una hora," Skye said.

They strolled Monterey, aching in every joint. Skye examined a village tinted with primary colors, cleansed by fresh sea breezes and populated by the most colorfully dressed people he had ever seen. To his eye, the women wore very little; their golden arms were bared to the blessings of the sun, and their bosoms were barely covered. They were mostly jet-haired, and had glowing brown eyes that raked his person as he strolled by.

The caballeros, on the other hand, vied with the ladies to be noticed, wearing short coats, red sashes, and gleaming white shirts festooned with lace. They were, to a man, possessors of proud steeds, which they corvetted and paraded. Victoria could barely contain herself, and gasped at every new sight.

"What a people!" she breathed, after watching a horseman dance his horse past, the equipage jingling and the tassels shivering. "Sonofabitch!"

Skye was glad Victoria was more interested in the horses than the horsemen. And that she had not paid attention to the dazzling beauty of the senoritas, whose glowing smiles had set Skye's heart to tripping.

They passed open-air markets and beheld fruits and vegetables and grains in crockery bowls and baskets, sold by Indians along with rural people. They clambered up narrow and crooked streets, past houses with inner courtyards and tiled or flagstoned patios behind black ironwork, where they could glimpse the domestic life of these handsome people.

Skye was impressed. Everywhere, the Mexicans had created their domestic and commercial life with artistry and beauty in mind. But when he had gauged an hour had passed, he steered Victoria down the long slope to the warehouses on the strand, and found the enterprise belonging to Baromillo.

The trader welcomed them cautiously, and bade them enter a spare cubicle where the clerk huddled over a ledger.

"Senor Skye," he said cautiously. "I do not expect to see you any more ever."

"The navy didn't want me," Skye said without further ado. "And now we need your help."

Baromillo frowned.

33

The bleakness and impatience in Emilio Baromillo's gaze didn't encourage hope in Skye. Nonetheless, he plunged in.

"I am thankful to find someone who can speak my tongue, sir. My wife and I are stranded here and need your assistance."

Baromillo stared, not a muscle of his face moving, not even a blink of his warm dark eyes.

"We wish to return to our own land."

"You're an Englishman. I think your navy was attempting to do just that."

"My wife's land is in the Stony Mountains, as the Yanks call that country. We haven't the means."

"Then you must wait here. You might earn passage on some Yankee coastal ship."

"How often do they come?"

The man shrugged. "Who knows? Tomorrow? A year from now?"

"Where do they go?"

"Sandwich Islands, usually, and then around the Horn to Boston."

"Is there a route overland?"

"A perilous trail from the village of San Diego, across deserts, to Santa Fe."

"What about northeast?"

"It is late in October, senor. It is already too late, even if you were properly outfitted. The mountains are a great barrier, with no open passes except briefly in the summer."

"What about up the coast?"

"A hard journey, but possible. Hudson's Bay sends trapper brigades south, even into California."

"I led a fur brigade for the Yanks, and Hudson's Bay was planning on employing me. Outfit me and I'll bring you beaver all winter until the passes are clear."

Baromillo smiled thinly. "And what is to insure that I would ever see you again?"

"My word."

"Your past does not suggest that it would be a wise thing for me to do."

Skye fought back his anger. He had always been as good as his word. "There's profit in it."

"I think not. You have nothing—nada. I would even have to clothe you. Horses, traps, saddles, a rifle, camp gear, skinning knives, everything. Beaver bring but little. I buy whatever comes to me, but I get nothing. Not like the sea otter, big beautiful pelts. I could sell every sea otter in California, and for a good price to any trader who sails to our bay."

"I could catch sea otter, then, if you'd advance something."

"Ah, no, senor, that is a vocation much coveted by our own laborers. My company has certain understandings."

"Horses, then. Where can we get those?"

"Ah, horses! We have horses in Méjico. Every estancia has a thousand horses and mules. But good horses are rare and command a price. Bad horses, bad mules, these are given to the Indios for meat. Every rancho has horses and saddles and leather tack. It is what we do best."

"I'll give a shilling for a decent horse, and another for a decent saddle. Three horses and two or three mules."

"Would that remove you from Méjico, where you illegally visit?"

"Yes."

"A shilling is worth about twice our real. You offer too little. Make it three shillings for a horse, four shillings for each saddle and tack, and one shilling for a mule. I will have them here mañana. Do not put much faith in the horses."

"That's sixteen. I will give you four more—make it almost a pound—for good sound stock, good hooves and not unruly, and for your kind service."

Baromillo nodded. "I arrive here with livestock when the bell tolls ten, senor, senora . . ."

Skye left the warehouse, heartened.

Weary as he was, he put the rest of the day to good use. He and No Name visited the mercados. He discovered that prices, in cash-short California, were low for anything locally manufactured. A few reales would buy amazing things. His lack of Spanish was no impediment and fingers served as well as words. The merchants eyed his coins, hard money, and smiled broadly. They were accustomed to barter.

By the time el sol was skimming the Pacific, he had acquired an ancient longrifle of the Kentucky variety, some dubious, locally made gunpowder, powder horn, a pound of precast balls, wads, and two spare flints. He bought a few trade goods, including awls, ribbons, cloth, knives, beads, two worn but thick Mexican blankets, and used canvas ponchos. At that point his few coins were almost gone.

He and Victoria stowed the gear in Baromillo's warehouse. She was absorbing the world of Europeans and kept her thoughts to herself.

His remaining coins, given him by McLoughlin, went for food: flour, dried beans, fresh loaves, coffee, all stored in coarse gunnysacks, as well as one battered tin cook pot that would suffice for them both.

He felt rich. He and Victoria gobbled baker's sweets. She had never tasted such things and smiled. The dog received a one-centavo bone. Then they headed for the shore again, wrapped themselves in their blankets and ponchos, and awaited the dawn.

Late the next morning Baromillo and a pair of vaqueros showed up with the horses, mules, and tack. Baromillo stood dispassionately while Skye and Victoria examined the beasts. Two were bridled and saddled, and these at least had some passing acquaintance with a rider. The others were obviously straight out of the great herds and unfamiliar with anything other than a halter and braided leather rope.

Risking a kick, Skye lifted hooves, discovering one that was seriously cracked. That was on the unbridled horse, and he rejected it. The mules sidled away. He climbed onto the uglier of the two saddlers. The horse humped its back and refused to move. But the other saddler seemed more obedient.

"All right," he said. "I'll take all but the grulla with the cracked hoof. I'll trade that for two packsaddles for the mules."

He ended up with one packsaddle, which the vaqueros strapped to the sullen mule after roping it down.

It was going to take plenty of work to transform this lot of evil-minded rebels into a good saddle-and-pack string, but Skye figured he had plenty of time and trail to do it.

Then, suddenly, it was all over. He and Victoria had an outfit of sorts. He loaded their paltry supplies onto the back of the wild-eyed mule and tied the burlap sacks down with thong. He wasn't happy with that. The first rain would ruin much of his food and damage his tradegoods. There came over him not joy, but an ineffable sadness.

"Senor Baromillo, I have one last thing to do," he said. "I want to write a letter and I want you to post it on the next English vessel. It is to my father. I wish to bid him goodbye. I don't have a centavo left, but I'll trade you a few of these goods I bought."

Something softened in the don's stern visage. "Write your letter, senor. Your story is a hard one."

Skye clasped the man's hand and held it a moment.

The words came hard, and he wrote with difficulty, forming letters and sentences out of his schoolboy learning.

Dear Father,

I had high hopes of returning to England to see you and my sisters. But those hopes were dashed by the Royal Navy here in Mexico, which discovered my presence and made mischief. I am unable to return to England and unable to restore my good name.

It is painful to me that we won't meet again in this lifetime. But I am grateful to Hudson's Bay Company for conveying word of me to you, however late it came. Too late for my beloved mother to know. You had thought me dead when all the while I was the Crown's miserable prisoner, unable to escape, unable to contact you.

So, Father, I am destined to spend my days here in North America, without the solace of your company. I am grateful to you, sir, for bringing me into this world, and for your kindness, and for your nurture during my salad days in England.

I am grateful for your love and for equipping me to face a hard world. If we don't see each other again, be assured for the rest of your days that I honor you above

all else, honor my patrimony, treasure your love and proffer my own, and I will devote myself to the good conduct
you instilled in me both by instruction and example.

> Your loving son,
> Barnaby
> Monterey, Alta California, Mexico,
> October 30, 1832

Skye dipped the nib into an inkwell and addressed an
envelope and handed the letter and envelope to Baromillo.

"If you can read English, please read this, sir, so that
you might know the kindness you are doing me by letting
me send this letter."

The fur trader did, and quietly folded the letter, in-
serted it, and sealed it with candle wax.

"Now you must leave Méjico," he said.

Skye clambered aboard his unruly horse, which humped
and threatened to pitch him off, while Victoria mounted
hers and adjusted her voluminous skirts. Then he heeled the
sullen horse, which refused at first to go, but No Name
intervened, nipping at fetlocks until eventually the train
moved, two green horses and two half-wild mules, along
the shore of the bay, never far from chaos.

Thus ended a dream. He would never fulfill his desire
to live as a free Englishman without stain upon his honor.
Nor reunite with his beloved family. He saw no future.
His spirits did not lift.

34

Victoria was too busy wrestling with her rebel horse and the balky mules to notice the glory of the Monterey coast. So was Skye.

Her mare wouldn't turn unless she yanked hard on a rein. It stopped repeatedly, tried to run off, kicked at the mules trailing her, bit at her shoes, waited for the chance to buck her into the ocean, and refused to trot or run. If her horse was bad, the mules on the jerkline were worse. The one carrying the packsaddle, from which their few possessions hung, would stop dead every few yards, jolting her procession to a halt. The other mule occasionally ran forward, threatening to break free. Only the dog, nipping at fetlocks and stifles, managed to keep the horses moving.

Skye, ahead of her, was having his own troubles with a horse that would trot a few yards and stop, try to break for Monterey, pitched on the slightest excuse, and shied at every shadow or bird or for no reason at all.

They came at last to a willow grove, and Skye dismounted.

"Hold this rein while I whittle a couple of switches," he said.

He extracted his Green River knife from its belt sheath and began whittling two stout willow switches. He handed her one and kept the other.

"You lead with the mules. I'm going to walk behind your horse, leading mine," he said. If your horse or the mules cause any more grief, they'll answer for it."

"Sonofabitch," she said. She had heard the trappers use that expression many times, and found it highly satisfying and useful and a valuable addition to the English tongue, especially when dealing with horses. She had the notion that it was vaguely prohibited by some of the white chiefs and that made it all the better.

She attempted to start her mare, without effect until the sharp smack of the switch jolted the mare into a trot. Resounding cracks of the switch behind her let her know the mules were receiving the same discipline, and so the procession north began again, this time with more success. Skye, walking beside her mare or the mules, did not spare the switch, and the three beasts of burden settled into grudging compliance.

Thus they actually made some time that afternoon. Skye eventually mounted and employed the willow on the croup of his own saddler, even when the result was a fit of bucking and rebellion.

The yellow dog bore down, and any foolery by any mule was met with a quick nip. Somehow, No Name evaded the wild kicking that always resulted when he vectored toward the rebel. Victoria marveled. The dog was as good as another herder, maybe better, and the Skyes began to pick up some speed. She squinted at Skye's spirit-dog and thanked the mascot for his great kindness.

Now at last she began to notice the golden panorama before her. At a point well north of Monterey the trail left the bay and headed inland. Skye took it. Trails always led somewhere, and this probably would take them to Yerba

Buena. Soon the green ocean vanished and they rode between golden, autumnal hills covered with waxy-leaved green shrubs and junipers.

She had marveled at Monterey. These Mexicans had built their lodges of earth bricks, daubed them white, and covered them with bright red tiles, cleverly designed to drain off the rain. At every hand she discovered marvels: carriages with wheels on them, drawn by burros or mules. Handsome horses, caparisoned with carefully tooled saddles. Women who wore perfumes, amazing scents that invoked envy in her. Great trading buildings heaped with good things: barrels of wine, sacks of grain, shelves of ironwork, and everywhere leather goods. They made leather do for everything, from ropes to vests and riding pants.

But the women fascinated her most. They were honey-fleshed, not as dark as she was, not as fair as Skye, but warm-colored, with glowing eyes and swift, sweet smiles. And they wore mountains of clothing, one skirt over another, as if they did not wish to show the contours of their bodies from waist down. They were mad for jewelry, too, and wore copper and silver and sometimes even gold, or polished stones, and ribbons in their hair, and soft slippers rather like moccasins.

She thirsted to learn everything there was to know about this tribe called Mexicans, and she knew that at the campfires on the trail, she would think up questions to ask him. He seemed to know all about them and she marveled that he knew so much, or could walk into a trading place and come to an agreement with the fat brown clerks without even understanding their tongue. She marveled at prices. How did anyone know the price of anything? Why were some things so cheap and others so costly? Who set these prices and why?

Skye scanned the heavens, constantly alert for rain. They had little to protect their food and bolts of trade cloth except the ponchos, and that worried him.

"If it's clouding up, look for shelter, Victoria. Anything. Those burlap sacks aren't much use in bad weather."

She marveled at the sacks, having never seen one, hoped she might receive them all from Skye some day.

That evening they camped in a peaceful notch in the hills, watered by a clear, sweet spring that wrought a comet's tail of green vegetation down a gentle grade. The place showed signs of frequent use, and she had to travel a way to find deadwood for their cookfire, but she didn't mind. She liked this Mexico place, and its peace, and the sweetness of the air, and the mildness of the climate.

Skye unloaded the surly horses, put them on improvised pickets where the golden grasses grew thick, and sat down. She studied him closely and knew the sadness had not left him. For many moons he had thought of nothing more than sailing across the big waters to his home and his father and sisters and family. Of repairing the wrong and winning a good name. All this had possessed him, inspired him, driven him from the mountains to Oregon, and then down to this place called Mexico. And now it was gone, destroyed in a few hours by a chance encounter with the Royal Navy, the very ones who had stolen his liberty from him in the first place.

Now he looked weary, and she saw something else in his weathered face: a great sadness. She did not know whether she could comfort him. What could some woman of the People do to console this man, whose family had been ripped from him forever?

What was she to him? Was she still his beloved woman?

After they had eaten some beans she had boiled, and some hard biscuits he had purchased, she knelt beside him while he smoked a pipe of precious tobacco, actually part of the trade goods he had purchased to succor them along the way. He drew deeply and let the fragrant smoke eddy out of his lungs, even as he stared at things invisible to her. He handed her the pipe and she sucked deeply, enjoying the smoke in her throat.

"Skye," she said. "Would you talk?"

He didn't reply at first. "I am a man without a country," he said. "And without a future or a past."

"Without a future?" She was hurt.

"I had always, in the back of my mind, thought of returning to my home; England, some day. I've always wanted to receive my good name back; to be honored among my people. Even if I chose not to stay there, but make my home here with you, I wanted to clear that up. Now I can't. I can never go home, never make the name of Barnaby Skye an honorable one in England.

"A man wants a good name. A man wants to be honored by his own people."

"But you have a good name, Skye. You have a good name among my people, and among the Yankees. You even have a good name with Hudson's Bay, or at least the big man, McLoughlin."

He sighed. "Yes, and that is good. But my heart cries for a good name among my people."

"Ah, it is truly so. I understand this thing. I would not wish to have a bad name among my people. My heart would feel bad even if I had a bad name among your people. This I understand. When you have a bad name, there is no future."

He took the pipe from her and drew long, and exhaled slowly. The smoke was good. The smoke was making him calm, and maybe taking his suffering away. Tobacco was a good thing and the messenger of peace among the tribes.

"You have a very small country," she said. "Your country is me and this dog that lies beside us. We are your country for as long as you will have us."

He smiled and handed the pipe back to her. "That is a very good country," he said.

But there was something in his tone that troubled her
and she fathomed what lay behind his words. He yearned
for the things she simply didn't understand. He sometimes spoke of books. She had scarcely seen a book, and
they were great mysteries to her. How could anyone get
something from all those tiny black marks on a thin sheet
of paper? He spoke of art and politics and ideas and philosophy and the sciences and applied arts, and she knew
she was like a child and knew nothing of these things.
What she fathomed, at bottom, was that her life was too
small for him, and that he would always be a little sad,
even when he was closest to her and they seemed almost
happy. She would always give him what she could, and it
would never be enough.

35

The next dawn Skye tried out the old flintlock. He rested the barrel on a boulder, sighted on a knot, and squeezed. The flint snapped sparks into the pan, ignited the charge, and the patched ball whumped the tree trunk, but about two inches lower and to the right of where he had sighted. He tried again, with almost the same result, and knew he must compensate.

The night had been mild, the California slopes peaceful and empty. He saw little evidence of passage along the trail, and concluded that this province of Mexico was lightly inhabited; a sunny wilderness wanting only water to make it a paradise.

He and Victoria had worse trouble with the green horses and mules that morning than the previous; it was as if the beasts had learned nothing from yesterday's discipline. He saddled his balky mount, which reared back and snapped its halter rope and dodged him. His temper heated until No Name herded the horse toward Skye with snapping jaws. Victoria's mount accepted a saddle but threatened to buck. The yawning packmule humped when the packsaddle fell over its back, and lowered its head, ready to buck the burden off. Skye sighed and cut fresh switches from a live oak, and handed one to Victoria.

After some mighty cursing and lashing, they got their unruly transportation moving. The dog helped, nipping at the heels of the stubborn mules. The saddling had cost them an extra hour and slowed their start. But by the time the sun was pouring merry warmth upon the brown slopes, and the hawks were circling the blue sky, the Englishman and his Crow bride were making headway, ever northward, through a land too sweet to permit gloomy thoughts.

This day, at least, the rebel animals settled faster into a routine than the previous day. Skye didn't mind. Where else could he acquire four-footed beasts of burden for a few shillings? Any horse or mule that had received the benefit of the great equestrian skills of the Californios would have cost fifty times as much.

And so they passed a magnificent November day, pushing ever northward, inland from the coast but never far from a salty sea breeze. They wound up and down great golden hills, and even crossed low coastal mountains, seeing no one but enjoying the abundance of life at every hand: deer, fox, an occasional stray longhorn bearing an elaborate Mexican brand that had been burned into a thigh or shoulder; and always the crows and gulls and songbirds wheeling in flocks as they rode by.

For two days they traveled north, making better time as the livestock settled down. The dog trotted ahead, an outrider alert to danger, and Skye was glad to have him along. The trail crossed few rivers, but offered many springs that emptied down a cleft or rose in a slough. The aching emptiness of this northern Mexican province astonished Skye.

Then, while nooning at a sweet spring purling from a gray cliff, No Name growled quietly and they found themselves in company. Several beaming Mexicans on fancy ponies, dressed in charro clothing, white-stitched black pantalones, soft leather boots, splendid embroidered waistcoats, and extravagant high-peaked hats with broad brims, drew up. Among them was a girl dressed entirely differently, in a plain skirt wide enough to permit her to sit astride her horse, and a well-filled but begrimed white blouse.

What struck Skye at once was the weaponry carried by these seven jolly Mexicans: dragoon pistols on each man; rifles in scabbards dangling from each saddle; a sheathed sword on several.

"Hola! Hola!" said one, smiling broadly. This one was barely five feet high and almost as wide, but somehow looked much larger.

"Jesús Santamaría," he said, driving a thumb into his own chest. Then he rattled on in Spanish, and Skye comprehended not one word. "El Grande Santamaría," he concluded, "Santamaría gordo, Santamaría borracho, Santamaría magnifico."

The others dismounted from their groomed steeds and surveyed Skye's animals or washed their faces in the rivulet flowing from the spring. All except the girl. But Santamaría eventually gestured to her, and she silently slid off her horse and walked around a bend and out of sight.

Skye waited warily. Victoria stood, uncertainly, but neither spoke. He thought this might be trouble, but probably was not. Men bearing so many arms might be up to no good, but perhaps this was dangerous country. Skye realized he hadn't been very watchful. So tranquil was this province that he had scarcely kept up his guard.

The visitors seemed to be waiting for something and it was only when the girl reappeared and Santamaría began jabbering, in harsh staccato, that Skye began to fathom what this visit was about. Smoothly, Santamaría pulled his big pistol from its leather nest, and instantly the other six hombres did also, and Skye found himself peering into the huge black bores of seven cannons, the flintlocks cocked back and ready.

Santamaría was obviously shouting directions, but Skye couldn't fathom a word.

"He says put up your hands," the girl said in flawless American English.

Skye did, slowly, seeing his imminent death. Victoria did also.

The weary girl slowly translated Santamaría's next outburst.

"He says he is the great Santamaría, unsurpassed in all of Mexico for robbery, terror, murder, torture, crucifixion, and rape of women, young and old, virgins and whores. He says he is a legend, the scourge of all California, the only man spoken of only in whispers. Men die of fear, of heart failure, when he approaches, and he wants you to know that."

She listened to another outburst, while the fat bandit minced back and forth.

"He says you are being robbed and maltreated by the king of all bandits under the heavens and on earth and upon the seas and under the ground. No pirate has half the reputation as Jesús José Santamaría for murder and torture. That the name of Santamaría will live forever, and be whispered over graves, and put down in history books by those who can write."

Santamaría pointed a finger at Skye and shouted endlessly.

"He says he has killed forty-three men, sixty-one women, eighty children, countless animals, and seventeen priests, but you are a foreigner and wouldn't know these things, so he will have to demonstrate his great prowess to you so that forever more you will know that Santamaría robbed and pillaged you and left you for dead."

That was the first ray of hope. Skye believed until then that he and Victoria would die. Not that being left for dead was much to hope for.

Skye addressed the girl: "Ask him how he came to be a great bandit."

Santamaría listened to her, and smiled, baring gold teeth, and began that staccato again.

"He says that he was the son of a rich man, and got bored because everything came so easily to him. Beautiful senoritas waiting in his bed, fast-blooded horses, heaps of gold, cattle too numerous to count, everything. He lacked for nothing. He got fat from good eating. He says he is a bandit and outlaw because he has everything and is bored, which is far more wicked than being a bandit because he is poor or unhappy or unjustly treated. The only thing that counts is fame. He wants to be the greatest of everything: have more women than any other man in Mexico, more money, but reputation is all that matters. He says he wants to live forever."

"Who are you, miss?"

She looked hesitantly at him.

"I am his woman."

She explained that to Santamaría, who retorted at length.

"He says I should correct that; he has had a thousand women, and he will pitch me to the wolves . . . soon."

She looked frightened.

Skye said, "Tell Santamaría the great bandit that I will have a shooting contest with him. Rifles, pistols, anything. And if I win, we go free, and we take you with us."

Hesitantly she translated, only to meet with wild laughter.

"He says you are loco, crazy. He will not give you a fair contest. He is even now thinking of ways to torment you."

"Ask him for a duel. Any weapon of his choice at ten paces."

Apparently he understood without translating, because he laughed at length, and then fired his pistola at Skye's feet. The ball plowed dirt inches from his boot, just missing the dog. The bandit casually sheathed that weapon and plucked out his second as acrid smoke drifted past Skye.

"He says you are a fool. What do you take him for? Someone who would submit himself to your good aim? Because of this it will go all the harder for you."

Skye laughed, not knowing from what strange corner of his soul the laughter came from. "Tell Santamaría he is nothing, a fraud and a fake, a fool, and no match for any serious pirate and bandit."

Hesitantly the girl translated, this time into a dead silence. The quietness stretched to forbidding length, and Skye wondered whether the execution squad would dispatch him with a single crash of the pistols.

Instead, the bandit made one small left-handed gesture. His cohorts untied the two horses and mules from their pickets, rummaged through Skye's goods, and told Skye to remove his frock coat.

He did, and they poked through it, as well, and then rudely poked around Victoria's skirts until they were satisfied that no further booty was to be gotten from Skye and Victoria.

Then they gestured Skye and Victoria to a large shagbarked tree and had them stand before it. Skye's heart sank. They formed a ragged line and lifted their huge pistols until seven muzzles pointed at the Skyes.

Skye's pulse soared. The end, then. He saw the dog, the hair of its neck poking up, crouched and waiting to spring at Santamaría.

Victoria turned flinty and silent.

Santamaría stood to one side, sword in hand, arm raised.

He brought the sword down.

A ragged eruption of explosions deafened Skye.

He felt bark slap him, and shattered lead sting him in a dozen places about the neck and shoulders, and the bandits' laughter lacerate his soul. Victoria sagged to the ground and for a terrible moment Skye thought they had murdered her as a joke. The bandits hooted, gathered the Skyes' horses and mules and outfit, mounted, and rode away like a posse of carrion birds.

Victoria wept. Skye comforted her in his arms, but she could not be comforted. Then the dog squirmed close, and began licking them both, the steady scrape of its tongue its way of comforting them. It took an hour for Skye's pulse to settle.

36

The sun still shone. Skye stared at the heavens, amazed. He led Victoria to the spring and washed her face and his, sluicing drops of blood away from tiny wounds where shattered lead had seared them. They sat in the grass, dumfounded, not wanting anything but to sit stupidly and behold the sunny world.

He saw hurt in Victoria's face and something else: banditry was something new to her, something she scorned. In time, after the mild breezes had restored order to his soul, he began taking stock. Now they had only the clothes on their backs. He stood, recovered his grimy frock coat and dusted it off. She rose also and began shaking dirt off her skirts. He recovered his beaver top hat and discovered a bullet hole in it. He pushed a finger through both holes and wiggled it at her. She smiled at last.

He donned his frock coat and top hat, looking once again the dashing gentleman, and noted that she looked the fashionable lady. They were city-dwellers out on a stroll with their dog. He smiled and she caught his humor and smiled back. It was the best thing to do at a moment when they had nothing. No food, no shelter, no protection, no coin, and no tongue in common with those who lived in this vast province.

"I don't know where we're going or what we'll find, but we may as well head north again," he said.

"I don't know this land," she said, and he understood her meaning. An Indian woman could find foods in the wild if she knew them: roots, berries, nuts, bulbs, stalks. But everything in this Mexican province was new to her, and she would be almost as helpless as he.

They lacked so much as a piece of string. So they were a pair of swells, promenading through the wilds, and somehow that caught their fancy and they started hiking the elusive trail. They would live or die, be rescued or find succor on their own, as Fate would dictate. What else was there but to laugh?

They trudged along the dirt trail, pausing at each of the numerous springs to refresh themselves. The dog was often out of sight, but always scouting. Gentlemen's and ladies' shoes weren't designed for hiking, and their feet felt pinched and blistered. But there was no help for that except to pause frequently. Skye knew that they would soon be lame, and that the lameness could kill them along with all the rest.

So he squeezed her hand and they limped along the trail and hoped for miracles. Maybe the dog would bring them food.

Twilight found them at a comfortable spring, surrounded by choking brush in arid hills, and Skye decided that they had gone far enough and their feet needed respite. He was starved, and knew Victoria was, too.

They pulled off their shoes and bathed their tormented feet in the cool water. The dog had vanished, perhaps hunting.

That's when they heard the snort of horses, and moments later a dozen fierce-looking Mexicans rode in, surrounded them, and stared. Skye rose calmly, hoping that these rough customers might be their succor.

"*Manos arriba!*" bellowed a skinny one with huge mustachios, a cocked eye, and a puckered scar that ran across his jaw to his left ear. He wore a peaked leather sombrero that barely contained an explosion of curly black hair.

Skye didn't quite grasp the Spanish. "Manos arriba," he replied cheerfully. "Nice evening."

"Manos arriba! Arriba!" the skinny man on a ribby bay horse bellowed.

Skye saw the dragoon pistola in his hand, and started laughing. He turned to Victoria. "The man means to rob us."

She started laughing, too.

"Manos arriba!"

This time a shot stopped their laughter cold. One of the horsebacked riders raised his hands, as a demonstration.

Skye and Victoria lifted their arms.

The leader unloosed a furious barrage of Spanish invective that Skye couldn't comprehend, but he got the drift: Where are your horses, where are your goods, where are the others? You couldn't be here alone.

Skye thought a moment. "Jesús Santamaría," he said.

"Santamaría! Santamaría!"

The leader turned sullen. "Santamaría," he snarled.

Two of the bandits dismounted and frisked Skye and Victoria, doing it insolently and rudely.

"Sonofabitch," Victoria said to one.

He laughed.

"Nada," said the other. "Nada."

"Santamaría," said the chief. There followed a furious debate among them, with the name of the other outlaw prominent in it. But Skye could not fathom what they were talking about.

"Comida," Skye said. "Succor, help, food, horses. Get us help." He pressed a hand to his stomach, pointed at his blistered feet, pointed at their horses.

The sinister bandit king paused, stared, and laughed, baring yellow teeth with black gaps between them.

"Succor," he said, and the rest chuckled.

He pointed to himself. "Raul Sacramento del Diablo," he bellowed. "Bandito primo," he announced.

Skye didn't believe him. This cur didn't compare with Santamaría.

"Santamaría, primo," he said. "Numero uno."

Sacramento howled, gesticulated, bawled, and snarled.

Skye pointed north. "Take us to Yerba Buena," he said. "Yerba Buena!"

"Si."

The bandit snarled something and at length.

"Comida," said Skye, glad he remembered that word.

"Comida! Comida!"

They laughed.

"I will tell everyone that Sacramento del Diablo is the greatest of all Mexican bandits," Skye said.

The bandit squinted malevolently.

The gang stayed, built a fire, and roasted a flyspecked haunch of beef they had loaded on a burro, while Skye and Victoria sat quietly. It took an hour to cook, while Skye sat there, salivating, hungering, itching to put meat between his teeth.

At last they ate, and served Skye and Victoria first, and then the dog, after sawing off tender beef with grimy knives. Skye fingered the hot beef gingerly, and tried to let it cool, but his ravenous appetite overcame his prudence and he wolfed the food. Victoria was downing hers just as enthusiastically.

The food was fine, but the company wasn't. Something bad was in the air, some sort of anticipation that radiated from the swarthy faces of his captors. They eyed him and Victoria with faint amusement and no more compassion than they would feel for a mosquito. A rank odor of dried sweat fouled the air around the cookfire. No breeze blew, not even an eddy of air to cleanse the hollow of the foulness of this bandit outfit. Skye thought he smelled vomit, blood, sweat, and something rank, like a festering wound or two among these watchful birds of prey. Whatever the case, Skye sensed the evening's entertainment was not over and that the next minutes could be dangerous and even fatal.

Victoria sensed it, too, and kept glancing at Skye, sending her silent message of fear and worry.

Then the vulture leading this vicious pack, who styled himself Sacramento del Diablo, Sacrament of the Devil, wiped his lips with the grease-stained sleeve of his leather shirt, and rose. His eyes were on Victoria as he approached, and Skye knew suddenly what was about to happen.

The dog growled low in its throat. Victoria froze. She had no weapon, not even the small and secret hideout knife she normally carried, because the last gang of bandits had stripped it away. She was as helpless as a baby chick.

Skye stood. There were a few things he would die for; a few things in his soul that he regarded as more important than life. His freedom, for one. Avoiding torture, for another. And the sanctity of his woman.

The gaunt, hollow-chested bandit clasped Victoria's arm and lifted her up, his face swimming in anticipation.

Skye slammed into him, sending him reeling backward. They landed on the grass together, Skye on top, and Skye began hammering the chieftain brutally, heedless of the shouts around him, the sudden rush of men determined to pull him off their leader. Berserk rage loosed in him and he fought with the powers of a madman, his great fists smashing everywhere, his thrashing legs booting at any target, his elbows hammering into the chieftain. He felt blows rain on his head and back, turned and booted a man in the groin. He saw the flash of metal and felt a searing pain across a forearm. The snarling dog leapt at the attacker and pulled him down, biting him on the arms and legs and lips.

But now he was beyond subduing, and thrashed about so violently that the bandits could not pin him. Skye traveled to some distant shore where the howls of men and the thud of his fists grew remote, where the taste of his own blood didn't matter.

Vaguely, he heard the savagery of the dog and the shrieks of clawed and bitten men. But he was losing ground. And then, finally, they pulled him off the chief and pinned him down, eight of them against his writhing strength and the snapping, slavering dog, which was sinking canines into flesh until they were all soaked in blood, and howling great oaths at him.

Skye drifted into a haze, but he could see the bandit chief rise slowly, clasping his crotch where Skye had smashed him, and stand, bent over, his face in agony.

Skye peered about, through puffed eyes, and discovered Victoria standing apart, a flintlock rifle at her shoulder, cocked and ready. Other firearms lay at her feet. The bore of her rifle aimed squarely at the bandit chief, and the man was taking her seriously. Diablo straightened up and let go of his crotch.

Then he muttered a command.

The bandits pinning Skye let him go. He sat up slowly, and then stood, fighting back the dizziness. Victoria's rifle never wavered. Some of the bandits could not stand, and lay in the grass oozing blood from dog bites. The ones that could stand made no effort to rush her.

But strangely, the chief smiled, dripping blood from a corner of his puffy mouth. He bowed, laughed, and issued a stream of orders to his men. The four standing bandits brought two saddled horses to Skye.

"Vaya, Yanqui diablo," the bandit said. "Adios, muchacho."

Skye plucked up one of the pistols and poked it into his waist, another loaded rifle, and helped Victoria mount one horse. Then he managed to pull his tortured body up and into the saddle of the other.

They watched silently. They had defeated him, pinned him down, and yet they had lost, and every one of them was bleeding from dog bites and suffering from the mayhem.

The only happy man among them was the chief, Raul Sacramento del Diablo, whose face was wreathed in joy. Skye did not entirely grasp what had happened, or why the bandit king set them free instead of killing him. Least of all did he understand why the man was smiling with some sort of ethereal joy—unless the bandit simply cherished a good brawl, win or lose.

And Skye and Victoria and No Name fled into the night.

37

Guided by a gibbous moon throwing lantern-light over the dim trail, they rode north a mile or so. Then Skye stopped. The dog was limping. Skye dismounted and gathered No Name into his arms. He lifted the weary creature into Victoria's lap.

"Hand him to me when I get into the saddle," he said.

"I'll carry him, Skye. Damn good dog."

"Yes."

"He's like ten warriors."

"He's got war honors, Victoria. Counted coup many times."

"Spirit-dog," she said. "You must never name him."

"You all right?"

"I am all right. You?"

"I don't know."

He surveyed himself. His frock coat was filthy and busted apart at the shoulders. His britches were torn. His body had survived without serious damage except for the knife slash across his forearm. When they reached the next spring he would wash it.

"You are a great warrior, Skye."

"They wrestled me down."

"Dammit, Skye, eight men. It took all of them to do it.

And you humbled the chief. That dog's a great warrior, too. Every one covered with his own blood."

She stroked the head of the recumbent dog, which lay across her skirts. Something about that stirred him.

"You're a great warrior woman, Victoria. Everything changed when the chief saw the bore of your rifle. You were ready to kill him and he knew it."

"You were ready to die to save me." She was peering at him so intently that he felt embarrassed. "I am loved," she said. "You give away your life for me."

"We all risked our lives, including that mutt, for each other. That dog was dodging kicks and dodging a few big knives, too. But he never stopped biting."

This moment was an affirmation, and Skye treasured it.

He found a pair of leather rings, designed to carry a rifle, and slid the weapon into them, freeing an arm at last.

"We got a rifle and pistol out of it, but no powder or balls. Two shots. It'll help."

They started their horses north, and rode another mile until they found a spring. There they watered and washed, and then withdrew into brush to await the dawn. Skye rolled under some manzanita and slept, letting the silence and coolness and darkness of the California night heal body and soul. The dog lay quietly beside him. They were warriors together, bonded by blood.

As he lay hurting through the fretful night, he realized that something had changed. This ordeal was another passage in his life. He had fled from Monterey feeling utter loss, loss of his birth family, loss of a nation, loss of everything familiar. And now, after this ordeal of banditry, and their survival against all odds, he was discovering that he had a new family. He studied Victoria who lay inert a few feet away. Always before, in the recesses of his heart, he had wondered about the future: could he, an Englishman, find bliss with this Crow woman? Would he ever grow restless for another, one of his own kind? Some sweet English-speaking lady, in lilac cologne, who might share everything that had been his inheritance from the Island Kingdom? Would he grow bored with Victoria, who knew nothing of that life? And until now he never had an answer.

But now an answer was forming. Yes, he told his doubtful soul, yes, I can live with her always. I can cease being the Englishman. We can become a new nation, she and I, not English, not Crow, not Yank, but children of the American mountains. And now the dog had joined the family. Strange beast, often out of sight, obscure, unmastered, and alone. But now the yellow dog lay beside him, bonded by war and blood.

Skye stared at the dog, loving him more than ever, feeling at one with the creature. He reached across the weeds to clasp the dog's injured foreleg, and felt its heat rise in his hand. He stroked the foreleg gently. The dog stirred and licked Skye's hand, and sighed.

And Skye knew that he had passed from one realm into another, and that these beloved allies, his Indian woman and his dog, were partnered with him along the long, lonesome road ahead. For the first time in years, he didn't miss his native land.

The next day they starved. Skye rode dizzily, wondering whether he could hang onto his horse long enough to reach a village. Victoria was stoic, and rode in resolute silence, while the dog seemed oblivious of the famine that was tormenting the human beings. Occasionally Victoria dismounted and collected some object or other from the ground. Skye discovered that these were arrowheads, and one old and rusted spearhead, abandoned or lost by the Spanish.

"Go hunt," she said that afternoon. "I can cut meat with these things."

He examined the charge in the flintlock rifle. Some of

the powder had slipped out of the pan, but it probably would fire. He would have only one shot, so it had to count. He had the pistol in his belt, but he would need that for other purposes.

He heeled the bandit horse ahead. It responded swiftly. He had never hunted in an arid, hilly, monotonous land like this, and scarcely knew what sort of game to look for, but he set out, riding ahead, figuring that all game had to water somewhere. The dog did not go with him, which darkened his spirits. But the dog was still limping.

He spotted a spring far up a slope a mile to the left of the trail, a smear of greenery that indicated water, rode cautiously in that direction, and then dismounted. He tied the horse and crept forward until he had a good field of fire overlooking a tiny rivulet that burst from dark rock. Then he settled the rifle barrel over a downed juniper trunk and waited.

But nothing came there. He wondered if his own rank odor had driven game away, or whether this region lacked game entirely. When it grew too dark to make meat he retreated to his horse and rode quietly down to the trail, where Victoria would be waiting for him. He felt faint with hunger and miserable with defeat.

He found her and the dog at a tiny marsh-lined pond well ahead. She had an animal hanging from a limb and was butchering it slowly, with the ancient spearhead, a hard and miserable task, while the dog lay waiting.

Amazed, he unsaddled and picketed the horse beside hers.

"How?" he asked.

She nodded toward the dog. "He brought it. Dragged it. Yearling red deer. I have never seen a red deer."

The deer's windpipe had been mangled.

The dog, again.

He gathered firewood, which lay abundantly about this tiny marsh area, and slowly peeled shreds of dry bark until he had a small pile. Then he gathered small sticks, broke them into fragments that would catch easily. And then he pulled the big pistol from his waist and studied it. He had no worm or other means to disarm it, but he worked powder out of the pan and hoped that would do. Then he nestled a cottony bit of tinder below the frizzen, cocked the flintlock, and squeezed, aiming the weapon away from camp. It didn't fire, but neither did the rain of sparks, as flint struck steel, ignite his tinder. Five attempts later, using various bits of tinder, he was able to transfer a few glowing embers into the little mouse-nest of tinder on the ground, and blew gently upon it. In a few minutes he had a flame. In an hour they had cooked meat.

The yellow dog ate first and best, and settled into a supine languor.

That evening they continued to butcher and cook the meat until they had roasted it all. They ate the whole while against the starvation to come, feeding bits to the dog, which soon surfeited itself and settled into a nap. Skye watched the skies restlessly. This was November, the monsoon season in this Mexican province, and his small family had no shelter at all.

He talked Victoria out of her petticoat, and wrapped the cooked meat in it and hung it high in a limb, fearing bear or wolves.

He did not sleep. Their vulnerability worried him. He had the rifle for protection against predators or mortals, and for food. One shot. And yet he was glad. His mood had slowly risen, like yeasty dough, since fleeing Monterey.

They made good progress the next day, seeing no one. But the following day, when the trail wound close to the great inland bay and away from the coastal mountains, they beheld traffic on the road. They passed coppery peasants with creaking ox-carts laden with hay or melons, and women bearing baskets on their heads, old people in black who were standing and staring at the world. They passed corrals and strings of burros and flower-bedecked graveyards.

They had somehow left a dangerous wild behind and were approaching a more civilized country along the endless shore of a vast and shimmering freshwater sea. Skye traded the pistol for melons and beans and goat meat, and still had enough for an ancient flea-infested blanket.

They exchanged cheerful greetings with all these warm-fleshed people, but beyond that they understood nothing and could not convey their slightest thoughts. They knew they were closely observed, and with great curiosity, especially by women and children. They realized that Skye's stubbled face, torn and stained frock coat, and Victoria's ripped and soiled skirts occasioned much clucking among the Mexicans. The Californios wore clean clothing, much of it snowy white, or black, or dove-colored leather, and numerous gaudy rings, bracelets, and necklaces made to glitter.

The trail occasionally lifted them over majestic hills only to dump them into cloistered valleys verdant with waxy-leaved shrubs. But eventually it led past an ancient mission called Mission San Francisco de Asis, though the people didn't call it that. Skye thought it had been named after some woman.

But it was the first truly formidable building Victoria had ever seen, so he paused there and let her gape at this holy place of the Mexicans, and exclaim at the candles and gold and lovely images. She could not fathom the bleeding Christ, crowned with thorns, or why mortals knelt before him.

"Sonofabitch," she muttered, along with other imprecations. What sort of god was this? She began eyeing Skye suspiciously for signs of adherence to this strange belief.

Late that afternoon, they reached the cold and misty

village of Yerba Buena, chilled to the bone, and discovered a settlement of three or four hundred, and a grimy Yank brigantine bobbing lazily in the harbor, riding the ebb tide.

38

Yerba Buena sprawled so widely that it gave the illusion of being larger than it was. But Skye swiftly discerned a thriving commercial port perched on the chill peninsula. Burros, dogs, chickens, hogs, and sheep rambled across the village. No Name eyed them carefully but did not contest the neighborhood. Seagulls perched on every roof. The tang of the sea lay in the fresh breeze, a clean scent as old and familiar to Skye as his own name. Old women in black shawls hung on benches, and old men in dark woolen homespuns lounged in the feeble sun.

But it was the brigantine that captured Skye's attention. Where was it headed? The Stars and Stripes stirred lazily from its mainmast. Stain had long since reduced its white hull to a patched tan and brown. The grimy sails had been furled slovenly, bulging loose on every spar. Skye looked in vain for a name. A fine spread eagle, gilded and fierce, decorated its stern. Once it had been a proud ship. Now it probably hauled stinking seal pelts to New England.

He saw no one aboard, but a grubby longboat was moored to a small wharf on the waterfront that extended just far enough to keep a small boat afloat at low tide.

"I want to book passage if it's going north," Skye said to Victoria.

"I don't like that big canoe."

"It's Yank. We'll be safe enough."

"It's a bandit ship. I am tired of bandits."

"No, just a coaster picking up sea otter and selling stuff from the East Coast."

"We have horses. Let's walk on the earth."

"This is where we either catch that brig or get ferried across the water to the north side of the harbor."

"Let's do that. We got horses."

"And nothing to live on."

She didn't respond. He knew she was unhappy, tired of this long ordeal, and above all, homesick. He knew all about that malady. He had been homesick for years in the Royal Navy. The offer from Hudson's Bay had wrought a whole new wave of homesickness. But the navy had cured that in Monterey.

She was plenty homesick now, having seen a large chunk of the world beyond the foothill kingdom of the Absaroka people. The odd thing was, he was beginning to share her yearning, not for England but for her village, and maybe even the company of the Yank fur brigades. And for the great Rocky Mountains, where he had found himself, his manhood, his wife, and his liberty.

"Victoria," he said quietly, "we'll go to the mountains and your people just as fast as we can. I miss them as much as you do."

She eyed him, this time with a certain wonder, and with an infinite trust. He saw that trust form in her face and smiled.

"We'll get there, and maybe in three moons be sitting in your father's lodge."

He stirred his horse and they rode quietly along the waterfront, past obscure adobe buildings that looked abandoned but probably weren't. A taberna near the dock beckoned. That would be the place of food and drink and most dockside transactions in Yerba Buena.

They rode to the taberna and dismounted, hitching their reins to a rail. The dog settled smack under his horse, as if to prevent it from departing without him.

Skye lacked so much as a shilling. He surveyed his dress ruefully. The sleeves of his frock coat were half-ripped from it, and the rear seam had come undone half up the back. The fabric had been hopelessly stained. His toes bulged through cracks in his boots. The battered beaver top hat now had a bullet hole through it. His shirt was vile. Weeks of stubble decorated his cheeks and his hair hung in strings. His nose had blistered in the California sun and looked like a red mountain between his small blue eyes.

Victoria had managed to do better. Her dress hung limply without its petticoats, but she had somehow kept it relatively clean. The shawl had survived and hung loosely over her shoulders. But the rents in her skirts showed hard use, and her Vancouver-made slippers had virtually fallen apart. She wore her black hair braided, and it shone from the frequent washings she had given it, milking the stalks of yucca for a sort of soap. She was quite the lady, even if he looked the ruffian. Why was it that Indians could endure the wilds and look their best in it, while white men deteriorated the moment they were beyond the reach of civilization?

No matter. He would try to find out about the brig, and about ferries that would take them and their animals across the amazing water gate that almost sliced California in two.

He took her arm and escorted her into the taberna, carrying his rifle with him because he didn't entrust it to the horse outside. The door hung on leather hinges, and the windows lacked glass, though they could be tightly shuttered in squalls.

If anything, the place was colder than the village without.

A Mexican man motioned him to an empty trestle table, but Skye resisted. He couldn't afford a meal or a drink, as much as he pined for both. Instead, he studied the half dozen patrons, settling at last on a bearded Yank in the corner, sitting lazily over a mug of cerveza with a Californio. The master, probably, but there was no way of knowing. This one sported a beard such as Skye had never seen; it bulged outward like a sunburst, reaching his lap and haloing his face with a salt-and-pepper aura. The man's mouth was not visible, and that orifice lay buried beneath a matt of stained hair.

Skye doffed his top hat and approached.

"You the master of that brig?"

The man surveyed him. "Abner Dickens."

"Barnaby Skye, sir, and Victoria. Mr. Dickens, you headed north? I'm looking for passage for my wife and my dog and maybe one horse."

"That was my intent. But if my dickering with this gent here is successful, I'll be heading around the horn."

The Mexican knew English and was following the exchange.

"What would be your price?" Skye asked.

"I don't reckon I'd take your horse. Nuisance and a danger at sea. The rest of ye?" He studied Skye's clothing. "How'll ye pay me? In coin?"

"We have to sell one or two horses here."

"Fat lot of money you'll get. The last thing a Californio needs is another horse. Sit," he said, nodding toward the bench.

Skye and Victoria sat. The scent of cooked meat dizzied him, and the sight of good brandy on the wood table shot hungers through him.

"I'd also sell the rifle if I have to."

"Fat chance of that. No one can afford one. Where do you want to go, exactly?"

"Astoria, mouth of the Columbia."

"You willing to work?"

"We both will work for passage."

"I'm short of men. Ship's company down seven. Two scurvied and died off Chile. One ran into a whore's stiletto. Four deserted, Callao, Diego . . . Can she cook?"

Skye didn't answer. He was having second thoughts. "Where are you bound?"

"Sandwich Islands to get some Kanakas. Good seamen and cheap. But you need to keep a whip handy."

Skye knew that once he boarded that brig he'd not get off it until it reached its home port. He didn't want to go to the Sandwich Islands. "Sorry, mate," he said.

"Mate? I thought so, Skye. You've shipped before. I could use a bosun."

Skye didn't answer. He could not conceal his past even if he tried.

"You're an Englander," the master said.

"London," Skye replied.

"Long way from home," Dickens said. "You hire on and I'll take you and your lady to Boston and see to your passage across the Atlantic."

It stirred him. Passage to England. His dream fulfilled after all, but not on an HBC schooner. Passage to his father and sisters, and kin. That royal pardon, a good name. He sighed, and then felt Victoria stirring unhappily beside him.

"No, thank you," he said. He had already crossed that bridge and would never turn back.

The master's cordiality cooled, and Skye could almost hear the man thinking of ways to shanghai Skye and ditch the woman. He would be on his guard.

"A thousand pardons, senor," said the Mexican. "That fusil—that rifle. I know it. How did you get it?"

Skye weighed an answer and decided to conceal nothing. Half truths and untruths never sat well with him. Silence was sometimes a refuge, but not deception. "It belonged to a bandit in a gang south of here," he said. "Horses did, too."

"Sacramento del Diablo," the man whispered. "How did you get this piece?"

"That was the second bunch robbed us, and I got mad."

"Mad? Loco?"

"Plenty loco."

The Mexican involuntarily made the sign of the cross. "And you live to tell of it. You were coming from Monterey, si, and that is the worst trail in California. Why you are alive I cannot imagine."

"How'd you know this rifle?"

"It was stolen from my son, senor."

"They stole the rifle from him?"

"After they killed him. That trail, it is infested with bandits. No one in his right mind goes by land; always by sea. I begged Andres not to go that way."

Skye sighed. "The rifle's yours. I don't want stolen property."

The man was touched. "A thousand thanks. Ask me any favor, senor. It is Carlos Sepulveda you address."

Skye considered. "We need to go to Fort Vancouver in Oregon. How can we outfit and do that?"

Sepulveda shook his head. "It is too late by land, senor. The mountains to the north are impassable in the winter. Only by sea . . ."

39

Skye didn't like that news. This remote province of California was walled by alpine snow much of the year. Not until May could he escape it by land. He sat there, in the taberna, wondering what blow would strike next.

"There is one way, senor, but it is arduous, si?" Carlos Sepulveda continued. "Sail south to San Diego. There one can take a wandering trail across arid wastes to the City of the Holy Faith in Nuevo Méjico, Santa Fe, and from there go north through fierce lands . . ."

Skye nodded. He lacked the means, the patience, and the time. Fort Vancouver lay only a few hundred miles away; not two thousand.

"I'll take ye to Astoria, Skye, for wages," Dickens said.

"It's Mister Skye, sir."

"Mister, is it? How do ye collect a gentleman's title?"

"Because I'm here in the New World, mate. For much of my life I had only a surname and never even a mister. All the officers called themselves mister or sir, but that didn't apply to Barnaby Skye, who was pressed off the streets of Wapping, near the London dock, at the age of thirteen and held prisoner until he escaped here in this free land seven years later. Now I am called a deserter.

"No one will ever take my freedom away again. They may capture me, but not alive, sir. My freedom is worth my life. Put me on a ship against my will, sir, and I'll fight to death. Take me where I will not go and I'll fight to the death. My freedom is worth my life. I spent all those years with no liberty, mostly a powder monkey and then an able seaman, living only to obey and avoid a flogging and given nothing for it but my gruel. That's no life, sir. It's living death. I was a brute, a beast of burden, to be reined and spurred and whipped, and tossed to the sharks if I did not bend to their will."

Dickens' eyebrows arched.

"So, a warning, sir. I am Mister Skye, not Skye. If you sail for the Sandwich Islands against my will, you'll have a mutineer on your hands. If you're as good as your word, you'll have an able seaman, working hard and true, and an able cook, working hard and true. It's life or death for me, Mr. Dickens, and not all the whips of all your bosuns can subdue that."

Dickens stared. "I'll take you up the coast. I've recruited two boys here, but they're green. We'll train them. I'll do some trading for otter pelts along the way, and sell the last of my trade goods, so it makes sense. We'll deliver you to Astoria and then head for the Sandwich Islands for some Kanakas. You and Mrs. Skye willing?"

Skye studied the man. "Is that your bounden word, and are you good as your word, Mr. Dickens?"

"I'll oath it, Mister Skye. Upon my honor, we'll go directly up the coast to Astoria."

"And release us, Victoria, my dog, and me, there?"

"Upon my honor, sir."

Skye swallowed back the anxiety. "Then we'll sign on. When do you pull anchor?"

"First thing in the morning."

"Time for me to sell the horses and outfit, then. All

right, Mr. Dickens, we'll be waiting at that jetty at first light. You'll not be disappointed."

"Far from it, Mister Skye."

They shook on it.

The trader, Sepulveda, helped Skye that afternoon. One of the horses, unmarked, traded easily for ten reales. The other bore a brand no one would touch, and the Mexican finally agreed to drive it out of town and abandon it.

Skye bought worn blankets and two knives with nine of the reales; a supper and shelter on the floor of the taberna with the last. A blanket and knife apiece from Sepulveda. He threw in some cowhide and thong and an awl as well. Victoria smiled. A blanket and a knife was treasure. And she could resole his boots and make herself some moccasins.

The next dawn they waited in the chill while Dickens' crew rowed a longboat to shore. Along side them were two solemn Mexican youths, one of them accompanied by his father. The boys looked frightened and ready to bolt.

Skye and Victoria boarded and settled on the hard bench as the seamen backed the longboat and rowed toward the brig. It was a fateful moment: there he was, a seaman again, though he had vowed he never would be. He eyed the motley sailors, mostly white Yanks, but some half-castes he thought might be Caribbean or drawn from the dives of New Orleans. They looked hung over and surly and he supposed it would be a day or so before they sweated the booze of the sole grogshop in Yerba Buena out of their pores. The ruddy bosun in command eyed the Skyes and the two newcomers closely.

The brig, *Dedham*, looked even worse close at hand than Skye had supposed from shore. Dickens, dressed shabbily in an ancient sweater, nodded them aft, and Skye poked around until he found above-deck quarters that had obviously been vacated by a bosun or master's mate just previously. The two-bunk compartment was little different from the one on the *Cadboro*, except this was filthy.

Victoria grunted. Skye knew that in short order this tiny place would be immaculate, unlike the rest of this creaking two-masted trading ship.

Skye doffed his battered frock coat and reported to work.

The deck hands were reeling the longboat aboard and the seamen were scaling the rigging, heading for the spars on the foremast where the square-rigged sails were furled. Men crawled out on the spars, oblivious of the height, and waited to release the gathered canvas which they would not do until the brigantine had passed through the gate and was at sea, because of adverse winds.

He watched sailors hoist the fore-and-aft mainsail, drawing it up from the boom to the gaff atop the main-mast. That one looked well-used, much-patched, and heavily stained as it caught the air of the great bay.

All this had proceeded in silence, which told Skye that this was a veteran crew needing no direction from the bosuns or master. That was the first good news.

The brigantine heeled in the wind. The helmsman steered it north, and Yerba Buena swiftly vanished behind hills and mist, and the great gate lay ahead, cold and bright and mean. A small ugly thought wormed into Skye's mind. He would know within the hour whether Dickens was a man of his word. Once they reached the sea, there were three directions the brig could go: south, west, or north. They passed the jaws of land, hit choppy waters, and then burst out upon the great Pacific, sparkling green and blue under a cloudless heaven.

The men up on the spars of the foremast dropped the canvas with heavy thumps, and they swelled with the wind. These were as badly mended and worn as the mainsail. Dickens would be lucky to make his home port without losing his sheets. He wondered why the man ran such a ship unless he was very nearly bankrupt.

Dickens approached him. "All right. You've seen the drill. I've good men, veteran seamen, but we're shy right now. Ship's company should be thirty-two; we're at twenty-five not including the new boys and you and Mrs. Skye."

"At your service, sir."

"I'm making you a boatswain. Don't ask me why; I'm just doing it. I'd thought about making Mrs. Skye a cook, but I need a sailmaker worse. That's been part of the trouble. My sailmaker's boy died of scurvy."

"She'll take to it, sir. What do you want of me?"

"You'll do first watch. You can start by putting those boys to work holystoning the deck. After that, I want you to examine the ship stem to stern and report. After that I'll introduce you to the crew."

Skye found the Mexican boys, Armando and Pio, hunted down the equipment and found it in a dock locker, and showed the boys how to scrape the good teak deck of the brig with blocks of soft sandstone. It was high time. The deck was slippery and gummy with the accretions of the sea and the animal cargo. The brig would be a safer place when the deck was immaculate.

Skye inspected the brig, estimating it to be a hundred and five feet from stem to stern, and twenty-eight at the beam. The foremast had been spliced; a sign of sure trouble in times past. He found neglect at every hand, and thought maybe if given his freedom he could bring the ship around before reaching Astoria.

'Tween decks he found a sailmaker's and carpenter's shop, a galley and mess, forecastle berths, storerooms, bosuns' quarters, and abaft these, two cabins, housing the master's mate and helmsmen. Below, in the cargo hold, he found stacked sea otter hides on racks well above the cargo deck, and a small collection of trade goods in crates and barrels. This brig was sailing half empty, which may be why Dickens was cutting every corner.

It would get him and Victoria to Astoria. Whether the decaying bark would take Dickens to Gloucester, Massachusetts, his home port, was a question.

He returned to the spar deck and found Dickens and two bosuns. Wind swelled the sails. The ship laid a course due west. The California coast lay small and dark.

"Mister Skye, meet your watch officers, Lars Pedersen, first mate this watch, and Amos Carter, second mate. The other lads are below. Gents, Mister Skye, here, likes to be addressed as I've addressed him, so that's how we'll proceed. He's been in the Royal Navy and knows the ropes. His wife, Victoria, will work in the sail loft. And the dog will—what will the dog do, Skye, for his keep?"

"He will keep watch over us, Mr. Dickens."

"Ah! I imagine that's worth the salt beef. Very well, gents. There's work to do, and two new boys to bring along."

Skye noticed the shadow of the foremast sliding across the teak deck. The brig was swinging north.

40

Victoria knew at once what to do. Making a sail was very like making a new lodge. But instead of stitching with other women of her tribe, she was working with a strange little gnome of a man who talked so fast she couldn't understand him. All she knew was that he was very fierce and had a leer that offended her.

She found herself in a large room between decks, the sail loft. Great rolls of heavy fabric the little man called linen, or sailcloth, lay about, along with coils of manila rope, and scissors and knives and needles and thimbles and rolls of thick sail twine.

"This here, she's a new fore top sail. Foremast, top yard, that's how you name them. Now I got her laid out and cut into panels according to pattern, and what you're gonna do is sew them panels up with a real fine double stitch and no wrinkles that let the air through, got that?"

She didn't, but she nodded. "Now this here's how it's done. You take this big needle and thread it with twine like so, and then wax it so the right-hand twist lies true, and then you stitch like so, good straight line, double so she stands in a good gale."

On the floor, the pieces of the new sail were arrayed like the hides going into a new lodge cover, all carefully cut.

"All right, you tackle them seams and I'll sew patches on the corners. We get this sewn up, and we do the hems, the luff first—the forward edge—and then the foot, and then we put in the luff rope and the foot rope. Those help keep the sail from stretching out of shape, you see?"

She didn't, but she nodded.

"Then we sew in the bolt ropes on the luff and foot, and add the grommets, reef points, and the rest."

Maybe, she thought, this wasn't so much like sewing a lodge after all, except that the great pieces were on the floor, and cut according to a pattern.

Two portholes, without glass in them, threw white sea-light over the floor. She could see the benign sea shimmering there, and hear the creak of the ship's timbers as it skimmed the cold waters. She could scarcely imagine how white men had created these giant canoes, big enough to roam the seas and sturdy enough to weather storms. The whole ship had been a wonder to her.

The little man, whose name she learned was Perkins Gouge, never stopped talking and she hadn't the faintest idea what he was saying.

"Them Mohawks was thick with them Redcoats, and the Hurons and Oneida were in the middle of it, too, and we was marching up there near Lake Champlain when we come upon Prevost's column, and next thing was, they formed into a red wall, Brown Betsys poking out at us, bayonets on 'em, and they got on their knees and laid a volley and it sailed clear over us.

"We took cover and begin snipin', but they just march forward in that line, like they is brushing off flies, except now and then a Redcoat topples like a tree, and they cut loose with more volleys, one rank moves up and fires, and then backs off and the next rank moves up and fires, and they're driving us back right into the arms of them miserable Iroquois and that's when hell breaks loose and I'm about to lose my topknot."

Victoria sewed, at least until the little man peered closely at her work and got mad.

"That's not the way, damn ye red hide, it's done like this, see here?"

"Goddam," she said and waited for his instruction.

He made her cut out her stitches, wax the twine again, and start over. The ship creaked, and her mind drifted. She wanted to be up above, on the deck with Skye, free in the morning air, the dog beside them.

He was doing well, he said, training Armando and Pio, putting the rotting ship in shape, scraping away the neglect. He said the repaired sails and new sails were important. Without them Dickens wouldn't make it to his port.

They were following the coast but sometimes it was so far from the ship she couldn't see it, or could see only a thin and mysterious blue line. But then Dickens veered toward shore, reaching a settlement of some sort. He went ashore in a longboat rowed by crewmen, and returned with a stack of sea otter pelts, lifeless, eyeless furs that made her feel cold. She was not allowed on deck, so she knew almost nothing of what transpired, but Skye filled her in.

He said there were settlements along the California and Oregon coast, some Indian, other half-breed, that did business in otter and sealskins, and Yank merchant ships like this one, along with the HBC, bought every pelt they had to offer and paid with trade goods not unlike those her own people acquired in the Rocky Mountains.

She finally rebelled at the little tyrant who worked her until her hands went numb, and took breaks when she felt like it.

"Lazy, worthless redskin," Gouge bawled.

"You sonofabitch," she replied, remembering trapper words with joy. "You ain't worth spit."

She needed the air, and relief from him and his grisly stories of butcheries, massacres of Indians, battles at sea, great fires, roasted flesh, on and on.

Perkins Gouge was asking for a scissors in his belly, she thought. She'd do it, too, and then jump into the sea so as not to shame Skye.

All the while, she was getting an education in sailmaking. They completed the tight-stitched double seams welding the panels of the great sail together, and he actually smiled. Then he showed her how to table the sail: sew hems on its edges, beginning with the luff, or top, and then sewing the rope tightly into the luff. The task was just as intricate and artful as sewing a good buffalohide lodge together, and she began to enjoy making everything tight and strong.

"We finish this, and then we start on a mainsail," he said during a less bloodthirsty moment. "She's got a rip from gaff to boom, and we got to cut out the rotten panel and sew in a new one. That sail, she's too big to stretch in here, so we gotta do it a piece at a time."

But mostly he talked of war and blood and beheadings and amputations, and surgeons with saws, and mortar, and canister, and chain shot. When he was tired of that he talked about swords, dirks, stilettos, and beheading axes. He favored beheadings one whole day. He had seen several, or so he led her to believe.

He was the bloodiest little man she had ever encountered, but she knew she would soon be rid of him. His leering never stopped, but she ignored it. Skye would deal with him if it came to that.

One good thing came of her labor. She discovered that scraps of new and rotten sailcloth were available to any seaman who wanted them, and these leftover pieces were constantly being fashioned into britches and jackets and shirts and even slippers by industrious seamen in the fore castle. She and Skye had nothing, scarcely the clothing on their backs, so she set out to manufacture some. As weary as she was of sewing, she worked hard during their half-day rest, and made him some britches and shirts, a thick blouse for herself, and several sailcloth moccasins for them both.

The sea rose and fell in eternal calm, and she wondered when a storm would come. Whenever they were beyond landfall, she grew taut and upset and cursed these white men for taking her so far from her home. But then the blue rib of the continent would rise out of the mist. It was beyond swimming, but she comforted herself with the notion that she could somehow reach there if she had to.

One twilight the second watch discovered a bonfire on the distant shore just before dusk, and Dickens steered the brigantine shoreward. That was usually a trader's signal. The twilight offered safe passage and they made the coast in a half hour and beheld a great crowd on the distant shore. Black cliffs leapt up behind the settlement.

Skye and Victoria watched as the crew dropped anchor and prepared the longboat for Dickens. But even before the seamen could winch the longboat to the water, a swarm of giant canoes set sail for the brigantine, their high prows brightly painted and the paddling oarsmen stroking the dugout canoes to a great speed.

She thought there were two or three hundred villagers on the beach, and she wondered what people they were. She didn't know the people here on the edge of the world. Behind them was a village consisting of giant longhouses of bark, and racks for drying fish, and carved poles with spirit-figures on them to ward off evil. At least that was how she interpreted them.

These people were barechested even in this cold season, but wore leather skirts or pants, and great necklaces of gleaming things she couldn't make out.

"Good trade, many skins," she said to Skye.

He grunted.

A dozen canoes were closing on the ship, each canoe with twenty or more men in it.

She caught glints of metal things in the bellies of the canoes.

And no furs. No skins, unless it was too dark to see them.

Dickens had pulled the longboat up and lowered the Jacob's ladders so the visitors could clamber aboard and trade.

"Damn, Skye, I don't like this."

"Like what?"

"Them warriors."

"Warriors? They're trading."

No Name's hair bristled.

"Look at the dog, Skye."

"Mr. Dickens," Skye bawled. "Raise those ladders."

The master turned to glance at Skye. "What are you talking about, Mister Skye?"

"War," Skye cried.

But it was too late. The first barrage of arrows from the bows hidden in the dugouts found their mark. Dickens took an arrow through the mouth, tumbled, and fell over the rail.

Another arrow caught the bosun.

A whirling axe struck a seaman who was trying to raise one of the rope ladders. Then, with a ululating howl, the warriors scrambled to the deck, dealing death at every hand.

41

Skye hurried Victoria aft, deep into darkness. The big, stocky tribesmen poured aboard, their faces hideously painted with red ochre, scaling the rope ladder with breathtaking speed. Volleys of arrows from the high-prowed dugouts felled most of the deck hands. Indians clubbed and stabbed others racing from the forecastle up the gangway. Still others raced to the pilot house and butchered the helmsman and master's mate with sickening speed. A howl of red joy bloomed among them, sending chills through Skye.

"Drop the Jacob's ladder off the stern and go," he whispered to Victoria. She slid to the rail, tossed the manila-and-wooden rung ladder over while he grabbed a belaying pin, the seaman's first and last recourse, and braced to fight two of the naked savages who were bearing down on him. He parried the lance of one easily and ducked under the war axe to club him hard. Skye whirled toward the other as a spearhead blurred by him, tearing cloth. The dog leapt, clamped jaws over an arm, and bit furiously. The red-painted warrior howled and tumbled down. Skye caught him across the head, knocking him senseless. The cur let go and leapt at another huge warrior thundering toward Skye.

Too many warriors. Skye whirled his belaying pin at one, the dog bit another, and then it was time to leap or die.

His heart pumped hard. He leapt over the taffrail, fell a sickening distance, hit brutal cold, and rose again to the surface. The sea swelled high about him. He caught his breath, realized he couldn't swim with his boots on and paddled desperately.

"Skye," cried Victoria.

He could scarcely see her in the blackness. She clung to the slippery rudder. He grabbed it too, feeling the icy water numbing him. Neither of them could endure that blast of cold for long.

Above, the dog howled, lonesome and eerie.

"Jump!"

The dog whined.

"Jump!"

The cur gathered itself and leapt, just as dark demons loomed above, and fell in a graceful dive. The dog slid easily into the briny, and Skye grabbed him by the nape of the neck.

The huge swells of the ocean poured over them. The ship had anchored at a roadstead, there being no sheltered water at this place, and the full might of the Pacific beat on her.

"My shoes," Skye growled.

He managed to lift a leg out of the whirling water, and Victoria undid the laces. It fell away. With struggle they got his other shoe off. Skye was still half-snarled by clothing, as was Victoria in her voluminous skirts.

Above them the shrieks and thumps of struggle diminished and Skye believed not a soul of the ship's company remained alive, save for himself and Victoria. It had all taken three or four minutes. The howling of the victors sent chills through him and he wondered what mad celebration was occupying them as they stomped rhythmically upon that newly holystoned teak. Who were they? He did not know. The brig had passed the Klamath River and Dickens thought he would be trading with the Yurok or possibly the Hupa as he dropped anchor. But there were also the Tolowa and Karok thereabouts. Maybe even Clatsop or Chinook.

One by one, butchered bodies of men he had known splashed into the sea. He gasped at the roiling body of the Mexican boy, Armando, who had only just signed on, and at a second-watch bosun he'd smoked with, bobbing lifelessly in the swells.

He took stock. They were protected by darkness and the curve of the hull at the stern, but he knew this ship would be a ball of fire ere long. They were far from shore and could not swim it. Their bodies were weighted by clothing and their arms would eventually give out and they would no longer hang on to the rudder or that lifesaving bottom rung of the Jacob's ladder that kept them alive.

Darkness! When the ship started to flame, they would be exposed. No time at all.

He guided Victoria's hand to the dog, released his hand from the rudder and felt a surge of the sea lift him. He needed to swim around the stern. Once he could look down the side of the hull, lit by the huge bonfires ashore, he saw the great red-nosed dugouts poking into the ship like piglets suckling at the sow. They were empty but tied up, and that was the sole chance.

Up above, he heard frenzy and looting. He swam back.

"Got to get a canoe," he gasped. "I might be seen. Enough light there to be the death of me. I'll get it. Hang on here. If I can't paddle it, come to it."

"Sonofabitch," she said.

That was her way of saying everything. He borrowed her knife, let go of the rudder again, and swam through the brutal cold to the nearest canoe, which bobbed violently on the swells of the ocean. He clamped his hand on the gunnel. No one spotted him. He worked toward the prow, staying in shadow from the coastal fires, found a braided leather rope and severed it. The canoe banged into the ship, almost crushing him. He gathered strength, heaved himself mightily, and fell in a heap into the canoe, flat on his back, peering upward, water rivering from him. A warrior stood at the rail straight above him, scarcely ten feet, staring down.

He lay still in the black belly of the dugout. He was lying on some paddles, and slowly extricated one. The man above him turned away. Skye saw the beginning of a blaze up there, pale light. Too late, too late.

He sat, paddled furiously, barely moving the heavy dugout.

No alarm went up. The victors were celebrating. Skye realized they would burn this ship and all its contents, the cargo of pelts as well as the trade goods and everything else that might be useful, in a frenzied celebration of their prowess. What mattered the otter pelts, the hatchets and knives and awls and blankets and flannels and cottons and canvas when measured against victory at war?

He paddled furiously, unable to make headway against the huge swells of the Pacific that lifted and dropped him, and pushed him farther from the brig even though he tried to stay close.

"Skye!"

He spotted Victoria swimming, the mutt beside her, and paddled desperately, unable to turn the dugout toward her. He thought he was losing ground, but she was gaining bit by bit. The swells separated her from sight, and he feared he had lost her, but then suddenly she was there in the faintest of light, and he wrestled her up and into the bottom, where she lay soaked and cold and gasping. He found No Name dog-paddling beside the hull, and got him aboard.

"Victoria, paddle!"

She was weeping and out of breath. She clambered up and took the big paddle he proffered and they stroked hard, even as the sails and ribbing bloomed orange and the crackle of flame raced up the rigging and into the yards, snapping like giant firecrackers.

He thought they were naked there, light upon them, but maybe not. The victors were still whooping, their eyes blinded to the small struggles of two mortals and a dog in the blackness beyond the holocaust. A ship was dying, and these devils were celebrating it.

No Name shivered, shook water off, and padded to the prow, where it set itself a guard over the ocean.

The surf heaved much too powerfully for Skye and Victoria to steer the massive dugout away, so they drifted shoreward against their will. The best they could manage was to paddle the dugout north of the village even as they closed with land. They might be caught instantly when they reached shore. But for the moment they lived.

All their work had brought them only a hundred yards or so north of the village, but at least blackness cloaked them there, and they were somewhat shielded by a rough and rocky shore.

"Save our strength," he muttered.

They let the dugout drift until it struck an obstacle, and began careering violently as the high surf toyed with it, lifting and dropping and finally rolling it over.

They were pitched once again into the sea, but this time there was rock under foot, and even as breakers crashed over them with frightful force, they crawled to land and lay, panting, in the blackness on the stony and hostile continent.

He clamped Victoria's cold hand.

Skye peered into the sea, beholding the murder of a merchant ship. Twenty-seven merchant seamen had perished. Now the warriors were descending the ladders and gathering in their canoes. They would soon discover one was missing.

No time, no time.

Skye stood, pulled off his battered frock coat and wrung it. Victoria stood, undid her skirts, which were weighting her down almost to the point where she couldn't walk, and squeezed water out of them. The mutt shook and shook.

They were barefoot and maybe in worse trouble than ever. Sharp rock stabbed him with every step. They had nothing.

There was little they could do but wait. He led them back from the beach and into a rocky defile where blackness swallowed them. He clambered up the rock, cursing it whenever it lacerated his feet, but eventually he found a perch where he could look down the strand at the shoreside village. It nestled around a creek that tumbled from the inland coastal range into the ocean, providing the village with fresh water.

The warriors had loosed most of the dugouts and were paddling back to the village with easy strokes. There was no sign that they were looking for a lost canoe.

One by one the dugouts beached on a sandy strand where a crowd swiftly dragged them beyond the high-tide line. And there the entire village stood, transfixed by the pyrotechnics on the black waters. The ship's small store of gunpowder blew, shivering the coast with thunder as the whole burning deck lifted upward and fell sizzling into the sea.

Maybe there was a raw, slim chance in this.

He ducked down to Victoria, who huddled miserably.

"We've got the whole village to ourselves," he muttered.

She didn't need encouraging. They were as good as dead the way they were, desperately cold and barefoot, with nothing more than a small knife and no hope of rescue.

They had recovered their breaths and made steady but

slow time toward the inland side of the village, suffering the wounds of sharp grasses, driftwood, and rock on their feet. Victoria did far better than Skye, having lived in moccasins all her life.

But at last they made the outskirts, and beheld in the dull orange light a number of cedar-planked longhouses, apparatus for drying fish, some things suspended high above the paws and teeth of animals, and much that they couldn't fathom.

"You ready?" he whispered.

"That first big lodge," she said.

They walked in, plainly visible to anyone on the shore who might bother to turn around. But no one did.

42

Exhaustion beset Skye. The ice water had sucked the heat from his body, and now his muscles barely worked. He stumbled toward the longhouse, helping Victoria, who shivered with every step.

Then he paused, took hold of her and drew her tight to him, cold and wet. He hugged her.

"Worst still to come," he said. "Whatever happens, I just want you to know you are the greatest gift."

She was weeping and clung to him fiercely.

They let go, knowing every moment counted. They found the open entry of the big cedar-planked longhouse, and penetrated fearfully. A fire burned lazily in a central pit, its smoke dissipated through portals in the plank roof. Surely this was the home of several families, or a clan. Raised sleeping areas lined the walls, and a vast array of food and equipment hung from the rafters above.

They were not alone. Skye froze when Victoria pointed. An old man gazed at them from a pallet. An elderly woman stared. Two others, apparently ill or old, lay swathed in blankets or skins.

None of them said anything.

The small warmth of the longhouse revived Skye's spirits and body. He and Victoria needed everything, but most important were moccasins. Tentatively, they moved about, watching the old ones. The dog patrolled the dusky room, sniffing and whining.

Victoria found moccasins, calf-high, lined with seal-skin, and richly dyed. She tried them, found them loose, but kept them. She found a cedarbark skirt, and swiftly dropped her own soggy skirts and put it on, sighing.

Skye's search took longer, but he found some good otterskin moccasins that fit, and gratefully pulled them over his bruised feet. The warmth was welcome.

Swiftly they gathered more: sealskin robes, artfully sewn together; a fine bow and quiver filled with arrows; a bone awl and a bone ladle; bags of thick fat, whether whale blubber or something else Skye could not say. And a prize: a broken flintlock, the barrel twisted but the lock intact. Flint and steel made fire.

Cedarbark rope, a fowling net, and that was as much as they could carry. One of the old men was mumbling, whining in anger, and Skye sensed it was time to flee. They had the means to live—if they could escape.

He peered swiftly out the door, beholding the shocking sight of the brigantine burning almost to its waterline, the villagers rapt along the sandy shore. But soon they would weary of the spectacle and Skye intended to be long gone before they did.

He nodded to Victoria, who hoisted her plunder on her shoulders and followed him. He noticed that she wisely took her soaked white-woman skirts with her, leaving little trace of their visit to the longhouse.

He headed straight toward the coastal mountains looming not far back, and plunged into a terrible thicket of brush and vines and fallen deadwood, vaguely lit by the great fire offshore.

Painfully they fought their way uphill into deepening blackness, feeling their way along, scarcely knowing where they were going.

The dog tagged along, then vanished and returned, and then began an odd mewling and whining. Skye's heart was laboring and he paused, exhausted, as the dog trotted off and returned, back and forth. Wearily, he followed the dog on its sideways course, until they burst into the creek bottoms and a clear trail mounting ever upward into the coastal mountains.

The going went easier then, with the dim form of the yellow dog piloting them. A little moonlight cast pale hope across their path, and they continued until neither of them could walk another step.

Skye stopped, his heart pummeling him, his legs quaking. Gratefully Victoria sank beside him.

"We've come a piece," he said. It was all he could do not to fall instantly asleep.

"We can't stay here, dammit," she said. "Daylight, they come."

She was right. But they could rest a while more. No one would come up that steep trail this night.

A misty fog built up, shutting away the view, and Skye feared they would make no more progress and might get soaked all over again. But the moon had vanished, and now there was nothing but Stygian darkness.

No Name whined.

"Can't even see you, old boy," Skye said.

Silently, Victoria found the coil of cedarbark rope she was carrying, and tied a loop into one end. This she slipped over the dog's neck.

"Trust the spirit-dog," she said.

It was all Skye could manage, just to stand and shoulder his load. But in a slow fashion, one small step at a time, they let the dog lead them where it would take them. Skye dreamed of ditching the burden on his back, dreamed of rolling into that sealskin robe, dreamed of being warm. He could hear Victoria before him, her breath laboring, bearing a terrible load of her own.

But then they stepped onto level land, a flat rocky area devoid of vegetation except for patched grass, and here the fog did not hide the moon. The dog turned away from the trail and took them toward the base of a mist-obscured cliff, to a thin dry recess in the dripping rock. The rear was barely four feet from the overhang but it would do. No mist brushed his cold-numbed face. A small animal whispered away as they ducked in.

"Dog, I owe you my life again," he muttered.

Victoria sank to the rubble-strewn floor of this protected place and lifted the loop of bark rope from the dog's neck, muttering strange Absaroka songs to the mutt.

Wearily, he worked himself out of his soaked clothes, inch by inch, setting the torn frock coat aside, along with a ragged shirt and britches, and then rolled himself into the luxurious coil of the sealskin robe, and felt its gentle heat at once. Victoria had wrapped herself in her sealskin, and was sighing joyous little breaths of happiness. Or maybe she was crying.

In the moonlit gloom, they inventoried their new possessions: the precious moccasins, a coil of cedarbark rope, a fowling net, a horn ladle, the battered musket with a working flint and steel lock, and the smooth, masculine bow, quiver chocked with iron-tipped arrows, and even a spare bowstring of some sort lying coiled in the quiver. One of the leather bags contained several pounds of blubber or seal fat. The other was stuffed with fishmeal, a good coarse flour that could be cooked into something.

Victoria found her sailmaker's knife and whittled some of the blubber and gave it to the cur, who gnawed happily on it.

Skye found himself filled with euphoria. Soon he would drift into sleep. He had never been so exhausted. In the space of two hours they had survived the apocalypse. Death swarming over them in red-ochre masks; terror;

the bitter sea that sapped their energies; an exhausting ride to shore; a time of lying numb and helpless on an alien beach; and then succor, taking from this warmaking people enough of the essentials that mortals needed to keep hearts beating in their bosoms.

It rained just beyond their noses, a dripping whisper of discomfort. An occasional gust drove moisture upon them, but nothing could dampen their joy as they lay against the back wall, collapsed into each other, surrounded by velvety and warmth-giving fur, and alive, all three of them, against all odds.

It was a miracle.

Sleep overtook Skye, but a fretful one in which a hundred anxieties tormented him. He woke up frequently, afraid of the red-ochre masks of deadly hunters. But no one came in the night, and when dawn broke gray and cold and dripping, they were alone.

His body ached. No part of him felt good. In spite of the robe, he felt chilled and wondered if he would be fevered here and die, having only escaped the very jaws of death the night before. Within his sealskin moccasins his lacerated soles pumped pain into him, and he knew the going would be hard this day. He dreaded sloshing through muck in those precious moccasins, wearing them out prematurely as the leather weakened.

They would not have a fire. There was not a stick of dry wood or tinder in sight. Victoria stirred, threw off her robe, and stood, which was more than Skye could do.

She eyed her soaked dress and camisole, and then set them down.

"Too damn cold," she muttered.

She looked fetching in her woven bark skirt and nothing else but her moccasins, but Skye was too exhausted to respond to the stirrings of his body.

"I'll not wear anything," she said.

He enjoyed the sight of his half-naked Diana throwing

the quiver over her thin bare shoulder and rolling up their few provisions inside her sealskin robe.

It wasn't raining, but the morning would be icy and mean. He forced himself up, discovering more aches than he had muscles, and tried to wrestle himself into his clammy britches, which clung to his hairy legs and wouldn't pull up until he yanked violently at them. He, like Victoria, elected not to wear anything else of their wet duds, and so they started once again up the trail under a glowering heaven, making good progress until their stomachs rebuked them and they grew dizzy for the want of food.

Yesterday's ordeal had sapped today's strength. They rested and trudged forward once more, going as long as they could as the trail slowly vanished and the rivulet beside them diminished into a spring, and then a dry gully. But they were nearing the crest of a mighty ridge, so Skye pulled onward, and Victoria doggedly kept up, until at last they stood at the ridgetop.

Skye's spirits dropped. He had hoped to gaze down upon a mild and grassy land beyond the coastal mountains. Instead, he beheld a jumble of more mountains as far as the horizon, densely forested and impenetrable.

They rested on the ridge, silent and bitter and lost. He hadn't the faintest idea where he was. They needed to escape this dense forest that snared them in its thickets, but he saw no boulevard, no highway, taking them to easier places. The valley below looked impassable, so thick with brush that he knew they could never hack their way through, especially without so much as a hatchet.

But the ridge itself looked better. It trended north and south, and was open in places where rock crowded out life. And north was the direction he was heading. North to Fort Vancouver, the nearest speck of civilization in many hundreds of miles. Walk north. Walk to the Columbia, wherever that was.

The ridge was negotiable. Some spots were easy; some were tough, especially the steep slopes, the defiles, or the thickets of dense brush. A winsome sun improved their mood, driving the moisture out of the air, and they paused to dry their soaked duds on a black, hot, sunbaked slab of rock and rest.

Victoria sliced thin slivers of the seal fat, but she and Skye could barely swallow the stuff. She opened the other leather bag, mixed some of the fishmeal with clear water in a small rocky pool, and made a paste. They managed to down enough of this to keep their hunger at bay, and then fed some of the fat and meal to the dog, who licked every last crumb of it and waited for more with soulful eyes.

"I don't know where Oregon is," Skye said.

"Dammit, I don't care," she said. "You, me, and the dog. What else is there?"

43

They toiled through a trackless wild, the sun often hidden from sight by a dense pine canopy above, or a ceiling of brush lower down. Skye's heart was as shadowed as his body, and he knew Victoria was wrestling with the same darkness that afflicted him. Noble firs rose higher than he had ever seen a tree grow, and water fled downslope from a myriad of springs. But they were lost in a growth so thick they could not even fathom their direction.

They saw no game at all because this tangled forest crowded it out, and their tiny larder diminished alarmingly. Periodically Victoria paused in an open glade to let them escape the heavy weight on their shoulders, and absorb the fleeting sun while they could, and then she whittled fat for each of them, or mixed a mash of fishmeal. Even the dog seemed despondent.

At least it didn't rain, Skye thought. A cold pelting rain just then would have sunk Skye's spirits to the bottom of hell.

But then, as they wrestled across a slope cut by a brook, the dog drew himself up, peered about, and pointed downslope. Skye thought the dog smelled an animal below, and struggled onward. But No Name refused to budge, and stood there quivering and whining and yapping.

"Dammit, Skye, he's telling us to go back," Victoria said.

Skye, in a bad mood, refused, but when Victoria turned back he had no option but to follow along like some pack mule born to obey.

The dog waited until his companions had gathered, and then plunged straight down a terrible slope.

"We'll just be trapped in brush down there," Skye grumbled, but he let himself be led.

Victoria's attitude changed radically. "The spirit-dog will lead us out," she said resolutely.

Skye doubted it.

They skidded down mossy slopes, stumbled on debris, stepped over fallen slippery timber, dodged dense and prickly thickets, and then the land changed subtly and they found themselves on fairly level ground, still surrounded by green hell. Here the dog found a clear game trail, and big animals had obviously used it. Except to duck now and then, Skye had no trouble following it. The dog trotted ahead of them, his tail lifted, barely deigning to see whether his mortal friends were walking behind.

The filtering light brightened, and then the trail veered smack into a riverbank. They beheld a considerable stream glittering over rocks and splashing around a bend hellbent for the ocean. Foliage hugged its banks, but here was light and hope, and a path to somewhere. The dog marched upstream, following multiple game trails that braided the bankside, and they progressed easily that day, covering many miles.

Skye saw big, silvery salmon waggling just under the surface of the crystal water, and ached to catch them. He thought of the fowling net, and supposed its mesh was too large. But maybe not. They paused at a grassy park in an oxbow, and rested for a while in an idyllic and enclosed wild, a terrible distance from other mortals.

He unrolled his sealskin robe and extracted the net tucked in it. Victoria tied a tether to it, using the coil of cedarbark rope. And then he cast the circling net over the busy water. It settled and sank slowly, barely heavier than the water. Skye watched silver shadows vanish and supposed they had failed. But one didn't vanish. It hung in the water with the net over it.

"Don't pull it in," Victoria commanded, as she pulled out of her skirts and moccasins and waded gingerly out on slimed rock. She slowly settled the net over the fish until it was well wrapped in cord, and pulled it out.

Skye swore the salmon was the size of a small shark. He could scarcely guess the weight, but it felt fat and meaty in his big hands.

"Aaiee!" she cried.

The dog sniffed and Skye watched a long canine tongue lick a chop.

While Victoria filleted the big fish, cussing at having to eat such a foul thing, Skye experimented with his broken musket. He pulled some fine inner bark from a dead tree and stuffed it where sparks would shower over it, pulled back the flint, and let it smack the frizzen. Soon he had a smoldering bit of tinder that he nursed along with soft breaths until a tiny flame erupted. Then he added the smallest imaginable sticks to build a lilliputian fire, which burned lazily, yielding no heat. Cooking that salmon would take a while.

They wrestled rock to the fire to make a firepit, and there they roasted the fillets, spread out on the encircling slabs of rock, while the cur munched cheerfully on the fishhead and offal. Dark clouds blotted the sun periodically, and Skye sensed they were in for a drenching, but he resolutely fed the hot little fire.

That's when Victoria glanced up and muttered, "Sonofabitch!"

A silvertipped grizzly was standing on its hind legs, its

little eyes staring at them, his nostrils sniffing his dinner and wondering what to eat first.

"Dammit," she cried, and Skye heard terror.

Victoria snatched her bow, and attempted to string it but found it too strong for her. Skye barely managed, and his respect for the coastal warrior who owned it leapt. He handed the strung bow to Victoria, who nocked an arrow. She would not use it except in desperation. Only an arrow straight to the heart, missing the ribs, would stop that humped brown monster from doing whatever it chose.

The grizzly sniffed, studied the scene, lowered himself on all fours and padded swiftly toward Skye and Victoria. The dog snarled. Skye and Victoria eased back, back, into the rocky bank, and then into the cold tugging stream. The bear halted at the firepit, swatted the sizzling fish off the rock with claws as long as human fingers, and sniffed the salmon lying in the grass. It was too hot, so the big bear settled on its haunches and waited, while Skye and Victoria cooled their heels in the ice water of the big river.

No Name watched, crept forward by wiggling along the grass, heading straight for the grizzly, until Skye thought the mutt was daft. One swipe of a claw would shred him and make another meal for the hairy brown giant. The bear sighed, slobbered, and began nipping at the still-hot fillet, tearing it apart with its deadly black claws and feeding small steaming pieces to himself.

That's when the cur nabbed the other fillet, which was lying on the grass a few yards from the bear, and raced away. The grizzly paid no heed, enjoying his feast.

Victoria cursed mightily. Bears scared her. Skye was sweating, in spite of the brutal cold water reaching high up his thighs. The water was poor protection. That bear could splash in, not even feeling the cold under its shaggy pelt, and land on them long before they made the opposite shore.

But it didn't.

The dog dropped the hot fillet, whined, picked it up and carried it to the riverbank, and waited.

The bear ate, poked around, sniffed the Skyes' gear, tore at it with its paws, while Victoria cussed it in English and trapper tongues, invoked her deities, and threatened to puncture the beast with arrows.

About the time Skye's feet were losing all sensation, the bear shuffled away.

Skye and Victoria made haste back to their camp, rebuilt the dying fire, dried themselves, and then, at last, shared the fat fillet with No Name.

Skye laughed, a big and hearty thunder rising within him. Bears were good news. This was game country. The menacing beast had left them alone.

Victoria looked at him soberly. "You got bear medicine," she said. "All the rest of your life, you and bears are brothers. I have spoken this."

"Aw, Victoria . . ."

"I have spoken!" she snapped.

Skye had always wondered how she knew these metaphysical things, but she seemed absolutely certain. The beliefs of the Plains tribes had always been a great mystery to him. How did she know that No Name was a spirit-dog destined to look after him and his family?

They devoured the whole fillet. Suddenly the world was a better place. This great ripping river poured out of the continent. It had cut through the coastal range en route to the sea. They would work upstream, find abundant game in this sunnier and grassier country, and at last head for home.

The scattered clouds thickened and joined until a gray ceiling hung low upon them, sawing off mountaintops and shooting cold through them. But the rain held off. Skye began hunting hard for a place to hole up, but this valley offered little to anyone escaping a storm.

They hastened along the river, sometimes along its

bank, sometimes distant, and then they rounded a bend and beheld a fishing village: bark houses, an elaborate pole trestle over the rushing water where spearmen could harpoon the salmon, great drying racks, and piles of fish offal. Not a soul stirred. This was a site used seasonally by some tribe or clan, and then abandoned to sleep as it did now.

They reached the first of the bark-clad houses just as fat cold drops of rain splattered on them. They stepped into a gloomy interior, spared the rain by a deftly shingled bark roof and walls, and welcomed the gloomy refuge as the storm swept over them, rattling rain and hail on their shelter. An icy wind eddied through the building, and Skye knew that it would be none too pleasant within even though mostly dry. The accommodations might be primitive, but the hand of man gladdened him. He had been half mad for other company in that silent, treacherous woods.

"The one I shall not name brought us here," Victoria said.

Skye gazed gently at No Name, who lay contentedly at the door, keeping watch.

44

They stood in the twilight of a winter's day at the end of a year beside the Columbia, staring across a misty sweep of water to a shrouded island. Beyond stood Fort Vancouver, which lay hidden from them even though they knew it was there across the father of western waters.

For weeks they had toiled over the mountains of the Oregon country. One day they reached a divide, and beyond it water trickled east, and after that they descended into a long valley with a river running north.

The Willamette.

Now, near the confluence, they stood gratefully, so gaunt and worn that they scarcely fit the rags they wore. The dog's ribs poked through his yellow hair, and a hollow had formed behind his ribs. Winter had taken its toll even in that mild land. Game had been scarce, and often they had paused to hunt or fish. Victoria's bow and the fowling net were all that stood between them and starvation.

Skye marveled that they had come this far, after so many disasters and so much trouble. He would have died but for Victoria, and the dog. Often it had pointed toward game or frozen before bobbing ducks on water. The salmon had come and gone, and when they left so did their meals.

Silently Victoria gathered dry wood, what little she could find, for a signal fire while Skye peeled back dead bark and scraped the soft fibers within. Once again he would have to build a fire. He doubted that the post would see the bonfire while veiled by the fog, but the fire would warm them.

Fort Vancouver probably lay a little to the east, and it would be quite possible that no one would come when summoned.

The old flintlock was worn, and Skye was having more and more trouble striking flint to steel, but he managed this one last time, after a heart-stopping moment when a piece of the old flint shattered away.

At least there was no wind to thwart his every effort. Wearily he added sticks, and then branches, until the smoky fire rose well into the evening. He saw no lamplight on the far bank as dusk settled.

There was little to do but wait. They had no food. Victoria had turned dour these last weeks, as much because the sun came and vanished swiftly as because they were starving to death. But they had made it here, somewhere around the first of January by Skye's dubious reckoning.

The warmth felt good, and stayed the damp cold. They sat on the bank, huddled together with the dog, and waited. But nothing happened and Skye resolved himself to spending the night there, awaiting the time when the fog would lift. He scratched around for deadwood and debris to keep the fire going, not an easy task without so much as a hatchet, and built up a pile of wood to warm them during a hard night.

Then he and Victoria, worn with cares and exhausted by months of barest survival and threat, dozed lightly in their battered sealskin robes.

"Allo, allo!" came the voice.

Skye awakened with a start, and rolled away from the fire.

"Allo," came the voice again, from the riverbank.

"Here," said Skye.

Moments later two dark figures emerged from the fog.

"We are make come by ze bourgeois, McLoughlin," said one. "It is a signal, oui?"

Voyageurs. "Yes, a signal, and you are welcome, friends," he said. "Can you take us across?"

"We 'ave a petit bateau. You 'ave horse?"

"A man, a woman, and a dog."

"Ah! Bien. Allors. Gaston," he said, pointing at his chest. "This is Honore, oui?"

The pair of them, stocky Canadians, squatted at the fire, examining the Skyes.

"I see you before, le nom est . . ."

"Mister Skye . . ."

"Ah! Mon Dieu!" Gaston, the one addressing the Skyes stared at them as if examining ghosts. And then he stared at the dog and made the sign of the cross.

"We had trouble," Skye said, "but by the grace of God, we're here alive and together."

"Sacre bleu!"

They led the Skyes down to the shore, where a rowboat was beached.

Skye was uneasy. "How are you going to find your way across and not just be swept downriver?"

The voyageurs laughed, which didn't comfort Skye any. But one of them cupped a hand to his ear, and they stood silently for a while. Then, faintly, the sound of a distant gong, muffled by mist, reached them.

Skye nodded. Away from the fire the blackness cloaked them so that he could not even see the faces of his company in that small, wet-bottomed rowboat. But the voyageurs set out upon the river with confidence, and rowed steadily, guided only by the distant gong, which rang every two or three minutes. It seemed a poor device by which to navigate, and Skye wondered whether they would end up far downstream.

The crossing seemed endless, but just when Skye started to despair, the voyageurs reached the opposite bank, and began rowing upstream so close to land that it lay barely beyond the oar. That leg of the journey seemed endless, too, and Skye realized that in spite of the bell, the rowboat had indeed been driven downstream.

But at last the faint lanternlight of the post blurred through the mist, and the voyageurs drove the little boat onto a sandy strand, then leapt out and dragged it with its passengers half out of water.

"Vancouver. The White Eagle awaits," Gaston said.

"What time is it?"

"It makes huit . . ."

Eight. That early. It had darkened at five that time of year.

The dog leapt out easily, but the Skyes were slower gathering up their robes and truck. They plodded wearily through the opened double doors and into the post. Soft light glowed from several windows. The factor's house had real glass windows, not thin-scraped hide or an open window shuttered at night. It amazed Skye to see yellow lamplight pierce through a window, after so many months in the wilds.

Gaston and Honore escorted them into McLoughlin's home.

Warmth and light and comfort smacked Skye palpably, as if he were stepping into a new world.

The White Eagle, towering over them all with his crown of snowy hair and raptor's nose, simply gaped, first at the Skyes and then at No Name, who settled comfortably on the polished plank floor.

"I am seeing ghosts, or am I mad?" he asked.

"We had trouble."

Marguerite McLoughlin rushed into the bright room and gasped. For there were Victoria, wearing the same skirts that had been fashioned by Marguerite's needle, but now in rags; and Skye, wearing a frock coat sewn together in that very post, but now unrecognizable, and the mark of starvation upon their gaunt and shrunken frames.

She clapped a hand to her mouth and cried.

"They are back, Marguerite, and now we shall hear their story," the chief factor said. "But first, my friends, food and drink, eh?"

"That would comfort us, sir."

At once, Marguerite hastened off to pull a meal together.

"The *Cadboro*—is it all right? Has there been a disaster?"

"The schooner's fine, sir. Last we knew, anyway. We sailed as far as Monterey, Mexico, with Mr. Simpson, and there ran into a squadron of the Royal Navy. Why we're not in the schooner, we'll tell you in due course."

"Ah! Already your story comes clear. And I rejoice that the *Cadboro* and Emilius Simpson are preserved. Our whole annual take in furs was aboard. That dog," said McLoughlin. "Start with the dog."

Skye did not dare sit, knowing his filthy clothes would soil the good furniture, and so he stood wearily.

"Do sit down, Mister Skye, and you as well, Mrs. Skye. You'll do this battered furniture no harm, and I fathom you're at your wits' end."

Gratefully, Skye sank into a horsehair sofa, with Victoria beside him. He had not sat upon something soft for months.

"The dog, sir, ran beside the ship, hour upon hour, day upon day, down the river. Mr. Simpson kept assuring us that the mutt would give up at the rivers it had to swim, and go back. But it didn't . . ."

The story of the heroic and indefatigable dog mesmerized McLoughlin. "We did our best to pen him before the *Cadboro* left, sir. But next we knew, he was gone, and I've heard no more since. But I told my people the dog and his master would be parted nonetheless, for what dog can walk on water? I seem to have been in error."

Skye described the miraculous dog, and how its heroic chase finally persuaded the master, Emilius Simpson, to permit the creature to board at least as far as California.

Then Skye turned to the desperate events in Monterey, his discovery, the chase, the headlong flight, the difficulties in provisioning, the weary trek north, the two sets of bandits, the reception in Yerba Buena, the discovery of the Yank merchant trader heading north, and their signing on . . .

"Dickens. I know of him. He's never brought that brig in here, but my people on the coast compete with him."

"He suffered a lack of hands, sir. Lost some to scurvy and others deserted, so he was glad to take me on, if only for a way. He had two new Mexican boys aboard, and after delivering us to Astoria, he was headed for the Sandwich Islands to find some Kanakas. But we never made it."

Marguerite rushed in, bearing hot tea and some scones.

"Here you are, and there's more. And plenty of jams and jellies."

Skye marveled, and was reminded again that this post operated farms and orchards and diaries. He ate greedily, scarcely believing the goodness of the scones. Victoria tasted them tentatively, and smiled.

Then, at last, he turned to the attack on the Yank brigantine, describing the swift assault and desperate defense that lasted but a few minutes, and the ultimate destruction of the entire ship and its contents, with a loss of twenty-seven men, including the two Mexican boys recruited in Monterey.

"Terrible, terrible," McLoughlin muttered. "This must be dealt with. Do you know the tribe?"

"No, I don't. Dickens showed us the Klamath River when we passed it, and we had sailed another day and into the evening when we spotted the bonfires and Dickens decided someone wanted to trade."

"We'll look into this! We'll deal with it! HBC and the Yanks always stand together on matters like this! We have men in that country, trading along the coast just as the Yanks do, and we'll find out! By God, this is insolence!"

And then, to the amazement of both Skye and Victoria, McLoughlin told them that Professor Nutmeg and Nat Wyeth and his men were there, at Fort Vancouver.

45

Skye and Victoria listened incredulously to McLoughlin's news. Nat Wyeth's brig, the *Sultana*, had been lost at sea. The news reached Fort Vancouver shortly after the Skyes had sailed on the *Cadboro*, brought to the post by another Hudson's Bay ship in from the Sandwich Islands.

Because of the disaster, Nutmeg had not returned to Boston, and Wyeth's enterprise had foundered. All the equipment to preserve and pack salmon and send the casks east had perished. What's more, most of Wyeth's men had abandoned him, discovering choice farmland up the broad Willamette Valley. Skye and Victoria had unwittingly passed several rude farms operated by the Americans, and also a few run by Creoles retired from HBC service.

"And what are the professor's plans?" Skye asked.

"He's looking for a way east."

"And what are Wyeth's plans?"

McLoughlin smiled. "He's a man of great enterprise. A setback merely spawns a dozen new ideas, so he runs hither and thither here, getting ideas. He talks now of visiting some of our fur posts, no doubt to master the business and compete with us. But withal, he is good company and I admire the man."

Skye marveled. Here was a man who had lost everything, was a continent away from Boston, and yet brimmed
with schemes to make his fortune some new way.

"I should like to see them both, if the hour is not too
late. I scarcely know Wyeth, but Nutmeg, that's quite another matter."

"He'll be pleased to see you, Mister Skye. He is worried about returning to his university."

Skye sighed. "Perhaps he should sail out on the next
brig."

McLoughlin laughed. "That, sir, would deprive him of
the chance to pluck up more plants and roots and but-
terflies."

"That's what I was afraid of."

"And what of your plans, Mister Skye?"

Skye stared disconsolately into the fireplace, watching
orange flame lick a log.

"Dr. McLoughlin, we will return to the mountains."

McLoughlin pondered that. "HBC can employ you as a
trapper, but not as a brigade leader. We've several men in
our ranks who've eluded British justice, but they're invisible and not even Simpson knows of them. I've quietly put
them to work with traps at small posts. But we can't put
you in a visible position in HBC. You understand, of
course. Simpson not only runs the company; he's the king's
man." He paused. "I still want you. You've rare skills and
courage. This escape . . . this resourcefulness. We've few
men of your caliber, Ogden, Ermatinger, one or two others.
I say, Mister Skye, let me give some thought to this."

"Things have changed, Doctor. Victoria and I and
this yellow dog who's been our companion and our help
in time of need . . ."

Those great eyebrows frowned, and Skye felt the piercing stare of a powerful man.

"Mister Skye, a man's name is of little account here.
It's of little account at the Yank rendezvous. I hear there's

men among the Yanks whose real names will never be known. There's a career in Hudson's Bay for, say, a man who bears any name other than Skye . . ."

The great factor waited expectantly, filling his parlor, so formidable that Skye quailed slightly before him. But Skye knew what he must answer.

"I have a good name in the mountains, no matter how matters rest in England and at the admiralty. That, Doctor, is worth my life. Beyond that, it wouldn't take long for my true name to be revealed to Governor Simpson's ears. I am not unknown, after six years in the wilderness."

Simpson sighed. "You know, Mister Skye, the very nature of your response only adds to my esteem. I'm afraid your honor is Hudson's Bay's loss, but there is something in it: it is my gain, for I have found a man among men, a man I admire. And I wish to emphasize the esteem I hold for you, my dear Victoria, intrepid woman and able hunter and loyal consort."

She smiled.

"You'll be going to the Yanks, then, I suppose."

"We plan to go back to the Americans, sir. The next rendezvous. Where is it, do you know?"

"At the head of the Green River, I hear. The Yank Captain Bonneville's building a post there."

Skye nodded. Once he got to the Seedskedee, as he preferred to call the Green, he'd find it.

Marguerite summoned them to her table. In the space of a few minutes she had loaded her table with cold beef, bread, potatoes, and beans.

"Please eat," she said. "You look like you might need a bite."

"Madam McLoughlin, that is an understatement," Skye said.

He settled into a real chair at a real table, and Victoria joined him. This was no campfire meal, hastily swallowed while resting on their own heels, but a meal served on china.

Skye sighed, and dug in, pleasuring himself with real salt on his meat, and real butter and jam on the biscuits set before him. Victoria watched, swiftly copying his manners, and managed to feast with barely controlled haste.

He dosed the rib roast with salt and sliced off juicy pieces, and then slathered butter over a biscuit and felt it crumble under his touch. He sliced some boiled red potatoes in two, inundated them with butter and a little salt, and felt his teeth clamp the delicate red skin. He returned to the beef, sawing slice after slice, feeling them leak juices into his mouth. He spooned huckleberry jam over a muffin, and let the concoction settle on his tongue. It was too good to swallow. He beheld, before him, a goblet of ruby port, as clear as stained glass, and sipped delicately, and then quaffed mightily. Ah, the things that food and wine did to a man's spirit!

Victoria smiled at him. When had they feasted like this? And rested in a safe, warm place like this?

He turned to the chief factor. "This is too good to be true," he said. "Our diet has largely been whatever the dog dragged in."

The thought galvanized him.

"Would it be possible to feed the pup?"

Marguerite smiled and pointed toward the door of the kitchen.

"He has a bone with lots of beef on it," she said.

Skye could not remember the last time his belly felt comforted. They had eaten raw mallard, a goat, various seeds and nuts and roots Victoria had scrounged, a marmot, assorted fish, often raw and barely edible because they often could not start a fire.

McLoughlin sipped tea and waited for the Skyes to finish, but Skye knew he had much more to discuss.

"How are you going to the Rockies?" the doctor asked at last.

"I should like to work for you, sir, and earn enough for an outfit."

"We're always short of men. There's plenty to do, especially for someone who knows about peltries. They need to be sorted and graded and baled. You up to it?"

"Yes, sir."

"What about me? I work," said Victoria.

"There is work to be done, Mrs. Skye. Consider yourself employed by HBC." He turned to Skye. "Now, the matter of Professor Nutmeg is much on our minds here. You see, Nat Wyeth absolutely refuses to take the man east. He says he lost days trying to find the wayward botanist, and sent search parties out in all directions, and finally supposed the man was dead until he stumbled on one of your messages. That suffices, in his mind, to refuse the naturalist. Nutmeg, of course, is most desirous of returning by any means. You willing to take him to rendezvous?"

Skye didn't really want to, but nodded.

"There's more, you know. He's not, ah, welcome. What we hear is that the Yanks won't take him back to St. Louis when their supply train leaves rendezvous. What'll the professor do then, eh?"

"Maybe he should wait here for the next Yank trader, and go by sea."

McLoughlin stared into space. "I like Professor Nutmeg and admire his great enterprise. Come, Mister Skye, let us find some way of getting the man safely back to Boston, eh? He has no funds here but eventually he'll pay you, no doubt sending a credit out with the next supply train from Missouri."

"If you're thinking I should escort the professor clear back there, sir, I must respectfully decline. Mr. Nutmeg has means by sea."

"And by river, Mister Skye. What I have in mind is taking him to that new American Fur post, Fort Union, at the confluence of the Yellowstone and Missouri. From there, if you reach the post in time, the professor can go downriver on the fur company's river packet, eh? Safe aboard, unless they let him loose and he wanders out of sight while they're cutting wood, in which case it's their own fault."

"Have you proposed this to him, Dr. McLoughlin?"

"No, because there's been no one to take him to Fort Union, and Nat Wyeth wants nothing to do with the man."

Skye thought about that and liked it. He could drop the professor and then accompany the American Fur Company men to the rendezvous. And better still, he could talk to the factor there, and see about employment.

"The flower collector is a good man," Victoria said. "I will keep an eye on him."

Skye knew she was urging him to say yes. He grinned. A trip to Fort Union would take them right past her Kicked-in-the-Belly people, and there would be a joyous reunion.

"I like the idea," he said. "But we'll have to see if Professor Nutmeg likes it, too."

46

John McLoughlin liked to warm himself in the bright winter sunlight streaming into his office through small glass windows. Those windows were the only glass he knew of in the western half of the North American continent, and he considered them a luxury beyond price. What other room, in a thousand miles in any direction, possessed glass windows?

He spent some of that morning wrestling with the problem of guests. The post, an isolated island in a vast wild, offered succor to any passing white man. Nat Wyeth and his men, for instance. He arrived there only to discover that disaster attended his plans, and suddenly the Hudson's Bay Company became his only refuge.

McLoughlin did not turn him—or any other Yank or Canadian or Englishman—away, no matter that the directors in London strictly forbade him to succor or cooperate with any of the company's rivals, especially the Yanks. The Oregon question had not been settled and the company did not wish to act in any fashion that would deprive England of territory, or deprive itself of a secure and permanent monopoly of trade.

But what seemed logical in London was not feasible in the midst of a vast wild. Dr. McLoughlin had no intent of turning stray and desperate people away in their moment of need. So he had permitted Nat Wyeth to make himself at home, even though Wyeth's plans for a salmon fishery and some trade in peltries ran against HBC's own interests. Who could turn away a man who had lost a ship, and a dream, at sea?

So the post was burdened with several people who consumed its meat and produce and grains, burned its firewood, ate its fish, lived within its shelter, and earned HBC not a shilling. He liked Wyeth, and didn't quite know why. The New Englander bubbled with enthusiasm and enterprise, throwing one or another wild idea into the air, striking sparks to McLoughlin's imagination and setting the tinder aflame.

Skye was another sort. From the moment he arrived the previous evening, gaunt and worn and destitute, Skye had assumed that he had obligations. No sooner had he told his tale and eaten Marguerite's swiftly wrought meal, than he offered to work for his living. And so did his lovely Victoria. He was not a man to accept endless hospitality and return nothing. Even now, as weary as he was, Skye was employed in the warehouse grading pelts with an expert eye, and helping with the pressing and baling. Victoria had given herself over to the women of the establishment, to mend and sew and make the rags they all wore about the post endure a while more.

Thus it was that Skye, from the day of his arrival, was contributing to the company, along with his good wife. There seemed to be not a thought in his keen mind that he should enjoy the hospitality of the company and return nothing.

To be sure, he and his lady needed an outfit, but McLoughlin would have provided one whether or not he worked for it. The factor had given numerous men, defeated by wilderness, an outfit sufficient to take them wherever they were headed. The outfits he gave away at a dead loss at least had the virtue of lessening the number of people dependent on the enterprises of Fort Vancouver.

But not Skye. That man, no matter that he was half sick from starvation, was earning his way in the world, and McLoughlin set him apart in his mind as a sterling Englishman who had been dealt one cruel blow after another by the nation he still called his own.

The Skyes would leave Fort Vancouver better off for their presence. Hudson's Bay could use men like that, and it grieved the factor that Skye would not have a chance to contribute to the company. But Skye was doing the right thing. He would have a better chance among the Yanks than within the company, doomed to be an obscure trapper beyond the Cyclopean eye of George Simpson.

The doctor finished his eggs and breakfast kippers, and now it was time to invite Professor Alistair Nutmeg to a small but vital meeting of the minds.

The man was not lazy, but neither had he contributed to the company that succored him. He had drifted out upon the fields and forests day by day, plucking up his botanical specimens and beginning a new collection after losing the old, pressing his plants between precious papers he had begged. That was, indeed, a good thing for science and knowledge. It might even have the practical result of giving the world new herbs and medicines.

There had been several alarms when the good man had vanished for days at a time and was feared lost. But just about when McLoughlin was readying a search, the half-starved savant would drift in, utterly unaware of the mounting concern about him. A pleasant man he might be, and civilized, and a fine companion over dinner wine, but not a man to be let out of the academy, except with a warder. No wonder Wyeth, and every other son of the mountains, would have nothing to do with him.

McLoughlin summoned the man, and the professor

duly appeared in the chambers, looking as gentle and distracted as always.

"Please sit down, Professor. We've a little something to discuss," he said.

Nutmeg perched like a butterfly upon the edge of a wingchair, alighting for just as long as necessary before fluttering off.

"The Skyes are here," he said.

"No! How could that be?"

"A long story, and you'll learn it. I've taken the liberty of discussing your plans with them. I think we've found a means to restore you to Harvard College."

"Oh, indeed, capital, capital."

"Overland travel is pretty much confined to seasonable climates, but in the spring, at the appropriate time, they will take you east to the confluence of the Yellowstone and Missouri rivers. And from there, you'll travel by river packet to St. Louis and civilization. After that, it will be up to you to arrange river passage up the Ohio and to New England."

"Why, sir, that's most kind, but I must resist. How am I to collect specimens and put this continent in botanical order from the confines of a riverboat?"

McLoughlin ignored that. "You have two choices, Professor. Leave here by sea, on the next coastal ship of any flag, or go with Mister Skye and Victoria."

The professor blinked, not liking it. "All for nothing," he muttered. "I can't complete my work on a wooden deck."

McLoughlin stared into the fireplace, where a thick log burned lazily. He decided not to respond, for anything he might say would seem a rebuke to the professor. He had never met a man so devoid of practical sense, and even the ordinary courtesy by which one makes commerce with others. There could be no arguing with a man oblivious to the strains he created upon all those who suddenly were forced to look after him.

"The Skyes have volunteered to take you," McLoughlin said. "They'll leave in early April, or maybe late March if the weather's good. They need to make Fort Union, the new American Fur Company post there, before the riverboat turns around and heads for St. Louis in June or early July."

"Is there no other choice, sir?"

"Mr. Wyeth has his own difficulties, and lacks the time or men to look after you when he heads for the Yanks' rendezvous."

"I see. Well, then, I shall go, and count it a loss, this wretched trip."

"I think it's really a great advance in your work, sir. You have in your head, and in the notes you've written here, a major start to a North American botany."

But the professor was lost in his own world, so McLoughlin led him out of the study.

"Really, Professor, you ought to say hello to your companions. They're about the post now, Skye in the warehouse, Victoria with the women, and the yellow dog somewhere. He and your mutt are friends, I take it."

"Oh, the dog, too? Yes, rather. I shall welcome them. Thank you for reminding me. I admire the rough chap and his squaw."

McLoughlin bit back a retort, and saw the man off.

The Skyes would have a burden once again, but McLoughlin intended to make it up to them with a good outfit; a better outfit than their labors could purchase.

Later, McLoughlin found Nat Wyeth out in the shops, surrounded by cordage, weights, floats, pulley devices, and sketches tacked over a workbench. He was attempting to make a new sort of gill net with floats on top and weights at the bottom that would harvest salmon by the boatload and earn him several fortunes.

"See here, John, I've got this vee-shaped net, you see. It folds in on itself with a tug of the rope, and the salmon won't be able to duck out. Oh, what a fortune, what an improvement in the ways we fish!"

"Nat, the Skyes are here. Returned last evening, worn out."

"The Skyes? Did the *Cadboro* go down?"

"No, it's a long and bloody mean story, and I'll tell it in time. But they're here, and they've agreed to take Professor Nutmeg with them to Fort Union in time to catch the AFC riverboat. So you're free from that matter."

"I always have been free. I absolutely refuse to shepherd a half mad fool through dangerous country again. I simply thought you'd pop him on the next brig to sail up the river."

McLoughlin nodded. Nat Wyeth entertained his own grand vision of the world and its glowing opportunities, and would not, given his tinkering and enterprising nature, be inclined to help an innocent and somewhat daft professor from his home city if that meant slowing things up. Not that he didn't like Wyeth, whose Promethean enthusiasms struck sparks and lit fires in every mortal who came into contact with him.

It had been a profitable morning, and he had resolved the matter of the fort loafers. He would mention it all in his regular reports to Governor Simpson, of course, but he would be a little vague about certain aspects of it. Such as the names of those who would take the professor to the Missouri River.

47

Barnaby Skye found pleasure in his daily toil. He graded pelts, and then pressed and baled them for shipment, a task that required muscle and patience.

After that he split cedar shakes from thick logs hauled and floated great distances by the post's woodsmen. Like most seamen, he understood wood and how to shape it. With axe and wedges and maul, he snapped shingle after shingle free, and day by day built a great pile of them for Dr. McLoughlin's perpetual building projects.

Once in a while the factor paused in the yard outside the post, watched him at work, and wandered silently away, making Skye wonder whether his work was adequate.

The skilled work heartened Skye, but even more pleasant was the knowledge that he was earning his keep, and maybe collecting some credit for an outfit. He saw little of the illustrious visitors. Professor Nutmeg had visited with Skye briefly but obviously was restless, preferring the company of better educated men, or at least idle men. Nutmeg and the post's second in command, James Douglas, had become fast friends, each of them starved for the company of literate men.

Victoria had been working hard, too. A community of

two hundred consumed clothing, and there were too few women at hand to mend the heaps of torn shirts and britches, and to transform all those bolts of English wool and linen and cotton into shirts and skirts and britches and gloves and underwear.

When the women weren't sewing they were knitting, an art that totally eluded Victoria, and which fascinated her. First they ran sheep's wool through a spinning wheel, and then knitted the yarn with a great clatter of needles, so fast that Victoria marveled. Out of all this effort rose a pile of stockings and some sweaters.

Skye watched the winter elide into spring, which came early in that mild land. Then, as March dwindled, he knew it was time to settle accounts with Dr. McLoughlin and go.

He found the factor out in a sunny field watching a Canadian plowman scratch the earth behind big mules.

"I'd like a word, sir. It's nigh the time for us to leave and settle our accounts."

"Of course, Mister Skye. I've been meaning to ask you about it."

Skye followed the factor through the great gate of the post and into his study.

He opened a ledger book and examined it through oval wire-rimmed spectacles.

"You and Mrs. Skye have a credit of fifty pounds and a few pence," he said.

"And what is the cost of our board, sir?"

"We haven't charged Wyeth or Professor Nutmeg board, sir, so why should we charge you? There is ample."

Skye twisted his hat around in his hands, scarcely knowing what to say.

"You'll need some sort of outfit, I imagine."

"Yes, sir. And something for the professor."

"He's made his arrangements with us. We'll outfit him and he'll send a draft to our secretary in London."

That was good news. Skye didn't know how he could afford to outfit the botanist.

"The horses we bought from you are fat and sound, and you may have them again," McLoughlin said. "We'll add a greenbroke pack animal and you can break him on the trail."

That pleased Skye.

"Come along, now. We'll go to the store."

Skye always relished the sights and smells of that place. He drank in the pungent scent of leather, the scents of bolts of woolen cloth, the scents of blankets and dried fruits and the iron scent of traps and axes, and the scent of a well-oiled rifle.

The factor found the clerk at a desk.

"Mr. Rutgers, I'll want you to outfit the Skyes. They'll be wanting saddles and tack, including a packsaddle; two pairs of four-point blankets, flint and steel, an axe, a good rifle, powder, powder flask, bullet mold, lead, and spare flints; a cookpot and a few kitchen utensils, some cord suitable for picketing horses, and whatever else . . ."

Skye objected. "I can't afford all that, sir. I have no means to repay."

McLoughlin stared down upon Skye from his Olympian height.

"Your sole obligation is to treat our HBC men fairly out in the trapping country. Ogden despises the Yanks who tricked him and failed to keep their word. You're an Englishman. That's all I require."

Skye was so gladdened that he fairly danced. "You have that promise, sir."

"Very well, then. Get everything together, and I'll get the professor started. When do you wish to leave?"

"As soon as possible."

"Tomorrow, then. We'll miss you, Skye. It will be my regret that we couldn't employ you. I've never seen a better man to help us along."

Skye marveled at the compliment.

That fine fat afternoon Skye selected his equipment, testing each item piece by piece. He decided on a good English military rifle converted to mountain use with a shorter barrel. He selected a pound of precast balls, wadding, powder, a flint and steel in a leather pouch, two pairs of thick, heavy, well-carded Hudson's Bay blankets, gray with black stripes so as not to advertise their presence.

He chose two used English saddles, a sawbuck packframe, three saddle blankets made of unmarketable pelts, three halters, fish hooks and line, two bridles and bits, picket ropes, a light copper cookpot, two metal ladles, two bowls, a fine-edged steel axe made in Manchester, an awl, patch leather for boots and moccasins, sugar, coffee, beans, flour, tea, a ball of real soap, a big belt knife and two smaller knives, some metal arrow points for Victoria, two used blanket capotes for rough weather, and an oilcloth cover for emergencies.

That was a fine outfit, and its price ran twenty pounds higher than the credit. He owed McLoughlin all that the man had asked: proper treatment of HBC brigades in the wilds.

He had learned, over the long visit, something about wilderness war from McLoughlin and Douglas. Bridger and his men had played a deadly trick on the newer American Fur Company men by leading them into Blackfoot country and setting the rivals up for an Indian ambush. In fact, the Blackfeet did attack the American Fur brigade, killing its partisan, William Vanderburgh, a West Point man who had made a fine name for himself in the fur trade.

It was true, McLoughlin added, that the American Fur brigade dogged the steps of the Bridger outfit, horning in on the beaver grounds. But the result was very close to being murder and certainly was an act of putting the rivals in harm's way.

The news shocked Skye. Would the fur brigades resort to extremes in the course of their rivalry? His opinion of the men in the Rocky Mountain Fur Company diminished sharply on that news, and that was a very good reason to find his employment elsewhere. No commerce was worth such a price and he vowed then and there that he would never, for as long as he lived, work for any firm that behaved in such a fashion.

That meant saying goodbye to old friends: Jim Bridger, Tom Fitzpatrick, Milt Sublette, Henry Fraeb, and Baptiste Gervais. As individuals, he treasured them all. But as a company, they had crossed the borders of honor. He knew they would try to justify themselves to him; tell him that American Fur's Vanderburgh and Drips were horning in and following them. Argue that in the wilds, a savage law prevailed and had to be heeded or the company would go under. But none of those arguments sufficed to justify what Bridger and his colleagues had done. They had sullied their souls. A man had to draw a line somewhere, and Skye drew it right there.

So, maybe this time he would not go to rendezvous. It was something to think about.

The next morning he and Victoria said their goodbyes to Dr. McLoughlin, collected their ward—for that was what he seemed to be—and began the long trek up the Columbia River. They crossed new-plowed fields, splashed along a muddy trail, and soon left the brooding Hudson's Bay imperial city behind them, slumbering in a tender sun.

The season at Fort Vancouver had repaired their bodies, allowed them to live in comfort, and restored their outfit, and thus their chances of surviving and earning a living. Skye knew that the wilds would shock his body and mind, but he also knew Victoria would slide easily into living in nature and probably be happier away from the great post than within it.

He let Professor Nutmeg catch up and ride beside him.

"Well, Professor, we'll get you to Fort Union safely—if you wish to get there and you wish to be safe."

"How do you mean that, Mister Skye?"

"If your passion for collecting samples overcomes your common sense, you are likely to lose not only your samples and notes, but also your life. This time, it will be up to you. That is a decision that you, as an adult man, must come to."

"Why, forgive my wanderings, my dear Mister Skye. I never really saw the harm in them."

Skye didn't reply, for there was nothing more to say.

48

They pierced inland without trouble, following the right bank of the Columbia. Professor Nutmeg was never so happy as when he could capture new-minted leaves and twigs, or sketch an odd plant. Skye didn't mind so long as the naturalist stayed in sight and used ordinary cautions. There were so many ways to get into trouble.

Maybe the professor was going to do better.

They passed occasional fishing villages and from these the Skyes obtained dried salmon for the larder, with a few treats for No Name. They were in no rush: it would not be until May that they could negotiate the snowbound continental divide and enter the Missouri watershed.

Within two weeks they had reached Fort Walla Walla, and enjoyed the hospitality of its factor, Pierre Pambrun. Skye remembered the post all too well; he had come within an inch of losing his life there during his desperate flight from the Royal Navy. But that was another factor and another time.

At a hearty salmon feast that night, Pambrun questioned the naturalist closely.

"Monsieur, does your lovely wife suffer from your long absences?"

"No, no really," Nutmeg replied. "The old dear's used

to it, and anyway she considers me a nuisance about the house."

"But surely you're eager to resume lecturing at Harvard."

"No, I can barely stand those musty amphitheaters and bottles of formaldehyde and alcohol. No, my good man, what makes my heart sing is simply wandering, free as a meadowlark, plucking up whatever strikes my fancy."

"But where will it all lead, monsieur?"

"To a cataloguing of all that grows in North America."

"And what good is that? Will it earn anyone a living?"

Nutmeg gazed at the factor as if he were a freshman. "My dear man, it's for the sake of knowledge. There may be some slight practical advantage in it—a new medicinal herb, or a decorative new bloom for a garden, or maybe even a new tuber or nut for food. But that's not it. It's the glory of getting the natural world straightened out and understandable."

"Ah, food. Yes, we've sampled every berry here. I look for purgatives, you know. The banks of the Walla Walla River lack digestive aids, which is a great lack for me. But maybe you'll find one. Do you know of any?"

"I can't say that I do, Mr. Pambrun. My task is to advance science."

The factor was not quite satisfied with all that and regarded Professor Nutmeg as an odd gent, but Nutmeg didn't seem to mind. His thoughts were always elsewhere, as if mere mortals didn't much matter in the natural world he was cataloguing.

They proceeded up the Walla Walla River in a tumult of spring, with flowers rioting at every hand. Now Skye found himself being slowed by the professor, who abandoned all thought of catching the riverboat that would carry him home. He took to ignoring his horse, leaving its management to Victoria while he dashed here and there, up slopes, down to the river, examining everything from thistles to cattails, and never forgetting a tree, many of which the dog had already marked.

"Professor, we'll need to move fast now. I'll want you on your horse and keeping up. We've an appointment in early June, and we're slipping behind."

"Yes, of course, my dear Skye. We'll carry on, eh? March, march, march."

But it did little good. Skye realized that he could really not influence the trajectories of his naturalist friend any more than he could command the dog to heel. Not any more now than on the trail going west. This man's vision was not focused on anything but the leaf or root in hand. He was in his own Eden: gentians, buck beans, marsh fel-wort, milfoil, mares-tail, mulberry, four-o'clock, white water lilies, evening primrose, juneberry, silverweed, blue-eyed Mary, Queen Anne's lace, oxeye daisy . . . each day a dozen new treasures for the naturalist.

Increasingly, Nutmeg vanished from sight, over the brow of a hill or around a bend, often with No Name watching over him. (Nutmeg had left his dog Dolly at Fort Van-couver.) Sometimes he vanished for hours on end, leaving Skye and Victoria uneasy. Even in that warm valley dan-gers lurked at every hand.

At dinner one evening, as they were penetrating the Blue Mountains, Skye decided enough was enough.

"Professor, tomorrow I'll want you on your horse, and from now on Victoria will lead it."

Nutmeg was aghast. "But that would keep me from my work!"

Skye didn't respond. They had been through all this a dozen times.

The next morning, after rolling up their blankets and saddling the horses, Skye silently led Nutmeg's nag to him and waited. Nutmeg sighed, put a foot in a stirrup, and hoisted himself upward.

They made good progress that morning, but Nutmeg

sank into reproachful silence. At one point he did cry out, so Victoria let him dismount, dig up a reed growing alongside the Grande Ronde River, and scribble some notes. Sullenly he mounted again after discovering that the Skyes would not permit him to walk.

Skye worried plenty now. He figured they had six weeks to reach Fort Union, and that wasn't time enough unless they could persuade the professor to abandon his researches altogether.

"Mr. Nutmeg," he said, as they sat under a makeshift shelter that turned away a drizzle, "beginning in the morning, we're going to make a dash. We've got to make thirty or more miles a day up the Snake, over the divide to the Three Forks. We're stopping for nothing."

"But—"

"Next time, Professor. Do it next time. Consider traveling with the army's mapping parties. They send out topographical outfits all over the American West, and you'd be safe and at your leisure. Part of Captain Bonneville's business is reconnoitering the West."

The professor nodded curtly and turned to his blankets.

The silence that followed stretched into the next day and the next. But at least the professor was obediently getting aboard his horse and letting himself be drawn up the Snake River with all the speed Skye could muster. By the beginning of May Skye was working up Henry's Fork toward the Missouri headwaters, and he was thinking that, with luck, he could make it. The professor had fallen into perpetual anguish, and began complaining constantly.

They crossed a snow-patched divide into the Missouri drainage, followed the Gallatin River and plunged into the vast, rolling intermontane basin where the Gallatin, Jefferson, and Madison rivers formed into the great Missouri. But this verdant grassland was prized Blackfoot country, and Skye knew he would need to be cautious. Puffball clouds scraped shadows across the hills making it difficult to spot the ancient enemies of the trappers, and even hard to spot game because the whole world seethed.

Skye kept his party low, reconnoitered from ridgetops, and raced ever eastward to Jim Bridger's pass to the Yellowstone. They made few fires, shot no game, rode apart from visible trails, and never moved without examining their flanks, rear, and what lay ahead. The dog stood guard, roaming out on the flanks to detect trouble, and watching the shadows of the night with such acuity that Skye came to feel safe in the dog's custody.

They reached some steaming hot springs, the banks white-rimmed with minerals, the odorous water draining through pools into a small marsh alive with cattails and sedges and lilies. Stately cottonwoods, in new leaf, guarded the oasis. The dog sniffed suspiciously, detecting the faint spoor of ancient enemies. Skye watched the dog, every sense alert.

"I should like to stop here for a while," the professor said. "Unique, you know. There'll be a dozen variants or new species here, and I've never had a chance—"

"Sorry, mate, but this is Blackfoot country, and they come here. It's a favorite spot. This is not safe."

Nutmeg looked so bitter that Skye almost relented. But the thought of a party of Blackfeet drifting this way to enjoy the hot waters, hastened Skye away. They proceeded another two miles before dusk caught them, and settled under a low cutbank carved eons earlier by a creek now a quarter of a mile away. The surrounding brush would conceal them and their horses well. The dog sniffed out the territory and settled just outside of the camp.

They were depending entirely on Victoria's powerful yew wood bow. That afternoon, she had driven an arrow through the neck of an antelope and they had hastily butchered it, taking only the hindquarters and leaving the rest to the wolves and the dog, who stayed behind for a feast.

They were in a good spot, invisible, out of the wind, far removed from the creek, and shielded by brush and trees that would dissipate the smoke from Victoria's hot fire. Victoria cleaned the ground for their bedrolls, taking care to remove the smallest rocks and twigs, and then laid a mat of sedge over the cold earth while Skye climbed a nearby slope to reconnoiter. Early night was always an excellent moment to spot distant campfires. He waited for his eyes to adjust to the blackness, found the North Star, and began a quiet study of the country. Spring breezes steadily raked the area, and he drew the air through his nostrils, seeking the slightest scent of smoke: sour smoke if it came from cottonwood, sweet smoke if from pine.

He could not tell. His skills weren't the half of Victoria's who had been born to this life and whose instincts were often intuitive. He saw, smelled, and heard nothing, and then retreated to his own camp, satisfied, the dog a shadow behind him.

He always slept lightly, in part because hard ground didn't foster deep sleep, and partly because his ears were attuned to subtle changes in the rhythm of the night. He and Victoria always slept close, but the professor usually unrolled his blankets at a distance, out of a certain delicacy.

Skye awakened in the gray half-light before dawn, sensing something was amiss. He glanced about fearfully. The horses stood quietly. The camp gear was undisturbed. He padded over to Nutmeg's blankets and found them neatly rolled beside his gear. But he was not present. Skye waited a moment. The man might merely be in the bushes. But the professor did not return and Skye knew at once that the naturalist was heading back to the hot springs and the unique flora that grew there.

Annoyance built in him.

"What?" said Victoria in a voice that carried only a few feet.

"The professor."

She rolled out of her blankets, stretched, and padded over to the professor's ground.

"At the springs," Skye said. "He wanted to go back there, collect and sketch, and return before we broke camp."

"We gonna wait?"

"I suppose. Country's empty, far as I could tell."

"This is no damn good," she said.

Skye wasn't so sure. "He'll be back soon," he volunteered. "The dog will find him."

"And if he don't?"

Skye had no answer to that.

49

No one was at the hot springs. Skye and Victoria and the dog searched the area and found nothing. The only hoofprints were those of their own horses. Eerie silence greeted their calls.

"Well, dammit, let's circle around," Victoria said.

She and Skye had broken camp, packed the professor's kit and loaded it on his horse, and searched the campground area thoroughly before returning to the hot springs. Plainly, the professor had dressed—his clothing and boots were gone—and gathered his collection bag and sketch paper and drifted away just before first light.

But he wasn't at the springs or in the marshes below it or along the creek racing to the Gallatin River a few miles distant.

Victoria studied the moist earth, looking for the professor's bootprints, but saw nothing she was certain were his.

"I'll go down one side, you the other," Skye said. "If we're separated, meet at the campsite, and if we're in trouble, head for Bridger's Pass."

She nodded, wove her pony in and out of thickets, her eye keen and focused, her senses tingling with all the sights and smells and sounds reaching them. The dog came with her, sniffing, pausing, growling now and then.

"Nutmeg," she cried, her low voice reaching just as far as she wanted it to. "Professor Nutmeg."

But all she managed to do was stir up the magpies and startle two crows. The dog paused, sniffed, whined, and then trotted on. Victoria studied the spot where the dog had paused, finding nothing.

She turned the pony out of the river brush and rode to a nearby hill to reconnoiter, squinting hard at distant horizons, trying to separate the fleeting shadows of clouds from the movement of armed men or drifting herds of buffalo. The May morning was benign, a copy of the previous day.

From her vantage point she spotted Skye now and then, working down the creek, until at last he turned toward the springs. She met him there, and the dog burst out of the bush, panting.

"Vanished," he said.

"Not Siksika," she said. There were no moccasin prints in the soft spring soil. No Blackfeet or other People had wandered by.

"No prints of his boots, either," he said, awakening to something. "He never came here."

The realization startled them both.

They rode cautiously back to their abandoned campsite. But only silence greeted them when they reached the cutbank.

This ground was higher and harder than the ground around the hot springs, and less likely to reveal Nutmeg's tracks, so they dismounted and began their search on foot.

Victoria wondered once again what sort of man would drift away, scarcely aware of those who were shepherding him, obsessed with his work. Beyond the creek lay the grassy slopes of the first foothills of the Spanish Peaks, and she scanned them for the familiar image of the man.

One could not know what interested him: one day he would be hiking ridges, the next day studying river bottoms, the day after that wending through rock at timber-line, yet another day studying the life in a still pond. He had no favorite haunts; he sought to open the whole natural world to his understanding.

She climbed a ridge and cautiously peered over it, always alert, and saw only the magpies.

Magpie. Her spirit-helper.

She lifted her arms, a thin young Crow woman sitting in the white man's saddle, reaching upward and outward with a prayer:

"Fly over the man. Lead me to the man," she asked.

But the magpies did not fly.

She slumped in her saddle and closed her eyes and beseeched the Old Ones of the earth and sky and under the earth.

"Old and Wise Ones, have pity on your poor daughter; bring this man who collects all the growing things of Mother Earth to put in his books, bring him safely to us, and keep him safe, and answer the mystery," she whispered.

She opened her eyes and beheld a land warmed by a gentle spring sun, empty and peaceful. The dog lay beside her, questions in his eyes. She watched a soaring hawk far distant, and crows talking in shrill alarms, and the eternal breezes whispering the leaves and rustling the verdant grasses. And not a sign of the professor.

If he did not go to the hot springs, then where?

She circled the campsite again, hoping to cut his path, but saw nothing but a fresh track of a young grizzly bear. She turned to follow the tracks as they drifted toward the foothills along a rivulet that would soon dry up in the summer's inferno. The bear would be cross and hungry after the winter's sleep, and ready to kill. She would be wary. It could run faster than her pony, at least for a short stretch.

The bear had descended into brush, so she followed it

there, reaching a larger stream where it had fished, or eaten a rotten carcass and left. She smelled death, and hunted the ground carefully. The dog sniffed and whined and poked his nose into the brush.

But the professor wasn't there, nor could she find the remains of any creature. Relieved, she backed out of the brushy cul-de-sac and headed back to the campsite, where she found Skye, his face like a thunderclap.

"We've left enough hoofprints here to bring the whole Blackfoot nation down on us," he said.

"But the prints go every direction, back and forth, here and there."

"That'll make them all the more curious. We've got to move."

She wondered if he was about to abandon the professor.

He led them up the middle of the creek to a long slope leading toward a spring high in a grassy notch, and then settled their horses, along with the professor's, in the notch and out of sight, and waited. The dog had vanished again, and returned.

He had chosen well. Her man always chose well. From this high point they could see much of the surrounding country. They could see the sky, and read the weather, and prepare for distant storms. From this vantage point they could peer straight down upon their campsite, a tiny spot in the distant emptiness, but close enough to reveal the movement of the professor should he return there.

They picketed the horses and let them graze, watched clouds build over the peaks to the south and east, and waited. All that day they waited, often misled by scudding shadows racing across the great basin of the Three Forks. The dog lay beside them, not interested in the hunt.

That day passed. In the evening they descended. On foot, they searched the slopes and creeks, pawed through brush, sniffed the air for the iron smell of blood and decay. They padded by moonlight toward the hot springs again and probed the area, smelling the rank sulfur of the mineral water, studying earth and brush and secret places, and even trees.

The dog whined and shivered.

Nothing.

Skye grew morose. Victoria watched him sink into bad humor. He was hating this vigil now, and itching to leave, but she knew he wouldn't. These white men stuck together, and that was often their salvation. He had told her about the time Jim Bridger had abandoned the wounded and feverish Hugh Glass to his death, and how Glass had miraculously survived and heroically dragged himself hundreds of miles to succor. He would not be a Jim Bridger. He would not abandon a man, or lead rivals into the deadly arms of the Blackfeet, as Bridger had done just last winter.

They retreated to their small aerie at the top of a slash in the foothills, and slept uncomfortably, with Nutmeg's ghost haunting them. The dog was gone all night.

The next day passed slowly and silently, and the next. Each day they scoured a broad area, riding quietly through meadows and groves of aspen or cottonwood, poking around brush, studying streambanks, only to return mystified to their high lookout. Their food was running out along with their patience. But still Skye stayed put, studying their campsite far below for any sign of the missing naturalist.

Four days had passed. Skye's temper was not far behind his eyes now, and she could say nothing to temper it.

"He's either dead or faint with hunger and wandering wherever his collector's eye leads him," he said. "The way he did to Wyeth after the rendezvous."

"He is a good man, but a child," she said.

"He's an irresponsible fool."

"Making bad words about him does no good."

Skye subsided. The anger in his face slipped into

desolation. He had lost a man in his charge. He had lost a friend. He had lost a man who was attempting to bring new knowledge to the world. Only the intervention of the Above Ones would ever bring Professor Nutmeg back to them.

She knew that in the morning Skye would leave and she knew that if he gave up and headed over Bridger's Pass, this would haunt him all of his days. He would blame himself, feel the sting of failure. But she knew that none of this was his failure. Nutmeg had made his own choices. He had been severely warned over and over.

She brimmed with curiosity that itched and scratched at her. Where did that man go? What was his fate? Did he live? Skye was half-crazy for knowledge, too. They both knew that this was the worst of all endings because it didn't end. He was alive or dead or wounded and immobile. He was a captive or slave or not. He was sick or not. He was wondering across meadows, looking for specimens, unaware of time—or not. They would never know, and that was a burden that could scarcely be borne.

In the night the weather changed, and Skye and Victoria awakened to overcast and the iron scent of rain in the air. Their unprotected ridge-top aerie was no place to weather an icy spring storm. Birds no longer tarried in the sun, but flew with purpose. The breeze no longer toyed with their clothing, but stabbed icy fingers into their flesh.

Darkly, Skye saddled his pony, and then the professor's, and loaded the gear onto the horses while Victoria made ready to leave. They had not eaten, and were out of food. The dog was spending more and more time rummaging a living. But they would make for Bridger's Pass this day and leave Professor Alistair Nutmeg, lecturer at Harvard on the natural world, to the fate he had carved for himself.

Darkly, they rode away.

50

Barnaby Skye was enjoying a hard-won peace. The disappearance of Professor Nutmeg still haunted him, but he believed that the man himself caused his misfortune, and the Skyes had done everything within their power to look after him.

Still, they missed the man, missed his innocent cheer, missed his boyish enthusiasms and the ecstacy in him whenever he added a new plant to the catalog. No one could know whether he was dead. They found no body, nor any place where carrion-eaters congregated. They had scoured the whole country, finding not a trace of the man. If he had been taken captive, it was by men on foot because they found no hoofprints marking the passage of any large party.

And when they left, at last, they put a message into a cairn at the campsite, telling Nutmeg to head east over the pass and into Crow country where Victoria's people would be alerted and ready to care for him.

That was all anyone could do.

He and Victoria and No Name arrived at the Green River rendezvous on June tenth, and found that many of the free trappers, along with Wyeth's party, Bonneville's group, and the rival outfits, American Fur and Rocky

Mountain Fur, had set up shop. There was even an English noble named Stuart, along with his entourage, camped in colorful tents with coats of arms flapping in the wilderness winds.

Victoria discovered that several lodges of Crows were present along with many Snakes, and she discovered friends among her people, which gladdened her heart. But Skye roamed the gathering restlessly. His mood was not helped by a heavy overcast that carried occasional cold showers and hid the tops of the distant mountains, turned the world gray, and made dry firewood a scarce item. There were times when he pondered the stupidity of living out of doors year-round; times when a hearth, a roof, a soft bed, an easy chair, and a good kitchen seemed more inviting than this wild life.

He lacked so much as a cent and hadn't a single pelt to trade, and often roamed hungrily through the two trading posts, or even through Captain Bonneville's crude fort where other goods might be purchased. But a penniless man could only yearn and study, and sometimes scheme of ways to squeeze some small item out of these ruthlessly commercial enterprises.

He passed knots of his old friends, talking and smoking their pipes, enjoying the luxury of tobacco after most of a year's privation. Sometimes he joined them, and they always welcomed him, and once he even sucked some smoke into his lungs when they passed a pipe around. But he was famished in a dozen ways, and sat irritably as they spun yarns, bragged about the pelts they had gathered, the bears they had subdued, the icy rivers they had crossed, the Blackfeet that had chased them, the rattlesnakes they had captured by hand, the Indian maidens they had conquered, the tribes that had adopted them, the buffalo they had eaten, and the jugs of trade whiskey they had demolished . . .

He could not bear any of it and retreated, a solitary

misfit, as itchy and angry as he had ever been. What had the year brought him? It had started so high, a chance to recover his good name, word from his father, a trip across the sea followed by a high position in a company spawned by the nation of his birth. Then it had sunk so low, so dangerous, so desperate, so impoverished, so devoid of succor. Only the kindness of John McLoughlin had rescued him and Victoria and enabled them to reach the mountains again. And then the final blow, losing a great naturalist and friend, as if he had stepped off the edge of the earth.

His old comrades at Rocky Mountain Fur greeted him amiably but not with the whoops they reserved for their old brethren. His departure for the Hudson's Bay Company had changed everything, even though he had ended up not joining the British concern. So he and the mutt drifted through the vast grassy flat along the icy river, choked with snowmelt out of the mountains, poking into Bonneville's fort and trading post, visiting the tented stores of the rival companies, and studying the vast herds of Indian ponies and white men's mounts.

He felt again like a man without a country, especially when he spent time with Sir William Drummond Stuart, a Scotsman, actually, and captain in the Royal Army. In the presence of the Empire's military, Skye was wary and did little to promote a friendship with Stuart and his men. But that only left him all the more bereft of comrades.

Then one morning Andrew Drips approached him, and invited him for a little stroll along the purling river. Drips was somewhat older than the run of the mountain men, a veteran of the fur trade, the head of American Fur Company's mountain operations, and backed by the powerful Chouteau family of St. Louis, which had the means to muscle into the Rocky Mountain fur trade.

"I hear you're a free agent," Drips said. "Tell me what happened. Last I knew, you were accepting a tender from McLoughlin."

Skye told him the story as they hiked past Snake lodges, and the dog shuttled back and forth ahead of them.

"Ah! That naturalist was a man who could not help himself, Mister Skye. He went under. You bear no blame. You never abandoned him."

"But I feel bad, and I've lost a friend."

Drips stopped, peered into the crystal river as if to discern the future in its waters.

"Mister Skye, you are well known as a veteran, resourceful, and gifted mountaineer. I've been watching for years, but never more so than this rendezvous. You've survived circumstances that would put other men under. You're a natural leader. We need you. We've lost our best brigade leader, Vanderburgh, and I've settled on you to replace him. Would you consider an offer?"

"I would, sir."

"You would be our brigade leader, second only to me. I'm in charge of all the mountain operations. We'll pay you five hundred a year, deposited in St. Louis, plus your outfit. You'll avoid trouble as much as possible, gather peltries, and see to getting them either to McKenzie at Fort Union, or here, where we can pack them back. I'll be with you much of the time but at the post in the winter."

"We accept, sir."

"We?"

"Victoria, this dog of mine, and me."

"Good, good. We've good relations with the Crows. We even have good relations with dogs."

He laughed. Skye knew he was going to like this graying man. He knew that Drips had been born in Pennsylvania in 1789, worked in the fur trade since 1820, and was much admired. At age forty-four, he was a decade older than most of the three hundred white men gathered across the bleak prairie cut by the Green River.

Five hundred was good money.

They drifted back to the American Fur Company store,

where mountaineers traded peltries for jugs of whiskey, if that is what pure grain spirits, mixed with water and flavored with a plug of tobacco and a little pepper could be called. Here, spread over the grass or on makeshift tables, were bright bolts of flannel, iron traps, bits and bridles, packframes, thick blankets bearing two to four stripes that indicated their weight; here were shining mountain rifles, powder, awls, knives, canvas, gaudy calicos, powder horns, spare flintlocks, percussion caps, vermillion, beads, bells, mirrors, and all the foofaraw with which to trade with the tribes.

"Mister Skye, let me introduce you around—Pete Fontenelle especially, my right-hand man—and then you just take what you need on account. Outfitting items we'll provide; drink and other items, such as gifts for your wife, we'll post against your earnings. Later, we'll make some plans for the next campaign, and you'll let us know what you have in mind. We've forty trappers, more or less, plus more men at Fort Union."

Just like that. It was as if all this had been destined by some hand of Fate. As if Andrew Drips had decided on Skye long before Skye arrived at rendezvous. As if a man without a country had been given a home once again, and esteemed not for his connections or ties, but solely for his abilities in the mountains and among men.

Skye accepted the trust and esteem accorded to him.

Drips left him there. Skye ducked under the canvas shelter of the store, watching rain slide off the edges of the canvas. What riches lay at hand! All this meant warmth, dry feet, sugar for his sweet tooth, coffee and tea to hearten a man in icy weather, a caplock rifle to replace his flintlock, which usually didn't fire in rain; powder, lead pigs and balls, woolen long underwear, skeins of beads for Victoria and anything else to delight her heart. Oh, good times were coming!

The rain lifted and he beheld a sinking sun gilding the

grassy flats, poking under the pancake clouds and silvering their edges. To the west the clear blue sky promised a great day, a sky warm and transparent and infinite. A sky as wild as the land, without ceilings or the cramping of clouds.

He patrolled the Crow lodges where smiling Absaroka people nodded to him, watched fresh-killed elk roast over fires. An evening breeze swept away the moisture. He found Victoria with some Crow women sitting in a circle and gossiping.

She rose at once, and he led her back to the American Fur Company store.

"I'm a brigade leader with AMC," he said. "Quite a talk with Drips. We'll have everything we could ever want. Tomorrow, I'll get a good caplock rifle, and you'll get my flintlock."

She eyed him, a faint expectant smile twisting up the corners of her mouth. "And tonight, Mister Skye?"

"Well, I was getting to that," he said.

He stopped at the rude bench, a plank atop two stumps, where a clerk was doling out trade whiskey.

"One gallon, Mr. Privet," he said. "Put it on account. Also, two tin cups and a jug if you have one."

"No jugs, sir, too heavy, but I could lend you a kettle."

"That would be just fine, Mr. Privet. One measured gallon, one kettle, and two tin cups. Put the gallon on my account and we'll return the kettle and cups."

"Very well, Skye."

"It's Mister Skye, mate."

"Sonofabitch," said Victoria. "Tonight, the rendezvous begins."

No Name laid back on its haunches and howled.

AUTHOR'S NOTE

Most of the fur trade characters in this story were real people. All the Californios are fictional. Dr. John McLoughlin was a formidable force in the Hudson's Bay Company at the time of this story, and he and his wife and James Douglas are portrayed accurately.

Nat Wyeth, the inventive Boston ice merchant, met defeat time after time, and yet remains a major figure of the era, and perhaps the most important reason that the Oregon country is now under the American flag.

Peter Skene Ogden was the most formidable of the HBC men, and I have portrayed him as he was. He did not, however, attend the rendezvous where I have placed him. He was at that time far to the north, dealing with the Russians.

Professor Nutmeg is loosely based on the British naturalist Thomas Nuttall, whose trips west, one of them with Wyeth, contributed greatly to North American botany. He was as careless about his safety as his fictional counterpart, but survived.

—Richard S. Wheeler

Downriver

A BARNABY SKYE NOVEL

For my fine grandson, Remi Trottier

1

Gloom hung over the rendezvous on the Popo Agie River. Evil rumors wormed through the gathering, furrowing brows. They were saying this would be the last gathering of the mountain men. The American Fur Company wouldn't buy a beaver plew at all, or if it did, it would pay so little that the mountaineers would starve. A man couldn't keep body and soul together in the mountains anymore. There were whispers that the company's tent store would have fewer items and these would be more costly than ever.

It had reached Barnaby Skye's ears that the trapping brigades would be pared down and free trappers released from contracts; that long-term company men would be let go and that it didn't matter how good a job a man had done. He heard that the engagés would find themselves as useless as a lame horse. He had heard that prime beaver pelts wouldn't bring fifty cents, and an entire year's hard work wouldn't keep a man in gunpowder. Those bleak rumors had built up an awful thirst in Barnaby Skye. A jug usually solved his problems, at least until the fat moon turned skinny.

Just so long as they brought spirits, everything would be all right. Whiskey fueled each rendezvous. Without it, the trappers might as well go back to loading cotton or blacksmithing or plowing prairie soil or tallying waybills in a warehouse. But not one man among them believed that the year's supplies, now being packed in from Fort Union, would not include the pure grain alcohol that would be mixed with Popo Agie River water, a plug of tobacco or two, and some Cayenne pepper, that set the old coons to baying.

One thing wasn't a rumor: fashion had shifted. In 1833, John Jacob Astor himself had discovered that silk top hats were the vogue; that hats made from beaver felt had vanished from the shops of Europe. In 1834 he had sold out his American Fur Company, and now the Upper Missouri Outfit was really Pratte, Chouteau and Company, though no one called it that. It was said that Astor, the great fur magnate, had known exactly what he was up to, and had gotten out of the fur business in the nick of time, richer than Midas and safer than Gibraltar.

That was the dark talk those June days beside the Popo Agie, where it met the Wind River, among dour trappers waiting for the fun to begin and the trade whiskey to flow. The rest of the bad tidings wasn't rumor at all. No one had done well this year. Beaver were just about trapped out, except maybe on the streams controlled by the dangerous Blackfeet, and the competition of small outfits and free trappers had made life in the wilderness tougher than ever. No one had many plews to trade, and those few wouldn't bring much more than a few grains of DuPont powder and a bar of lead. There were men in camp who had put in a hard year's work and wouldn't get fifty dollars for it.

And so, that June of 1838, Barnaby Skye waited for what life would bring, but without much hope. Maybe this would be the last rendezvous. He would have to find some other way to survive, and so would all the rest of the mountain men gathered together for the customary trade festival and summer fun that year. What would he do? What would he become? Who would he be in the hazy future? Was this the end of his sojourn in the wilds? Would he return to the sea, from whence he came?

At least the American Fur Company had sent an outfit upriver, and it was due at any time now. The trappers could buy the traps and gunpowder and flannels and blankets they needed, and keep on going for another year if they had a few packs of skins to peddle. Maybe there was hope in that. Maybe things would get better.

The trappers knew that much, because an express rider from Fort Union, located at the confluence of the Yellowstone and Missouri, had told them the *Otter* was thrashing its way upstream with an outfit, a cargo of trade goods. But no one knew what bleak news would accompany the outfit, and not a man in that camp believed that the news would be very good. The St. Louis owners of the company had made it clear a year earlier they were losing money on the beaver business. Silk was in; beaver felt was out.

Skye had been a brigade leader, a salaried man, one of only five in camp, so he had weathered the bad times a bit better than some of the trappers. They had numbed their legs for long hours in freezing water while baiting traps with castoreum and collecting beaver, found small comfort in winter's darkness, fought their way into obscure corners of the Rockies, only to find that other, equally determined trappers had cleaned out the streams. And now the beaver had all but vanished.

Lucien Fontenelle, the veteran fur man in charge of field operations for the American Fur Company, was more optimistic.

"Beaver may be trapped out, but the company's not just in the beaver business," he confided to Skye as they lounged under a cottonwood, staring at snow-burdened peaks. "It can sell any pelt or hide we can ship."

"For less plunder," Skye said.

Fontenelle nodded. "Hard doings now," he said. "But we'll keep on going. That's what Pierre Chouteau himself told me; they'd keep on going. There's fur here and markets there. Maybe it'll be ermine or mink, deer and elk hides, weasel or otter, maybe even buffalo hides, but there's a market in the States."

Skye was not a gloomy man, nor a pessimist, but all the bad talk was eroding his joy. For a dozen years he had been in the mountains, and was considered a veteran and even an old man by the trapping fraternity, though he wasn't far into his thirties, and just beginning life.

They considered him an odd duck, perhaps because of his British ways and his peculiar looks. He had been a pressed seaman, dragooned into the Royal Navy when he was a boy in London. He hadn't escaped the iron claw of His Majesty's Navy until he jumped ship at Fort Vancouver, on the Columbia River, seven years later, and made his way into the interior, with little more than his wits and a knife and belaying pin to keep him alive.

Maybe that's why he was a more serious and somber man than most of the mountain fraternity; why he was more diligent and careful and willing to learn anything of value; why he treasured his liberty so much that he would die rather than surrender it. He had spent seven years in bondage, subservient to the whim of assorted boatswains, midshipmen, masters, captains, and lords of the admiralty, and freedom meant more to him than it did to anyone in the mountains.

Maybe he seemed odd to the fraternity because he insisted on being called *Mister*, or maybe it was because of his burly barrel-shaped body, or the seaman's roll in his gait. Maybe it was because of his giant misshapen nose, which had suffered much pulping and pounding in innumerable brawls, a hogback that now dominated his face so that his small blue eyes and thin lips shrank to nothing in comparison. Or maybe it was his battered black top hat, pierced by arrow and shot, which he wore with determined dignity in all seasons, perched on a full mane of ragged brown hair that reached his shoulders.

Or maybe they found him odd simply because he wasn't an American, and didn't speak the trapper lingo, and addressed others with politeness and civility, which were things he was born to and couldn't help. He was a man without a country; not able to return to England, yet not a westering man out of the States, so he lived in some sort of limbo, his only nation the trapping fraternity of the mountains—and his wife Victoria's people, the Crows.

But he didn't mind. What counted was their respect as well as his own respect for himself, and what else they thought of him didn't matter. He had mastered the wilderness arts in a hurry. And never stopped learning how to subsist himself in a world where there was nary a shop on any corner to sell him beef or pork or bread or greens, and nary a tailor to sew him a suit of clothes, nary a smith to fashion a weapon, and nary a doctor to tend to his ills and aches and broken bones. He had mastered the Arkansas toothpick, the Green River knife, the Hawken percussion rifle, the war axe and throwing hatchet, the savage's bow and arrow, war club and lance because there were no constables in the wilds to protect him. He knew how to build a smokeless fire, how to read the behavior of crows and magpies, how to sense an ambush around a bend. He had graduated summa cum laude from the Rocky Mountain College, where one either won a baccalaureate or died in some obscure gulch, his fate unknown.

So he, along with two hundred others, lingered in the verdant meadows where the Popo joined the Wind, awaiting whatever the lords of their fate in distant St. Louis had to offer. It was a sweet land, at least in summer, with cool evenings, and vast panoramas in which grassy benchlands surrendered to dark-timbered slopes, which in turn stretched upward in bright blue distances to snow-capped peaks that fairly cried "Freedom!"

The blue haze of campfires lay in the air, and the pungent aroma of wood smoke. In addition to the trappers, the dusky tribesmen had gathered once again to trade their pelts for all those treasures brought from afar by the white men: powder and lead, blankets, hooks, traps, mirrors, beads, and especially, the trade whiskey the wily traders concocted and sold by the cup or jug for furs.

Skye could see the tawny buffalo-hide lodges of the Crows arrayed in a circle, and those of the Shoshones and Nez Perce, and some plenty of other tribes as well, dotting the verdant meadows. Here, on neutral trading ground, even hereditary enemies enjoyed a momentary peace, though they were all fair game for one another once they departed from the legendary trappers' fair.

Skye waited restlessly, his eyes on the low divide that would someday soon reveal a string of heavily burdened pack horses and mules, and some gaudily bedizened mountaineers driving them into the rendezvous.

He did not know what he would do if the news was bad, which is what he fully expected. There weren't enough beaver pelts in camp to pay for the enormous expense of shipping all those goods from St. Louis, much less earn anyone a profit. He had two skills: he was an able seaman, and could always ship out on any merchant vessel, and he was also an able mountaineer. He suspected he might just need to learn another trade, and he wasn't sure what it might be.

His wife Victoria was visiting with all her friends and relatives, some of whom she saw only at these annual fairs. At rendezvous time, he often went for hours, even a day, without seeing her. But whenever they were together on the trail, leading a brigade, she and he scrubbed and cooked and hunted together, lived and loved together with a unity of purpose and spirit that transcended their radically different upbringings. They were friends and lovers, hunters and warriors, and boon companions upon life's sweet walk. Except when he was enjoying his annual binge. The thought made him thirsty.

He was still young. He'd suffered hardship in the mountains, but his body was strong, and hardship had annealed the steel in him and wrought a man of rare courage and intelligence and something else: honor.

Ten days passed, then eleven, and finally on the twelfth, Joe Meek, who had been scouting up the trail for news, returned with news: The American Fur Company pack train would arrive the next day. From the crest of the ridge where he had observed the distant train, he could see it was a small one, poor doings compared to the outfits the company brought in during the heyday of the beaver trade. But an outfit, anyway, and maybe there would be a few casks of spirits on the backs of those mules to gladden the hearts and bodies of the trappers.

So the next day, that June, Skye might learn his fate.

2

Barnaby Skye harbored an awesome thirst after a hard year in the mountains. He knew exactly what he would do the moment the American Fur Company store was in business: he would dicker for one quart of trade whiskey and begin sipping, and not quit until the elixir had burned a fine hole in his belly.

Ah, the joy of it. In some small patch of Eden, every ache in his battered body would vanish, every worry, every fear, and every ancient irritation; and he would know only blossoming bliss and blooming brotherhood, daisies and roses and bagpipers, visitations from angels, advice from saints, hallucinations and corporeal joys. The trade whiskey was ghastly, a devil's concoction that corduroyed the throat and shrank the gullet and assaulted the brain and shriveled the intellect, but what did it matter? After a few sips, he never noticed. A year in the mountains was a lifetime; a year without a sip was an eternity.

Keenly, his dry throat anticipating the debauch, he watched the American Fur pack train trot in, bells jangling and hooves clopping, punctuated by an occasional gunshot and many a neigh, whether from a four-footed horse or two-footed animal being uncertain and immaterial. Old Andy Drips was leading it; the gray-haired,

weather-stained, plaid-wrapped veteran of the mountains
had been with American Fur for years, and was second
only to Fontenelle.

Along with the rest, Skye crowded about the pack
train, observing its diminished size, but he was heartened
by two mules carrying pairs of sturdy casks. These partic-
ular oaken kegs glowed and shimmered, as if lit by divine
light, or a blessing from Saint Jerome. At least Skye
thought so. The spoilsport United States government had
been doing its indecent utmost to interdict shipment of
ardent and rectified spirits into Indian Territory, but somehow the company always managed to supply its trappers
with the nectar of life.

As famished as these gentle nobles of the wilderness
were for whiskey, they were even more famished for
news, news of any sort, even the topics of recent Boston
sermons, and as Drips genially braced the rough knights
who clustered around him, he dispensed a few St. Louis
newspapers. Every word in them would be read and studied and squinted over. Every scrap of information about
the States would be digested and regurgitated.

Skye had seen many a rendezvous, and remarked at
once the subdued nature of this one. In times past, the arrival of a company outfit had occasioned a frenzy of shooting, whooping, mock combat, gaudy Indian parades,
reckless horsemanship, and inane hollering, all intended
to whet thirst. This was different. Drips was smiling, shaking hands, slapping backs, posing like a Saint Bernard
with a brandy cask, but it wasn't the same. Hardly any
trapper had fired his piece in welcome, because DuPont
powder was scarce and costly. Even the Crows and Shoshones were watching quietly rather than curvetting their
horses or dressing in feathery ceremonial regalia for the
big whoop-up. The excitement swiftly subsided into watchfulness as Drips's engagés began to unload the packs and
set up shop.

"Skye, you old varmint, good to see you," Drips said, embracing the Englishman.

"It's Mister Skye, mate."

Drips laughed. "Forgot. Mister Skye it is. Did you have a good hunt?"

"Beaver's scarce, Andy."

"What did you boys get?"

"Not two packs."

Drips sighed. "Same for the rest?"

"Worse, I think."

"That's what we guessed, judging from the returns at Fort Union." He eyed Skye sharply. "I want to talk to you later. Privately. Don't touch that jug until I do."

"That's a tall order."

"You let me get the store set up, and collect some news from the other brigade leaders, and then we'll palaver."

Skye reluctantly agreed. A year-long big thirst would have to continue an extra hour.

"You seen Alexandre Bonfils?"

"He's around."

Bonfils was another of the company's brigade leaders, related in half a dozen ways to most of the company's St. Louis owners. Bright, young, canny, wise in wilderness ways, and ambitious. Skye had never much cared for him, but had nothing against him, though other men did. The young man sported a tricorne and wore a medal on his chest, to let the world know he was a man of parts.

"Good. You wait for me, and we'll pow-wow."

"In one hour I'll be waiting in line with a cup, Andy."

The master of the revels laughed.

Drips, a busy man with heavy responsibilities, turned swiftly to the tasks at hand the moment he finished greeting his mountain companions, the AFC men and free trappers.

Skye waited irritably. His Crow wife, Victoria, stood

with her Crow friends, studying this latest caravan from the white men's world. His mangy yellow dog, No Name, sulked at the fringe of the crowd, suspicious of any disturbance and almost invisible to most mortals. No Name was even more independent than Skye, but the dog and the man had come to an understanding about life, and formed a mutual protection society.

He eyed Victoria fondly. She was wiry and glowing, with raven hair and an unblinking direct gaze that sometimes unnerved others. She liked a good bout with the trade whiskey as much as he, and now he saw her grinning in anticipation. Only the dog, among the Skyes, scorned the annual bacchanal, and had taken to nipping and snarling at Skye whenever Skye had put away too much nectar, for which offense Skye bellowed at the dog and threw rocks at him.

The ranks of mountaineers were pretty depleted this time, but he saw Jim Bridger waiting patiently. Like everyone else, old Gabe, as he was called, worked for American Fur now. Chouteau's outfit was the only sizable company left in the Rockies. And his friend Christopher Carson was on hand, out of the southern plains, to enjoy the party. Carson usually worked with the Bent Brothers, down on the Arkansas, but this time he had drifted north.

Then, suddenly, Drips was at his side again.

"They'll be trading in a few minutes." He nodded toward the Popo Agie. "You good for a little walk?"

Skye nodded unhappily, feeling deprived. The pair distanced themselves from the hubbub. No Name spotted them and followed, stalking them as if they were game, not the source of his meat and protection.

"You winter all right?" Drips asked.

"Had some scrapes with Bug's Boys," he said, alluding to the Blackfeet.

"Anyone go under?"

"No, we got out of there. But mostly we wandered up streams looking for beaver and finding nothing. Even the beaver dams have been pulled apart."

"That's what they expected in St. Louis. Maybe it's a blessing."

"Things pretty bad?" Skye asked.

"Yes and no. The beaver trade's over. They've been wondering what to do. Pierre Chouteau thinks he might send an outfit one more year; there's still some demand for beaver felt and trim on clothing. But mostly, he's cutting back." Drips eyed his old friend sharply. "They're letting almost all the brigade leaders go, Mister Skye. Including you. They'll send a small outfit next year, but only to trade with free trappers. No more company brigades. You'll all be on your own if you want to stay out here. Myself, I'd think about doing something else."

"That's hard news. I don't know what I'll do."

"Well, that's why I'm pulling you over here for a little pow-wow. The company's not getting out of the fur and hide business, but we're shifting operations. We can sell every ermine and otter skin we can find, and there's a market for deer and elk hides, and buffalo too."

"Forget beaver, then?"

Drips smiled.

They had reached the riverbank. The icy snowmelt gurgled past them, crystal, sweet, and delicious. A fine cool breeze eddied through the verdant spring grasses, like a mysterious finger writing the future.

"The company has plans for you—if you're interested." He waited for an affirmation. Skye nodded.

"Tulloch is leaving Fort Cass. They're looking for a replacement, a new trader for the post. You're an obvious choice, with a Crow wife. That gives you some power within the tribe, and helps the company lock down the Crow trade."

That interested Skye. Cass was a small log post, a satellite of Fort Union, located on the Yellowstone River at the confluence of the Big Horn. It did a modest trade with the Crows, Victoria's people. But the Crows weren't ardent beaver trappers and the post never did a large business.

"I might be," he said.

"There's a few hitches. One is that you're not the only man they're considering. Bonfils is another contender. And he has relatives from one end of the company to the other. There's another factor, too, which Pierre Chouteau himself urged upon me, old friend. They don't know you in St. Louis. You're a shadowy Englishman to them, known only through reports from those of us who keep an eye on the mountain trade. You'd have to go to St. Louis, meet Chouteau and his colleagues, tell them how you'll improve trade, and let them decide."

"St. Louis? That's a piece."

"No, not so long. You'd go back on the *Otter*. It's leaving just as fast as we can get these furs to Fort Union. The spring flood's already peaking and there's not a moment to waste."

"When do you leave here?"

"Tomorrow at dawn."

"Tomorrow! You just got here."

"We'll pack whatever furs we can for the riverboat. Fontenelle will haul the rest to Fort Union after the rendezvous."

"Tomorrow!" Skye didn't like that at all. He would miss the rendezvous. Miss the precious time with old friends. Miss the gargantuan drinking bout that would begin as soon as the traders could mix a kettle of whiskey.

"Bonfils will be on that boat," Drips said. "If he goes and you don't, you and the company will come to a parting of the ways. He's bright, fluent in two or three Indian tongues, knows the business inside out, has a Hidatsa woman, and their tongue is almost the same as the Crows'. He's junior to you by ten years, but he's well connected—maybe too well connected, to put it politely."

"Not even time for a drink," Skye muttered. "A miserable bloody little drink."

Drips grinned.

"Do I even stand a chance against him?"

"Certainly. Old Pierre Chouteau wants the best man, absolutely the best, and knows more about you than you might think."

"How long in St. Louis?"

"One or two days. You'll need to get a trader's license from General Clark if you're selected. Whoever they choose will start west at once. Reach Fort Cass before snow flies and relieve Tulloch. We'll be sending the *Otter* back up the river as far as it can get in low water. Whoever gets that position at Cass will be on it, and then head west from Bellevue with a small pack train, out the Platte River."

"Tomorrow!" Skye said. "I'd better talk to Victoria."

"Tomorrow at dawn. We're going to be weighing and baling furs this evening, writing chits the trappers can spend at the store, and we'll pull out at first light, moving as fast as we can. Be ready, packed and saddled and fed."

The whole business dizzied Skye.

"I'll let you know," he muttered, unable to absorb so much so fast.

Drips looked at him sharply. "One thing more. You may not want to be a trader. A man like you."

"What do you mean?"

"Just what I said. Think it over. And do it fast."

"Would you explain yourself?"

"No, and forget that I even warned you. The company will require certain things of you. That's all I can say. Some men there are who should not be traders for Pratte, Chouteau."

Skye searched the face of the man, uneasily, but found only a mask.

Andy Drips slapped him on the back. "For my money, you're the man they should turn into a trader."

That left a lot unsaid.

3

Many Quill Woman heard that her man, Mister Skye, was looking for her, but she was in no hurry to respond. He probably wanted someone to roast some meat. He could easily cook his own, but men liked to make women do it, and it didn't matter whether they were men of the People, or white men. Usually, she didn't mind, for that was what had been ordained from the beginning of the world, but at rendezvous things were different. Skye could cook his own damned meat. She was occupied.

She usually spent rendezvous apart from him. All year she toiled at his side, making camp, dressing hides, sharing his hard life and dangers, along with the brigade of trappers. But by the time rendezvous rolled around, she was weary of white men, and yearned for time among her many friends who always came to the great trappers' fair.

So she did not hurry. She had visited old friends in several Absaroka lodges this day, as well as fat grandmothers in a Shoshone lodge and some chunky Nez Perce women, and even visited with some treacherous and thieving Bannocks, who usually were at arrow's point with the Crows. That had been an act of great charity and munificence on her part; normally, an Absaroka woman never conversed with such trash. But an iron law of peace prevailed at the white men's fairs, and so it was that hostile tribes camped side by side, and even visited with one another, so she had deigned to talk briefly with a squat, ugly Bannock woman who was missing half her teeth.

She would talk to anyone at rendezvous. All except the Blackfeet. If Blackfeet had ridden to the banks of the Popo Agie at this time, much red blood would be lying on the green grasses.

Skye called her Victoria, after the princess, now queen, of his people across the sea. She did not know what that was all about, but being named for a great woman was surely an honor, and she loved her man for it. The more names one had, the more honor. They had an uneasy relationship, divided by all the things they didn't grasp about each other, and the lives they came from. And yet, she counted herself the happiest and most fortunate of women, the envy of all her sisters among the Kicked-in-the-Belly band of the Crows.

Who else had such a man? Had not Barnaby Skye the biggest, most mountainous nose in the world? Was he not a mighty warrior, a prodigious eater, a man big across the chest and belly, though not very tall? Was he not a leader of his people? Did he not survive perils that would sink lesser men? Was he not more tender and kind and caring than any Crow man she knew? Did he not consult her and imbibe her wisdom?

Yes, she was fortunate, and she would eventually go to him and cook some meat . . . but not for a while, dammit. He deserved to wait. Rendezvous brought out the worst in him. Anyway, the traders were mixing up a great batch of whiskey, and everyone she knew was waiting eagerly to trade pelts for cups of the fiery brew that made a man or woman happy and mad, and took away the pains and sorrows of the world. Soon she, too, would bay at the moon, howl like a wolf, and laugh all night and rub her hand through Skye's whiskers.

For an hour she resisted, even though the gossips told her that her man was wandering through the lodges, bellowing her name, seeking her company. She had laughed. Let him bark at her like a lonely coyote; this was her summer time with all her friends, her People, and women from other Peoples. This was the time to see all the new babies and sorrow that she had none and probably wouldn't ever have any because this gift had just not come to them.

She loved Skye. He was in his mid-thirties, and in the prime of his life. His body had borne many wounds, and he had suffered from all the miseries that life brought; cold, starvation, sore bones and muscles, poor food, and great thirst. Yet, she had never seen him healthier or stronger or more in command of himself, of his men, or of life. A dozen winters now he had been in this country, and he bore the marks of this hard life upon every limb, and yet no warrior was stronger.

"Your man is calling again," said Arrow, her brother, testily. "Why do you defy him? You are a bad wife."

She laughed. They were watching her to see if she would ignore her man, but she wouldn't give them anything to gossip about. She rose quietly, crawled through the lodge door, and beheld him three lodges away.

He looked troubled.

"Come. We have to talk privately, away from everyone," he said.

She followed, faintly annoyed but concerned.

"When will the traders open their store?" she asked.

"It's open now."

His tone of voice was brusque.

He led her to a fallen log, once a noble cottonwood but now the home of crawling things.

"This may be the last rendezvous; maybe one more next year. I'm out of work, Victoria."

"Work? What is this? You don't have to work. We will live with the People and be happy."

"But there's something new . . ."

She gathered her spirits together. Skye was acting very strange. Maybe he just needed his jug. He was always strange until he had a few drinks at rendezvous. He was known to be crazy in the days and hours before rendezvous.

"Maybe I can be the trader at Fort Cass," he said.

"The trader? What happened to, what is his name, Tulloch?"

"He's heading for the States. The position's open. I'd be a trader, trading with your people, trying to keep all your Otter clan happy. I'm going to apply."

"I would be close to my people!"

"Yes, always close. Not roaming all over the Rocky Mountains all year."

"Aiee! This is good."

"I may not get the position, though. And even if it is given to me, I might not want it."

She waited patiently for him to explain. He did try hard to explain all these things white men do, and how they think, but often it didn't make sense. They had no gods and did not listen to the spirits. She would never understand the pale-eyes, and their ways. But that was all right. He was absolutely boneheaded when it came to understanding her people.

"There's another candidate for the job, maybe more than that. We both know him. Alexandre Bonfils."

"A boy," she said.

"He's done well, Victoria. His trappers brought back more fur this year than mine, and they got it up in the Blackfeet country without getting into trouble. I can't say as much."

"He was lucky. Good medicine. He make the beaver come to the traps, and he don't get caught. But maybe his medicine won't be so good next time."

"He's bold and young and intelligent; he may get that position. Having a Hidatsa woman who can talk your tongue helps, too."

"He has many women, not just her. And he sells her to any trapper for a pelt or two. I would not want to be the woman of Bonfils."

He smiled. She did love that smile, which wrinkled flesh around those buried blue eyes.

"Is it time to buy some whiskey?" she asked, hopefully.

He lifted that battered beaver hat, scratched his long locks, and set it back again. "No, we're not having any whiskey this year."

That jolted her. She thought he was crazy. He would have some credit at the store. They could have lots of whiskey at the rendezvous.

"You got some big reason, Skye?"

"We're taking off at dawn for St. Louis. At least I am. They want to see me. The big chiefs, the owners, they've never met me, and they don't want to put a man they don't know in a position like that. Big doings. They want me to hear how they operate."

"St. Louis?"

"On the fireboat, the paddle wheeler at Fort Union. They need to take the returns downstream before the river drops. Andy Drips will collect and bale all the furs he can tonight, and start at dawn for Fort Union. With me. With us, if you want. If you'd rather stay with your people, you could—"

"St. Louis? The many-houses place?"

"Many houses, many stores, the big river."

"And white women!"

He laughed. The biggest mystery in her life was white women. For many years she had seen these white trappers, all of them without white women, and it puzzled her. She hadn't the faintest idea where they were hidden, what they wore, or what they did. The white men said their women were back in the many-buildings places like St. Louis, and were too frail to come into the mountains like the men. They would not survive for long in lodges, or in bad weather.

All of that astonished her. She thought that white women must be greatly inferior to any other kind, and had secretly nursed a great contempt for them. No wonder white men left them behind! They were a frail and miserable and pale sex, always dying and shivering and getting themselves buried.

"When are you coming back?" she asked.

"Fast. The riverboat goes downstream much faster than upstream. We can be in St. Louis in a couple of weeks after we leave—ah, maybe fifteen or sixteen sleeps. We would spend only a day or two in St. Louis. Then we'd outfit and ride back. If we go light, maybe three moons. Back here before it gets cold."

She squinted at him suspiciously. "Is this where the white women are?"

He laughed. "I imagine. I've never been to the States."

"Will I see what they wear?"

"You'll see everything they wear. They all dress differently."

"Will I have to ride on the fireboat? It is a beast."

"Yes."

"I could walk along the bank while you ride the boat."

"No, it goes much too fast."

"I don't want to put my foot onto a boat with fire in its belly and steam coming out. Bad medicine."

"That's up to you, Victoria. It's safe enough, but once in a while one does hit a snag and sinks. I have to go. I don't want to. I was looking forward to rendezvous. Looking forward to . . . a jug or two—"

"Sonofabitch!" she yelled. "I can't even see my friends!"

"You could winter with the Kicked-in-the-Belly people. Your mother and father would enjoy that."

"And leave you all alone? Skye, dammit, I want to see these white men's buildings worse than anything. I want to see your pale sickly women! I want to see where all these beaver furs go; where they all disappear to. I want to see where all this metal comes from, guns and powder. How do they make that? I want to see how they make blankets. Where does the wool come from? You tell me these things, but I have to see them.

"But most of all, Skye, I want to see the women. Goddamn, if I don't go along, maybe you'll throw me out of the lodge and marry one of your own kind."

Skye began to laugh. She loved his laugh. It began deep in his belly, a great rumble that shook his barrel frame, and then slowly rose up his throat and burst upon the world like a grizzly dance or a wolf howl.

"We'll take a few jugs and drink them on the fireboat," he said at last.

4

Skye woke up in a foul temper. It was going to rain; he could smell it. It had rained all June. They would be traveling in an icy drizzle.

But that wasn't the source of his ill humor. He had waited all year for rendezvous, waiting for fine times, big doings, roaring, ripping, *hooraw*ing fun, belly-tickling yarns, and now he was cutting out before it started.

Victoria wasn't faring any better. She dressed sullenly, as irritable as he, her eyes accusing, her glare daring him to say one word, just one word, so it would all blow up and she would stay at rendezvous. They had the good sense not to say anything to each other.

He pulled his thick-soled moccasins up, tugged his fringed buckskins over his blue shirt, and stepped into a gray and hateful dawn. The rendezvous slept sweetly. Even the revelers had surrendered to Morpheus. He saw Gabe Bridger snoring peacefully beside a dead campfire. The rain would wake him up soon. Even Bridger, one of the partners of the defunct rival fur company, was now working for Pierre Chouteau and his St. Louis capitalists. Where else could a mountaineer go? To Mexico? No one was making a living farther south, trying to drown a few beaver for

Bent, St. Vrain and Company. The good times were over, and the mountain life was going under.

Smoke from a couple of fires hung lazily over the camp, layering the air. This was the time of day of surprise attack; of hordes of vermillion-painted savages sweeping into a vulnerable and sleeping village. But that would not happen here at the great trade festival. Mountain men had fangs and two-legged predators knew it. The mountaineers and Indians guarded the horse herds well, night and day. And years ago, a few Blackfoot and Gros Ventre raiders had bumped into the rendezvous and started a war, and they weren't likely to try it again.

He headed for the river, splashed brutally cold water over his stubbled face and battered hands, dried himself with a handful of grass, and headed for the breakfast fire, walking painfully, as if on pebbles, because the chill had stiffened his limbs. Over at the store, Andy Drips's clerks were furiously baling plews, while others loaded packs onto mules.

"We'll be out of here in an hour," Drips said. "Have some breakfast. Real coffee."

"Don't touch it."

"You limeys. I suppose you want tea."

"Just some meat."

Drips pointed to a slab of buffalo loin that had been rotated on an iron spit over cottonwood flames until it was scorched outside and succulent within. Skye pulled out his Green River knife and began sawing, feeling the hot pink juices leak over his scaly hands. Buffalo was a satisfying meat, tender at the hump and loin, tough and chewy elsewhere. This was stringy meat, old bull, but tasty. It would give his teeth something to do and put some strength into his belly.

"You do a good trade last night?" Skye asked, around the meat.

"No. Not three packs of beaver from the free trappers.

Few more from the Injuns, and some weasel tails, ermine, mink, and otter."

"What happens to all these trade goods if they don't sell?"

"It'll all get packed back to Fort Union."

Skye looked at the hardware, blankets and cloth, a pathetic fraction of what usually arrived in the annual packtrain. "Don't think there'll be much to take back, mate."

"Fontenelle will bring whatever doesn't sell, and whatever furs he can still buy. We've got most of the pelts loaded. This ain't much of a rendezvous. You can feel it. Maybe it's the last. Who knows? Makes a man feel bad about things."

Skye nodded, feeling an autumnal chill, like the falling of aspen leaves, even though it was June.

He spotted the young Frenchman, Alexandre Bonfils, approaching, and studied his rival. Together they would go to St. Louis, but only one would win the trading position at Fort Cass. Bonfils peered at Skye with quick dark eyes, and then at the wavering fire. If getting up at this hour was hard on Skye, it was plainly worse for the disheveled younger brigade leader, whose lax discipline often got him into trouble.

Bonfils's life in the mountains had been a series of narrow escapes from weather, cold, starvation, Indians, and sickness. And yet the man's daring and genius, his uncanny ability to bring in the beaver was even more formidable than Skye's. Bonfils did not hesitate to take his men into Blackfoot country, moving swiftly from stream to brooding stream in virgin beaver waters, and escaping before Bug's Boys got wind of his presence.

The man affected a certain patrician elegance that shouted his superiority to the world. One of his oddities was the ever-present Royal Order of Chevaliers medal pinned to his breast. This device, a bronze medallion chased with gold, featuring the bas relief bust of Louis

XVI hanging from watershot blue silk, announced the magnificence of the Bonfils name to all the mountain men, as well as stray savages. His other idiosyncracy was to have his family coat of arms sewn in gold lamé thread to his parfleches. By and large, the mountaineers enjoyed the gaudy display; beaver men could accommodate almost any attire, and the more bizarre, the better. Skye didn't mind any of it; did he not insist on wearing his own battered beaver top hat like a bishop's miter?

Bonfils poured steaming coffee into a tin cup, nodded at Skye, and grinned.

"So, my *ami*, we will go seek our fortune together on the *bateau-à-vapeur*."

Skye nodded. He knew if he opened his mouth he would regret what might come out. Bonfils had been drinking all night, yet here he was, showing no effects of the binge, while Skye, sober even after a parched year, was aching, irritable and as friendly as a lame grizzly coming out of hibernation.

"Is madame coming?" Bonfils asked.

"Yes."

"Ah, is it wise? I am lending Amalie to a friend. She would be an encumbrance in St. Louis, you know."

A mountain marriage, Skye thought. A temporary liaison between a trapper and a red woman, swiftly abandoned whenever the need arose. A man like Bonfils would have a dozen belles in St. Louis dancing in attendance, and would not let himself be embarrassed by the possessive arm of a squaw.

Bonfils's Hidatsa woman was pretty, bright-eyed young, vivacious, and a commodity the brigade leader sometimes lent to others for a favor. The young man's approach to life was to treat everything as a marketable commodity: loyalty, men, beaver, nature, women, and power. But that didn't disturb Skye. Bonfils's approach to native women was much the same as that of most trappers. Skye's enduring and committed marriage was the real oddity.

"I'm sure, monsieur, that Pierre Chouteau will want to discuss the trading business out of earshot of your squaw. There are certain aspects of the business that are not for savage ears," Bonfils said. "Profit is everything!"

Skye nodded dourly, and sawed at the haunch of buffalo, sensing that Bonfils still wanted to palaver. For reasons Skye couldn't fathom, he had never much cared for the young Creole. The man was well educated, interesting, witty, brave, adept at survival in wilderness, a great raconteur, well liked and respected among the mountain fraternity. Skye couldn't fathom what was irritating him.

Within the hour Victoria had sullenly loaded their small seven-pole buffalo-hide lodge onto a travois, harnessed the packhorses, stuffed the panniers with their few things, fed No Name, their mutt, a buffalo rib, and was ready to go. Skye used to try to help, but she had always shooed him off, saying it was woman's work.

Drips's men were almost ready, too, and some of them were masticating meat before heading down the trail. Fontenelle, who would be in charge of the store, watched quietly.

Skye suddenly had a wrenching premonition that he would never see a rendezvous again. It tore at him so violently that he walked away from the hum of activity, down to the bank of the Popo Agie River, which ran through sedges there, and peered into the flowing waters that dully reflected in silvery images the distant mountains, their tops sawed off by a heavy overcast. Around him the rendezvous slept sweetly. Few men rose early during the summer festivals, and rare was the mountaineer who greeted the sun at any time.

An ache filled him. These mountain rendezvous were the only home he had had for many years. No matter where the site might be—Green River, Cache Valley—the great reunions were his hearth and parlor and kitchen. He was a man without a country.

He watched smoke curl sleepily from a few lodges, saw the mist obscuring the dark brush arbors where his friends whiled away joyous days, knew that if he walked through that quiet camp, he would see scores of men he cherished, like Joe Meek, or Black Harris, or Gabe Bridger, or Kit Carson, lying in shaggy buffalo robes, or between dirty blankets, or in lodges like his own, or under canvas, all of them with their Hawken or mountain gun within easy reach, trappers and warriors, storytellers, drunks, fiercely loyal colleagues, rough and violent and young and bold.

"Mister Skye," Drips called. "You think about what I said last night? About being a trader? You ready for all that?"

"No, I didn't think much about it. I don't want to think about it."

"You and old Pierre may have some different ideas about how to do things. He isn't going to let you trade your way. Only his way. The company way. You got that clear?"

Skye nodded. "We'll see," he said, cautiously. The camp tore at him; the future tore at him.

They wanted to look him over in St. Louis. It dawned on him that he wanted to look them over, too. What sort of men was he working for? Who were they, these distant lords whose command stretched even to here, in utter wilderness? Were they good men and true? Were they honorable? Did they possess that special quality of the English—moderation? Were they ruthless?

Suddenly this trip took on a new dimension. He had always been curious about the Americans, and now he would find out about them. For years he had thought about becoming an American citizen; the republic stood for things he admired. And yet, the Americans he had met were a mixed lot, some of them scoundrels and others fierce and implacable and merciless. But there were fine men among them too, men like Bridger, Carson, Fitzpatrick, and Jedediah Smith. He liked most of them. What had started a few hours earlier as a quest for a job, now loomed larger. He would see about these Yanks, and whether they were worthy of his esteem. And whether he would some day join them, swearing his fealty to them and their laws and Constitution. This trip could result in more than a job; much more. Or much less.

"Well, Mister Chouteau," he said aloud. "You'll look me over, and I'll look you over. I hope you're the man I want you to be, and your nation is the United States of America I dream it should be."

Few trappers and Indians had awakened to see them off, and these few stood silently. Scarcely one man of the mountains cared to think about what was happening: a company pack train leaving the day after it arrived and unloaded a handful of goods, after paying a lousy fifty cents a plew for what few beaver were available.

Skye didn't want to think about it either. He stepped into the high-cantled Indian saddle Victoria had gotten for him, and reined his buckskin into the procession. The caravan required no word from Drips; it simply started moving. Not even the crack of a whip was needed to start the packhorses. Twenty well-armed engagés of the American Fur Company, Skye, Victoria, and No Name, who mysteriously appeared when Skye stepped into his stirrups, Bonfils riding a handsome bay and leading a single packhorse, and Drips, gray and weather-whipped, his every motion economical.

Slowly they toiled up a long grade and then, at the last bend Skye turned, his heart wrenched once again by the sight of that beloved, sorry gathering, and then they rounded a spur of foothill and history fell behind them. Within minutes they had entered fog, and then icy mist, and finally they rode into a cruel drizzle, the kind Skye hated most.

All that long, cloud-shrouded day Skye grieved, while his horse plodded dully ahead. The rain quit but the overcast did not, and by noon they were chilled to the marrow. Drips stopped them in a piney glen and had his engagés boil up some broth over a smoky fire while the pack animals rested.

Two days later they cut around the foothills of the Big Horns and headed northeast. For a while Victoria was on familiar ground and bubbling with cheer, but soon they would cross into the lands of the Sioux, and then there might be trouble.

Drips drove them hard the next days, but the weather was fine and they reached the Yellowstone nine days later, covering as much as forty miles in a stretch. Then the sun besieged them, and man and beast suffered under the glare of sun that burst into the heavens at five in the morning and didn't set until ten.

They saw no Sioux, or Assiniboine either, but they fought an enemy that was even worse: black flies devoured them and stung the horses, and if not flies, then mosquitos, droning viciously at most of their camps. Bonfils, ever brave, made jokes and won the admiration of the engagés with his gallantry, but Skye bore the maddening insects dourly.

They faced two difficult crossings. The first would carry them to the left bank of the Yellowstone, and the second would take them across the mighty Missouri to the portals of Fort Union. The post had flatboats, mackinaws, to help with that enterprise, but they would be on their own crossing the swollen Yellowstone.

Drips chose a broad and gravelly reach of the river, negotiable except for a twenty-foot channel, and they spent a whole day swimming horses across that narrow but treacherous current. But the old master knew what he was up to, and by evening he had assembled his caravan on the far bank.

The next evening they reached the Missouri, and Skye beheld a great post, one he had never seen, squatting on the north bank, and bobbing in the river, the paddlewheel vessel *Otter*.

5

Skye scarcely knew which sight galvanized him more: the white enameled *Otter*, tied fore and aft to great posts set into the levee, or the imperial American Fur Company headquarters, Fort Union, set on a yellow bench above the Missouri River.

It took some while for a pair of mackinaws, poled and paddled by sweating engagés, to carry the entire pack-train, horses and mules, one dog, and various pilgrims and voyageurs, across the sparkling river.

Here was the seat of an American empire, stretching from St. Louis up the river clear to British possessions and the walled borders of Mexico. He saw a snaky pennant flapping airily over the stockaded fortress, but knew even at that distance it wasn't the Stars and Stripes, and the national flag would probably fly underneath if it flew at all. No doubt the masters of this fur empire considered mere national sovereignty of much less importance than their company banner.

Victoria didn't like the look of that fireboat, even though its boilers were cold.

"Dammit, Skye," she muttered. "I will walk."

He laughed. "Twin chimneys," he said. "Thirty-two

horsepower of high pressure steam to spin those paddle wheels."

"Bad spirits, and don't give me no guff."

He studied the vessel with a seaman's eye, noting the flat, bargelike hull, which probably had only five or six feet of cargo space; the freight booms fore, the cabins aft, and the privies ahead of the wheelhouses. The white enameled superstructure rose amidships and looked the worse for wear, with soot staining the woodwork. The riverboat looked hard used.

"We will die," she said. "The water spirits will reach up and smash us against a rock because this offends them."

Skye didn't argue. It would take skills beyond reckoning to steer that monster, the first steam vessel he had ever seen, though he had heard enough about it on the long, hasty trek from rendezvous. Andy Drips had waxed lyrical about this steamboat, and the others in the planning stage or being built for the company. "And we have a whole carpenter and smith shop on board. If anything breaks, we can fix it," Drips had said.

Skye had wondered about that. It would take more than a blacksmith to fix a ruptured boiler, he thought.

When their turn came, they loaded their horses and travois and gear aboard one of the mackinaws, while No Name watched suspiciously. At the very last moment, as the engagés pushed away from the south bank of the Missouri, the old dog howled and leapt, landing aboard and shaking himself. Skye remembered another time, long before, when the strange yellow cur had followed a schooner mile after mile along the Columbia River, determined to go wherever Skye went . . . or die. Skye could not think about that without feeling his throat tighten.

The engagés bantered in French with Alexandre Bonfils, who smiled a great deal and made friends easily. Skye wondered how he could possibly win a post from his

French rival, in a company that was almost entirely French. Bonfils exuded the optimism that is natural to well-connected young men in their early twenties who have the inside track to everything good in the world.

The flatboat, or mackinaw, passed close to the huge riverboat, and Skye marveled that this machine had fought its way fifteen hundred river miles, against the current, often against the wind, pausing only to load cordwood. It carried a cargo that would supply not only the rendezvous, but also the entire needs of Fort Union and its satellite posts, including Forts Cass and MacKenzie, as well as Fort Pierre and its satellites. And that within this boat's hull would lie a fortune in peltries: beaver primarily, but also otter, mink, weasel, ermine, elk hide, buffalo robes, buffalo tongues preserved in salt, and more.

They debarked at a crude wharf and were met by a crowd of people, including the Fort's factor, Kenneth MacKenzie, James Kipp, his second in command, and assorted Assiniboine ladies, got up in high fashion. These were mountain wives, the mates of traders, the paramours of engagés, and servants who were casually traded from man to man to make the long winters go by swiftly. Many bore the cruel mark of smallpox on their faces, as did most of the engagés. The disease had obviously scythed through this place and left its calling cards.

The post itself rested on an arid bench in a yellow-rock country, a site far less handsome and inviting than Fort Vancouver, the great Hudson's Bay post on the Columbia. Here were no orchards or cultivated fields or granaries or gardens, but only naked rock and sagebrush. Even so, by all accounts, the masters of Fort Union had found ways to fill their lives with amenities, including fine wines imported upriver, along with splendid furniture, spices, condiments, china, silver, handsome woodstoves, bolts of silk and cotton and flannel, and infinitely more.

Skye studied Victoria to see how she was managing,

and found her surveying everything, assessing the dark, boisterous Frenchmen engaged to the company, examining the dusky Assiniboine women, famously dressed like tarts in striped silks and glossy satins, their hair beribboned, their feet in dainty moccasins so heavily quilled or beaded they looked like rainbows on each foot.

"Sonofabitch," she said, echoing the trapper vernacular she had picked up. She loved the trappers' expietives and used them with rich imagination, especially when she was in the company of anyone who disapproved of them.

"Greetings, gents, greetings, Mister Skye," said Mac-Kenzie, the huge chieftain, so formidable it must have taken an extra yard of fabric to cover him. Skye thought the man must be six and a half feet, and would weigh sixteen stone. MacKenzie himself was dressed in somber black and looked like an outsized minister or mortician. He had built the post, got into trouble years earlier for operating a still and was removed, but had returned to his familiar haunt once again, the absolute Lord of the North.

"And you must be Victoria. You are a legend, madam. You are the queen of the mountains!"

"Whatever that is," she said. "You gonna put up our horses or must I do it?"

"Tonight, madam, it would be our honor to care for your nags. Tomorrow they'll be boarded."

"On that fire canoe? The horses?"

"Your two saddle horses and equipage. They'll go as far as Bellevue, where you'll pick them up when you return."

"That dog, he goes with us, goddammit."

"Of course. A dog and his mistress cannot be separated."

It all made sense to Skye. Downriver, at Bellevue, on good prairie benchland near the confluence of the Platte River, the factor, Peter Sarpy, would board the Skye saddle horses until Skye headed back upriver, and provide him with packhorses in exchange for the ones he would leave here.

"Kipp here," said the second in command, a short but powerful gent with an iron grip. "Come along now, and see the post."

James Kipp hurried the Skyes and Bonfils and others up a steep path to the fort, which stood close to the Missouri. The interior yard was about what Skye expected, ample and solid, and the tall picketed walls stilled the blustery wind so that the air was quiet within. The great Kenneth MacKenzie, who had built the post, had built well. Encased by the cottonwood walls were warehouses, barracks, a kitchen, a chief factor's home with eight real glass windows and a shake roof. At opposite corners were bastions sporting small cannon for defense, and something more . . . an air, a feeling, a sense of imperial power that Skye hadn't felt since leaving Fort Vancouver, the Hudson's Bay post.

Below, the sweating engagés were loading the packs and bales of fur directly into the *Otter* under the gaze of a man Skye would soon meet, its master, Captain Marsh.

Kipp showed the Skyes to guest quarters.

"Dinner at eight in the chief factor's dining room," he said to Skye. "Mrs. Skye will eat with the women."

"Mr. Kipp, my wife would enjoy the company of the traders."

Kipp paused, scratched his whiskers. "I'm sorry. It's tradition here. The dinner table is set for gentlemen, and includes those of higher rank. There's a dining hall for the engagés—"

Kipp was plainly discomfited.

"I think perhaps we'll eat with the engagés," Skye said.

"Dammit Skye, you go eat with the men," Victoria said.

Skye knew the arrangements bothered him more than her. Many were the functions and meals within her Crow tribe that divided the sexes. He didn't know why he was so unhappy with this arrangement here, but he was.

"All right," he said, reluctantly.

"I'm sure Mrs. Skye will enjoy the company of our many ladies, most of them Assiniboine, but she'll be meeting my Mandan wife, some Sioux and Cree ladies, and so on . . ."

"Hell yes," she said. "Goddammit, Skye, go eat."

Kipp grinned. Barnaby Skye's wife was a legend in the mountains.

At the appointed hour, which seemed very late to Skye, he approached the chief factor's residence and was immediately invited into a sunny parlor for cordials, which turned out to be a robust port wine. Skye drank greedily, remembering all the joys of rendezvous he had surrendered to come here, but thinking that as the chief trader at Fort Cass he could have his nip each evening. Being a trader, with his own table and own wine casks, enough to last a year, enchanted him.

And so he met the great men of the American Fur Company, assessing them even as they assessed him. He met the bewhiskered red-faced master, Benton Marsh, natty in a blue uniform, and his mate, Trenholm. Marsh looked to be a choleric man, but one who smoothed things over out of long practice. Skye found himself peering into cold gray eyes, and felt a certain wariness.

He remained quiet, as was his wont, but Alexandre Bonfils was circulating gregariously, making friends, offering bon mots, and bragging not a bit modestly about the pelts he had acquired at great risk in the heart of Blackfoot country, pelts now resting in the bowels of the *Otter*.

At the stroke of eight, sounded by a handsome pendulum clock in a cherrywood cabinet, MacKenzie escorted his black-clad clerks and motley guests into his long dining room, where a splendid table awaited them. Here were furnishings Skye had not seen in the West, except at Fort Vancouver. A snowy linen cloth and napkins, elaborate silver, Limoges china, crystal goblets, a table groaning with condiments and awaiting the platters of food being prepared by all those pox-marked Assiniboine women.

MacKenzie seated them all by rank, the junior clerks at the far end of the great table, ascending to the most senior men and senior guests at the head of the table, above the salt. Skye and Captain Marsh were seated at MacKenzie's right and left, and that was how the trouble started.

"Ah, my friend Kenneth," said Bonfils, "how is it that Skye sits above me?"

MacKenzie reddened. "Because I have arranged it."

"But I am senior, monsieur," he said blandly.

"I believe, sir, that Mister Skye has been in the mountains far longer than you, and we are pleased here to honor that."

"Ah, you are mistaken. I have been in service to Pratte, Chouteau quite a bit longer than he has, having begun my engagement seven years since."

The room quieted. Young Bonfils, so well connected to the company's owners, was asserting rank.

MacKenzie, the strongest of men, decided to settle the matter. "My young friend, you are my guest here—"

"I will resolve this," said Skye. "Mister Bonfils, by all means, take this seat. I will join my wife."

Skye smiled gravely at this august assemblage, and walked slowly out the door.

6

Skye brushed off the trouble, but Victoria didn't.

"Why didn't you stay?" she asked in the quiet of their small chamber.

He threw a big hand over her and drew her tight. "Some men want rank," he said. "I don't worry about it."

"But dammit, Skye, you should have let the big chief MacKenzie decide."

"Maybe so," he said. "But I did what I did, and it's over."

"It's not. That man Bonfils, he will put this to good use. He will tell the world that you are not big man enough to be a trader."

Maybe she was right. He had felt something sinister brush him as lightly as a feather; something lurking just beyond his understanding.

After Bonfils's outburst, Skye had nodded at MacKenzie and stalked out while the others stared. MacKenzie had started to protest, but let him go. Bonfils was grinning amiably, and the instant Skye neared the door, the young rival edged toward the vacated place near the head of the table. Captain Marsh and the senior men seated at that table like a row of penguins had said nothing, but their gazes followed Skye.

He had headed for the mess hall where ordinary men

ate, and was able to catch a meal just as the cooks were clearing away the trenchers. No one there said anything either. He felt more comfortable among them than he did with those zealous men of rank and all their pretensions. There was something stinking and fraudulent about all that faked opulence, so far from the true seats of power and commerce. Everything had been imported, from the casks of wine to the table linens. The Assiniboine women decorating that post, tricked out in bright taffetas and the latest Paris styles, were there to foster the illusion of civilization, but they were merely concubines and servants, the company's pox-marked whores.

Skye dismissed the episode from mind; it was not important. Obviously, Bonfils regarded rank as something so important that he made a public protest. The man had a point: he had been with the Chouteau interests much longer than Skye had. And his trapping brigades had done brilliantly, bringing in more beaver than anyone else's. Maybe he deserved the honor. Maybe it was a passion of the very young, like Bonfils, to enjoy rank. He wore a medal on his chest, and had his family crest veneered to his equipage, so rank obviously meant everything to him, even a thousand miles from any world where rank meant something.

Had Skye casually thrown away the esteem of those substantial men when he bowed out? Company politics were new to him. He had never entertained ambition. He had been too busy surviving in a mountain wilderness even to consider advancement within the company. But now, suddenly, a trading position meant a great deal to him. With it, he would have a future. Without it . . . he didn't know.

Skye remembered his life in the Royal Navy, where he was the lowliest of the low. Rank had been important to everyone with any ambition, and men zealously guarded their rank, and all the manifestations of rank. A lord admiral wanted every honor and prerogative associated with his high position. Even a lowly jack tar might want the ship's company to know he had been in his majesty's service longer than those young whelps.

Skye breakfasted with the engagés the next dawn, and then watched the rivermen build fires in the boilers and get up steam. He watched intently as the deck hands boarded his saddle horses and penned them in a cage on the foredeck. Even as firemen started to build boiler steam, woodcutters were carrying the last of the cottonwood logs they had stacked bankside. An amazing eight or nine cords of firewood rested on the deck, handy to the firemen, and Skye wondered how long that would last. That riverboat would eat wood.

"Ah, so it's you, Skye," said Bonfils, drawing up beside. "An exciting adventure, *oui*?"

"It's Mister Skye, mate."

Bonfils laughed. "So I've heard. A fine cachet for a mountain man."

That sally from a man who wore a royal medal on his chest. Skye remained quiet. That *Mister* was, after all, the rank he had insisted on ever since escaping the Royal Navy.

"Well, *Mister* Skye, we missed you last night. Talk turned to weighty things, including the future of the fur business, the decline of beaver, the advances in firearms, the sonnets of Shakespeare, the means by which redskins can be persuaded to part with furs and pelts for less and less of value, and the ultimate ownership of Oregon. I ventured the opinion that anything dyed a gaudy color, no matter how trifling its value, would fetch a good price from the savages, and I must say, the gentlemen at table largely applauded my observation. But I suppose those things are not of any consequence. You aren't a citizen, I gather, and have no interest in the republic or its commerce, or in belles lettres either."

"And how would you conduct trade at Fort Cass, Mister Bonfils?"

"*Monsieur* Bonfils, if you can manage it. I am for profit, by whatever means, and so I loudly proclaimed. Why hire trappers and hunters when we can engage the Indians to do these, for the price of a few dyed turkey feathers?"

Skye began to grasp the sharp-edged drift of banter like this, and dismissed the young man. "It's time to fetch my wife, sir."

He headed back to the post, hearing Bonfils's easy chuckle behind him.

MacKenzie stood just inside the post, and hailed him:

"Mister Skye—"

"Mister MacKenzie, don't apologize. Young men seek their moment of glory. I had a fine buffalo feast with the engagés."

"No, that doesn't do. I regret the whole business." He hesitated, and then spoke. "If you had stood your ground, I would have made it clear who's the host and who's commanding the post. You would have given me a chance to say a thing or two."

MacKenzie offered a meaty hand, and Skye shook it.

Skye found Victoria in their gloomy room, perched on the soft bed which owed its comfort to its tick, which was stuffed with the thick beards of buffalos. Her cheeks were wet. No Name, their yellow mutt, sat at her feet guarding her against a world neither liked.

"Victoria—"

"Dammit, Skye! Something bad's gonna happen! Maybe we won't see the mountains again!"

He knew enough to keep quiet. Over the years he had come to understand her mysterious, sometimes uncanny sense of the future, something she called her medicine. Her spirit helper, the magpie, often darted before her, telling her what lay ahead. And now she sat on the edge

of the bed, her honeyed cheeks wet with tears and fore-
boding.

"You may be right," he said. "Riverboats get into trouble fast. Boilers blow. They snag. Some catch fire. They're
always trouble—"

She pressed his hand and stood. "Dammit, we'll be
late."

He lifted two battered parfleches, and she grabbed two
others, and thus they transported most of their worldly
possessions through the yard of the post, out the narrow
gate, and down the steep grade to the levee, where the
Otter rocked and vibrated like a rabid wolf. A palpable
fear swept over Victoria, but she walked determinedly beside her man, and they boarded amidships, on a gangway.
The dog sulked, bristled, and followed, sniffing the deck
and everything on it, and then wet some firewood.

Bedlam prevailed. Everywhere, engagés and sailors
were loading goods; buffalo haunches for the cooks, bales
of buffalo robes and deerskins and elk hides which had to
be lowered with a boom and spars and tackle into the low
hold, where another crew pushed and hauled the cargo to
spead its weight evenly. A cabin boy threw a pail of slop
overboard. A crew rolled casks of water aboard, not to
drink but to replenish the boilers.

Skye and Victoria found their way aft to a cramped
cabin and entered it, finding several small compartments
around a central hall where meals would be served on
folding tables. There was a small woman's compartment
aft, farthest from the boilers and thus the safest, but Victoria scorned that and chose to bunk with her man.

The quarters were spartan, trimmed in oak but walled
with plank. A small glassed window provided the only
light. A simple washstand with an enameled tin basin and
pitcher supplied the only bath.

No Name whined, sniffed the corners, and vanished
into the cabin, and then out the door onto the deck, where

he sat, quivering with dread. Skye followed him, feeling suffocated by that tiny dark compartment, and knowing that Victoria would snarl at him if he stayed longer. She was plainly having a bad time of it, wrestling with a thousand new things as well as a terror beyond describing.

Now he could hear the rumble of the firebox and smell the billowing smoke as it descended over the vessel. The escapement pipe, which released used steam, began to pop and hiss as the boat turned into a living thing, a monster trembling on the great hawsers that pinned it to Fort Union.

A crowd gathered at the bank; the gaudy Assiniboine women in their finery, the engagés, mostly wearing leather and wool, the breed children scooting about, the black-clad monkish clerks, and scores of tribesmen and their squaws solemnly wrapped in blankets to ward off a sharp dawn chill, the low sun gilding their bronze faces.

Skye had put his mealtime with the ship's company to good use, asking innumerable questions. This riverboat ran 120 feet and needed four feet of draft loaded, which was too much, especially with the river lowering almost daily as the spring floods receded. There would be sandbars just a foot below water level, sinister sawyers, the broken limbs of sunken trees, waiting to tear the hull apart, currents whipping the boat into rocks and obstacles, and always the desperate need of wood.

Ten cords each day this monster burned. And many hundreds of miles along the Missouri where there was not a tree in sight. A single trip up the river and back consumed the wood of over fifteen hundred trees: hardwoods down near St. Louis; softer woods, such as the prolific cottonwoods and willows upstream. A full load of wood weighed thirty to forty tons.

Then, suddenly, a shrieking whistle blew, and the mate bellowed in the megaphone. No Name laid back his head and howled. Captain Marsh stood on the upper deck, called the texas, and watched his sailors loosen the hawsers.

Skye marveled that such a complex piece of equipment could pierce so far into utter wilderness. From the jackstaff a triangular American Fur Company pennant fluttered, and a Stars and Stripes hung from its staff at the rear. There were shouts, men winding hawsers on capstans, and then the boat shuddered free and into the swift cold current, its speed sickening.

Victoria caught his hand and squeezed it. The dog bristled. The cannonade of the escapement pipe deafened them now as the wheels rumbled inside their housing and thrashed the river. Fort Union began to shrink into a blurred blue horizon.

Up above, standing next to Captain Marsh like the Angel Gabriel, was Alexandre Bonfils, whose uncles owned this vessel.

7

Alexandre Bonfils lounged beside the helmsman in the pilothouse seething with importance. He had perched himself at this lofty station so that he might view the passing world from the best perspective, yet didn't see the shaggy old buffalo bull lapping water at the bank, or the soaring golden eagle, or the kingfisher diving for minnows, or the stretching green distances of the northern plains, as the river passed through mysteries.

His vision was focused elsewhere, no matter what the world brought to his empty gaze. He wanted that position at Fort Cass, and knew he could not win it unless he took certain measures. Fort Cass wasn't much of a post, merely a satellite of Fort Union, and the Crows didn't do a large trade. But it was the only trading position available because there were so many senior men, all veterans, in the company; the only one likely to open in the next several years, the only one that would advance his ambitions. Some day, he would take over the firm from his mother's cousin, Pierre Chouteau, and be the Emperor of the West, and the Prince of St. Louis.

He had been a brigade leader, but what did it matter? Any seasoned mountaineer, like the barbarous Skye, could reach that position with a few trapping and survival skills, and a way with men.

But being the factor at a trading post, being a licensed trader for the company, that was something else. A trader was advanced up the chain of command if he did well. A trader could swiftly take his share of the profits and retire in St. Louis a wealthy man, high in the ranks of the fur company, an annual annuity comforting him. A trader operated a wilderness enterprise, lived in solid comfort within a building instead of freezing or boiling or starving or thirsting or running from savages. A trader was a weighty man, not some hireling bought and sold by the company. A trader was noticed; an engagé lived in obscurity. And a trader could do whatever he had to do far from prying eyes, the sovereign of his own kingdom.

He knew all about traders, having grown up in the business. The man who put his thumb in the cup while measuring out sugar or flour or whiskey or coffee was the man who tweaked a profit. The man who watered the second or third gill of spirits sold to the savages was the man who got good robes at less cost. The man who sent agents skulking into the night to bribe chiefs away from the opposition was the man who got the furs. The company that sold cheap cast-iron hatchets and axes, instead of steel ones, was the outfit that pocketed the profits, not only from the cheaper tools, but because the savages returned again and again for more soft-metal tools. Poor red devils never grasped the difference.

It all amused him.

Bien. He would be a trader, and it would not matter that Skye was senior in years and experience. Skye would be dealt with, and that is what occupied his every thought, even as he stared, unseeing, at a stationary horsed Indian on a distant bluff, without seeing the man; why he scarcely noted the riverboat slowing and stopping. Why he didn't watch the steersman in the yawl row ahead, make soundings, and then direct the packet toward a newly washed channel where the riverboat would not ground on a bar.

It would have struck a stranger observing Bonfils that this was an odd man, stationed exactly where he could see everything, but gazing on the day's events with a blind eye. Bonfils didn't even hear the quiet exchanges between the pilot, the captain, and the helmsman as they negotiated a dangerous passage where the murky Missouri broadened, the shifting sands built new barriers, and murderous sawyers, dead trees, lurked just out of sight under the placid sun-washed surface of the river.

How much did Skye know, and how much would he tell in St. Louis? It came down to that. A word from Skye would carry weight in the Gateway to the West. Bonfils had no illusions about family connections. The fur trade was exacting, brutal, cruel, risky, and precarious. Pierre Chouteau and General Bernard Pratte wanted the best men in the field; profit depended on it. Men without an excess of honor, which certainly qualified him.

He laughed softly. Being a relative wouldn't count for much, at least not at a certain level of responsibility. The hard-eyed seigneurs who ran the Upper Missouri Outfit would not permit mere blood or lineage to affect their choice—but neither would his connections hurt him. The company was closely held.

Alexandre Bonfils had advanced with breathtaking speed; a brigade leader after only one year in the mountains! And now he would be celebrated as the man who brought the most beaver packs to St. Louis, a fortune snugged in the gut of this riverboat!

But certain matters needed to be concealed, and certain rumors squelched. He had no way of knowing how much Skye knew, or what the gossips at the rendezvous had been whispering, or how much of all that Skye would drone into the ear of old Pierre Chouteau, thus ending

Bonfils's career in the mountains, and his hopes of being a dashing dauphin of Creole society in St. Louis, with an unending supply of supple and eager mademoiselles to brighten his life and warm his bed.

Both the Chouteaus and the Prattes knew why he had escaped to the distant fur country in the first place at the tender age of seventeen. He had gotten Marie Therese Lachine with child, and faced with marrying or fleeing St. Louis for the fur country, he had fled, spending time clerking at Fort Clark and Fort Pierre before drifting west to the beaver country.

He was a father, but had never seen the child, for the maiden had swiftly been sent downriver to Baton Rouge, where she was hastily married to a Robidoux cousin. What a relief! He might have been stuck with that whiny and simpering little snip for the rest of his life. All she had to offer was a pubescent sweetness, which no doubt had already vanished under layers of lard. He smiled. He fancied that the little episode had made a man out of him. It would not count against him. What man in the mountains hadn't just that sort of difficulty in his past?

He spotted Skye leaning over the beak of the boat, watching the mysterious river eddy by, the man's black beaver hat glued to his unkempt locks. What a comic figure the barrel-shaped man was, ruffian to the core, ill-kempt, his body webbed with scars, his little pig eyes caught between a glacier of a nose. And yet the man evoked fear in Bonfils. That disreputable slug from the Royal Navy had hamlike fists that could pulverize a foe, a catlike grace that belied his awkward top-heavy carcass, and a withering stare that caused most men to turn away.

But that wasn't what evoked fear in Bonfils. There was something uncompromising about Skye; something simple and solid and unyielding that set the man apart. Skye would do what he had to do, and say what he had to say, without a scintilla of social grace or cunning. Maybe it was some sort of brutal honesty, exactly the sort of transparency that Bonfils detested in a man. He himself was more civilized and saw life's nuances.

He wasn't sure just why he feared Skye. He didn't fear anyone else. And that fear cropped up every time he encountered Skye, turning him into pudding.

Skye probably knew everything there was to know about Bonfils; all the rumors, all the gossip that passed quietly from man to man in the mountains, especially when they were sharing a jug of mountain whiskey. He would know . . . about the dead Blackfeet. He would know . . . about the losses of trappers. He would know . . . about killing the Piegan woman. He would know . . . about that business with the five Cheyenne women. He would know about the sly coup against the Hudson's Bay Company, and how he snatched twenty-three packs of beaver just by taking them when the fools weren't looking. Surely he would know everything, and that was rankling Bonfils now, as he stared down upon his fellow passenger.

Maybe Skye hadn't heard a word.

A shudder ran through the boat, followed by a lurch, and then sudden immobility. The *Otter* had struck something.

From his aerie he watched deckhands peer over the bow, beside Skye. One had a pole, and when he thrust it into the brown water, it hit bottom only eighteen inches or two feet down. They were grounded. Men peered over the side, looking for damage. Others scurried down the hatch, seeing whether they were taking water. Behind him he heard the captain and the pilot shouting directions. He heard a clank and a thunk, and then the snap and hiss of steam rattling out of the escapement pipe, and the rumble of the pistons. The paddle wheels thrashed thunderously, churning up foam. The *Otter* backed away from the bar, and soon floated free.

These crewmen knew what to do. They lowered the yawl from its davits and the steersman and his fellows began taking soundings, looking for passage around that new sandbar, a barrier that hadn't existed only a few weeks before when the boat had thrashed upriver. The riverboat slowly backed upstream, propelled by the reversed paddle wheels, and waited for the crew in the yawl to find a way, if a channel existed.

Bonfils didn't much care. What was all this to him? He studied Skye, who was observing the whole operation with the experienced eye of a seaman.

Bonfils knew suddenly how to proceed. He badly needed to befriend Skye, share confidences, reveal the soul, and maybe find out what Skye knew or suspected; find out what his adversary would do in St. Louis—if he ever reached St. Louis. There might be an accident, man overboard in the night, plainly drunk. And his squaw too, dead from the effort to save her lout of a man. Bonfils had a splendid cache of Kentucky bourbon in his kit; maybe he could put it to use.

He smiled. Who could offer more bonhomie than the young man who had invented the art? He abandoned his post near the helmsman, tipped his straw hat to the mate, and clattered down the companionway to the boiler deck. Bonfils then went forward to the place where Skye leaned over the rail, his moccasined foot on the coaming, his shoulder pressed against the jackstaff, his mutt watching warily.

"Ah, there you are. A close call, eh, Mister Skye?"

Skye nodded, his gaze quietly measuring his fellow passenger.

"They know how to proceed. I imagine they'll find the channel, and we'll be off."

"What brings you down from the pilothouse, mate?"

"We haven't really had a chance to talk, *mon ami*. I want you to know that whoever is chosen, I will abide amiably with the decision of the company officers. You're a man I've always admired, Mister Skye."

"What do you want?"

Bonfils laughed. The man was so crude. "Want? We have a fortnight of travel before us, time to enjoy the adventure. Perhaps we'll shoot buffalo together, or drop ducks for our supper, or saddle these horses and hunt . . ."

Skye didn't reply. The crew in the yawl had found deep water, and he was watching them jab their sounding pole deep into the river, and measure an opening for the ship.

"Actually," Bonfils said, "I've always regarded you as my mentor, and studied your ways. You're a legend, Mister Skye, and now at last I have a chance to learn more about you, how you think, what you do, how you approach the company throne at St. Louis . . . and what advice you have for a poor, young supplicant."

Skye shrugged, his smile contained. "I'll meet them, we'll palaver, and they'll decide," he said. "And so will I."

In that artless answer, Bonfils found menace.

8

Through much of that first day on the river, Skye suffered the unwanted company of the young brigade leader. Bonfils made a show of patrolling the vessel, acquainting himself with its operations, but sooner or later he arrived again at Skye's side, there to flatter the older man with small, adroit compliments, admiration that Skye supposed was more feigned than real, and all of that combined with a peculiar humility, in which Bonfils derided his own skills while inflating those of the man next to him.

Skye had had no experience with flatterers; they were unknown in the mountains, and he had never heard a word of flattery aimed in his direction during all the time he spent in the Royal Navy. But here was this honey-tongued Creole admiring Skye's hunting skills, his ability to survive in bad weather, his handling of tough scrapes, his skilled dealing with Indians, his bluntness. The man had plainly inquired about Skye, and seemed to know more about Skye than Skye knew about himself.

What did it mean? Skye imagined that the young man wanted his approval; maybe a kind word given to General Pratte or Pierre Chouteau. Maybe he wanted to find out something to use against Skye.

At one point, Skye pointed at a distant cliff where half a dozen Indian women stood.

"Ah! What fine vision you have, Monsieur. I would not have seen such a sight, myself."

"I think you would have, Mister Bonfils."

"Ah! No. Now I am beginning to understand why you are a legend in the mountains. You see around corners and over the brow of hills, to the war party lurking on the other side."

Skye felt annoyed, but held his peace. Whatever Bonfils was up to would become clear in due course. In the space of half an afternoon, Skye had received more compliments than had come his way over an entire life.

But once in a while, Bonfils probed a bit. "What are your plans, Monsieur? If you become a trader, I would envy you. A good life, settled in a comfortable place, *oui*?"

"Yes, a good life. I would see to it that the company has the loyalty of my wife's people . . . and I would see to it that they receive good value for the skins and furs they bring me. The Crows aren't numerous, and they need weapons and powder and everything else white traders offer. The Sioux and Blackfeet outnumber them. So, sir, my loyalties would be evenly divided between the company, and the Crows."

Bonfils smiled brightly. *"Quell magnifique!"* he said, but Skye knew that his own words would be used against him in the privy chambers of St. Louis, where profit mattered most and fairness to the Indians was a consideration only so far as to keep their allegiance. But he would not alter his position.

He was a stubborn man. If he traded with Victoria's people, he would see to it that they were generously treated. There would be no fingers or thumbs in a measuring cup, and no extra river water in the spirits, and no weaseling down the price of good furs placed on the trading counter, in order to pay less. Not for Victoria's people. Not for any people, anywhere, ever.

The *Otter* rounded a sweeping bend flowing between low gloomy bluffs, and headed for a notch on the left bank where the green of a wooded patch bloomed brightly in an ochre world. The vessel slowed, and the thunder of the wheels muted into a soft sloshing, and the rattle of steam popping out of the escapement dwindled to a mutter.

"Wood stop," yelled the mate. "All able men report."

Skye had heard of these episodes. The crew and every male passenger would soon be debarked at that patch of trees, to chop, saw, cut and haul seven or eight cords of firewood aboard.

"Ah! A chance to stretch!" Bonfils said.

Skye wondered whether the young man would contribute. These wood stops would be a good test of a passenger's character. There would be slackers, and there would be workers, and he wondered which category Bonfils would fill!.

The boat drifted into shore, and bumped gently into the bottom. Two boatmen, one fore, one aft, slipped into the muddy river and waded ashore, carrying manila hawsers, which they tied to tree stumps. Other deckmen lowered a gangplank. It didn't quite reach shore, so they added a few loose scantlings to the gangway until a small dry passage ran from the coaming to the grassy riverbank.

A deckhand gave each parting crewman an axe or a saw, and the crew, save for the master and pilot and engineers and firemen, fanned into the cottonwoods and willows and box elders.

Skye received a huge two-man crosscut saw, and headed onto shore.

"Monsieur, that's a two-man saw; we can work together," Bonfils said, catching up.

Skye grunted.

Behind him, the last of the crewmen abandoned the vessel, and he saw Victoria slip down to land, along with No Name, and begin to hike upslope. He knew her thinking: here were all these stupid white men cutting wood, vulnerable, not knowing who or what lay just over the brow of those yellow bluffs. She would look. That was her nature, bred into her by generations of her ancestors, whose life and safety depended on just such caution. He blessed her and loved her. Maybe, on one of these wood-cutting stops, her vigilance would spare them disaster.

Four deckmen with axes headed for green trees and began girdling them, chipping through bark and cortical fibre so that these trees would be dead and dry next riverboating season. But the rest headed for the gray skeletons of trees killed the previous year and now ready to fell and burn.

"*Ici, monsieur,*" Bonfils said, pointing at a gray giant that once was a noble cottonwood.

Skye stared up at the noble ruin, a tree so grand he was sure a dozen cords of firewood might be gotten from it. But it was close to other less noble trees, and would be dangerous to fell so close to so many toiling men.

"Maybe we'd better pick something smaller. It'd take an hour just to saw through that trunk," Skye said.

"We shall do it. We shall show them what we're made of."

"That's what I'm hoping to avoid," Skye said gently.

Nonetheless, Bonfils grabbed one end of the long saw and stationed himself beyond the gray trunk. Skye peered about, decided a warning or two would clear the area before the tree fell, and they began to work.

Bonfils didn't shrink or slack. The saw bit fiercely through cottonwood as they scraped it back and forth. They cut a notch in the direction they hoped the tree would fall, and then attacked the other side, the keen-edged saw ripping noisily into the dry wood. Skye began to sweat, even in the coolness of the woods.

In the distance he saw Victoria clamber the last fifty feet to the edge of the bluff and stand there, a tiny statue against an azure sky, with No Name beside her. She was beautiful, he thought; a guardian of her family, and all these other blind white men.

A breeze eddied through the woods, carrying the scent of grass and sun and the day's heat. Bonfils sawed furiously, and Skye wondered whether the man regarded this as some sort of competition; whether the man, in his own soul, would brag to himself that night about how he sawed harder and produced more than old Skye. How odd that was to Skye. How odd that Bonfils had to prove himself, if that was what he was doing.

The cottonwood teetered on its dwindling base, and Skye shouted at the deckmen nearby, pointing the way the giant would fall. For his efforts he received only curses: it meant that the deckmen would have to abandon their own valuable labor, and perhaps deal with the giant tree. Skye privately cursed his luck, and vowed never to let Bonfils draw him into trouble again.

They sawed furiously while the sweating and sullen sailors backed away, and then with a creak and a snap, the giant toppled down, carrying four smaller trees with it. The crash shook the earth, and caused others to pause fearfully, until the mate roared at them to get busy.

Just as Skye expected, the downed giant was so tangled with the lesser trees that the hands had no choice but to cut up the larger one. Skye heard them muttering; the blame came in his direction, and he owned up to it. It had been a stupid and vainglorious act to fell that tree.

But swiftly, the experienced crew hacked and sawed the giant into usable pieces, most of them four-foot lengths that could be stuffed whole into the fireboxes under the twin boilers. A crew toted the heavy logs aboard, while the firemen arranged them into neat stacks adjacent to the maw of the hungry fireboxes.

The trunk of the giant cottonwood was so thick it was useless, so the crew reduced the limbs until there were no more, and then returned to their own felling, their glances sharp and unkind. If Bonfils had attempted to cover himself with glory this afternoon, he had failed.

Within an hour, the teeming crewmen had loaded all the wood aboard that the ship could hold. Skye stood, sweating, as he watched the last of the limbs and trunks go up the wobbly planks. Some short blasts of the whistle alerted those on land, including Victoria, who had returned to the riverbank. She and No Name boarded, the dog sniffing every stanchion and post. Skye reached over and petted the yellow dog, his boon companion along a thousand wild trails, and the dog licked his hand.

Silently, keeping her thoughts to herself, Victoria studied the ruin of that wooded notch in the bluff, the site of a tiny spring-fed creek, and then she wordlessly headed aft to the fantail, the place she had anointed for herself, even as Skye had chosen the prow. It was as if he loved the future, while she clung to the past. He didn't doubt that this trip was a disturbing change in her life; she was witnessing great changes, and knew that these things would soon disrupt the ancient, timeless traditions of her people.

Two short blasts of the whistle. The deckmen loosened the hawsers and scrambled aboard even as deckhands slid the gangway past the coaming. The ship drifted free, soon was tugged by the current, and then Skye heard the great splash of the paddle wheels rumbling inside the wheelhouses and felt the vessel shudder.

Bonfils had vanished somewhere. Skye headed for the prow, where he hoped to cool off. But a deckman waylaid him.

"The master wishes to speak to you, sir."

Skye clambered up the companionway to the pilothouse and found Marsh.

"Mister Skye," Marsh said without preamble. "We

think perhaps you lack experience felling firewood. You dropped a tree with a worthless trunk—much too large for us to use—and disrupted the work of a dozen men. Some judgment is involved in collecting the wood."

Skye nodded.

"From now on, sir, please report to Haines when we fetch wood. He's the one down there at the capstan. He's a veteran riverman, and he will put you to more productive use."

Skye started to salute, and then remembered he was not in the Royal Navy anymore. "As you wish, Captain," he said, and retreated, his thoughts focused on that clever Bonfils and his schemes. Marsh's opinion of Skye would count in St. Louis.

9

So many were the mysteries of the white man that Victoria thought she could never fathom them all. The greatest of all mysteries was the absence of white women. Before she had boarded the fireboat, she thought maybe she would find white women on it, but that proved to be wrong.

That was puzzling, because Skye had told her that white women were frail and lived in houses. Here was a house on water, with rooms for frail women, but she saw none at all. Only men. Somewhere, there had to be white women, unless these white men sprang from the bosom of the earth, or were borne here by strange beasts who lived in the East. Were there such things as white children? She had never seen those, either. Aiee! What a strange tribe these pale men were!

She was determined to get to the bottom of this, and hoped that in this place of many houses, St. Louis, all might be revealed at last.

The fireboat wasn't a mystery. That first day she had gingerly studied it; had seen how the roaring fire in the metal box had made steam, which was captured in a great iron kettle until it acquired great power, and she saw how this great power drove the paddles and made this fireboat go against the wind, against the current, against nature, wherever the white men made it go. That was no mystery at all.

But Captain Marsh was a mystery. The Big Chief of this fireboat wore a costume of dark blue, plainer than any other costume. He wore a small cap with a little beak on it, but that was dark blue also, and without honors. If he was the Big Chief, why did he wear no honors? Where were the marks that told the world that he was the Big Chief? No feathers or quills or beads or paint. No stripes or chevrons. He did wear a close-cropped brown beard, trimmed almost daily to the contours of his red face, she supposed. But he never painted his face and never carried a lance or shield or staff. He wore nothing around his neck; no bear claws like her man Skye; nor an amulet.

He should be acting like a chief; wearing eagle feathers, painting his face. He should begin each day as father sun climbs over the horizon by seeking his medicine from the sacred medicine-givers, and then exhorting the men under him, pacing back and forth, his oratory inspiring them to make this great steamboat go forth into the world. But he did none of these things.

And instead of inspiring his men to great efforts and feats, he said almost nothing, and with hard eyes, merely watched everyone from his aerie they called the pilot-house. If he was commanding, why didn't he command? And yet, somehow, his will got done and that too was a mystery. How did those sailors know what to do when no one was telling them? Did white men have some secret sign language she didn't know?

She had asked Skye this and he had laughed, and she had gotten angry at him. He explained that the men knew what to do without being told. But that didn't explain the mystery. What made them do it if no one told them to?

She and No Name had padded about, learning everything they could about this strange boat. No one paid her the slightest heed, except Bonfils, who eyed her with frank admiration and invitation, as if he wanted to sample Skye's woman! No, the machinery was no mystery. It was wondrous, but she understood it. She understood the speaking tube by which Marsh directed the engineers to do something. She understood the black metal chimneys that drew the smoke up. She understood the davits that raised or lowered the little yawl. She understood the six-pound brass swivel cannon that was like Skye's rifle but bigger, and made much more noise. It could slay twenty men at once, and she feared it.

Once she understood, she stopped worrying so much. Magpie, her spirit helper, hopped along the riverbanks, or flew over, keeping an eye out. Her fears diminished, and now she began to enjoy the boat, and study the mysterious shores of the river, where unseen eyes studied the boat as it passed.

That evening Captain Marsh stopped at a long wooded island, which afforded fuel and protection from marauders. She knew exactly what to do. No sooner had the gangway been lowered than she took the haltered Skye horses out of their pen on the foredeck, and led them down to the island. They drank thirstily, and she could see the muscles of their necks working the water up their throats and into their bellies. There was plenty of good grass there, and no place for the horses to go, so she would let them graze all night if Captain Marsh permitted it.

These were good Crow ponies, selected with care by Skye and her family. The Crows were the finest horsemen of the northern plains, and these horses could carry Skye's bulky body easily, and heavy packs as well. They weren't the fastest horses in the great Crow herd, but they were chosen for a more valuable trait: endurance. They would continue onward, while fast horses faded. They could run away from trouble, and there were times when she and Skye had been grateful for their strength.

They had hooves of iron, and never grew footsore even on gravel and rock, unlike so many of the horses brought from the land of the white men. And they could make a living on almost anything green, and didn't need all the grain and hay required by white men's ponies. Good horses had saved their lives, and would again, which is why Skye and Victoria treated them well.

In the soft summer twilight, the crew and passengers cut firewood. Here were willows and cottonwoods, and a great heap of driftwood at the upper end of the island, awaiting the axe and saw. They made short work of the task. There would be ample wood to fire up the boilers the next morning.

And they could sleep this night without a guard, because the river protected them. Deep channels isolated the island from the sere and lonely plains beyond. She strolled the island, relishing the feel of soft, warm earth beneath her moccasins, rejoicing that she had survived this day upon the fireboat without mishap. Skye finished his woodcutting and joined her while the cooks prepared a meal.

"Marsh says we can hunt tomorrow, you and I; he'll put us ashore with the horses, hour or two before they launch. Trick is to keep up. That boat's traveling fast, downstream, we have to stay ahead of it. If we shoot a deer or a buffalo, we should try to drag it to the bank. They'll see it and send a yawl for it. He said his hunter, Drouillard, hasn't had luck. He has a crew to feed. Tomorrow he'll put Drouillard on the left bank and we'll take the right."

"Ah, dammit Skye, I like that."

"So will our animals," he said. "No Name will get himself a run; the horses never did like that pen and all that noise."

"We got damn good horses, Skye."

He peered into a lavender twilight, pensively. "When I first came to this country, I didn't know a good horse or a bad one, and didn't care. Now I care more than anything else except for you and that worthless dog. Someday, I'd like to train up a colt my way, make him do what few horses do. Teach him how to make war, and when to run, and how to run. Get your brother and father to help me."

"My brother can teach a horse those things."

"Then we'll give him a gift and have him start a colt for me when we get back."

She loved those moments with Skye. They were bonded so closely that often they knew each other's thoughts without speaking a word.

The next idyllic days, she and Skye hunted the right bank of the river, plunging into giant coulees, topping bluffs, poking into copses of willow or cottonwood, under a cloudless azure dome of heaven. No Name slithered ahead, pretending not to notice or care, but pointing at game, or stopping cold to signal his allies—no one would ever accuse No Name of being part of Skye's family—of the presence of something or other nearby.

But hunting for a river packet proved frustrating. Twice they shot a buck and dragged it to shore, only to see the faint smoke of the vessel far downstream. Once they shot a pronghorn only to scare away several elk they hadn't seen.

By nightfall of the first day of hunting they were thoroughly humiliated, and the thought of returning to the vessel empty handed gnawed on them. Then, No Name stiffened, and she saw a buffalo cow and calf watering in a slough back from the mighty river. Skye shot them both, the boom of his Hawken echoing hollowly in the silent wild. They approached the dying cow gingerly; buffalo were dangerous. But she was supine, and leaking blood from a chest wound into the waters of the slough, lying in a bed of crushed sedges. The calf had died instantly, and lay on muddy land.

They rode to the riverbank just in time to hail the boat,

which was probing through the waning light as Marsh looked for a place to anchor and refuel.

The yawl showed up promptly, and a crew of six cook's helpers and deckmen began butchering the massive buffalo while Skye and Victoria mounted to the ridge to keep watch. This was dangerous country, not a place to be caught off guard. The *Otter* slid as close as the channel allowed, and idled there at anchor in the purling purple waters, while the cook's crew butchered, nipping and tugging back the bug-ridden hide, cutting the huge tongue out, and then sawing the tender flank meat, and the delicious hump ribs, the most succulent part of the bison. No Name sat patiently next to the butchering and was rewarded with offal, which he devoured gluttonously to the sound of boatmen's laughter. From the hurricane deck, the tight-lipped Captain Marsh watched silently, and Victoria felt ill at ease whenever she glanced at that man.

"Ah, we'll feast tonight!" bellowed a deckhand. "Fat cow! And it was them Skyes that finally brought in the meat!"

Victoria sat on her restless horse above, a lone mortal on a mournful sunset ridge, listening to them rejoice below, knowing that one buffalo and one calf wouldn't feed the men on that boat more than a day. The fireboat slaughtered wood and buffalo. White men lived prodigiously.

"Cap'ain says there's an anchorage mile down," the cook yelled up at them.

Skye nodded.

But the next day, Marsh called off the hunt.

"We'll reach the Minnetaree villages tomorrow," he told them. "They like to trade for corn and vegetables, and they usually have plenty of meat, too."

Victoria seethed with excitement. These people called themselves the Hidatsa, and they were ancient friends of the Absaroka, her people, and spoke a tongue so close they could understand one another. They lived in houses of mounded earth, and raised crops, and hunted buffalo, and were allied with the Mandans, just downstream.

"Is that not the people of Amalie, Bonfils's woman?" she asked, knowing the answer but testing Skye.

"Believe it is," Skye said neutrally.

"I wonder why he didn't bring her here," she said, wanting to gossip.

"We'll know tomorrow," he said. "Alexandre will be among his wife's people. See his wife's family."

Victoria felt a chill creep through her.

10

As the *Otter* rounded a bend, Alexandre Bonfils beheld the largest of the Hidatsa villages on the right bank of the Missouri. He had been there before; it was Amalie's home. The arrival of the steamboat excited these bronzed agricultural people who mostly wore white men's cloth, and they flocked to the riverbank. There would be fevered trading and excitement and dances to celebrate this wondrous event.

The river packet was too distant for him to make out faces; he would have to wait. Amalie's large and powerful family and clan would be present, as would the man she had been married to before Alexandre wandered into the compound of earth-mound communal houses. That brainless hulking brute, a village soldier, would not welcome him. The thought evoked some merriment in him. He had pilfered her from him just for amusement. She had been a gorgeous young mademoiselle, sloe-eyed, of sinuous figure, with a bold gaze and a come-hither smile embedded in her coppery cheeks. He had known at a glance she was his for the taking.

But that had been the easiest part of it. Fending off the affronted husband, if indeed these savages actually married, proved to be more entertaining. The Hidatsa cuckold had not been content to fight alone, but had sent kin and clan after Alexandre, including Amalie's brothers, one of whom had met his demise in a small hollow in the prairie, where Alexandre had ambushed him; the hunted stalking the hunter.

So this visit would be an adventure. He loved adventure and danger, and never felt fully alive unless he was walking the edge of some abyss. He provoked danger, sought it out like a lover, and toyed with it, which is why some of his more timid confreres in the fur business avoided his brigades, even though his luck held and always would because the advantage always fell to the audacious.

Little did Marsh know that there was bad blood between one of his passengers and these Minnetaree people, bad enough blood to evoke a pitched fight if it came to that, which Bonfils hoped would be plain to Marsh. He had plans and ambitions.

Alexandre was the last of seven children, of whom four still lived. His mother had cried, Enough! and taken refuge in a separate bedroom. From then on his father had seemed distant to the child, and was more and more absent from the white porticoed redbrick family manse on Rue Papin, for reasons unfathomable to one so young. His mama, Alexia, had indulged him wantonly, a fact he appreciated only because of the whining and pouting of his older siblings, who had not seen their every whim gratified the way this youngest and last child was cosseted.

So he had grown up unchallenged and thus bored, and swiftly discovered that life in St. Louis, where he was a dauphin of the merchant class, awakened his senses only when he was doing something absolutely scandalous, such as seducing Creole virgins or in one case a plain and swooning convent novitiate, or drinking absinthe in waterfront dens while fondling the lush hard breasts of serving girls, or copulating with languorous and gorgeous

black slave women in the carriage houses of his Creole
friends.

Now, as the boat slowed and the steersman eased it toward the right bank, he anticipated new amusements, and
perhaps a chance to make impressions. He headed for the
rail and stood prominently there, a dark, bright, insouci-
ant figure who would galvanize attention on the shore, as
soon as one or another of Amalie's clan discovered him.

This early July day had scorched every scrap of moisture out of the close air; the heat bore down like rolling
thunder over the dun earth-mound houses and the tawny
fields of maize and squash and melons and tobacco. It
raised mirages and made images waver drunkenly. The
crowd of virtually naked brown males and bare-breasted
brown-fleshed women rippled with excitement as the
Otter hove to, and seamen cast anchor well out. Marsh
had said he always traded well away from shore, for safety's sake. There was little forty crewmen and a few passengers could do against four or five hundred visitors, if a
showdown ever came. The dugout canoes of the village
would ration visitors and impose some sort of control.

A shrill blast of the whistle paralyzed the Indians for a
moment, and then they danced and jostled their way to
the riverbank, a hideous gallimaufry of savages, many of
them carrying woven baskets laden with maize and other
grains and fruits. On board, the mate and a few sailors
doubling as clerks were organizing a trading store, with
blankets, bright bolts of cloth, packets of vermillion, sugar,
knives, awls, axes and hatchets, beads strung in loops,
and assorted smoothbore muskets and flintlock rifles
for hunters, all of it jamming the foredeck near Skye's
horses.

A dozen dugouts, each hollowed from a giant cottonwood log, launched simultaneously, chocked with Hidatsi
people, the men with pomaded hair rising high above

their faces, the women with straight jet hair hanging loosely over golden shoulders.

Bonfils discovered Victoria Skye staring at him, her face guarded. But what did she know? If he couldn't have a Hidatsa girl tonight, after lubricating matters with a little good whiskey from his silver flask, he might try her.

Even as the first wave of dugouts sped across the choppy blue waters of the river, other craft were being prepared, as these river-dwelling people brought baskets of maize, or haunches of buffalo swarming with flies, or dead fowl hanging on a pole by their legs, to the floating store on the foredeck.

Marsh nodded to several sailors who were standing at the gangway, ready to board a few dozen Hidatsa at a time. The traders—experienced men, Bonfils thought— had swiftly set up their shop, even including some bushels and a scales.

"About twenty at a time," Marsh yelled through a megaphone from the pilothouse.

They swarmed in, the dugouts nosing into the low coaming of the riverboat, and clambered aboard, some on the gangway, but most simply over the rail or under it.

Bonfils knew the tongue.

"Ah, we shall buy a knife! Oh, look at that blanket. I will sleep warm in the winter! Ah, what will they give me for a basket of corn?" The women were gabby; the men taciturn, lithely patrolling the deck of the boat, their quick knowing gazes settling on the heaped firewood, the horses, the master watching these proceedings with caution, the Skyes, who stood aside, with that mutt at their feet; and then at Bonfils, who had gauded himself up for the occasion in fringed buckskins, a bone necklace, a bright red calico shirt, quilled moccasins, and a flat-crowned black hat decorated with a band of rattlesnake skin.

He recognized none of them. These Hidatsa were friendly people, not armed with anything other than a sheathed knife; carrying bows and quivers of arrows would have been considered a hostile act.

It was, actually, an old crone who recognized him. She wore a simple frock of patterned purple calico, which hung from a bony body topped by a seamed brown face and a mouth lacking most teeth. But she walked directly at him, stopped, frowned, and he knew the woman was one of Amalie's many grandmothers, venerated for her medicine and wisdom.

"Ah!" the woman said. "And where is she?"

"She is not here, grandmother."

"You have put her out of your lodge?"

He wasn't really sure. He'd grown tired of Amalie and had lent her to a friend. But the old crone's challenge, which was not at all friendly, decided him.

"I gave her away to a great white chief. She is honored to be the woman of a mighty trapper, grandmother."

"She lives?"

He smiled and shrugged.

She pursed her lips, spat, and turned away. Bonfils was aware that Victoria Skye had listened and probably understood the Hidatsa tongue, so close to her own.

He smiled at her, and wandered toward the trading, which now proceeded furiously a few yards away.

The old woman had not been silent. Now as he approached, others turned and stared at him. He smiled and doffed his splendid chapeau, so they might see him in sunlight and confirm that yes, it was the legendary Bonfils, who had arrived in their village, wooed many a maid, and made off with the wife of Barking Wolf, a clan leader with much medicine and a bad temper, and then dispatched her brother when he came after her with a war party. *Sacre Bleu*!

Allors, it was time to greet them. "See, it is Bonfils," he said in Hidatsa, jabbing a thumb into his chest. "The very same. I am going to the village of many houses now, on the fireboat, to be given a higher position. I will become a trader, you see. Maybe I will trade with you. Ah, I see you now, Barking Wolf! How swiftly your clan brothers have whispered of my presence here! See me now. I am going to return, and all your people will trade with me."

That wasn't quite exact. These people traded at Fort Clark, and sometimes Fort Pierre, and rarely got to the Yellowstone Country, where Fort Cass stood. But he wished to impress them. He wished to laugh merrily.

Barking Wolf was a soldier not much older than Bonfils, stocky and short and smouldering. He had always smouldered. He had smouldered in the company of Amalie, smouldered with his clan-brothers, smouldered while hoeing corn in the fields, smouldered toward his rivals in the buffalo hunts that kept the Minnetaree villages in meat.

"Monsieur Bonfils, what is all this?" asked Marsh from above.

"It is my mountain wife's family and her former mate, *monsieur le capitaine.* They are discovering that I am present, without my Amalie, and they are looking forward to whatever trouble they can cause me."

Marsh didn't like it. "Bonfils, we are trading for food, and you must retreat to your cabin at once. I will not have trouble, and trouble is what I see here."

Indeed, the Minnetaree people had stopped their frantic trading and jostling, and were observing the exchange.

Victoria Skye whispered something to her man, and the pair of them retreated aft. Bonfils watched them sidle away. Skye had always been too prudent for his own success, he thought.

A subchief Bonfils knew, old Standing in Water, snapped an order, and the trading ceased altogether. The clamorous crowd slipped away from the traders, until a no-man's land stretched between the crew and the Hidatsi.

Harshly, the hawknosed elder orated, gesticulating toward Marsh, who stood above, staring at this confrontation on his boiler deck.

"What is he saying, Bonfils?"

"He's saying that they will not let this packet leave if I am on it."

"Why do they want you?"

"I haven't the faintest idea," Bonfils said, amusement playing with the corners of his mouth.

"What is the trouble?"

"Offer them a big damn gift," Victoria Skye said.

"Don't give them a feather," Bonfils said easily, loving the confrontation.

And there it stood.

11

Skye smelled trouble, and began easing aft with Victoria. None of the sailors were armed; most of the Hidatsa wore sheathed knives. Marsh must have scented trouble too because he gestured sailors to the capstan to pull anchor if need be. Others gathered casually around the six-pounder at the prow, where an enameled chest contained powder and grape.

But there was Bonfils, a charismatic, mesmerizing figure talking volubly to the Indians, a vast smile wreathing his face, his body arched and confident and somehow larger to the eye than it really was. Skye had never seen anything quite like it: this young Creole was gradually defusing the moment, pawing about like some giant cat, the sheer force of his voice and will subduing every spirit within earshot.

The man radiated something Skye couldn't fathom, some mysterious and commanding force that derived from his sonorous, compelling voice, the easy tenor of his tongue, a smile, warm dark eyes that feasted carnivorously upon whoever was in his sight; a line of clean and regular white teeth, not to mention that costume, the elaborately fringed buckskins, the quilled moccasins, the red shirt, the bone necklace, the splendid beaver hat with its rattlesnake band, and not least, the bronze medal on blue watershot silk decorating his chest. No Indian ever paraded in ceremonial clothing more effectively than Bonfils.

"What's he saying?" Skye asked Victoria.

"I don't get it all. But he's telling them that in himself lies their future. Treat him as chief and they will be chiefs; treat him badly and there will be no more blankets, shot and powder, awls, knives, axes and hatchets, for the window of the trading company will be forever closed, and the people will be ruined."

Whatever it was Bonfils was saying in easy oratory, the tension seeped from the charged moment, and those brown hands that clutched the hafts of knives relaxed.

Marsh, above, obviously knew enough to say nothing, and simply waited for events to play out, his relentless glare on Bonfils. The sailors ready to pull anchor—the farther from the village, the safer the *Otter*—no longer stood at the ready.

Then, at last, with a sweep of his red-shirted arm, Bonfils invited the Hidatsa to trade once again.

Skye watched the angry ones closely. Were these warriors somehow related to Amalie? But even those most likely to spill blood seemed to retreat into themselves. Soon the trading was going again; the sailors and clerks accepting baskets of maize, pelts, squash, buffalo robes, and tanned hides, while the shoppers were examining awls, feeling the edges of hatchets, fingering flannels, and studying the three-point blankets heaped on the boiler deck.

"Sonofabitch," Victoria said. "He did it."

"Did what?"

"He has big medicine, Skye. Those warriors, they were going to kill him. That one there—the one called Barking Wolf, he was Amalie's husband once. And that one there; he is a brother of Amalie, and made medicine to kill Bonfils."

"But they didn't."

"Big goddam medicine."

Even now, Bonfils, slim and confident and springy on the balls of his feet, greeted the Hidatsa like some potentate. The crowd swelled as more dugout-loads of Hidatsa arrived, clambered on board and deposited their pelts and baskets of grain and vegetables before the traders.

Marsh, red-nosed and irritable, appeared on the boiler deck, and corraled Bonfils. "Monsieur Bonfils, what was all this about?" he asked in a dulcet and icy voice.

"A private matter, *mon capitaine*. Some wretches in this friendly village have taken umbrage, and I reminded them forcefully that the entire village would suffer if they acted rashly."

Bonfils smiled, and Skye felt the presence of galvanic energy, almost lightning, shooting and sparking out from him.

Marsh was not placated. "And what was this private matter?"

Bonfils laughed softly. "A woman, of course. What else?"

"Is that all? Is there more? Are you telling me everything?"

Bonfils laughed easily. "All that matters."

Marsh struggled not to say something or other, and finally subsided. "This is a profitable stop," he said grudgingly, swallowing back whatever was on his mind.

Bonfils smiled that galvanic beam again.

Marsh turned to Skye. "He rescued us; a cool man, wouldn't you say? I saw you heading aft, out of harm's way."

It hung there, this gentle insinuation of cowardice.

Skye might have argued that he and Victoria were preparing for war by fetching some weapons. Not for nothing had he been in the Royal Navy. But he saw the captain's mind snap shut, and let it go. This was the second time he had incurred Marsh's disfavor. And maybe it would not be the last, given the length of the trip and the difficulties a steam vessel on the upper Missouri would surely encounter.

"Yes, sir. Mr. Bonfils has turned the tide in his favor," he said.

"A remarkable young man," Marsh said, satisfied with Skye's response.

"Goddamn reckless sonofabitch, get us all killed," Victoria said.

Marsh, taken aback, stared at her, and then smiled wolfishly. "They will enjoy you in St. Louis," he said to her. It was not a compliment.

The trading continued for another hour, and by its end Marsh was well provisioned with meat and grain and had added scores of pelts and robes to his cargo. Skye and Victoria watched closely, alert for trouble that never seemed very far away. The unhappy young men with Barking Wolf hung together in sullen knots, refusing to leave the boat, and glancing boldly at the unarmed clerks and sailors.

"They haven't quit," Skye said to her. "This isn't over."

Bonfils, either recklessly or with incredible courage, meandered toward the sullen clique and began addressing them in the Hidatsa tongue, his confidence glossing them all like sunlight. Most tribesmen loved a show of confidence and courage, and Bonfils was oddly welcomed even among those schemers seeking his doom.

The traders were totting up ledgers, stowing unsold goods, hauling pelts and skins to the hold, or carting maize and meat to the kitchen. Most of the Hidatsa had left, and the remaining ones were stepping gingerly into their dugouts.

Firemen began stuffing big willow and cottonwood logs into the firebox, and a cloud of acrid smoke blew downward over them all. Steam began popping from the escapement.

"Mr. Bonfils, would you invite your guests to depart?" Marsh said through his megaphone from above.

The young man nodded, and gestured toward the remaining dugout snugged to the side of the packet. But this last group of six men didn't budge. They ranged in age, the eldest showing gray in his loose-hanging hair. That one bore the marks of war: a puckered wound along a forearm; a rough-healed gash across the left side of his face. His gaze focused unblinkingly on Bonfils. The young man who had once possessed Amalie as wife was declaiming.

Skye didn't like it.

Around him, the crew prepared to sail. Men gathered at the stem to raise a kedge that had steadied the vessel offshore.

Victoria jabbed Skye in the ribs. Startled, he followed the point of her finger. These six Minnetarees had spread slightly, two of them quartering around Bonfils. They all looked poised for action of some sort.

Slowly, the elder one slid a long and rusty skinning knife from a sheath.

Skye and Victoria edged toward the group, with No Name advancing ahead of them. Skye saw that Victoria had her own little knife in hand.

They surprised the warriors, who turned, too late, to discover the company.

Skye never paused. His massive hand clamped over the wrist of the man holding the knife; Victoria pressed her blade hard on the neck of the one on the other side. And No Name, his hair pricking upward snarled, baring a pair of canines that could only win respect.

The moment passed. No one in the work crew readying the packet to sail had seen any of it. The older man twisted around, his eyes brimming with rage, and Skye strengthened his grip with one hand, and prepared to knock the man flat with the other.

At last Bonfils grasped that he was in mortal peril, and backed out of the circle of fire.

"Tell them to get in their canoe," Skye said, in a voice that didn't carry.

Bonfils did.

The Minnetarees left reluctantly, in stiff, proud spasms that told the world this was not over; Alexandre Bonfils was a marked man in that clan, and maybe in that tribe. These people might have been farmers and hunters, living sedentary lives beside the great river; but they had not neglected the arts of war.

Skye released the wrist of the older warrior, probably a clan chieftain, ready to block a thrust with the knife. But it didn't come. No Name crouched, ready to go for the man's throat. The warrior, seething now with something so foul and raw it landed palpably on them all, backed off to the coaming and stepped over, and into the dugout.

The mate barked a command. The crew at the capstan twisted up rope until the boat drifted in the current. A shout from the pilothouse down the speaking tube energized the engineers, who engaged the pittman rod to the flywheel, and the giant paddles sliced water.

No one else on board, least of all the powerful master or his mate, had registered the last taut drama at the riverside village.

The vessel soon rounded a bight and left the Minnetaree village in memory.

Bonfils smiled brightly, but that charismatic quality that made him look larger than life had vanished. The smile was veneer; he was a shaken and angry young man.

"Well, you certainly made me look bad," he said.

"What we made you look, Mr. Bonfils, is alive," Skye said.

12

Lame Deer hoped she would not be too late. For days she had hastened along the Cheyenne River, ever eastward toward the house of the rising sun, the happiest of the four winds. No war parties had molested her and she had seen no fresh pony tracks. The buffalo were elsewhere, and so were the hunters. If she had come across Lakota, she would have been welcomed and protected, for those were ancient friends of her people. If Pawnee or Arapaho, she might have suffered a cruel fate, including captivity.

She rode a gaunt red roman-nosed pony, swaying steadily step by step, her velveteen purple skirts hiked high to seat herself in the high-cantled squaw saddle that was one of her proudest possessions. In her bony lap sat her daughter of two winters, Singing Rain, and behind her rode her boy of four winters, Sound Comes Back After Shouting, on a sore-backed gray packhorse burdened with precious robes and pelts and a parfleche with a little pemmican and jerky in it.

Her man, Simon, had given Singing Rain another name, Molly, and had called Sound Comes Back, Billy. She was going to the place of many lodges to find her man, whom she had not seen for an autumn and winter and spring and now summer; four seasons too long. Simon MacLees was his name; he was a trader. He had a partner in the place of many lodges he called St. Louis, a man named Jonas. He had called himself the Opposition, and she gathered that meant he was a rival of the American Fur Company, like a fox pup among wolves.

He had built a sturdy log trading post on the Belle Fourche River, within sight of the sacred mountain of the Cheyenne People, Bear Butte, and there had done a good trade with the Cheyenne, the Sans Arcs, the Blackfoot Sioux, the Hunkpapa, and sometimes other peoples as well, but that business was fading because so many of her people had moved south to trade at a great fort called Bent's.

For five winters she had been his woman, sharing his life in the post built of big cottonwood logs and chinked with mud against the winter winds. She had always been happy there; never far from her people. But she knew he had fits of loneliness and was sometimes restless, especially when the snows trapped them in their wooden lodge and there was no one else to talk to, and he paced the flagstone floors.

Four springtimes in a row, his partner Jonas had shown up in the moon of the flying geese, sometimes with other white men, bringing new tradegoods—bright-colored blankets, awls, knives, hatchets, rifles, lead and powder, and bolts of red and green and blue flannel. Then Jonas would load the packs of robes and the pelts on the big gray mules he always used, and vanish to the east.

Then last spring, Jonas didn't come and there was little to trade. And then in the autumn, her man Simon left for the place of many lodges, St. Louis, with many promises that he would return. But he hadn't returned. She lived alone, with her little children, waiting for his boots to print the dust.

Her kin among the People told her to forget him. White

men were like that. But she could not. She had sold the last few goods in the store and then waited as the summer faded into yellow leaves, frosts and bare limbs, and the winter howled, and then the sun burned away the snow and green grass burst through the drifts. Surely he would come with the warm tide of the sun, but he had not, and she knew that some bad thing had happened, and he was detained.

She had subsisted as long as she could at the post, sometimes given a haunch of venison or elk by the Sioux, because her people rarely stopped by. The Cheyenne had moved south. But he didn't come. She roamed the hills for wild onions and greens and edible things—but never fish, the unclean water creature. And still he had not come.

"Ah, return to us, and some good Cheyenne will take you," her friends said. But she had always shaken her head. She wore the rope, as she had as a maiden, so that she might remain inviolate; no Cheyenne man would touch her for as long as she wore it. She belonged to Simon, for all time, until they were gone from the earth and had become stars in the heavens. And she found in her children the proofs of his presence within her heart, and she bided her time.

Simon had made her proud. She had been the wife of a trader, a man who brought precious and magical things to her people in exchange for something as ordinary as a pelt. By what mysterious power could white men conjure metal pots and knives and awls and hatchets? How did they make blankets? Where did Simon and his partner get these marvels?

But that was only the smallest part of it. Cheyenne men ruled their women, and sent them away if a woman was not obedient, for it was a grave offense to defy him or the elders, and a woman faced unspeakable evils if she did. Simon was different. He was *Hoah*, a friend. What Cheyenne husband consulted his wife as Simon did? A woman kept the lodge and raised the children and answered his every beck and call. But Simon MacLees had been a companion and she liked that.

She did not know of any other woman of the People who had a male friend; they had husbands and sons and fathers, but that was different. Their entire life consisted of visiting with their sisters and mothers and other women. So she considered Simon MacLees a treasure beyond price because he was a friend as well as husband.

He was strange; all white men were strange. He had no medicine and worshiped nothing visible. He never sought the help of the *Ma i yun'*, the Powers who governed the fate of mere mortals. He never talked about where he had come from, or what his people were like back in the place of many houses. It was as if he had been born from a whirlwind, without a family. And now he had gone away as mysteriously as he had arrived one day at the village of Red Robe and opened his packs to show the People what he would offer them for beaver pelts, ermine and fox and deer and elk and buffalo robes.

She had been standing right there, in a whitened doeskin dress with fringed sleeves, and high beaded moccasins. She had many suitors but was not yet taken and her parents had bided their time, wanting the best young warrior for their daughter. Like all Cheyenne girls, she had been a virgin, wore the sacred rope about her loins, and was carefully chaperoned. Nothing was worse for a Cheyenne girl than to be used by several men.

Ah, what a moment that was, when his gray-eyed gaze settled on her, paused to see into her, and swept over her young figure, and then back to her face, where his warm gaze seemed to pierce right to her heart.

Ah, Simon! She would track him to the ends of the earth. She would bring his children to him, and help him escape from the troubles he was in. It didn't matter what the People thought: she would go to the place of many lodges. Even her spirit helper the raven *Okoka* told her not to, and old Four Braids, the elder with great wisdom and an eye upon the mysterious future, the keeper of a medicine bundle, had warned her sharply.

And yet she had come because she had to come, and she would find Simon MacLees and joyously show him how the children had grown, and how much they had learned, and how beautiful they were, partly pale and partly brown like herself, golden children like sunrises in the Moon of First Frost.

She knew all the news, for such things were cried to the entire village of Red Robe. She knew that the fireboat had come to the trading post where the Big River and the Elk River—the white men called them by different names—came together, and soon would go down to the place of many lodges.

She had inquired how she might ride on that boat, though her father had told her not to set foot on it because it offended the evil spirits under the water. But she did learn that she might find the boat and board it if she hurried. She resolved to go at once. Nothing remained within the cottonwood logs of the post. She had nothing to sell, and Simon brought her nothing to eat.

She packed the skins and robes she possessed on one of her two scrawny horses, one sore-backed with a cracked hoof, the other a sullen mare that would not move unless she lashed it. That was all she had, but that would do. She would go to the Big River and wait for the fireboat. She had no idea how she might obtain a ride; but she knew that white men traded almost anything for furs, and of furs she had a few.

She did not think about the chance that the boat might have passed by. If that was true, and it didn't come after many sleeps, she would walk down the big river to this place where white men lived. Simon had said the river would take him there; it would take her there too.

It would be a hard walk. She would walk past the Arikaras, sometimes enemies of her people, but this was the land of the Miniconjou and Yanktonai, and there she would be safe. What power would a woman with two small children have against an enemy? And yet, most would respect her, for a woman of the People, traveling alone, was a wonder, and would be honored except maybe by the Pawnee.

For Simon she would risk all that. She and Simon had talked of many things. He had told her about schools and buildings made of red blocks of fired earth; of wagons, and theaters and books. He had shown her some books, and the mysterious little signs within them had intrigued her. Now she would see where these came from!

It was because Simon was a friend, and few other women of the People had a male friend, that she would go to Simon now. She was very proud to have a man friend; not just a husband who gave orders and expected much labor and then went off to smoke with other men, or pray to the powers together, or perform secret dances, or drum for victory, or ride away to hunt and fight.

Once she had yearned for just such a proud husband; a slim, brown, sharp-eyed man with long braids, a man who would win great honors in war, count many coups, save his people, bring them plenty of meat, ride first in the parades, wear many eagle feathers in his hair, find favor with the elders and the shamans. Oh, how she had yearned for such a man, so she might be proud and looked upon as the most fortunate of the Cheyenne women.

But then she discovered friendship. Simon made her laugh. He rarely forbade her anything. He showered gifts upon her; a new awl, a skein of beads, a blue blanket with black stripes and four bars on it, indicating the heaviest weight.

Ah! What woman among all the bands of the People had such a friend?

Now she hastened her reluctant four-foots eastward, toward the Wind of the Rising Sun. Sound Comes Back was always hungry, and she could not feed him enough. Singing Rain was docile, and sat quietly behind her mother, accepting whatever life visited upon her. Lame Deer made do with cattail roots, which she mashed to pulp and boiled into a white paste that filled the belly and sufficed for food.

The Cheyenne River flowed lazily eastward through lonely steppes and grassy bluffs. At least there were willows and cottonwoods in the bottoms, and plenty of places for a small woman to hide from distant eyes, though no one tracking close or hunting her would fail to find her.

The weather that moon of the ripe strawberries grew hot, slowing the horses, but she would not let them pause except for a while to graze, or lick water, or scratch themselves by rubbing against a willow to rid themselves of fleas and flies.

The Cheyenne widened into a formidable river as its tributaries added their flow, and then she descended long coulees choked with brush, and passed through a dense forest, and beheld the Big River, a vast expanse of shimmering blue water.

There was no sign of anything or anyone, except some hard-used trails along its vast valley. She feared the fireboat had passed. She feared it might came and not see her. Or maybe the white chiefs who steered it would not accept her gifts; several robes for three passengers; some smaller pelts for the ponies.

And so she made a small camp that sunny and quiet afternoon, and waited.

13

Victoria saw the woman first as the packet rounded a bight, and motioned to Skye. His eyes weren't as keen as hers, and he almost missed her. But the woman was making herself known to the crew by waving a red banner on a stick, the sweeping flourishes of crimson brightening the right bank across the dull water of late afternoon.

"She's got horses and some children," Victoria said, and once again Skye squinted into the shadowed spit of land where she stood, until he could make out the small buckskin-clad figure of a boy, and a smaller child grasping the woman's leg.

"She wants something," Victoria said.

"Trade, probably."

"One woman? Trade? Dammit, Skye."

Skye nodded. The distant woman's signaling was urgent, even violent, her flag on a stick describing great arcs, her whole body twisting with the intent of being seen.

Skye touched Victoria's hand, and headed up the companionway to the hurricane deck and the pilothouse.

"We see her," said Marsh. "Can't stop for a lone trader."

"That doesn't look like a woman trying to trade, mate."

"Squaw alone like that. A white man would be different. We can make another six, eight miles before dark. Boilers eat wood, Mister Skye."

"Six miles? Suppose you let Victoria and me off, with our horses. We'll see what she wants, and then hunt along the way to your night anchorage."

Marsh said nothing. The riverboat was passing the woman, who waved her banner ceaselessly, almost furiously. Skye knew the woman was calling, maybe screaming; he could see it in her face, though the rumble of the paddle wheels and the rattle of steam from the escapement kept him from hearing anything resembling a woman's voice.

The pilot and helmsman were following the channel, veering toward the right bank. Below the left bank was a vast shallows dotted with snags and gravel bars, and the helmsman was cautiously edging the vessel closer to the steep bluffs of the right bank.

They passed the woman, who leapt and jumped and cried out, and Skye suddenly felt bad.

"All right," Marsh said. He pointed to a place where the channel cut close to a sharp grassy bluff. "Get your horses; we'll be six miles down. There's a creek there with a good patch of timber. Bring us meat."

Skye heard the clanging of a bell as he raced down the companionway to the boiler deck. He motioned to Victoria, who had been standing at the rail, her small foot on the coaming, looking unhappy.

"We'll see," he said. "Talk to her, make meat, meet the ship downstream."

That's all it took for her to race to the pen, throw her small pad saddle on her nag, and fetch her bow and quiver. No Name circled restlessly, ready to go wherever his partners went. Skye saddled his ugly, roman-nosed grulla horse and led it to the gangway amidships.

A few minutes later, the ship drifted into the right

bank, bumped bottom, and pulled away. The gangway didn't reach, but it wouldn't matter. The crew dropped the far end into the river and Skye and Victoria rode down the incline and urged their ponies toward the steep bank, which the horses took with violent leaps that almost unseated them both.

Marsh wasted not a moment. The boat was already adrift, the gangway drawn up, and the helmsman steering it back into the channel. With a shudder the paddle wheels engaged, splashing water, and the boat raced downstream again.

In an amazingly short time, the world was veiled in silence. Smoke hung in the quiet air. The bluff cast a long lavender shadow over the water. The sinking sun colored the world orange and gold and dun. A streak of green filled the eastern sky.

The woman came running. She was leading a saddled ewe-necked pony and a gaunt packhorse, dragging a child, and carrying a smaller one in the crook of her arm.

"Cheyenne," Victoria said sourly. Enemies of her Absaroka people.

Skye always marveled that Victoria could read the tribe in a glance. He couldn't, and never got the knack of it. They waited for the Cheyenne woman, and when she did finally stop before them, she was out of breath, and Skye sensed a wildness and despair and defeat in her.

"Fireboat. I want to go," she cried.

This Cheyenne knew a little English.

"Well, maybe so," Skye said. "Who are you?"

"The woman of Simon MacLees," she said, half gasping it out between gulps of air.

Skye knew the name. Opposition. A trading partnership. He sat uneasily on his restless, dripping horse. "You want to trade, is that it?"

"No, go on fireboat. To . . ." she paused, searching for words. "Place of many lodges."

That surprised Skye.

He would get the story en route. "Tell us. Maybe you can go. Fireboat's going to stop a way down for the night. Wooded flat with a creek on it."

The woman gulped air and nodded. She handed the smallest child, a girl, to Victoria, and pointed to herself. "I am named Lame Deer," she said. "That is the People's name, as I am born. Simon MacLees gives me other name. This is Singing Rain, called Molly by him, and Sound Comes Back After Shouting, my boy, he calls Billy."

Skye beheld a solemn child clinging tightly to his mother's hand, half afraid, half truculent.

"I am Mister Skye; this is my wife Victoria, Many Quill Woman, of the Absaroka.

"Aiee, those are names I know," the Cheyenne said, suddenly wary.

She lifted her generous velveteen skirts and clambered aboard the gaunt horse. The boy clambered behind her, sitting on the rump behind the high cantle of the squaw saddle.

"We go to the fireboat?" the woman asked.

Skye nodded. They followed a dusky and difficult riverbank trail, circling marshy flats full of sedges, until Skye found a way up to the tableland above where the going would be easier and straighter. They pierced from indigo shadow into golden light from a horizontal sun that raked the land and painted every bush and tree.

"My heart is big with the dream of my man," the woman said in a voice that sang of music. "He walks across the mountains; he fills the valleys. He comes into our lodge and brings meat and comfort. He has stars in his eyes, and he lights the night like a big moon. He smiles and all my fears fall away like the leaves of autumn. He floats high in the sky like an eagle, walking over clouds, seeing what is to come from afar, and it is so. He says one soft word, and it is stronger than a hundred men shouting.

When he sings, the wolves sing too. When he laughs, the coyotes laugh too. He gathers the blossoms, and gives them to me, and my heart grows big. Now I am called to him, and I go."

Skye marveled. She had few English words, and yet she used them so sweetly, and with such lyrical power that he believed she was a born poet.

In the space of a half hour, Skye got her story. She was going to find MacLees, who hadn't returned after a trip east. She had a few robes and pelts to trade for passage.

Skye suspected that if MacLees lived, and indeed, if he had reached St. Louis safely, he would not want to see his squaw. Traders and trappers had routinely formed temporary liaisons with Indian women, often serially, even bigamously. These were called mountain marriages, and many was a trapper or trader who simply abandoned his dusky bride and his breed children when the urge came over him to head back to the States. Many a mountaineer had married a white girl and never spoken a word about the half-breed family he left behind in the impenetrable reaches of the West.

He had heard nothing of MacLees's death, though the names of all trappers and traders who were killed, or died of disease, or had vanished, were bruited through every camp in the mountains. He suspected the man lived. He suspected the partnership had gone broke, trying to buck the powerful attractions of Bent's Fort, which had drawn the Cheyenne southward and had captured most of the trade with that tribe. He suspected that MacLees and . . . yes, Jonas, that was his partner's name, had quit the mountains. And now this beautiful and poetic Cheyenne woman, probably in her early twenties, was determined to find him.

But of all this he said nothing. He gauged Victoria's sharp glances, and concluded that her thoughts largely paralleled his own. This ragged family looked hungry.

Skye found some jerky in his kit and handed a fistful to the woman, who took it gratefully and gave each child a piece. Jerky was an unsatisfying food that left one hungrier than before. It took a while to soften in the mouth, to become edible, and then it vanished down the throat with one small gulp. But it could keep a body alive.

They rode steadily into a descending twilight. The sun set, momentarily illumining the bowl of heaven with salmon and pink, and then they pierced through the long summer's twilight, the heavens from north to west a bold blue band. There was light enough to travel; light enough to spot the vessel. Ahead a mile or so he discerned a dip in the hills and a dark patch at its base, next to the river. He could not see the packet, but it would be there.

He felt cool night breezes eddy over him, the colder air rolling down the long slopes to the river bottoms. He heard terns and sandpipers, and watched crows gossip. He spotted the streak of a black and white magpie, and wondered whether Victoria had seen her spirit helper.

Victoria had; her gaze followed the bird, and her face radiated serenity. The Cheyenne woman might be an enemy of the People, but sisterhood formed a stronger impulse.

He saw two does drinking at river's edge, far below, too far to shoot at; he didn't feel like hunting anyway, and rode past them. If he had veered in their direction, they would have vanished into the wrinkled slopes.

They descended into the creek bottom at dusk, and could hear the whack and thump of axes before they saw the riverboat or the woodcutting crew. Skye led the uneasy Cheyenne woman to the vessel, which rocked gently bank-side, tied stem and stern to trees. They waited while the crew manhandled cordwood up the gangway. The Cheyenne children looked terrified, but their mother solaced them with soft words. She looked ill at ease herself, her black eyes focused on the white superstructure, the busy white men, the smoke eddying from the chimneys from the dying fires under the boiler.

Skye led her and the children on board, while Victoria held the horses, and then up the companionway to the pilothouse.

Marsh stared sharply at the young woman and her brood.

"She's Lame Deer—Cheyenne—and wanting a ride to St. Louis," Skye said. "She'd like to take the two ponies, too. She's looking for her husband. I guess he's there all right."

"I can't take her."

Skye studied the master, finding him in a testy mood, wanting to finish the day's work.

"She brought twelve fine-tanned robes, some beaver plews, and some ermine. Says she'll trade it all for the ride."

"I don't want a squaw and some breed brats."

Skye felt the rumble of anger building in him. "Maybe I'll ride horse down to St. Louis with her. You can tell Chouteau why."

Marsh backed off. "Deck passage."

"No, women's quarters. She needs shelter for the children."

"They're not used to it. Never saw a chamber pot."

"She's a trader's wife."

Marsh sighed. "I'll regret it," he said, but he nodded.

14

Benton Marsh was an irascible man, and now he was even more so. He didn't like vermin-ridden Indians on his packet, a view he kept private because the American Fur Company depended entirely on trade with the savages.

He peered out upon the world from behind a brown beard which he kept neatly trimmed to within an inch of his sallow face. Some might have called him handsome. His composure was so total that few guessed that behind his quiet calm raged a man of harsh and savage judgments, which he kept entirely private, veneered with a faint smile on occasion.

His ability to ferret out the frailties of every mortal had earned him the respect of Pierre Chouteau and the other chiefs of the American Fur Company, who treated him as a sort of privy counselor and consulted him about personnel. He found more pride in that role than in his mastery of the river.

If the trip upstream was perilous, the trip downstream was even more so. The paddle-wheel boat was carried along by the seven- or eight-mile-per-hour current at uncomfortable speeds, at the very time when the water levels were dropping daily as the spring runoff vanished. It was on the downstream trip, when the boats were burdened with a year's prize of peltries, that they most often succumbed to assorted disasters.

He stood in the pilothouse, along with his pilot and helmsman, studying the treacherous river, reading the currents, examining the heavens for rain and wind and storm, all dangerous to navigation. Not to mention Indians, who could amass along the bank at any point where the channel took the boat close to shore.

Simon MacLees's squaw!

Marsh was appalled. Of all the wild strokes of bad fortune! But maybe not so bad: knowledge is power, he thought. He could deal with it; with her.

If he had known who Lame Deer was, he would have flatly rejected passage. But Skye had brought her aboard and settled her before the whole story emerged. Now there was trouble, and Marsh fumed. This was a personal matter, affecting his family, as well as a business matter.

The red slut was going to St. Louis, and she would get there one way or another unless he found a way to prevent it. He wished he had never set eyes on her. She was Simon MacLees's mountain woman, and that spelled trouble right in the bosom of his family. His stepdaughter, Sarah Lansing, was soon to be married to MacLees; in fact, within days of the time he expected to return to St. Louis.

Marsh had known MacLees and his partner, Jonas, for years. St. Louis might be a bustling and brawling city of thousands, but the fur business was a small, closed circle. MacLees and Jonas had been an opposition firm until Pierre Chouteau, with his usual ruthlessness, had crushed them every way possible—by undercutting, by causing them license problems with the Indian superintendent General Clark, by filing complaints about the use of alcohol, by establishing a rival post nearby, where American Fur Company traders bought pelts for more, and sold goods for less, even at a temporary loss, until MacLees had virtually run out of options. The drift of the Cheyennes down to the southern plains and Bent's Fort had been the final blow.

And here came his filthy squaw! When he got to St. Louis he would have the squaw's cabin fumigated and scrubbed down. For that matter, he would have the Skyes' quarters fumigated. Victoria was another squaw he couldn't do anything about until he got his boat back. This was Chouteau's bidding; if Marsh had any say about it, the dirt-crusted redskins would be allowed only on the boiler deck for trading, and that as little as possible. And never, not ever, in the cabins.

Marsh grunted. There were going to be some explosions in St. Louis. He was privy to some things no one else on the boat knew. The American Fur Company was about to offer MacLees a position, which is what it often did with defeated rivals. Unknown to Skye and to Bonfils, MacLees, a veteran trader, was Pierre Chouteau's first choice for the Fort Cass position. The man knew Indians, knew trading, knew how to make a profit, and that was more than Skye or Bonfils knew.

It helped MacLees that he was betrothed to Sarah Lansing, daughter of a Chouteau company attorney, August Lansing, who was once married to Marsh's wife, thus adding to the threads and connections that gave him the inside track for a high position. Sarah Lansing was Marsh's own stepdaughter; his wife's child by the earlier marriage, raised by the Lansings.

And now, along comes MacLees's mountain woman! Just in time for the wedding! How delighted Sarah would be to learn about this red whore and her breed brats! Marsh smiled sardonically. What a fine scandal it would be . . . if the woman actually reached St. Louis. It would break Sarah's heart. But that would not happen.

Marsh hadn't decided what he would do about her, but

he knew that he would unload her somewhere and send her back to her people, with a stern warning never to set foot in Missouri. If he took that squaw clear to St. Louis, and raised a scandal, his friend Pierre Chouteau, and his acquaintance August Lansing, not to mention his own wife and step-daughter, would land on him and he would never hear the end of it.

So MacLees had himself a red woman! And that red woman was riding the *Otter*! Marsh enjoyed the irony.

Mountain wives were an unspoken part of the trade but one didn't hear about them in polite society—unless they showed up on someone's doorstep. MacLees had abandoned his, and never dreamed he would see her again.

MacLees was the obvious choice to trade with the Crows. That Cheyenne squaw wouldn't help matters. Not that Sarah would go west into an utter wilderness. MacLees would do what so many traders did: impregnate her and leave for a year; and then return and repeat the cycle. After a few years, he would have his fortune and his children and would retire in St. Louis, while she would be busy managing a family in St. Louis.

Marsh watched carefully as his pilot and helmsman negotiated a broad shallows, pocked with a thousand stumps and other debris. The channel ran straight through the middle of it, braiding itself around islands and bars. It was one of the most treacherous spots on the upper Missouri, and the doom of half a dozen captains before him, all of them running Opposition boats.

That took the better part of an hour, with only one crisis, when some invisible sawyer scraped along the port side, banged on the wheelhouse, and levered the entire packet sideways. But no damage was done and the boat drifted through another hundred yards of trouble before striking a clear channel again.

"We made it, no thanks to you," he snapped at his pilot.

He rang a bell, signaling the engineers to open the throttle, and was rewarded with a chatter of popping steam from the escape pipe.

The crisis over, he returned to his musings. Somewhere, he would unload the Cheyenne woman. Fort Pierre was next. It was Chouteau's new fort, the headquarters for the whole region, and the supply depot for the satellite posts the company had established in the area. Chouteau himself had picked the site several years earlier on his first excursion up the river.

He wondered what to say to the woman, and decided he would not say anything: he would simply put her off and tell her to go home. He would have liked to put Skye's squaw off too, but thought better of it.

He had little use for Skye. The man might have a reputation as a mountaineer, but he was a cockney oaf, without the brains to make anything of himself. He was doomed to the life of a mountain exile, attached to that barbaric Crow woman, and St. Louis would swiftly mock him and send him back to the wilds.

He had even less use for Bonfils, primping dandy, reckless fool, but Marsh could do nothing about it. Bonfils was connected by blood to the owners. Nonetheless, Marsh intended to catalogue Bonfils's follies during this voyage south, and make mincemeat of the young man in the privacy of Pierre Chouteau's study.

Chouteau was particularly eager to learn the weaknesses of his relatives; and Benton Marsh had been his primary source for years. Just why Chouteau cherished the salacious news about his cousins and uncles and nieces and nephews more than any other gossip, Marsh could only guess at. Amusement, probably. Pierre Chouteau loved to offer witty toasts at family affairs that harpooned one or another of his Creole kin.

Tomorrow, if the wood and water and weather held, they would dock at Fort Pierre, the most splendid edifice on the river save for Fort Union. It stood on the right bank, upon a generous plain well above high water level, a rectangle of pickets encasing a dozen or so commodious buildings. Its factor, Pierre Papin, traded with the Teton, Yankton and Yanktonai Sioux, and sent a great harvest of buffalo hides and robes southward each year, an increasingly profitable trade for the company.

The *Otter* would take on as much of this wealth as it could, and catch the rest on a return trip this far up the river if there would be water enough. The Bad River, which flowed into the Missouri just below Fort Pierre, usually made the difference, supplying the water for late-season navigation.

Marsh turned the vessel over to the pilot. This stretch of the river offered no obstacles and cut serenely across open flats guarded by distant amber bluffs. It was a monotonous land, suited only for the savage spirit. White men required a country with more amenities. The entire area was useless, save for cattle raising, whenever the buffalo were exterminated along with the tribes who fed on them.

Yes, Fort Pierre would be the end of the journey for the squaw, who even now was circling the deck, gazing at wonders beyond her sullen comprehension.

He would tell her at Fort Pierre to debark; she and her brats and those two scrawny ponies. Yes, that was all that was required. A word. If necessary, he would have Skye or his squaw put it into the finger-language of the plains. But that probably would not be necessary. He would send Trenholm to her cabin and have him evict her.

He would like to debark the Skyes, too, but they would be another matter. Skye was no fool. Marsh knew he would need a good reason to debark them; something that would stand up with Chouteau. He would come up with one. Bellevue, downstream, would be the obvious place. That was where the Skyes would leave their horses and pick them up again en route to the Crow country.

That would narrow the field to MacLees and that reckless fop Bonfils. The master of the *Otter* would make sure MacLees was selected—for the good of the company, of course. And for Sarah.

15

Victoria found good company in the Cheyenne woman, Lame Deer. The young mother could understand English well enough. Apparently Simon MacLees had been able to converse with her in Cheyenne, and they had employed both tongues.

The Cheyenne and Absaroka might be hostile, but that did not wither the blossoming friendship between them as they roamed the decks of the riverboat, sometimes leaning over the rails to watch the turbid river flow by; sometimes sitting on the hurricane deck where they could see the majestic stream in all its grandeur flowing between distant slopes.

For Victoria, the chance to coddle the little ones was a moment precious beyond words, for she had borne no child and felt that she would be forever barren. She scarcely knew which one she loved more; the bright girl, Singing Rain, with red bows in her glossy black hair, or the feisty boy whose name she shortened to Echo. To Lame Deer she explained that Echo was the English word for sound coming back, and Lame Deer repeated it with a smile.

It was good to have a woman of the People for company; they could be together all the way to the big place where all the white men's wonders came from.

Victoria wanted to see where metal came out of the earth, and where the powder that exploded came from, and the little brass caps Skye slid over the nipple of his rifle. She wanted to see how cloth was woven and how blankets became so thick, and whether a thousand frail white women were employed making these things, out of sight.

But those things didn't interest Lame Deer at all.

"I will find my man, and he will be gladdened. His heart will grow when he sees the children we have made. He will stand taller than the others. He will look upon me with wisdom. He will walk with the footsteps of a great chief of his people. He will touch me and I will shiver with gladness.

"He will take me to his father and mother, and they will welcome me. I will present our children to them, and they will make blessings and do the sacred things of their people, and sprinkle them with sacred waters, for this is what Simon MacLees told me once, when the night was very black and our robes were very warm.

"They will tell me the story of their people; where they came from, and how they were made, and who this Christ is, just as I have told him about Sweet Medicine and how he teaches the People. And we will all be friends and kin together, in a moment of great feasting. And I, Lame Deer, will be very proud and my heart will sing. And after that we will go back to my people again, and he will be great among them."

Lame Deer spoke these things almost in a dream state, as if she were in the midst of a vision quest. She made the white men's words so beautiful that no white man could ever match her. If she were an Absaroka woman, she would be revered as a story-giver, and given much honor by the People because she could see beyond vision, and hear beyond what the ears knew.

But Victoria listened sadly. She had been around reckless white trappers a long time, and she sensed that the happy young woman's dream might be dashed on the rocks of things the Cheyenne didn't grasp. Such as that the white men got tired of living so far away from their own kind and often abandoned their Indian families and married white women; the very white women that neither Victoria nor any other Crow had ever seen.

"It is a big place, this St. Louis. How will you find him?" she asked the Cheyenne.

Lame Deer only smiled and shrugged. "I will say the name, and the town crier will take me to him," she whispered. "For all the world knows that name.

"I have been to Monterrey, a city far to the west, the place of a people called Californios, so I have seen a place with many houses," Victoria said. "There are more than can be counted. And they have habits we do not know. There was no town crier there, to tell them about those who come. There are some places a woman can't go. And they have a religion that is very strange. To enter a place where they hide their God, I must wear something upon my head.

"I will find MacLees."

"I'll help you," Victoria said. "I know white men better. I'm not afraid to ask. I will see a man in the street and I will ask him if he knows Simon MacLees. And if he doesn't, I will walk into a place they have called a taberna, and ask the men there. That is the Californio word; it is a place to drink whiskey. And maybe they will tell me."

"You will help me, then. You know them better than I do."

They were standing at the blunt prow, watching the river part before the flat-bottomed boat. There was little to see; the far shores revealed no life; the water was blank and told her nothing. The children peered at the murky tide, at the solidly built boat, and accepted it all, though Victoria was not at ease surrounded by water-spirits and white men's mysteries.

"What did your man tell you when he left?"

Lame Deer puzzled that shyly. "He said he was going to St. Louis, the place of many lodges, to do business."

"Did he say when he would be back?"

Lame Deer slowly shook her head, a sadness in her brown eyes that touched Victoria. "He come back sometime."

Victoria didn't want to say what she thought, but she needed to prepare this girl-woman for rejection. "What if he will not come back?"

"He come back. Simon MacLees, he come back. For he has held me in his arms, and touched my lips, and gazed into my heart. He is like a lion roaming the hills for food for us."

But Victoria caught the doubt in her tone.

"What if he can't?"

Lame Deer stared. "Why do you say such things?"

"This company, American Fur, it is big medicine. Very strong. MacLees, little medicine. Maybe this big outfit, it says no to MacLees; he can't trade no more with your people."

Lame Deer's lovely face crumpled. "Sometimes I think that," she said sadly. "But he come back. He's my man. These be his boy and girl. See how they have the look of us both. No good man leave behind his own child."

Victoria wondered whether to suggest other possibilities, and decided she had a whole trip of many days to do so, and it would be best to prepare Lame Deer for bad news a little bit at a time.

The riverboat was making good time this day, plowing the river under a cloudless blue bowl. She felt a change in the rhythm suddenly, a slowing of the engines, and saw the boat veer toward a patch of willows and alders and cottonwoods ahead. The master would stop for fuel. She had seen so many of these stops that she knew the drill: soon the bell would summon every able-bodied man to the boiler deck, and when the gangway was lowered, these men would fan out and begin sawing and chopping carrying wood. Soon there would be no trees left along the big river, because these men always killed several more for future use, by girdling them.

She saw Skye present himself to the mate, who handed him a crosscut saw. Skye was always one of the first off the boat and last to return. No Name always joined him, his tail wagging slowly, eager for a run and a chance to wet a few trees. Skye worked hard. This was women's work; no Absaroka man would stoop to such a thing, but that didn't bother him. White men were different.

The boat slid close to the bank, bumped something and rocked in place while the deck crews shouted, threw hawsers over the rail, and slid the gangway outward. From where Victoria sat high above, she could see that this woodlot had been much depleted by other visits.

She followed Skye until he vanished behind foliage, and then she studied the brooding slopes for danger, squinting as her gaze swept ridges and gulches, pausing at anything the slightest bit unusual or strange. But she saw no sign of trouble. She glanced forward toward the pilothouse and saw Bonfils there. The young man had ceased to go on the refueling trips, and Marsh said nothing. She wondered about it: was that an honor, not being asked to cut wood? Was Skye being dishonored? She could not know, but resolved to ask Skye about it.

She loved the quiet, when the fireboat idled in the lapping waves and the steam made no thunder and the big paddle wheels did not rumble and slap and splash. This machine of the white men ate trees, and someday that would all come to a stop because there would be no more trees.

It didn't take long. The further they progressed into this trip, the faster were the woodcutting stops, as passengers acquired skills and organized themselves better. She watched the deck crews carry the fresh logs aboard and stack them neatly, within reach of the firebox. A bell summoned those on shore, and soon she saw Skye and No Name walk wearily to the deck. She was always careful about No Name, remembering how that dog had once followed a boat carrying Skye and Victoria for a long distance, never giving up. No Name was a spirit-dog, and he made Victoria feel chills sometimes when she gazed at the mangy creature.

They progressed easily the rest of the afternoon. Skye clambered up to the highest deck and sat with the women, watching the shoreline slide by. They passed a woodlot where white men were sawing planks and others were cutting logs, and the mate, Trenholm, told them they would reach Fort Pierre in a little over an hour.

It seemed a greener land than upriver; verdant grasses shivered in the breezes, and the hills weren't so arid. Then, far ahead, she saw the thinnest veil of smoke, and in a bit, a distant palisade, the famous Fort Pierre, a rectangular stockade like the others she had seen, composed of pickets, a massive gate in front, and various buildings within. But this post was on a broad flat, and around the trading center rose more lodges than she could count; smoke-blackened buffalo-hide cones, one after another, a sea of bright-painted lodges built after the manner of the Lakota, with distant people running now to the riverbank to greet the fireboat.

She saw a small puff from a corner bastion, heard the crack of a cannon, and knew the white men at the post were welcoming the fireboat. Another crack, and then the deck hands fired the little brass six-pounder on the foredeck in response. The penned horses stirred nervously. The fireboat slowed and shuddered as the big paddles stopped revolving and the boat slid quietly toward a muddy levee, where it would soon be tied to posts.

She could not yet see individuals who were gathering and jostling at the riverbank, but she knew who they were: enemies of her people. These were Sioux, mostly the Dakota ones, Yanktons, Yanktonai, but also some Tetons, or Lakota. Many was the Lakota scalp dangling from an Absaroka lance! Lame Deer stared raptly at the gathering crowd of Sioux.

Now a few of the post traders appeared, men in black suits and stiff white shirts, quieter than the frenzied Sioux but no less delighted to see the fireboat.

A shrill blast of steam announced the arrival, and now every living person in the whole area was crowding the shore, cheering the boat as the pilot and the master and helmsman eased it home. Finally the deckmen tossed the hawsers to waiting hands on shore, and the boat slid to a halt.

Aiee, she wondered whether she had the courage to walk down to the boiler deck and onto land, with so many Sioux waiting to separate her from her hair!

Then the mate, Trenholm, appeared on the hurricane deck and addressed Lame Deer.

"End of the ride," he said. "Captain's putting you off."

The woman stared.

"Got your stuff on the deck. Bring the young 'uns. We'll unload the nags in a bit."

The Cheyenne woman looked bewildered. "Is this the place of many houses called St. Louis?"

"Nope, but this is as far as you go."

Victoria intervened. "She paid robes to go to St. Louis."

Trenholm laughed. "Off she goes! Come along now."

Slowly, Lame Deer gathered her little ones in hand and followed the mate to the companionway.

16

Skye stood at the rail watching the hubbub. On shore, a crowd jostled and pushed. The arrival of a riverboat was a great event at Fort Pierre Chouteau. The Sioux added to the press of bodies, studying this amazing machine of the white men, their thoughts private and unfathomable. Skye thought them handsomely formed, and taller than most tribes. Most of the males wore only breechclouts that hot day, but many wore white men's shirts and britches, and stovepipe hats. The calico-clad women stood back, knotted into clusters, holding their children close. Dogs circled crazily; No Name watched them from the deck, his neck hair bristling.

When the deck crew finally slid the gangway to the levee and the boat was snubbed to massive posts set in the earth, a great traffic commenced on the gangway; passengers heading for land, and a few company clerks fighting the tide to reach Marsh, their hands clutching manifests and bills of lading. Skye thought he would wait. There would be time enough to roam the post, meet Laidlaw, its factor, and patrol the Sioux lodges to study the ways of these powerful people.

Fort engagés were hurrying bales of buffalo robes,

beaver pelts, and other furs to the bank. The *Otter* would carry a fortune in furs and hides back to St. Louis. On its upstream trip, it had dropped off a year's supply of trade items and household goods for the post; now, en route to St. Louis, it would carry the annual returns, as the fur trade called the accumulated peltries.

Deckmen opened the cargo hatch and several dropped below to begin the mighty business of storing tons of furs in the cramped hold and moving all the furs brought from Fort Union aft to make room for the new load. The boat drew four feet of water loaded; the hold was only five feet high, and a man had to stoop. Other deckmen swung a cargo boom toward shore, where a fort crew waited to load the bales of fur.

Two deckmen were in the horse pen, sliding hacka-mores over the Cheyenne woman's wild-eyed ponies, and that seemed odd to Skye. Maybe they would exercise all the horses, including those belonging to the Skyes. But they didn't halter any other horses. He spotted Tren-holm leading Lame Deer, the Cheyenne woman, and her children down the companionway. He was carrying her things; two parfleches, some blankets, and a canvas sack. Behind, a cabin boy was carrying her packsaddle.

Was she getting off?

He spotted Victoria, looking agitated, and he headed toward the companionway, curious about this turn of events.

Lame Deer passed him, her face granitic and proud, but her eyes betrayed sorrow.

"Say, mate, what is this?" Skye asked.

The mate grinned. "Cap'ain's putting her off. Don't want some lice-bait squaw on board."

Victoria appeared at the foot of the stair. "He's making her go!"

"Why?"

"He says he don't want her."

The mate continued toward the gangway, passing the lounging firemen and stacks of cordwood.

"You sure she isn't just getting off because she wants to?"

"I saw it. The big chief, he just tells the little chief to unload her."

"Is he giving her back her fare? The robes?"

She shook her head angrily.

He pushed into the crowd. Lame Deer was waiting near the gangway.

"You getting off?" he asked.

"He make me go."

"You want to go to St. Louis?"

She nodded. She stood resolutely, tall and straight, her face blank and empty as an August sky.

"Want me to talk to Marsh?"

She stared silently, and now he saw an edge in her. The boy clung to her skirt; she held the girl on her hip.

Skye did not understand any of this. "Don't get off until I see about this," he said.

She looked fearfully at the mate, Trenholm, who was getting her horses readied to lead down the wobbly gangway.

Skye vaulted up the companionway to the pilothouse, which was now jammed with company clerks in black suits. Marsh looked up, his face showing displeasure at the unauthorized presence of a passenger.

"Why are you putting that woman off?" Skye asked.

"Because I choose to," Marsh snapped and returned to his examination of a paper the clerks had handed him.

"You returning her fare?"

Marsh, already choleric, exploded. "Get out!"

"I said, you returning her St. Louis fare?"

Marsh wheeled about and faced Skye. The captain was

about the same height and build, and probably was just as hard as Skye.

"This is my ship, Skye. I will do what I choose, when I choose, and for whatever reason I choose. Now get out."

Skye didn't budge. "Not until this is settled. And it's *Mister* Skye."

He wondered what it mattered to him. Why did he care about the Cheyenne woman? Was it because Trenholm had called her a louse-ridden squaw? Or was it simply his ancient hatred of injustice, a tidal wave of feeling that went straight back to the Royal Navy and the endless cruelties he had seen there. He remembered those naval officers, their arrogance and contempt, and with the memory came a hardening of his own. Damn the consequences. The heat rose in him, even as it filled the face of Marsh, who glared at him furiously.

"You owe her a fare. Get those robes back to her, or let her stay," Skye said quietly, an unmistakable menace in his voice. The pilot and helmsman stared. The fort's clerks gaped.

Marsh pointed. "Off," he said. "You and your filthy squaw. Off my boat!"

"Give the Cheyenne woman her fare back."

Marsh was totally unafraid, and Skye knew the man would fight, and fight brutally if it came to that. The master closed in, his fists balled, his hard gaze steady.

The pilot and helmsman circled to either side, ready to help. A dead silence pervaded the pilothouse, a silence so profound that it seemed to blot the hubbub on the boiler deck and riverbank.

Then all three leapt at Skye simultaneously. Skye didn't fight back; there was no point in it. They escorted Skye to the companionway and pushed. Skye stumbled downward, caught a rail, and tripped down to the boiler deck.

"Aiee!" Victoria cried. She had obviously seen at least some of it.

"We're getting off. Get the horses saddled. I'll get our truck."

The second mate followed, ready to throw them off if they didn't leave on their own. Above, Marsh watched from the pilothouse.

Skye headed for the cabin, filled with regret. What had he done? Had he ruined his future with American Fur? Were his old feelings about injustice, feelings dating back to his slavery in the Royal Navy, still governing his conduct? Had he not grown since those youthful days?

It was too late to have regrets. Marsh had ejected him from the *Otter*, and that was a captain's absolute right. Marsh hated the Indian women. His boat was for whites, not redskins. But that puzzled Skye. There was something else at work here; something he didn't know about; something connected to Lame Deer, or her husband, Simon MacLees. Marsh was a choleric man, but that explained nothing. A minor incident had exploded into something darker. Skye wondered whether he would ever know the answer.

He stuffed their few possessions into Victoria's handsomely dyed parfleches, checked to see if he had left anything in the gloomy little cubicle, and emerged on the boiler deck—right into Bonfils, who was lounging aft, watching the furious business of loading the packet.

"Why, Skye, you leaving us?" the young man asked, delight in his eye.

Skye ignored him.

"Handsome ladies out there. I suppose I'll go see what a few trinkets will purchase," Bonfils said, following Skye past the firemen to the midships area where the gangway stretched to land. "You are abandoning us. Is it that you have given up your little, ah, quest to impress your magnificent virtues and skills upon my uncle Pierre?"

Skye stared at the handsome brigade leader, and then returned to his business.

It took a few minutes for Victoria to prepare the horses, and then they led the nervous, whinnying animals down the wobbling gangway and onto the levee, where scores of Sioux eyed them solemnly. Here they were safe; beyond the fort, Skye and Victoria would be fair game. No Name slunk along with them, his neck hair bristling.

Skye stood at the levee, rein in hand, while Victoria finished loading the horses. He was looking for Lame Deer, who had vanished in the hurlyburly of the crowd.

"You see the Cheyenne?" he asked Victoria.

She squinted. "What for?"

"Take to Saint Louis."

"You still going there?"

He nodded, lifted his battered topper, and settled it on his long locks. "Got unfinished business there. And the least the company can do is get the Cheyenne woman there safely, long as she paid her fare."

"You still with the company?" Victoria's gaze bore into him; she was confused.

"Haven't resigned," he said. "Maybe I will in St. Louis."

"How we going?"

"I've got a little credit. We didn't have time at rendezvous to drink up the last of the salary." He grinned. She grinned back.

"Maybe they got some goddam whiskey here," she said, cheer leaking into her hard glare like sun bursting into an overcast sky. "We got to find that Cheyenne. They treat her bad."

"Marsh doesn't like Indians."

"Well, sonofabitch, I don't like Marsh!"

They found Lame Deer at the fort, her horse tied to a hitch rail, her children clutching her. She might be a trader's wife, but a post of this size was plainly intimidating.

Victoria approached. "Hey, you want to go to St. Louis? Place of many lodges?"

Lame Deer looked uncertain. "My heart is two hearts now. My mind flies away from my spirit. My children weep."

"We'll take you," Victoria said.

"Long walk. Marsh, the big chief, put us off too," Skye said. "But we're going to St. Louis."

Lame Deer studied Skye with knowing eyes, and a determined look in her soft young face. "I will put wings on my feet. I will walk and leave no footprints upon the meadows. I will walk beside the river, and the fish will play beside me. My feet will carry me to the end of the world, for there will I see Simon. He gives me a big heart. I will go with you."

17

Skye wasn't very sure about what to do. Maybe he should just hightail it for the mountains, and see what came of that. But all his instincts told him to finish what he had started: he would submit himself to the directors of Pratte, Chouteau and Company and if they made him a trader to the Crows, that's what he would do.

Marsh's conduct puzzled him, but since he could not fathom it, he dismissed it. Marsh probably favored Bonfils, and this contretemps was as simple as that. The captain would tell Chouteau that he had been forced to put the disobedient Skye ashore, and that would be the end of the contest. A ship's master was a law unto himself. There was little he could do to change that.

He headed for the store, intending to provision, and glad he had not spent all his hard-won cash at rendezvous. He would have to provision for Lame Deer and her children too. He had no great wish to take her to her wayward husband in St. Louis, and wished the woman would head back to her people. But she was as determined as he was to reach St. Louis, and so they would make common cause. The more he thought of it, the better he liked the idea. If her arrival in St. Louis upset some powerful people, that was all the more reason to take her there.

The trading store at Fort Pierre Chouteau stood just inside the big river gate, and was open for trade but largely empty because the throngs at the fort had clustered around the *Otter* to gape at its white enameled hull and cabins, its elaborate fretwork, its twin black chimneys, and all the wonders of civilization aboard. It seemed so improbable, this traveling city anchored in a wilderness; so defiant of nature and nature's God, that he found his own gaze drawn to it over and over, as the crew walked its plank decks, and gangs lowered bales of fur into its smelly hold.

He steered Victoria into the post and the trading room, which was crammed with every imaginable item that might appeal to the Indian imagination. What he wanted mostly was staples: tea, powder, lead, percussion caps, and some canvas tenting for shelter, since he had left his lodge with Victoria's people.

The sole clerk on duty, a sallow Creole in a black suit, was provisioning two Yank frontiersmen, one skinny, big-toothed and redheaded; the other short, stout, freckled, and jittery. They both wore broad-brimmed, low-crowned gray felt hats that kept the fierce sun out of their faces. They were both armed with wicked-looking knives and other lethal accouterments, including horse pistols and boot knives.

"All right, Leblanc, bring 'er out to the flatboat," the redhead said. A heap of goods, ranging from flour sacks to tins of sugar, lay on the rude counter.

"*Oui, monsieur*," the clerk said.

Skye waited to see what sort of payment would be required, but the man offered nothing, and no bill was laid before him by the clerk. Probably Company men, requisitioning goods, Skye thought.

The redhead turned around, studied Skye a moment, and unwound himself, his gait so languorous and catlike that he exuded sheer menace. Skye supposed that the

Yank frontiersman in the blue chambray shirt had won a few scrapes. The other, whose step was oddly swift for one with rolls of fat rolling off his jaw and belly, was no less a menace. The pair weren't ones to trust.

The clerk summoned a breed boy to tote the mound of goods out the door, and turned to Skye.

"Sir?" he said.

"I'm provisioning," Skye said. "Now first, how many leagues is it to St. Louis?"

"By land or water?"

"Land."

"You're not on the riverboat?"

"We just got off it."

The man blinked. "A great oddity, sir. You will need cash to provision."

"Got it. Company credit, on paper."

"But they put you off the boat?"

"How many miles?" Skye asked, an edge in his voice this time.

"Ah, four hundred and some—"

"That far?"

"In leagues, monsieur."

"A thousand two hundred miles, then?"

"Ah, oui . . . one thousand and three hundred, more or less."

"Twenty days on a flatboat," said a voice behind him. Skye turned and discovered the redhead, lounging at the door. The man had been listening.

"We're traveling by horse."

"Mighty strange thing to do with a river to float you there in comfort."

Skye nodded. How he traveled was not the stranger's business. He would need provisions for seven or eight weeks for his entire party. He hoped to supply much of his provender with his heavy, octagon-barreled mountain rifle. Buffalo, deer, antelope, maybe some elk. . . .

Skye turned to the clerk. "You have any mules or pack-horses for sale?"

"Ah, no, only mustangs. Subdued horses are scarce here and valuable. They are hard to keep; hay, feed, and there is always the, ah, shall we say embezzlements of the Indians. . . ."

That was bad news. Skye needed two more pack animals. St. Louis was a long way.

The redhead was grinning. "You want a ride, easy trip, you got a ride. Me and my partner got us a mackinaw."

Skye turned. "Who are you?"

"I'm Red Gill; him out there, he's Shorty Ballard."

"And what is your business?"

"Independent company out of St. Louis."

"What are you carrying in your mackinaw?"

"Some hides, tallow, buffalo tongues . . ."

"What did you bring upriver?"

Gill grinned, revealing gaps where incisors should have been. "Oh, I reckon a few tradegoods for the Opposition, but not on that there mackinaw. We bought that boat at Fort Clark from the Chouteau interests."

Something didn't sound right. "You running an account here, I see."

Red Gill grinned. "We're teamsters. We brought some stuff by packtrain, and now we're taking some robes back by water. There's just two of us, and that ain't enough to man a flatboat proper, much less fight Injuns. You come along, and we won't charge ye but a little."

It was a temptation. Thirteen hundred miles of horse-back would be an ordeal, and without pack horses and supplies, it would be reckless.

"I'm Mister Skye," he said. He motioned them out the door and into the hot July sun. "Maybe you can persuade me," he added.

"Show you," Gill said, motioning Skye. Ahead, a breed boy and Shorty were toting sacks down to the riverbank, where a small mackinaw was anchored well down-stream from the riverboat.

Skye had never been on one. He found himself board-ing a scow made of thick handsawn planks still oozing sap, with a beveled prow and a squared off stern. A rudder on a long tiller dangled from the rear. Amidships was a cargo box, and behind it a small cabin with plank walls and a doorless entry at the rear. For a roof, a chunk of old, tallowed buffalo-hide lodgecover stretched over curved ribs. The mackinaw was perhaps forty feet long, with a beam of twelve, and it rode lightly in the water, drawing scarcely even a foot though it was loaded.

This was a one-way craft, to be sold for scrap at its destination. There were oar sockets forward, and various poles and oars lying on the planking. There was one odd-ity: a glorious bouquet of prairie asters, red mallow, and prairie evening primrose poked from a holder in the prow, a rainbow-bright and startling gaud upon a utilitarian scow.

"It beats riding," Gill said. "Have a lookaround."

The craft was sturdy enough; that didn't worry Skye. The nature of the company was what troubled him.

"I think we'll take our horses," he said, watching Shorty and the breed boy stuff a sack of corn, a cask of flour, a keg of tallow, some salt and sugar and pepper and mustard into the rude cargo box.

Skye edged toward the box and discovered it was full of packs of buffalo hides, and some casks.

Red shrugged. "We're just a pair of entrepreneurs out of Saint Louie," he said. "We've had our fun; Yankton women and all. Delivered upriver, and going back now."

"Delivered what, and to whom?"

Gill laughed until he wheezed, and Skye watched the adam's apple bob in his skinny throat. "You sure are choosy," he said. "Them squaws, they'll be safe with us, and the little ones too."

"The Cheyenne woman is returning to her husband," Skye said carefully.

"Oh, who's that?"

"A trader," Skye said.

"Well, we're pulling out in a little bit. You want a ride, we'll charge you ten apiece; the wimmin cook and take care of things; you help pole and row and steer, and if there's a fracas, have that piece ready to help. We got a little protection here," he said, waving at the plank-walled cabin. Several rifle ports had been shopped into its sides.

Skye laughed shortly. "Not much protection for the man on the tiller," he said.

Gill laughed. "It's been thought of."

"It's not Indians I'm worried about."

Gill straightened, fire blazing in his blue eyes. "Well, then, you just go get yourself to hell on a horse," he snarled. "We offered you a cheap ride if'n you share the load, and that's all I'm going to say. If we ain't for you, quit palavering and wasting our time. We got to make St. Louis with these hides or we don't make a profit."

Skye refused to budge. "You have an account with Pratte and Chouteau?"

Red Gill turned wary. "No, not as I know."

"How was all this truck paid for?"

"They owed us, and that's the last damned question I'll answer."

Skye pondered it. "I'll talk to the women and let you know. We have to provision, too."

"*You* got an account?"

"Brigade leader with the company."

"Mister Skye, is it? I heard of you. Now I got a question for *you*. How come you ain't on that riverboat?"

Skye smiled.

Gill waited, cheerfully, until it was plain to him he would get no answer. Then, "I got me a one gallon jug in there, and it ain't mountain whiskey either; it's good Kentuck I been presarving."

Barnaby Skye felt his resolve sliding from under him, and headed for the women to talk things over. Captain Gill—the name fit perfectly—had made a proposition he couldn't turn down.

18

Benton Marsh was worried. His hold was crammed with furs, and an additional nine packs had been stuffed into the women's cabin. He had a full complement of passengers, too, mostly Creole engagés who were returning to St. Louis after fulfilling their contracts with the company.

The *Otter* was drawing a full four feet of water, and that spelled trouble this late in the season. Worse, he would be loading forty cords of wood at Farm Island, just downstream; wood cut for his use by the post because there was so little of it in this area.

Once he left the island, he would be overloaded, though that burden would lessen as fast as the wood was burned. Within an hour after the Fort Pierre returns, as the company called its fur harvest, had been stowed away and the ship properly balanced, he was sailing toward the island for the fuel.

He was an irritable, irascible man, and his worries didn't improve his disposition as he stood in the pilothouse watching his pilot and helmsman ease the ship into the glittering river. Nor was it improved by the presence of the well-connected Alexandre Bonfils, whose professed goal was to become a trader, but whose constant presence in the pilothouse suggested that he might have other motives. Was he Pierre Chouteau's eyes and ears?

Marsh held his temper, but just barely.

The vessel moved sluggishly into the channel, leaving the post behind. There were no visible snags or bars ahead, no sharp bends to whirl the boat toward shore, and Marsh relaxed.

"There," he said, pointing at a rude levee at Farm Island.

The helmsman was already steering in that direction.

"How many new passengers?" Bonfils asked, peering at the motley crowd on the boiler deck.

"Twenty-seven," Marsh said, wondering why he answered; indeed, wondering why he permitted this scion of the owning families to be there. But he knew why.

"Minus a few." Bonfils laughed. "Thank you for the great favor."

Marsh stared coldly.

Bonfils met the gaze. "Skye and his squaw, left behind. That eliminates the only real problem I face. He's formidable in his way, but of course has his little difficulties."

"What difficulties?"

"He's a deserter from the Royal Navy and makes no bones about it. Ah, *mon ami*, I think that is a black mark upon him."

"It doesn't improve his chances," Marsh replied curtly.

The pilot pulled the bell cord, and soon the rumble of the paddle wheels lessened and the rattle of popping steam from the escapement died. The vessel slowed, drifted toward the woodlot, while Trenholm readied the deck crew and instructed the passengers, who were about to perform their first wood duty.

The fort's engagés had stacked the four-foot cordwood in orderly piles next to the landing, and in short order the crew and passengers were hauling it aboard and noisily stacking it on the foredeck under the direction of the burly firemen who could each lift an entire four-foot log and jam it into the inferno.

As usual, Bonfils had escaped the task by standing there in the pilothouse like some laird. Marsh was tempted to direct the young man to go to work, but bit back the command. He seethed at his own frustration; why couldn't he summon the courage to put this dubious princeling to work like ordinary mortals?

The task was going smoothly but would require two hours, even with so many hands. It took two passengers to lift a single four-foot log aboard. Marsh didn't much care for this softer upriver fuel, mostly cottonwood, willow, box elder, and even driftwood, though the driftwood didn't burn well and had to be mixed with other wood or burned with resin. Occasionally he burned some ponderosa pine, which worked better.

It took twice as much upriver wood to feed his boilers than the better hardwoods downstream, such as the solid, heavy, oak and hickory and walnut and maple. No one had found coal. In three or four years, every tree here on Farm Island would be gone, and then what?

It was during this fuel stop that the pilot spotted the mackinaw bobbing up from behind, and pointed at it. Marsh picked up his spyglass to see who it was; he knew most of the rivermen.

This one was newly made of raw wood; maybe at the Navy Yard north of Fort Pierre; its planks not yet weathered. It had the usual cargo box amidships, and a rude cabin. He focused on the man at the tiller, and knew him: Shorty Ballard. Red Gill and Ballard were teamsters and boatmen licensed by General Clark to transport goods in the Indian country. They supplied the Opposition, and as far as Marsh knew, had no connection to Pratte, Chouteau and Company. But they had never lacked cash, which they spent unwisely in St. Louis, and there had always been question marks surrounding them.

His glass then revealed some unpleasant news: the Cheyenne woman was en route to St. Louis after all, and the Skyes as well, and even their damned dog. The Skyes must have sold their horses for passage, because there were no beasts of burden aboard.

They were continuing downriver!

So his efforts to protect his daughter and wife might well come to naught after all. There might be a scandal. MacLees might find his future clouded and his marriage in distress.

Irritably he glassed the whole flatboat, wondering what was in the cargo box, and wondering whether he ought to overtake the craft downstream, bring it to heel, examine the box, and confiscate the goods if there was the slightest sign of illegality. Maybe he could stop them all in their tracks. Not for nothing did he have a six-pounder and a large crew.

He'd see. Meanwhile, he'd arrive in St. Louis a week or ten days ahead of the flatboat and would have time to warn MacLees, and influence Chouteau. It would be tricky, but it would protect the company. And protect Sarah Lansing.

The flatboat drifted by, riding a relentless current that averaged seven or eight miles an hour, and its passengers waved lazily. They would be a half hour downstream before the *Otter* was ready to go. But there were ways . . .

"There go your passengers," Bonfils said.

Marsh grunted.

When the wooding was done, Marsh set out again, pushing hard through the midday heat until he sighted the flatboat a couple of miles ahead. The *Otter* would overtake the flatboat in an hour, about four in the afternoon. He knew all about flatboats. They could make excellent time going downriver, and could more easily travel at night because they drew so little water they didn't need to stick to the channels. Many a flatboat had been navigated by moonlight on the shoulders of the mighty river. Neither did a flatboat have to make wood stops.

He eyed Bonfils irritably. "Perhaps you wish to retire from the pilothouse for a time?"

"No, this is the place to be," Bonfils said. "Best perch on the boat."

"You may take our leave," Marsh said directly.

Bonfils looked startled, and then cloudy, as if this was something to remember and make use of in the future. Nonetheless, he retreated to the hurricane deck and down the companionway, his brow furrowed.

Marsh turned to his pilot, Lamar DeWayne. "Give that flatboat as much grief as you can."

The pilot stared a moment. The helmsman turned to peer at the master. The command jeopardized DeWayne's federal pilot license.

"We are far from St. Louis. I don't wish for you to swamp the flatboat. Just brush it and make sure it's caught in our wake."

DeWayne reddened. "Why?"

"Because I told you to."

Marsh could see the pilot wondering whether to obey, or whether to face the master's wrath and ability to make his life miserable.

"I don't suppose you would supply me with a reason," the pilot said.

"Smugglers and rivals."

"If they're smugglers let's pull them over and have a look."

"I am considering it."

"Weren't those our passengers on it?"

"Yes, unfortunately."

"Is this connected to them?"

Marsh exploded. "Do it or give me the helm."

DeWayne glowered and ordered the helmsman to ease to the right edge of the channel, where the flatboat was proceeding. Unfortunately the channel was plenty wide there; the episode could not be dismissed as an unfortunate navigational problem.

"Add steam," Marsh said.

DeWayne clanged bells. Moments later the chimneys billowed black smoke and the thunder of the paddle wheels noticeably quickened. The current gave them seven miles an hour; the thrashing wheels doubled that. That speed would be safe enough until they reached the bight a mile ahead where the channel cut to the right bank and then swung hard left.

"Slow as soon as you pass the flatboat," he said.

DeWayne nodded.

They gained on the flatboat, loomed behind it. Shorty Ballard peered behind him and eased toward the right bank. The helmsman followed, closing on the flatboat.

Now the people on the flatboat leapt up in alarm, and Ballard yanked the tiller hard heading for shore. Skye had removed his topper and was waving hard at them, even as his squaw was shepherding the Cheyenne woman and her brats to the right side of the flatboat.

The *Otter* overtook the flatboat and the helmsman spun his wheel until the steamboat was veering back to the channel. The flatboat rocked violently, toppling its passengers and taking water. Ballard was thrown into the river, and Marsh watched him surface, shout, and start swimming. Gill threw him a line, Ballard caught it and crawled back, hand over hand, to the pitching flatboat.

"Make a log entry, DeWayne. 'Collision with flatboat in channel narrowly averted by skillful maneuvering of the *Otter*.'"

"Write it yourself," DeWayne retorted.

19

Skye picked himself up from the slimy floorboards, found his top hat, and stuffed it over his stringy hair. Murky water sloshed about, floating debris with it. His britches were soaked on one side.

He checked Victoria. She was sitting with splayed legs, her skirts in a pool of filthy water, a sober expression on her features. He offered his big rough hand and helped her up. Water dripped from her fringed buckskins. No Name peered at him inquisitively and with some vast resignation.

Gill was helping Shorty over the transom. Water was rivering from the helmsman's blue chambray shirt, and it plastered his dark hair to his skull. With a grunt, Shorty landed in the slop, cursing violently, fulminating great oaths against the pilot, helmsman, captain, company, and all steamboats in general.

Gill was all right, smiling thinly, and taking stock of the flatboat. But Lame Deer was not. She crouched before the crude cabin, her whimpering children clinging to her, worry glazing her warm brown eyes.

"The river devils have reached up from under the water to pull us to them," she whispered. "We ride on top of the dead, over the waters that want to pull us under and hold us down. Ahhh . . ."

Victoria reached the woman and began jabbering in some sort of Indian lingua franca, but Lame Deer only nodded, her face grave, and her gaze trailing the steamboat as it diminished far ahead and finally swept around a bight. The children remained stonily silent, as most Indian children did in a crisis.

Gill unbuttoned his soaked shirt and wrung it, his grin returning as he surveyed the vessel.

"Close one," he said.

"You think the pilot didn't see us?" Skye asked.

"Not a chance of that. You ever been in a pilothouse? You see the whole layout."

"It was deliberate?"

"Couldn't have been other; channel's two hundred yards wide here." Red squinted at him as he pulled the soaked shirt back on. "He got something against you?"

"Not this big a something. Not the sort of something that would overturn a mackinaw."

"Marsh sure had something against someone, brushing us like that. What do you suppose he meant by that?"

"Warning," Shorty Ballard said, getting a grip on his tiller and steering the boat back into the channel where the current would be fastest.

"Who's he warning?" Red asked.

No one could answer that.

Skye thought he saw a wary look pass between Red Gill and Shorty, but he couldn't fathom what was inspiring their caution. It puzzled him. Why would Marsh do that? The man didn't want Indians on his boat, but that hardly explained it.

Lame Deer lifted her soaked children onto the dry and sun-warmed planks of the cargo box, and there the two little ones rested solemnly while the sun pummeled moisture from their clothes.

Gill found a collapsible leather bucket and motioned everyone to his front corner of the flatboat so he could scoop up the filthy water accumulating there. He couldn't get much at a time, and Skye thought the sun would evaporate it faster than Gill could dip it out, but Gill kept working.

Even though the sun shone brightly, a cloud hung over the boat. What had been a cheerful start down the river had deteriorated into silence and caution and fear. The bravado wasn't working; Lame Deer's fear was palpable, a tense terror that contrasted sharply with the quiet certitude and courage that had brought her so far from her home and tribe.

Gill quit dipping and sat down. "If Marsh's got something against you 'uns, me and Shorty want to know about it. This here's dangerous country. Why'd he put you off his boat?"

The question was aimed at Skye.

"He put us off after we tried to help the Cheyenne lady," Skye said. "We arrived at Fort Pierre, and without a by-your-leave had his mate tote the woman's gear from the cabin and put her and her nags off. She'd paid in furs for passage to St. Louis, and Victoria, she got her dander up and we went to talk to him about it. I was thrown out of the pilothouse, and they put us off too."

Red shook his head. "He's an ornery sonofabitch, but that don't make sense."

Skye didn't argue the point. He didn't like being on any boat, helpless, under the control of others. He didn't like being on the riverboat, and didn't much care for the trip on the flatboat either, at the mercy of a pair of men he didn't know and whom he suspected of being less than forthright.

Skye figured maybe it was his turn. "What did you say you do for a living, mate?"

"Rivermen."

"Where'd this flatboat come from?"

"They built it at Fort Pierre, up in their yard north of the post."

"How'd you get it?"

Gill paused, for the first time growing wary. He shrugged. "Deal we did with the company."

"And how did you get up here from St. Louis?"

Gill grinned. "Forget it, Skye."

"Whose furs are these in the box?"

"Them robes and pelts are ours, lock, stock and barrel."

Gill turned away. Shorty was frowning. Skye had the distinct feeling a lot was left unsaid.

Skye tried another tack. "I think you'd better report this to General Clark, if that's the man to talk to. Someone should be pulling that pilot's license. That was a deliberate act, I think."

"Aw, Skye, it wasn't nothing. Just forget it."

"It's Mister Skye, mate. And it's not something to forget. You'd better report it. Or I will."

Red shrugged, and once again Skye sensed there were things unspoken.

"You just mind your business, Skye," Shorty growled from the stern.

Between the warm sun and the labor of crew and passengers, the flatboat dried out. Gill and Skye spent the next hour putting gear in order, coiling hempen ropes, checking the cargo box for leakage, mopping river bilge out of the boat. Shorty steered in the exact center of the channel, swearing profusely, a low monotone of cussing that Skye found inventive and odd. The women vanished into the cabin, and when they emerged Lame Deer was wearing a dry skirt and Victoria's buckskins had been wrung out and smoothed.

Skye wandered to the prow, peered into the water, and tried to put it all together, but he only ran into mysteries. Something more than Marsh's ugly temper and powerful racial antagonisms had caused him to put the Cheyenne family off his boat; and the Skyes too. What was it? And what was this outfit's real business? Why were Red and Shorty so secretive?

He discovered a heavy stubble of beard on his face, dug a straight-edge out of his kit, lathered with a sliver of soap, and scraped carefully. He lacked a looking glass, except the rippling surface of the river, but his fingers served to tell him what surfaces had been missed. Victoria loved his smooth cheeks and she grew testy about his bristly facial hair. The little Cheyenne children, Singing Rain and Echo, as he called the boy, watched solemnly.

"Bet you watched your father shave," Skye said.

The boy stared, and turned away.

The boat creaked with every swell, but Lame Deer never quite accepted the groaning, and he saw her studying the planks, the oakum calking, the crudely joined corners, doweled together for the want of screws or nails. Often they were a hundred yards from a bank; a hard swim in swift cold water, especially when dragged down by doeskin clothing.

They made another twenty miles that day and camped on a gravelly bar stretching out from an ash grove. Skye wished he had a horse to reconnoiter the country; they were vulnerable not only to predatory war and hunting parties, but also to bears, migrating buffalo herds, and wolves. He cradled his mountain rifle in the crook of his arm and hiked in his soaked moccasins across a grassy flat and up a ravine until he topped the bluff guarding the valley, and saw only a silent plain, undulating westward toward the sunset, shrouding its secrets. No Name patrolled before him, acknowledging only that he and Skye were bound by Fate, but not by affection. No Name lived by his inner lights, which Skye had never fathomed or changed.

Skye felt incredibly lonely there, so far from other

mortals. Loneliness was nothing new; he had been lonely ever since the moment a press gang had hauled him off the London Dock and stuffed him into a warship. He had been thirteen years old, and never saw his family again.

This vast plain reminded him of the sea; desolate, hollow, but grand and ever-changing too. He hoped he might hear coyotes this night; he wanted life around him. He knew there would be deer and antelope and all manner of small creatures patrolling the riverbanks this evening, and maybe he would make meat. But in this twilight he felt not life, but a deadness, a forsakenness in this solemn and flat land without landmarks. He preferred the mountains.

He found Victoria and Lame Deer boiling cornmeal. They would have corn mush again, tasteless and dull but filling. It satisfied the belly, but not the tongue.

Shorty and Gill insisted that people sleep on the flatboat at night, rather than on dry land, and maybe there was reason in it, Skye thought. When everyone had eaten from the mess tins, and done their ablutions in the brush, Gill herded them back aboard, and he and Shorty maneuvered the boat twenty or thirty feet offshore, and set anchors. Skye slept on a buffalo robe, wishing for soil which he could sculpt into a decent bed. The planks of the flatboat were unyielding. The bunks in the cabin were occupied by the women and children, luckier than he by virtue of sex and age.

But the starry night passed, and even before dawn Shorty was stirring, and soon Red was too. They pulled anchor as soon as Shorty could see to navigate, and drifted through another humdrum morning, watching the plains march by, the bluffs change from tan to orange to white, the tributary creeks tumble into the Missouri, and the fishing birds wheel through the sky, dive for minnows, shrill their warnings, and flap away from carrion.

Then, midday, they spotted the *Otter*. She lay crosswise

of the channel, her deck tilted sharply, her chimneys askance and emitting no smoke.

"Will ya look at that," Red said. "She's run aground."

"Hit a bar," Shorty said, squinting.

"Hit a bar and it twisted her around so that bar runs along her keel, looks like," Red said. "They're gonna need some lighters to clear that hold and float her over."

That's when the six-pounder cracked, a puff of white smoke ballooning from its barrel even before the sound reached Skye's ears.

20

Shorty Ballard ignored the shot and steered the flatboat straight ahead on a trajectory that wouldn't come within a hundred yards of the marooned riverboat. Crewmen stood on the sloping boiler deck, but other people, passengers mostly, had splashed across a gravelly shallows to the left bank and stood on a knoll.

Skye didn't like it. "He means for you to stop and render assistance," he said.

"After what he done?" Shorty's bellicose retort was intended to settle the matter instantly.

"You'll see your license pulled," Skye retorted. Failure to render assistance was a grave matter.

Red Gill grinned, and motioned to Ballard.

"The hell I will!" Ballard spat. Skye sympathized. The wake of the riverboat had pitched Shorty into the Missouri and endangered his life. But Skye could see a deck crew charging the cannon, and this time with more than just powder. He nodded to Victoria, and both of them lay flat on the warm boards, as close to the plank side of the hull as they could. Lame Deer vanished inside the cabin, herding her children with her.

Marsh's voice, amplified by a megaphone, boiled

across the water. "Gill and Ballard, bring that flatboat in at once!"

"Go to hell," Ballard yelled.

Time slid by, while the flatboat approached the point where it would pass the grounded steamer.

"Bring her here!" Marsh bellowed. "Or face the music."

Shorty bristled. "Go to hell, Marsh."

The response this time was another crack of the cannon. Skye watched someone with a fusee dip it to the touch hole. Skye ducked and covered his head, knocking off his topper in the process. The ball crossed the bow and hit water near the right bank. Skye slid his head over the gunnel and stared. A crew was frantically recharging the piece.

"Gill, pull over," Marsh bawled. "Next time we won't miss."

Red crawled back to Shorty. "Give me the tiller," he said.

"Hell I will. They won't shoot a hole in a boat they need."

Skye lifted his head. "It will be cannister, and it'll clean you right out of the boat."

"Then I'll lie on the planks and let this sonofabitch drift by; it's in the current anyway."

They were opposite the riverboat now, and Skye heard the snap of small arms, and felt lead pop into the planks. He'd had it with this pair. They were up to no good. He gathered himself, crawled aft under cover, and then sprang at Shorty, catching him unprepared. He heard the pop of rifle fire, and then he landed on Shorty, ripping him loose from the tiller and landing on him in one swift motion.

Red dodged sideways, not wanting a part of this, but Skye spotted a drawn Arkansas Toothpick in his hand. The blow knocked the air out of Shorty, who gulped for breath, gasping on the floorboards. Skye leapt for the tiller and stood up, braving the pistols of crewmen, and swung it hard toward the left bank. The flatboat had already passed the *Otter*. For a terrible moment the bore of the six-pounder followed him as the crew swung it, but then they saw the flatboat veer sharply, its skewing wake showing them the sudden turn.

Shorty recovered but chose not to fight. Red, his furious gaze darting from Skye to the riverboat, crouched ready for action. And then he did an odd thing: He dug into a tackle box at the prow, and with his back to the riverboat, dropped his jug of Kentuck overboard.

Skye mourned, but at last had an inkling of the business this partnership was in.

He studied the riverboat, watching the six-pounder swivel in his direction; watching Marsh up on the hurricane deck watching him; watching the crew watching him. Everyone on that steamer had seen the whole business.

Red slid his Green River knife into its sheath, and grinned.

Shorty started cussing again, a nonstop, profane damning of everyone's ancestors, parents, animals, connections, children, grandchildren, businesses, profits, and anything else that caught his wrath. Victoria was so fascinated that she crouched beside Shorty, blotting up locutions for future use.

"Goddam," she said, her face wreathed in joy.

"Skye, run that flatboat into the bank there," Marsh bawled.

"It's Mister Skye, mate."

The captain looked even more choleric than usual. Behind him on the hurricane deck stood the helmsman, hefting a rifle.

A party of boatmen had stepped off the riverboat and advanced down a spit of gravel to the point where Skye was steering the flatboat, and in moments they caught the lines that Red pitched to them. Red eyed Skye, his gaze so odd, so twisted, that Skye couldn't fathom what was going through the man's head.

Shorty oozed sheer hate, and Skye knew he had made an enemy, and when this pair got their flatboat back, Skye and Victoria and the Cheyennes would not be aboard.

The flatboat bumped gravel, but the crew pulled it upstream to the looming riverboat. Skye stepped to land, and helped Victoria. The riverboat rode on a sandbar, canted prow and starboard down, stern and port side up, entirely in water. The gangway provided a bridge to a gravelly driftwood-littered island, one of many separated by shallow flowage of the river, which formed a huge oxbow there. Even when unloaded, it would be a hell of a thing to float that ship and ease it out to the current in an area of braided channels.

The starboard paddle wheel had shattered.

"Skye, why didn't you stop as directed?" Marsh bellowed.

Skye ignored him. Marsh knew perfectly well who had stopped the flatboat to render aid, so there was nothing to say, not one damned word.

"Trenholm, examine that flatboat and bring me a manifest."

The mate and two crewmen boarded, probed the packs of robes in the cargo box, poked around in the cabin, and emerged.

"No manifest," Trenholm said to the man above.

"Then what's in there?"

"Nineteen bales of robes and pelts and some loose furs."

"Whose pelts?" That question was directed at Red Gill.

"Reckon they're ours."

"We'll see. If you don't have papers, they're contraband."

"Contraband hell!" Shorty yelled.

"We'll take this to Gen'ral Clark," Gill said.

Marsh laughed. "You will, eh? Get those packs out of there and tow that flatboat around to midships and tie up. Get busy. We're losing time."

Skye watched, wondering whether Gill and Ballard would end up with their buffalo hides when they got their vessel back. For that matter, he wondered whether he and Victoria would be stranded two or three hundred miles from anywhere.

"You can't do this," Gill said hotly.

"Get busy," Marsh yelled.

Crewmen from the riverboat swarmed over the flatboat, hoisting the hundred-pound packs out of the cargo box and onto gravel. Lame Deer drew her children away, hurried them across wet rock and settled them at a distance on a gravelly spit. Skye knew she didn't understand any of this and was finding safety in distance.

That afternoon sweating boatmen hoisted pack after pack of furs out of the hold of the *Otter* and into the flatboat, and then poled the flatboat to a point just downstream where the cargo could be unloaded on dry ground. There, the furs could be reloaded onto the flatboat and lightered back to the steamer after it had floated over the sandbar.

The riverboat didn't budge. The pressure of the current pressed it to the bar. Evening came, and still the boat didn't float free. Crewmen built bonfires downwind, and continued to lift cargo out of the hold through the twilight and into darkness, while Marsh paced his hurricane deck furiously, emanating rage but saying nothing.

Ballard and Gill, helpless against this armed commandeering of their boat, glared at Skye, who was the author of their misfortune, and Skye figured he and Victoria would be walking to St. Louis when all this was over. Ballard cussed nonstop, softly, profanely, witheringly, his wrath washing over Marsh, Trenholm, every deckman in sight, as well as Skye and Victoria. Skye wasn't worried about him: a man venting his spleen in such fashion was less dangerous than one bottling it up, like Red Gill, whose silent assessing gaze hid calculations and bitterness.

His stomach told him it was time for some good biscuits and corn, but no one started a meal. Marsh paced relentlessly; his mate, Trenholm, oversaw the operation, the steersman stood at the pilothouse, rifle in hand, and the crew worked silently, saying nothing about food or rest under the palpable rage of the master.

Then, when the flatboat was poled away with yet another mound of peltries, the boat ground against gravel once, groaned, creaked, and floated over, gradually righting itself. The crew anchored just below the bar but well away from shore, just downstream from the heaped cargo on the gravel.

At last Marsh halted for a meal. A cool night wind whipped the light of the bonfires. He and Trenholm and young Bonfils descended to the gravel spit to examine the shattered right paddle wheel along with his carpenter and blacksmith. Skye quietly splashed across a flowage and joined them. In the dim light of a distant bonfire, and the ineffectual light of a bird's-eye lantern, Skye thought he saw half a dozen shattered paddles, each of which would need to be unbolted from the wheel and replaced.

Marsh fumed. "Get busy. I want this repaired by daylight," he snapped at his carpenter.

The man started to protest, and then held his peace.

Marsh noticed Skye. "What are you doing here?"

"Looking."

"Go back with the others. I'll deal with you later."

Skye lifted his battered top hat. "Deal with us?"

"I'm busy. Don't get in my way."

"We'd like to get some of our food out of the cabin of the flatboat. We have hungry children to feed."

"Skye, get the hell out of here."

Bonfils laughed. "You're out of luck. It's the company you keep. Those gents are smugglers. Maybe you are too."

So that was it. Skye wasn't in a mood to argue with the master or his ham-fisted mate or the scion of the company.

He splashed across the shallows again, headed straight to the flatboat which was riding the water loaded with the last of the ship's cargo.

He walked up a plank, boarded, headed aft to the cabin, all without protest from the deckmen. No one stopped him. Inside, he opened a food box, pulled out a sack of cornmeal, found a kettle, a firesteel, and other items, and returned to shore. An hour later Victoria and Lame Deer fed cornmeal mush to the children, and then the rest.

Lame Deer sang, this time in her own reedy tongue, smoothing the hair of her children, her voice soft and melodic, the cursing of the nearby rivermen contrapuntal. The children nestled, and she held them close, blanketing them with her courage as the darkness enveloped them all.

Skye sat in the dark, his belly full of fried corn mush, wondering whether to make his fate or wait for it.

21

A low growl from No Name awakened Skye. He peered about, disoriented, a thick ground fog obscuring everything in the gray predawn light. He could not remember where he was; then the hard gravel he was sleeping on reminded him. He was on a spit of land on the left bank of an oxbow of the Missouri River, an island of sorts but only for the moment. When the river dropped another few inches, it would be shoreline.

He had learned to respect No Name's warnings. The dog was an ally rather than a pet, an independent, cantankerous, wily peer who made common cause with Skye and Victoria, but whose tail rarely wagged, and whose affection was fleeting and reserved. But the very qualities that had made No Name a master of survival had been offered to Skye; and now the dog was softly warning his human companion of trouble.

Skye glanced about. He and Victoria had spread their robes beside some red willow brush, next to a stack of driftwood. She did not stir. And yet he felt a moving presence in that camp. He remembered that the Cheyenne woman and her two children were closer to the shore, nestled in the roots of a cottonwood. He didn't know where Gill and Ballard were and didn't care. The flatboat bobbed nearby, a gray blur, with some of Marsh's crew aboard. Just downstream, on the other side of the gravel bar, floated the *Otter* in shallow water. The ship was obscured by fog. The noise of repair had ceased in the middle of the night, either because Marsh called a halt or the carpenter and his mates had finished installing new paddles.

Skye lay quietly on his back, listening closely, seeing nothing but sensing trouble. He pulled back his robe, collected his mountain rifle, pulled his powderhorn over his neck, and then lifted his hightop moccasins over his feet and laced them. He nudged Victoria, who sat up in one lithe motion, glanced about, and silently collected her bow and quiver.

The dog was pointing toward the mountain of fur bales stored on the gravelly spit, and Skye thought perhaps the rank smell of the furs and uncured hides had drawn a predator, maybe even a bear. He sensed but didn't hear motion around the pile.

Then he saw the shapes of moving men, walking single file, filtering through the foggy dawn, so close he thought surely he and Victoria would be discovered. *Indians.* That much he knew. Now there were more, scores of them peering and poking, examining the flatboat without boarding it, and vanishing in the fog downstream, where the riverboat rode the night on tethers tied to trees.

Many Indians. Victoria was cussing softly. "Lakota," she whispered. "Goddam war party. Painted up."

He couldn't fathom how she knew, but Indians could recognize one another far better than whites.

Painted for war. But probably not against whites. The Teton or Lakota Sioux as well as the Dakota Sioux had been at peace with the traders for years.

He couldn't put numbers to this crowd, but there were plenty of Sioux around, poking, probing, reconnoitering, maybe looking for easy plunder. They would find it.

Marsh had posted no pickets and had assumed he would be safe enough in this friendly country. Not that Marsh was equipped to fight a war. He knew there were but five or six rifles aboard, and maybe a few pistols, and even those weapons were largely owned by passengers, mostly engagés returning to St. Louis. There was the six-pounder mounted on the foredeck, maybe still loaded—and probably useless. Anyone trying to aim or arm it would be mowed down in a hail of arrows.

Skye sighed, wanting to act. For much of this trip he had been under the command of others, his own will counting for nothing. His fate was not in his own hands. He was at the mercy of the company, and its factors in the posts, and then its riverboat captain and his crew, and was finally in the hands of the operators of a flatboat; men apparently engaged in some sort of illegal traffic.

He had, moreover, taken upon himself the protection of a Cheyenne woman and her children. So there he was, unable to give a command and see it followed, as he had when he was leading a trapping brigade. Quite the reverse: here he was expected to obey instantly. Even Gill and Ballard expected it. Ever since he had landed in North America, he had controlled his destiny; and now he was not in command, either of himself or others.

He had no friends among Marsh or his officers; and no friends on the flatboat either, not after tackling Shorty Ballard and seizing the tiller and steering the flatboat toward the *Otter*.

He watched more shadowy figures patrol the site as the light quickened noticeably. At any moment, these Sioux would be discovered and all hell would break loose. And yet the Sioux had not engaged in bloodletting. Their tomahawks and knives rested in their sheaths. They probably had not yet figured out what this camp was about, and what they might do without resistance if they chose.

Skye supposed the best bet for his people would be the

flatboat, which could be unloosed quickly and supply them with the safety of water as well as the drift of a current. He nodded toward it, and Victoria nodded back.

Barely forty feet away, obscured by the fog, a knot of warriors huddled, whispering furiously, plainly at odds, confused, and wary. There was traffic now, warriors walking back and forth, splashing across the gravelly shallows between this meandering spit of gravel and the one lower down, where the riverboat bobbed on the quiet river.

Victoria slipped back into the brush and disappeared, and Skye knew she was awakening the Cheyenne woman and maybe reconnoitering.

Skye had a decision to make and only moments to make it. He knew somehow it was portentous, and the wrong move could cost him his life, and maybe Victoria's too. He could shepherd Victoria and the Cheyennes out of the area before the daylight pierced the veil of fog, using the braided gravelly islands as their escape route. Or he could try to save the furs and boat and ultimately, Pierre Chouteau's company. Almost half of the annual returns were stacked there on the gravel. A fortune by any measure. He could try to keep hotheads, including Bonfils, from starting a fight they would only lose. These warriors, after all, had yet to lift a war axe, fire an arrow, or lance a sleeping boatman.

He knew what he had to do, and finished dressing, clamping his black beaver topper to his head. Then he whistled, and then he called.

"Gents, come visit me; I'm right here, plain sight if you move a little closer. Welcome, Lakota!"

His voice seemed muted in the choking fog; had anyone heard?

"Hey, Lakota! Dakota! Here I am!"

Now at last shadowy shapes materialized, and in moments he found himself surrounded by warriors, eight, ten, fifteen, armed and dangerous. They were Sioux all right; tall, sinewy, light-skinned, wearing war garb, which is to say, very little but paint. Some wore eagle feathers in their hair; war honors. Others wore medicine bundles or amulets suspended from their necks. Most wore summer moccasins. They were vermillioned and ochered, in chevrons, stripes, handprints, and mystical designs.

Skye felt the prickle he always felt when he considered how easily an arrow could pierce him. But he lifted his hands and made the peace sign, the brother sign, the friend sign. They stared.

He identified himself with the sky sign, and some recognition filled their faces. His name had come to mean something among the western tribes. He had fought for Victoria's people, the Crow.

Finally a headman of some sort emerged from the thick fog, and stared at Skye. This one was a long-nosed giant, a foot taller than Skye, built like a bear.

"Who you?"

That was English. The chief had been around a trading post.

"I am Mister Skye. My wife and I and others are assisting the captain of that fireboat. He is making repairs."

The words didn't register. This one knew all too few.

So Skye told him again, simple words, many signs.

"What will you give us?"

Ah, there it was.

"Gather your warriors here and I will give you food and a gift."

He wasn't sure what sort of gift. The headman weighed all that, eating up time.

"Be quick about it," Skye said. "They will shoot you if they see you." If those aboard the riverboat weren't all dead.

He heard some of the crew that had spent the night on the flatboat talking. The daylight was intensifying. He heard a scuffle, some grunts, and then the boatmen, along with Gill and Ballard, appeared, prisoners of still more Sioux. They looked frightened but knew enough to shut up, their gaze fixed on Skye, who stood in the center of a mob of fifty warriors.

"Who are you?" Skye asked the headman.

"Bull Calf, a war leader of the Sans Arcs, as we are called by the white men. We are going to kill the lying Pawnee, and bring back slaves and many horses."

Bull Calf was a noted war leader, a force to be reckoned with. "How many are you?" Skye asked.

"We are many. Ten times the fingers of my hands."

Skye gambled. "You will need to cross the Big River to go to the Pawnee."

"Yes. That is why we are here; this is a good place. But we found you and the fireboat."

Skye calculated swiftly. "We will give you a gift. We will take you and your ponies on the fireboat across the Big River. Then you will be strong and fresh. If the fireboat is not fixed, we will take you across the Big River in that flatboat." He pointed. "A few at a time. Then you can kill the Pawnee."

Bull Calf translated for his warriors, who listened solemnly, craning their necks to see Marsh's boat slowly emerge from the fog in the morning sun. He saw curiosity, fear, anger, and awe on their faces. Most had never even seen such a boat, much less ridden on one. And here was a chance to cross the Big River without getting wet or losing horses or endangering themselves.

Bull Calf nodded.

But even as he nodded, he saw Bonfils and Marsh's boatmen on the fog-shrouded riverboat swing their sixpounder around until its muzzle was a black hole facing this throng.

22

Skye yelled. The Sans Arcs fled, stumbling over one another to escape the bore of that six-pounder on the hurricane deck thirty yards distant.

Dawn light glinted on the brass barrel. Bonfils, wielding a punk, jammed it into the touchhole. Smoke erupted. Skye felt grape blow the top hat off his head, sear his ribs, smash into his thigh. Felt himself punched backward, flying through air.

A sharp boom reached his ears as he fell. He heard screams; saw warriors bloom red; saw Ballard fly backward and tumble to earth; heard a child's sob and then his pain deafened him and he heard nothing but the roaring of his pulse.

He heard, from some vast distance, the roar of the six-pounder again; horses splashing across the gravelly flowages; the ululating howls of the Indians; the crack of rifles and carbines, and again, the bark of the cannon. He writhed on the ground.

Victoria raced up to him, weeping and cursing.

"Where, where, dammit?"

Skye ran his hand along his ribs, and found blood there and seared flesh, and hurt that lanced him and stopped his breathing. He tried to suck air but raw pain stopped his lungs. His shoulder hurt viciously and shot pain along his arm, numbing his hand. His right thigh stung—pounding, throbbing, relentless pain shot up his leg and into his belly. Nausea engulfed him; he wanted to puke, but couldn't move his lungs. Dizziness engulfed him.

He gasped for air; wheezed and sucked, but the pain paralyzed his diaphragm. Something had shattered ribs and torn him up. He felt his bones click and scrape when he moved. He felt himself whirl out of consciousness, and fought his way back. Stay awake. Blackness hovered. Sticky blood soaked his shirt, hot, red blood. His bad arm stopped working. He needed sweet air, and his lungs were quitting.

"Goddam, goddamn," she sobbed.

"Can't breathe."

Skye drifted in and out of the world. Once, when vomit rose in his throat, he tried to puke, but he couldn't. It settled down his gullet, sour and obscene.

Sobbing and fierce, Victoria poulticed the wounds, all the while giving Skye a running account of the battle. The Sans Arcs fled to the left bluff, carrying three or four wounded and maybe some dead. A few of them formed a rear guard, shooting their carbines at the riverboat crew on the hurricane deck.

He heard shouts, howls, sobs, and anger. He tried to sit up, and fell back, with Victoria snapping at him to lie still. He wanted to orient himself. His pain had melded into rage at Bonfils, who had destroyed a peaceful parley, wounded him and others, and made enemies of the Sans Arcs and other Sioux.

He lay defeated, sick, nauseous, wondering if he was dying, feeling the pain stab in and out of his body with each breath. Then he turned his head and saw Ballard, lying still, with a blue hole in his forehead. Gill was sitting beside his partner, dazed, silent, and bitter.

Painfully, Skye rolled his gaze toward the sobbing he

heard behind him, in the cottonwoods. There, Lame Deer sat, weeping, the still form of her son, Sound Comes Back After Shouting, in her lap, while Singing Rain clung to her mother.

Victoria was weeping.

The grapeshot, fired at that distance, had spread into a broad pattern, scything down every living thing in a twenty-yard swath, including a Cheyenne child.

"He dead?" Skye gasped.

"Through the neck."

Skye sagged into the earth, desolated, hot tears collecting in his weathered face. Two dead. Others injured. He felt too nauseous and weak to do anything but lie quietly and listen to the ebbing sounds of flight. Soon, all he heard was flowing water, and all he felt was pain and the warmth of the sun.

Victoria was working on him, shooting pain through him as she dabbed at the rib wound.

"Stop it," Skye muttered, but she didn't. "Can't breathe . . ."

A shadow crossed his face, and he looked up to find Marsh and Trenholm and Bonfils staring down at him.

"You alive, Skye?" Marsh asked.

Stupid question. Skye glared.

"This is a mess," Marsh said. "I don't know what happened. You're welcome to ship's stores. We've some morphia."

"Go away," Victoria snarled.

Gill rose, faced Bonfils. "You killed Shorty," he said in a low and deadly voice.

Marsh stared at Bonfils.

"Didn't know you were in that mob of thieving redskins," Bonfils said.

Skye struggled to focus on Bonfils. "They weren't thieving."

"They were painted up. I saw them from my cabin; painted up, carrying bows and tomahawks, creeping through the fog, getting ready to jump the *Otter*, steal every pack of fur sitting there on that spit."

Skye listened quietly, too sick to talk, but Red Gill wasn't silent.

"Goddammit, Mister Skye had them quieted down. They were going after Pawnee, and planned to cross the river here and ran into us. He offered them a ride across, and their chief, Bull Calf, agreed. It was all settled, peaceful."

"A ride on my boat?" That was Marsh's voice, waxing indignant.

"It or the flatboat," Skye mumbled.

"What gave you the right to tell them that? I wouldn't have a bunch of filthy warriors and their crowbait horses on my boat. It was a trick. Once aboard, they'd loot it and kill us all."

Skye didn't argue. Blackness crept through him.

"Marsh, they was just looking for a ride and maybe a meal and maybe even a trade or two," Gill said. "Now, I'm going to St. Louis, and I'm gonna visit Gen'ral Clark, and he's going to hear the whole story, and I'm going to blame Bonfils here, you can damn well count on it."

Marsh snarled something.

Bonfils began to snap, like a crackling fire. "I drove off marauders. I spotted them in the fog, sneaking up. I saved the company's furs. And that's how Clark and the company will see it. . . ." Bonfils sounded excited, his voice harsh and pitched. Skye felt his wounds throbbing.

"You killed that little boy. Simon MacLees's boy," Skye said. "And MacLees is going to hear about it, I promise you that."

Marsh and Trenholm and Bonfils stared at the distant Cheyenne woman, registering her grief, and the dead child in her lap for the first time.

"Accident of war, couldn't be helped," Marsh said. "Just an incident. I'm sorry about it. Sorry about Ballard, there."

"An incident?" Skye struggled to sit up, wrath driving him, struggled to stand. It was foolishness. Pain and nausea engulfed him. Dizzily, he tumbled back to the gravelly ground, gasping for air, willing his lungs to pump.

Boatmen from the *Otter* had gathered around, though a few patrolled the area, rifles in hand.

"Start loading those bales," Marsh snapped. "We'll sail as soon as we have our cargo stored." He turned to several of them. "Gather driftwood. There's plenty here."

"Give me my flatboat back," Gill said.

Marsh laughed shortly. "You're a smuggler and you'd just better get used to what we'll do to you."

Gill cussed helplessly.

"At least, bury Ballard," Skye said.

"You can manage. We don't have time," Marsh said.

Skye struggled against the blackness engulfing him, and when he opened his eyes again he peered up at the confident-looking Bonfils, Marsh's hero of the day. "Look for me," Skye said, swallowing back his vomit.

Bonfils smiled broadly and tipped his hat.

The rest of that morning passed in a haze of pain and confusion, but he knew the boatmen were ferrying bales of furs back to the steamboat and loading them, using Gill's flatboat. He knew they were confiscating Gill's bales because Gill was raging at them, and they were holding him at gunpoint.

He knew that poor Ballard lay in the sun, unburied and unmourned, and that the bereaved Cheyenne woman had retreated into the willow brush with her dead boy, to be alone with her grief and out of sight of the authors of her sorrows. He heard her singing; a low, monotonous, strident wail unlike the sweetness he had heard earlier.

He knew that Victoria hovered over him, slid water into him, put compresses and plasters on him to cool the mounting fevers. He felt her tears fall wetly on his cheeks, and felt the gentle touch of her fingers, sending love, willing him to heal, comforting him. He felt himself being rolled onto a softer robe so the gravel would not stab his back.

He smelled woodsmoke, and knew the firemen were building up steam. That meant that the paddles had been repaired and the steamboat was being readied to travel. He knew that Bonfils was parading about, the company-certified hero of the hour, the man who had saved the *Otter* and all its precious cargo, not to mention the entire crew.

He knew that three of those balls in the cannister shot by Bonfils hit him; others had butchered a child, murdered a St. Louis frontiersman, and wounded or killed several Sans Arcs.

Marsh pulled out mid-morning. Skye heard the snap of steam exiting the escapement, and heard the rumble of the wheels and the splash of the paddles as they thrashed the river. Then they were gone.

He saw a blue heaven above him, and magpies flicking over him, and crows sailing the breezes. He heard the soft lap of the river. He moved and felt his ribs scrape against cartilage, and felt Victoria's tight bandage. He coughed, shooting wild pain through his torso, and then sucked air desperately. The poultice comforted him.

It was very quiet, save for the angry muttering of Red Gill. Skye turned, and could see Gill poking around in the flatboat. At least Marsh had returned it, raped and empty, to its owner. It rested just off the gravel spit, moored fore and after by hempen hawsers to the willows.

Gill approached him after a while, squatting down.

"How you doing?" he asked.

"I'll live."

"I can't hardly navigate without another man. You up to it?"

"Victoria can help you."

Gill looked about to say something, but held his peace. "You ain't up to it."

"Soon," Skye said.

"I got to bury Shorty."

"You might offer to help Lame Deer first."

"Bury a redskin?"

"She will wrap the child in a robe, put it in a tree, and offer it to the sun."

Gill pondered that. "Maybe I should do that with Shorty. I don't hardly know how to bury him around here, on gravel, a foot above the river."

Skye nodded, feeling delirium wash through him. He hoped it would be a long time before he was carried to the flatboat. He hoped the gentle rocking of the flatboat wouldn't make him any more nauseous than he was.

Victoria had vanished and he knew she was consoling the Cheyenne woman, the pair of them just as far from white men as they could get on that gravelly island.

He wondered what MacLees would think upon hearing the news that Bonfils had killed his boy. Maybe MacLees wouldn't care. Maybe Marsh and Bonfils wouldn't say anything. Maybe the log of the *Otter* would show nothing, nothing at all . . . Maybe Marsh and minions would spread their own carefully wrought version among the powerful. At any rate, the steamer would reach St. Louis weeks before the flatboat did—if Gill managed to reach St. Louis at all.

Skye pondered that, and amended it: if he and Victoria and Gill and Lame Deer and Singing Rain ever reached St. Louis at all, and were allowed to see the general, or were welcomed into the offices of Pierre Chouteau. There were too many ifs and ors.

23

The river glistened; nothing stirred. The sun beat mercilessly upon that place where so recently the horrors of war had carmined the gravel with blood.

Victoria's heart lay heavily within her, but she pushed aside her desolation to help those in need; her man, Skye, gasping and nauseous; and Lame Deer, the stoic mother, staring helplessly at the body of her son, killed by a thoughtless act of fear by that Creole sonofabitch.

She brought cold water to Skye, who sipped it gratefully. He didn't want much; only to be left alone. But he was lying in full sun.

"We got to get you into the cabin," she said.

"Leave me."

She ignored him, and found Red angrily putting the flatboat in order, his own cursing a match for Shorty's. He had dragged Shorty aboard and wrapped him in an old blanket.

"Thieves! Killers! Wait 'til I tell Chouteau!"

"Ah, Mister Gill, I need your help."

He stared at her and then nodded.

"I got to get Skye into the cabin. Out of the sun or he maybe die."

"He's too shot to move."

"We carry him together in a robe."

"You?" He eyed her slim frame doubtfully.

She didn't reply but dug around in the cabin for a blanket, and waited for him.

Together they rolled Skye into it and half-dragged, half-carried him up the wobbling plank and into the flatboat. Skye groaned. She settled him on the bunk, checked his bloody bandages to see whether this passage had reopened the wounds, and then went back for his rifle and top hat. Tenderly, she settled his possessions beside him, his rifle within easy reach, just as it always was.

He reached up and clasped her hand in his. She saw tears in his eyes. His cold hand, weak as his grip was, spoke to her of profound love. She fought back the roar of anguish in her, and smiled. She would not let him see her own tears.

The shade of the cabin would protect him from Father Sun. She pressed her palm to his brow and found it fevered. Soon she would give him herb tea if she could find what she needed.

She found Red Gill slumped on the deck. "Now you got to help me with Lame Deer."

Red nodded morosely. She plucked up the small robe the boy had slept in and brought it, along with some thong.

Lame Deer sat silently in a private bower she had found, screened by red willow brush, a place to be alone with her grief. She stroked Singing Rain absently, calming the fretful child, but her spirit was far away, and Victoria thought her mind's eye was gazing upon her homeland, her Cheyenne people, the lodges of her kin.

"We send Sound Comes Back After Shouting to the place of the spirits now," she said gruffly.

Lame Deer stared, saying nothing.

Victoria motioned to Red. The child lay on the gravel, flies collecting around the fatal wound, a thin layer of browning blood covering the boy's neck.

She spread the small robe on the gravel, lifted the child onto it, and pulled the robe over the boy. She lashed the bundle with thong, driving away the swarming flies, and nodded to Red.

She found some box elders flourishing on a slight rise, and a place where one might anchor some crosspieces to a low fork in one of the trees. It took her and Red Gill a while to complete the little scaffold, but at last she was satisfied. Here the Cheyenne boy would lie, under the rustling leaves, while his soul climbed the long trail.

She returned to Lame Deer's bower and tugged at the woman's hand while Red gathered the bundled body of the boy. That was the funeral procession: Red, carrying the bundle, Lame Deer and her daughter, and Victoria, her sharp quick gaze checking distant ridges for trouble even as she grieved.

Red lifted the bundle onto the scaffold, as if the boy weighed no more than a feather.

Lame Deer stood before the scaffold, her countenance solemn but composed.

She was plainly seeking English words, and then did speak.

"This was good child. MacLees, him and me, we make him one winter night, very cold, and then I see the owl float by, and so this is the owl prophesy. This I know long ago, that this good boy would not be alive for long. But I put that in my heart and kept it until now. It make me sad now.

"MacLees, he love this boy, want to make him a trader like himself. Now MacLees will be sad. This boy, he was going to be in white man's religion; big medicine, bigger than maybe Cheyenne medicine. This child, the one whose name is known, he walked with big steps, a little man so soon. He comes into the earth lodge and now he goes, and leaves an empty place inside of me. Where he goes, he will be a great one, with many honors."

She wept then, tears leaking from her warm brown eyes.

"MacLees, now he must be told. I go to Many Houses to tell him. He will do what he will do when he learns this."

What was Lame Deer saying?

Red was listening impatiently, some innate courtesy keeping him from returning to the flatboat. Victoria watched him, read him well. Hard man, good man, wild and reckless, not a man to live in Many Houses place but out where no elders and chiefs curbed him.

Lame Deer reached upward and placed something on the bundle.

"Turtle stone," she said to Victoria. "It says who he is to the spirits."

An amulet.

She led the way out of the grove, and into the blinding sunlight, with the subdued girl, Singing Rain, beside her, hobbling across the rough gravel.

Red and Victoria followed.

"Got to wait until Skye's up," Red said. "I can't handle a flatboat alone. Need a strong man up front with a pole, among other things."

"I will steer," Victoria said.

He considered it and shook his head.

"You steer, the Cheyenne and me, we pole or row or whatever you want, dammit," she said.

"You're too small."

"All right, sit here and starve!"

She had touched the sore point. The cornmeal wouldn't last long.

He grinned suddenly. "Can't get into a worse jackpot than I'm in now," he said. "But we got to hold a little service for Shorty first."

He headed for shore and began collecting the larger stones from the gravel banks, and these he carried aboard and placed next to Shorty's wrapped body. She fathomed his intent, and collected stones herself, but Lame Deer retreated to the front of the bobbing boat and settled on the planks.

When Red had collected enough stones, he opened the blanket and placed them alongside Shorty, who lay there open-mouthed and sightless, and then tied the blanket tight, using up all the thong.

Then, grunting under the heavy load, he lifted Shorty and slid his partner into the river, and stood, panting. The soft splash radiated outward and vanished in the flow. Somewhere, not far below, a mortal lay, perhaps tumbling slowly downstream. Victoria didn't like it; giving the body to the water demons, which were the worst spirits of all, as any Absaroka knew. But maybe white men were demonized by other things, from the sky.

Red stood at the side, panting, somber, upset.

"Don't know what to say, Shorty, so I'll say good-bye, and good luck wherever you are. I'm proud to know you, proud to ride the river with you, Shorty Ballard. I guess, well, I'm not good at prayers, so I'll just say, like the Spanish, *vaya con Dios*."

Skye's muffled voice rose from the cabin. "I can lead you," he said.

"I'd be obliged."

"The Lord is my shepherd, I shall not want . . ."

Victoria listened to these familiar words, so different from the medicine of her people, but a great comfort to white men. Even to a smuggler like Red Gill, if that's what he was. She wasn't quite sure what Red Gill did and why it was considered so bad, or what else was wrong with him that the big chief of the riverboat would treat him with such contempt, and without even a moment's regret.

Skye finished reciting, his voice soft and gentle and barely audible in the afternoon quiet, and then Red thanked him and untied the front hawser from the bankside brush.

He loosened the rear rope and scurried aboard as the current caught the flatboat and nudged it away. He yanked the plank into the boat and headed for the tiller. The flatboat, unburdened by cargo, floated high and skimmed into the river.

She watched the place of death and darkness fall behind.

"Where's No Name?" asked Skye from within the cabin.

Fear lanced her. She hastened around the flatboat.

"Stop. The dog is not here," she said to Red.

Red immediately pulled the tiller and the flatboat drifted toward shore. Even before it bumped the riverbank, she leapt out and began trotting back toward the place of death, swallowing back her fears.

She reached the flat and saw nothing.

"No Name," she cried. "Spirit Dog, where are you?"

She discovered only silence.

Maybe it wasn't so bad. No Name lived his own life. If he felt like it, he would keep up with the flatboat while hunting along the shore. But the more she tried to persuade herself of all this, the worse she felt.

She began a thorough examination of that brushy flat, visiting the places where Skye had fallen, Shorty had died, the little Cheyenne boy had breathed his last, and several Sans Arcs had either died or been gravely wounded. She saw nothing but blood on gravel.

Then, some distance back from the river, she spotted the familiar yellow, and pushed through thick canebrake to reach the dog.

No Name lay under brush, in a small hollow. He was very still.

"Aiee!" she whispered.

She crawled under the brush to the dog. It lay unmoving. A bloodless hole pierced its chest. She reached, frightened, to touch the dog, find breath, find life. But there was no life.

Bonfils's cannister had snuffed out yet another life.

She gathered the dog in her arms, and staggered to her feet, carrying a heavier load than she had ever known.

24

Alexandre Bonfils stood in the prow of the *Otter*, congratulating himself. Had he not rescued this ship and all its crew? Had he not saved the entire cargo, half the company's annual returns, from the theft of savages? Had he not acted with speed and decisiveness? As a result of all this, had the company not halted smugglers and confiscated nineteen bales of pelts? And while it was unfortunate that some ruffians and savages got shot, he could scarcely have hoped for a better result.

The riverboat gathered its muscles and plowed downstream, leaving the savage squaws, Skye, and the smuggler to mend themselves, and maybe mend their ways if they had any sense. Bonfils doubted that Skye or any of the others would reach St. Louis now; in any case, if they did show up in a few weeks, Pierre Chouteau and General Pratte would have long since awarded the trading post position to him; how could they not? And once he showed some skill there, dealing with the Crows, some sharp improvements in the profits, he would swiftly advance to greater things.

Trenholm appeared at his side.

"Marsh wants you," the mate said.

Bonfils smiled and nodded. The commendation from

the captain would be music to his ears. A kind word from the powerful captain in St. Louis would assure success.

He hastened up the companionway to the hurricane deck, and forward to the pilothouse, where he found Marsh dourly writing at a small desk. The captain peered up, and the look in his red face was not pleasant.

"Let's get something straight, Bonfils. You will never again touch that cannon or fire any sort of shot from this vessel without my permission."

Bonfils was taken aback. "But there was no time . . . we were on the brink of disaster."

"Disaster!"

"*Mais oui*, the savages were about to overrun us."

Marsh sprang to his feet, his face reddening.

"You endangered my ship. You acted without permission. You started a war! You ruined the company's trading with the whole Sioux nation! And all because you didn't wake me, ask me!"

Bonfils resented the outburst. "*Monsieur le capitaine*, I beg to remind you the savages were gathering on the riverbank, only ten yards away; scores of them, ready to plunge into the water and overwhelm us and strangle us in our sleep! I beg to remind you that on that gravel beach, just a few yards distant, lay half the wealth of Pratte, Chouteau and Company! And that is where the savages collected, right there, ready to commandeer that flatboat, ready to pitch the bales into the river if the spirit moved them! I saved the day; I drove them off! I collected two of your crew and we defeated them. We are safe here, we have more pelts than when we started! We—"

Marsh waved a hand so forcefully that Bonfils abruptly stopped.

When the master spoke, the tone was low and deadly.

"If I had irons I'd put you in them. As it is, you'll be confined to your cabin the rest of this trip."

"Confined!"

"You will learn, Bonfils, that dangerous passengers are confined."

"Dangerous!"

"From now on, every trip I make up this river will be frought with danger from the Sans Arcs and maybe other Sioux. And from now on, every robe and pelt from that band will go to the Opposition."

"But I saved your life!"

Marsh barely whispered. "This is not the mountains; you are not leading a trapping brigade and fending off Blackfeet. Those you shot are our trading partners. They were not about to pillage this ship; far from it. I have confirmed that indeed, they were looking to cross the river, as Skye said. One of the Fort Pierre engagés who knows the tongue listened to several of the Sans Arcs who were collecting their wounded, and got the story. Skye had no business offering them this vessel, but at least he didn't mow them down with grapeshot. Nor did he murder a white man in the process."

"It was an accident of war!"

Marsh peered into the sunlit waters ahead. "There are things you don't know," he said.

The helmsman and pilot cast furtive glances at Bonfils, and Trenholm stared away from them.

"Maybe this should be dropped. It is a mere incident."

"Dropped? It is already in my logbook. An unauthorized discharge of my cannon, twice, into trading partners standing peacefully yards from this boat. And I have named you. This will scarcely go unnoticed. I plan to discuss it with Pierre Chouteau. I'm sure that when that flatboat reaches St. Louis, Skye and Gill are going to say a few words, not only to Chouteau, but General Clark. And there may be a warrant issued against you."

Bonfils's mind raced. This could hurt him with his family, with his petition, his life, his career.

"I see it differently," Bonfils said. "I will not sit in confinement the rest of this journey, a punishment I don't deserve. Put me ashore."

Marsh laughed meanly, and nodded to Trenholm. The burly mate laid a hand on Bonfils, who violently threw it off. Then Marsh himself grabbed a fistful of shirt.

"Bonfils, you may be connected, you may be your family's choice, but here on my ship you're a piece of manure. Get your revenge in St. Louis. Whine all you want."

He nodded to Trenholm, who led Bonfils out of the pilothouse and down the companionway.

"Do I post a guard, or do you give me your parole you'll stay in?" Trenholm asked when they reached the cabin.

Bonfils hated the moment, hated the indignity. How had his life come to this? He wouldn't let some river rat tell him what to do.

"Say it."

Bonfils stood rigidly.

"All right, if you won't give me your word, you're confined. I'll post a deckman outside your door," Trenholm said.

Bonfils slammed the door behind him. He peered through a small porthole at the passing shore, and suddenly realized he had lost not only his freedom but also his reputation. And for what? Rescuing the ship from those idiots.

The *Otter* was two weeks from St. Louis. Two weeks confined to this miserable cubicle! Told when to eat, when to relieve himself! He paced; he flopped onto his bunk. He peered out the porthole at a free and serene world. He raged at the master, the mate, and everyone else aboard. He plucked up his Hawken Brothers .53-caliber rifle, a finely wrought octagon-barreled weapon that could drill a ball through a buffalo.

This was madness! He would draft a report and deliver it to his uncles and cousins. He would take this matter straight to the powerful families who ran St. Louis. He would have Marsh's scalp. He would ruin the man. He would see to it that neither he nor Trenholm ever served on another American Fur Company ship.

His rage, his fevered visions of revenge, lasted twenty minutes. Then he stood wearily, paced his compartment. Three paces door to wall. Two paces across. He peered out the window again. The scenery was exactly the same as before: nameless bluffs, empty skies, every blade of grass free to live as it could.

He flopped onto his bunk again, and tried closing his eyes. *Mon Dieu*! How could any mortal submit to such confinement? And all because he rescued the ship and cargo and crew from a pack of savages!

He tried thinking of women, ah, Emilie, ah, Marguerite, ah, Bridget, ah, sweet Cherise, ah . . .

And what of the future? Was he disgraced? No, never, not after he had had a chance to explain himself, tell people what had happened. But would he lose his chance? Would Skye now have the inside track? Ah, there was a new pain on top of all the rest.

In an abstract sort of way, he was sorry Skye got shot, though in fact it amused him. His rival, the London lout, just happened to be in the path of the cannister! Still, it was another thing to explain to his uncles. The fog! Yes, of course, the fog! How could any man tell what lay in the fog?

And if he could not tell what he was shooting at, then why did he fire that six-pounder?

Ah, *mon pere*, it was necessary to save the ship, save lives, save the cargo by which we all grow rich!

He endured an hour more, then opened the door a crack. A deck man stared at him.

"I am going to the closet," he said. The man didn't stop him. He walked forward, entered the cabinet that hung over the river, just ahead of the wheelhouses. There was a bench within, with three holes in it. The river skirled below. The blades of the wheel slashed into the river, spraying water about.

He lingered there, just because he hated to return to his cabin, but finally he stepped out into sunlight, relishing it, relishing liberty. But the burly deckman was waiting, lounging against the rail, his bare foot on the coaming.

Bonfils returned to his room, his eyes hungrily raking the boiler deck, the firemen, the sunny prow, the broad river glinting in the bright sun. He entered his cabin and shut the door behind him, knowing what he had to do: escape. No innocent mortal could endure two weeks cooped up like an animal!

A cabin boy brought him some slop in a bowl. Marsh wouldn't even give him proper food! He caught the boy.

"Marcel, bring me food, eh? Much food, wrapped up in a bag. I will slip you a few pieces of eight."

The boy looked frightened, but finally nodded.

The chance came at dusk, when Marsh stopped for wood. All hands reported to Trenholm, who handed the crew and passengers axes and saws. Bonfils discovered that his guard had vanished to shore with the rest. Even Trenholm had gone ashore.

Bonfils gathered his rifle, his powderhorn, his kit. He pushed his straw hat over his long locks and stepped out. No one stopped him as he walked down the gangway and into a grove of willows, past the work party and up a game trail leading to the top of the bluff.

He turned at last to look down at the *Otter*, only to discover the master's spyglass upon him. Marsh waved casually, an exaggerated flap of his arm. So the master had foreseen it all, and let Bonfils walk.

25

The fever and nausea departed abruptly, and Skye grew aware of the world once again. His shoulder and thigh ached numbly, but the wound that still tormented him was the one that shattered his ribs. That one hurt so much his body refused to breathe, and he gulped air in pain.

He heard the lap of water against the plank hull, and the gurgle of the river. Somewhere forward, the Cheyenne woman crooned softly. She had been crooning all day, a low, melancholic song that tugged at the roots of his heart. He wondered what it would be like to lose a son, and was overcome with a sadness that he and Victoria had never conceived one.

The woman sang her sadness, and her melancholia suited him. She had lost a boy; he had lost a dog. He had loved that dog like a son. He had tried to put the dog out of mind; what was No Name but a miserable cur that had attached himself to the Skyes and kept its distance? And yet he could not. No Name was a magnificent dog, fierce and loyal, great-hearted, mysterious, independent, and sometimes tender. Now he was gone.

When Victoria had stepped aboard carrying that limp yellow bundle of fur, her lips pressed tight and her face etched with sorrow, Skye's own spirits had plummeted to that netherworld where the Dark Prince guarded the gates of hell. No Name dead. For that little while, Skye didn't care whether he lived or died. He had loved the dog. Even now, days later, the numbing loneliness he felt when he thought of his faithful animal was more than he could endure. They had wept, buried the dog in the river with songs and prayers, and set out upon their journey. For days afterward, Skye had the eerie sensation that the dog was running along the riverbank, beside the flatboat.

From his bunk he could see Gill at the tiller, looking dark and vacant-eyed, his thoughts upon his partner and not the currents that shouldered them ever southward. The boat carried no load, drew only a few inches of water, and scarcely needed steering. Skye grew aware of Victoria beside him, and reached out to her. His hand caught hers and squeezed it.

"You better," she said.

He nodded.

She began to change his poultices, which hurt. But when she had pulled loose her dressings, he could see that the hard red inflammation had subsided. Somewhere along the way, she had gathered her own medicinals from alongside the river, and had packed the wounds with them. He did not know what herbs and leaves she had used, but the presence of green moss over the wounds surprised him.

Gill shadowed the door, and then he entered.

"Heard you talking. You some better?" he asked.

"Who's at the tiller?" Skye asked.

"It'll take care of itself a while."

"Better," Skye said.

"Anyway, you made it; Shorty didn't."

Skye didn't respond to that. He knew what was on Red Gill's mind: if Skye hadn't wrestled Shorty down and steered the flatboat over to the beached steamboat, none of it would have happened. Maybe he was right. But maybe the next cannister shot from that six-pounder would have cut Shorty to pieces; maybe the next shots after that, fired from the looming riverboat, would have raked them all. In any case, the iron law of the seas and rivers was to stop and render assistance. Red was bitter. He'd lost his partner and his cargo, which was to be his profit, and had unwanted passengers as well, and nothing but debt back in St. Louis.

"I'm sorry about Shorty, mate."

Red glared, watched Victoria work on the wounds, and then retreated to his post at the tiller.

The dolorous song continued. Lame Deer was singing away her sorrows.

They drifted through a quiet and partly cloudy day, sun bright one moment, and obscured the next. He saw Red turn over the tiller to Victoria and heard him pacing the boat. The singing stopped.

By afternoon he felt well enough to sit up a few minutes, and he pulled himself upright in the bunk, resting his head on the forward wall of the cabin, which was the rear wall of the cargo box. The Missouri had grown into a majestic flowage, drawing waters to it from a vast basin. He felt he was traversing a lake rather than a river.

A rifle crack shattered the peace, and as his body jerked in response, his wounds stung him.

Gill yelled, and Skye saw him peering over the water, trying to locate the source of the distant shot.

Victoria stood beside Gill at the back of the flatboat, and finally she pointed to the left bank.

"Some sonofabitch standing there," she said.

Skye strained forward until he could see out of the small porthole sawn into the side of the cabin. Indeed, a man stood on a high prominence forty or fifty feet above the river. He was waving his hat and beckoning the craft to him.

Skye watched Gill pull the tiller, and watched the

shadows and sunlight move across the floor of the cabin, and knew that Gill was heading for shore. Even as the flatboat veered toward the riverbank, the man scurried downslope to the water's edge and waited, rifle cradled in his arms, with a sack in his hand. He looked vaguely familiar.

Skye sank back on his bunk, unable to stand the pain of sitting, and waited restlessly for news.

Then Gill began cursing, a low monotone cussing that his partner Shorty had employed to voice all manner of opinion from hatred to joy.

"Who?" asked Skye.

"Bonfils."

"Bonfils!" The author of his wounds. The man who killed No Name. The author of the death of Shorty. The author of the death of Lame Deer's boy. "You going to stop?"

Red grunted.

Skye lifted himself from the bunk for a look, and discovered Bonfils thirty yards across water, his rifle at the ready across his chest.

Skye fell back weakly. Victoria swept into the grimy cabin and worked feverishly, loading Skye's rifle from the powderhorn that hung over the corner of Skye's bunk.

"Bonfils got that rifle pointing at Gill, almost. I'll kill that sonofabitch," she muttered.

Skye held up a hand and she subsided.

He waited patiently, listening to the water lap and gurgle. Then he felt a jar, and the flatboat bumped shore.

"How about a ride?" yelled Bonfils.

"What are you doing here?" Gill asked.

"I left the riverboat."

"Why?"

"Felt like it."

"I said, Why?"

"Had a little trouble with Marsh."

"About shooting us with the goddamned cannon."

"I want a ride to St. Louis."

"You killed Shorty."

"How was I to know he was in there with all those redskins?"

"I think you can walk," Gill said.

"Is Skye in there?"

"You're going to walk, Bonfils."

"I think you are going to take me and be glad of it. In fact, my friend, this rifle says so."

"The hell with you."

Skye heard Gill pick up a pole to push the flatboat farther away from the riverbank.

"Gill, you don't listen. This rifle is pointing at you. Your fate is in your hands. What a pity. The two smugglers go upriver and never return! Now listen: Would you like to get your cargo back?"

Gill paused.

"Monsieur, I know things. All day, many days, I talked with Marsh in the pilothouse, and from his lips come many things. I will tell you something I know. The one who employs you is not the Opposition, but Pierre Chouteau, is that not so?"

Skye heard only dead silence. He wished he could take a good look at Gill. The assertion was so astonishing that Skye could barely fathom it. Chouteau? Why would the company employ Gill and Ballard?

"What else?" Gill asked neutrally.

Bonfils laughed. "There is much. I can help you. A word in the right ears in St. Louis will return your cargo, yes? I will tell you as soon as I step on board; as soon as we are heading for St. Louis. This I promise you."

Gill must have changed his mind, because Skye felt the boat bump bottom, heard the brigade leader step aboard, and felt a faint rocking of the flatboat. Moments later the boat was riding the current again.

Bonfils slipped into the cabin, laid his rifle on the other bunk, and smiled. "Ah! So you are alive and in good flesh!"

Skye was too worn to resist the man, so he kept quiet.

"I will tell you something, Skye—"

"It's Mister Skye, mate."

Bonfils laughed. "The *homme* with the best chance for the trading post, he is in St. Louis now preparing to marry a niece of General Pratte, the stepdaughter of Capitaine Marsh. Her name is Sarah Lansing, and her beau is Simon MacLees, and he is a great favorite of the capitaine."

"MacLees?"

Skye lay on his back, contemplating that. "If he's the choice, why did they want us to come to St. Louis?"

Bonfils shrugged. "I do not read minds, Skye. But when we arrive with MacLees's mountain wife, and there is a fine fat scandal, the unexpected may happen, *oui?*"

Bonfils abandoned the cabin and headed aft to talk to Gill. They palavered in such low tones that Skye could not catch it all, but he knew Victoria was hovering about. She had a way of being invisible to white men. He needed only patience and he would know.

A while later she slipped into the cabin.

"They going to St. Louis day and night. No stop. They gonna pass the riverboat. It ties up at night. It can't see nothing in the dark, so this boat pass them up some night soon, and get there first."

"Why, Victoria?"

"Get to Chouteau ahead of Marsh."

"But why?"

"So Chouteau gives the robes back to Gill. I got that much, anyway. Gill and the one who is dead"—she avoided naming the name of the dead, as always—"they take whiskey upriver by pack train, many mules, make big circle around Fort Leavenworth where the bluecoats watch the river.

"They get pay in robes, bales of robes and a flatboat to bring them down the river. No record is ever made. Gill and the other, they talk about working for the Opposition, but that is not so. Bonfils says he get the bales back for Gill."

Skye pondered that and thought it might be true. But he didn't doubt that Bonfils had private designs that would affect him and Victoria, and Lame Deer too. But he could only wait and see.

26

Alexandre Bonfils held the aces. He knew things. And the few things he wasn't sure of, he could guess at with all the shrewdness of a wealthy young Creole reared in St. Louis society. Odd, how the affairs of St. Louis threaded westward into an utter wilderness. He had discovered secrets! And now this flatboat was drifting toward St. Louis, brimming with them! Oh, ho, the ways he knew to embarrass Pierre Chouteau!

The *capitaine*, Benton Marsh, had not said a word to him about the Cheyenne squaw, or why Marsh had abruptly ejected the woman and her children from his steamboat. But Bonfils knew! Ah! It was delicious to think about it. Scandal! The Beaujolais and brie of St. Louis society!

The Cheyenne woman was a threat to Marsh's future son-in-law, and an embarrassment. Children, too! Ah, proof of dalliance far away from prying eyes. Her arrival in St. Louis would trigger a splendid scandal that would embarrass Marsh's stepdaughter, Sarah Lansing, and wreck Simon MacLees's chances in Pratte, Chouteau and Company, and probably wreck the nuptials. Ah! What fun it would be to arrive in St. Louis ahead of the steamboat, and make sure that the Cheyenne woman and her brat were properly introduced! Especially the little breed girl, whose papa everyone in St. Louis knew!

And of course, MacLees's downfall would clear the way for the appointment of Bonfils to the trading post. MacLees was the rival to worry about: a shrewd trader, experienced in the art of running a trading post, a man of great talents—and a little squaw no one in St. Louis knew about!

Bonfils chuckled. The woman was his ace. She sat there in the front of the flatboat, her back to the cargo box, fussing with her daughter, oblivious to the white men behind her. Little did she know she was a future debutante, and Bonfils would arrange for her coming out, right down to her ball gown.

Skye could be easily dealt with. A simple visit with General Clark would do the job. Clark was the man who issued permits and licenses. Anyone trading with Indians in United States Indian Territory had to have a license, and had to be an American citizen to get that license. Skye was an Englishman. That detail had been overlooked by Pierre Chouteau. Bonfils laughed. It was all so simple, so easy. General Clark might even eject Skye from the United States. A pity. Poor devil might have to rejoin the Royal Navy.

Still, it would take some doing. A flatboat was scarcely the speediest mode of travel. But if it progressed continually, night and day, it would indeed reach St. Louis ahead of the river packet, which could not navigate at night unless the moon shone bright. It was crucial to get to Pierre Chouteau first, tell him that Marsh stole the packs from Gill. That would put Marsh on the defensive. Uncle Pierre had gone to great lengths to transport spirits to the posts far from the prying eyes of the government, and now Marsh had ruined the fragile and private arrangement. Ah, what fun to know how things worked. If Uncle Pierre dreaded anything, it was the exposure of his whiskey-running.

The other matter would be more entertaining, like watching a Molière comedy. Introducing the lice-ridden Cheyenne squaw around town, as MacLees's mountain lady, and her breed child with the blue-green eyes and light brown hair, would start things in motion. That would be the *coup de grace*.

He meandered back to Gill.

"We must never stop. Night and day, we must never stop."

"Got to eat, rest, sleep—" Gill said.

"Non, non, we must catch up. Marsh is leagues ahead of us!"

"Don't know that he is. He's got to take on wood once, twice a day, and we just keep on a-going."

"You sleep; I will steer at night. I am not afraid of night. And this bateau, it draws only four, five inches. We go over bars, over snags, over the top. We get to St. Louis ahead of Marsh, and I will get your furs back from Uncle Pierre."

Gill shrugged.

Bonfils paced restlessly, back and forth, from stem to stern, aware of the gazes following him. The river had broadened into a noble stream, carrying a vast burden of water from the distant mountains and the everlasting prairies ever south and east. The country had become monotonous. Who was there to talk with? The only interesting person was Skye, who lay abed.

He would talk with Skye anyway. The man had been sitting up; his fever had vanished. He was taking some broth. Bonfils ducked through the low door and into the dark and grimy cabin where Skye lay. His squaw sat across from him, silently watching the river.

"*Bonjour, mon ami*, how are you this day?"

Skye nodded curtly but said nothing.

Bonfils tried again. "Soon we will be in St. Louis, eh? Now what will you be saying to Uncle Pierre? I will tell him that we had a little bad luck."

Skye looked better; less flushed, quieter. But he didn't respond.

Bonfils felt faintly defensive and annoyed. "Ah, it is that you do not wish to talk with the one who put some grape into you. This I understand. But of course it was purely an accident. No harm intended. And it did stop a war party from pillaging the company furs, or capturing the riverboat."

Skye would tell Pierre Chouteau a different story, and it was necessary to find out what the Englishman would say, so it could be dismissed. But Skye wasn't cooperating; he just lay there, eyes closed, as if he wanted Bonfils to leave.

"Madam, your man recovers nicely because of your care," he said to Victoria.

She made no sign of having heard.

"Truly, he will be almost fit by the time we reach St. Louis. Well enough to hobble around, don't you think? Pierre Chouteau will admire him for his courage, coming clear down the river with a body in such need of repair and rest. Do you suppose he will need to winter in St. Louis, where he can get good care, before he ventures back to the mountains?"

She didn't respond; didn't smile, didn't nod, didn't speak. He felt as if he were being examined, not by some savage woman but by a surgeon, or maybe by a confessor listening through the grille.

"The Cheyenne squaw, she sings well, *oui*? I am listening to her send her boy along the spirit trail, and am filled with utmost admiration. She sits quietly at the front of the boat, like a goddess, watching the river and singing. Truly, she will be the queen of St. Louis! I myself will present her to society, letting all the world know she is Simon

MacLees's wife, and that the pretty little creature is his daughter!"

Neither of the Skyes responded, which annoyed him. So that's how it would be! Here he was looking after them, making sure they got to St. Louis ahead of Marsh and his vitriolic accusations, but they showed no appreciation. Very well, then.

"Bonfils," Gill yelled.

"Ah, pardon, *mes amis*, the man wants me," he said, rising to leave. He ducked through the low door, into sunlight, and headed for Gill, who was steering for shore.

"Why is it that you stop? Are we not trying to keep on going no matter what? Go on, go on!"

But Gill just shook his head and pointed.

Ahead was a great turmoil. Bonfils strained to see what Gill had spotted. On the left bank was a swarming brown mass, slowly undulating toward the broad, sparkling river. And clear across the river, forming a barrier, was a brown band, quietly and powerfully moving from shore to shore, a thousand snouts and horns and heads; buffalo. And on the right bank were thousands more, clambering upslope, rivering the water out of their brown hair, and following the rest of the gigantic herd up and up and over the crest of the bluff, as if they were all marching into the heavens.

"Buffalo crossing," Gill said.

"It's amazing. There must be tens of thousands."

"All of that."

"How long will it last?"

"Who knows? Hour, day, several days."

"*Mon Dieu*! I have heard of such a thing, but never have I seen it!"

He clambered up on the roof of the cargo box to see better. Countless bison were moving sinuously down the far slope, driving into the river at a good launching place that had turned into muck, and were slowly paddling a third of a mile across the water, their heads and horns and snouts making vee-shaped waves. They were six, ten, twenty, fifty in a rank, and the ranks spread like a brown carpet clear across the Missouri.

Gill was heading for the right bank, and he clearly intended to hole up until the herd had crossed. But that was foolish.

"Just go ahead, go ahead. The beasts will let you through."

Gill shook his head. "Them buff'lo, they can hook a horn right through the planks. Don't matter if they're in water. Get into the middle of them, and the buff would cut this poor flatboat to splinters."

"How do you know that?"

"Just do."

"We're losing time!"

"Nothing anyone can do about it."

Bonfils could see no end of the herd, no stragglers topping the left bluff; only a vast brown column of animals appearing on the ridge and working downslope to the river. He had never seen such a sight; more buffalo in this one herd than he thought existed in all herds everywhere. None of the beasts bawled; yet a faint rumble, the impact of thousands of hooves, the struggles of tens of thousands of animals to swim, the shuddering and labored climb up the mucky right bank and the walk up the slope, made a faint hum, but what struck him most was the odd silence in the midst of so much motion.

Gill reached a point a hundred yards upstream from the crossing and close to the right bank, and there he turned the flatboat into the shore until it ground to a halt. He eased off the gunnel with a rope in hand, and splashed to shore in a foot or two of water, to tie the rope to a sapling.

Bonfils endured it for a while, growing more and more restless. The great flow of animals never ceased, never slowed, and with each passing minute, his patience eroded and his temper mounted.

27

Barnaby Skye struggled to sit up so he could see the herd swimming the Missouri. He fell back weakly, the shattered ribs shooting pain through him. He gasped for breath, and tried again, this time struggling upright. Ahead, he saw the procession slowly wending down the left slope, swimming across the river like some brown tide, and emerging slick and wet on the right bank, just a hundred yards below where the flatboat was tied to river brush.

The sight awed him. He was seeing a majestic wave of buffalo that vibrated the boat even as it lay quietly beside the shore. He scarcely heard the noise of passage, and yet the air was not still, and some obscure thunder filled it, and some suffocating force seemed to draw the oxygen out of it. The herd possessed within it so much energy that it was unfathomable; all the energy of thousands of square miles of grasslands; more muscle and breath than the whole human race. He thought that never in the rest of his days would he see such a spectacle, and he counted himself privileged to witness it.

He had never felt so helpless. His body was not obeying him. He could not will his pain away. He could not exist now without the help of others. Victoria spooned broth into him and changed the poultices on his three wounds. Red Gill steered the flatboat and looked to its safety. Even the Cheyenne woman, Lame Deer, took her turn looking after him.

This weakness was new to him. He had been helpless in the Royal Navy, too; imprisoned and dependent on others. But not ill, not so drained of vitality that he could barely manage to sit up. That was different. He had never before been gravely injured, and now he realized how fragile was his flesh, and how much his very life depended on others.

The only person who no longer visited him was Bonfils. Maybe it was just as well that the aristocratic Creole stayed away; whenever Skye contemplated his wounds, and the unending ache in his shoulder and thigh, and the sharp pain that rose and ebbed every time he breathed, and his dead dog, he knew he could not endure Bonfils; not for an instant.

How strange it was to be weak; to be cared for, to be so helpless.

As soon as Gill tied up, he collected his Pennsylvania longrifle from the cabin, along with his powderhorn.

"Gonna have some good cow for supper," he said.

Skye nodded. He might manage some broth, and a few bits of meat, but he would not be able to eat even the most succulent of the parts of the cow, the humpmeat, one of his favorite foods.

He watched Red Gill progress down a plank he had run from the flatboat to the sedge-lined shore, and then walk downriver toward the awesome herd. A while later he heard a crack, oddly obscured by the gutteral noise of the passage.

Gill had gotten his cow.

Skye watched the vast herd, wondering when it would end. He had heard somewhere that sometimes they tied up a riverboat for two or three days.

Gill shouted toward the boat.

"Bonfils, ladies, help me butcher," he said. "The cow strayed out from the herd; we're safe enough."

Skye heard movement forward, and low voices. Then he watched Victoria and the Cheyenne woman, with her little girl, edge down the shaky plank to shore, and start toward the carcass somewhere ahead, beyond Skye's vision.

Where was Bonfils?

Skye heard footsteps toward the front of the flatboat, but plainly the young brigade leader was not leaving the boat, even to cut up the buffalo or start a fire to cook it. Skye was on the wrong side of the cabin to see much of what was happening on shore. But he knew the women would be gutting the cow, cutting out the tongue, and sawing away at the shoulder hump, which made the best of all roasts. It would take a long while to butcher the huge animal and cook a haunch or boil the tongue.

He drifted in and out of awareness, as he often did in his sickbed. Some moments, he smelled the sharp, rank odor of the herd, or listened to the muted rumble of its passage, or followed the soft patter of footsteps on the planks of the flatboat. Other moments he was far away, in the past or future, his mind roaming far from his wounded body.

Sometime soon he would be in St. Louis, facing a powerful and ruthless man he had never met, seeking a position that would ensure him a life of relative comfort and ease, as well as the prospect of a good future. Or maybe not. He had heard enough to know that he might not be appointed; Bonfils or MacLees might well receive Chouteau's favor. Maybe this trip would all be for nothing. Maybe these wounds, which had bled the strength out of him and rendered him little more than a bedridden wreck, might defeat his purposes.

He heard footsteps, and knew his rival was heading

aft. A moment later Bonfils darkened the door and stepped in.

"Ah, Monsieur Skye, we are alone at last. How do you fare?"

Skye stared.

"Truly it was regrettable that you were trapped in the middle of those thieving Sioux."

Skye was tempted to argue that Bonfils had been a damned fool, but he held his peace. The man was obviously here for a purpose.

The young Creole found a seat on the opposing bunk, which was nothing but a stretch of planking, like that which supported Skye. "You are progressing?" he asked politely.

"No fever. No infection."

"A blessing. You have a gifted woman."

"She packs the wounds with a blue moss she scrapes off the north side of trees."

"The Indians, they are crafty healers, *oui*?"

Skye nodded. These pleasantries were not why Bonfils had settled his lean and dark self in the cabin. Skye wondered what would come next.

"I myself am mad with eagerness to go again. These buffalo are an unexpected frustration," he said.

"Most amazing thing I've ever seen," Skye said. "I'll remember it the rest of my days. More buff than I've ever seen in all of my life; brown river of them."

"Ah, you are a sentimentalist! I see only hides and meat."

Skye settled deeper into his robes. Speaking taxed him and made his ribs ache. "I think you're here for some reason," he said. "I am very tired."

Bonfils smiled brightly. "You are discerning, *mon ami*."

"Now I'm your friend, am I? Would I be more of a friend if you had put four holes in me instead of three?"

Bonfils laughed easily. "You have wit, monsieur. No, what I wish to discuss with you is simply your future."

Skye waited. Breath came harshly because his lungs rebelled when his ribs ached.

"I shall tell you exactly what my plan is. First, I must overtake the riverboat and reach my mother's cousin, Pierre Chouteau, before Marsh does, to settle certain accusations he will make against me, things that might damage my chances. And of course, introduce him to the Cheyenne woman, MacLees's squaw. That will be a very pleasurable moment, taking her and the little breed child in hand and into that handsome house, where the women will stare at the squaw and see whether there really are lice in her hair." He laughed softly.

Skye was hurting from his attempt to sit up, so he lay very still, listening.

"I think that once Lame Deer is known, MacLees will no longer be a contender for the post on the Big Horn River."

"I didn't know he was a contender."

Bonfils laughed. "There is much you don't know. MacLees abandoned his squaw and is soon to marry a lovely white girl, Sarah Lansing, stepdaughter of Captain Marsh, and related to General Pratte. But when Lame Deer reaches St. Louis, I suspect the outcome might change."

"And?"

"That brings us to you. You are an Englishman, *oui*?"

Skye nodded.

"A deserter from the Royal Navy, is it not so?"

Skye waited for whatever was coming, staring at Bonfils, who was enjoying himself.

"You know, if you become a trader for the company, you must become an American citizen. General Clark does not license foreigners for the fur trade, or people of bad character such as deserters. Nor does he permit them access to Indian lands held by the United States. You are here illegally."

That was a revelation to Skye.

"My design, Skye, is to tell the general that you are not an American. . . . should you arrive in St. Louis."

Skye absorbed that. Chouteau must have known, must have counted on him becoming an American citizen. Still, the subject had never been mentioned, and it irritated him.

"We are rivals, *mon ami*. And I will do what I must to acquire the post. It is the boulevard to success. A little while out there, earning the company a good profit and befriending the Crows, and I will have the credentials I need. Chouteau insists on practical experience. The senior men are very rich, monsieur, and so shall I be."

"And what's your design for me?"

"Bellevue, Skye. Get off the flatboat at Bellevue and head west with your woman. You will be safe. No official will know of your whereabouts or try to remove you from Indian Territory. You see? What I propose is in your interests!"

Bellevue was the site of an American Fur Company post near the confluence of the Platte River and the Missouri, a trading center run by Peter Sarpy for the Omahas and other plains tribes, a depot for the furs coming down the Platte River, and a supply point for much of the mountain trade. It would be only a few days away once they were traveling again.

"Sorry," Skye said. "We're going to St. Louis to try our luck with Chouteau. We'll not turn back now. And there's no way Clark can keep me from returning to my wife's people if I choose to go there."

"Regrettable," Bonfils said. "You force my hand."

28

Victoria ripped hard through the brisket until the guts burst out into a steaming heap. The cow was scarcely dead. Red Gill waited a few yards distant, wary of the stream of buffalo that were shaking, snorting, dripping water, shivering the very earth. Victoria didn't like it either, and wondered whether some minor excitement would send the vast herd trampling over her. She and Lame Deer worked only yards from the riverbank, and only yards from the undulating edge of the herd.

A calf bleated nearby and refused to meld itself into the herd. Victoria felt a moment's sadness, for this dead four-foot was its mother. But the calf would live; it was three months old, and nibbling grass.

Lame Deer had sliced open the flesh behind the jaw of the cow, and was carefully sawing off the massive tongue, a great delicacy, while Victoria was scooping out the brisket, aiming for the huge liver, another delicacy. A cloud of black flies whirled and whined over them all; with the herd came every vicious biting fly on Mother Earth, and all types of them were swarming over this dead animal. Victoria knew that by nightfall other predators would congregate, and by dawn this cow would be bone and hide. She shivered.

Red Gill retreated irritably, leaving the filthy work to the women, but he hovered not far off, and began gathering driftwood and brush to build a fire. The flatboat bobbed and bumped land just a few rods distant. Victoria paused to examine the skylines; all sorts of predators followed the herds, including the two-footed kind, and it paid to be wary. But she saw nothing.

She reached into the warm, pungent, slippery carcass and clamped her hand over the liver and tugged, while gently nipping away tissue with the other hand until she released the dark and slippery organ.

Her hands dripped blood, and the black flies swarmed in thick clouds, and she wished this ugly task were done and she was feeding the mighty strength of Sister Buffalo into her wounded man.

She sliced thin strips of raw liver and popped one in her mouth, feeling its succulence between her teeth. She sliced another and handed it to Lame Deer, who gave it to her daughter, and then bit into a second piece. What finer meat was there than buffalo liver? It carried the strength of the buffalo in it, and made one strong.

She set the liver aside in the grass and began sawing along the backbone, working toward the hump. She would not try to save this hide; she could scarcely harvest a day or two of meat before night fell.

She parted the hide along the ridge of the back, releasing swarms of worms and beetles buried in its thick brown matting. This cow must have been tormented, and no doubt the long swim across the river had helped cleanse some of the nesting parasites.

Lame Deer sliced with sharp, deft strokes, working from the incision under the jaw, until at last she had freed the tongue and it could be pulled out of the mouth. Oh, there would be a feast this night! Boiled tongue would put power into them all. Sister Buffalo would give her strength to the two-legged ones.

When Victoria had exposed the humpmeat which lay over the dorsal ribs, she motioned to Lame Deer and they grabbed the legs of the animal to flip it over so Victoria could work on the other side of the hump. This took a mighty effort, but the two women succeeded, and soon Victoria was skillfully slicing out the hump, which lay at the base of the neck, and which contained the most tender and edible of all the flesh of a buffalo. It was no easy thing to cut the humpmeat free.

She peered up and found Bonfils staring at her, but he didn't venture into the cloud of vicious black flies, and she wished she didn't have to feed him.

Gill set up an iron tripod, hung a black kettle from it, and then collected the tongue, brushing off the black flies. He dropped the tongue into the kettle and fed more wood to the fire.

But Victoria and Lame Deer slipped liver into their mouths, licking up the salty blood, nurturing themselves and little Singing Rain, even as they worked. Let the men have the tongue. The women had the liver. And tomorrow there would be a hump roast.

The herd made her uneasy. Every little while it undulated close, and the dripping buffalo trotted by, churning up a muddied slope, so many that the earth quivered under their countless hooves, and the air was filled with soft noise, breathing, pent-up energy, and their sharp odor.

Then she noticed other animals nearby. Half a dozen wet wolves sat on their haunches on the riverbank, their coats glistening after the long swim across the broad river. A chill shot through her.

She picked up a rock and threw it at them. She liked wolves; they looked after her people, and some of the Absaroka warriors had wolf medicine. But she didn't want them there, twenty yards distant, contemplating her and the other women, smelling meat and death. The rock bounced between two of them and they lazily parted a few feet, undeterred.

She returned to her work, wishing she had her bow and quiver. She would drive an arrow into the big one who watched her with a feral and patient gaze. She turned to Gill.

"Wolves," she yelled.

Gill nodded, looking around for his weapon, when a rifle cracked. She saw smoke erupting from Bonfils's weapon. A wolf catapulted backward, yapping, shivering, and then dying. The others retreated sullenly. She and the Cheyenne woman held this ground for a little while, but the instant they abandoned the buffalo cow, the wolves would be upon it.

She stared at Bonfils, who stood grinning, proud of himself. He set down his rifle, poured a fresh charge of powder down its barrel, patched a ball and drove it home with the hardwood rod that clipped under the barrel. Then he cleaned the nipple with his pick. The rifle was armed, except for a new cap.

It took another stint of hard, filthy work to saw through bone and gristle and meat, but she and Lame Deer freed the hump and laid it in the grass. Victoria severed enough of the filthy hide to cover the hump and liver and the rest of what they had cut loose, and together they dragged it away from the carcass.

Even before the women reached the cookfire, gray wolves swarmed over the carcass; not just the six she had seen, but a dozen more, snarling and tearing, their feasting drowned out by the mutter of the passing herd, which still stretched from the distant bluffs across the river to the bluffs on this side of it.

She and Lame Deer dragged the bloody meat aboard and laid it near the front of the boat. Lame Deer began crooning in her own tongue, and Victoria knew she was giving thanks again to the animal that had been sacrificed to feed her and her daughter; and to rejoice in the goodness of the bountiful world, and the kindness of Sweet Medicine, the sacred brother and lawgiver who looked over the Cheyenne people.

Victoria washed herself at the riverbank, floating away the slime and blood, cleansing her brown face, slapping the black flies that still swarmed around her. The fragrance of the boiling tongue reached her nostrils, and she was ready to feast again. But first, she would feed her man.

She sawed off some half-boiled tongue and dropped it into one of the wooden trenchers Gill kept on board, and then headed for the cabin. She found Skye gazing up at her, drawn and ill.

"This is tongue," she said. "Good for you. It will put the strength of the buffalo into you. Eat!"

He struggled upward, breathing hard, wincing with every movement, but eventually sat up. He looked haggard.

"Eat buffalo, goddammit! It make you feel good."

But she had to cut each piece because he was too weak to saw at the dimpled tongue meat. He ate slowly, a few tiny slivers, and then waved the food away.

"Eat!" she cried.

He tried another piece and then stopped.

Outside, Bonfils and Gill were devouring the tongue and contesting something in low tones. They were on the riverbank. She could not make out what they were saying, but their words were cross even though they were filling their bellies.

Dusk was settling over the flatboat, plunging the cabin into darkness. Skye drank some broth, and then pushed aside the tin cup she had given him. He hadn't eaten enough.

"You got to eat and get strong!" she said, irritably.

The muted hum of the herd, the vibrations reaching her even in the flatboat, the mutter and snort of the animals, was wearing on her, rubbing her raw. The snarl of the wolves was irritating her too. Was there no end to this?

"Learned a few things from Bonfils," he said. "He says I'd have to become an American citizen to get a trading license."

She didn't understand any of it. "What is this license?"

Skye translated the idea to her in jargon she would understand, as he often did. "It's like a yes. I have to have a yes. Big chief in St. Louis says I got to join them or they won't let me trade with your people."

"How come?"

"They say the fur trade's for Americans. Not for others. Especially not for English. Makes sense, I guess. Maybe I won't be a trader if I can't get a license from this General Clark."

"We come all this way and you don't be a trader?"

He sighed. "Lame Deer's man, MacLees, he's likely the one going to be made a trader to your people . . . if Bonfils knows what he's talking about."

"MacLees?" she marveled. "He's the Opposition."

"He's been driven out. Now it looks like maybe they'll give him a job, put him to work. He's a veteran trader. That's how they do it. Drive out the opposition and then hire the best of them. They're even employing Gabe Bridger now."

She understood only part of it, but fumed at the very idea.

"Him I don't trust," she said, gesturing toward the dark shore where the two men sat at the fire.

"Bonfils, he's got his own schemes going. He says we should get off at Bellevue. That's a big post down the river some. He says I should stay out of St. Louis for my own good. That's what he talked about a while ago. You want to quit?"

"Hell no," she snapped.

He grinned in the obscure light. "Thought so," he said. It was the first time in days he had smiled.

29

Lame Deer awakened to deep silence. Not even crickets were chirping. Her hand found Singing Rain beside her, sleeping peacefully in the bunk across from Mister Skye.

She understood the silence. The buffalo brothers had crossed the Big River at last, and had vanished to the west. And the wolves had vanished with them. The night was no longer restless, and the very earth did not tremble under the impact of so many dark hooves.

She could see nothing. No moon lit the landscape or glinted off dark waters. She stirred, wanting to step outside into fresh air. Skye's sour breath filled this dank cabin, and she wanted to escape it and suck sweet fresh air into her lungs. Her friend the Crow woman slept across the floor of the cabin, rolled into a robe. The men slept outside.

She heard stirring in the fore part of the flatboat, and knew Bonfils was awakening. She hated and dreaded Bonfils, and marveled that such a one could be here in this flatboat with those he had hurt. She thought again of Sounds Come Back After Shouting, and grieved, the pain so sharp and so bitter that she wanted to scream in sorrow and cut her hair and deface herself as an act of mourning.

She had not known at first that this man, Bonfils, was the killer of her only son. That awful moment when the Sans Arcs had gathered around Skye, in the fog of dawn, she had seen two men aboard the fireboat dancing about, sometimes obscured by the whisps of fog, dark obscure figures she paid little attention to because Skye was conferring with the Sans Arcs, and she was listening to all of that.

Then the shocking blast came, and she heard screams, and beheld her boy tumbling to the cold earth. He fell onto his back, and she saw a dark, wet hole in his neck and another in his head, and his lips moved once or twice and then his spirit departed for the long trail. His eyes did not see her. Sound Comes Back After Shouting was gone, after four winters of life, and she heard another blast of the cannon and more screams, and white men's cursing, and then the Sans Arcs shouted, raced about, gathered their fallen, and vanished . . . and she began to weep.

It was not until the Crow woman told her about Bonfils that she learned who had killed her son. And now this very killer was aboard. She could not fathom it. That man had also killed Shorty Ballard, partner of the owner of this boat, and put three wounds upon Mister Skye, gravely injuring him, and yet that man walked the planks of the flatboat, lorded over them all, and acted as if nothing had happened. He had even been saying he had done a good thing and had rescued the company's furs.

She had thought often of killing Bonfils. But she knew she wouldn't. It was not in her to do such a thing, though sometimes she longed to stick her knife deep into his ribs and let him see what a woman of the People could do to the killer of her beloved son.

But she had chosen another course. She would tell MacLees about it; tell him everything, let him grieve for Billy, as he called the boy he doted on, and then Simon would be filled with wrath and seek justice against this man Bonfils, after the manner of the white men. And then this Bonfils would be driven from the midst of the white men.

But here he was, walking among the aggrieved, and she could not fathom it. Why had the boat chief, Red Gill, permitted this man to board? But she knew the answer to that: Bonfils had held a rifle on the boat chief.

She heard Bonfils walking rearward, heard him awaken Gill, who yawned and cursed after the manner of white men. She heard subdued voices, and Gill's snarl, but then the owner of this big canoe arose, and she could hear him making water over the side of the flatboat, and talking with Bonfils.

She threw off her robe, caring tenderly not to awaken her child, and stepped out upon the deck. A chill night wind caught her hair and an overcast hid the stars and Brother Moon so she could not fathom the time. But some intuition told her that Father Sun would soon appear upon the horizon.

It was much too dark to navigate, but she realized they were untying the boat from the bankside brush that tethered it, and a moment later she felt the craft bob and move slowly into the bleak darkness. She knew only that Gill had turned it outward from shore. He had great medicine, that man, and maybe he would steer the flatboat just by keeping it in the swiftest current. The boat rode high, carrying so little, and he feared nothing.

How impatient these men were, and how little they saw. All the trip, she had seen a world unfold that they never perceived; the black bear, the ravens, the Arikara women digging roots, the black snake swimming, the minnows, the turtle that paused to watch them, and the eagle climbing the stair to the sky.

But Gill saw things she could not; the way the water ran, the place where currents drove ahead, the meaning of the lines of foam, the snag that made a vee-shaped pattern in the water, the changing color of the river as it took on more mud and silt. She respected Red Gill, not only for his river medicine, but because he was strong and shrewd and watchful.

So they were once again moving. She exulted. Soon she would come to this place called St. Louis, and she would find Simon and his heart would be gladdened. The sharp breeze reminded her that it was not long before dawn, and she was hungry. Roasted hump meat hung from a mast forward; to fill herself she needed only saw at it with her skinning knife. She worked forward, through an inky darkness.

"The buffalo, they let us go," said Bonfils, materializing beside her.

She did not speak to this man; neither did she look at him or let him peer into her spirit. There was something possessive about him. She could not quite fathom his interest in her. It was not like a man's desire for a woman, but something else, as if she were something to use; something that would help him. She wished she knew what was in his mind.

"Don't want to talk, madame? Very well. It is not necessary. We will watch over you all the way to St. Louis, and then we will present you to the world." He laughed softly.

She found the meat hung well above where a creature could nip at it, and she reached upward, standing on the tips of her moccasins, to cut off the cool and succulent flesh of the blessed buffalo. She gave thanks again to this mother who gave herself to feed the two-foots, and then sliced a piece and popped it into her mouth, and then several more. And then she sliced a few small pieces and carried them back to the cabin. They would suffice for Singing Rain, and keep her strong.

She felt her way back, entered the cabin, and discovered that Victoria Skye was awake, and crooning softly to Singing Rain.

"We're on the river," she said.

"Buff gone?" Skye asked from the darkness of his bunk.

"Yes, the brothers have passed by and the wolves too."

She handed a slice of meat to her child, who began to mouth it. The girl would gum the juices out of it but eat little.

"Can Gill steer?"

"No, he is letting the boat go where it will go. He can see nothing."

"Sort of like my life," Skye said. "No one at the tiller. But the river's taking me somewhere."

She heard Bonfils and Gill far forward, trying to see what they could see. She liked the dark, and the soft gurgle of the water on the hull, and the closeness of the cabin.

"You any better?" Victoria asked Skye.

"Some."

"Want to sit up?"

He grunted. Victoria wrestled her man upward until he was resting against the cabin wall. She gave him a tin cup of water, which he drank slowly.

"Maybe I'll walk today," he said. "Need strength, if they put us off at Bellevue."

"What is this?" Victoria asked sharply.

"I think Bonfils is going to try to put you and me off at the next post. I'm guessing if I don't go voluntarily, he and Gill will put us off by force. He figures the fastest way to get rid of a rival is to keep me out of St. Louis."

"Sonofabitch," said Victoria.

"Why would he do this thing?" Lame Deer asked.

"Get me out of the way. That leaves only Simon Mac-Lees," Skye said.

"My man?"

"Your man." Skye looked uncomfortable.

Lame Deer could make no sense of it. White men were mysterious to her, and there were undercurrents that she knew she would never understand.

She did not want to ride in the flatboat with only Red Gill and Alexandre Bonfils. The Skyes were a comfort to her. Victoria had become a friend and also a mentor, explaining the strange ways of white men. And Skye himself was a great chief among them, well known to her people and all the Peoples.

"My man no work for American Fur."

Skye stared into the gloom. She could barely make out his face. "I hear that Chouteau—he's the big chief—is going to hire your man. He's got trading experience with your people."

A faint light began to pervade their universe, a light so false that she dismissed it. Yet she knew dawn was not far off.

Simon had said nothing to her about any of it. Maybe he didn't know. But he could have sent word up the river with the men who brought messages.

"If you get off the boat, then we will too, and we will walk to the place of the many lodges."

Skye peered at her. "I don't think Bonfils would let you," he said.

"Let me go? Him?"

Skye shook his head. The light had thickened, and she could see him clearly now, staring at her from those intent blue eyes. He coughed and turned his head away, clearly letting her know he didn't wish to discuss what he knew. He was hiding things.

She felt an unnameable fear crawl through her. Something strange and unknowable and evil was crushing her. She thought of this place Bellevue, and thought that she might escape there—if she could. And then walk to St. Louis.

30

Red Gill was in a sour mood. His annual trip upriver had been ruined and his partner killed. He would arrive in St. Louis penniless after a summer of hard and dangerous work—unless he could get his furs back. He scarcely knew who to blame, but Skye was one, Marsh was another, and now Bonfils.

If Skye hadn't knocked Shorty down and steered the flatboat toward the stricken *Otter*, the trouble wouldn't have happened. Shorty was going to take his chances with that six-pounder, and he was right. All of Gill's troubles were launched when Skye steered the flatboat toward the steamer.

If Skye hadn't intervened, Shorty would be alive . . . probably, anyway. Marsh wouldn't have confiscated the bales of furs as smuggler's contraband. Skye wouldn't be lying in the cabin recovering from three wounds, Bonfils wouldn't be on board, goading Gill onward like some madman.

It was that goddam Skye's fault. Probably, anyway. Gill didn't want to think about what might have happened if Shorty had continued to plow past the stranded steamer under the mouth of that cannon. Well, he'd never know whether Marsh would have fired or not, after putting a ball across the bow. Just one ball from that cannon would have blown the flatboat to bits; one cannister of grape could have killed everyone aboard.

But Red Gill refused to think about it. He would have taken his chances, just like Shorty. He'd been taking chances all his life, and this was just one more chance—until Skye wrecked everything.

But a small voice in him kept whispering that Skye had done the only thing, and he had saved lives doing it. Gill hated to admit it, and pushed the thought out of mind.

Damned Skye.

Gill manned the tiller, not wanting Bonfils or the squaws to do it. And Skye was too weak, even though he was wandering around the deck now. They hadn't overtaken the *Otter*, and Gill didn't expect to, even though Bonfils insisted on floating day and night in pursuit, like some madman.

And that brought up another matter that was irritating Gill: what the hell difference did it make if the flatboat arrived in St. Louis after Marsh did? Bonfils had been saying he had to reach Pierre Chouteau ahead of Marsh or Gill would never get his furs back, but the more Gill thought about it, the less sense it made.

Gill intended to have it out with Chouteau: return them furs or get into big trouble with the government. Chouteau would understand. Gill was not above going to General Clark and telling the Indian superintendent the whole story, how Pratte, Chouteau and Company had employed Gill and Ballard to sneak ardent spirits to the trading posts, and were being paid off in buffalo robes and other furs, all off the books.

Chouteau would make sure the furs were returned, and probably chew out that damned Marsh for seizing them. So why the hell was Bonfils in such a rush? Why was the Creole pacing the boat, urging Gill to find the fastest current, talking like a wildman of overtaking the steamer, looking for the *Otter* at every wood stop, lamenting every minute the flatboat stopped to cook a meal or hunt for game to put in the pot? What was the matter with the man?

They had been drifting downriver for days, through a hot summer, enduring flies and mosquitos, seeing no one except for the occasional Opposition post, shabby little affairs, along the way.

But now they were approaching Bellevue, or Sarpy's Post as the company was calling it. It wasn't much of a trading center, but it served as an entrepôt, storing furs coming in from the Platte River, and tradegoods destined for the upper Platte and upper Missouri.

The closer they got, the wilder Bonfils became.

"How soon?" he demanded.

"Soon as the river takes us."

"Can't you hurry? Put up a sail?"

"What's at Sarpy's Post?"

"*Otter.* We'll pass them there."

"*Otter*'s down in Missoura now, near to Independence."

"No, it can't! Ah, my friend Gill, when we arrive at Bellevue, there are some small matters to take care of; very important for you and for me, *oui?*"

Gill glared. He was tired of all this.

Bonfils drew himself up, and whispered intensely. "Under no circumstances must the Cheyenne squaw be allowed off this boat."

"And who's to stop her? I sure won't."

"But you don't understand."

"Damn right I don't understand."

Bonfils smiled. "Monsieur Gill, there are things beyond your knowledge that affect you. Just trust me."

"Bonfils, that woman goes where she wants to go, because I ain't stopping her."

Bonfils smiled, nodded, and retreated. "Very well,

but there is another matter. I want you to eject Skye and his squaw. Put them off."

That flabbergasted Gill. "Why?"

"As a favor to me, one that will benefit you, as you will see."

Gill didn't mind that idea so much. He had no use for Skye or that sharp-tongued little Crow woman he called his wife. Still, Bonfils was obviously a man full of schemes, and Gill wanted some answers.

"I want to know why, because if I don't like it, I ain't going to do it."

Bonfils sighed. "Ah, friend, when Skye arrives in St. Louis and meets Pierre Chouteau, I fear he will say things unflattering to me, and reduce my influence. It is because of my influence with my relatives that I can make sure you'll get your furs back, and your name will be cleared, and Capitaine Marsh, he will suffer for his rash conduct in seizing your cargo, *oui*? Trust me, my friend."

Gill didn't believe a word of it. "And what am I supposed to do?" he asked.

"Very simple. Tell him he must get off your boat."

"Let me get this straight. You want me to keep Mac-Lees's woman aboard at all costs, but dump Skye."

"Ah, you have a discerning mind, monsieur."

"And for this I get my cargo back."

Bonfils smiled broadly, something velvety and soft in his brown eyes.

"I'll think on it. But I'll tell you one thing, Bonfils. That steamboat's a week ahead of us by now, and you won't see it again unless you've got wings. That buffalo crossing wrecked your little plan."

Gill fumed. He didn't trust the sonofabitch. He didn't need Bonfils. He needed one quiet word with Chouteau. And he didn't doubt that Pierre Chouteau would give him whatever he wanted. If the company lost its trading license for smuggling spirits into Indian Country, that would be the end of an empire. Gill had his own lever. So Bonfils could go to hell.

No sooner had Bonfils headed forward than Skye appeared at the cabin door. He looked weak and pale, but he was standing now, and the pain was gone from his eyes.

"I heard that, mate," he said.

Gill didn't reply.

"You want the story?"

Gill nodded, ready to discount everything the mountaineer said. He'd be just as bad as Bonfils.

"Well, there's a position open . . ." Skye said, his voice so low it scarcely carried to Gill's ears. Skye laid it out in simple terms: he and Bonfils were being considered for the trading position at Fort Cass, and maybe Simon Mac-Lees too, though Skye said he had no direct knowledge of it.

As for MacLees, Bonfils believed that the arrival of his mountain wife in St. Louis would embarrass the former Opposition trader and ensure that Bonfils got the position, which was why he was obsessed with getting her there.

Gill cussed softly, a long, gentle stream of epithets that substituted for rage or amazement or sometimes wild humor. But he wasn't laughing now.

"How come you know this?"

"I've told you what I know. And what Bonfils said. I don't know the truth of it."

Gill believed the English sonofabitch, leaned over the transom, and spat. It was clear now. Alexandre Bonfils wasn't interested in doing Gill a favor; all he wanted was to get to St. Louis fast, with the Cheyenne woman he could use like some chess piece to embarrass a rival.

Gill spat again. He had Bonfils pegged now; should have seen it long ago. The Creole was a smooth, flattering bastard who made everything he did sound like a favor, even while he was using everyone in sight. Next thing

Bonfils would do is tell Gill that shooting Shorty was a favor, too, because Gill would end up with all the furs, instead of half.

Gill had a redhead's temper, but now he held it in check. He wanted to think. If it came to trouble, he could knock that Creole right over the gunnels and let him swim. Gill wondered why he believed Skye, and realized there was something in the man that commanded respect, and that was the difference between Skye and Bonfils.

The country was changing now; more trees, some hardwoods, lower hills. The river had accumulated the waters of a dozen more streams and had grown majestic. Above the confluence of the Platte, they passed various Opposition posts and the ruins of several others. Fur outfits had fought over this country from the beginning. He even saw some stacked cordwood, offered by local woodhawks to steamboats for a price. The river was changing.

He knew he would make Sarpy's Post at Bellevue by sundown or soon after, and there he intended to stop. He was no longer in a rush. What difference did it make if Marsh got there first? Pierre Chouteau was no fool. He hadn't built the most powerful fur empire in the world by being gullible or reckless. The hell with Bonfils.

As if in response to the thought, Bonfils appeared aft.

"Is this it? Is this Bellevue?"

"Couple hours, maybe three."

"Are you ready?"

Gill spat, making a white dimple in the muddy brown river. "Guess we'll take our time," he said. "I want to visit with old Peter Sarpy, eh?"

"But we must hurry!"

"Not we; you. I'm going to stop for a good visit."

Bonfils smiled, even laughed, but Gill didn't miss the fleeting calculation in those liquid brown eyes.

Benton Marsh was so pleased with himself that he neglected his daily tongue-lashing. Normally, he selected one or another boatman who had shirked his duties, and rebuked the man in sardonic, withering language intended for as many ears as possible. The boat ran better because the crewmen never knew who would be next.

He had driven the *Otter* up a treacherous, shifting river to the farthest reaches of the unknown continent and returned bearing a fortune in furs and hides, along with the usual riffraff out of the mountains, plus precious information, worth plenty to the right parties.

Now he was negotiating the lower Missouri, still cautious even though the volume of water was greater, because of the many snags lurking just below the innocent surface, ready to tear out the hull of his boat and shatter men's dreams. Soon he would be in St. Louis, and then he would ride a hack triumphantly up the slope to Pierre Chouteau's ornate home, and whisper things into Chouteau's funneling ear, strictly in private. Benton Marsh knew himself to be an invaluable asset to the entrepreneur.

There, in a private warren of Chouteau's home, he would whisper the news. Such as that he had saved the company a great embarrassment. And that he had confiscated nineteen bales of buffalo hides from smugglers and scoundrels. And that he had concluded on good evidence that Skye was an ignoramus, an East End London hooligan, unsuited for so demanding and diplomatic a profession as trading; and alas, the company's favorite nephew, Bonfils, was impetuous and reckless.

With relish, he would tell Chouteau about Bonfils's rash and unauthorized use of the cannon, its fatal results, and its deleterious effect on trade with the Sioux. So much for that wretch! He would add that in his estimation, MacLees was the only man fit for the trading position. He wasn't sure whether he would say anything to Chouteau about the Cheyenne squaw, or that Marsh had rescued the young man from a scandal. He would decide about that when the time came.

Marsh could well envision Chouteau's response; always subdued but appreciative, the gravity of the man evident in his intent gaze, and his odd humor blooming in the small, almost smirky smile that would soon build in his dark face. There would be a bonus, of course. Maybe even a partnership share in the firm, at last. Chouteau knew whom to count on.

Soon Marsh would be seeing his lovely stepdaughter, Sarah, and would relish her happiness as the nuptial day approached. He had bought her a new pianoforte, and she was mastering it and singing, too. Her voice was a little less than sublime, but no matter. She could hold a tune as long as she didn't get into the upper ranges.

He watched the riverbanks roll by. They were tree-lined now, and the forests closed down upon the great stream, with rarely a patch of grass in sight. For two days he had been traveling through settled country. Now fueling was easy. He had only to pull up at one or another woodhawk's lot and load the heavy hardwood logs aboard, pay the man or leave a chit that was as good as cash anywhere. Sometimes the woodhawk's wife had fresh potatoes or carrots or greens, and these he bought too for the mess. His passengers had grown weary of buffalo and elk and antelope.

The *Otter* churned past rude hamlets, which always erupted whenever the boat passed by; dogs, children, adults, all of them waving, shouting, barking. Sometimes horses shied, and once in a while his passage sent a herd of cattle thundering away from the frightful apparition on the river. The passage of a steamboat was no small thing.

Now, fifty miles out of St. Louis, Missouri seemed totally civilized. Farms dotted the slopes. Towns of red brick and whitewashed cottages clustered along the banks. River traffic increased: ferries, sailboats, rowboats, fishing ketches, flatboats, and keelboats, all hauling goods and people up and down or across the broad river. Civilization at last.

He marveled that only a few weeks earlier he had reached a point near British possessions far to the north, after passing through an impenetrable wilderness that would remain that way for a century. Only a few days before, red-skinned savages had congregated about the boat, dumbstruck by its power, superstitious and frightened when he rang a bell, shot steam up the escapement, blew a whistle, or ordered the great paddle wheels to thrash water. White men understood such things; red men never would.

He would arrive in St. Louis at dusk, maybe at twilight, but with just enough daylight to reach a safe anchorage. Word of the *Otter*'s arrival would have reached the pier ahead of him, carried by horsemen, and by the time the packet eased to shore, a hundred lamps would light the way, dimpling the black waters with pricks of light. And a crowd would be gaping at the boat that traveled clear to the unmapped land of savages, some unimaginable distance away, and safely back.

Maybe even Chouteau.

Yes, he hoped Pierre would show up to celebrate Marsh's triumphant journey. It would be fitting.

Just as he hoped, he raised St. Louis just as blackness was lowering, and his pilot edged the riverboat through the inky waters until it gently bumped pilings in the levee. The rumble of the paddles suddenly ceased. At that moment, his pilot blew the whistle, and the engineers shot a great bang of steam through the escapement, and he could see the throng recoil, and then shout and cheer. Hats sailed, bull's-eye lanterns swung crazily, ladies in black lace sitting in ebony carriages watched demurely from behind their accordion-folded fans, well apart from the hoi polloi. Maybe one of those shining vehicles contained his wife or even Sarah Lansing. He would welcome the hugs, the exclamations, the sweet perfumes, the promise of bliss, the domestic hearth, the sweetness of one's own home.

He watched his crew run the grimy gangway to the levee, watched others tether the boat fore and aft with great looped hawsers, making it secure. He was in no rush. In fact, he was observing the crew: this was a test. The better men worked faithfully until dismissed. The worse ones were looking for ways to bolt for the nearest dive, or head for their wives, or paint the town. He had the answer to that, though. The pay envelopes would not be distributed until he was good and ready.

He saw a carriage drawn by a pair of dappled drays clop down the cobbled grade to the levee, and sensed that this time the chief officer of Pratte, Chouteau and Company would soon appear in his cabin instead of waiting for his arrival up the hill. The coachman drove straight to the gangway as the crowd parted, and indeed the man who emerged, stocky, dark, square-set, and splendidly if a bit casually dressed, set foot on the glistening cobbles, and then upon the gangway. He looked up at the master, and waved languidly.

Marsh beckoned him up and set out a bottle of cognac and some glasses on the small walnut table within. He lit the hanging oil lamp with his striker, and awaited the emperor, who swept in grandly.

"Ah, Benton, so good, so good, *mon ami*. You are back safely, and we see the vessel is heavy-laden and rides low. How do you fare? How is your health? Did we lose anyone?"

"No one I didn't intend to lose. And your health?"

"We are well, though madame struggles with gout, and there has been dysentery again. The whole city smells of excrement."

"Well, Pierre, we're in St. Louis with good news aplenty. You are rich, once again. Very, very rich."

"Ah! We shall see. In New York they speak dolorously of dropping prices. They have us by the throat." Chouteau plucked up the cognac and poured a generous dollop into the captain's cut-glass snifter.

"Tell us everything! But first, what do you carry?"

For an answer, Marsh pulled out his papers and ledgers and lay the cargo manifest before Chouteau. The entrepreneur donned his wire-rimmed spectacles, and began reading the watery black script, lifting the ledger pages up close to the soft light.

"*Manifique, c'est marveloux*. So much. Is there insect damage or soaking?"

"No, no trouble this time."

Chouteau read and reread the manifest. "There is more here than we were led by the expresses to believe we possess."

"Ah! Some nineteen bales of buffalo hide, and odds and ends I picked up along the way from savages."

"We are sure there is a story in it."

There was indeed.

Trenholm knocked politely. "We're secure. Crew wants to go," he said.

"No, not until every bale is safe in the warehouse."

"They're grumbling."

"Let them. Every bale accounted for, and a receipt for it. They'll be freed in a few hours. Except for you, of course, and a half dozen men you select. They stay."

"Aye, sir."

Trenholm left, and they heard him clatter down the companionway.

Oddly, Chouteau's smile had vanished.

"Monsieur Marsh, is there anything urgent we should know?"

"Oh, a few small matters, an incident or two, and some action on my part that will save the company from embarrassment."

"Really, we shall relish the story."

"Yes, it'll take a bit, but we have time."

"Ah, my captain, was that not your wife and the lovely Miss Lansing we saw on the levee, awaiting your presence?"

"Yes, it was. They can wait a little. That's the fate of the wives of sailing men, I'm afraid. The lamp in the window."

Chouteau smiled gently. "We see things differently. A man who returns to his wife after a long absence should fall into her arms—assuming, of course, she is of a certain age and not infirm."

They laughed.

Chouteau stood. "You have mail from the posts, we presume?"

"Yes, as always. Quite a packet of it."

He handed Chouteau all the letters he had collected en route, reports and complaints that would give the fur magnate a fine idea of the situation at each fur post, and the preoccupations of each trader.

"We will read these, my friend. Come to our house at ten, and we will have a cigar in our study, and you can tell your anecdotes, eh?"

"Very well, sir."

"*Bien*! And tell your passengers, Bonfils and Skye, to come to our offices midmorning."

"They are not aboard, sir."

Chouteau stood stock still. "You have much to tell us, then. We will read this correspondence while you put this bateau in order and embrace your enchanting wife and family. Then, *mon ami*, we will see."

32

Sarpy's Post, on the right bank of the Missouri at the confluence of the Platte, looked different from any other post that Skye had seen. This one was simply a hilltop farm, with a farmhouse and a few buildings scattered about. It was not fortified.

Were they that close to civilization? Or were the tribes in the vicinity, such as the Omahas, that pacific? Gill had steered the flatboat past several posts, mostly Opposition outfits, in the Council Bluffs area, but now he pulled the tiller and steered the boat toward the bank, where a few people stood watching.

"There's more to it than it looks," Gill said, reading Skye's mind. "This place—Bellevue—been in the middle of the fur trade from the get-go."

"Will we see white women?" Victoria asked.

Gill grinned. "Not as I ever heard. Some comely Omaha ladies, maybe."

"Where the hell are your women?"

"There ain't any. We get borned a different way. We cut off a toenail, put her in whiskey, and it grows."

Victoria laughed.

Skye saw that the people on shore were Indians after all, but dressed entirely in white men's duds, duck cloth pantaloons and chambray shirts, mostly. And the sole woman was in printed calico. Tame Indians, the mountaineers called them. Not the furred and feathered variety in the far West.

Gill steered the flatboat toward the crude landing, and tossed a hawser to one of the men, who wrapped it around a post poking up from the mud. Bonfils threw the plank gangway to the bank, stepped ashore ahead of the rest, grinning broadly. For once he didn't seem to be in a rush.

Lame Deer followed, her walk wary and cautious. She carried her girl in her arms, and then set Singing Rain on the damp earth. She was dressed in a fringed buckskin skirt and moccasins, and a blue cambray shirt, all quilled in the Cheyenne tradition, and sharply different from clothing of the tame Indians.

Skye followed, still weak on his pins and wobbly, but Victoria helped him alight. He wondered how he could manage the hundred yards upslope to the store, but taking a few steps at a time he worked his way forward, glad to be walking. Gill secured the boat, wrapping another hawser forward, and then joined them in the trek to the store.

"There's a mess of Sarpys in the fur business," he said. "Pete here, he's the son of old John, and coming along smartly in the company. His pa's a partner in the company, got a thirty-second of it, I think. Tom, an uncle, got himself blown up a few years ago, messing around a powder barrel."

By the time Skye reached the store, he was exhausted, and settled on a plank bench to catch his breath. He wasn't healing as fast as he had hoped, and was still just about useless. At first it had been the rib wound that tormented him; now it was the thigh wound, which ached mercilessly and drew the strength right out of him. Still, the wounds had scabbed over and weren't infected, and with some time he might recover his health. Victoria had taken good care of him, but he was still just about worthless.

The view was handsome from up there, and he studied the sparkling blue river while his heart thudded and slowed, and a dry breeze toyed with him. Victoria headed into the store, along with Bonfils and Lame Deer.

"I got some private business with Sarpy," Gill said, heading for the farmhouse.

Skye guessed it had to do with smuggled alcohol. Red Gill struck him as a bold, likeable, daring frontiersman who would make his coin any way he could, no matter what the rules were. He might well have supplied Sarpy's Post with ardent spirits, if indeed that was Gill's real business.

After Skye recovered his breath, he wobbled to his feet and entered the post, which looked more like an ordinary store for white people than most trading posts. But he spotted the usual blankets, awls, trade muskets, shot and powder, knives, pots, skeins of beads, along with sacks of cornmeal, sugar, coffee, and all the rest. He loved these stores, with all their small sweet luxuries, and meant to buy Victoria something. A black-suited clerk hovered behind a plank counter, keeping a wary eye on customers, but his eye betrayed a lively curiosity as he looked over these latest specimens from the far West.

"Out of the mountains?" the clerk asked.

"From the Stony Mountains," Skye said.

"You've come a piece." The man was itching to find out Skye's business, but Skye wasn't in a talking mood.

"We got good prices, better than mountain prices," the clerk said as Skye studied the stock.

What struck Skye at once was Bonfils, who was holding up a gaudy red and blue blanket for Lame Deer. Her eyes shone with pleasure.

"Madame, it is for you!" he said with a gallic flourish. "And now I shall buy one for the *petite fille*!"

He dug through the two-point blankets and plucked up a green one for the child.

"Ah! I see smiles! Now, how about a little paint, eh?"

He led the Cheyenne woman toward a shelf filled with small, papered cubes of vermillion, and handed one to her. "There's this, but perhaps you'd like some ocher too! And of course some lamp black, and some cobalt!"

"Ah!" she cried.

"And let us not forget some big beads, and thread and needle, and a string of jingle bells! Now, how about some tobacco? Ah, a few plugs, and a clay pipe! You shall have a good puff or two, all the way to St. Louis!"

Lame Deer was laughing and shaking her head. Skye had not seen her laugh for weeks.

"Now, madame, what about a hatchet, and some velveteen for a skirt? You'll have time to work it up, and when you find Simon MacLees, you'll look like a Cheyenne queen!"

"What is queen?"

"Very beautiful and important lady. MacLees will go mad with happiness!"

"Ah! Ah!" she cried, fondling the purple velveteen.

Bonfils raised two fingers to the clerk, who cut two yards of it and folded it neatly.

"You got a little lard?" Bonfils asked.

The clerk nodded, and pulled a tin off a shelf.

"Good. We'll mix us some paints!"

Swiftly, Bonfils heaped the goods on the counter, and then added cornmeal, coffee beans, parched corn, sugar, molasses, and chocolates.

Even as the clerk was totting up the cost of all that, Bonfils was mixing vermillion with the lard until he had a shiny red paste, and then he began painting Lame Deer, a thick red streak down her forehead, chevrons of red on her brown arms, while she laughed and squealed. When Bonfils was done, he stepped back to study his handiwork.

"Yes, yes," he said, "you'll be the belle of St. Louis. Ah, the perfect savage!"

"Goddam," said Victoria, approving. "Skye, why don't you get me that stuff?"

"With what?"

"You gonna take me to the city with all the lodges dressed like this?"

Skye grinned. "When I get that job, I'll dress you in satins and silks, like all those Assiniboine ladies up at Fort Union."

Victoria grunted, not certain she liked that.

Skye found a barrel to sit on. He could scarcely stand up for five minutes.

Bonfils pulled real gold out of some inner pocket, and paid the clerk with yellow coins so bright that they stole sunlight from the room.

"Where's Sarpy?" Bonfils asked.

"At the house, talking with your friend."

"Well, say hello to him, *mon ami*, and help me load this stuff."

The clerk lugged sacks of food and the heap of Lame Deer's goods down the steep slope, and left them in the flatboat cabin, while Bonfils added a few yards of gaudy ribbon to his purchases, and then handed the ribbon to Lame Deer.

"You come along, *ma cheri*, and we'll tie some ribbons to your hair, *oui*? Then we'll have a big smoke!"

Lame Deer's eyes lit up again. She had turned into a wild beauty, with the vermillion striping her face and arms, and the gaudy blanket drawn around her, and the clay pipe in her hands.

Soon, Lame Deer, her little girl, and Bonfils retreated to the flatboat, and the clerk finished his hauling and returned, winded, to the store.

"Haven't seen gold out here ever," he said, fingering Bonfils's ducats. "I had to do some calculatin' as to the value."

Victoria was sulking. "How come he bought all that

stuff for her, eh? Maybe he could buy some for me! You gonna fix me up for when we get to this place of the lodges? You gonna make me happy, or am I gonna look like some damn Injun around all those white women in all their silk stuff, eh?"

Something about all this puzzled Skye, but he had no answers, and figured he would find out soon enough. Was Bonfils courting the Cheyenne woman? Did he plan to steal her from MacLees?

Skye had some residual credit with the company, but he wasn't inclined to spend it on foofaraw. When he returned to the mountains, it would be with a new percussion rifle, made by the Hawken Brothers of St. Louis, some good DuPont powder and shot and caps, some real cowleather boots, and a load of necessaries. And a jug or two if he could manage it. Not just trade whiskey, either, but some real, potent, smooth Kentucky.

He was out of sorts, had been ever since he was wounded, and his spirits were darkened by uncertainty. He wanted that trading job badly. It would provide him with a living, and put him in daily contact with Victoria's people. But as much as he wanted that, he felt doubts gnawing at him, things just beyond the pale, things unfathomed, a thundercloud just over the horizon.

There was the question of his health. Would he ever recover? And if he were offered this job, and took it, he would become a company man, and that meant obeying instructions and doing things he would not otherwise do. . . . Would he be required to cheat? Put a thumb in the sugar cup, the way he had seen traders do? Water the whiskey, adulterate the flour with clay, all for a profit? Would he be at the beck and call of Chouteau? He had been a free man of the mountains for many years, but would he still be free? Would he still be honorable?

While he was fretting over that, and Victoria was poking her way through the tradegoods and muttering happily, he heard Red Gill yelling. The boatman stepped into the trading room, peered wildly at the people within, spotted Skye, and beckoned.

"He's gone!" Gill roared at the puzzled Skye. "Bonfils!"

Skye hastened to the door and peered down the steep path to the riverbank. The flatboat had vanished. It was so far gone that Skye could not even spot it down the long sweep of the river.

33

Benton Marsh was feeling testy as he stepped from his cabriolet and faced the front door of the brick Chouteau residence, which he privately regarded as a grotesque melange of porticos, gargoyles, dormers, cornices, motley architectural styles, and gallic gaud.

For some reason, Pierre Chouteau put him on the defensive and he didn't like it. For that matter, he didn't like that frog, Chouteau. After months on the steamboat, where he was absolute master of his universe and his word was law, he suddenly found himself back on the ground, and in a world where there were masters of men, chief among them the man he was about to visit.

A handsomely liveried house slave appeared out of the darkness and led the cabriolet off. The trotter's hooves clopped hollowly on the glistening cobbles as Marsh headed for the enameled door of the famous house where all the spiderwebs of ambition in St. Louis were spun. It was an ostentatious house, though actually a large, homey and comfortable one.

The door swung open even before he reached it, and a graying slave in black brocaded silk with white ruffles at the collar and sleeves let him in and took his top hat and umbrella.

"He's off there in the parlah, suh," she said.

Marsh trod over an Aubusson carpet with bold golds and blues in it through the parlor to the lamplit study, Chouteau's private and secluded den, where much of what happened west of the Missouri River was decided over snifters of brandy or glasses of amontillado. The captain saw no signs of other life in the house, and supposed that Madame had retired to her chambers.

Chouteau was standing, a certain smile on his face. That smile, which always resembled a smirk, had always annoyed Marsh. No one but a dark-fleshed Creole frog would smile like that, as if in amusement or disdain. But Marsh had endless experience smoothing over his own choleric temper, and smiled warmly as he and the master of an American empire shook hands and proceeded through the wine-pouring and cigar rituals.

Marsh was no good at small talk, and wished that this St. Louis Midas, this bilingual Western Caesar, would get on with it.

"Anything in the mail?" Marsh asked, impatiently.

"Ah, *mon ami*, why is it that our traders complain that they have too much of this and not enough of that one year, and the opposite the next year? We have a time supplying them with whatever feathers and beads and trinkets their tribes demand at the moment. Fashion, it is ephemeral, *n'est pas*?"

Chouteau swirled a stiff drought of ruby port in his glass and swallowed it in a gulp.

"Ah! We have discovered the cure for aches of the body," he said. "But my dear *capitaine*, we believe you have some stories you wish to divulge, in strictest privacy?"

At last, the cue, Marsh thought impatiently. He scarcely knew where to begin. But the Cheyenne squaw was a good enough place. Later, when Chouteau had imbibed more wine, Marsh would talk about such disasters as firing a cannon into the Sans Arcs, killing a boatman and wounding Skye, jettisoning Chouteau's own relative Bonfils, booting Skye off the boat, and a few small items like that.

"Well, yes, in chronological order. We were proceeding homeward when we were flagged by a squaw on the riverbank. I was reluctant to stop, but did so because Skye pressed me to. A *squaw*, after all. The squaw, a Cheyenne woman, spoke a little English. She wanted a ride to St. Louis for herself and her little brats, and had some robes and a few fox and otter pelts to trade. . . . So I offered deck passage; nothing to lose, of course. . . ."

Marsh described what he learned from Skye. "The squaw was the mountain wife of Simon MacLees! Imagine it! Going to St. Louis to find out what happened to her man!" Marsh laughed darkly. "When I found that out, I put her off at Fort Pierre, along with her brats, fumigated the cabin, too. Camphor works well. And so . . ." he spoke softly, "I saved you and also my family embarrassment. Poor Sarah! How agitated we all would have been! Imagine that squaw and her little breed brats showing up at his doorstep on the eve of the wedding! And of course," there was a question in his voice, "I saved embarrassment to the company too. You were considering MacLees for the Fort Cass position. Am I not correct?"

Chouteau nodded softly, and said nothing. That was one of the maddening things about the man. He funneled vast amounts of information through those hairy ears poking from his wavy black hair, yet offered none; not even his reaction to events. Marsh swallowed back his choler but nursed a grievance. Chouteau had not yet said one word to him about his successful trip up that dangerous river. Not one word thanking him for all his devotion and skills.

Chouteau whirled the red ambrosia around his wineglass and waited, quizzically.

"I must tell you candidly, the Skyes took the squaw's part, and so vehemently I was forced to eject them as well," Marsh said. "I will not have mutiny or rebellion on my ship."

This time the whirling of the glass ceased altogether. "Tell us more," Chouteau said softly.

Marsh did, stressing the insolence of the man, the sheer stubborn arrogance of this common slug off the docks of London. But Chouteau simply stared blandly, his odd smirk gone, and Marsh had the feeling he had displeased Chouteau.

"I will not have anyone interfering with my command of the ship!" he said firmly, "Any more than you would tolerate someone meddling with your operations."

"Did Skye ask anything of you?"

Marsh shook his head, not wanting Chouteau to know that he had kept the squaw's fare to St. Louis, the robes and pelts.

"We will get his story," Chouteau said. "Is he coming?"

"I suppose so. Don't put much credence in anything he says; the man is utterly unreliable."

Chouteau arched an eyebrow, and that smirky smile emerged on his face once again. "And?" he said.

"I'm afraid I had some difficulties with Alexandre Bonfils as well," Marsh said reluctantly. This interview was not proceeding as he had hoped.

"Ah! Tell us!" Suddenly Chouteau was all ears.

Marsh sighed. "It's a complex story, my friend. And I must backtrack a bit. You see, Skye and the squaws arranged passage with two flatboat operators, a pair of scoundrels named Red Gill and Shorty Ballard. Do you know them?"

Chouteau's gaze turned opaque, and Marsh could not fathom what was passing through the skull of that man.

"Well, one day we hit a gravel bar that hadn't been there before, and far from help, too. The usual procedures didn't lift us over, and along came that flatboat with Ballard at the tiller . . ."

He went on to describe how it had taken a shot across the bow to bring in the boat, saying nothing about Skye's role in the process; the unloading of the cargo to a gravelly island just the other side of the bar, and the refloating of the boat.

"We were about to reload, having passed over the bar and repaired the paddle wheels and anchored in safe water, when at dawn, in fog, we were beset by a Sans Arc war party, which was filtering around the shore opposite the boat, obviously dangerous.

"Bonfils discovered them. They had collected around the camp of the flatboat people, and it turned out that Skye was negotiating with them. What they really wanted was a ride across the river; they were in hot pursuit of the Pawnees. Skye, without authority, offered them the use of the riverboat. But Bonfils was unaware of that. He rounded up a crewman or two and charged the cannon with grape and fired, scattering and wounding the Sans Arcs, killing Shorty Ballard, injuring Skye, and killing one of MacLees's brats."

Chouteau pursed his lips.

A silence stretched out, and Marsh listened to the tick-tock of the grandfather clock.

"Of course the shots awakened me. When I found out about it, that Bonfils had done this without authorization, risking the company's trade with the Sioux and killing a white man, I of course put him ashore at once."

Chouteau's liquid eyes seemed to flare and then the light in them faded. "Skye is alive?"

"I suppose."

"Ballard is dead? And of the Sans Arcs what is known?"

"Nothing."

"Ah, *c'est mal*. And where is our young relative?"

The words were meant to remind Marsh there were

blood connections between the brigade leader and Chouteau, and Marsh didn't like to be reminded of that.

"Coming down the river, obviously," Marsh retorted crisply.

"Is that all, then?"

"No. It was obvious to me that Ballard and Gill were hauling cargo gotten in illegal trade, no doubt supplying spirits to the Opposition, so following many precedents done by this company and encouraged by the army, I seized their cargo, which is why we have more bales of pelts than were on the manifests supplied by the posts. A fine coup, if I may say so. You are more than a thousand dollars richer."

Chouteau's soft white hand went still again, and the wine stopped its mad whirl around the glass and settled into a placid red pool. "And you are going to report this smuggling and seizure to General Clark, we suppose?" he said at last.

"Of course! That pair were up to no good; and we have an extra thousand dollars of profit from it. And we have, to borrow your phrase, erased the Opposition."

"My capitaine, please go to the levee at once and arrange that those bales, the confiscated ones, be separated from the rest and put in another part of the warehouse and guarded carefully."

Marsh nodded curtly. The command was a rebuke.

"We think it would perhaps be best for us to discuss matters with Red Gill when he arrives. Say nothing to General Clark."

"My navigator's license requires me to report such matters promptly."

Chouteau's smirky smile appeared once again, and he nodded.

"Very well, monsieur. Go report to General Clark in the morning. We would not want you to lose so important a thing as your livelihood."

Marsh started to stand, but Chouteau stayed him with a wave of his soft hand. "How far behind you are they?"

"I don't know or care. I have done everything in my power to preserve the good name, profit, and influence of this company, and what a boatload of smugglers and malcontents do is not my business."

Chouteau merely smiled, a response Marsh did not like. There still had not been the slightest commendation of his considerable efforts, or his good judgment, or his formidable skills.

"Is your report now complete, my *capitaine*?"

Marsh nodded.

"*Alors*, Hannah will show you out."

Marsh retreated, seething.

34

Bonfils gone. The flatboat gone. The Cheyenne woman
and her daughter on that renegade boat.

Skye squinted, hoping to see the distant vessel, but
he saw nothing but a broad blue stream wending its way
to the sea. It was very quiet at Sarpy's Post.

Red Gill cursed softly, a string of oaths that seemed to
vent his anger the way a valve hissed steam from a
boiler. He wheeled around and headed for Sarpy's house
again.

"I'll fix this," he said.

Skye felt weary; he was far from healed, and an hour's
sojourn here had exhausted him. He wanted only to find
refuge in his bunk. He had nothing but the clothes on his
back. His mountain rifle, powderhorn, beartooth necklace, blankets, and robes and spare clothing lay in that
flatboat, along with all of Victoria's spare gear and duds.
He wore only a blue calico shirt, duckcloth trousers, and
summer moccasins.

He hadn't the faintest clue about the future. By rights,
he should stay here and heal up, and then try to arrange
some credit with the company. He still hoped to get to St.
Louis but that prospect was looking bleak now, and the
chance of winning that trading position was leaking away

with every mile that Bonfils put between himself and his rival.

He turned to Victoria, who was standing beside him.

"Don't know what to do," he said.

She wasn't even cussing. Instead, she was studying the river.

"Maybe Sarpy would hire me long enough to get well and earn an outfit."

The thought discouraged him. An outfit would require a year of hard labor.

"You any ideas?"

"Horses."

"Don't know how we'll pay, but I'll go talk to Sarpy after Gill's done with him. They owe us a couple of pack animals, at least."

She squinted at him. "You going back?"

"No. We've started something. Let's finish it."

"You think Bonfils, he gets to be the trader?"

"I think Bonfils thinks we're going to quit and go west. He's counting on it. And I'm not going to satisfy him."

"You got some wounds ain't healed up, but you ain't quitting."

"No, not quitting. Never quit. Just keep going. People who quit, they just betray themselves."

She reached over to touch him, and he felt her hand press against his forearm.

They would go on, never quit, never surrender. Even in failure, it is a good thing to know you've tried with all your strength.

Which reminded him that he didn't have the strength of a baby, and he needed to sit down before he toppled over. He eased to the earth, and she joined him, watching the river to St. Louis flow by.

In a while, Gill appeared, and with him a short, thin young man.

"Mister Skye, this is Pete Sarpy, the trader here. I told

him what happened. In fact, I told the whole story. I told him about Bonfils, and Lame Deer, and the riverboat, and all the rest of it."

Sarpy extended a smooth hand, which Skye shook. "I've heard of you," he said. "Upriver, Skye's a name to be reckoned with."

"And so are your family," Skye replied.

"You going to talk to old Pierre, eh? He keeps to himself pretty much. Gill here, he knows Pierre better than I do."

Something passed between Gill and Sarpy that Skye couldn't fathom.

Sarpy looked at Skye and Victoria. "Your outfit went down the river, eh?"

Skye nodded.

"Go in there and pick up a new one."

"With what?"

"On my say-so. I will forward the bill to Pierre Chouteau. Gill's getting an outfit too. Then you'll take that sailboat down there."

Skye saw a small craft tied to the levee. A sail was wrapped around the boom. He doubted the homemade boat reached twenty feet stem to stern.

"We use it to get across the river, pick people up," Sarpy said.

"You won't need it?"

"Sure we'll need it, but we'll get it back."

Skye felt a stir. He knew sails and he knew wind, and he saw that the little craft below could maneuver easily in the broad river.

"I can sail it," Skye said, even though he had never set foot in so small a sailing craft.

"Royal Navy," Sarpy said.

Gill was grinning. Skye knew intuitively that all this was Gill's doing, and he wondered what hold the boatman had over Sarpy. There were mysteries about Gill. Maybe someday Skye would get the story.

Skye and Victoria hiked down the slope to the little boat, discovering a hand-crafted vessel made of hand-sawn planks caulked with oakum. The flat bottom would be unstable in a wind, but he could see nothing else wrong with it except that it had no cabin, no shelter against the elements. There was nothing within; no oars, no anchor or rope. Just some flat benches. A tiller operated the rudder at the rear.

"Does it have a keel?" he asked Sarpy.

"Small one, about a foot."

"It'll do," Skye said.

Wearily he hiked up the steep slope, wondering whether his leg would give out, but he made the hill and paused to catch his breath at the store. Victoria was already within, piling blankets and gear on the counter.

Gill came in, grinning. "Guess I got some pull, eh?" he said.

"I don't know how you arranged it. This is the only boat they have here."

"Like I say, old Red Gill's got a way to get around in the world. You'd better remember it. You ever sailed a small boat?"

"No, but I know I can."

"They flip over easy, just a freshet will do it. This has a squared bottom, and it don't lay over like a round-bottomed hull."

"We'll manage."

Skye headed for the rack of rifles, and plucked up each one, hefting it, finding them unbearably heavy. He knew when he was stronger they would feel lighter. But for the moment, his still and sore arm was crying out whenever he lifted a weapon.

He tried several, some of them old longrifles from the

eastern states, knowing they would be clumsy in the mountains. They were all flintlocks, and he wanted a percussion lock. But the only percussion weapons were brand new.

He found a Hawken .53-caliber mountain rifle, heavy, half-stocked short-barreled, built to endure the abuse of the wilderness. He knew that he had a quality weapon in his hands. The rifled barrel looked clean to the eye, and the oversized lock looked like it would survive all manner of battering. He checked the nipple within the wire mesh protective basket, looked at the hickory ramrod, cocked and lowered the hammer gently, testing the trigger mechanism.

It would do.

His arm hurt like the devil.

He found a used powderhorn, a pick with which to clean out the nipple, and a box of fulminate of mercury caps, good quality ones of brass rather than copper. He picked up a bullet mold, and some small pigs of lead, but also a pound of pre-cast balls. A one-pound can of DuPont would do for the time being, and he added some patches.

Victoria's heap on the counter grew at an amazing pace. She had added flint and firesteel, a butchering knife, a tin cookpot, a skillet, some tin messware, a ball of soap, an awl, thread, a hank of hemp rope, thong leather, and a dozen other items.

"Victoria, we can't pay all that back. Not with this too." He hefted the rifle.

"That's a damn pretty gun," she said.

"We'll see if it shoots true."

She eyed him. "You can hardly lift it."

That was true. All of this hefting of heavy metal objects had started his arm howling and his rib wound aching so badly he was having trouble breathing again.

"You get down to the boat, dammit," she said.

He didn't. He stubbornly helped gather the outfit, even as Gill got his together, along with plenty of parched corn, sugar, coffee, tea, cornmeal, and other foodstuffs.

"They're not going to let us walk out of here with this," he said to Gill.

The boatman grinned. "I got ways," he said.

"You got powers beyond mortal knowledge," Skye retorted.

It proved to be true.

When the clerk tallied up the goods, Skye's outfit came to over two hundred dollars, and Gill's came to a hundred fifty, including food for the three of them. But the clerk offered no quarrel. Gill began grinning.

"See what powers I have, Skye?"

"It's Mister Skye, mate."

"Then it's Mister Gill, if that's how it is."

They laughed. Skye's ribs howled.

The clerk helped them tote the heavy loads down to the levee and even helped stow the goods in the little sailboat, under the neutral stare of a few Omaha women.

When the stuff had been settled in the hull, the clerk stepped to shore, and stood by.

Gill undid the ties, while Skye unrolled the sail and ran it up the mast and tied it off. A summery beeze ballooned the linseed-oiled linen, and it tugged the little boat outward.

From above, Sarpy waved.

Gill replied with a casual dip of the arm.

And Skye marveled at the hold Red Gill had over Pratte, Chouteau and Company.

35

Alexandre Bonfils had exactly the cargo he wanted, and had put his rival behind him. For as long as he could peer backward, toward Sarpy's Post, he had seen no one on the levee. The Skyes were within, dickering for some goods, and Gill was off visiting with Sarpy.

To be sure, the Cheyenne squaw glared at him darkly, and he knew she was angry about all this. She paced the flatboat, knowing she was a prisoner. But he would deal with her after he put a few river miles between him and the fur post. Just then, he wanted to keep the flatboat in the fastest current and make his escape so successful that Skye would never catch up.

Poor old Skye! Bonfils laughed. He had Skye's outfit aboard, effectively stopping hot pursuit by horseback or canoe or any other means. He also had Gill's possessions, a kitchen outfit and some sacks of meal and old clothing. Gill could not move until he replenished everything needed for river travel.

But best of all, Bonfils had the squaw and the brat, and once he arrived in St. Louis, he would play that card for all it was worth. And that was going to be pure fun. He could hardly wait to see the shock and embarrassment on the faces of the bride's family; the astonishment with which MacLees would discover his mountain squaw and brat.

Oh, the secrets would tumble out, and St. Louis would chuckle up its sleeve and gossip about it for months. And old Uncle Pierre would come to laugh secretly at MacLees, and enjoy the whole spectacle. The Creoles would make much merriment out of it, but the miserable Protestant English-speaking population would cluck, cluck, cluck and whisper the scandal from ear to ear.

It was usually easy to find the channel and he had no trouble steering the flatboat to that fast-flowing heart of the Missouri. It was only on the long sweeping bends that he found he had to steer the flatboat into the swift current and keep it from being swept toward shore.

The squaw's relentless gaze disconcerted him. She never looked elsewhere; always at him, as if assessing his very soul. Not that she would know what a soul was. Savages wouldn't fathom such a thing. And yet that unblinking examination of him was a little unnerving. She had drawn her brat to her, and was absently comforting the child with her hand as she studied Bonfils. Would the woman never even blink?

At last the squaw studied the shore, and Bonfils wished to know what thoughts passed through her head. He would have to be careful not to let her escape. She was the prize. St. Louis was a vast distance away, and she would have her chances every time they cooked a meal or otherwise approached a riverbank. Islands! He would make sure they anchored only at islands so she couldn't just pick up the brat and hurry away in the night. Ah, there was always a way!

She probably entertained only one thought in her head, and that was to find Simon MacLees and present her little girl to him, and begin nesting with him again. Well, Bonfils would help her do it! And that was why she would stay with him. She could not get to St. Louis unaided.

A few hours elapsed, with the woman alternately staring at him from a blank face, and viewing the shore. When the time to stop and rest and eat had passed and twilight lowered, she grew agitated but said nothing. Bonfils found the travel easy: the river took them along without effort or even steering. The empty flatboat cleared all snags and bars, and seemed unstoppable.

Then, at twilight, the woman arose, negotiated the passage alongside the cargo box and cabin, and confronted Bonfils.

"You left them behind," she said.

"We will go to St. Louis faster this way. You will see your man sooner."

"Why did you leave them?"

"Because Skye and I want the same job as trader. If I get there ahead of him, I will get it."

He wasn't very sure of that but it sounded good. He still had to deal with whatever Marsh told Chouteau about the Sans Arcs.

"Why am I here with you? Why did you not leave me back there with the others?"

"So that I can take you to your husband."

She stared at him again, her warm brown eyes unblinking.

"It is not so," she said.

"Of course it is so, *madame*."

She sighed. "We are hungry. My girl need food." She pointed. "There is a place. See, many trees. We will have a fire and eat."

"No, we have to get to St. Louis."

She stood silently a minute. "I will walk to this place, St. Louis," she said. "Let me go."

"Too far to walk."

"I will walk for many suns. I am not afraid."

"No one can walk that far."

She seemed puzzled. "I can walk as far as I want."

"Well, you just wait. Maybe after dark I will find a place."

He could use some food himself but there had been no islands.

He took another tack. "If you walk, you won't be able to carry all the things I got for you."

"Why did you get those things?"

"So you can look pretty. When we get to St. Louis, you must wear your paint, and put feathers in your hair, and wear the jingle bells on your feet, yes? Then you will look like a queen of the Cheyenne, and all the white men will look upon you with wonder."

She did not reply for a moment. Then, "Is that what the white women wear?"

"Oh, yes, feathers and beads and warpaint. They are all savages at heart."

He felt her stare raking him again, and didn't like it.

"Marriage is sacred among the People," she said softly, carefully choosing words. "We mate for life. My man MacLees is mine forever, and I am his. I will go to him and give him all that I can. All that I am. He will be sad because we have lost a son. But he will be glad to see our daughter again, and see how she has grown. She walks in beauty. She is a wise child. He will rejoice to see me. See? I know how to say these things in English."

They sailed into dusk, and then Bonfils did discover a wooded island. A swift survey revealed a thin strand of wooded land, dividing two sweeping branches of the river.

He pulled the tiller and the flatboat headed for a clear area of the shore, where there seemed to be no tangle of submerged limbs.

She watched him, studied the island, studied the shoreline, looking like a caged eagle wanting to fly away. He would have to be careful. Keep his rifle in hand, keep her away from it, keep her away from the boat, compel her to gather wood, build a fire, and start a kettle of cornmeal boiling while he watched over her and the girl. The girl, that was it. The girl was his hostage. He wondered whether she would resist when it came time to travel again. The girl would solve that, but he didn't want to be so obvious. In the morning he would step aboard with the girl. Lame Deer would come because she had to.

They bumped the shore, and she leapt gracefully to land, carrying her baby in one arm. He followed, tied the flatboat to the thick brush, and unloaded some kitchen goods. She and the child had vanished into a thicket. He swiftly cased the island; it covered perhaps two hectares and neatly divided the river. The banks seemed a vast distance away, low black walls across moon-silvered water.

She took an interminable time, but finally she did emerge from darkness carrying an armload of dry kindling. She carried flint and steel in a small beaded pouch at her waist, and after much effort—a moist breeze discouraged fire-making—she nursed a small flame. An hour later they were eating yet another meal of cornmeal mush; if it were not for some salt he acquired at Sarpy's store, it would have been almost unbearable.

She ate with her fingers, dipping them into a bowl, and fed MacLees's brat the same way.

"It was an accident," he said. "I didn't see the boy—"

She stared at him.

"I didn't know your son was there. There were the Sans Arcs, and the fog, and we were being attacked, and I drove them off."

"The one who died," she said, "he was my man's son. I will tell my man about it. Yes, I will tell him that you put powder in the big gun and aimed it, and killed the one who we are talking about, and also the boatman, and wounded Mister Skye very badly. This I will tell my man with a tongue filled with fire. I will speak words of smoke and flame, like the crackling of wood. He will know what to do."

Bonfils heard the threat in her voice. "You haven't grieved. You should grieve. Don't women who lose a son or husband cut half their hair off? Isn't that the sign of grief among the Cheyenne? A woman's hair cut on one side?"

She nodded. "It is the way of my People. But not Mac-Lees's people."

"You should do that. Ah, yes, it would truly tell MacLees that you grieve." And make her even wilder looking and more barbaric to St. Louis sensibilities, he thought.

Lame Deer suddenly looked desolate.

She scooped the last of the mush and slid her laden fingers into Singing Rain's mouth. Then she walked to the river and washed her hands and Bonfils could barely see her in the blackness. She stayed there a long time, while the moon climbed and then vanished behind clouds. He scanned the night sky and decided it would not rain; not for a while. He was uneasy about sharing the flatboat cabin with her. In fact, he thought he might disarm her; especially that knife she wore and used so deftly.

He heard loons calling on the water and a disturbance on shore. Unseen creatures swept through the air about him, and he wondered what they were, and what they were hunting. And still she did not return.

He kicked the fire to pieces and poured water over the ashes, not wanting to be the cynosure of any eyes.

The moon emerged from a silver-lined cloud, and he beheld her again, a dim figure in the pale light. He intended to travel at once, and motioned her toward the flatboat, which rocked quietly in the river, shedding sickly moonlight from its dull hull, thunking softly against a submerged log.

She followed him, stepping into the boat, helping the little girl, offering no resistance.

It was then that he noticed: she had sawed away the left half of her jet hair. On the right, it hung loosely braided over her breast; on the left, it dangled in crude strands to ear-level. The barbaric sign of mourning. She turned to him, letting him see her disfigurement, her head thrown back in faint disdain, something proud and savage in her ravaged face. Perfect! He exulted. It would add to the sensation she made in St. Louis.

36

Violent gusts threatened to tip the crude sailboat and swamp it. Skye had to drop the sails during windy moments for fear of capsizing. A south wind at times checked their progress.

They drove downriver for two days without spotting the flatboat. The plan was to sail night and day, taking turns at the tiller. But the second night a massive cloud cover obscured the shores and plunged them into inky blackness, and they could only drift across the currents until they struck land, and wait for better visibility.

The next day they started downstream under cast-iron skies that soon began to drizzle, chilling them all. Victoria kept glancing at Skye, worried that the cold rain would further weaken him.

"You all right?" she asked.

Skye nodded from his pallet.

"You ain't," she said.

Skye agreed. He was maddeningly weak and the numbing rain was bringing on a fever. She nodded to Gill, and they headed for shore again. Gill dropped the sail and wrapped it around the boom, while Victoria pulled a tarpaulin over the boom and anchored its corners to the gunnels, supplying a shelter of sorts, open at both ends but at least a haven of dryness.

The rain pelted down, spattering the river about them, dripping through a hole in the canvas, gusting inward from the aft end of their tentlike shelter. It chilled all of them. It drizzled into the belly of the sailboat and Skye knew they were going to have to bail soon, or slosh around with inches of water on the planks.

He remembered the crude comfort of the flatboat with its enclosed cabin, and he knew that Bonfils and Lame Deer and her daughter were enjoying some measure of comfort.

Gill, cussing softly, scooped water out of the boat using a cooking kettle and a skillet. Skye wished he could help, and at one point sat up to take over the bailing. But then he fell back upon the stacked supplies.

"Don't do that," Victoria said.

"Got to help Red."

"You get sick."

Skye was feeling plenty sick. The rain had halted his healing and left him weak and shaky. "I have no fire in me," he said.

"You'll get better."

"I wonder."

"It take long time; you got three wounds, two very bad."

Skye sighed. Would he ever get well? What if he sank into sickliness, and became dependent on Victoria to keep him going? Was his life going to change because of his wounds? He'd seen plenty of shot-up men fumbling through hopeless days.

"You stay in there, Skye. I'll pitch this damned water out," Gill said.

"You'll get sick yourself."

"Been sick before. I don't have no holes in me."

Gill scooped another thin load of water with his sheet metal skillet.

They could not manage a fire that day. Skye felt a ravenous thirst for tea. If he could have a few cups of steaming tea his soul and body would be repaired. But there wasn't a dry stick of wood in sight. So they all starved.

"I'm ready to eat a catfish," Gill said. "You got to understand that's the sickliest flesh ever I ate, but I'd eat one now and lick my chops too."

Skye lost his hunger and lay quietly, a blanket over him that only partly subdued his shivering. Wet gusts bulged the tarpaulin, spraying water within. He wondered if he would ever be warm again. This was worse than trying to get through an arctic night in the mountains rolled in a pair of buffalo robes.

Red sat inside the shelter, only to bolt outside every few minutes, never happy. He dripped water. His coppery hair was plastered to his freckled face. He looked like a trapped animal. Finally he began untying the boat.

"I'm steering out and letting it drift," he said. "I'll watch the bends and keep a hand on the tiller sometimes."

Skye nodded. He would have done the same thing.

The boat slowly drifted into the channel while the shores fell away, veiled by the rain and mist, and they were nowhere, sailing through a private world, going wherever the current took them.

Skye felt a chill settle in his bones. Victoria discovered it; she was always checking on her man. She piled her blankets over his but this did not stop the shivering.

"You ain't well yet," she said crossly.

"I'm too cold."

He shook until he could shake no more and slumped into stupor as the heap of blankets gradually warmed him. He did not know how long he lay like that, but when he returned to this world the rain had stopped; the distant riverbanks were clearly visible, and the cast-iron overcast had given way to light cloud cover.

"Some way to get a job," he said to her. He was sick of travel, sick of weakness and pain.

"You get better."

He didn't feel better. Gill was at the tiller again but not employing sail because the tent shelter still stretched over the boom.

He heard Skye and came forward, ducking under the canvas. "You mind if I raise the sail?"

Skye shrugged.

Gill undid the canvas at the gunnels, pulled away the tarp, untied the sail and raised it. The unstable craft heeled and then settled. They were plowing downstream again, driven by a steady northwest wind.

Skye watched the world roll by. His life seemed to be out of his hands.

"I'd like to see the mountains again," he said.

"I don't like this country neither," Victoria said.

"Hope to get shut of it soon."

"We'll dry out," Gill said. "Clouds getting lighter all the time."

Skye felt a little better, and not so fevered. But he was not fooled. Injuries left their mark.

He felt Victoria's small hand on his forehead, and then felt it run through the stubble of his beard.

"You gonna be strong soon," she said.

She knew what he had been thinking even though he had spoken not a word of it.

The trading position meant everything to him. He would have a living and a future. She would be comfortable. He would be able to help her people. The Crows would have a friend in the trading room. With the beaver trade fading, the position was his bright, sweet tomorrow.

That is, if he ever recovered his strength. He had been so gravely wounded that he might not recover the strength of his youth; this might be the great divide, separating the strong young man from the weakened older one. This

terrible assault on his body might force him into a different and sedentary life, or one filled with chills and sickness, such as he had experienced here in this rainy prairie
land, where the vegetation grew thicker, and moist breezes
dampened everything.

He rose shakily. "I'll take the tiller," he said.

Red grinned. "Long enough for me to stretch," he said.

Skye liked Red Gill. The man was simultaneously secretive about his livelihood and open, brash, straightfor-
ward about everything else, including his passion for
flowers. Let there be a bloom along any shoreline and
Gill was steering toward it to have a closer look. Sometimes the man collected asters or daisies and decorated
the prow of the little boat, with all the pride of a Venetian
gondolier.

"You regret going to St. Louis, given as how you got
shot and robbed and all?" Gill asked.

"Nothing is without risks," Skye said. "And the more
something is worth, the worse the risks."

"You gonna get that job?"

"I hope I do."

"Me, I'm going to put in a word for you, and a word
against Bonfils."

They sailed through the rest of the day under a cloud
cover, and then headed for an island.

"Maybe we can get a fire going," Gill said, eyeing the
long, thin strand of woods.

When they bumped into the shore, Victoria made the boat
fast, and they strolled along the narrow place, scaring up
ducks. There were plenty of campsites visible, some of
them recent, and even some gathered wood. But only with
great difficulty was Victoria able to nurse a glowing ember bedded in the underside of some bark she peeled from
a cottonwood into a tiny flame.

They ate hot food that night, and Skye drank what he
thought was a gallon of tea. They set off as the light was

fading, and a half hour later Victoria spotted a small orange glow on another island.

"Bonfils," Gill said.

"You want to stop and take him?" asked Victoria.

Gill said, "It's a temptation. Get our stuff back from that sonofabitch."

"You sure that's him?" Skye asked.

"I can make out the flatboat."

Skye pondered it. "What I'd like most, mates, is to pull over, wait for dark, take down our sail so we're less visible, and slide by. We'll get to St. Louis days ahead of him. I think there's advantage in it. We've got the sail and we've got three people to navigate all day and night. We'll get our outfits back when he gets there."

"You think he's expecting us to follow?"

"You, maybe. You live in St. Louis. Not me. He probably thinks we quit and headed back to the mountains," Skye said.

"I'd like to take the bastard."

"Then what?"

"Get my stuff back. And the boat."

"Are you ready to keep him prisoner? I can't help much. You'd have to steer, ward off Bonfils."

"Me, I'd just put him off, like he put us off, go on without him."

"You figure you can take him?"

The boatman reflected. Bonfils was larger, harder, and had just spent several years in the mountains. "I don't know," he said.

Gill was plainly tempted to surprise Bonfils, but in the end, acquiesced. They all wanted to talk with Pierre Chouteau before Bonfils did. They swiftly dropped the light-colored sail and headed for the shadowed right bank where they waited until the night was inky, and then steered out into the current. In an hour they had passed the wavering orange flame and left it far behind.

37

One day they passed a settler's cabin. Smoke issued from a rock chimney. Tilled fields planted to corn and wheat surrounded it. A pole fence held some cows in a paddock.

"Is this a white man's village?" Victoria asked.

"Nope," said Gill, "just a farmer."

"What is a farmer?"

"One who grows food for a living."

"But there is food everywhere—"

"Farmers, they plow and plant, and work a heap for nothing much except feeding the grasshoppers. You ain't ever catching me behind a plow, looking at the south end of some mules."

Victoria absorbed that, without grasping much of it. "Is there a woman in that house?"

"Most likely."

"But she never comes out? All white women live inside the logs and never come out?"

Gill, who was at the tiller, smiled. "Where'd you get that notion?"

His attitude annoyed her. "I know about white women. They are weak creatures who have to stay in their lodges and are afraid of the sun. That is why they don't come with their men."

"They're busy cooking and caring for the little ones, I guess."

"No, they are weak. They faint away, make the little death, in the sunlight. So it is said among my people."

"Reckon we'll see one soon, and outside, too."

"What is 'outside?' "

Gill looked startled. "Why, there's the outdoors, like we're in, and there's indoors, like inside a lodge."

"But no white woman ever came to my land or visited my people. It is because they are frail and die."

Red Gill grinned. "Now, I reckon you have a case."

That day they sailed past several more cabins and on each occasion, Victoria studied the homestead, trying to see a white woman.

"There ain't any," she said after passing a large log house on the left bank. She eyed him skeptically. "You don't have one. Where's yours?"

"I don't want one. I run away from a dozen, and I'll keep right on running."

Skye had been listening idly to all this from his resting place near the bow. "Is this Missouri?" he asked Gill.

"Left bank, I suppose," Gill said. "Right bank's Indian territory."

"Who says this thing?" Victoria asked.

"Gover'mint drew a line; this here is civilization to the east, and that there's unsettled country to the west. We're fixing to pass Fort Leavenworth. That's where the soldiers control the river, look for smuggling and all that."

"We're stopping there?" Skye asked.

"Don't have to. Not going downriver. But they'll be looking at us in their glass."

"Are there women there?" Victoria asked.

"Yep. Mostly officers' wives."

"Then we will stop. I want to see them."

Gill looked uneasy. "I reckon you'll see white women aplenty down the river a piece. No need to stop at Leavenworth."

The way he said it alerted Victoria to his discomfort. "You do something the soldiers don't like?"

Gill clammed up and glared at her. They were sailing a vast expanse of river, wider than most lakes she had seen, with thick forests on either bank. Clouds had settled over the whole country, turning it all flat and gray. She didn't like this moist Missouri land.

"You need a woman," she said to Gill.

Gill grinned again.

"I'll get you a good woman. Maybe Lame Deer. She makes a good woman for you."

He stared at her. "She's MacLees's woman."

Victoria laughed triumphantly. "She was. But white men don't keep their mountain wives. Gabe Bridger told me all about mountain wives and how they ain't the same as real wives."

Gill eyed the shore uneasily.

"Some do," said Skye, from his forward perch.

She turned to look at her man. He seemed earnest and yet she was worrying about this trip. Maybe Skye would abandon her and find a white woman, frail and sickly so he could take care of her. That dark possibility had bloomed in her mind and the closer they got to this place of many lodges, St. Louis, the more the fear gripped her.

"Maybe you gonna take some damned weak woman with pale skin, and send me back," she said, an edge in her voice.

Skye didn't reply. He beckoned to her, and she slipped forward, around the boom and the chattering sail, watching out for her head if the boom swung in a breeze, and stood before Skye.

He still looked sick and most of the time he simply lay there, letting Gill operate the boat.

"When we leave St. Louis," he said quietly, "you'll be with me."

She wasn't so sure of it.

There, in the prow of the boat, was a leather device that Gill had rigged up to hold flowers. He picked a fresh bouquet of them each day, and they brightened the whole boat with their various colors. Yesterday he had picked a number of tall stalks with pastel-colored blooms on them, flowers she had never seen before, and now the pink and blue and purple blossoms decorated the boat. Whenever Gill spotted a patch of color on shore he steered the sailboat to that place and anchored long enough to replenish his bouquet.

Ah, Red Gill. She liked him. He was a strange and secretive man, but she adored his flowers. He called these hollyhocks, and said they were white men's garden flowers, not wild ones. She didn't know what wild flowers were. Garden flowers and wild flowers were as confusing as indoors and outdoors. She had asked him why he gathered the flowers and put them in his boats, and he had said he was an artist at heart, and he liked flowers, and they reminded him of women.

"Them flowers are pretty. That's reason enough."

"Are they just to look at? The People make medicines and spices and food from them, too."

"We have flowers for that," Gill said. "Women have herb gardens. Women especially got a whole list of flowers that cure things. Like foxglove and skunk cabbage and red pepper and mandrake and goldenrod."

"Damn, white women, they good for something anyway," she said, evilly.

At midafternoon, they approached a settled area with white frame buildings that looked very strange to Victoria, all snugged on a bench just above the river, in front of wooded bluffs.

"Leavenworth," Gill said. "Just a little of it's visible

from the water. Most of it's up, top of that bluff. Parade ground, officers' quarters, barracks, all that. This here, the levee and the warehouses, that's where they do business."

Skye lifted himself from the prow and examined the oncoming post. "Inspections?" he asked.

"From stem to stern, everything going upstream, from canoes to steamboats."

Something in Gill's voice registered worry.

"I want to stop," she said.

"Ain't a good idea."

"Why, mate?" Skye asked.

"You ain't even a citizen, Mister Skye. They'll be wondering how come you're around here, coming out of Indian Territory, without being no citizen."

"Mister Gill, are you saying my presence here is illegal?"

"I don't rightly know. Everyone in Injun country's supposed to be licensed. Me, I'm licensed for the river."

Skye glowered at the distant post, which slumbered in a pale sunlight. "All right, let's get past it then," he said.

Victoria heard strength in his voice. Her man was beginning to come alive again. She had sung many songs over him and driven out many devils.

She spotted men in blue coats standing along the levee, and one was glassing them with a brass instrument. She had seen a few of these in the mountains and marveled that they could make everything come close.

Then she spotted a white woman. She stared, uncertain for a moment, but yes, it was a woman, in brown skirts. Victoria could even make out the pale face, and the straw hat the woman wore, and the woman's hair, which was the color of cornmeal. She had rarely seen hair like that. It seemed to glow yellow, even though the sun was obscured by light clouds.

This woman was staring at the sailboat and talking with the three men in blue coats. At last she had seen a white woman. For years she had wondered why the trappers came to them without women. She itched to talk to this one. She had a list of questions to ask. What did they wear? What powers did they have? How did they raise their children? Did they care about their men? Were they proud of their men, the way the People were?

She watched the blue-coat men move about on the levee, suddenly in a hurry. Two of them approached a small brass cannon and fiddled with it. Then a ring of white smoke erupted from it, followed by a sharp crack.

Gill sighed. "Dammit all to hell. They want us to report," he said, pulling on the tiller until the boat hove around and headed toward the right bank.

"What for?" Skye asked.

"Who the hell knows?"

Skye pulled himself up, lifted his top hat and settled it over his unshorn locks, and waited for the little boat to dock under the mouths of cannon.

38

A half a dozen blue-coats stood at the levee. To Victoria, they looked all alike in their uniforms and visored hats. But one wore a sword and had more marks of honor sewn to his clothes. A chief, she thought.

Cussing softly, Red Gill steered the little sailboat toward the bank, while Skye dropped the sail. Gill tossed a line to one of the soldiers, who wrapped it around some pilings set in the muddy earth.

"Mawning," said the man who'd caught the line. "Going downriver are ye?"

"St. Louis," said Gill.

The soldiers were eyeing the cargo, what little there was of it.

"No hides, I see. Is this all personal gear?" the man asked.

"Yessir, corporal," Gill said.

Victoria wondered what a corporal was. The man's honors were sewn on his coat, but she didn't know one from another.

"Any pox you know of upriver?"

"Pox?"

"Smallpox. There's a fright about it."

"Nothing we heard of."

"Who are you gentlemen?"

"Red Gill. I got papers, only they're not with me."

"Gill, yes. And this man?"

"Barnaby Skye, sir."

"Nationality?"

"Formerly a subject of the crown—"

Victoria heard a tightness in Skye's voice, and knew he was tense.

"Canadian, then."

"No, not Canadian."

"Your squaw?"

"My wife."

Several soldiers chuckled.

"What are you stopping us for?" Gill asked.

"Pox. We're vaccinating everyone up or down; there's a scourge in St. Louis, and some of the tribes upstream have succumbed. It's a vicious and highly contagious disease."

Victoria had heard of it, this dread sickness brought by white men to the Peoples, with deadly results. Fear clamped her.

"Kindly step out and we'll innoculate you with Jenner's vaccine."

"You mean scratch us, like I heard is done?"

"That's the idea," the corporal said.

Skye helped her step out. The sailboat bobbed lightly behind them. White men's buildings and equipment crowded the space. She saw only the small brass cannon here, but above, away from the river and higher, she saw the mouths of several big cannon, and felt the power of this place.

Whitewashed buildings with glass windows. She ached to see what lay within, and how all that wood had been so cunningly joined together. A livestock pen with a pile of hay. Wagons and carts, buggies and carriages, such as she had never before seen.

But what riveted her was the woman. Were all white women so beautiful? This one was young, and frankly curious, eyeing Victoria with as much fascination as she was eyeing the woman.

What Victoria had thought was milky hair proved to be the lightest yellow, silky and soft, drawn back into a bun under her straw hat. And her face; what a face, her flesh creamy and rosy, her soft eyes the color of the heavens, and her nose thin and white. She had lips that formed naturally into a smile; she was a happy woman, with her daughter clinging to her soft white hand.

They both wore brown. The white woman was adorned in deep brown muslin trimmed with white. Her generous skirt was gathered tight at her slim waist. Something like a men's jacket completed the ensemble. Her daughter, who might have been five or six, wore a miniature soldier's costume, with brass buttons.

Victoria stared enviously. No wonder white men hid their women from the world. They didn't want anyone else to see them! This one didn't look weak or sickly. Her eyes shone and her countenance was lively. A dread crept through Victoria. If white women were like this, she would lose Skye. So riveting was the sight of this woman that she scarcely paid attention to whatever business these soldiers were conducting.

"Captain Rosecranz, army surgeon," the corporal was saying.

The older one had brown muttonchops and small spectacles perched on his bulbous nose, and his gaze darted from one man to the next, finally settling on Victoria.

"This will only take a moment, gents," the surgeon said, opening a black pigskin bag. "You won't regret it."

"Have we any choice?" asked Skye.

"No, sir. We're vaccinating everyone going up and down the river. For their sake. My good man, until we learned to vaccinate, England alone lost forty-five thousand a year. And Boston was practically depopulated for years on end. It's a vile disease, high fever, followed by lesions on the face and then all over the body, which suppurate and disfigure for life—"

"Is there danger to my wife?"

Rosecranz paused. "Some savage women are more vulnerable. But I assure you, most do just fine."

"How does it work?"

"You'll be infected with cowpox, a mild version of smallpox. Jenner discovered that people who had the cowpox didn't get the smallpox. I have a phial of lymph from cowpox sores and we can perform this procedure easily enough."

Fear burrowed through Victoria. "Sonofabitch!" she snapped.

The doctor stared at her, startled.

"I ain't going to do this!"

"You have no choice."

"I'm going to my people."

Rosecranz addressed Skye. "Hold her. I'll scratch her and it'll be over."

"No, sir. If she's going to take the pox vaccine, it will be her choice."

"We can't let you pass if she doesn't. She could carry the plague—"

"It is her body and her decision, Doctor. If she declines, I'll head upriver with her."

Skye seemed formidable, except that he was surrounded by soldiers and helpless.

"Well, let's get on with it," Rosecranz said. He turned to Gill. "You ready? Best to remove your shirt."

While Gill tugged his shirt off, Rosecranz opened a velvet-lined black box with shining medical tools in it. One was a needle on a little stick.

He unstoppered a phial that contained a thick liquid, and then took hold of Gill's arm.

"I don't like this," Gill said. The fearless boatman suddenly looked liverish and upset.

But the doctor had the arm firmly in hand, and squeezed one drop of the terrible liquid onto Gill's arm midway above the elbow and shoulder. Then, with the needle at a low slant, he mauled the flesh, abrading it but not piercing it, drawing no blood.

"Hey, are you sure . . ."

"You'll thank me," the surgeon said, releasing the arm. "All done."

"All done? That's it? Am I gonna die or get sick now?"

"Some feel sick a few days. A mild fever. Most don't. A sore will develop at the site of the inoculation, but it'll go away."

Gill exhaled, as if to release a mountain of tension, and pulled his shirt back on.

The physician turned to Skye. "Next?"

Victoria saw the trapped look in Skye's face.

"Don't do it!" she hissed.

But Skye was unbuttoning his chambray shirt. He pulled it off, and stood hairy and bare-chested. The white woman stared, and then turned away.

The doctor spotted the barely healed wound in his shoulder, and then the deep flame-colored furrow across his ribs. "Those are recent," he said.

The soldiers gazed intently.

"Few weeks," Skye said.

"Where did you say you came from?"

"I didn't."

"How did you suffer these?"

Skye shrugged.

The corporal bristled. "You would be well advised, sir, to answer the doctor. Unless you wish to be detained."

"Shot from the cannon of the *Otter*."

"From Marsh's cannon! And how did that happen?"

Red Gill boiled. "Because some reckless fool named

Bonfils thought we were being raided by some Sans Arcs one foggy morning and didn't look at who he was shooting at, that's why, dammit all to hell, and killed my partner and a little Injun boy too, along with some Sioux."

"And what were you doing with the *Otter?*"

"Helping them get off a sandbar."

"In that little boat?"

Skye and Gill explained, as best they could, that they were on a flatboat at the time, but the army contingent looked skeptical.

"We'll report this to Gin'ral Clark," said the corporal, since there wasn't much anyone could do about it. "I'd like to hold you, but there ain't grounds. But believe me, don't think this is settled."

"I don't suppose it is," Skye said, mildly, settling his top hat. "It would be kind of you to care about the injured more than caring about your report. You must have all the details from Captain Marsh, isn't that correct?"

The corporal bristled, itching for a fight, and Victoria thought they would all end up captives.

But the surgeon clamped Skye's uninjured arm to him, released a drop of that evil fluid, and again pressed the needle into the fluid and flesh ten or twelve times. Skye watched, grimaced, and then dressed methodically.

The surgeon turned to her.

Victoria knew she would perish. She had not seen her spirit helper the magpie for many suns. She fought back terror and tears.

Skye gazed kindly, but left everything to her. She knew he would go upriver with her at once if she refused. But she hated the very thought of it, sacrificing himself for her, even as she dreaded sacrificing herself for him. But then she found her resolve.

She pulled up the buckskin sleeve as high as she could, baring her thin brown arm. The white doctor held her brown arm, released a single drop of the fluid, and pressed the needle hard a dozen times, never breaking the flesh. She winced and studied the place where Death had entered her.

It was done. The evil liquid had been pressured into her.

The doctor was putting away his instruments.

She felt a great despair as she rolled down her sleeve. She had to say good-bye to her man. In the boat she would sing her death song.

39

The closer they came to St. Louis, the lonelier Skye felt. That was odd, and he couldn't fathom his own feelings. Here at last, in North America, he was seeing familiar things: brick buildings, handsome frame houses, neatly tended farms, bright gardens, cobbled streets, men and women in ordinary attire, and not the exotic buckskin garb of the mountains.

People like himself, speaking the English tongue as he did, engaged in occupations he understood. A branch of England, really, even though this robust young nation had fought free of the mother one, and was absorbing thousands of immigrants from other parts of Europe.

How could he possibly be lonely, just when he was coming into contact with people like himself, after so many years? Maybe it was the dog. He grieved for No Name. Maybe it was Victoria, who was acting strangely, perched in the rear of the little sailboat singing softly, dark dirges that sometimes attracted his concern. She had a stricken look upon her; a bleak, desolate gaze he could not fathom, and sometimes tears in her eyes.

Maybe he was lonely because she had pulled into her own world.

Red Gill had turned quiet too. The memory of his partner Shorty was haunting him. This time, instead of floating down the river with his partner and a fortune in furs, he was coming back to St. Louis without any returns for his effort, and the other half of the partnership had been committed to the riverbed, a long way away.

For days, Skye and Gill had traded stories to while away the boring hours on the river. They had both turned brown and blistered under the relentless sunlight bouncing off the murky river, and pummeling them from above. There was no shade, save for the sail itself occasionally, on that majestic waterway that sluiced through the wooded green shores of Missouri.

A place called Westport Landing, near Independence, had interested him because for all the years of the rendezvous, it had been the jumping off place of the packtrains heading west. It was more of a town than he had realized; handsome redbrick buildings around a square, the simple, plain American architecture yielding its own practical beauty.

It was there that Victoria had finally seen white women going about their daily business, some with baskets in hand on the way to the butcher or baker; others strolling with their children, or hanging their wash on lines, an occupation that intrigued Victoria.

At last, Victoria had come to understand that white women were neither fragile or weak or sickly; they didn't come west with the trappers because this was a different culture, not a bit like hers, and women simply played a different part.

Here, too, she saw her first black men and women, except for swart Jim Beckwourth, the mulatto mountain man who had lived with the Crows for years. But Beckwourth hadn't been very black, and these in Missouri were as dark as ink. She studied them, exclaimed at them, and marveled that so handsome a people could be white men's slaves.

Skye himself bloomed and he was beginning at last to put his wounded body out of mind. He could breathe without feeling sharp pain. His shattered ribs and cartilage no longer grated at his side whenever he moved. He had not yet recovered the full use of his wounded arm, and sometimes it prickled clear down to his fingers, but each day he managed to increase the range of movement. Someday soon he could hold up a rifle again, and even aim it. He walked with a small limp when the torn muscles in his thigh balked at their task, but he worked at healing that, too, by walking round and round the boat, and as much as he could on land whenever they docked.

But what worried him most was Victoria. The farther they plunged into settled America, the darker was her visage. And she had never stopped her private singing.

Once he had observed her studying birds that swooped over the water, or patrolled the shores.

"Magpie is not here," she said.

Gill had confirmed it. The western magpie did not exist in this central part of North America. That news had brought a sharp intake of breath from Victoria. Her spirit helper, the chosen guide she had met during a spirit-dreaming session as an Absaroka girl, was no longer present, no longer flying before her. Maybe that was why she was singing. She was alone, bereft, like a white man so far away he was beyond the visibility of God.

They had no cash, but sometimes stopped at a riverfront town anyway, bartering a few items from their outfits for fresh vegetables, berries, or beef. Oddly, Victoria refused to leave the sailboat, desolately sitting there at the levee, or on a dock, when Skye and Gill tried to trade something for fresh food.

Numerous islands provided safe campgrounds. Missouri was thinly settled, and often they traveled for miles without seeing any sign of habitation or human existence on those brooding wooded shores. Skye sensed that the vast rural areas, still devoid of homesteads, harbored twisted and vicious border men who would stop at nothing. He had seen a few in the mountain camps, and knew that the young republic seemed to breed malcontents and murderers along with the many yeomen who were building a nation.

They were meeting river traffic now; fishing boats, scows, keelboats, and once a proud white steamer, the *Antelope*, along with innumerable rowboats, used by Missourians to cross the river. All these local people used the islands as havens, including runaway slaves.

Still, he wasn't at home in this place. The weather had turned sultry and his clothes stuck to him, glued on by the sweat of his body. The moist air suffocated him and left him yearning for the sweet, dry comfort of the mountains. It stormed frequently, and not even the hastily rigged shelter of a tarpaulin spared them a miserable drenching and sodden moccasins and boots. He had taken to rubbing grease into his Hawken to keep it from rusting, and polishing the steel of his knives each day to fend off corruption of the metal.

He could not fathom why any sane mortal would abide in wet, dank, gloomy Missouri, as hellish a place as he had ever seen. He would have preferred the jungles of Burma to this sweaty, overcast, choking place.

It amazed him that he was willfully traveling all this way just to seek a position. Why was he doing it? He no longer could answer that piercing question. For the sake of a trading position he had endured two thousand miles of travel, three nearly fatal wounds, seen the brutal murder of his beloved dog, watched Victoria slide into fear and isolation, and discovered insult and rivalry and contempt in unexpected places, among unexpected fellow travelers. He could not even explain to himself what the trading position meant to him, or why he was willing to come so far, at such cost, to apply for it. All the reasons fell away.

But oddly, one remained. He wanted to see the United States and fathom its robust people. Was it truly the hope of the world? What a curious reason to travel so far, and yet that wish to see the new nation had grown stronger than any other. He would see the land of the Yankees, and meet the people, not the wild ones who came to the mountains but the ordinary yeomen and burghers and their wives and children. Then he would know. And then he could weigh the grave matter, which was oddly affecting him with such passion, of whether to become a citizen.

They camped one night on a narrow island that showed signs of other visitation; ashes, chopped wood, garbage and bones. Red Gill wandered off, down the long strand, leaving Skye and Victoria alone. Skye was plenty worried about her. His Absaroka wife was shrinking into a shadow of herself in this dank place.

He took her hand. "Let's walk some," he said.

She pulled her hand away.

"You've got something hanging around your neck," he said.

She eyed him sharply and tried to distance herself.

"Let me see your arm."

She stopped struggling, and rolled up her sleeve. The last crust over a small sore clung to the flesh where she had been inoculated.

"This looks just about healed," he said. "Just like the doctor said. Mine's healed up. You'll be fine, and now you won't ever die of that disease, which gladdens me right down to my bones." He tugged at a sleeve, having trouble rolling it up his massive arm, but finally he was able to show her a small, white dimpled area that was the sole remaining sign of the smallpox vaccination.

He began to fathom her torment. She had been singing a death dirge all these days.

"Victoria, Victoria . . ." he said, clasping her to him.

She resisted at first, but then her arms clamped his body and she hugged desperately. He ran his hand over her jet hair, his gesture awkward, and she buried her face in his chest and sobbed.

"Soon we'll go back to our country. I don't much care for this place."

She lifted her head. "No, you will stay here."

He lifted his top hat and settled it, perplexed at her mood, and aching to lift her out of it. "The land of the Absarokas is my land now," he said. "Those mountains with the tops white with snow; the pine forests, the good horses and endless prairies . . ."

She shook her head.

"We'll be heading up the river in a few days."

"I have seen the white women."

He could not make sense of that. "They're not so different from women of the People," he said.

"They are like you, and you will go to them sooner or later. I know this. I have looked at them. They are beautiful, not like some old savage. They dress in skirts, many fine stitches, that no damn savage ever sewed. They got all these things, manners, you got and I don't. You and me, what do I really know about you? You are stranger to me. But they know you, all your thoughts, because they were born like you."

She buried her face in his chest, and then whispered more.

"We get to St. Louis, and they'll all come to you and entice you and show you their white skin, and this old savage woman, she gets put aside. Even black women are better than savages."

At last he had some inkling of what was desolating her. It hurt him that she didn't believe in his love and esteem for her anymore.

"Have you seen me flirting with the white women?"

She didn't answer.

"You think that because MacLees abandoned his red woman, and Bonfils probably will, that I'll do the same?"

"The white men all go back to their kind," she said, her voice smothered in his shirt.

"Have I told you that I love you, Victoria?"

"Sonofabitch," she replied. "In a few suns, you won't say it no more."

40

Red Gill steered the little craft toward St. Louis in almost steady rain, a relentless drizzle that chafed at Skye, soaked his clothes, bred mold on his leathers, rusted every steel surface on his Hawken even when it was sheathed, and made the air hard to breathe. Victoria had taken to bailing out the sailboat with a tin cup, while saying nothing at all.

The windless wet air made the sail useless. It flapped and dripped rain, and rarely collected a breeze. Skye finally lowered it, and they depended on the steady river current to take them to the great city. Victoria's nose began running, and Skye pitied her. In all the time they had shared together in the dry West, he had never seen her nose run, and had rarely seen her sniffle. But now something in the very air was disagreeable to her, and making her sick. She said not a word, but he knew she was increasingly ill and maybe fevered. It worried him.

The closer they came to St. Louis, the more animated Gill became, and he often jabbered about one landmark or another. The Missouri ran slate gray, its water murky and barely potable, the gloomy banks crowded with osage, locust, sycamore, shagbark hickory, oaks and elms, all of them cheerfully identified by the boatman. He, at least, was glad to return to his home. Skye wondered what sort of home Red Gill had. A room, probably, or maybe no quarters at all. The frontier was filled with vagrants.

"This here's the grand prairie back of St. Louis," he said, waving a hand toward the right bank. "Mostly wooded, but plenty of parks too. Farm land now. There's a limestone bluff near the river, and below that's a bench where the city sits, most of it. The city's bursting up the cliff now, and spreading out."

They drifted past two large islands and then into a vast and confusing confluence with the Mississippi, so enormous that Skye was glad he wasn't navigating because he couldn't tell one shore from another, and often there seemed to be no shore at all.

"The Father of Waters," Gill said, with a grand sweep of his rainsoaked arm. All Skye saw was gray mist stretching into obscurity. But Gill seemed to know where he was going, and hewed closely to the right bank, where a swift current propelled the little boat southward.

At last Victoria stopped her bailing long enough to stare at this strange place where the Big River joined the Father River. She wiped rain away from her face, trying to fathom landmarks in this gray and featureless seascape. Her rain-drenched chambray blouse was plastered to her small body, and once Skye caught Gill staring at her with half-masked hunger.

"We're pretty near there," Gill said. "If the fog lifted, you could see it now; biggest city in the West; biggest north of New Orleans, and still pretty much French, but that's changing. Yanks like me setting it right."

The fog at the confluence gave way to a low gray cloud cover and lighter rain, and in time the ghostly city did emerge from the dark mist, a gloomy prospect of warehouses and other buildings crowded along the levee. But what astonished Skye was the number of steamboats, one after another, as far as he could see, tethered to pilings along the levee.

"Pretty busy place, eh?" Gill said, some pride welling up in him. "Those there boats, they're from the Alleghenies, come down the Ohio to here; or up from New Orleans, or down from the north, Illinois and Iowa and up there, or like us, down from the west. This is where it all comes; the goods, the commerce, the people. A New Englander can ship a cargo down the coast, around Florida, to New Orleans, and up here."

The magnitude of the city stunned him. It seemed almost a London, and this seemed more than a Thames.

"There now, you can see the new cathedral of St. Louis, that spire yonder where the Frenchies worship. That's on the south edge. We won't go that far. I'm going to head for LaClede's Landing, the old dock where it all started, because near there's where I've got my room. That street the church is on, that's called Church Street, *La Rue de l'Eglise*, and this street on the riverfront, along the levee, it's Main, *La Rue Principal*."

"The streets have two names?"

"Yep, you can't expect Yanks to twist their tongues like that speaking French. Next in is Barn Street, *La Rue des Granges*, and that cross street, heading up the slope, that's Tower, *La Rue de la Tour*. See, it ain't so hard."

Skye wiped rain off his face, and glanced at Victoria, who was staring in rapt bewilderment at something unfathomed in her mind, and beyond imagination.

The slap of water on the hull reminded Skye that Gill was steering the craft across the current now, toward a small, stinking dock area where keelboats and flatboats crowded so tightly that they were tied to one another instead of to land. Gloomy warehouses and mercantile buildings lined the levee like black teeth, disgorging and swallowing the contents of the riverboats. And amid them, he saw grog shops, low, sullen buildings with rough characters lounging around their doors. Not a woman was in sight.

"Rough quarter," he said.

"Roughest in the world," Gill said, heading for a small opening between two flatboats. "They'd as soon slit your throat as let you pass. Unescorted woman has about as much chance as a shoat on a butcher block."

He eased the boat into an awkward corner, where projecting boulders threatened to hammer the hull, and the boat jammed suddenly against the levee. Victoria grabbed a line and jumped out. There was nothing to tie to, so she tugged the prow up a muddy incline.

"Goddam," she said, squinting at a scene so alien to her that she might as well be on another planet.

The whole area stank of sewage, dead fish, effluent, rotting food, and decay. Skye stepped onto the black mud of the levee and stretched. For this had he come two thousand miles. This was the United States. He had never been in the United States before, at least its settled region. And even this was barely settled, though French and Spanish had been on this river for nearly a century.

The rain mercifully ceased. A breeze immediately rose, the air chilling him as it cooled his soaked shirt and buckskins.

St. Louis! From here had come his succor for many years, and here would his future be decided.

Everywhere, drays, freight wagons, buggies, carriages, carts, and even a few elegant victorias and landaus crowded the waterfront, with the cacophony of neighing, whinnying horses adding to the din. Black stevedores hefted enormous bales of cotton, or massive crates, or heavy casks, in and out of shadowy interiors. Great noxious puddles silvered the cobbled street. Rain had blackened the backs of horses, and still dripped noisily from eaves.

Victoria gaped at the hubbub, the wagons, the Negro men, the white men in handsome suits, the roustabouts in duck cloth britches and loose blouses, and blue uniformed officers on the river packets. Skye thought she looked frightened but determined; a native woman trying to absorb the fantastic and show no shameful fear.

He stepped toward her and slipped an arm about her waist, his hand clasping her and sending assurances toward her. She turned away from him, not toward him, and he sensed she did not want him to see her face, or the fear and awe and fascination in it; things a Crow woman would marvel at for the rest of her life; things too fantastic to repeat to her sisters around the lodgefires of her people; things that would make the Absarokas call her a liar if she tried to describe them.

She said nothing, but found his rough hand and squeezed it.

Behind them, Gill was shuffling goods forward in the sailboat and raising the dripping sail just enough to let it dry. It would rot if he wrapped and tied it wet.

Skye watched, absorbed, and stayed on guard, knowing waterfronts well. He eyed his outfit lying in the prow, wondering how to store it and where. He was penniless.

"Red, are we saying good-bye?" he asked.

Red grinned. "You going to see old Chouteau, like I am?"

"Yes, but we need to find a place to camp."

"Nearest camp, I suppose, is four or five miles up that cliff and out on the grand prairie. All privately owned, but you could get permission. And it's gonna be wet."

"We'll find a spot," Skye said. He was worried. They had too much gear in their kit to tote on their backs for more than a few hundred yards. Those vultures lounging across the mucky street would pounce on anything lying loose in that open sailboat the moment the boat was not guarded.

"Come with me," Gill said.

Skye divided the load, giving Victoria the lighter things, including the blankets, while he loaded the sacks of staples and tools on his shoulders. The weight strained his wounds, and he felt flashes of the old pain course through him, making him want to drop every burden. But eventually he and Victoria and Gill shouldered their gear and wobbled northward, past the frenzy of the levee and up a slope to a dirt street hemmed by tawdry tenements. Gill grinned, led them around a mucky path to the rear of a grimy building, and dug an iron key out of a flowerpot. Moments later he ushered them into a dank room, with one small window admitting light. A narrow iron bed occupied one wall; a commode and dresser the other. That was it.

"Home sweet home," Gill said. "Leave your duffel here. It's safe enough, long as I lock up. I ain't got anything to eat, but we can boil up some cornmeal. There's a little kitchen down below."

A sorry home for a man who risked life and limb to smuggle whiskey for the Chouteaus, Skye thought.

Skye wasn't hungry. His fate was about to play out, and he didn't want an ounce of food or drink to deaden his senses. This was it. His fate would become clear right here in this grubby city.

Victoria shook her head. He watched her touch the rough plaster walls, examine the iron bedstead and try the cotton-filled tick, study the commode, with its vitreous porcelain pitcher and basin atop it, and then swing the cabinet door back and forth, admiring the brass hinges that held it up.

She stared at everything, probably repelled by this dreary little hovel, but she had slipped into deep silence and he knew enough not to disturb her. They heaped their outfit in a corner, apart from Gill's, and Skye headed outside to a washstand and outhouse he saw in the tiny rear yard, there to freshen himself as best he could before heading toward the mansion of the man who would decide his fate. But he put that thought at a distance, not wanting to deal with it. Not yet.

"You ready to meet the man?" Gill asked, combing his matted hair with his fingers, and shaking the grime from his pants.

"I don't suppose I'll ever be ready," Skye said. "But we have business to do."

41

The vaccinations went better than Alexandre Bonfils thought possible. When he learned at the Fort Leavenworth levee why he had been compelled to stop, he envisioned nothing but trouble with Lame Deer. But instead, she had assented at once, and submitted herself and her daughter to the surgeon.

"My man had this thing done," she explained. "He showed me the little place on his arm, and told me he was safe from this pox disease. We will have it done too."

And so they continued down the Missouri in the flatboat with minimal delay; the whole business had taken scarcely half an hour. The assorted enlisted men and officers had scarcely bothered to examine the empty flatboat.

He exulted. For days he had sought out islands as night camps, fearing that his doe would flee if he chose to camp on one bank or another. The only bad thing about steering a flatboat alone was that there was no relief when rain or night fell, and he had to be at the tiller most of the time. Lame Deer and Singing Rain wandered the vessel, or settled in the cabin during the heat of the day. The Cheyenne voiced not the slightest protest at any of Bonfils's conduct and didn't even seem aware that she was a virtual prisoner. And yet . . . her conduct made him uneasy.

Skye and his squaw were stranded back at Sarpy's Post and out of contention, while the squaw would guarantee that Simon MacLees would not be selected. So it would be that the toast of St. Louis, Alexandre Bonfils, would win the trader position, and he would soon head west with the comfort of Fort Cass ahead of him.

He would abandon Amalie, of course. He had grown weary of her. The Crow women were said by the mountain fraternity to be the most wanton of all, and he thought one or two, or even three, such savage ladies would make his winters fly fast. What did they want but a bit of ribbon or a few beads for their devotion? Ah, he could see himself as the dauphin of the Yellowstone, living in wild luxury for a few years, until he wearied of it and uncle called him back to St. Louis and a full partnership in the firm.

The land had changed. Walls of majestic trees hemmed the Missouri: sycamore, locust, shagbark hickory, elm, oak, osage, and many more. The air had turned soft and velvety with moisture, and in his estimation more pleasant than the harsh dryness of the West. It showered almost daily; by afternoon, clouds built up into towers, their bottoms blackened, and a lightning-charged storm crashed through. In those moments, he tied up and waited out the deluge in the cabin with the savage woman.

There was about her a certain dignity that sometimes annoyed him. She spent those rainy moments asking him questions: how do white men raise their children? Do white men have more than one wife? Who is chief among the white men? What do women wear in this place of many lodges?

He responded sullenly. He was aware that she was preparing herself for her sojourn among a strange people, and he didn't want that. He wanted to present her as a wild savage—and MacLees's squaw—and make her a laughing stock and MacLees the cynosure of a thousand tongues.

They arrived one day in Independence, and Lame Deer insisted upon examining the village.

"Why? What is there to see?" he asked.

"I will see the people."

Reluctantly, he stepped aside and let her clamber onto the levee. She helped her child step to land. He intended to shadow her, ever fearful that his hen would escape the coop. She walked slowly among the citizens, drawing some stares even from a frontier population used to wild Indians. It was her ghastly sawed-off hair that drew attention. Lame Deer noticed, and gazed reproachfully at Bonfils, who had taunted her into a display of grief more familiar to her people than to these white people.

"Hurry up; we must be off now," he said. But she chose to take her time, quietly examining the brick buildings, the lovely town square, the glass-fronted mercantiles with all their goods displayed. But above all the people. She paused frequently, absorbing every aspect of men's and women's dress; the fullness of the skirts, the whiteness of the men's shirts, their boots and slippers, their hairdos, the wicker baskets the women carried while shopping, the clothing worn by children.

"We must be off!" he announced, but she simply turned to him and smiled.

"I like this place," she said. "I am seeing things that my man told me of; things I could not imagine. The people are like cranes and herons whose feet never touch the earth. They are all chiefs; this is many-chiefs land. Even the little ones and the women are chiefs. Strong and good are the chiefs. Even like MacLees, these chiefs know all things, and their wisdom is before my eyes, and now I am joyous because I have seen the mystery of MacLees."

They paused at a church, red brick like so much of Independence of the 1830s, with a white spire.

"Is this a store?"

"No, this is a church."

"And what is that?"

"A place where people come to the Creator."

He was getting testy. The last thing he wanted was to discuss white men's religion with her, or dwell on the differences of the churches.

"I wish to see."

"We should be off to St. Louis. There are better churches in St. Louis."

She ignored him, climbed some steps, and opened the door and found herself in a sanctuary, dark and empty.

"I have seen this sign before," she said, pointing to a wooden cross above the altar. "Sometimes there is a man upon it."

"He is a man like Sweet Medicine," he said, invoking the Christ-figure of the Cheyennes.

"Ah! So this is a teacher. Sweet Medicine taught us all the virtues, and how to live in beauty. This is the One that Simon MacLees told me of?"

"I will tell you when we start down the river," he said.

"It is something for me to learn of, so my man can be happy with me and share his life with me."

Bonfils smirked.

It took three hours before Lame Deer was ready to set foot in the flatboat, and when she did, she rummaged about in her parfleches in the cabin, showing sudden signs of industry.

Alexandre Bonfils cast loose the lines, clambered aboard, joked with several rivermen on the levee, and poled the heavy boat away from the bank and into the gentle current.

Lame Deer stayed largely within the cabin, even though the day turned out to be a glorious one. Once she headed forward, and strangely enough, dipped her head into the river, lathered it, and washed her hair. Then she vanished into the cabin again. Later that afternoon he discovered that she was sewing.

They passed other vessels; mostly rowboats, but once a keelboat with a large crew poling their way upriver close to the far bank. All that while, she remained within the little cabin, and this cloistering of herself piqued his curiosity. From his position at the tiller, he could see in, and knew she was sewing, but he knew nothing else of her busy day.

At dusk he found a fine island and steered the flatboat toward it. The boat scraped over a snag, and then another, and he thanked his luck that it was not loaded. He anchored at the island, which showed no signs of habitation, apparently because river men had feared the snags.

He tied up to some sycamores growing at the bank, and stepped ashore, grateful for a respite from the navigation of the great river.

Then she stepped out of the flatboat cabin, tugging her child with her. The sight astonished him. She had trimmed her hair until it lay almost evenly around her neck. One side was still short, but even that had been carefully cut and shaped, and now her glossy black hair framed her strong features with balance and regularity. And her dress! She had modified one of her crudely sewn squaw dresses into something closely resembling a white woman's afternoon gown of teal cotton, with much tighter sleeves and an even hemline.

"Will Simon MacLees like this?" she asked.

"Madam, it is a great mistake. You must wear just what your people wear, and on the occasion of your meeting, you must be gotten up with paint."

She looked puzzled. "I do not think so. I have seen white women, and that is how I will be. I will be his wife in this place of many lodges, and I want to make him very happy with me, and our girl."

"Madam, he did not marry you because you were like the girls back home, but for your fine savage beauty."

"What is this word, savage?"

"Ah, different from us."

"Yes, we are different. But he is my man, and over many winters we have come to be more alike. I am happy. I have seen how the women dress, and I will make my clothes like that. And when the sun comes in the east, I will make clothing for Singing Rain too, so that he will be pleased with her when he sees her in this place of the white people."

He felt himself growing petulant, and masked it with a smile. "Ah, madam, just this one time, wear your finest ceremonial clothing. Heap big medicine! Wear the elk's tooth blouse! Wear the quilled doeskin! Wear the elk moccasins! Wear your paint! Wear feathers! Vermillion! Ochre! Let him and all of St. Louis know you are a woman of the Cheyenne!"

"Why do you want this?"

"Because . . . because it will be a great moment."

She smiled. "I think you have other reasons."

He made camp sullenly, realizing that his cheerful fantasy of scandalizing and shocking St. Louis had quietly filtered away with the breeze. All that paint; the vermillion he had purchased, the jingle bells he had expected her to wear, the earbobs, the silver rings, the foxtails, the blue garters, the red and green cock feathers, the blue and white barleycorn beads, the pigeon egg beads, the white and purple wampum, the hawk bell, the hairpipe beads, along with the fine brutal mess of her hair, the unfashionable squaw dress, the clay pipe and plug tobacco, all gone a-glimmering.

He discovered within himself an odd and unexpected emotion. Envy. This squaw cared so much about her man that she was transforming herself into a white woman, believing that her runaway lover would welcome her all the more. Amalie would never have done that; nor any other woman of the tribes he had encountered. Not for Alexandre Bonfils.

His thoughts amused him. In St. Louis he would seduce one or another Creole beauty, maybe several, and none of them would ever hear a word about Amalie.

Lame Deer was gazing on him, and the serene and accepting look in her face was unsettling.

42

Red Gill led the way, and Skye was grateful because he hadn't the faintest idea where in St. Louis he would find Pierre Chouteau, Jr. The man had an office, of course, in his warehouse down near the river, but no lamplight shone in the arched window at that hour.

"We'll hike up to his house," Gill said. "It's a piece. Will you be up to it?"

"I don't know," Skye said. "Leg still hurts and I can't pump my bellows much."

Gill nodded. He led Skye and Victoria through dusky streets with brick buildings crowded cheek by jowl, with only pools of light from windows to guide them.

"I guess you figured out Shorty and me by now," Gill said.

"No."

"We pack wet goods for Pierre Chouteau. Not the company. Just him."

Skye sensed he was about to hear secrets. Gill was a smuggler; that much he knew.

"It's the inspection at Leavenworth causes the trouble," Gill said. "The company can't get a drop of whiskey to the posts. Congress even tightened the law. Used to be there'd be a boatman's ration, one gill a day allowed, but no longer. Them puritans in Congress, they don't want nary a drop going up to the posts, or down the gullet of a redskin."

They walked a while more, through narrow streets, and Skye got the impression their direction was southerly, where the land was flatter.

"I shouldn't be saying a word. Get myself into trouble, only I'm gonna quit. I'm done for good. Shorty getting killed, that did it for me. I don't want no part of this anymore."

Skye nodded, saying nothing. But he was certainly listening closely.

"It takes a mess of spirits to fuel the fur trade," he said.

"Damn right," said Victoria.

"We had to get it to the posts. Every factor at every post knew us and waited for us to show up."

"How'd you do it?"

"Different way each time. This last time, we got us a good pack string, good Missoura mules, and had big tin casks soldered up, and we took it out to the posts that way, never even getting near the Missouri until way up near Council Bluffs. Until then, we just headed north, bunch of mules, through barely settled country. Well, we dole it out as we go, cask here, cask there, and then a flatboat's waiting for us at Fort Union, and it's got our payment in hides in it; just hides, all off the ledgers, and Shorty and me come on down to this here town, sell the hides to wholesalers and cash it out for our profit. It's a trade. They get some good mules up at the posts; we got a flatboat to sell too, so old Pierre, he likes it, we liked it, and them traders liked it. And the flatboat, it brings us extry cash. Someone always buys it to haul stuff down to New Orleans."

"I thought it was something like that, mate."

"Pretty risky. We never done it twice the same way. Some times we headed out like we were going to Santy

Fe, and then swung north. The patrols out of Fort Leavenworth cover a heap of country, so that was a bit troublesome. If we get caught, we lose everything. But we always done it."

"Never got caught?"

"Never. People knew we was smugglers, so we let it be known we was hauling for the Opposition." He glanced sharply at Skye. "I'm getting out, so it won't do you no good to go spill it all to Gen'ral Clark."

"Not even on my mind," Skye said.

"The company got into trouble once, you know. When Kenneth MacKenzie had himself a little old still shipped upriver and brewed his own likker, buying maize from the Mandans. Nat Wyeth tattled on him, and they durned near pulled the company trading license, and it was all old Chouteau could do, yanking strings in Congress, to stay in business. But he's got to have spirits. All them others got spirits, and with spirits you just walk off with the business."

Victoria laughed.

Skye didn't laugh. He really hadn't known much about the politics of the fur trade, never having been in the States before or getting some notion of its laws. He thought of all those times when he and Victoria enjoyed a good jug, scarcely aware that every drop of it had been brought illegally into Indian Country.

"That going to continue?" Skye asked, thinking that as a trader at Fort Cass he might himself be doling out illegal spirits, and hiding his stock of it from an occasional traveler or Indian Bureau agent.

"You ask old Pierre that. He shore don't say nothing to no one. Me and Shorty, we smuggled his spirits out there for six years, and no one ever caught on. Only ones that knew for sure was Chouteau and the traders at the posts. Everything was hidden. Buying spirits was off the ledgers. Getting the mules and the tin casks was off the ledgers. Paying us, that was off the ledgers, and in hides, not cash."

"What are you going to say to Mister Chouteau?"

"Well, we'll just see. I got a few levers, including a big mouth, specially since I'm getting out, Shorty dead and gone, my old friend wiped out by that sonofabitch Bonfils. Makes a man plumb bitter, and I ain't walking in there feeling any too kindly toward that Creole and his six thousand relatives that run the whole damned fur business in the country, save for a few independents."

Skye wanted to ask a lot more questions, but Red Gill had clammed up, and the grim set of his mouth warned against any more talk about a matter so incendiary.

Skye found himself wondering about Pierre Chouteau and his methods. For all his time in the mountains, he had heard tales about the ruthless Mr. Chouteau, and his effort to erase the Opposition, especially the Rocky Mountain Fur Company, Jackson, Sublette, Bridger, Fraeb, and the rest of the old coons. Chouteau had succeeded, too. Nothing remained in the northern and central plains but the American Fur Company, technically the Upper Missouri Outfit, now called Pratte, Chouteau and Company. And the Bents were almost the sole survivors in the southern plains.

It had grown very dark, and houses no longer rose cheek by jowl, or even with their doors on the street.

"Getting close," Gill said. "It's that there."

A brick-walled enclave rose before them.

"You think he'll see us now? Not at his chambers in the morning?"

"Mister Skye, old Pierre, he'd be mad at me if we waited one spare minute. I've come all hours, sometimes right in the middle of dinner, or he's been in bed half a night, or when he's having some Frenchy priest saying the mass to the family, and he just excuses himself and glides out and we go to his study and he lights the wick and we palaver until he's squeezed everything I know out of me."

Skye noticed that Victoria was uncommonly quiet, but she was cruising not only through utterly new turf, but also through a world she didn't understand.

Gill reached an iron-grilled portico, and rattled the closed gate. An old black man in black livery emerged at once from the darkness.

"Got to see old Pierre," Gill said.

The man squinted, surveyed Skye and Victoria from liquid brown eyes, and opened the gate.

"Massah's in," he said.

A slave. Skye hadn't much thought about slavery until he was suddenly confronted with it here in what the Yanks called a Border state. Skye had been a slave; the Royal Navy had made him one, pressing him off the streets of London and locking him into ships of war for seven years. He hated slavery in all shapes and forms, whether open and blatant, like this oppression of Africans in America, or just slightly less blatant, like pressing seamen into the navy and paying them a bare pittance and keeping them for as long as it pleased the lord admirals.

But of course Chouteau would have slaves. A man like him would think nothing of it.

They walked through a flower-decked yard, past magnolias and chestnut trees, toward a gleaming, black lacquered door with a brass knocker. Within, laughter erupted. Light spilled from casement windows, some of them open to the evening breezes. The tongue was French, fluid and soft and amused. Skye saw men in brocades and silk, black pantaloons, waistcoats, high collars, and women in summery white cottons and Brussels lace and pleated muslin.

Gill knocked.

A black woman opened to them. She was ancient, white-haired, sharp-eyed, sorrowful. She wore a black cotton gown rimmed with white, and a large porcelain crucifix on her heavy bosom.

"Mr. Chouteau," Gill said.

"Cadet?"

"Yes, junior. I'm Red Gill."

Skye wondered what that was about.

The black woman nodded and ushered them into a white foyer gilded with gold leaf and lit by six oil lamps in a crystal chandelier. The woman limped heavily, with a world-weariness that could not be concealed.

Another slave. Skye watched her lumber toward the salon where all the festivities were brightening the world, and saw intuitively a will not commanded by her own self; a dream lost and hope squashed by a terrible institution. And what for? Because the Chouteaus chose to keep her as chattel rather than pay her a wage for a lifetime of servitude? Suddenly he hated the abominable institution of the Americans, and thought ill of any human being who enslaved another, including the man who had employed him.

The venerable slave reappeared, this time with stocky, jet-haired, square-faced Pierre Chouteau, Jr., in a handsome blue waistcoat with brass buttons.

"Ah, ah!" he said, a small smirk lighting on his lips. "Ah, at last, messeurs and madame."

He motioned them toward another part of the manse, this area black and shadowed, and steered them into a chamber lit only by a faint light from outside.

"One petite moment," he said, scratching a lucifer. He lifted a lamp chimney and lit the wick and blew out the match with a small, whimsical puff.

"Here we can meet in private," he said, his soft assessing gaze raking in everything visible about Skye, Victoria, and Red Gill.

43

"**P**ermit us," Chouteau said in a soft, gallic voice, shaking hands. "We are Chouteau. And you, *mon ami*, are Mister Skye. And madame?"

"This is my wife, Victoria," Skye said.

"Ah! Enchanted, madame. And Mr. Gill we know."

He shook hands with Gill, neutrally, revealing nothing. "We trust you had a pleasant and uneventful trip?"

Skye found himself wary of this man who was setting snares. It was not an uneventful trip, and Marsh would have told him so, long since.

"I fear we've interrupted a party. We can return in the morning," Skye said.

"*Non, non*, you must tell us everything. Leave out nothing. We have private business with Mr. Gill here, for some other time—"

"No, it ain't private, Mr. Chouteau. I'm getting out of my business and want to settle up."

Chouteau stared at the riverman, not entirely blandly. "Ah, some other time, our friend Gill. Now we must celebrate the arrival of our colleague and his beauteous wife, yes?"

Gill turned surly. Skye was certain that there would be some harsh exchanges, with Gill demanding his peltries back and maybe threatening Chouteau with exposure if he didn't get them. But if trouble was looming, Chouteau was too much of a master to reveal it.

He smiled graciously.

"My friend Skye, we have heard much of you for years; the reports of our bourgeois in the field, the brigade tallies that reach my desk, the impressions of our men, all add up to the best of recommendations. When it came to choices, your name was at once placed high on our list, and over the names of so many others who have neither your experience nor your judgment. You see? We meet for the first time, but *mon ami*, we have been keeping watch over you and know more than you might expect. That is the privilege of the senior partner, *oui*? But tell us about the long trip? And where, *mes amis*, is Alexandre Bonfils? Did he not start out with you?"

"He's coming along on a flatboat belonging to Gill," Skye said, wondering if he could ever sort out for Chouteau just what happened.

"Extraordinary! Your flatboat, Gill?"

"Yes, with a Cheyenne squaw and her girl," Gill said. "We were all together until Sarpy's Post."

"We are astonished. You must explain this," Chouteau said, directing himself to Skye.

"The Cheyenne woman's the wife of an Opposition trader named Simon MacLees," Skye said. "She hadn't heard from him for some while, and found the courage to come out of the mountains to look after him. She brought her children . . . her child now. I understand he's my rival for the trading position."

Chouteau pursed his lips, stared into the flame, and sighed. "Your information is very old, and you must have heard it filtered many times over many tongues, beginning perhaps with our Captain Marsh, and maybe others?" He paused, seeing Skye nod. "We did consider Monsieur MacLees for the position. He's a veteran trader and a gifted man, and gave us a very difficult time in Opposition.

"But you see, when we first approached him, he told us he was soon to marry the lovely Sarah Lansing, one of the great beauties of this city, and had no wish to go out into the West again. He tells us he will live in St. Louis. He has secured work elsewhere, we understand with Robert Campbell, brokering hides and pelts."

"Goddam," said Victoria.

Chouteau's gaze flicked in her direction, and then away, some faint amusement in his face. "Fort Cass will go either to you or Alexandre Bonfils. You are both eminently qualified to trade with the Crows. It is not a large post, but an important one to us, because the Crows are good buffalo hunters, and the future of the fur trade lies in hides, not beaver. And how is your health, Mister Skye?"

"I am doing better."

"You received injuries, did you not?"

"Captain Marsh has been here ahead of us, and you must have the story, sir."

"Ah, indeed, one story. But we like to hear the story from each person."

"Maybe that should wait until morning, sir. We've come a long way."

"Non, non! We have all the time in the world. Who is here tonight? My Gratiot relatives, whom we see all the time. They are partners in the company, you know. We don't see our men from the field but once in a long while, and so, our friend, we want you to divulge the whole story of the trip down the river, beginning at the time you and Bonfils boarded the *Otter* at Fort Union. But first, may we pour you some brandy? And by all means, sit yourself."

Skye nodded. A snifter would drive away some of the aches and cares of travel. And that yellow silken settee looked inviting.

And so the story came out. Skye didn't know what to

say, or how much to say, and decided on a bare recitation of the facts, without the slightest shading. He would be especially careful describing Bonfils, and the reckless discharge of grape shot into the Sans Arcs—and others.

Chouteau settled himself in a wingchair with crewel-work covering it, and sipped his brandy, listening intently, and no doubt forming sharp impressions. Skye knew he was being assessed, measured, weighed, and examined. He described the moment when he and Victoria spotted the Cheyenne woman and persuaded Marsh to pick her up; the moment when Marsh ejected her from the vessel without repaying her, over Skye's protests. The moment when Skye and Victoria found themselves afoot at Fort Pierre, and their meeting with Red Gill and Shorty Ballard, and their switch to the flatboat to continue their journey.

"Ah! My *capitaine*, he told us he was beside himself when he discovered that the Cheyenne woman was Mac-Lees's mountain wife! MacLees was about to become his son-in-law! He did what he had to do to prevent the woman from ever reaching St. Louis—scarcely realizing you would take the woman's part!"

Pierre Chouteau seemed much amused, though none of it had been very funny.

Skye saw the moment looming when he would have to describe his rival's reckless conduct at the place where the *Otter* had grounded and the Sans Arcs had appeared one foggy dawn, and decided to let Red tell that part of it.

"Red," he said, "please tell Mr. Chouteau what happened during the time we were helping the steamboat."

"I damn well will," Red snapped, in a voice that wiped Chouteau's perpetual smirk off his face.

Red's bitter story flooded out, beginning with the shot across the bow of the flatboat; Shorty's determination not to stop; Skye's intervention; the rescue operation, in which the *Otter*'s cargo was removed until the boat floated; the arrival of the Sans Arcs before dawn on a foggy morning; Skye's negotiation with them to ferry them across the wide Missouri; Bonfils's reckless cannoning of the group with cannister; the dead and wounded; the harsh treatment of the wounded and dead by Marsh, while the steamboat was reloaded, and then the grief-laden trip downriver.

Pierre Chouteau sipped brandy, twirled the amber liquid in his snifter, stared into the lamp, and grunted.

The rest of the narrative came easily to Skye. He described his own struggle with grave wounds and nausea and pain; Bonfils's astonishing appearance and presence among them; the man's scheming at Sarpy's Post, the theft of the flatboat, and the acquisition of the small sailboat from Sarpy, with which they passed Bonfils in the night and beat him to St. Louis.

The more Skye talked, the more agitated he became. And when he finished his narrative, that shadowed study was plunged into a portentous silence.

"My dog is dead. I came close to the brink. We buried Shorty Ballard in a canvas shroud, weighted with rock, and said good-bye to a good man. We buried my dog. We buried that Cheyenne boy, Sound Comes Back After Shouting, innocent child, eager to see his father. The Sans Arcs took their own with them, but I'm sure they'd buried a few."

"Four," said Chouteau. "Seven more gravely injured. Eight more less injured. We've received an express. They are agitating the Teton Sioux against the company." He cocked his head. "Marsh said you were negotiating ferry passage for that war party on the *Otter* without authority to do so."

"Yes, sir."

"You might have asked him."

"I did what I had to do."

Chouteau waved a hand. "It was the right thing to do.

We just wanted your answer to Marsh's accusation. Exactly the right thing to do. Most admirable, and it shows what a veteran of the fur trade you are, Mister Skye. Now, if you will excuse us, we will closet ourselves with Monsieur Gill for a few minutes. We will have Bertha show you to the foyer, where you may wait. We wish to talk further. Meet us at the offices, tomorrow at ten, yes?"

"Ten, at your firm," Skye said.

Chouteau rang a bell, and the ancient, stooped servant slave appeared.

"Take them to the foyer, and Mister Gill will join them shortly," Chouteau said.

The woman silently led them back to the foyer, and they could hear the festivities in a nearby room, where light spilled from a dozen lamps.

Gill joined them in a few minutes, and they plunged into a dank night.

"Old Pierre, he didn't even wait for me to speak my piece. He says my pelts are in the warehouse and I can pick 'em up anytime. He had Marsh put them in a separate place. I guess Shorty's family gets half of the price, when I get them sold. I told him that sonofabitch Bonfils was a disgrace to the company, blood relative of his or not, and that if he had any goddam brains, he'd better put his chips on you."

Skye listened to all that, but he felt detached, as if this was all about someone else. They plunged into the night, and Skye wondered where he and Victoria would spend it. Chouteau's hospitality had not extended to accommodations. Even his slaves had a bed.

44

Skye reported to the brick headquarters of Pratte, Chouteau and Company the following morning, feeling tired. He and Victoria had ended up in Gill's airless cubicle, making a bed by stretching out their blankets on the hard grimy floor.

Victoria intuitively chose not to accompany him this morning, and he resolved to tell her everything that transpired. He had no secrets from her, and the company would not impose any if he had his say about it.

He felt an odd trepidation about the position, not at all what he expected so long ago at rendezvous. But he refused to let those worries rot his resolve or spoil the moment he had struggled toward for so long. If all went well, he would soon be heading for the mountains with a paid position, bonuses for meeting or exceeding goals, the chance to bless Victoria's people, and the prospect of success in the company. Not bad for a poorly schooled refugee trapped in a world not of his making.

He found the warehouse and factor's rooms hard by the riverfront, an austere brick building that radiated none of the opulence of the Chouteau residence. A small plaque, gilded letters on black, announced the company. The cathedral bell struck ten as Skye opened the creaking door and pierced into an unfathomable gloom. The acrid odor of furs and hides permeated the dark corridor. A varnished oak door beckoned, and it opened upon an austere office that shouted business. Chouteau was not present. A porcine clerk hunched over a rolltop desk, putting figures into a gray-backed ledger book, by the gloomy light of a wall of tall windows of wavery glass that faced west, away from the majestic Mississippi.

Skye hesitantly lifted his top hat, which was as well brushed as he could manage, and waited. Eventually the clerk deigned to study him.

"Tradesmen use the other door," he said.

"Mr. Chouteau is expecting me. I am Mister Skye."

"I can't imagine why," the man said, surveying Skye as if he were a side of hanging beef.

But the man sidled off his stool and vanished through a door with pebbled glass in it, and soon emerged from it and beckoned Skye.

"Monsieur Chouteau has arrived and will see you," he said.

The fur magnate's inner sanctum was as spartan as the warehouse, save for large windows admitting generous light.

"Ah, Skye, close the door please," he said.

Skye did, gently. What secrets had spun out here, behind that closed mahogany door?

"We should like to know exactly how you would proceed with business at Fort Cass," Chouteau said, after the barest of preliminaries.

"I would proceed, sir, with an intent to earn a profit. This requires loyalty, I to the Absarokas, and they to the company. I intend to give them good measure, exactly what the company has agreed to give for each sort of pelt and grade. As is usual, I will give the chiefs and headmen gifts of some value, to assure that they do not take the tribal trade elsewhere . . ."

Skye noted that Chouteau was dimpled up again, that amused, impatient look he had seen the previous evening. He looked bored, as if he had heard all this many times.

"Yes, yes, yes, Skye. But we are in the business to make a profit. To spend as little as possible to get as much as possible. That requires a certain, ah, delicacy."

Skye waited silently for more, and Chouteau did not disappoint.

"My friend Skye, there is only one goal: profit. Get us every pelt you can, drive off the Opposition by whatever means, and give as little as you can for what you get. It is clear, is it not? Crystal clear. If an Opposition trader arrives, you must drive him off: temporarily, offer more for pelts than he does; and don't hesitate to use other measures. Your post will be supplied, as always, with the means to attract Indians and affect their judgment. Entertain, my friend, entertain lavishly and buy every pelt in sight even as the savages dance and sing."

Spirits.

Only Chouteau wasn't saying it. In fact, Chouteau was speaking in Aesopean language, charging his instructions with much more than the words would, on the surface, suggest.

"Is that good for the tribe, sir?"

Chouteau was nonplused. "The tribe? The savages? What does that have to do with it?"

"They are my wife's people."

"Ah, but what does a mountain liaison matter? They come and go. Yes, look after the savages, of course. They will come to your door in times of war, wanting arms and powder, and you will be their savior. Eventually, Skye, you'll come to St. Louis and live in splendor. We reward our best traders very well, we assure you."

"I understand I must be a citizen to get a trading license from General Clark."

"A trifle. Don't go to General Clark. They've no reason to assume you aren't a citizen. We shall list you on our rosters as a citizen."

"I think I should go to the general—"

"No, don't do that. It would take too long. You would have to swear allegiance before a federal judge, and even then you would not yet be a citizen. No, let it lie. We have a great advantage. There is no record of you, yes? They cannot prove you are not a citizen."

He smiled, obviously enjoying the thought of putting one over on the authorities.

"Ah, Skye, you are well known to us here. We have watched you from afar, but not without interest. No man comes to us better recommended. You are resourceful. You avoid fights with the Indians, so that your brigades have lived and trapped. But you are a mad dog when you're cornered and then, beware, for Skye will perform the miraculous." He paused, dimpling up again. "It shows in our records. More beaver pelts, better cared for, less loss of matériel, more men coming into rendezvous, and in better condition. Ah, yes, we know of these things, and we are pleased to behold the author of such profit and value in our company!"

Skye scarcely knew how to respond, so he just ran a weathered hand through his unwashed knots of hair. There had been no place to lave himself for this interview, and he wore just what he had worn for a thousand miles of river travel.

"You will go far," Chouteau said, and paused pregnantly. "But of course there is always a condition—absolute loyalty. Your heart may not be divided, Skye. Not in little pieces, one for your wife, one for her tribe, one for England if you still care, one for your dear friends who organized the Rocky Mountain Fur Company, one for Hudson's Bay or another company. Ah, no, your loyalty will be toward us. In the field, you will think only of us, and the profits we require to stay in business. The fur trade is the riskiest of all enterprises, my friend. The profits seem high, but that is how we cover the inevitable disasters.

"So you will wring every cent out of a yard of ribbon or an awl, and every dime or bit out of a blanket or packet of vermillion. We have clerks here assiduously buying these things from all over the world—vermillion from Asia, beads from Venice, fine blankets from England, knives from Vermont.

"We gather these, and ship them out to you at enormous cost, and expect you to turn them into hides, beaver pelts, bearskins, elk, ermine, and now especially buffalo, which makes greatcoats, carriage robes, and a host of other things, including belts for pulleys.

"And all our labor is focused on you, at the trading window, taking in furs, examining and grading them carefully, and then offering no more than their real value. Ah, you see, it is the most important of all vocations! You can make or break us!"

Skye listened to the lecture, not doubting most of it, but there were things here that he ached to understand, undercurrents, ideas unspoken, commands and instructions never made explicit but certainly present. Pierre Chouteau was talking about the underside of the fur trade, yet not really saying anything about it. The finger in the cup, the thumb on the scales, the cheap cast-iron tools that shattered, and especially the whiskey, watered and rewatered and offered for every robe in a lodge, even in the middle of winter.

Skye liked and yet didn't like him. Chouteau was good-natured and filled with humor. But he was also the man who had destroyed everyone in his path. He wished Chouteau would put it on the table, get it out in the open: Would Skye be required to chisel, or could he deal honorably in all matters?

That was the crux of it. Suddenly, in Skye's mind, the tables were turned. He stood there, weighing the man, gathering together the understanding he would need to come to a decision: Would he work for this man or not?

Chouteau talked a while more, but the words were veils, and the purpose was to probe and plumb the bulky, big-nosed Englishman who stood before him, on one foot and then the other. It was odd, finally, how few questions Chouteau asked. Nothing about Skye's background or family; nothing about his service in the Royal Navy; nothing about his philosophy or religion or experience or connections.

It came down to an examination of a man thoroughly known to Chouteau by reputation, if not in person. And the real purpose of this endless interview was instruction, by subtle and indirect comment, about what the next trader at Fort Cass would do and not do.

Then suddenly it was over, and the dimpled, amused master of the fur empire rose, clapped Skye on the back, and told him to report daily. There would be no decision until Chouteau had a chance to review the merits of other candidates.

"And where shall we find you, Monsieur Skye?"

At last, some recognition that Skye was far from home.

"With Red Gill."

"That is not desirable. Can you not find some other billet?"

Skye stood silently, awaiting what would come.

"Ah! Gill works for the Opposition, so naturally we are concerned. Don't believe anything he tells you."

That was not true. Skye made note of it.

Skye wandered through gloomy halls and out the door, into a rainy day, splashing through silver puddles and dodging dripping eaves, intending to find Victoria. He would have to barter something that he had gotten from Peter Sarpy to feed them.

He wandered along the waterfront, heading toward Gill's quarters, when he saw the familiar flatboat nosing to the levee, steered by Alexandre Bonfils.

45

Bonfils maneuvered the big flatboat toward a berth on the levee, a delicate task for a man alone at the tiller. But his luck held; a generous slot had opened because of the departure of a steam packet.

From within the cabin, the Cheyenne squaw watched, bemused, as the city emerged from the mist like some ghostly presence. He would have given his last sou to know what was on her mind as she discovered the legendary place of many lodges before her very eyes, and saw the stained brick structures and grimy frame buildings rising rank upon rank before her.

He was soaked and chilled, even though this August shower had scarcely cooled the summer heat this gloomy day. He did not know quite how to proceed; whether to take the squaw to see Simon MacLees, or bring her with him to Pierre Chouteau's chambers. He was leaning toward the latter. Uncle Pierre would be amused, smile that smirky little smile of his, and elect Bonfils for the job before the whole scandal blew up.

Bonfils laughed with anticipation.

He swung the tiller hard, needing to angle across the steady current of the mighty Mississippi to harbor his awkward boat, but he succeeded, driving it straight toward the mucky stone-paved levee. The moment he bumped shore, he would leap from the flatboat with a hawser in hand and wrap it around any of the numerous pilings sunk deep into the levee, and make fast the vessel.

It was just then that he saw the apparition.

It could not be Skye. He had left the man far back at Sarpy's Post, below Council Bluffs. The sight rendered him witless for an instant. Someone else! He could not fathom it. How did that mountaineer arrive here ahead of him? Impossible! *Sacre Bleu*! But it was Skye, in his top hat, thick-nosed and ugly as sin, limping along in the rain. And then Skye saw him.

With a roar, Skye raced toward the waterfront, the limp slowing him scarcely at all, and suddenly Bonfils knew he was in trouble because Skye was not going to stop on land; he was going to leap straight into that boat.

Bonfils let go of the tiller, confident that he could whip the older man if it came to that; a man barely out of the sickbed, with all-but-mortal wounds weakening him.

Then in one bound, Skye was over the transom.

"Got you," he growled. "Want my outfit back."

"Get off the boat," Bonfils retorted.

Bonfils swung a haymaker that hammered only the air, and Skye landed on the younger man, knocking him to the floorboards. He glimpsed Lame Deer peering out of the cabin at them, her hand to mouth, starting to keen.

Bonfils sprang upward, tossing Skye aside, and confidently began pummeling the older man, but Skye bore in, unafraid, though breathing hard while Bonfils had scarcely started to suck air.

But Bonfils had not met such a man as this, and sensed that all those years as a tar, in shipboard brawls and war, had taught the Englishman a thing or two, because he felt blows rain on him, catch him in the liver, the groin, the jaw, the ears, almost as if Skye were playing with him.

Skye quit pounding, grabbed Bonfils by the shirt, and

tossed him to the planks again. The Creole leaped up, but Skye was looming over him. The flatboat had caught the current and was drifting into the side of a steam packet.

Skye stepped back, pulled the tiller to twist the boat away from collision just as Bonfils flew at him. Skye tripped him; Bonfils landed in a heap, bloodying his lips when his teeth cut them as he landed. He wiped the blood away.

"We're going to see Chouteau," Skye rasped.

Bonfils didn't want to. Not just then. Not until he could concoct something to explain things.

Skye was breathing hard. The brawl had drained him. Maybe there would be some advantage in that, Bonfils thought.

The boat had drifted into the channel, and Skye steered it past the packet, where fifty faces stared into the flatboat, and several men with pikes stood at the rail, prepared to push the flatboat away.

Skye chose a spot several hundred yards downstream, well below the warehouses on the levee, and docked the flatboat. Bonfils tied the hawsers to a tree stump left there for the purpose.

"Come with me," Skye said, retrieving his top hat from the slimy floorboards.

"What if I don't?"

"Then you'll take what I give you. You can walk or I can drag you."

Bonfils knew he could sprint faster than the barrel-shaped, wounded man, and nodded.

"Lame Deer, come with me," Skye said roughly.

The Cheyenne woman edged from the cabin, looking fearful of what might occur. She tugged her daughter with her, and they stepped to shore. She had dressed herself as closely as possible to what white women wore, and had succeeded.

"We're going to see Red Gill first," Skye explained to

her. "To get this boat and his gear back to him. Then Victoria and I will find the house of Simon MacLees and we will take you there so that you and he can see one another. We will help you."

Lame Deer nodded.

Skye turned to Bonfils, puzzlement on his face, as if he didn't quite know what to do. "It doesn't matter what I do with you," Skye said. "You're done for. I was going to drag you to your uncle and toss you in his lap. But now I don't know why. Chouteau knows the whole story. All I want is my outfit and Gill's." Skye lifted his top hat and settled it. "I'm going to unload our gear, and Red's, and Lame Deer's, and you can do what you please. Go visit your uncle if you wish. Or head for Tahiti. I'm not holding you."

Skye was dismissing him. How peculiar! Bonfils exulted uneasily.

The Londoner simply turned on his heel and stepped into the flatboat. Little by little, he emptied the cabin of its burdens: Gill's clothing and rifle and trunk; Skye's and Victoria's robes and Skye's mountain rifle, Lame Deer's beautiful summer robe, and the parfleches containing her few things.

Bonfils thought feverishly. He hadn't expected the Skyes ever to come to St. Louis, and he wondered how they did, and how they passed him. And what he should do.

"I have connections," he said to Skye.

Skye stopped his unloading. "Yes, you do," he said. "And you'll rely on them instead of on yourself. If you want anything of yours from the cabin, get it."

The suggestion had an eerie quality to it, and suddenly Bonfils wanted nothing but to get away from there.

"I leave the squaw to you," Bonfils said. "Seeing as how that's where you set your sights, squaw man."

Somehow it sounded hollow.

Skye barely nodded, as if further concourse with Bonfils was no longer necessary. He was straightening the gear on the levee, and at the same time looking for a cart or a hack.

Bonfils nursed his sore lip, wondering what to do. He had come this far, confident that he had eliminated Skye as a rival, and could embarrass MacLees out of contention. He stood there on one foot and the other, unable to decide, and then cockily started toward Pratte, Chouteau and Company, two hundred yards upriver. With each step, his confidence returned. He was family. What were families for, but to nurture and protect their own?

He brushed himself off, laughed, knew he could silver-tongue his way out of trouble, and hiked jauntily toward his distant uncle's lair. He had been there many times, watching his mother's cousin fling his resources into a wild and unknown land, and many months later, watch the furs float down the mighty rivers and into his warehouse.

The blood on his lip tasted salty, but the minor bleeding would cease by the time he was sitting in Pierre Chouteau's office. He glanced behind him. Skye had summoned a hack, and was dickering with the hack driver. Lame Deer stood aside, her daughter clutched to her.

Bonfils gathered courage, strode toward the dreary brick edifice that formed the heart of an empire, turned into its gloomy corridors, and then presented himself to Pierre Chouteau.

"Alexandre, we've been expecting you," Chouteau said, after studying the young man standing in his doorway. "Is your lip still bleeding?"

"Bleeding?"

"When you landed in a heap after Skye hit you in front of our warehouse."

Bonfils laughed nervously. He should have known that everything of consequence that happened on the St. Louis levee would reach his uncle's ears in moments.

"I am back from the mountains, and ready to assume whatever position you have in mind for me," he said, and then remembered his manners. "I trust you are well, and the family is in good health?"

That dimpled little smirk built on Chouteau's face, and Bonfils knew all would be well.

"New Orleans," Chouteau said.

"I don't follow you."

"New Orleans is where you should go. But of course, we leave all that to you." Chouteau shrugged, a gesture imbued with gallic charm.

"I would like a trading position. Wasn't that why you summoned me?"

"It was. A most regrettable decision, it turned out."

Bonfils didn't like the gist of all this. "I wish to inform you, sir, that no matter what the captain said of me, my swift action that morning saved an entire cargo of furs, and ensured a profit for you."

Chouteau looked amused, but behind that humor was a dangerous glint.

"We would suggest, young man, that you remove yourself from this city before we do it for you. You could take that flatboat if you wish. It belongs to Gill, but we'll make it up to him. We trust you have returned his outfit to him, and returned Skye's?"

"*Mais oncle—*" Bonfils was aghast. "You have not even let me tell my story."

"If you should see Skye on the levee, tell him we wish to see him. We will offer him the position. A great step upward for the man. *Au revoir, mon neveu.*"

"I never really wanted that lonely job in that lonely post anyway," Bonfils said. "It was all a game."

46

Skye found Victoria on the waterfront, quietly blotting up the ways of white men. She took one look at the hack, loaded with so many possessions as well as Skye, Lame Deer, and Singing Rain, and ran to it, clambered aboard and hugged Lame Deer. It was the first carriage ride for either woman, and they sat spellbound as the hack driver steered the dray horse over the wet cobbles.

"So?" Victoria asked, waving at the mound of goods.

"Saw his flatboat come in. I talked him out of our possessions."

Victoria glanced at him sharply, noting the torn clothing. "Where is he now?"

"Seeing the uncle."

"What did you say to him?"

"I didn't. I ran at him."

She smiled at him. "Where are we going?"

"Find Red. He's in the warehouse grading his buffalo hides, I think."

"Driver, the Pratte, Chouteau warehouse first," Skye said.

The man nodded, stared sharply at Victoria, just as he had stared sullenly at the Cheyenne woman, tugged the lines and steered the blindered dray leftward to veer across the wet expanse of the cobbles to the brick warehouse. Skye hadn't a cent to his name, but the man accepted a blanket for an hour's time.

The hack pulled to a halt, and the old, wet-backed dray sagged in its harness.

"We'll be out directly," Skye said to the weary man.

He led the women into a cavernous and ill-lit place, redolent of fur and hide and the acrid odor of ancient dried flesh.

They found Gill immediately, off in a separate bay, examining his hides one by one.

Gill looked up, spotted Lame Deer, and started.

"What the hell?" he asked.

"Ship came in," Skye said. "Got your stuff and ours in a hack."

"Where's that sonofabitch?"

"He's gone to talk to his uncle."

Gill eyed them, dropped the robe without examining it, and sighed. "You want to store the stuff in my place?"

"Just long enough so that it doesn't walk away."

Gill nodded. "We'll get it over there. You got everything of mine?"

"Your stuff, Shorty's stuff, and whatever was lying around that flatboat."

"You got the boat, too? How the hell did you persuade him to give it up?"

Skye smiled, flexing his fists. Gill looked alarmed.

"You get hurt?"

"Some."

He nodded at Lame Deer. "She all right?"

"Ask her."

"Yes," she said. "It was a long trip."

"He hurt you or . . . do anything?"

"No, because I showed him my skinning knife and told him he would not sleep well if he touched me."

Red Gill hoorawed.

They clambered aboard the groaning hack, and the driver took them to Gill's room, and even helped unload the gear. When they were done, there was no space left in that small place. Lame Deer studied the gloomy chamber closely, her lips compressed.

"I like a lodge more," she said softly.

"So do I," Skye said.

The bewhiskered hackman wasted no time whipping his bony dray away from the tenement and back toward the levee, clutching Skye's good blanket as his pay.

"Tell me the story," Gill said, settling on a corner of his narrow cot and pulling out a pipe that Skye had never before seen. "And if I forgot it, thank you. This is a big bundle of stuff, me and Shorty's gear, and worth something. Them rifles alone cost a month's pay."

"A lucky break," Skye said. "Red, you know this town?"

Gill nodded.

"MacLees's place?"

"Think so; if not, I'll find out."

"Think you could take us there? Lame Deer has some business to attend, and I don't aim to leave her alone here in St. Louis."

Gill tamped yellow leaf tobacco into his pipe and struck a lucifer. After he had a fire blooming in the bowl, he nodded. "I think we owe it to her, she being alone and under our care." He gazed at her. "You want to pretty up?"

"I'll help, dammit," Victoria said. "She don't know nothing about big places."

"Skye, let's you and me leave these ladies alone. I'll fetch them some water and good lye soap."

Lame Deer trembled, and Skye realized that this ordeal was coming to its conclusion, and that she was a lonely, frightened, desperate woman of the plains caught at last in the strange and mysterious world of white men. She had borne her troubles well, but he saw in her face a whiteness and exhaustion that bespoke her true condition.

"Go, dammit," Victoria said, pushing them both out the door.

"First time I got booted out of my own room, and by a damned squaw," Gill said, and then apologized to Skye with a grin.

They lounged about under a small portico, awaiting the women. The rain had almost stopped, but water dripped steadily from eaves.

"Tell me where MacLees lives," Skye said.

"He lives with his pa. I'll take you there but I ain't going in," Gill said.

"With his father?"

"Yeah, since he come back from the mountains. I knew him some. Pretty fancy house. They ain't poor."

"What does the father do?"

"Brian MacLees is a banker and what they call an arbitrageur, buying and selling money mostly. St. Louis, it's got no one money, so it's dollars, pence, shillings, state bank notes, pieces of eight, ducats, reals, francs, guilders—you name it, after being part of Spain, France, and the United States. And there's English coin out of Canada to deal with too. Old MacLees, he's made him a pile just straightening the mess out."

"Brian MacLees put his son in business?"

Gill shrugged. "Simon got the money somewheres, but went through it. Chouteau don't let no Opposition company last for long, let me tell you. Now Simon's getting married, I hear. Benton Marsh's stepdaughter, Sarah Lansing."

"Getting married?" Skye was thunderstruck.

"So I heard at the warehouse. Next Saturday, too. Big wedding, pretty fancy goings on. The Lansings, they're rich, and they ain't sparing the horses, I heard. Sarah lives with her real father, not her mother. Nasty divorce a few years ago, rocked St. Louis. Benton Marsh has had his share of women, and then some."

"And Simon MacLees abandoned Lame Deer without a word, never let her know."

Gill shrugged, uneasily. "Mountain weddings, them don't count for much."

Some things about the trip were dawning on Skye. "You think that's why Bonfils was so eager to bring Lame Deer here? Embarrass MacLees? A scandal that could cost MacLees a position?"

Red grinned. "That's how it slices up," he said. "Say, you don't think maybe we should get the women to hustling, do you? They're taking forever."

"I reckon when a woman wants to pretty up, it doesn't matter whether she's a white or an Indian. They're going to pretty up at their own speed." Skye astonished himself with that bit of wisdom, since he had never waited upon a white woman in his life.

Getting fancied up for nothing, he thought. Nothing but a lot of hurt. He wished Lame Deer had never come here; he wished he could whisk her away before this cruel meeting afflicted her. She had already lost a son on this long trip; and now she would find a man who had abandoned her. He felt helpless to stop this terrible reunion, but he didn't have the faintest idea what to do, except to let it play out.

They fidgeted another while, and finally the door to Gill's room creaked open. Skye beheld a beautiful and solemn Cheyenne woman, dressed largely as a white woman might dress, with Victoria trailing behind.

Lame Deer had made herself lovely. Her jet hair looked odd, but it glowed, and there was a red ribbon tied in a bow on one side of it. She wore a green calico dress, with a bone necklace. On her feet were the traditional high moccasins of the Cheyenne, these exquisitely embellished with quillwork. Her soft eyes were alive with joy.

Suddenly Skye felt very bad. He must have shown it, because he caught Victoria staring at him.

"What?" she said sharply.

Skye shook his head.

"No sense in standing in the rain," Gill said. "I'll take you, but I ain't hanging around, no how."

The child had been cleaned and groomed too, and wore a green dress that matched her mother's. Skye stared at the pair of them, and thought of their doomed journey and the mortification they would soon endure, and felt bad as they splashed through mucky lanes that soon soaked their moccasins.

The slow drizzle fit his mood.

Gill led them upslope to the neighborhood where the Chouteaus and so many of their relatives lived, where the air was better, the shade trees majestic, the views generous, and the city they owned lay supine before them.

They reached a two-story Georgian home of red brick, with a shining white veranda across the front.

"MacLees's house," Gill said. "And I am gonna vamoose."

"Red—"

But Gill was hurrying away, just as fast as he could walk.

47

A black manservant opened, and stared at the motley
people on the veranda. The man was a slave, but
Skye got the distinct impression that the haughty servant was sitting in judgment, and the visitors were found
wanting.

"Simon MacLees, please," Skye said.

"Ah will fetch him directly. And who are you?"

"Mister Skye. He will know the name."

"From?"

"From the West."

The man vanished into the dark recesses of the house,
made even gloomier by the slate sky and slow drizzle.
Victoria as usual was studying, gauging, marveling at
what white men had wrought. But Lame Deer's face was
a mask, unfathomable to any observer. If she was curious
about all these comforts, she showed no sign of it.

Skye had the sense that more than the heavens would
be weeping in a few minutes. After a considerable time, a
lean, hawkish, raptor-eyed man in a fine silver-embroidered
waistcoat and black pantaloons appeared, jaunty until
he discovered who was standing at his doorstep. He stared,
visibly startled, and then his good humor faded behind a
hard mask.

"Mister MacLees, I'm Barnaby Skye, and this is my wife Victoria. And this woman you know."

MacLees stood stock still, not even drawing breath, some wild alarm in his bright brown eyes. "I—don't know you," he said at last, his gaze darting madly from face to face.

"Simon," said Lame Deer. "I come."

"Who? Who?"

"Me. I come. See the child we made, Singing Rain." She herded the girl forward. The little one looked upward at her father, her face solemn, and clutched her mother's hand.

"Who . . . ah, who are you?"

Lame Deer was puzzled. "A long way we have come, Simon. A long way from the People, with many suns on the big river, always toward the East Wind, Simon, my own." Her composure crumbled. "I have bad news. The one who was our firstborn . . ." she was carefully avoiding the name, as was her tradition about those who were dead, ". . . he is gone up the pathway of the spirits."

Lame Deer stood there, yearning, open, vulnerable, and brimming with tenderness.

"Ah, ah," MacLees looked utterly disoriented. And no wonder, Skye mused. The young man had thought he was a safe fifteen hundred miles and an entire civilization away from his Indian wife.

"See, see how your girl has get big," she said, urging the child forward again.

The girl clung to her mother.

"It was a hard trip," Skye said, "but she bore it bravely, her thoughts always on you. She has been worried for many months, because you did not return. She never heard a word."

"I don't have the faintest idea who this squaw is," Mac-Lees said, his voice wavering. "Or why you are here."

Skye was disappointed in the young man, who was hiding behind a feeble and transparent lie.

"You might welcome her," Skye said, relentlessly.

MacLees seemed to harden. "Nor have I met you, sir. I don't quite know what you want or why you're here, but if you have no business with me, then I shall excuse myself."

Skye straightened himself and waited, unbudging. He would not help this spoiled young scion of a wealthy family out of his little dilemma.

A graying man emerged from the gloom of the house. "What's this, Simon?" he asked.

"Some people who think I know them," MacLees said.

"Mr. MacLees? I am Mister Skye; my wife, Victoria, and this is Simon's Cheyenne wife, Lame Deer, and Simon's daughter. They have come a long way."

The world seemed to stop in its tracks. Beyond, in the bleak interior, he spotted a stout woman hovering about, and the manservant standing erect and disdainful to one side.

The senior MacLees turned red. His glare settled on one, then another, and finally on Lame Deer.

"Blackmail," he said. "You are a blackmailer. You want money or you intend to embarrass us upon the eve of Simon's wedding."

"Wedding?" Victoria snapped.

"Wedding. And I won't stand for it. Leave at once, and if I see you in St. Louis again, you'll all be turned over to the authorities."

"Simon, I come long way," Lame Deer said, her hands lifting toward him. "How good to see you. I will be like a white woman to you, and learn all these strange things, and make you happy. It will be like it was, when we had our own lodge, and we were together. This I will gladly do—"

"Out!" The senior MacLees shook his fist.

The great oaken door swung hard, and snapped shut in their faces. But through the leaded glass windows at either side of the door, white faces peered at them.

"He gonna marry some white girl," Victoria said to Lame Deer.

The Cheyenne woman stood erect, summoning her courage, and wheeled off the veranda. Then she began singing, a lamentation that rose and fell in minor chords as she sang the music of grief and loss and stayed the ache of her heart. She turned, stared at the half-timbered house and the velvet lawn about it, and the manicured grounds, and closed her eyes for a moment. When she opened them, she was somehow different.

Skye reached her, clasped his big, scarred hand into hers, and led her into the rain. One bad moment had wiped out her dreams and hopes, and fifteen hundred miles of travel toward her lover. But when at last she reached the lane, and could no longer see the house, or those ghostly faces peering through the windows, she slumped, and he could not tell whether the wetness on her cheeks was raindrops or tears. Victoria caught Lame Deer's other hand, and held the child's hand too, as they retreated not only from a cold home, but also from warm hopes, dreams, and visions of a joyous tomorrow.

They slogged silently down a narrow lane toward the riverfront, scarcely knowing where to go. Between them they hadn't a cent for food, shelter, or transportation.

Skye didn't like St. Louis anymore, and wasn't sure he ever did. The place oozed with its grimy little secrets. The climate was foul, the soul of the city corrupt. When they reached the levee, he discovered that Gill's flatboat was gone. The little sailboat had vanished too. He steered the women toward the Pratte, Chouteau warehouse again, needing to find Gill.

Like it or not, he had several people depending on him for food and shelter, and no doubt, a means to go back to the mountains, and Gill was the only person he could count on.

He turned to Lame Deer. "You want to stay here?"

She shook her head sternly.

"You want to go back to your people?"

She faltered then, unsure of herself. "I do not know," she said. "My medicine . . . I have no medicine. No vision rises in me to light the way like a torch."

"You have good medicine," he said, but she looked desolate.

He steered them through open double doors into the pungent vaults where the company stored its peltries, and found Gill back at work, pulling each hide open and examining it.

"Told you so," Gill said, surveying the gloomy party.

"We need—"

"Yeah, I know."

"The flatboat's gone."

Gill stopped his grading. "Already? Bonfils didn't waste no time. Old uncle must have told him to vamoose. Chouteau come around here a few minutes ago and told me the same. Long as I was doing his dirty work for him, getting spirits out to his posts, he knew I'd keep my mouth shut. But now that I quit, now he's worrying maybe I'll talk too much, spill his secrets, cost him his license, like the last time the company got into a jam.

"So he wanders through here and asks if I'm satisfied, and I says yes, except Bonfils took my flatboat, and he says he'll pay for that, two hundred dollars, and he says he thinks maybe it's time for me to get away from St. Louis, and the ears of old General Clark, who is sitting there, not a hundred yards from here, governing the whole Indian country, and handing out licenses. So I says I'll think about it, and he says if I think fast, he'll sweeten the offer."

"Like what?"

Gill grinned. "Ain't decided yet. The longer I hang around here, the more he itches for me to vamoose and raises the ante. I could maybe go into the Santy Fe trade. Lots of teamsters making plenty hauling stuff out there. Them Messicans pay silver or tallow or hide for just about anything gets hauled out there, half starved the way they are by all them tariffs and duties and rules their government puts on 'em. I could clear two thousand dollars a trip, maybe more. I'm more teamster than waterman anyway." He nodded toward Lame Deer. "How'd she take it?"

"She is a courageous woman."

"You get in to talk with MacLees?"

"Only as far as the door. He pretended not to recognize us. There he was, facing his wife, the woman who had borne his children, and he said he didn't know her."

Gill spat. "Guess that says all that needs saying about him. Then what?"

"MacLees senior called us blackmailers. Told us to get out of St. Louis or face the constables."

Gill grinned. "More dirty linen no one wants aired."

Victoria said, "What are we gonna do?"

Skye was reminded that he was penniless in a strange city, and had two women and a child to care for.

"Red, would you look after these ladies for a while? I want to talk with Chouteau."

Red grinned. "Have a seat. Or help me grade these robes," he said. "All you got to do is open up the robes and let me have a look-see. When I sell, I want to get my money's worth, and that means looking at every robe."

The women nodded. Lame Deer settled upon a bale of robes and drew her girl to her.

Skye left them, and headed through the dreary warrens of that warehouse until he found his way into the company headquarters, and Chouteau's chambers.

"Ah, Mister Skye, we weren't prepared to see you, but it is just as well," Chouteau said, rounding his desk.

Skye nodded. "I am hoping you have news."

Chouteau's compressed smile emerged on those pouty lips again. "We have rid the city of my nephew. He's en route to visit relatives far away. We saw him only briefly, long enough to reject him for any position in the company—ever." Chouteau was not smiling now. "We have received an express from Fort Pierre. The Teton Sioux are, shall we say, angry. They lost four young men, and others lie in torment. They want revenge on Bonfils, and reparations—blankets, guns, powder, lead, and much more. That grapeshot into their midst not only injured you, sir, but the company.

"We have chosen you, Mister Skye. You will be our trader at Fort Cass."

48

How sweet it was. The unknown rival, MacLees, had declined the position, and sullied himself. The known rival, young, skilled, and connected in all the right places, had shown appalling judgment, damaged the company and many innocent people, and now was banished. And the position had settled upon Barnaby Skye.

He could, if he took it, greatly benefit Victoria's people, making sure they were well armed against their clamorous enemies such as the Sioux and Blackfeet, supplying them with good blankets to warm themselves on an icy winter's night, offering them all the tools and equipment they needed.

He could delight Victoria with a solid log home and garden and safety; vest her mother and father and brothers with great status among the Crow people; give Victoria a richer life as various visitors came by; and maybe even provide a place for children, if she could only conceive. All of that and security, and maybe down the line, a better position, more responsibility, more salary, and someday even a share in the company. That was how Chouteau did it. His best traders received a share in the profits, something that inspired them to diligence and enterprise.

He had come a vast distance, over hundreds of miles of

land, and over a thousand miles of river, for this. He had endured insult, and then life-threatening wounds, for this. He had endangered himself and Victoria for this. And after this, he would still need to take her safely home, up the Platte and North Platte in autumnal weather, past her tribal enemies, two vulnerable people in a harsh world . . . for this.

Chouteau was waiting, some small amusement building in his face, as usual.

Skye shook his head. "Sorry, mate. I'm not your man," he said, a slight roughness in his tone.

An eyebrow arched. "Not our man?"

Skye shook his head. He didn't know just where or how he had come to that decision, but he had, and now he was sacrificing every advantage being offered him, the one and only time in his hard life, because of . . . something.

He knew, painfully, what it was. Honor.

"Not right for me."

An eyebrow arched. "We never ask twice, Skye."

"It's Mister Skye, mate."

"May we inquire?"

"It needn't be spoken," Skye said. "I owe you my thanks for considering me. And bearing the expense of bringing me here. I trust horses will be waiting for me at Sarpy's Post, as agreed upon, in trade for those I left at Fort Union."

"*Certainment.* We will write a draft, just in case the matter is in question when you arrive."

"And I trust you'll provide river passage that far? The *Otter*'s going that far, water levels permitting?"

Chouteau nodded, and seemed to resign himself. "It would have been awkward," he said. "Your citizenship, General Clark . . ." A gallic wave of the hand dismissed that line of thought.

Skye let it go at that. There was honor and dishonor in the fur trade, and all parties had sullied themselves at times, especially with illegal spirits. Skye did not consider himself any loftier or better than the rest. He had drunk illegal spirits at the rendezvous. He had given spirits to his Indian wife—also illegally. And yet, there were others he knew, among the mountain men, who hewed to honor. Jedediah Smith was one, killed by Comanches in '31, but a man to remember. Skye knew he could never be a man of Smith's caliber, but in a smaller way, he could try. He could do what was right.

He stood reflectively in Chouteau's chambers, upbraiding himself for playing the fool, throwing away all that had been offered. Chouteau sat, reached for his quill, dipped it, and began drafting a requisition for four horses, the quill scratching noisily on the soft paper. The brass pendulum of a cherrywood grandfather clock swung metronomically, reminding Skye of the passage of his life, time gone irretrievably, and the passage of once-in-a-life opportunity from the one powerful personage who cared enough about him to offer him a chance.

"Please make it passage for me and my party. I want to take MacLees's wife and baby back to her people," he said. "And please direct Marsh to accept us."

Chouteau nodded.

Skye hadn't the faintest idea what he would do or how he would support himself. He might be able to keep himself in galena and DuPont by shooting buffalo and skinning off the hides. Beyond that, his life was a blank. Had he been the ultimate fool? He knew most of his mountain friends would think so; most of the world would think so.

It seemed amazingly quiet for a midday encounter in the busiest quarter of St. Louis, and yet he could not even hear the clop and rattle of a dray outside those tall windows.

Chouteau finished with two drafts, and handed them to Skye. The first granted him and his party passage upriver.

The second gave him his choice of four of Peter Sarpy's saddle or packhorses, and tack.

"There, Monsieur, there. A petite surprise, all this. We are mystified. And curious. What will you make—ah, what will you do?"

"Turn into a savage, I imagine," Skye said, a faint amusement building in his face.

"*Sacre Bleu! A sauvage!*"

Then Pierre Chouteau was laughing, this time with big, boisterous gusts. "We make plans, and Fate makes other plans! We will give you some counsel. Don't go into Opposition."

"Don't plan to."

"Ah, they all say that to me, and then they secretly put together a small outfit and head west, thinking that we will never know. But we know. The company has a thousand ears, and ten thousand special ways of triumphing . . ."

Skye lifted his battered top hat, settled it, and grinned.

Chouteau nodded, a sudden dismissal, and Skye found himself alone, unemployed, unprotected by powerful interests, caught in a strange and gloomy city, and with several Indian women to shelter in a cruel and sordid town.

He stepped outside, and discovered that the storm clouds had at last slid by, and a golden sun painted the world, glinted off the puddles, and warmed the breezes. The world was a good place. Even St. Louis was a good place. He sucked fresh air into his lungs, surveyed the awesome river that drained much of North America, which ran most of a mile wide there, and felt at peace.

He decided to make one small call before breaking the news to Victoria. The plain, utilitarian one-story redbrick United States government house stood just a few yards distant, and he had in mind a visit to a man revered by all the world for his exploration of this continent early in the century; a man who held the fate of so many in his hand.

He crossed the stone-paved street, passed a staff with a red, white and blue flag dangling from it, and entered. General William Clark's chambers were located at the end of a short hall. He was actually not a general in the United States Army, but of the Missouri Militia, but the title, as so often was the case in this republican country, seemed interchangeable. He and Meriwether Lewis had both been called captains at the time they led the Corps of Discovery. Skye opened a plain, varnished door, entered, and found two clerks slouching at battered desks situated by the tall windows to catch the sun.

"General Clark, please," Skye said, removing his topper.

"And who is calling?"

"Mister Skye, sir. Barnaby Skye."

The clerk made Skye's presence known. Clark himself opened his inner office door. The old, weary, redheaded man with a military bearing beckoned. The legendary American wore an ordinary suit of clothes, not a uniform, and wore them carelessly as well. He looked unwell.

"Ah, you are Barnaby Skye. Your reputation precedes you, sir," Clark said, offering a big, solid, meaty hand, which Skye took in his own. A tremor spasmed Clark's hand.

"I can't imagine it," Skye said. "A man like you paying attention to a man like me—"

"Come in and visit with me."

Skye was heartened by this unsteady old American with a hospitable instinct, and settled uneasily in a chair opposite the general.

"I am surprised to see you in St. Louis, sir. You are one of the legends of the mountains."

"How would you know that, sir?"

"Through these chambers, my British friend, come the masters of the fur trade. Both Sublettes, Campbell, Drips,

Mitchell, most of the upper echelon of the Chouteau company . . . shall I name a dozen more?"

"No, sir. You probably know more about me than I know about myself."

Clark laughed easily. "It is quite possible."

"I came here at Mr. Chouteau's request. He thought to offer me a trading position."

"I see." Clark's affability had suddenly vanished.

"I turned it down."

Clark took some while registering that. "You turned it down? I knew you were coming, and I expected you to inquire about United States law governing the Indian country. Citizenship, especially. You are not an American, I take it."

"No, sir."

"Then I am puzzled."

Skye sought the words he needed. "I am married to a Crow woman, and have been many years. I want to know two or three things. One is whether I am legally entitled to be in your territory. The other is what nature of business I might engage in, if I am lawfully present."

"Simple. A squaw man's entitled to live with his spouse, as part of a tribe, no matter what his nationality. And you can engage in any business you wish, but only within that tribe and to others in the tribe. Save, of course, the purveying of ardent spirits, which are totally prohibited in the Indian territory now."

"I could actually do some limited trading?"

"Within the Crow tribe, yes. It would be no different than if a Crow himself were engaged in business with his tribesmen."

Skye brightened. "That's what I need to know."

"Ah, Mister Skye, I take it that you will not become an American citizen?"

"I am thinking on it."

"I regret that you find it necessary to weigh it, but I understand the case."

Skye nodded, not wanting to pursue that any further. He was still, in some lingering way, an Englishman at heart, and maybe he would end up somewhere in the Empire, such as Canada. And besides, he wasn't so sure about these Americans.

"How else may I serve you?"

"Those are the things I wanted to know, sir."

Clark stood at once, and Skye realized that this official was not one to lounge about. "If you are in St. Louis for a while, come visit me. We will share stories of the mountains, and grizzlies, and Indians over some brandy. And do bring your native wife."

"Victoria, sir. Many Quill Woman to her people."

"Ah! Bring her, then."

"I will consider it an honor."

Skye left, feeling heartened by this old man, but also wary of him. He headed back to the Chouteau warehouse, knowing Victoria would be waiting, and would want his portentous news.

He felt sublimely happy, but he wasn't sure she would.

49

Victoria listened intently. "You said no?"

"Yes. I just couldn't accept it, and I may regret it, but I had to."

She nodded. "That which guides you inside of yourself, it is always true to you, and that is all there is to say. I am content."

"I would have hurt your people."

"Some other trader will come, and he will hurt them."

"Let it be someone else, then."

"We have come a long way."

"Not for nothing. All this had to happen."

"Aiee, it is so. I have seen this land and this many-lodges, and now I am wiser than I was before."

"We'll get a ride part way back on the steamboat."

She processed that a moment. "With the captain, Benton Marsh?"

"Yes."

"He is a bad man. Maybe I walk."

"Chouteau gave me passage for me and my party. We can put up with him for a week or ten days."

She laughed. "He will put up with us! I will make it hard for that sonofabitch."

Skye laughed too. "We got a long trip ahead. You up to it?"

"My People call me. My country, the mountains, in the foothills, with the prairies rolling away, call me."

"I arranged passage for Lame Deer and her girl. Take 'em with us."

"If she wants to go. Maybe she stays here."

"I suppose we should ask," he said.

The rejected Cheyenne woman was sitting quietly in the cool gloom of the warehouse, watching Red Gill grade his hides and prepare to sell them.

Gill looked up as they approached. "You got the Fort Cass trader position?"

"It was offered. I turned it down, Red."

"Turned it down you say? Ain't that the craziest thing I ever heard. What'd you do that for?"

Skye just shook his head.

"Well, I wouldn't work for the company, neither. That's a rough outfit, and a man can't call his soul his own."

"Something like that," Skye said.

"What're you going to do?" Gill asked.

"Start a little trading store. Long as I'm married to a Crow woman, it's all right," Skye said. "That's straight from the general himself. After I got loose of Chouteau, I hiked over there and talked to him."

"How you going to stock it?"

"I've got two outfits now. I'll sell one for horses and a few trade items."

"You figure that's a living?"

"No," said Skye.

Gill dropped the robe he was examining. "You want to partner?"

"Doing what?"

"Santa Fe trading."

Skye shook his head. There were twenty other outfits in the business, and more coming in each year, and all of them better financed. But it would not suit Victoria, and that was reason enough. And he wasn't sure about lining up with a smuggler.

"I guess not, Red, but thanks for the offer."

Red grinned. "I figured it'd be that. You're a man of honor; me, I'm an opportunist. Tell you what. I'll lend you some start-up if you want."

It was tempting. A few hundred dollars of trade goods would go far. But after a moment's reflection, he declined. He was a man without a country; also, a man who had to go it alone. He couldn't say why.

"I think I'll just weather the bad times," he said.

"Luck," said Red.

Skye and Victoria braced Lame Deer, who was sitting contemplatively, cradling her girl.

"We're going back west. We'd like you to join us," Skye said. "Take you to your people."

"We will walk?"

"Riverboat up to Sarpy's Post, and then horses and pack mules out the Platte River. Long trip, and the weather will turn."

"The same fireboat?"

Skye nodded.

She seemed to harden before his eyes. "I will go. This is a place like a cloudy night. I see no stars. The stars are like friends, and I see no friends. I come to give myself to my man; give my child to him. He sees me and then I am a stranger to him, and they close the door and I am standing with his little girl!, and the door is closed."

She shuddered, and then focused on some distant place beyond all horizons.

"He will walk in darkness. He will pass meadows blooming with flowers and not see them. He will stumble when there is no rock to stumble on. He will look behind him to see who is following, even when no one follows. He will smile, but his spirit is sad. He will have friends, but will not be a friend of himself. He will be with many, but he will be alone. I cannot help him. This path he choose for himself; me, I am not welcome in his lodge. His medicine is bad and mine is good and I will walk along soft trails covered with pine needles and my feet will not hurt."

Skye marveled again at this woman's images. Where did they come from? What artesian well, of what sweet water, rose within her? Was this a curse or a prophecy?

"We'll be your traveling companions, and you can call on us," Skye said.

She seemed to come out of some trance, and stood. "We go now?"

"I'll find out," Skye said. "I hope we have some time. I've got some trading to do."

Two days later they boarded the *Otter* under Marsh's baleful eye, and settled in their staterooms.

First Mate Trenholm appeared. "Captain wants you," he said.

Skye followed the mate up the companionway, wondering what more trouble the captain could inflict on his party.

Marsh stood in the pilothouse, massive and choleric as ever.

"You lost, Skye," the captain said, enjoying himself.

"I was offered the position and turned it down."

Marsh wheezed. "You make a poor excuse for a liar," he said.

"It's Mister Skye, sir."

Marsh laughed. "I knew you'd lose. I told Chouteau you weren't fit. You were better than Bonfils, but that's not saying much."

Marsh had called him a liar. Skye wondered whether to make an issue of it. He knew it was bait. Marsh was looking for an excuse to toss Skye and his women off the steamboat, and a brawl would do nicely.

"That it?" Skye asked.

"Behave yourself. The moment this boat casts off lines, I'm God. I'm the master of this boat and all upon it. You can leave now if you don't like it, or I'll put you ashore at the first woodlot on any excuse I can find, or no excuse at all if I feel like it. And don't go whining to Pierre Chouteau. He'll laugh."

Skye didn't move a muscle.

"I hear you tried to blackmail MacLees," Marsh said. "I got the whole story firsthand, over some good brandy. It's the source of much humor in that household. You and your slut and that squaw on their doorstep. The wedding, by the way, was splendid."

Skye grinned.

Marsh waited, poised like a cat, his huge red fists ready to hammer Skye. The helmsman was ready too, with a club. Trenholm hovered just outside the door, on the hurricane deck, a thick club in his hand. They were ready to kill him, hoping for it, and were looking for the slightest excuse.

Skye kept his mouth shut and his hands at his sides.

"I'm calling you a liar and a blackmailer, Skye," Marsh said. "I hear no objection. I guess you must agree."

Skye smiled.

"Very well, I get no argument from you about your character. You'll be deck passengers. I'll have a cabin boy get your gear out, and unload it on the deck. Then I'll have him delouse the rooms."

Now at last Skye spoke, softly and resonantly. "Tell the helmsman and Trenholm to back off and put down their clubs. Then I'll answer you, man to man," Skye said. "You want a reply? I'll give you one."

Marsh eyed the helmsman and the mate, and Skye could see him calculating. He waited calmly, on the balls of his feet. His gaze bore into Marsh. Then he edged forward until the length of a pencil separated him from the master.

"Well?" Skye asked. "What's your reply?"

Marsh didn't blink and the moment stretched long, but then there was a subtle change; nothing palpable, but a change even so, and Skye knew he had won. The master needed his armed thugs and they all knew it. The insults and taunts were dust.

"We're leaving as soon as steam's up," Marsh said.

Skye wheeled away, down the companionway, and back to the rear staterooms. He found the women all together.

"We're getting off the boat."

"Sonofabitch!"

Lame Deer was staring at him. "It is good. I love to walk upon the breast of the earth and feel the grass beneath my moccasins. I love the earth. It is honest and clean. My legs do not grow weary, and I can walk from sun to sun."

Skye nodded.

A preliminary whistle squalled from the standpipe. The chimneys belched black smoke. Steam was up. The fireboxes roared.

A cabin boy appeared, and Skye directed him toward the mound of gear. Skye and the women each collected all they could carry, and hauled it out upon the main deck, next to the gangway.

"All ashore that's going ashore," a second mate bawled at the crowd on the deck.

"Help us get this off," Skye said to the cabin boy. The lad looked doubtful. "There's time, and Marsh will wait if he must."

The lad nodded, and helped them move their truck to the levee, where a crowd watched silently, curious about Skye and his Indian women.

Up in the pilothouse, Marsh was smiling. The moment the boy was done, Marsh pulled a cord. Deckmen pulled up the gangway. Rivermen loosened the hawsers. The *Otter* slid away from the levee, and began to buck the current of the Mississippi. The wheels thrashed, and the boat shuddered forward, and the captain laughed. He had gotten rid of Skye's party after all.

But Skye, staring up at the man, didn't mind.

50

In a grove outside of Independence, the last caravan of the season creaked to life one early August morning, and headed out the well-worn trail toward Santa Fe. This one, thirty-two wagons strong, consisted of independent entrepreneurs, except that Ceran St. Vrain was among them with a dozen wagons destined for Bent's Fort and Taos. The Bent brothers and St. Vrain were partners in the other great fur empire, this one stretching across the southern plains, and reaping a harvest of buffalo robes that rivaled Chouteau's.

Skye and Victoria knew several of those travelers, including Uncle Dick Wooton, Kit Carson, and Lucien Maxwell, all of them veterans of the mountains. Some of them had been in St. Louis for one reason or another that spring and summer. It would be grand to see Kit.

Skye had traded his spare outfit for passage on a steamer, *Arapaho*, as far as Independence, and there was enough left over for horses as well, which they took with them on the steamer because there was an acute shortage of mules and horses in Independence, where the Santa Fe trade devoured livestock.

With Skye was Lame Deer and her daughter, sharing a small mare Skye had acquired for her. She was smiling, knowing that at Bent's Fort she would find her Cheyenne people, and maybe even her own kin. The Cheyenne, who had lived for years around the Black Hills and along the Cheyenne River, where MacLees had traded with them, had drifted south in recent years. And now she was going home.

Red Gill was taking a wagon west, loaded with hardware and satins and velvets for Santa Fe, and had put together his outfit just in time to join up with the others before the cold weather roared down on the plains. Even so, the last part of his trip would be tough, with snow on the peaks of the Sangre de Cristos in Nuevo Mexico.

But it was to St. Vrain that Skye was attached now.

"My friend, come work for us," William Bent's partner had said expansively in Independence.

"Maybe for the winter," Skye had replied.

And so Skye had hired on, and now, this fine hot day, the motley assemblage of foul-mouthed teamsters, adventurers, merchants, buckskin-clad mountaineers, trappers' children, and a few Indians, like Lame Deer, rode out. Skye and Victoria preferred their saddle horses, but Lame Deer was content to sit in the van of one of St. Vrain's lumbering, rocking freight wagons, and tie her mustang mare to the tailgate.

Skye drew up beside her wagon.

"You happy?" he asked.

"I go to my people," she said. "They are strong and good. They listen to Sweet Medicine, and obey his wisdom. My clan will care for me, and for Singing Rain. They will honor me, and soon I will find a new man with a true heart and I will be given to him, and I will make his lodge a good place. And we will follow the four-foots and the buffalo, and make our lodge warm in the winter, with many robes and much meat."

"You glad you went to St. Louis?"

Her face clouded a moment. "I have been where no

Cheyenne woman has ever gone, and I see many things. But my heart is big now that I see the grass and the sky, as far as my eye can see. And I will bring this knowledge of what I saw in St. Louis to my people, and help them know about white men. I am big in my heart, but in St. Louis I was small in my heart. Now you make me happy, and you are my friend, and I will sing about you to my people."

"Thank Victoria, not me."

"Ah, the Absaroka woman, she is a true friend too. She loves Singing Rain, and my girl-child loves her too."

Skye nodded, and spurred his lean, rough-gaited, nondescript nag forward to walk beside St. Vrain.

"You want to winter with me, up at my post?" St. Vrain said. "I could always use a man. You'd be closer to Victoria's people."

"Might. But only if you offer the jug. I have the biggest thirst I've ever had."

St. Vrain laughed. "It is possible," he said.

"I didn't get a sip all summer. First I got yanked out of rendezvous when they were just unpacking, and in St. Louis I didn't have even two bits to buy a refreshment. So I'll let you and William make offers. How many jugs do you bid?"

"I think William Bent could outbid me," St. Vrain confessed. "We don't have to smuggle spirits, you know. We've got Taos Lightning, brewed in old Mexico. Aguardiente, it's called. A fiery brandy, fermented from the agave leaf. Oh, Skye, it bites. It kicks. It makes a man howl."

Skye rumbled, the anticipation of paradise welling up in him.

And so the procession creaked west, the big wooden wheels hammering along rutted trails, winding through mixed groves and prairies, splashing through muddy creeks, and eventually out upon vast grasslands that spread to the mysterious horizons where the future lay, like the seas upon which Skye had sailed for so many years. It would be a good trip if the grass held up. Many Santa Fe caravans had already lumbered down the trail, and the grass had been well chewed down.

Maybe this was the future, he thought. The beaver were gone, and beaver felt wasn't in demand anyway. If there were any more rendezvous, they'd be melancholy affairs at best, a mournful echo of those grand frolics of yore. But a man could still survive out here, far from the cities, far from all the civilizing influences that he would just as soon avoid. There was a living to be had from buffalo, and he reckoned he could make some money someday just taking people where they wanted to go and looking after their safety.

That year of 1838, the Bents and the Chouteaus had divided up the West; the Bents controlling everything south of the South Platte, while the Chouteaus dominated the robe trade to the north. Only a handful of independent traders were surviving against the two giants. Skye had tried the Chouteaus; now he would see about these others.

He found Victoria, who was back toward the rear with Red Gill, enjoying the mild day.

"You happy?" he asked.

"This damned horse! It don't do nothing right. But I got him figured out. He was not gonna walk one more step, so I leaned forward and took an ear, and I whispered into his ear, 'You sonofabitch, you get moving or I'll eat you.'"

"And what did the horse do?"

"Well look at him! He's a prancing fool!"

Skye was content. Victoria wished she could be heading toward her people, but had settled into cheerful acceptance of the turn in their fortunes. She had brightened from the moment they left St. Louis. Skye planned to winter at the great adobe fort built by the Bents, enjoying the mild climate and the good company.

He was glad he had gone to St. Louis, even though the whole thing had come to nothing. The cost to his body had been terrible, but the trip had opened vistas to him. At last, he had seen the Yanks in their homeland. He no longer wished to work for Pierre Chouteau. Skye knew himself to be a man of honor, and if he paid a heavy price because of his beliefs, so be it. He could always live with himself; other men with more flexible ethics might not like what they saw in the looking glass.

He was no longer tempted to become an American citizen. Not now. Maybe not ever. How could a people with such noble ideals harbor so many cutthroats and ruffians? Skye grasped anew that he was a man without a country, and probably would live out his life that way, apart from the cabals and crowds and schemes of empire.

That was all right. Even if he belonged to no people, he belonged to a land, and that land stretched across the great prairies to the mountains, from British Canada on the north to Mexico on the south. Alone, yet not alone, for no man with stalwart friends is ever alone, and no man with a woman like Victoria is ever alone, and no man who harbors a bright vision of the way things should be is ever without comfort.

St. Vrain had promised him any position he wanted, and he thought he might take some trips out to the Apache and Comanche Indian villages on the Mexican side of the Arkansas River, where he need not worry about having a trading license from General Clark. There could be some danger in it, but Skye was born to danger, and thought he would be all right. Bent regularly sent small trading outfits to the surrounding villages to bid for buffalo robes, and Skye thought he might do that. He wouldn't earn much, but there were some things in life that were better than money. And if he hung around Bent's Fort, he and Victoria would be employed, fed and sheltered for as long as he wanted to stay on the Arkansas River.

That was good enough for *Skye. He and Victoria would* settle in, and maybe some twilit evening, up in that famous second-floor billiard room Bent had built for his men, he and Victoria would pull the cork on a jug of Taos Lightning, settle down on a thick buffalo robe against the adobe wall, gather his friends for some quiet good times, and rejoice that they had escaped secretive, scheming St. Louis. They were out beyond the rim of civilization, where life was sweet as mead and a man was always free.